A
WOMAN LOST
SERIES

T.B. Markinson

Published by T. B. Markinson

ISBN: 978-1-98-151083-2

Visit T. B. Markinson's official website at lesbianromancesbytbm.com for the latest news, book details, and other information.

A CLUELESS WOMAN

A novel by
T. B. Markinson

CHAPTER ONE

"I FEEL LIKE A LADY OF THE NIGHT." MEG CRAMMED THE WAD OF TWENTIES I'D JUST FURTIVELY handed over into the pocket of her jeans. "Of course, if things don't turn around for me soon, that might be my future calling. Do ya think William would pay to sleep with me? He was never shy about his desires."

I assumed she'd added that juicy detail about my colleague to bait me. No, to remind me of what she was capable of and to keep me in line. Years of falling for her self-pity and emotional blackmail had taught me to steel myself and ignore Meg to the best of my ability, but I still found myself saying, "I can't keep handing over wads of money."

"Why? We both know you aren't even close to draining your trust fund, not even a quarter of it." Meg leveled her deep-green gaze on my face.

"I'm not responsible for you."

"Responsible for me?" She laughed, bitterly. "Have you been attending Al-Anon meetings or something?"

I sighed. "I need to go." I hoisted my book bag over my shoulder. Meg feigned lunging at me, and I jumped back. We were in an alley behind a coffee shop, and Meg was blocking the street exit. The door to the coffee shop didn't have a handle, and I assumed it could only be opened from the inside. I moved back, against the wall, inching closer to safety.

"Must be nice to have the luxury of being a student." Her abrasive smile alerted me to tread carefully. My mind flooded with memories of invoking Meg's wrath. She crossed her arms, revealing she had no intention of budging. "How are William and Janice? It's been a long time since I was welcome to join the weekly study sessions." Her eyes lit up. "Hey, I know. I bet William would pay big bucks for me to tell him all about us." She ran a finger down my face, and I willed myself not to cringe. "The things you used to do to me and what you begged me to do to you." She reached for my belt buckle, but I backpedaled, much to her delight. "I bet that'd get him off." She squared her shoulders. "Or you could just meet me next week." Meg patted the wad in her pocket.

"Fine."

A car horn blared, and Meg spun to view the commotion, allowing me to sidle past. Once out of harm's way, on the sidewalk, I turned. "Keep going to your meetings, okay?" I said.

Meg's eyes softened but then quickly coalesced into anger. "Get off your high horse, Lizzie. You aren't perfect. And don't forget" — she stabbed a finger in the air — "next week."

Any retort would just egg her on, so I wheeled around and marched toward the shop's entrance.

"Lizzie!" a shout came from behind me. It wasn't Meg's voice, so I turned.

Janice strode up next to me, hooking her arm through mine. "I thought that was you. Why in the world are you hanging out in a back alley with Meg, of all people?"

"Were you the one who honked?"

She nodded. "I was looking for a parking space and considered the alley when I spied you two. Not sure what got into me. Shock, probably. Or fear."

"Whatever the reason, thanks."

"How much this time?" Her arm tightened on mine.

"Too much."

"You know, you aren't responsible for her."

"So people keep telling me. But it's —"

"Hard. I know. I get it. Meg and I had been best friends before she spiraled out of control. I can't imagine how hard it is for you, being her ex. Besides, she does it to me too." Janice tugged my arm and motioned to a bench outside the trendy coffee shop. "Sit for a moment."

I complied.

"Do you remember the three of us before everything? We were The Three Musketeers. The only girls out of ten students studying under Dr. Marcel." Janice unraveled a chunky knit scarf with a fringe, letting it drape over her shoulders like a shawl.

I laughed. "We had to band together to deal with all the machismo bullshit. Mostly from Jared and Trent."

"God, I was relieved when Trent left last year for Harvard. His leer." She shook it off. "And Jared thinking he was God's gift to all women, even with his lazy eye and stutter!"

"I still remember the night when you told Jared he turned you gay." I laughed.

"And he believed me. No offense, Lizzie, but women are way too much work." Janice nudged my arm.

I wholeheartedly agreed.

"I wonder how he's getting along in Arizona," I said in an effort not to dwell on Meg and the alley situation. My eyes feasted on the Rocky Mountain foothills set against a brilliant lapis sky. I'd rather be hiking to the summit, Horsetooth Rock. I longed to feel free.

"Still can't believe Jared scored a teaching gig before finishing his dissertation." Janice slapped her thigh.

"Come on. His dad is president of the university, and his mom is a state senator. Jared will never have to worry about a job — he'll be tenured in record time."

Janice placed a palm on my thigh. "You recovered from …?" She nodded her head toward the alley. Janice knew me all too well, but she played along for a few moments to allow my skittering heartbeat and ragged breathing to regulate.

I nodded. "Yeah, thanks again for saving me. Again."

"Don't thank me." She groaned. "I'm still mad at myself for not seeing the warning signs about Meg's drinking. Shit, the two of us used to go out together and get hammered." Janice covered half her face with the scarf.

"Hey. Stop that." I pulled her hand away from her face. "You can't blame yourself for Meg."

"I know, I know …" She looked away. I knew all too well the guilt swimming inside her head.

I stood. "We should get inside." She reluctantly followed, and I opened the door and motioned for her to walk ahead. Janice marched to the counter and ordered a beer. It was barely five o'clock, and I playfully rolled my eyes at her.

"Don't start. It's been one hell of a day already." She smiled. Both of us knew today was no different from any other day, and given the conversation we had just ended, it was a tad bit uncomfortable. "You ready for William?" She squeezed my arm.

"I better be. He just walked in." I leaned in and whispered, "Please don't mention you had to rescue me from Meg."

"Like I would." Janice plastered a fake smile on her face and greeted William. "Willy Boy, you ready for tonight's riveting discussion?"

William bristled at the nickname. He was from Rhode Island, and his full name was William Connor Abernathy Thornhill V. He'd actually introduced himself like that when we met at orientation several years ago. I soon learned that none of the Williams in his family went by anything other than William. Janice, though, never quite got that — or never cared much for it.

"Wouldn't miss it for the world," he sneered in his typical way.

With a frosty nod toward me, he ordered himself a beer. I wasn't a teetotaler; however, I wasn't exactly thrilled that we met at a shop that served alcohol after five to drum up business. Not that I never drank, but the three of us met for academic purposes, not social. And when Meg had been a member of the group — well, it made my life harder since she didn't know her limit. I rubbed my eyes to wipe away the memories.

"Shall we sit?" I asked, motioning to our reserved table in the back.

William gestured for Janice to walk ahead of him and said, "Lady first."

She gritted her teeth while I ignored his dig. Since Meg quit the program he went above and beyond to ruffle my feathers. My sole purpose for continuing these sessions was to finish at the top of our PhD program, which meant I couldn't get sucked into William's pettiness.

The three of us met each week at Chippie's Coffee Shop to prepare for our seminars. The name of the venue had never been officially explained, but I assumed it was a play on the chipped cups and pint glasses. Every one I'd been served over the years had been chipped or cracked. Superglue, or what have you, held most of them together, and each week the person with the most damaged cup had the privilege of leading the discussion. William was tonight's winner. It was going to be a long night.

"It's obvious you've never had mind-blowing sex," William said, and took a massive swig of his second beer. His swarmy smile conveyed that could change if I went to bed with him.

I blinked once. Twice.

Janice just gawped at him and then back at me. Her mouth formed an O, which was unlike her. A spunky San Franciscan, she was normally easy-going and unflappable. Although naturally brilliant, she was a free spirit who didn't give a damn about academia and had entered the history PhD program just to get her parents off her back.

Janice enjoyed the meetings purely as a form of entertainment. As long as she stayed in the program, her parents supported her and left her alone. So far, at least. She hadn't expressed any desire to find a rich guy to marry instead, even though it wouldn't be hard for her to succeed in that endeavor. She reminded me of Audrey Hepburn, just not as skinny. Collin, her on-again-off-again boyfriend since college days, was a decent guy, but Janice was in no rush to settle down, if ever. Whenever he pushed for more, she broke it off. As far as I could tell, her sole ambition was to float through life with no responsibilities or demands.

Seconds later, I was finally able to speak. "And how did you deduce that, exactly?"

"Deduce!" Janice slapped my thigh under the table and chortled. "Lizzie, you crack me up. Go on, Willy Boy." She faced William, who sat opposite of us. "Tell us how you *deduced* that."

From the beginning, he and I had viewed each other as the main competition in the program. His last comment, though, was a step too far and, quite frankly, rude.

"Anyone who says they'd ditch Humphrey Bogart at the end of *Casablanca* obviously hasn't had great sex," he repeated without a trace of humor.

Janice laughed. "Oh, I get it. You're quoting *When Harry Met Sally.*"

William and I both pivoted to her, clueless.

"Seriously? Neither of you have seen that movie?" Janice shook her head, an expression of humor and dismay on her face; she wore that look a lot around us.

Usually, William and I did a good job of keeping Janice on task, but when she'd veered toward *Casablanca* tonight, William couldn't help himself. Apparently, he thought himself a modern-day Humphrey Bogart. Not as an actor, but as a hard-boiled but ultimately good guy who rescues damsels in distress—his words, not mine. With his scrawny frame, I didn't think he could pull himself out of a wet paper bag, let alone another human.

"Just because I wouldn't want to stay in a Vichy-controlled city swarming with German and Italian officials during World War II doesn't mean I haven't had great sex." My voice faltered at the end, not because it wasn't true, but because I didn't want too many people to overhear. It came out sounding insecure.

"When's the last time you experienced The Big O?" Janice nudged me. She didn't seem at all flustered that she was grilling me about my sex life during a study session.

"Not since Meg, I'm guessing. Which was what? A year ago? Longer?" William said. "And I'm sorry, but it's hard to believe Meg was a giver. A taker, maybe, but not a giver. And The Big O … I don't see it with her. Not with her—"

The table jumped an inch off the floor. Janice must've really walloped William in the shins.

"Why are you kicking me? It's no secret that Meg and Lizzie used to date and that Meg—"

There was another scuffle under the table. Janice knew much more than William, and it'd become typical for her to act like my protective older sister.

I rolled my eyes. "Can we get back to business?" I flicked the pages of the three books we had to read for this week's seminars. "I'm sure Dr. Marcel won't ask any questions about The Big O. Only Goebbels, Himmler, and Göring will be up for discussion."

All of us studied World War II, concentrating on Nazi Germany. Our current reading seminar focused on the rise of the Third Reich and the leaders who'd made it possible.

"Now Joseph Goebbels, don't get me wrong or misinterpret what I'm about to say, since we all know he was evil" — Janice shifted in her seat — "but with his position as the Reich's Minister of Propaganda and the way he coerced actresses to date him, he was probably better in the sack. Yeah, he had a clubfoot, but I don't think that would have impeded him much. Hermann Göring, maybe during his WWI ace flying days, before he ballooned out and became addicted to morphine … but Heinrich Himmler, the scrawny former chicken farmer" — she shook her head — "that man was never a good lay."

This was why I didn't think it was a good idea to mix booze with studies. Two hours earlier everyone was focused. Now, Janice was wandering into dangerous territory.

To my amazement, William joined the discussion. "What about Hitler?" he asked without moving his lips. It had taken me days, if not weeks, to get used to that quirk of his, yet I still caught myself staring at his mouth from time to time.

"Hitler?" Janice's voice cracked. "No way. I bet he couldn't even get it up. Besides, didn't he only have one ball?"

"That's the theory. Apparently, the Soviets chopped off one of his nuts and it's somewhere in Russia." William raised his eyebrows. He had a long, narrow face and a sloped forehead, and the gesture made him resemble a cartoon character.

"I've heard he liked to play dress-up and ask, 'Do I look like the Führer?'" Janice giggled and then took a sip of her beer.

I groaned.

"That reminds me." She swiveled to face me. "You never answered my question."

I stared at her.

"Your last Big O?" She smiled. "Including when it was just you." Her exaggerated wink made me roll my eyes.

William's eyes glimmered with too much interest. Shit, that reminded me to get cash before next week's session. Knowing Meg, she'd follow through on her threat of spilling all the juicy details about our sex life. Not that we had much sex in the final months. Meg was usually passed out drunk each and every night.

Not answering, I started shoving books into my bag.

Janice peered at her watch. "Oh, crap. I'm late meeting friends for dinner. See ya in class tomorrow." Unencumbered by books or a bag, she made a quick escape.

William stood and stretched. I eyed his silk patchwork belt, which featured whales, fish, and crabs. His blue gingham Vineyard Vines shirt was untucked at the back. He crammed his books and notebook into a leather briefcase more suited to Indiana Jones than to a history grad student and then raised one hand. I wasn't sure if he was gesturing good-bye or motioning me not to speak. Then he spun on his heel and marched out.

I shook my head and made my exit. Outside, I unlocked my bike from the overcrowded rack and hopped on. It was dark, but it was only eight o'clock, so I still had time to cram in a few hours of work before crashing and waking at six for my morning ride.

It didn't take long to reach my apartment. I hung my Cannondale from the hooks in the entryway ceiling, walked past the bookshelves and stacks of paperbacks that inhabited every available space, and veered off to the side of the main room to a small dining room that doubled as my office. The books offset the starkness of the cotton-white walls and institutional-beige carpet in my one-bedroom apartment. They were the only personal touches since I was never big on photos or decorating. Who had the time for trivial matters?

There was no one to greet me. I lived alone, and had done so since Meg left. Not that Meg and I had officially lived together, but when we were dating, she had stayed over many nights. Besides weekly meetings with colleagues and a meet-up with my buddy Ethan at Starbucks once a week, most of my human interaction took place on campus. I taught classes three times a week, attended seminars, and held office hours twice a week. During holidays and school breaks, I could go for days without speaking to anyone. I'd always felt more comfortable around books, which was why even the walls of the hallway and bedroom were lined with shelves.

I wasn't close to my family, which was okay with everyone on both sides. I didn't like them, and they didn't approve of me. My mother loved to refer to me as "the Les-Bi-An," never her daughter. My father was silent. And my older brother, Peter, was too busy getting rich on the West Coast and conjuring up ways to steal my inheritance.

In the kitchen, I prepared my usual two ham and cheese sandwiches, snatched a banana and an apple from the fruit bowl, and rummaged around for a large bag of tortilla chips and hummus. Then I settled in at the dining room table. Time to get some research done for my Hitler Youth dissertation, which analyzed the youth movement that indoctrinated young boys so they would grow up to be perfect Nazi soldiers. I had been slaving away in grad school for the past few years, and my current goal was to finish my dissertation in two years. My advisor was convinced I needed at least three, but I'd show him. I'd completed my undergrad in three and a half years with a double major in history and politics and flew through my master's in two.

Still, the huge stack of books on the table elicited a sigh, which, for a brief moment, I was certain echoed through my apartment.

"Do you think I'm pathetic?" I asked Ethan as he added gobs of sugar to his Starbucks house blend.

He dipped his head almost a foot and peered at me through his spectacles. "How am I supposed to answer that?"

"Honestly. Do you think I'm pathetic?"

Ethan maneuvered his lanky frame past three untidy tables and I followed, grimacing at the messiness of the place, until we settled on one that was almost clean. It was a little after ten on Saturday, and although it was quiet now, the early morning rush must have taken the staff by surprise. Two teenagers leaned against the counter, dazed and confused.

"Okay, what's got your panties in a bunch this morning?" Ethan set down his coffee, took off his coke-bottle thick glasses, and cleaned them with a cloth.

"The other night, William and Janice got on my case about how long it's been since I experienced The Big O." I didn't bother whispering the last part. Aside from the employees behind the counter, the place was deserted.

"The Big O?" He hitched up one of his thin eyebrows.

"You know. In bed."

"Oh, you mean the last time you had an orgasm." He wiped both eyes with his fingers before replacing his glasses. "And?"

"And what?"

He snorted. "When was the last time?"

I scratched my chin. "Not sure really. Meg."

"That was well over a year ago."

"Good grief. Not you as well. For someone who doesn't like sex, I didn't think you would gang up on me, too."

"Gang up on you?" He laughed. "I'm just curious." He ignored my comment about not liking sex. With the exception of coffee, Ethan disliked fluids of all types, but especially bodily fluids. It made me wonder how he'd managed to get married. "And their comments got you thinking?" he added.

"Yes. I mean no. Maybe," I stammered. "I just keep thinking about it."

"About what? The Big O or not having anyone in your life?" As usual, Ethan hit the nail on the head.

"Just the other day, I ran into one of my former professors. This guy is ancient, in a wheelchair, and he smells like an old person who's about to move on to the next world. Out of the blue he started telling me about how he and his lady friend went to the movies. I was flabbergasted. How did he have a lady friend? I don't even have a pet. Not even a goldfish."

"Do you want a lady friend?" Ethan's tone bordered on teasing.

"I don't know. Maybe. It might be nice to have someone." I peered out the window and watched the commotion taking place on College Avenue. "Most days I'm fine, but…"

"My advice. Don't search for it. If you try to find a girlfriend, it won't happen. But if you're at peace with your life, it'll happen naturally, sooner rather than later."

"Naturally." I bobbed my head and repeated the word. "Is that how it happened with Lisa?"

He beamed. "Yes and no. We've known each other all our lives. I was so young I didn't even know I was looking." He laughed. "*C'est la vie.*"

"What if I meet someone who turns out to be another Meg?" The thought was more than unsettling; it was horrifying.

Ethan patted my arm. "Not everyone is like Meg. I know trust isn't your biggest strength, but you need to learn to let people in. Not everyone is out to hurt you."

I huffed. "Hurt me?" Ethan knew my relationship with Meg wasn't great, but he didn't have full disclosure. No one did. I couldn't confide in anyone about how bad it had gotten before I reached my breaking point. That night she'd gone way too far. I massaged my lower jaw.

He swatted the air. "Oh, I forgot. You're Lizzie-the-Indestructible." His carefully guarded Southern accent slipped in. Ethan hailed from Mississippi, but most of the time he controlled his twang.

I forced a laugh. "Whatever."

His moustache curled up with his smile. "Having someone in your life could be a good thing. You can't spend all your time with books or riding your bike. Human interaction — have you heard of it?"

CHAPTER TWO

ON MONDAY, I FINISHED EARLY. I'D ALREADY HAD A ONE-HOUR WESTERN CIV LECTURE AT eight, followed by two fifty-minute reading discussions before noon. At one o'clock, I attended Dr. Marcel's twentieth-century European history class as the graduate teacher's assistant, and I held office hours from two to four. By half past four, I was usually ready to jump on my bike and head home.

This morning, when I'd left a little after six for my normal forty-five minute bike ride, the sky had been dark as midnight. Around the tenth mile, the sky lightened and I could see half-bare tree branches against the gunmetal sky. Temperatures in northern Colorado at this time of year hovered between the thirties and forties in the early hours, which made for chilly but not unbearable rides. The heavy low-hanging clouds had spurred me to get going before flakes started to fly.

The snow had already melted as I suspected it would. I owned a car, but my preferred method of transportation was my bike. If I didn't ride each day, I was more stressed than usual, and I was already wound way too tight, according to Ethan.

"Lizzie, do you have a minute?"

I forced down an urge to refuse my mentor. Dr. Marcel was a gifted historian, and I was lucky to be under his tutelage. Ten students in the program had applied to work with him, and he'd chosen me after I completed the requirements for my master's. I could still remember the day I received the news. I knew I'd have to work my ass off, and the challenge hadn't terrified me at all. I thrived under pressure.

What I didn't know was how much of a chatterbox Dr. Marcel could be. Every time he asked me into his office, I lost hours. Typically, I didn't mind—after all, he was one of the greatest historians west of the Mississippi. But my plan was to enjoy a rare afternoon bike ride and then fine-tune a lecture for the following week. I preferred to stay a week ahead, and I had to work on an outline for my semester research project, which was due in two weeks. My PhD program was a twenty-four hour job eight days a week. I simply didn't have time for Dr. Marcel this afternoon.

"Of course, Dr. Marcel," I said as sweetly as I could, trying to quash my unease.

"I'd like you to meet Sarah Cavanaugh." Dr. Marcel motioned to a young woman sitting in a leather librarian chair inside his plush office.

She was stunning. Chin-length chestnut-brown hair framed her face, highlighting her penetrating chocolate eyes and alabaster skin. Worries about my lecture and paper slipped into the recesses of my mind.

"Hello." She stood to shake my hand. Her skin was soft, and I thought I detected a hint of lavender.

"Hi, Ms. Cavanaugh." I dipped my head slightly and smoothed the front of my sweater-vest, which had a habit of bunching and giving the illusion of a potbelly.

She colored. "Sarah is just fine. I don't even like it when my students call me Ms. Cavanaugh."

"Oh, do you teach here?"

How in the world had I not met this gorgeous professor? I needed to get my head out of my books —and out of my ass.

"Sarah teaches English at a local high school," Dr. Marcel interjected. "She's on a committee to inspire more high school grads to attend college." He stopped speaking, giving the impression I now knew the reason for the introduction.

"That's wonderful," I said, unclear as to why I was needed for this meeting. I was a grad student, not an admissions officer.

I think she understood my predicament. My eyes had a way of betraying every emotion. "Our plan is to bring a handful of students to campus for a day. Have them sit in on some classes to give them a taste of college life." Sarah smiled awkwardly.

"Unfortunately, the plan is for them to visit next Wednesday, and my class is scheduled to take an exam." Dr. Marcel continued to beam vaguely, like the lovable village idiot.

I knew all about the exam; I was the one who'd written all the questions and would be doing all the grading. Graduate students were, in reality, indentured servants to the top professors in the department.

"I'm hoping you'll agree, Lizzie." Dr. Marcel's grin lit up the room.

"Agree?" My voice cracked and flashes of heat crept up my face.

"For my students to sit in on your class," explained Sarah. Her voice was sweet, magnetically so.

"Oh, yes, of course!" My sudden enthusiasm embarrassed me, but Dr. Marcel seemed to appreciate it. Sarah elevated one eyebrow in such a way that I thought for sure she was trying to decide whether I was mentally unstable or a blathering simpleton like my portly but kind mentor. Surely she was used to affecting people this way—men and women.

Would it be too obvious if I released my hair from the ubiquitous ponytail holder that was tightly twisted several times, strangling the thin strands into compliance? I imagined flirtatiously tossing it about like in the movies.

"Great." Dr. Marcel joined his hands together as if he were praying and nodded his head absently. Anyone who didn't know him would have thought he was senile, but he had one of the sharpest minds and never put on airs. He could lecture for more than an hour without any notes, and his information was always spot-on. During my first year, I tried catching him in a falsehood, or even just a wrong date or name. It never happened. He swiveled his head to me and then to Sarah. "That's wonderful."

All three of us stood in his office, unsure where to go from there.

Finally, Sarah eased the tension. "Would you have time later this week to go over the plans?"

"I'm free this evening," I blurted.

"Uh," she uttered.

I put up one palm. "Of course, you probably have plans. Later this week works as well. Whenever. I'm at your beck and call." I wrenched at my collar to release the heat pouring off my face and neck. Why was I insistent on acting like a fool in front of this woman?

"Are you available now for a quick cup of coffee?" she asked.

"Yes!" *Seriously, Lizzie. Bring it down a peg or two.*

"Wonderful," Dr. Marcel said, not noticing that his star doctoral student transformed into a complete and total loser around a beautiful woman. I wasn't the smoothest person, but I usually had more composure in the workplace. Not around Sarah, apparently.

We said our good-byes to the professor and made our way to the student center.

My brain was going a mile a minute trying to come up with something witty to say. Nothing came to mind. It was as if a loose screw had flown into my mental machinery, causing a total system failure. Instead of speaking, I stared at the ground as we walked, wondering whether each step was quashing my chance of asking her on a date.

"I really appreciate you taking the time out of your schedule." Sarah threw me a bone.

"Not at all. The pleasure is all mine. How do you like teaching high school students?" *Really, I could only come up with a work question?*

"I love it. My tenth graders are challenging, but most days I enjoy it. Of course, it must be different teaching college students." Her full lips turned up into a smile, beckoning mine.

"I doubt it. I teach freshmen. Half of the students are either falling asleep or texting. The rest are still in bed." Then I remembered I was supposed to impress her students. "But I'll amp up my lecture for you."

She laughed. "Good to know things don't change much."

The sparkle in her eyes made me wonder whether she could be interested in a stodgy PhD student. Why did I have to dress so much like an uptight grad student today?

She ordered a coffee, and I opted for a chai.

"I've never tried a chai before. What's it like?" she asked when we took our seats.

I gaped at her as if she was speaking Latin. *Never tried a chai?* "Uh, it's quite good." I started to laugh. "I'm sorry. I'm not making a very good impression, am I?"

Sarah shook her head seductively. "It's kinda cute actually."

That emboldened me a little. "Here. Taste it for yourself." I handed her my drink.

She took a sip, nodded appreciatively, and then took another sip.

"You can keep it if you want." Again, searing heat seeped into my cheeks, and I thought my skull would crack from the intensity.

"You don't mind?" She raised both eyebrows.

"Not at all."

"What else can I get you to do for me?" she asked in a flirty tone.

"You name it." I hoped I sounded confident, not pleading.

"Hmmm … anything?" She tapped her manicured fingertips on the table, pretending to be deep in thought.

"Shall we start with dinner?" My voice sounded odd, probably because I wasn't breathing as I spoke.

She chuckled. "That sounds like a good start. When?"

This woman didn't mess around. I liked that about her. "Friday?" I asked, accidentally dragging out each syllable.

"Maybe. But first, we should talk about next Wednesday." Her body language switched from seductive to professional.

The giddiness leached out of my body. "Of course," I said with as much conviction as possible. "Hit me with your plan."

She smiled at that and then launched into the program and her role. "A recent study has shown the number of high school graduates who go on to college is declining. Our goal is to help students learn more about their options, including scholarships, work-study programs, and loans since the Great Recession has made it harder for some parents to help out their children by remortgaging their homes or whatnot. And to encourage them to go above and beyond to find ways to seek responsible funding, we want them to get a taste of college life to show them what they'll be missing. We've scheduled a tour, a couple class visits, a lunch with faculty members and student ambassadors, meetings with admissions and financial aid, and we'll even visit fraternity and sorority houses—not parties, of course."

Sarah continued discussing the program and dropping alarming statistics. I could tell she had the spiel down to an art form. And that she truly cared about the kids in her group. "It's a new program, and I hope next year to double the amount of interested students."

I nodded encouragingly all the while imagining her naked.

"What do you think?" Sarah said after her shtick.

I grinned enthusiastically. Not only did I think her plan was excellent, but I wanted to get her to agree to a date. If I thought it would help my cause, I would dip into my trust fund to set up a scholarship fund for the program. It had been a long time since I felt myself this drawn to a woman. And truth be known, it confused the hell out of me. What had happened to the PhD student who preferred being surrounded by books? Now, I was envisioning her legs wrapped around me.

"Sounds great. Sign me up." That was stupid since I'd already agreed for her students to attend my class.

Sarah glanced at her watch. Her wrist was delicate, her skin creamy. "Oh, look at the time. I'm meeting someone in less than an hour." She retrieved a business card and pen from her purse. "Here, this is my cell number. Call me about Friday." With that, she hopped out of her seat and rushed off. I didn't even have time to say good-bye.

I wondered who she was meeting.

CHAPTER THREE

A LITTLE AFTER FIVE, A KNOCK ON MY OFFICE DOOR CAUSED A MILLION BUTTERFLIES TO flutter in my stomach like it was the end of summer, and they knew they didn't have much time left. Via text, Sarah and I had made plans to meet at my office on Friday evening, when she said she had to be on campus anyway. Or maybe she just hadn't wanted me to know where she lived. Not giving out my address was something I would do. We'd only talked that one day and texted a few times, but I got the feeling Sarah was an open book. Not only was I a closed book, but I also had reinforced padlocks securely attached.

"Come in," I called, straightening my hair.

Sarah popped her lovely head around the door. "You ready?" she asked, making it clear we would be vacating my office immediately. Being a grad student meant my office was one of the worst rooms in the history wing, if not the worst room. It was barely larger than a closet and had a fusty, cellar smell. "Of course." I grabbed my jacket. "Where are you parked?"

"Can we take your car? Mine broke down this morning, so my mom had to drop me off." She smiled sheepishly.

"Sure." I motioned for her to take a left down the hallway. "I hope it's nothing serious." Thank goodness I hadn't ridden my bike this morning. I didn't want to smell like dried sweat for my big date. *Big date. Get a hold of yourself, Lizzie.* It was just dinner with a stunning woman. That was all.

She let out a puff of air. "I'm afraid it's time for a new one."

Not knowing what to say, I opened the door to the stairwell and motioned for her to go ahead. We were on the fourth floor, but after descending two flights, I led us down a dark hallway.

"Where are you taking me? This is creepy." She reached for my hand.

"A secret passage. Trust me, nothing will happen to you."

She whirled around. "That's a shame."

I squeezed her hand, and her smile made me wet. I didn't know whether I was coming or going around her. "Right here." I opened a door to another stairwell. Two flights down, another door led to the parking lot and to my car.

"Nice spot!"

"It helps that not many know about that hallway. So don't tell." I flashed my best million-dollar smile.

"Your secret is safe with me. For a price."

I unlocked the door of my Toyota Camry, which had seen better days as the missing hubcap attested, and opened it. "Really? What's your fee?"

"I haven't decided yet." She slid into the seat and shut the door in my face.

I definitely liked her style.

I got into the car and flipped the key in the ignition, immediately regretting it as a voice blasted over the speakers. I tried to punch the eject button on the CD player, but Sarah slapped my hand away.

"What are you listening to?"

"Uh, a book," I said.

Her eyebrows shot so high they almost reached the top of her skull. "Get out!" She continued to swat my hand away. It took some doing, but I was able to turn the volume down all the way. "What book?"

The Rise and Fall of the Third Reich," I said in a tiny voice.

Sarah flashed me a knowing, rather baffling smile. "I like that about you." Without further explanation, she fiddled with the radio. Soon, music streamed through the speakers. I didn't recognize the woman singing, but I was grateful for the distraction. I was certain I was the first woman Sarah had dated who listened to audiobooks in the car, and ones about the Nazis to boot; however, I wasn't brimming with confidence that it created the best impression on a first date.

Somehow I was able to concentrate on driving, even while mortified by the audiobook debacle and her mystifying smile. "Where shall we go?"

"Do you like Vietnamese?"

"I know of a place on Drake."

She slapped my leg. "That's the one I was thinking of." Instead of removing her hand, she left it resting on my thigh.

Luckily, it was a short drive. Having her so near, touching me, was sending my body into a tizzy. I envisioned wrecking the car and her mom having to drive both of us home—probably not the best first impression to make with her mother. Moms didn't like me much. Mine despised me, and my ex's mom had wanted to rip my head off for turning her daughter into a lesbian. I hadn't turned Meg, but I was the first woman she'd introduced to her family. That was pretty much all the experience I had with mothers. Dating had never been very high on my to-do list. I suppressed a chuckle as I imagined such a list: pick up requested items from the library, grade exams, pursue an attractive woman, edit journal article. Truth be told, I was such a dedicated student that even if I did have it on my agenda, it would have been repeatedly pushed to the bottom. Until I met Sarah.

The hostess seated us at a booth in the nearly deserted restaurant that resembled an Asian version of IHOP. Each setting had a paper placemat with a Vietnamese map. The food more than made up for the lackluster interior and harsh lighting.

Frigid temperatures and razor-sharp wind outside had clearly kept most people home. Winter hadn't officially arrived, but someone forgot to inform Mother Nature.

"I swear this place is usually hopping," Sarah said.

I surveyed the room. "Yeah, sure," I said lightheartedly. "I get to pick the next place."

"Next place, huh? Do you always make assumptions on a first date?" Her tone suggested there would be another date, but her dark eyes were harder to read.

A waiter approached to take our drink order.

Sarah winked at me and whispered, "Safe, for now."

That made me smile.

I ordered a Thai tea; Sarah, the house red.

My phone vibrated in the left pocket of my trousers, and my leg jerked involuntarily against the table, nearly spilling my water. I resisted the urge to see who it was. Technology wasn't my thing, and people only called or texted me when trouble was brewing, or in Meg's case, when she needed money. However, I always had my outdated flip phone on, unless I was in class.

"You okay?" asked Sarah, craning her neck over the menu.

I nodded, ignoring the situation to the best of my ability.

Sarah let it go. "Shall we get an appetizer?" she asked with the sincerest look on her face. Was this a test?

I nodded enthusiastically. "Yes, please. It's been a long time since" — I was going to say *since I had a meal that wasn't a sandwich*, but I changed it to — "since I've been here."

She ordered the appetizer combo, which included fried shrimp, two egg rolls, and steamed dumplings. My mouth watered.

My phone buzzed again. This time, I controlled my leg so it didn't whack the table. Right then, Sarah said she needed to use the bathroom. As soon as she was out of sight, I checked my messages. Dr. Marcel had called and texted twice, telling me he had to go out of town for an emergency and asking if I could teach his class on Monday. I quickly responded *yes* and to let me know if he needed anything else. As I punched in the last letter, Sarah was already heading back to the table. I anxiously hit send and surreptitiously slipped the phone into my pocket. I didn't want to give her the impression I was glued to my phone. Ironically, I had only recently learned how to text after Ethan poked fun at my texting incompetence. Luckily, Sarah hadn't seemed to notice.

The waiter arrived with the appetizers, plunked the plate down in the center, and then backed away, bowing subserviently.

"Thanks," I said, unsure whether I should clasp my hands together and bow. *Wait, isn't that a Japanese tradition, not Vietnamese?*

"You trying to solve world peace over there?" asked Sarah. She expertly plucked up a dumpling with her chopsticks and dipped half of it into the soy sauce.

"World peace? No." I smiled awkwardly. "Just trying to remember Asian etiquette."

"You can use a fork if necessary." She tilted her head toward the silverware, missing my point completely.

I laughed. "Do you think I'm a barbarian or something?"

She held another dumpling in the air. "Prove me wrong."

I snapped the wooden chopsticks apart and rubbed the area where they had been conjoined, eliminating any snags, which always bothered me. With my eyes on Sarah, I deftly picked up a dumpling, praying my shaking hands wouldn't betray me.

"There," I said.

"Go on. Dip it." She teased me.

I did, but before I could place it in my mouth, Sarah accidentally knocked over the sriracha hot chile bottle and it rolled into my lap. My dumpling popped out of my chopsticks and hit the table, splattering soy sauce all over my shirt.

"You cheated!" I stabbed the sticks in her direction and then fished the hot sauce from my crotch.

Sarah sniggered. "It slipped." She gave a mock shrug.

"Yeah, right. That was sabotage, pure and simple."

"We should have made a wager." Sarah's wrinkled forehead told me she'd never confess resorting to devious machinations.

"I'd be a fool to bet against you. You have no honor."

"Take that back." She jabbed her chopsticks toward my heart.

"Will not." I parried her sticks with my own as if we were dueling with swords. Sarah bravely fought back.

The waiter began to approach, but then froze, clearly baffled by our childish behavior.

We giggled, and set our weapons aside as the waiter whisked away the rest of the uneaten appetizers without uttering a word. Damn! I was hungry.

"I think we're in trouble," Sarah whispered.

"Totally improper Vietnamese etiquette to have a chopsticks clash at the table." I winked.

Sarah covered her mouth to stifle a snort. The waiter was already hurrying back with our main course, probably in the hope we'd bolt our food down and make a mad dash for our car.

During dinner, the weather worsened. Snowflakes swirled furiously, creating a soupy mess of the sidewalk.

Sarah stared out the window, a dreamy expression on her face. "There aren't many who could get me out on a date on a night like this." She dipped a spoon into her beef rice-noodle soup. I had opted for the beef rice bowl.

"That's Colorado for you. Unpredictable weather. Unfortunately, I can't promise nice weather for our next date either." I clacked my chopsticks in the air, happy that my shakiness was at a minimum thanks to the meds.

"So, there *will* be another date."

Placing my hand over hers, I then pressed it comfortingly. "That, I can promise."

"Now, here's the real test." She narrowed her eyes before continuing. "Shall we get dessert?"

"By all means, or what's the point of going out to eat?"

Her approving nod told me I'd answered correctly. "I like a woman who isn't afraid to eat."

It made me laugh. Sarah was slender, so I was surprised she wanted appetizers and dessert. I had a super-duper metabolism thanks to my Graves' disease, so I could eat everything on the menu and not gain an ounce.

"Ice cream or mini cheesecakes?"

"Why limit ourselves?" I spun around to the waiter and ordered the green-tea ice cream and cheesecake.

His fake smile spoke volumes. He wanted us gone, but he was too polite to say so. Another person kept poking his head out of the kitchen. I got the impression that once we left, they'd close for the night.

With the increasingly nasty weather outside, we didn't linger long after we polished off dessert. When the waiter set the bill down in the middle of the table, we both reached for it.

"You have enough going on with your car. Please, let me pay," I said.

"Only if you let me pick up the next time."

"Okay, but this could be a never-ending cycle." I smiled.

"Would that be a bad thing?" She seemed so relaxed, even though this was our first date. An uncomfortable tightness settled in my chest.

Sarah asked me to drop her off at her mom's, where she was staying until she figured out the car situation. Sitting in the car in her mother's driveway, I suddenly felt like a teenager. "Um …" *Should I say I'll call you?*

Sarah laughed, leaned over, and kissed my cheek. "Thanks for dinner. I'll call you."

The lights outside the house lit up as if it was Times Square. The water droplets on the windshield reflected the lights, making me feel as if I was under the lights in a police interrogation room. "I think your mom knows you're home."

"You think?" She shook her head, smiling. "Seriously, I'll call you."

"Not if I call you first," I yelled after her as she walked to the front door. Sarah circled around and stared for a second before retreating inside. *Really? Did I have to be such a moron all the time?*

I waited for a moment, just in case she forgot something.

She didn't.

The clock on my dashboard said it was eight. Our date was a short one. Was that a good or bad sign? I hunched over the steering wheel to get a better view of the sky. *Stupid snow.*

My stomach grumbled. Putting the car in reverse, I decided to treat myself by stopping at Taco Bell before heading home.

CHAPTER FOUR

TWO WEEKS LATER, SARAH CALLED. WE'D SEEN EACH OTHER BRIEFLY THE DAY WHEN HER students sat in on my class, and we'd exchanged a few texts since our date, but I hadn't heard her voice in over a week. As soon as I did, I relaxed.

"Do you want to get together for coffee on Thursday night?"

"Sure." If she'd asked me to go hunting for crocodiles stark-naked I would have readily agreed.

"I'm so sorry it took me this long to call," she said. "My schedule has been jam-packed. I promise to make it up to you."

She had a sexy phone voice, and I wished I had the courage to ask if that meant I'd be seeing her naked soon. Instead, I replied, "Can't wait."

"Tell me, Lizzie, who knows you better than anyone else?" Sarah asked and then broke off a piece of blueberry muffin and popped it in her mouth. She'd suggested a coffee shop around the corner from my office, a quaint place that reminded me of a cozy kitchen in colonial America rather than a modern-day joint.

Finding the question odd, I took my time answering. "Ethan," I said eventually, with no intention of elaborating. Me, secretive? Absolutely.

"What's he like?" She blew into her mocha latte.

I blurted out, "He doesn't like sex."

Sarah flinched. "Oh, did you two date?"

"What? No!" I blinked several times, trying to delete the mental image from my head. "No, we're just good friends." I tugged on the collar of my wool sweater. "I'm not sure why I spilled the beans about that. It's not like he goes around telling everyone." *Lizzie, stop rambling, you idiot!*

Sarah smiled sweetly. Too sweetly. Like I was a special needs kid.

It was making me uncomfortable. "Usually, I'm pretty good at keeping secrets."

Sarah let out a bark of laughter. "Thanks for the warning."

"I didn't mean it like that. I meant other people's secrets." I yanked my sweater off as casually as possible.

She slid her hand onto my leg under the table. "Getting a little warm?" Her fingers fondled my thigh. "Relax. You aren't in trouble."

"That may be true, but I'm not scoring any points either," I said in all seriousness.

"Are you trying to?" Her eyes twinkled.

"No. I mean yes, but you aren't supposed to know that." I nibbled on my bottom lip and tasted mint Chapstick. I never wore lipstick, but I'd applied some eye shadow and a touch of mascara moments before meeting Sarah.

"Says who?"

She had me there. It was becoming apparent to both of us that dating wasn't my specialty. If I were Sarah, I'd be racking my brain for an excuse to bail, and then I'd change my phone number.

I shrugged.

"I bet if I asked you to cite three reasons why you study history, you would be able to do so without hesitation."

"It's the greatest story —"

She put a palm in the air. "There. Now you're more relaxed."

It was true. All of a sudden my awkwardness had oozed out of me — well, at least 60 percent of it. I wiggled my head, trying to dislodge the other 40 percent. It didn't work.

"How about you? Who knows everything about you?"

"My mom."

I laughed … until I realized she was serious. "Oh, that's cool." My relaxed feeling started to ebb. I couldn't fathom telling my mom my favorite color let alone anything super-duper private. Nerves chewed their way back into my stomach, and I took a long tug of chai to quell them. "Are you hungry?"

Are you hungry? That was the only thing I could think of? I saw a big flashing red sign over Sarah's head: *Mayday! Mayday!* Followed by an image of me hurtling through the sky without a parachute.

Narrowing her eyes, she said, "Yeah, this muffin tastes like sandpaper." She pushed the plate away. "Where would you like to go? My treat."

I waggled a finger at her. "You paid for the drinks. If I remember correctly, you set the rules. It's my turn."

"Nicely played. Maybe you aren't a complete amateur." Color pricked her high cheekbones, and I suspected she hadn't meant to verbalize the second sentence.

I couldn't stop myself from laughing. "Only time will tell. Tell me, do many of your dates stay one step ahead of you? I feel like I'm consistently three steps behind." I leaned closer. "Of course, I like the view."

She swatted my arm. "I can't believe you." Her expression told me I'd finally scored a point. "Just for that, I'm picking the place for dinner."

"Fine by me." I stood and put out my hand to help her up. "Where to?"

Twenty minutes later, the hostess at an Italian bistro led us to a secluded table in the back of a dimly lit romantic hotspot — or so it seemed, since all the tables were filled with couples that only had eyes for each other. Sarah walked in front of me, the exaggerated sway in her step strained the pencil skirt provocatively, doing wonders for my libido. She casually rubbernecked over her shoulder to see if I was enjoying the show. Indeed I was. I hoped my foolish smirk let her know it.

After taking our drink orders, the server left us.

"Do you ever drink?" asked Sarah, placing a linen napkin over her lap.

"Not when I'm driving. One whiff and I'm drunk. On occasion, I enjoy a rum and Coke in the comfort of my own home."

"I'll have to remember that."

"Planning on taking advantage of me?" I asked in my most seductive tone.

"Do I have to? I saw the way you were checking out my ass." Her sexy, almost imperceptible grin made me yearn for more.

"Wasn't that what you were going for?" Two could play at this game.

"Maybe."

A waiter arrived with Sarah's glass of wine and a Coke for me. He announced the specials before waltzing off to take care of other lovebirds.

Sarah studied the menu. "I think I'll get the harvest squash ravioli. You?" She peered over at me.

"Chicken parmigiana."

"Nice. Hope you don't mind, but I plan on tasting it."

"You can taste anything you want."

She bit her lower lip and continued to peruse the menu. "We might be in trouble when it comes to the dessert. Have you seen all the goodies on offer?"

My eyes wandered to the smidgeon of cleavage her silk blouse exposed. "Not yet, but I hope to."

Sarah's eyes flashed downward, and then she slowly raised them to meet mine. "I don't think those are on the menu." She took a sip of her wine, watching me carefully and clearly noticing my disappointment. "Not yet, at least."

Not breaking eye contact, I said, "I think you'll find I'm very patient." It took every ounce of chutzpah to sound convincing. If she'd given me any inkling that I might whisk her out of the restaurant and straight to my bed, I would have pushed everyone over to make haste—even the old lady by the door.

The glint in her eye told me she knew it. The truth was Sarah was unlike any woman I had ever met. I had a feeling I was heading for some serious relationship trouble. She wasn't the type who just wanted a roll in the hay. She was the type who wanted love with a capital L. If I wasn't careful, I could fall prey to her charms.

The whole love aspect was new territory for me, really. Even though Meg and I had been together for a couple of years, we weren't all that lovey-dovey. Maybe in the beginning, but now when I reflected, the memories that popped into my mind were filled with turmoil and fear of her having that drink that'd push her over the edge into the mean-Meg zone. Tipsy Meg was flirtatious and fun. Drunk Meg was a scary, vindictive bitch.

Not that I was completely turned off by love. I wanted it. I mean I *would*—if the mere thought didn't make me want to find a secluded cave to live in for the rest of my days. Yet, when I looked into Sarah's soft eyes, I felt the tug of love.

I washed it away with a healthy dose of Coke.

Our small table was arranged so that Sarah and I sat right next to each other. She placed her hand high up on my leg, settling the panic attack that was forming inside me.

"This could get interesting. Very interesting, indeed," she murmured. Her hand rested between my thighs now, and I wondered if she felt my warmth. I wanted her, no doubt. Sarah was wearing a skirt, and I might have done my own hand inspection if I hadn't had a feeling she wouldn't let me. It wasn't part of her plan, and there was no doubt in my mind she always wanted to hold the winning cards. I was elated, terrified, perplexed. One question kept flitting into my brain: Could Sarah be the one?

I wiped the thought from my mind. It was way too soon for that. Besides, as I'd learned with Meg, people showed their true colors sooner rather than later. *Patience, Lizzie. See where this leads, but don't let your guard down. Ever.*

We finished our meals. "Well, it's that time," she said.

Her teasing smile and squinting eyes made me wonder if she was almost dripping with desire like I was. "What time is that?"

"Time to decide what to devour next." Sarah licked her index finger and then ran the finger over her lips.

At first, I was confused, which was no doubt her intention.

"Oh, dessert," I said, waving at our waiter before requesting a dessert menu. "What sounds good to you?" I asked once the waiter had retreated into the darkness.

"All of it," she murmured, without even glancing at the menu. In fact, I was pretty sure she wasn't talking about dessert. I needed to wrest back some control.

"Then it's decided." I got the waiter's attention again and ordered a sampling of every dessert on the menu.

Sarah didn't speak. She didn't need to. I was scoring points left and right.

"Would you like grappa?" asked the waiter.

"Yes, two please," Sarah answered for me.

I'd never had grappa, but I'd drink gasoline if she asked me to.

It didn't take long for the waiter to return, and I was amazed he was able to fit everything on our quaint little table.

Sarah raised an elegant glass of grappa, waiting for me to reciprocate. "To a chance meeting and to seeing where it goes."

I clinked my glass with hers before taking a sip. The liquor's unpleasant kick made my eyes well up, but I was determined not to show weakness.

Sarah set her drink down and reached for a fork, but I swatted her hand away. "Allow me." I prepared a bite of tiramisu and placed it delicately in her mouth.

"Oooh . . . that's good." She wiped her chin with a napkin.

We sipped our grappa again.

Next, I fed her the crème brûlée. The crack of the burnt top promised greatness, and from the moans coming from Sarah, she was in heaven. So was I.

Again, a sip of grappa.

"I think we need more." Sarah snapped her fingers, making me laugh. The waiter, pouring wine for another couple, watched Sarah point to our grappa glasses and raise two slender fingers. He nodded, not at all upset that she was ordering him about. I had a feeling Sarah got her way with almost everyone. The goofy grin on his face made me want to say, *Easy big fella. She's mine.*

"Shall we wait, or is the triple chocolate cheesecake calling your name?" I prepared a tiny portion.

"Whatever you do, Lizzie, don't stop."

I felt my pussy throb, imagining the same conversation in bed. "Anything for you."

Sarah's eyes rolled up in her head. "Oh, that's the best so far."

The waiter set down two more glasses of grappa and left without saying a word. I planned on leaving him a large tip as a thank-you.

"Well, well, well. What do we have here?" If Meg hadn't been standing right in front of me, I would have recognized her snide tone, even despite the fact that she'd dyed her once-blonde hair a rich, fiery red. "Getting drunk on a school night. Shame on you, Lizzie. What would Dr. Marcel say?" Meg's companion helped her slip into a coat. Hopefully, that meant they were leaving and pronto.

Approximately 150,000 people lived in Fort Collins, and the one person I didn't want to bump into ever, let alone with Sarah, was peering down at us.

"Hello," was all I could force out.

Meg's gaze wandered over Sarah's face and upper body before settling on me. "What happened to only drinking at home?" She crossed her arms.

"I'm afraid I'm a bad influence." Sarah came to my defense.

"I see." An older man tugged on Meg's arm. She wore a tight dress—not her usual jeans and J. Crew sweater. And she was with a man—very unusual. "Have a good night, Lizzie." She turned each Z in my name into a weapon. "Oh, I'll be calling you to discuss that financial situation you brought up last time." She gave Sarah a final glare and rolled her eyes. Red-hot anger raged through my mind and body as I clamped my lips together to keep everything bottled inside. How dare she treat Sarah so flippantly?

I counted to ten before I said, "I'm so sorry."

Sarah's eyes darted across the room to where Meg and her companion were exiting into the darkness. "Is she a friend?"

I snorted. "Former . . ." I'd been about to say girlfriend, but instead added, "acquaintance."

"I'd use another word for her."

I let out a rush of air. "Really? What would that be?"

"Bitch."

"That one works as well." I smiled.

"What financial situation?"

I shrugged. "No clue. It's not like . . . history students are wheeling and dealing." *Accept for the wads of cash I hand over each time Meg texts.*

Sarah eyed me, unsure. "You okay?"

"Absolutely." I forced the fury out of my body.

Sarah placed a palm on my cheek. "Who knew I'd have to protect you on a date?"

"Let's hope that's the first and last time."

"Way back in the day, I was addicted to Tae Bo. I'm sure I'd remember the basics in a pinch." She feigned a jab.

"Maybe you can show me some moves, just in case."

"Honey, I'll show you more than that." She winked, and I was fairly certain it wasn't just the grappa talking.

"Promise."

She kissed my cheek, sealing the deal.

"What about you? Do I have to protect you from any crazies in your life?" I asked.

Sarah started to shake her head, but then blushed. "In high school an ex-boyfriend kept slashing my tires."

"What? Why?"

"I think it was because I dumped him right before prom so I could go with another boy."

"Who?"

"Matt. We dated until I left for college. We're still friends, actually."

"He doesn't mind you're bisexual now."

"Who said I was bi?" Sarah hoisted an eyebrow and crossed her arms, pushing her goodies up in such a way I wanted to rip her clothes off.

"Uh … my apologies. I just assumed—"

She cut me off. "Relax. I'm just giving you shit. But, no, I'm not bi. Once I figured it out—life was so much easier."

I braced for the dreaded "when did you come out?" bonding question.

Instead, Sarah continued. "Matt was a doll when I told him. He gave me a hug and said 'I know.' Whenever we got close to"—she leaned in—"going all the way, I panicked. Once I blurted, 'I need to make cookies for French class' and left poor Mattie with blue balls the size of coconuts and not for the first time." Sarah laughed.

I needed to erase that image from my mind. "What happened with the guy who slashed your tires?"

"Oh him, he left me alone after Matt found out. Matt was the quarterback, and I think the whole team set the jerk right, if you know what I mean."

I wished I had a Matt who could set Meg right.

By the time we polished off the rest of the mini desserts, including a white-chocolate raspberry cheesecake and a cannoli, I was not only stuffed but also sufficiently drunk. I'd lost count, but thought we had two more rounds.

I paid the check and stood, and immediately the room started to spin.

Sarah draped an arm around my shoulders. "You weren't kidding when you said you get drunk fast." Her arm was stronger than I anticipated.

We made it outside, the cold autumn air sobering me up a little, but not enough to drive. Sarah pulled her cell phone out of her purse and made a call. I was too occupied with leaning against the side of the restaurant, trying to stay upright, to hear a word she said.

Was this what it felt like to be Meg—out of control, not caring about those around her? I pushed Meg from my mind. Sarah had her back to me, but from her body language, I could tell she was smiling. Sweet, caring Sarah. Tonight wasn't about Meg—at least I didn't want it to be. *Focus, Lizzie*. Sarah. It was about Sarah. And me. Me and Sarah. If there was to be a me and Sarah now.

"Okay, our ride is on its way. Are you warm enough?" Sarah cupped her hands and blew into them. "It's colder than a witch's tit."

"A witch's tit." The expression broke me out in hysterics.

Sarah giggled at my expense. "Where shall we take you?" she asked.

"Home."

Shaking her head, she laughed again. "I know. Where do you live?" she enunciated.

I told her my address.

Soon, a Cadillac drove up, and Sarah whisked me into the back seat. The woman behind the wheel was the spitting image of Sarah. Realizing it was her mom's car, I tried to sit up straighter and rubbed my eyes with the back of a hand. Sarah slipped into the front seat and told her mom my address.

Streetlights blurred as we whizzed through Old Town as Sarah and her mom chattered like I wasn't in the car. Given the situation, I appreciated Sarah's effort to shield me from further embarrassment. Occasionally, I noticed her mother checking me out in the rearview mirror, and each time I pretended to be riveted with their prattle; however, everything around me was twirling in super slow motion, and I didn't have a clue what they were discussing. I prayed she wouldn't ask me a question. I sensed I had a silly smirk on my face, but try as I might, I couldn't wipe it off.

We had arrived at the restaurant around seven, but when I peeked at my Timex sports watch, I saw it was almost midnight. Thank God it was Thursday, which meant I only had to stumble through one lecture the following day.

When we arrived, Sarah helped me out of the car. Before shutting the door, she said, "I'll be right back, Mom."

I mumbled "Thank you" to her mother, even though I was sure she couldn't hear, since we were already five wobbly steps away from the car.

With one arm wrapped around my waist, Sarah helped me stumble up the stairs. "Where's the kitchen?" she asked when we were inside and tottered off in the direction of my pointed finger as I slumped on the couch. She returned with a Nalgene water bottle I kept in the fridge.

She shook it. "By morning, this should all be gone," she instructed. "Trust me, you'll thank me." With that, she kissed my cheek and said good-bye. I stumbled to my bathroom, peeled off all my clothes, and sat on the toilet—and that was the last thing I remembered.

CHAPTER FIVE

THE BLEEP OF A TEXT MESSAGE JARRED ME AWAKE. I SAT UP IN BED, COMPLETELY NAKED AND befuddled. I wasn't the type to sleep naked, not unless I had company. And I hadn't had company in months. I hoisted the covers off my bed, searching for another naked body. There wasn't one. Rubbing the sleep from my eyes, I tried to piece together what had happened the night before.

I read the text from Sarah: *Are you up, drunkie?*

Drunkie? Murkiness clouded my vision, and no matter how hard I tried, I couldn't shake it. Closing one eye, I was able to punch in the three letters for *yes*. Less than a minute later, the phone rang.

"Morning," I answered. My voice sounded much thicker than normal.

"Good morning. I wanted to make sure you didn't sleep in and miss your class."

"What happened?" I massaged my right temple.

"Grappa."

"Grandpa?" I asked, even more bewildered.

She laughed. "No, grappa. It's an Italian brandy."

Brandy. I didn't drink brandy. Not even the Italian kind.

Then, things slowly started to come back to me. I remembered sitting in a restaurant with Sarah. Meg. And then…

"Oh, God. Your mom." I slapped my forehead.

"No worries. Mom actually thought you were cute, in a drunken buffoon kinda way."

Drunken buffoon! Definitely not the image I wanted to cultivate. "I'm so embarrassed."

"Don't be. It was nice to see you completely relaxed. We may have to do a repeat performance — after you recover, of course."

"You mean I didn't blow it?" I realized too late how pathetic that sounded. With Meg and the grappa, I was shocked Sarah still wanted to meet up again.

"Not one bit. I had a great night." I could hear the smile in her voice. "Do you need a ride to work?"

"Thanks, but I can ride my bike and then pick up my car in Old Town after class."

"You sure you can manage on your bike?"

"I think fresh air will help clear the bubbles in my head." I shook my head, but the movement was unsuccessful in clearing the fuzz.

"Bubbles. Never heard a hangover referred to that way." She laughed. "Don't get sick."

At first I thought she meant don't catch a cold, but the gurgling queasiness in my stomach told me otherwise. "Hopefully I won't. I really can't remember the last time I got soused."

"Soused! I love it. Next time, only virgin daiquiris for you." The playfulness in her voice made me feel better.

"Deal. Thanks for calling."

"Text me when you get to your office so I know you're still alive."

"Will do." The line went dead. It was well after six. Slowly, I made it to the bathroom, holding onto the walls all the way, and carefully stepped into the shower. The hot water revived me, but I was still dreading the bike ride to campus, let alone giving a lecture. Thank God I had all my notes and PowerPoint slides prepared. I stood under the stream of hot water, chanting, "Just get through your lecture." Afterwards, I could call it a day and go back to bed.

"Good morning, Lizzie."

I nodded to Dr. Marcel as we both stood awkwardly in the hallway. He cleared his throat, and I realized he wanted to speak to me. I hoped my voice wouldn't sound as booze-thick as it had when I'd spoken to Sarah earlier. The alcohol had worked its way through my system, but the nausea hadn't. I tilted my head, inviting him to speak.

"If it's okay with you, I would like to sit in on your class today."

"Of course, Dr. Marcel. It would be an honor." Internally, I was screaming my head off. I had thirty minutes until the lecture, so I immediately headed across the quad to the library to fetch a coffee. Normally, I drank chai, but a strong black coffee was in order for today's impending fiasco. While waiting in line, I texted Sarah to let her know I was safe and sound.

Might even have a funny story for you next time we meet up, I added. She responded quickly—with a question mark.

"Here's your coffee." The frazzled student barista set it on the counter. She looked as if her morning had been even rougher than mine, which made me feel somewhat better. At least I wasn't still drunk, as I suspected of her.

I arrived in the lecture room relieved to find more than half of my students in attendance; that wasn't always the case on Fridays. A quick glance revealed Dr. Marcel in the back, along with William and Janice. Janice gave me a boisterous wave and a broad smile that suggested that no matter what I said she'd tell me I'd done a great job.

William, on the other hand, would not be so kind. His body language made it perfectly clear he intended to pounce on any mistake, no matter how slight.

I stifled a groan and waved at Dr. Marcel and Janice, resisting the urge to flip William the bird.

On the blackboard on the side of the stage, I wrote the word EQUALITY in capital letters. Generally, I tried not to write too much on the blackboard. My hands shook as a side effect of my Graves' disease, so my writing was almost always illegible to others. I'd become used to deciphering my chicken scratch out of necessity as a student. Focusing, I did my best to make the word large enough and clear enough for the people in the back row to see.

My watch beeped, alerting me that it was eight o'clock on the dot. "Good morning, everyone. Shall we begin?" I switched on the PowerPoint presentation by pressing a couple of buttons on the high-tech podium. "Today, we'll be discussing the French Revolution and the radical new term that emerged from this time period." I underlined the word on the board.

After a few moments, I forgot about the guests in the back row and fell into my normal lecturing groove. My queasiness subsided, as did the heaviness in my head. Standing in front of my students, giving a lecture, always gave me a natural high. Before I started teaching, I was so shy I never talked in class. But once I was on the opposite side of the lectern, I discovered my passion for teaching. Still, I couldn't deny that preparing for my lectures was the best part of my job. Research was in my blood.

When the quiet beep of my watch alerted me that I only had a few moments left before the end of class, I opened the floor to questions.

John, one of my brightest students, raised his hand.

"Yes, John."

"I'm just wondering, you said even those who believed in equality still tried to justify class differences … I mean, even though they believed people should be equal, they didn't mean all across the board … Was this the genesis of modern-day racism? Without degrees of equality, you can't have racism, right?" He leaned forward and rested his chin on his fist, resembling Rodin's statue *The Thinker*.

If it hadn't been completely inappropriate, I would have kissed John. "What a fantastic question! And very astute of you, I might add. On Monday, we'll be discussing *The Declaration of the Rights of Man* and paying particular attention to the first article. Then, together we can analyze John's question. Did everyone write that down?" There were some moans, but most of the students were too busy gathering their belongings to care. I sighed, but then forced a confident smile. They'd behaved pretty well for a Friday morning lecture, after all. "Have a great weekend."

I started to collect my notes from the podium.

Angela, the annoying eager beaver, who approached me after every class, pirouetted through the exiting students. Her shiny, perfect hair and unctuous smile grated on my nerves.

"Lizzie," she purred. I insisted all of my students call me by my first name.

I raised an eyebrow, doing my best to feign interest. It was obvious she was off her game today and couldn't think of anything clever to say. "Big plans this weekend?" I asked. I glanced over her head and noticed Dr. Marcel gathering the troops. Did I manage to give a halfway decent lecture, or was I doomed? I pictured being lined up outside, blindfolded with a cigarette dangling from my mouth, as the order was given for William to raise his gun…

Angela's giggle brought me back to reality. "Going to read *The Declaration of the Rights of Man*, of course."

It was hard not to laugh in her face. I was a serious student at her age, but never an outright brownnoser. I didn't have to be, but Angela was on the cusp of earning a C, even though she'd made it clear to me on more than one occasion she'd never received a grade lower than a B.

"Don't study too much. It's bad for your health."

Her pinched face was priceless as she tried to figure out what I really meant.

I smiled and she reciprocated.

"I hope you manage to squeeze some fun in this weekend, Angela."

Luckily she realized I was giving her the brush-off. She waved a cheery hand. "Toodles."

Still giddy from the lecture, I parroted Angela, much to her delight, giving her the impression we'd just bonded.

My three guests sauntered to the front. The scowl on William's face was the best news of the day so far. I hadn't screwed up, and Dr. Marcel's glowing countenance confirmed I had knocked it out of the park.

What a relief!

"Well done, Lizzie. Well done." Dr. Marcel patted my back. "How about I take the three of you to breakfast?"

Janice never refused a chance to socialize, even if it meant having breakfast with our elderly teacher. William nodded, although I got the sense he'd rather have a colonoscopy. And Dr. Marcel grinned in a way that made it clear we would be discussing and praising my lecture. Although I hated attention, I also secretly craved it, especially from Dr. Marcel who was more like a parent to me than my own mom and dad. And to be able to watch William squirm in his seat would make it even better. He had to know his turn would be coming soon. Dr. Marcel usually sat in one of our lectures once a semester, but this was the first time Janice and William had accompanied him. I hoped that meant I would be sitting in on William's class, waiting for my opportunity to pounce.

Maybe I should drink grappa the night before every lecture. I made a mental note to thank Sarah —maybe by licking grappa off her entire body.

We sat in a diner across the street, and before I could take a bite of pancake, William said, "I read your article in the *Quarterly*, Lizzie."

I set my fork down so I wouldn't attempt to stab him in the hand knowing he was getting ready to rip my argument to pieces.

"Did you? I must apologize. I still haven't read yours from the previous issue."

Janice stifled a snicker. Dr. Marcel scooped up a massive bite of omelet, oblivious to the tension.

"I must say I'm shocked by your conclusion. That the Boy Scouts and the Hitler Youth both co-opted the Back-to-Nature movement for paramilitary gain. The Hitler Youth, I give you. But the Boy Scouts?" His thin lips curled slightly but still didn't expose his teeth. To this day I still hadn't seen his pearly whites, or were they gnarly gray? What would he do if I attempted to lift up one of his lips with my knife?

"Have you read any of their manuals?"

"Can't say that I have, but —"

"I've read them. Every single one. How do you describe a group that plays games such as cutting the enemy's telegraph wires? Is that not a form of military training?"

We went back and forth until William stabbed his fork in my direction. "I was a Cub Scout and take great offence to your comparison."

"You were a scout in England before World War I?" I asked.

Dr. Marcel laughed. "And here I thought you were decades younger than me William. I didn't know you were old enough to be my grandfather."

Janice tittered.

William cleared his throat. "My father knows the head of the Boy Scouts."

"Of the United States of America. I think you missed that I analyzed the *British* Boy Scouts from their founding in 1908 up until World War One." I almost added, "Willy Boy," but ignored the urge. "Do I need to tell you the dates of World War One? I'll give you a hint, it happened before World War Two, which is your specialty." I tapped my fingers on the tabletop.

A flash of anger lit up his face and eyes.

Janice nudged my foot under the table, and the victorious look on her face let me know I was her hero for the day.

"Does anyone need a refill?" The waiter hefted a pot of coffee.

"I do." Dr. Marcel motioned to his cup, as did Janice. When the waiter left, he said, "Raise your glasses so we can toast Lizzie on her excellent lecture."

Dr. Marcel and Janice clicked their mugs against my orange juice glass. William seethed.

Typically, when William's claws came out, I did my best to maintain some sort of professional composure, but this morning, I let my hair down, so to speak. And it felt great.

"Did you survive the day?" Sarah's voice was a blend of concerned and sexy.

I relaxed into my desk chair at home and gripped my cell phone between my shoulder and my ear. "I did. And actually I should thank you."

"For getting you drunk on a school night?"

"Yes. It relaxed me completely. My professor and colleagues sat in on my class. Sarah, I knocked it out of the park. I wish you could have seen me." I rapped on the table with my pen.

She laughed. "Who knew grappa was your drink?"

I laughed with her. "How about you? How was your day?"

"In-ter-est-ing," she said, splitting the word into pronounced syllables. She sighed dramatically.

"Everything okay?" I was genuinely concerned, which was out of the ordinary for me. Most of the time, I was accused of being overly self-involved.

"Yeah, everything's fine. No reason to worry." Her tone lacked confidence, which of course made me worry more.

In the background I could have sworn I heard a woman's voice say, "Sarah, I need you."

"Hey, Lizzie, can I call you back later tonight? Or will you be sleeping?"

"Either way, call me."

"Okay." The smile returned to her voice. "Talk later."

I couldn't stop my mind from racing. I knew she spent a lot of time with her mom, but the woman sounded much younger. Her mom hadn't said much in the car last night, but I was 98.55 percent sure it wasn't her mother's voice.

So who was it?

Around midnight, Sarah called back, sounding as though she'd just finished a triathlon.

"Sorry for calling so late, but I promised to get back to you," she said.

"No worries. I wish I was with you. I'd put you to bed. You sound exhausted," I said while I scrunched a pillow under my head.

She sighed contentedly. "That would be nice, but don't fret, I'm heading home now."

"Wait? Are you driving?" I bolted up in bed.

"Yes, but I'm using hands-free. I like that, though."

"Like what?"

"That you're worried about me." She sounded so much more relaxed, and I couldn't help grinning.

Finally, I said, "Stay on the phone with me until you get home. I don't want you falling asleep at the wheel."

"Okay, Mom," she said, but I was fairly confident she wasn't peeved.

"Tell me about your day."

"Where to begin? I woke up with a doozy of a headache. Why did you order so many grappas?"

"Me?"

Her giggling soothed me. "You aren't saying I did, are you? I'm a responsible high school teacher. I would never get plowed on a Thursday." She was enjoying herself.

"So, only PhD students do such a thing?" I played along, relieved that she wasn't mentioning Meg. I hoped that was the first and last time Sarah interacted with my ex.

"Seems that way. What other naughty things do you do?"

"Ah, I can't say over the phone. Top secret."

"Sounds promising." I heard her take a deep breath. "I'm home."

"Good. Now I'm ordering you straight to bed."

"Mine or yours?"

I paused, contemplating whether she would be too tired to come over.

"Don't worry, I was just kidding." My pause must have given her the wrong message.

"Too bad. I was trying to decide whether you were too tired or not."

"Really?" She sounded pleasantly shocked. "Maybe we should wait."

I almost blurted out, "Hopefully not too long," but instead said, "Good night, Sarah. Have sweet dreams."

"I will now."

I closed my eyes and imagined Sarah's naked body pressed against mine. My hand slipped into my panties. This was quickly becoming a nightly ritual, and I hoped the real Sarah would be joining me in bed, not just the fantasy.

CHAPTER SIX

"WHY, LIZZIE, YOU SOUND SMITTEN." ETHAN BATTED HIS EYELASHES AT ME.

"Smitten? Please. People like me don't fall in love." I waved him off.

"Interesting. I didn't mention the L-word." Ethan's curious expression unnerved me, or maybe he was hitting too close to home for my liking.

I rolled my eyes. "I just find her fascinating really. I mean, I'm no Don Juan, but she finds my clumsy attempts to woo her charming. For the life of me, I can't figure out why."

He laughed. "Stop trying to figure everything out. You'll drive yourself crazy. Just relax and enjoy."

Two concepts I wasn't familiar with. "But what happens when—?"

He put a palm in the air. "Good Lord! You could talk yourself out of a free cheese sample at a farmer's market."

"Free cheese? Why would I turn down free cheese? Is it not sanitary? No toothpicks?"

Ethan shook his head as if he was trying to determine whether I was a Martian. "What's wrong with you?"

I slapped the table. "That's what I'm telling you! What happens when Sarah looks at me like you're doing now?" I frantically circled my finger in front of his face.

He attempted to swipe his confusion away with his palm. It didn't work. "Just be yourself. So far it's working for you."

I nodded, even though I could detect a hint of caution in his tone. Be myself. I could try that for a bit. First time for everything. At first, with Meg it was easier, since she expected me to be a scholar first and foremost. And she was all about Meg. When things got bad, I spent more time concentrating on every word I uttered since Meg had become a pro at twisting everything and turning innocent words into an insult. Once, during a cold snap, I mentioned her lips were so blue she looked like a Smurf. Meg pounced and said I was making a dig about needing to drink to cope with her depression. To this day, I still can't wrap my head around that one.

Sarah was much less threatening, but I had a feeling she wanted to get to know the real me. Delve into my deepest desires, wants, needs, and fears—that thought stopped me dead.

Ethan leaned closer. "My advice is hold onto her. You won't find many who find such a clueless person endearing." He hooted.

"Thanks, buddy. *You* don't mind my company."

"True, true. Somehow I manage to make it through our weekly chats." He kicked my foot and grinned. Then he took a sip of coffee. "How are your seminars going?"

"Good, except for William."

"He still gunning for you?" He mimicked firing a gun with both hands, adding machine-gun noises.

"Every chance he gets. I swear that guy won't stop trying to destroy me until he's dead. Last week he attempted to tear apart my journal article in the *European History Quarterly*."

"You've definitely made an enemy of him."

"I didn't do anything!"

Ethan chuckled. "You sounded just like a squirrel. William will never accept that Dr. Marcel chose you over him. I'm sure he's convinced you used nefarious tricks, maybe even sex."

Why did everyone insert sex or sexual references into everything lately? It was tiresome. No wonder I preferred books.

I crinkled my nose, ignoring the last statement. "Nefarious tricks. I've published and co-written twice the amount of articles he has since we started our program."

"He doesn't see it that way. He's a Thornhill, and Thornhills always get their way. It was probably the first time he'd failed."

"Second."

Ethan quirked an eyebrow.

"Janice found out he wasn't accepted into Oxford's program."

"Really?" Ethan's pitch spiked to a near operatic level. "I remember when he introduced himself to me years ago, before I could say my name he had explained why he was in Fort Collins for school."

"Dr. Marcel?"

"You got it." He tilted his cup in my direction.

Dr. Marcel used to teach at Harvard. He was one of the top professors in the field, if not the top. However, his wife grew tired of Massachusetts' brutal winters and sweltering summer humidity, so they moved here. It was quite the coup for our school.

"I got the same spiel. He tells it to everyone. I've wondered if he has it recorded on his phone so he doesn't have to waste a breath on low-life academics like us. It's hard to tell whether he's actually talking." I mimicked the weird thing William did with his lips.

Ethan burst into laughter. "Every time I spoke with him, I used to watch his lips. I never saw them moving. Not once! Does he have teeth?"

"It must be exhausting expending so much energy to look like one isn't expending any."

Ethan shrugged. "I don't think it's much fun being William."

"Probably not. It's not much fun being the one he's always gunning for, either."

"Be careful. He's the type who'll shoot you in the back."

"At least I'll get a couple of weeks of peace and quiet soon during our research break—the best part of grad school. No classes so we can focus on our semester research projects."

Ethan leaned back in his chair. "I do miss it. While you'll be in hog heaven, my in-laws are coming." His pained expression made me laugh.

"Not looking forward to it?" I teased.

He shook his head. "Relationships do have some downsides: in-laws being at the top of most people's lists. When are you going to introduce Sarah to the fam? It's so much fun." He let out a fake squeal and clapped his hands together.

"Ha! It worked so well last time."

He tutted. "Well, the relationship is still new, so probably best not to make plans." He knew full well the idea hadn't crossed my mind.

I thought of Meg and how she'd used her knowledge of my family, especially the money, against me. Not that Ethan knew that.

As if in tune with my thoughts, he smiled. "It might be a bit early to show Sarah where you came from. Don't half of the Denver Broncos live in your neighborhood?"

I shrugged. "And a few hockey players."

"Any movie stars?"

"Nah. I think they have vacation homes in Aspen, not on the outskirts of Denver."

"You and William have a lot more in common than you like to think."

"Am I as much of an asshole?"

"It depends on the day." He winked to soften the blow.

It didn't.

CHAPTER SEVEN

It was a relief when the research break ended. Usually, I loved my alone time and used it to concentrate on the nitty-gritty aspects of my dissertation, but this time being away from everyone and everything had been lonelier than normal.

To make matters worse, I didn't see Sarah once. We spoke on the phone most days, but I swear her calendar was fuller than the president's. If she wasn't coaching or attending meetings, she was tutoring underprivileged kids or stepping in as the faculty member for the school's gay group. Her latest kick was volunteering at a food bank with some of her high school students. And it wasn't like I could make a stink about that. I loved Sarah's drive, but shit, where did I fit in?

I closed my eyes and pretended I was sitting on the couch with Sarah, nestling my head on her shoulder. Her intoxicating jasmine perfume filled my nostrils.

An annoying voice ended the daydream.

"All she did was party and eat." William flipped through the pages of his copy of *Berlin Diaries* by Marie Vassiltchikov. It was Tuesday evening, and I was sitting in my Daily Life in World War II reading seminar. "I don't see the merit in reading this." William hardly ever saw the merit of any book we read. This was one of the negative aspects of academia. Everyone wanted to "uncover" a diary, letter, or any type of evidence to shed new light on subjects that had been put through the scholarly wringer. So when something new came out, most academics jumped all over the author because more than likely it'd refute their own theories. I wished one of Dr. Marcel's books was on the list to see if he had the balls to tear into it per usual.

Dr. Marcel shifted in his seat, smiling but not yet ready to speak.

I twisted back to William. "How would you survive the war?"

"You think she was partying to survive?" William tsked skeptically. "She was a spoiled brat."

Takes one to know one, I thought. "I do. She was a white Russian living in Berlin under the Nazis. It wasn't like she had a lot of options. She couldn't go back to the Soviet Union because the Reds were in charge and she was an aristocrat. Due to her background, she knew a lot of wealthy and important people in Germany, so naturally she went to their gatherings and parties. She used that to her advantage. There were bombings, firestorms, and food shortages. Considering what methods others took, I don't understand your vitriol against her." I stopped, but then another thought struck me. "And she was working for the resistance and knew about—or maybe was involved in— the plot to assassinate Hitler. Would you have the guts to do that, William?"

He gawped at me, and then his eyes narrowed. "Oh, please." He waved a dismissive hand. "She cared more about name-dropping than about killing Hitler. This book is all about her."

I shook both hands in the air, imagining wringing his skinny neck. "It's her diary!"

"I think Lizzie's onto something," Janice said in a calm tone. "At first, I got tired of her name-dropping, but then I started to put the pieces together. Even if you don't like her, you have to admit she provided a wonderful glimpse into civilian life in Berlin during the war." Janice was the only other student in the seminar. If it weren't for William, the vibe would have been cozy and educational rather than confrontational. William was dead set on holding the opposite opinion to me. If we'd discussed *Mein Kampf*, would he insist it was wonderful and well written since I would be the one tearing it to shreds? I kept hearing Ethan's machine-gun sounds in my head.

William snorted. "You're just as bad as Lizzie — so practical you think everyone else is practical."

Janice and I exchanged an amused smile.

"What do you mean?" I asked.

William placed a palm on the table. "What I mean, Lizzie, is that you don't have any human emotions. You think like a robot, and you think everyone else is as logical as you. Do you remember our movie conversation?"

Janice bristled for me. "Something tells me you're mad about another thing, Willy Boy." She pinned him with a glare and jerked her head in Dr. Marcel's direction. Janice had also applied to work with our professor. Unlike William, she didn't hold any grudges.

"Are you talking about *Casablanca* … weeks ago?" I asked, stunned.

Why was he still thinking about that? I knew he considered himself a lot like Bogie. Had he taken it as a personal slight? I'd only stated what I would have done, speaking theoretically and pragmatically. Sometimes it was hard not to think like a historian. Hindsight's twenty-twenty.

"We all know why you're opposed to love, don't we?" William sneered.

Even though I tried to keep the tittle-tattle about my relationship with Meg to a minimum on campus, college campuses were rife with gossip and backstabbing. After the breakup, Meg had been forced out of the program. Soon after, she'd entered rehab. She'd never outright blamed me, but she'd never come to my defense either. Me, I stayed mute on the subject, which only made it look worse. No one except Janice knew how hard I'd tried to keep Meg off booze. No one knew about all the nights I'd held her and all the times I'd copped her abuse. Meg was a mess. I'd done everything I could, including getting her into rehab and paying for it, but I could never tell others what it was like behind the scenes, both out of respect for Meg and, truth be told, also out of embarrassment. What I'd put up with made my skin crawl, even today.

"You just love ruining academic careers, don't you?" William continued.

"That's enough!" Janice's glare suggested she wanted to rip his head off and shove it down his puckered mouth. "I'm so tired of your whining. You think Vassiltchikov was bad. You've been moping ever since Dr. Marcel made his choice. Get over it. If you can't, get out. In every discussion you try to humiliate Lizzie. It's time to let it go. It's been over two years. Get the fuck over it!" She slapped the table.

I pivoted to Janice, my mouth hanging open. She was usually so laid-back, not the type to throw down the gauntlet. Her face was beet-red, and she inhaled deeply, trying to regain her composure.

Our usually silent professor let out a puff of air as he drummed two fingers against his lips. His teaching method involved getting the ball rolling during the first few minutes of class and then sitting back to let us work our way through the discussion. Half the time we bickered about what we thought was relevant or pure drivel.

William's eyes burned with rage. "I don't know what you're talking about. I'm trying to engage you two in dialogue." By the end of the sentence, his voice was barely a whisper.

Dr. Marcel cleared his throat. "I think that's enough for this evening."

Janice stormed out of the room. As I packed my books and notebook into my bag, Dr. Marcel said, "William, do you have time to talk?"

I didn't have to study William's face to sense his resolve wilting.

"Yes. Of course, sir."

I left the room silently, without my usual adieu to Dr. Marcel.

Janice stood outside, opening a pack of cigarettes. She wiggled the box, asking if I wanted one.

I shook my head. "No thanks. I don't smoke." Janice, of course, knew that.

She lit hers and took a long, angry drag. "He's such a fuckstick."

"Has been from day one," I said. "Dr. Marcel is talking to him now, I think."

She blew a puff of smoke out her nostrils. "Really! About time. Don't let him get to you. I was friends with you and Meg." She studied me cautiously, knowing the topic made me uncomfortable. "I know you did everything you could for her."

Avoiding her gaze, I responded with a non-committal shrug.

"Have you seen her lately?" Janice flicked her cigarette.

"Just last week, unfortunately." I focused on the ash floating in the air, thinking of all the money I'd given to Meg disappearing into a black hole.

"I saw her yesterday. Not a fan of the red hair, and what's up with the black fingernail polish?" She took another hit, released the smoke, and said, "Looks like a prossie."

"Prossie?"

"You need a one-a-day calendar from the *Urban Dictionary*. Prostitute."

My opinion of Meg wasn't very high, but prostitute? No way. My belly growled, causing both of us to laugh.

"Do you have plans for dinner?" I asked.

She noted the time on her watch and then dropped her cigarette on the ground and pulverized it with her shoe. "Shit! Collin's in town, and I'm late for our date." She laughed and then sang, "I'm late for a *very* important date," and scurried away, reminiscent of the white rabbit from *Alice in Wonderland*. It was a relief to see her back to her normal self.

William stormed out of the glass doors, saw me, paused, and then waltzed off in the opposite direction, holding his torso ramrod straight instead of his typical end of day slouch.

Sighing, I walked to the bike rack and freed my Cannondale. It was a cold night, and for the first time in a long time I wished I'd driven my car that morning. I briefly wondered whether Sarah would come and get me, but the fear of her being with someone else held me back. Lately, every time I called, I got the impression she wasn't alone. There weren't any more voices in the background, but intuition told me to be wary. I sensed Sarah was being overly cautious about what she said and how she acted. Like she wasn't alone. I wasn't sure what to think about that. Besides, she was still having issues with her car.

"Get moving and stop feeling sorry for yourself," I snapped.

CHAPTER EIGHT

"WAIT, ARE YOU TELLING ME YOU WOULD RATHER BE WITH THE OTHER GUY THAN HUMPHREY Bogart?" Ethan covered his mouth with a palm as though he was trying to trap more shocked words inside.

The altercation with William still rankled. Stupidly I'd brought it up during our coffee date. Ethan honed in on the *Casablanca* part, not the Meg aspect, which was a relief, to some degree.

"And stay in Casablanca and be with a guy who owned a bar that's controlled by the Vichy and swarming with Nazis and Italian fascists? Are you kidding me?" I crossed my arms.

"What about love?" Ethan said.

"What about surviving?"

"What's the point of living without love?"

I sighed.

Ethan's smirk widened. "You know, you're Sally."

Sally?

What was he talking about? I motioned for him to fill me in, too exasperated to verbalize it.

"*When Harry Met Sally.*"

"Who are Harry and Sally?" I crinkled my nose as if Harry and Sally had body odor.

Ethan rolled his eyes so hard I thought they might roll right out of his head. "Seriously? You haven't seen that movie?"

"Is it a new release?"

"Uh, no. It's a classic."

"What year? I love classics." I sat up straight in my seat, like I did in class.

Ethan rubbed his chin. "I don't know. The eighties."

I laughed. "The eighties. That doesn't count as a classic! Sorry."

He waved his hand, dismissing me. "In the movie, Harry and Sally get into a discussion about *Casablanca*, and Meg Ryan, who plays Sally, says she would rather leave with the other guy instead of staying in Casablanca with the guy who owns a bar. She claims women are more practical than that."

"I'm not getting your point."

"You have to see the movie to get the counterargument."

I let out a huff of angry air. "Can't you just fill me in?"

"Okay, but you may not like it."

"Try me." I waved him on.

"Billy Crystal's character—he plays Harry—says he understands and his theory is … that Sally hasn't had great sex."

"And?"

"And what?"

I slapped the tabletop. "What does that mean?"

"Sex? Geez, do I need to get out the dolls or something?"

I shook my head angrily. "How does that apply to me?" I enunciated each word carefully.

"You really are clueless about some things, aren't you? I'm just saying you should be careful telling people you'd leave Humphrey Bogart in the dust for a passionless marriage. People might think you're more frigid than you really are."

"They'll think I'm a Sally." Realization slowly seeped in. Oddly, Ethan was way more comfortable talking about sex than I was. It seemed everyone was lately. Or maybe I was just noticing it more since meeting Sarah. I was pretty good about tuning people out when they ventured into topics I'd prefer to leave unsaid. Since Sarah, though, everything was reminding me of intimacy, and I'd been entertaining way more sexual fantasies than I ever had with Meg.

"Exactly! Most people our age have probably seen *When Harry Met Sally*. Not sure about *Casablanca*."

"Oh, come on. *Casablanca* is a classic!"

"It is. How many times have you seen it?"

"I don't know, half a dozen or more. I own the DVD."

Ethan eyeballed me. "Interesting. And each time you think she should leave?"

I nodded without any hesitation.

"Good Lord. That makes me worry about you."

"Why?" I raised my shoulders.

"I don't know how to explain it. How do you explain love to someone who doesn't feel love?"

"Doesn't feel love." I scoffed. "I understand love."

"Understand?" he asked.

I curled my lips. "What do you know anyway? Need I remind you that just the thought of sex and all the fluids makes you cringe?"

He jutted his chin before waving my diversionary tactic to the side. Damn.

"How did you feel about Meg?" He leaned in.

"Let's not talk about her, okay? Look how that ended." I pushed my chair back.

He nodded knowingly. "So, you would rather steer clear of love to avoid getting your heart trampled on again."

"I'm not avoiding love."

"When's the last time you saw Sarah?"

I paused and ran a mental check through my calendar. "Uh, last week, briefly." It was longer than that.

"I thought you liked her."

"I do."

"But not enough to pursue?" He turned his head to the side.

"What? No," I said too quickly. I was embarrassed to admit that Sarah was the one who was playing hard to get, not me. When we talked, everything seemed okay, but getting her schedule to match mine was almost as complicated as cracking the German code during World War II. "I like Sarah, I do. She's beautiful, smart, funny, and caring."

"But?"

"I think she's seeing someone else." The sentence slipped out.

"What?" Ethan's brow furrowed.

"Once when we spoke on the phone, a woman in the background said, 'Sarah, I need you,' and it was a young voice, not her mother's."

"Her mother?" He looked confused.

"She and her mom are really close." I raised my hands, indicating go figure.

"Don't read too much into what you heard. Just because she was with another woman doesn't mean they're dating. Normal people have friends." He stressed the last sentence for me.

I ignored his comment about normal people. "What if, though? We only see each other occasionally. For all I know, she could be dating tons of women."

Ethan ignored my comment and placed his hand on my arm. "Let it happen. Call her. Don't let that mind of yours ruin something before it has a chance to really start."

I had been calling her. And texting. All to no avail. Of course I would never tell Ethan that. That was why I avoided getting close to people. It opened me up to feeling like there was something missing when the other person was absent. I hated that feeling. It made me lonelier than when I was alone.

Later that afternoon, I sat at my desk in my apartment with my cell phone in front of me and contemplated Ethan's advice. Should I call Sarah and insist on a date? Okay, maybe not *insist*, but ask. Plead? Get down on my hands and knees?

Each time I reached for the phone, I stopped.

"This is bloody ridiculous," I muttered to myself. "Just call her."

Still I hesitated.

I decided to flip a coin. Heads I would. Tails I wouldn't.

It came up tails.

So I called her. Screw the damn coin.

"Lizzie, it's so good to hear your voice." Her welcoming tone put me at ease right away. "How've you been?"

"Same old, same old," I said as breezily as possible. "The life of a grad student is so exciting. Sleep, study, sleep, study."

"What about eating?"

"I do occasionally." I laughed, thinking of the many sandwiches I consumed daily.

"You need someone to take care of you. How about we grab dinner later this week?" She paused.

I gathered she was checking her calendar, and I tried to block out the fictitious female names that appeared on each day. "Would Friday work? Just in case we get drunk?" She giggled.

"Sounds great. See ya Friday."

"That, you can count on." Her voice implied "and then some," and a pulsing I hadn't felt in a long time stirred through my body. I set my phone down and inhaled and exhaled several times to steady my whizzing throb.

CHAPTER NINE

On Friday afternoon, I received a text from Sarah: *I'm beat. Can we do takeout and a movie at your place instead?*

I was surprised she still wanted to see me if she was that exhausted, but I wasn't going to argue. I missed her. That thought alone made me shake my head. If Ethan knew, he'd be fluttering his eyelids and saying some cockamamie thing about being smitten.

Around six, I heard a soft knock on my front door, and my skin sizzled as if I'd just fallen into a geyser at Yellowstone. Was that what love felt like: hot, beyond painful, and terrifying?

"Can you believe this weather?" Sarah kissed me on the cheek and walked in.

I stuck my head out the door. The rain was now a slushy snow. Within a few hours the roads wouldn't be drivable, the moisture on them freezing under the snow.

"Huh, hard to believe. It was sunny a few hours ago." I watched the snow fall until I remembered that Sarah was standing right behind me, upon which I slammed the door shut immediately, as if afraid she'd dash out of the place in protest at my rudeness. "Here, let me take your coat."

She spun around and I eased it over her shoulders. "Would you like some tea or hot chocolate to warm up?"

Her nose resembled a red button on a snowman.

"Yes, please. Hot chocolate." She rubbed her hands together. "I had to park over in the next lot. It seems everyone is tucked in for the weekend."

"Did you get a new car?"

"I borrowed my mom's." She avoided my eyes. Was she embarrassed about her car woes?

"I ordered pizza, but maybe I should order Chinese or something for the rest of the weekend."

"Yes. Or we'll starve!"

I eyed her questioningly, until I realized I'd said the Chinese bit out loud. I hadn't been thinking about the two of us. Then it dawned on me—the storm meant it would be safer for her to stay the night. From the increasing size of the flakes, Sarah might be here all weekend. I smiled foolishly.

"Okay. Let's go to the kitchen, get your hot chocolate going, and find some takeout menus to peruse."

She nodded and led the way to the kitchen. I barely remembered the night she'd practically carried me in here after the grappa incident, but her recollection seemed much clearer.

Soon the kettle whistled. Sarah leaned against the counter, examining a Chinese menu as if her life depended on it. It might. Before she glommed on to the menus she'd inspected my fridge and cupboards and found them entirely lacking, except for sandwich ingredients, hummus, and fruit.

"Do you only eat sandwiches?" she asked, still studying the menu.

"Or takeout."

She extracted her cell phone from the back pocket of her jeans and dialed. "Yes, I'd like to place an order ... for takeout ... oh, how much? Okay." She rolled her eyes at me and then rattled off my address. I was amazed she had it memorized. She ordered more food than I would have; it would take us days to eat it all.

I tried to stop my eyes from widening at her list of dishes, worrying I would get a headache from the strain.

"Wow! I'm putting you in charge of ordering from now on," I said when she ended the call. "It might be easier next time if you say *the entire menu, please.*"

She laughed. "I know you can eat. Better to be safe than sorry. And it's my favorite takeout place in town. Can you believe they're charging a fee for delivering in a blizzard? He said ours was the last order they were accepting. Apparently the roads will be closed by nine."

"Blizzard? Is it going to be that bad?"

Sarah whacked my arm. "Don't you follow The Weather Channel? They say we're expecting two feet."

"Why would I follow The Weather Channel?" I handed her a steaming mug of hot chocolate. Each day I peeked outside and assessed the weather. Of course, Colorado's weather was fickle. The saying was: don't like the weather, wait ten minutes and it'll change. So why bother following it when conditions would invariably change anyway?

Sarah didn't bother to answer. Instead, she bolted for the front room, responding to a faint knock on the door. "How did they get here so fast?" she asked.

"I think it's the pizza I ordered." I tried to hide a smile.

She smacked her forehead.

Sure enough it was. A boy barely old enough to shave stood on my front stoop with three large pizza boxes and several smaller containers of chicken wings, garlic bread, and cinnamon treats. "Forty-one bucks." He sounded pissed.

I gave him fifty. "Keep the change."

A brief smile crossed his face, but he sighed as he turned back to the near whiteout conditions. No wonder the Chinese place was charging extra. Capitalism at its best.

"And you said I ordered a lot." Sarah took the containers off the top of the pizza boxes, allowing me to see. "What did you get?"

Without waiting for a reply, she headed back to the kitchen. "Good thing your fridge is nearly empty; we'll have room to store all this."

"And you have to stay until it's gone." I had no clue why that slipped out, but I immediately felt like an idiot for saying it. Usually, I liked my alone time. But the longing in Sarah's eyes pushed those thoughts out of my mind making it clear that my head wasn't in control tonight.

"That sounds nice. I've missed you." Without further ado, she flipped open the boxes.

I handed her a plate, watching in amazement as she stacked four slices on it. "And I thought *I* ate a lot," I said.

She grinned guiltily. "I haven't eaten much this week, what with work and …" She avoided my gaze and didn't finish.

"Are you okay?"

Her eyes glistened with tears. "It's been a rough week."

I encircled her in my arms, and she rested her head on my shoulder. "You don't have to talk, but I'm here."

Her arms tightened around my waist, but she didn't try to speak, and I didn't force her to. We had all weekend, hopefully. Besides, I wasn't the type to pry.

After we carried our plates to the front room, Sarah powered up the stereo and dug some CDs from her purse. "I hope you don't mind, but I'm not in the mood for audiobooks." She winked.

"I won't give up, you know. I'll convert you yet."

Taking the CDs from her, I selected one at random. There wasn't any indication of the band name, just a date: May 10, 2011. I took that as a promising sign. What can I say? I was that much of a history nerd.

We settled on the couch, and I chomped into a slice of cheese pizza. Sarah regarded her plate with disinterest, as if her appetite had slipped away from the sand like a wave returning to the ocean. I set my slice down and took her hand in mine. "Talk to me. What's wrong?"

A floodgate opened, wetting her cheeks, but after a while she sucked in air and sobbed. "I'm sorry. It's just been a horrendous week. One of my students tried to kill herself."

I hugged her, unsure what to say — if anything.

"We're trained to see the signs, but no one noticed a thing. And I'm really close to her. I feel like such a failure." We both sank back into the couch where I rocked her gently, completely at a loss. Sarah didn't seem to mind. She held me back, tightly, and then, moments later, leaned away and wiped her eyes with a paper napkin.

"Do you want something to drink?" I asked lamely. "Something stronger than hot chocolate?"

Her eyes brightened. "Oh, I picked up some wine. And rum and Coke for you." She reached for her handbag, which was more like a piece of luggage, and hauled out the loot. "What do you say? Will you get drunk with me?"

"How can I refuse?" I said, rising to get some glasses.

"I'm surprised you actually have wineglasses," she said, when I returned from the kitchen holding a wineglass and my concoction. The look that flashed across her pretty face made my pulse quicken.

"I'm not a complete Neanderthal. I just don't cook." I picked up one of the bottles. "I even know how to use one of these." I held up my corkscrew.

"Knowing how to screw is important."

I flashed her my I-can't-believe-you-just-said-that smile.

She saluted with her wineglass as a thank-you. "This will help me some, but tell me what's new with you to get my mind off things."

"Have you seen the movie *Casablanca*?" I asked.

She scrunched her forehead. "Yeah, why?"

I told her about my confrontation with William. It paled in comparison to her story, but it was all I had, and I was feeling put on the spot. Since Meg, my life had been uncomplicated—just the way I wanted it to be. Or so I'd thought.

"Seriously? You wouldn't stay with Humphrey Bogart?" she asked.

I kicked myself for entering the *Casablanca* fray yet again.

"Don't say it." I put up my palm for emphasis.

Sarah cocked her head. "Say what?"

"Don't call me a Sally?"

She laughed. "A Sally? What are you talking about?"

I studied her face to see if she was holding back. "So, you haven't seen it either?" I shook my head, victorious. Ethan didn't know jack shit.

She placed a hand on my thigh. "What in the world are you going on about?"

"*When Harry Met Sally*," I said in all seriousness.

"Of course I saw *that*. Years ago, but what does this have to do—?"

It was as if I could see the thought invade her mind. She covered her mouth in a weak attempt to suppress laughter.

"Did William call you a Sally?"

I blanched at the thought. "No, thank God. Ethan did, when we had coffee last week. Now my best friend and my colleagues think I've never had great sex." In the beginning, sex with Meg was satisfying. It wasn't until her drinking became uncontrollable that every relationship aspect besides caregiver was left in the dust.

"Colleagues. You talk about your sex life with colleagues?" Her sour expression screamed *danger*!

"No," I waved both hands in the air. "The conversation got out of hand, but I nipped it in the bud. I don't even discuss it much with Ethan, my best friend."

"Is Ethan the one who . . .?" She seemed unsure how to continue.

"Yes. He's the one who can't stand bodily fluids."

For some reason that made her laugh. "And he thinks you aren't good in bed. Oh, that's rich."

"Hey now. Don't put those thoughts in my head."

She kissed my cheek, taking me by surprise. "Wait ... you haven't seen *When Harry Met Sally?*"

Taken aback that she'd disengaged to ask me about a silly movie from the eighties, I shook my head.

"Next time, we have to watch it."

"We can tonight. I picked up a copy to figure out what Ethan was talking about."

Sarah squealed with delight. I had high hopes she would squeal much more later, but I knew I had to go slow. She was still not her normal bubbly self.

"You know, ever since the first time I met you, I thought you were a bit clueless."

Clueless? Was she trying to compliment me?

"Uh…"

"Don't worry. I think it's endearing."

That relieved me a little.

"And then there's that smile of yours."

"What smile?" I knew I was smiling, but I couldn't help it.

"That one!" She placed a hand on my cheek. "I love that smile."

An uncomfortable silence hung between us.

I sipped my rum and Coke, while Sarah stared at my bookshelf across the room. Finally, she asked shyly, "What's your dissertation on?"

I paused, taken aback by the abrupt change of subject. "The Hitler Youth."

"The what?"

"The Hitler Youth. Nazis' version of the Boy Scouts."

"Oh, that explains it."

"Explains what?"

"Why you have so many books with swastikas on the covers." She waved at my bookshelves. "I have to admit, it's off-putting at first. I wasn't sure about you when I strolled in that first night."

"Ah." I refilled her glass. "Before I invite another woman over, I'll need to do a de-Nazification sweep of my apartment." I laughed; she didn't.

Her pinched face and tense shoulders told me I had screwed up again—or was she thinking of her student? Dating was a minefield. Afraid to ask what she was thinking, I thought over what I'd just said, hearing my own words again and understanding how she might have taken them. No wonder I was single. I lacked charm, conversational skills, and panache. A rattlesnake probably had more dating smarts. Was there a Dummy's guide for surviving dating?

Sarah must have felt sorry for me, because she asked, "How many women have you had since the big breakup?"

"Big breakup?"

"Just a guess, but I think I'm right, considering you're hedging." She winked.

I spoke into my glass. "None."

"Was it that woman from the Italian place?"

I squirmed in my seat, neither confirming nor denying.

"How long ago did the relationship end?" she asked.

"Over a year."

"And you haven't had…?"

I had to laugh. "You're inquisitive … and feisty. I like that about you."

That softened her up a little.

"What else do you like?" she asked.

Oh, God. I was going to have to try to stay one step ahead of her, or she'd eat me alive. "Ha! Smooth!" I leaned over, one inch from her face. "You're beautiful, intelligent, and you have extremely soft lips."

She didn't pull away. "How do you know? About the lips part? We haven't kissed."

Our mouths were almost close enough to smooch. I hesitated. Sarah beamed, daring me. I went for it. Her lips were soft and moist, and I could taste the wine on her tongue.

The doorbell rang and I broke away awkwardly. "The Chinese is here," I said. "I mean, the food is here."

The odd expression in her eyes made it hard for me to determine whether she was impressed by our kiss; I was, but I sensed my opinion didn't really matter. In this instance, only Sarah mattered.

During the transaction at the door, Sarah stood right behind me, so close I could feel her body heat. It was exhilarating.

"Thanks, lady!" the young man said when I told him to keep the change. Math wasn't my strong suit, so I always erred on the side of caution.

"What do you say? Shall we skip the pizza, since it's probably cold by now?" I said.

She nodded enthusiastically. I had to admit the aroma of the Chinese food was making my stomach cartwheel in anticipation.

"Pizza is perfect for breakfast," Sarah said as I directed her to the dining room.

"Would you like some silverware?" I asked, setting chopsticks next to my place setting; I'd prepared the table for us both earlier, even if only for pizza.

"Wait, are you going to use chopsticks?" She placed her hands on her hips.

I struggled to interpret her body language. "Uh, yeah. Unless you would prefer I use Western silverware."

"Western silverware!" She let out a snort of laughter. "Do you always talk like that?"

"Like what?"

"A teacher."

"I am a teacher."

The most beautiful grin spread across her face. God, did she know how sexy she was?

"Besides, you're a teacher," I pointed out, needlessly. Of course she knew she was a teacher. That was how we'd met, after all.

Sarah tipped her head in agreement. "I'm just impressed; that's all." She took her seat. "I've been on dates with people who wouldn't even try using chopsticks in a Chinese restaurant, and here you are using them in your own home."

I mentally ticked another point in my favor and then motioned for her to dig in.

"So, did you rush home and clean this place after my text?" She placed a linen napkin in her lap.

Shaking my head, I replied, "Nope. Why? Is it a mess?" I dished out egg-fried rice.

"Your apartment is always this clean?" Her eyes bulged as she took in the room. "There's not a speck of dust, and the surfaces in your kitchen have a Mr. Clean shine."

"Oh, that. I'm a bit of a neat freak." I laughed nervously. "I can't take the credit. Miranda"—I noticed her eyebrows join in confusion—"my cleaner does all the work a few times a week," I added hastily.

"You have a housecleaner?" She didn't try to hide the incredulous inflection in her tone.

"Uh, yeah." I shrugged. "Is that bad?"

Sarah shook her head. "No. But I haven't met anyone our age who does."

"I pay her well." I defended myself like a total moron.

She laughed. "I'm sure you do. I'm just surprised; that's all. No judgment, I promise." She crossed her heart before picking up her chopsticks and dipping into the orange beef.

"I love your rustic dining table and chairs. I'm betting you didn't get this at American Furniture." I shook my head. "Next time I'll bring a flower centerpiece. Oak?" She rapped her knuckles on the table.

"Russian oak," I scooped out a heaped portion of sesame chicken, enough to feed two people, maybe three. Sarah peered over the table at my overloaded plate.

"Sorry, I have Graves' disease." I motioned with my chopsticks to all the food and then rubbed my thyroid with my left hand, a habit that was hard to break when the subject surfaced.

"Oh…"

"It's nothing to be alarmed about, really. It just means I have a hyperactive thyroid, so my appetite is always out of control. I take pills," I explained, neglecting to tell her that I took them to stay alive; that freaked some people out. It had freaked me out when my doctor instructed me to go straight to the pharmacy and get my prescription filled after he'd broken the news. "That's why I'm relieved you ordered enough for four. I didn't want you to starve."

"I thought you just didn't want to share," she teased, relaxing into her seat. She bit into an egg roll and licked a crumb off her lip.

I wanted her tongue on me. I shifted in my seat, trying to ignore the warm sensation between my legs.

"Oh, don't worry, I'll probably dip into yours." I instantly regretted my word choice. I wasn't even going for a double entendre.

"I hope so." She didn't bother to play coy.

After the whole Meg debacle, I hadn't thought I'd ever want to be with a woman again. With my career, I thought I could stay busy and be reasonably happy and satisfied. Women were nothing but an emotional drain, I convinced myself, not that I'd had much experience besides Meg. The short flings during my undergrad days didn't count. But sitting across from Sarah, in my own home, I felt complete. *Not that I'm pursuing a serious relationship*, I chastised myself. Commitment wasn't on the to-do list.

"Tell me about your family," she said without any trace of malice. Not that there was usually any malice in the question; it was a perfectly normal question. Problem was I didn't have a normal family, and I couldn't think of them without malice.

"I have an older brother who lives in California. My parents live in Denver." I hoped she hadn't noticed I gave the barest of details.

"Are you close?"

I cleared my throat, unsure how to proceed. "Not really. How about you?"

"I'm an only child, and my father died when I was quite young."

I reached across and squeezed her hand. "I'm so sorry."

She squeezed back, holding onto my fingertips for a few seconds. The heat from her hand sparked sensations I hadn't felt in some time. Was it wrong that I was picturing her naked right after she'd told me her father was dead?

"I don't remember him really. Mom and I are very close. We go shopping together every Saturday."

"Every Saturday?" I choked on some fried rice and then guzzled rum and Coke to ease my blocked airway.

"You don't like to shop?" She smiled, considering my reaction.

I shook my head. "I even have my groceries delivered."

"You eat in the dining room, have a housecleaner, and have your groceries delivered. Where are you hiding Jeeves?" she joked. At least I think she was kidding.

"I gave him the night off."

She guffawed, and we ate in companionable silence for a few moments.

"Do you feel weird being surrounded by swastikas?" She pointed her chopsticks to a stack of books behind me.

"I guess I don't notice it. I've been studying Nazis so long I'm just used to it."

She scrunched up her face.

"Not that I am one, of course. I mean … I'm fascinated. When I started researching the Hitler Youth and the indoctrination of millions of children … well, it astounded me. Still does, even after all this time. I'm lucky … most grad students are sick and tired of their dissertation by this point in the program."

She leaned left to gaze around me. "You might be the first person I've known who has actually read *Mein Kampf*."

"From your tone, I can tell that doesn't impress you at all. Just think, though, if people back then had read it—I mean *really* read it, all of it—the war and the camps might have been avoided. All Germany had to do was kick Hitler out."

"Kick him out?"

"He was Austrian, not German," I explained, after swallowing a mouthful of sesame chicken.

"Oh." Her eyes clouded over.

"Hindsight is twenty-twenty. What's your favorite book?" I realized I had droned on too much about Nazis. Historians weren't known for being suave.

"*Cannery Row*."

"Steinbeck. That's a great book. My favorite of his is *The Grapes of Wrath*."

"You read more than history texts?" Frivolity returned to her voice.

"Shocking, I know."

"Of course, Steinbeck's novels do have a certain level of historical and sociological appeal."

"Very true and an impressive assessment." Was she always so observant?

She flashed a victorious smile as if answering my unasked question.

I wasn't sure how to broach the subject, so I dove in headfirst. "You've determined that I haven't dated much since the *big breakup*." I made quote marks in the air in hopes to convey the ending of my relationship wasn't all that dramatic. "How about you?"

"Trying to figure out if I'm a sure thing tonight?" She tapped her nails against a wineglass.

"Wh—you're pulling my leg, aren't you?" I closed one eye, praying to the dating gods I was right.

"Maybe. Maybe not."

"The suspense is killing me." I set down my chopsticks.

"I bet it is." She stared me down for thirteen seconds. I knew because I counted. "To answer your question, my last relationship wasn't all that special, really. No major heartache on either side. It was fun for a few months, but it wasn't going anywhere."

"How long ago did it end?"

"Right before I met you."

"Does that make me your rebound?"

"Do you want to be my rebound?"

"Ha! I feel like I'm on a therapist's couch. Do you always respond with a question?"

"I don't know. Do I?" She grinned, obviously enjoying toying with me.

Strangely, I liked it.

Again we grew quiet, enjoying the meal.

"Are you cold?" I asked, noticing her shivering.

"A little." She nodded bashfully.

"I'm sorry. I'm usually very warm, so I keep the heat low." I motioned for her to pick up her plate. "Let's finish in front of the fireplace."

Balancing her plate and wineglass, she asked, "Won't that make you too hot?"

"I'll just take off my clothes." My cheeks burned at my unintentional *faux pas*. "I mean my sweater."

"I preferred your first response." She nudged me with her shoulder.

"There's a price for that."

Sarah hiked up an eyebrow. "Really? And what's that?"

"You have to stay the night."

"Pour some more wine and it's a deal."

She settled on the floor next to the fireplace. Orange firelight danced in her dark eyes. It took every ounce of control for me to not to lean over and kiss her right then and there.

Maybe it was her, but it didn't take long for the temperature to get to me. I set my plate down on my coffee table and yanked my sweater over my head. My T-shirt underneath hitched up, and I was sure I had just exposed more than my stomach, taut by all the hours spent on a bike.

"I wasn't expecting that," she murmured in a tone that didn't give any indication what she was referring to.

"I told you I get hot easily."

She smiled. "Not that. I wasn't expecting you to have a sexy bra on."

I shrugged, embarrassed. Soon after meeting Sarah I went lingerie shopping. I almost asked Ethan to go with me, but luckily there are countless articles on the Internet about what turns people on.

"Soft, sexy, purple … did I spot some Chantilly lace?"

"Maybe."

Sarah put her plate aside and scooted over to sit right in front of me. "So you aren't completely clueless, then?"

She didn't wait for a response. Stroking my cheek with one fingertip, she traced down the side of my face and continued until she reached the top of my shirt. Playfully, she tugged the T-shirt up for a glimpse.

"This won't do," she muttered, and before I knew what was happening, she'd ripped it up over my head. "It *is* Chantilly lace."

"And you?"

"No lace."

"I have a feeling, though, that it's not your everyday bra." My breathing increased as I watched Sarah eyeing my chest as it moved up and down.

"I don't do everyday bras. Never ever."

She didn't instruct me to find out for myself, but her smirk screamed it. Gently, I pulled off her sweater and started to undo her button-up. She studied me as I patiently freed her body. I felt like I was at a museum, savoring the parts of a Grecian statue, revealing one inch at a time. Neither of us was in a rush. Spying a hint of red, I popped another button and revealed a crimson bra with black Japanese script on the cups. It sent my pussy into a tizzy, but I didn't want her to know that just yet.

The next button revealed her toned stomach. Finally, I popped the last one and eased the shirt right off. Goose bumps formed on her skin; I trailed a finger across her belly, and they multiplied.

"Cold?" I murmured.

She shook her head, her chocolate eyes imploring me to kiss her. I leaned closer, feeling her breath. This was the moment I had wanted since I met her: that moment before making love. Time to explore her body with my hands and tongue. It reminded me of Michelangelo's painting of Adam and God—Adam's lifeless finger reaching out to God's for the spark that would bring humankind into existence. That inch of space between Adam's finger and God's might be one of the most powerful blank spaces ever created.

There was an inch between my mouth and Sarah's. I smiled, knowing my grin exuded sheer happiness and so much promise.

"What are you waiting for?" she whispered.

I desired her spark. "You. I've been waiting for you."

Our mouths came together, soft and then hard. I deepened the kiss, and Sarah's gentle moan urged me on. She lay down on the floor, and I moved on top of her, her skin pressed against mine, electrifying all of my nerve endings.

I reached behind her and unclasped her bra. Her breasts were soft and full, her nipples resembling delicate pink buttons. Her left breast proudly bore one single freckle. My thumb circled the freckle and then her hardening nipple as we kissed again.

Moving to her other breast, I caressed her nipple with my tongue. Sarah's back arched, and she reached up and freed my hair from its ponytail holder. She ran her hands through my hair while my fingers trailed her stomach.

When she moved to undo her jeans, I stopped her. I wanted the pleasure of undressing her completely. Her panties matched her bra, as I'd suspected they would, and I teased a finger over the silk, feeling how warm she was, how wet, how almost ready for me.

I slipped the red panties slowly down her legs, noticing the wetness shimmering on her thighs. I wanted to taste her. Wanted to be inside her.

Not yet.

I raised her foot and sucked on her toes, then traced a hand up and down her firm calf. Her legs were smooth, supple, and stubble-free. She had prepared for this night, as had I.

The faintest smile played on her lips as if she had been reading my mind. Then she nodded. "Yes," she whispered.

My tongue slid its way up her leg, pausing right before her pussy. I could smell her—so sensual. I inhaled deeply. This was what it felt like to be completely alive, with all senses on high alert.

Moving to her other thigh, I licked my way to the place I could tell she wanted me. Her hips arched, calling me.

I opened her slick lips with careful fingers and eased a finger inside. Sarah let out a sexy, come-hither whimper.

Keeping my finger inside, I moved up to kiss her again, thrilled by the sensation of her tightening around my finger. We continued kissing, my finger moving in and out of her. Sensing she wanted more, I worked my way back down, detouring at one nipple and then the other.

Down and down my mouth explored.

I eased another finger inside her and flicked her clit with my tongue.

"Fuck, Lizzie. You feel so good." Her hands fisted my hair.

My fingers slid in and out slowly, my mouth and lips focused on her bundle of nerves. She was getting wetter by the second, and the movement of my hand was getting more frantic. Sarah's hips gyrated, forcing me to make an effort to keep my mouth where she wanted it. Truth be known, it would have taken a madman with a shotgun to get me to stop. Actually, even that wouldn't have stopped me from making love to Sarah.

I was falling for the way she moved. For her taste. For her soft moans.

Her breathing quickened; she was so close to coming. Her upper body jolted off the carpet and she let out a shriek that told me not to stop, even if the house caught on fire.

I plunged in as deep as I could go. Her nails dug into my back as she groaned and sighed.

Her body trembled, and I held my tongue and fingers in the same spot, relishing the vibrations of her orgasm as they progressed through her body. Sarah pushed my head deeper until I could barely breathe—not that I minded.

When the second aftershock stilled, she fell back onto the carpet. I plucked an afghan off the closest chair and spread it over us. She didn't move, so I held her; her hair smelled sweet, mussed on my shoulder.

"That was amazing," she said.

"Anything for you."

"I like the sound of that." She pulled my face to hers and kissed me. "I like tasting me on your tongue."

That got me going. I reached down to be inside her again, but she swatted my hand away. "No. My turn."

She flipped me on my back, hovering over me, her eyes feasting on my body. "Hard to believe you can eat so much and stay this fit." She stroked down from my neck to the waistline of my jeans. Without a word, she slipped my jeans off and removed my panties. "I wondered."

"If they matched?"

She nodded.

They did.

"Tell me. Is the cluelessness just an act?" She placed her hand over my crotch as if holding my pussy hostage.

"I wish it was."

Tilting her head back, she laughed heartily. She looked sexy as hell. I motioned for her to kiss me. "I can't get enough of you," I murmured.

The way she responded to my kiss suggested she felt the same.

I flinched as her fingers parted my lips below, and she entered me.

"And I have a feeling I won't ever get enough of you fucking me."

Sarah pushed in deeper, and I tossed my head back. "Please," I whispered.

"Anything for you." She nibbled on my earlobe, causing me to moan. My ears and neck were my favorite erogenous zones. She took note. I sensed she was an excellent student as well as a teacher.

Her tongue explored my body in a way no one else's had, each passing second heightening my emotions.

When she licked my clit, sucking it into her mouth, I nearly shouted in rapture. Sarah circled my bud, pushing me closer and closer to The Big O.

"Oh fuck, this feels incredible."

Her eyes flickered to mine; even with the firelight gleaming in them, they mirrored the intensity stirring in my body and mind.

CHAPTER TEN

"A GIRL STAYED AT MY PLACE LAST WEEKEND," I CASUALLY TOLD ETHAN AS HE SAT ACROSS FROM me in Starbucks.

"Is that what you call it?" was his glib reply.

I wrinkled my brow. "Call what?"

"Masturbation."

"Oh, hardy har har."

"What's your blowup doll's name?"

"You are on a roll today." I took a loud, angry slurp of my chai, just to annoy him.

"You keep setting them up, and I'll keep knocking them down." He tugged on the corner of his thin moustache.

"Please, I'm not easy."

"That's not what I heard." He mimicked smashing the cymbals of a drum kit and then said, "Ta dum da!'" His awkwardness made the action even funnier.

I sucked my bottom lip, trying not to laugh. "Just because you don't like sex doesn't mean the rest of us don't."

"Neanderthals. All of you!" He giggled foolishly.

"You sure do enjoy discussing my sex life."

"Because it gets you all riled up. I like watching you squirm."

"I don't squirm."

"Sarah might prefer it if you move more. Missionary lesbian sex, I imagine, doesn't impress the ladies."

"What?"

"You'll need to do more than just dry hump her leg."

I choked on my chai.

He mimicked a theatrical bow while staying seated, took a moment to catch his breath, and then said, "How cute that you said a girl stayed at your place."

"Why is that cute?"

"You're trying so hard to keep your emotions in check. Trying to separate your heart from Lizzie logic, but you're falling for her, aren't you? And I'm referring to Sarah, of course, not some random girl you had over." He winked.

"Lizzie logic?"

He didn't respond. Instead, he stared me down. He'd mastered this tactic back at school and it still worked.

"Whatever," I said.

"Ha! I knew I was right. Not that you would admit it. Feeling a little scared, Miss Lizzie?" Ethan let his Southern accent slip in, and then he chuckled maliciously.

"You're full of yourself today," I said, aware that he was making me uncomfortable. "What's going on?"

"I paid off my student loan last week. I feel free." He reached for the sky with both hands.

Ethan and I had started grad school together. Initially, he had been pursuing a PhD in Twentieth Century Literature, but he'd quit two years after earning his master's. I'd hoped he might go back and finish his doctorate one day. It seemed the chance of that happening just got slimmer. But I knew that debt weighed heavily on him. It was no secret he and his wife didn't make a lot of money.

"What? How?"

"My grandfather died —"

"I'm so sorry!" I hadn't even known his grandfather was ill.

"Don't be. He was an asshole. But a rich asshole." He tapped his fingers together Scrooge-like.

"That's great, then. I'm happy for you." I tried to pretend I wasn't still disappointed that he'd quit. During his master's, we'd been inseparable, helping each other through many all-nighters. We were in different departments, of course, but we both focused on the same time period and loved to bounce ideas off each other. When he'd given up, I'd felt abandoned and we even stopped speaking for a while. When we'd run into each other months later and gone for coffee, I'd discovered I still enjoyed being around him.

After my relationship with Meg crashed and burned, Ethan had been there for me. His marriage hadn't been stable at the time either. Before, we'd bonded over graduate-school stress. Now, coping with everyday life was the issue that brought us together once a week.

"Oh, are you still mad?" He waggled his eyebrows.

"What? No. Of course not. You want another?" I stood to order a second chai.

"Sure. My usual, please."

"One plain cup of Joe coming up."

When I returned, he set his book aside. Despite having quit his program, Ethan always had his nose buried in a book; I admired that about him.

"So, I have confirmation." I stared into Ethan's eyes, after retaking my seat. "I'm not a bad lay."

Coffee spewed out of one corner of his mouth, and he wiped it off the table with a napkin. "And who, exactly, confirmed this for you?"

"Sarah, of course." I took a careful sip of my chai, which was still scorching hot.

"How do you know *Sarah* isn't lying?" The trace of a sneer made the corners of his lips curl.

"Don't start with the whole Sally thing again."

He slapped the table. "I *knew* you'd watch the film. You are such a nerd! You'll *research* anything." Even though he didn't make air quotes, I felt them in his tone.

"I should thank you, actually. I watched the film with Sarah. And then we watched *Casablanca*. Of course, now she thinks I love romantic movies and she wants to do another marathon this weekend."

"Two movies don't equate to a marathon. Do you have to pick out the rom-coms?"

"What's a rom-com?" I frowned at him.

Ethan groaned. "Okay, let me help you. Rom-com is short for romantic comedy—films that are lighthearted, funny, and focus on true love no matter the obstacle. Think *Love Actually*."

My face betrayed me.

"You haven't seen *Love Actually*?" He was speechless. "Good Lord! How is it that I know more about chick flicks than you do?"

"Your wife, maybe."

"Lisa's not a fan of them, actually." His frown showed his disappointment.

"But you are?"

"I won't lie. I enjoy a good rom-com from time to time." Ethan seized my journal and clicked the pen. "Here's a list to get you through." He scratched the cap of the pen against his cheek after each entry, putting much thought into the selection. A few moments later, he handed me the list. No wonder people thought he was gay.

I scanned it. "I don't know any of these." I mouthed the titles as I read: *Moonstruck, You've Got Mail, Notting Hill, Bridget Jones's Diary, Four Weddings and a Funeral*.

"Why did you list the last one? That doesn't sound romantic or funny."

"You have to trust me on this." He thumped the list.

"What about *Bringing up Baby* and *The Philadelphia Story*? I like those. Surely screwball comedies count."

"Only as backup. Not as the only movies." He narrowed his eyes. "Do you understand? Not everyone loves classics like you do."

"Okay, geez. Whatcha reading?" I gestured to his book.

"*Thank You, Jeeves*."

"Funny. Sarah asked me where I hid Jeeves when she was at my place."

He sighed. "You mentioned Miranda, didn't you? Seriously. You need to stop telling people you have a cleaning lady." He punctuated each word with a nod of his head. "It's weird for someone your age."

"What's wrong with wanting a clean place?"

"Nothing. If I could afford it—"

I started to speak, but Ethan's glare forced me to suck my words back.

"Don't pimp out Miranda."

As per usual, he was dead-on. I had been about to offer to pay for her to clean Ethan's place once a week. He hated it when I did things like that. I'd never understood his sensitivities about money. Of course, I'd always had money. I had never known what it was like to live paycheck to paycheck. Last year, I'd helped him pay for a new transmission for Lisa's car. The conversation hadn't been pretty, but in the end, Ethan had let me help. He had to really.

"You act like an old lady sometimes. I'm surprised you don't wear lace shirts with frilly collars. Not that *that* is much better." He gestured to my outfit, and I had a feeling he was trying to steer the conversation to safer waters.

I peered down at my sweater-vest and jeans—my typical uniform on days I wasn't lecturing. "You're an old lady," I said, knowing full well how meek I sounded.

"Does Sarah dress like you?"

"No way. She's hot!" A grin spread across my face.

"You see!"

"But I can't dress like her. I'd feel foolish. She has the body for it." I outlined a curvy body to emphasize my point.

He laughed. "Maybe just ditch the sweater-vest for a while. Try wearing a normal sweater."

"I did the night Sarah was over."

"And you got laid. See how that works." He winked.

"She told me she likes that I'm clueless."

Ethan burst into a fit of chuckles. "Oh boy, that's funny. And lucky. Careful, Lizzie, you might actually keep this one."

"What do you mean?"

"I know you. All those years you dated Meg, even though she spent most of her time at your place, she never moved in with you. I bet she never even had a key." He boosted one eyebrow over the rim of his glasses.

I blinked and then swallowed hard.

"What did you say before, 'People like me don't fall in love?' I have a feeling commitment isn't your thang." His Southern twang twisted the final word.

"I don't remember saying that." However, I had to admit it sounded exactly like something I would say. I took pride in not needing others in my life. And I feared how Sarah would react if she found out about my obscene amount of money. Meg was still in my life because I was rich.

"Not too long after we met, when I told you I was married, you said it for the first time. You should have seen the disgust on your face." He waved liked he was shooing away a gnat. "I already knew you well enough not to be insulted."

"Do you think that's true? I'm a commitment-phobe?" Realizing I was blinking excessively, I tried to steady my eyelids. When my eyes started to water, I realized I wasn't blinking at all.

Ethan watched, bemused. "It doesn't matter what I think. It matters what you think, and how you react to a serious relationship. One word comes to mind: sabotage."

"Sounds like a Hitchcock movie." I rubbed my temple. "I think he made one called *Sabotage* and another called *Saboteur*."

Ethan gulped some air, rolled his eyes, and swiped a stray hair off his shoulder. "Sarah's right. You really are clueless."

"Have any of your students ever tried to kill themselves?"

"What?" He plunked his cup down.

"One of Sarah's students tried to kill herself last week," I explained.

"Oh. How awful." He shook his head. "Nope. Not to my knowledge. Is she close to the kid?"

I nodded. "I think she's close with a lot of her students. That's how we met."

"A high school student introduced you? You're kidding!" He chuckled.

"No, you idiot. She organizes visits to college campuses to encourage at-risk students to apply. She also coaches volleyball."

"Ah, she's one of those."

"What do you mean?"

"An overachiever. You two are perfect for each other."

"What? Don't you volunteer?"

"Volunteer? Teachers get paid for those things. Not a lot, though. Not enough for me to figure out how to coach some lame sport like badminton."

I tried picturing Ethan coaching any sport; I couldn't. Is that why Sarah was always so busy with school activities? Trying to earn extra dough?

"What about debate? You love to argue with me."

"Please. You're easy pickings!"

This made me laugh. "Do you think she's poor just because she's a teacher? She shops a lot."

He scratched the side of his nose. "Please don't ask her that. Not everyone is so flippant about money matters."

I sighed. Ethan was right. I couldn't ask her why she shopped so much when she couldn't afford a car. It was none of my business. A thought struck me. Maybe her mother paid for everything. Did moms do that? Mine was probably still pissed she had to feed and clothe me until I was of age, but maybe that wasn't the case for all daughters. Was that why Sarah spent every Saturday with her mother? Free shit? Okay, that thought didn't make it any better.

CHAPTER ELEVEN

"LIZZIE, TRY THIS ON," I SAT UP, NAKED, AND SLIPPED ON A LILAC SWEATER-VEST SARAH HAD retrieved from one of the spilled shopping bags. After her usual shopping spree with her mother, she had popped by my apartment. Before I knew it, we were in bed together.

"Oh, this is soft." I hugged the vest, loving the sensation against my bare skin.

Sarah held my arms to the side and inspected her purchase. "Not bad. Shows off your curves a bit more."

"Curves? Please." I crossed my arms.

She yanked them apart and cupped one of my boobs. "Yes, this is a curve. A very nice curve, I might add." Her other hand slipped under me to grab my ass. "This is another."

I responded by pulling her on top of me.

"I might have to buy you more gifts if you always respond this way."

"No need to buy me gifts. I know you're saving for a new car. I can think of other ways to get me revved up."

Sarah quirked a sexy eyebrow.

She was still wet from earlier, allowing my fingers easy access. Her eyes closed and she sighed as I nuzzled her breast with my nose.

"Now this is a curve," I said. Her nipple rose to attention. "And I love this." I took it in my mouth. Down below, I thrust my fingers in and out of her. "Oh, and the way your hips move when I'm inside you … it's … absolutely incredible."

Sarah slid her hands around my neck and pulled my face down to hers. Her ragged breath inspired my fingers to probe deeper. Biting her lower lip, she watched me intently.

"Come for me. I love your face when you come."

"I love —" She couldn't get the rest of the words out.

"Now, that sweater-vest looks good on you. Did you go shopping?" Ethan stirred more sugar into his coffee.

"Uh, no. Sarah bought it for me."

"Sarah bought you a sweater-vest? So you do wear them around her. I thought we talked about this." He waggled a wooden stir stick jokingly in my face.

I put my palms up in mock surrender. "I was wearing one when she met me, and the other night she surprised me at my place, so of course I had one on then." Actually, I'd worn them around her more often than I cared to admit.

"Of course." He smiled wryly. "How many do you own?"

"One more this week," I answered.

"*Touché,*" he retorted and leaned over to rub the fabric. "Soft. Cashmere soft."

"What? No. It can't be."

He motioned for me to lean over. When I did, he flipped the tag out for a better view. "Yep. Cashmere."

"What? That doesn't make sense. She doesn't have the money for this. Why is she buying me this?"

"How do you know she doesn't have money?"

"She teaches high school English," I said.

Ethan scowled; then a faint smile made an appearance. "I see. From my experience as a high school English teacher that's true."

"I'm sorry, Ethan. I speak —"

"Without thinking. I'm aware. Who does she shop with? I know it's not you."

"Her mom."

"Maybe her mom pays for everything. Mine still splurges on me once in a while."

"You think this is a gift from her mom?" The idea was unsettling.

"Not necessarily. I'm just saying you don't know how much of her own money she actually spends."

Several awkward seconds slipped by. "Should I give it back, just in case?"

Ethan was lost in thought. "What?"

I tugged at my vest.

"No. You should not give back a gift and say, 'You're a poor teacher. You can't afford this.'"

"I have to pay her back. Or maybe —"

He put his palm to his forehead to cut me off. "Or what? Trust me, whatever thought just popped into your head, forget it."

I grunted.

Ethan's eyes widened.

"I wasn't thinking anything." I spoke to my lap.

He brushed my hand, and I met his gaze, softened behind his thick lenses. "Listen, I know money holds no value for you, since you have more than God, but it's a sensitive subject for those of us who have to sell our souls to make a penny or two."

I remained mute.

"Do not offer her cash or a check. You have to trust her."

I shifted in my chair. He had no idea about Meg's demands for money. I pushed the thought out of my head. "But this doesn't make sense. Her car broke down, and she needs a new one. Why is she buying me this when she needs a new car? I have to pay her back. Her mom drives her back and forth to work. Maybe—"

He silenced me with a crisp shake of the head. "No. Do not think of buying her a car. Out of the question." Ethan chomped down on his lower lip.

"I wasn't thinking that."

He cocked his head, daring me to explain.

"I was going to rent a car for her," I said, still to my lap.

"Do not offer to buy her a car. Do not offer to rent her a car. She's a grown woman. You have to trust her."

"Am I allowed to drive her to work and pick her up? Sometimes she stays the night at my place," I mumbled.

"Do you ever stay at her place?"

"Rarely."

"Why don't you stay at her place more?"

"In Loveland?"

He shook his head. "Yes. You know that's where I live, right?"

"I didn't mean it like that. Her apartment isn't very nice, and it's old. I'm getting the heebie-jeebies thinking about it. Who knows how many people lived there before?"

My apartment was brand-new when I moved in.

"Are you afraid of ghosts?"

"No. Germs."

"Such a priss."

"Says the man who only shits in his own home."

He flashed his you-got-me grin.

"She says she prefers my place since its newer and sparkling clean." I did too, not that I would tell Sarah that, but I think she knew my true feelings. She had walked into the bathroom unannounced while I was squatting a good three inches over her toilet seat.

Ethan's forehead scrunched. "Okay, so how often is she staying over?"

"A couple nights a week." I squirmed in my seat. Ever since the first weekend she'd stayed, it was more than two nights.

"Oh, good Lord! Is this a U-Haul lesbian thing?" He chuckled.

"A U-what?" I cocked my head.

"A U-Haul Lesbian." He studied my face and then howled with laughter. "You don't know that term?" He lifted his frames and dabbed his eyes with the cuff of his sweater. "I swear I'm gayer than you."

"What are you talking about? Is U-Haul a gay-owned company?"

That made him bellow with laughter even more. When his mirth subsided, he explained. "Lesbians are known for moving in together after a couple of dates. That's why they're called U-Haul lesbians, because after their second date they move in together." He watched closely to make sure I was connecting the dots. "Understand?"

"That's absurd! Why would two rational adults rush into things?"

"That may be the case, but if you plan on getting back into the lesbian world, you might want to brush up on the lingo."

"Lesbian world? What do you mean?" I rubbed my chin.

"When's the last time you went on a date? Not including Sarah."

"Not since Meg. You already know that."

"You two broke up over a year ago." Despite the topic, he had a compassionate air. "I know she ripped your heart out, and it's good to see you're getting past it. Not all women are evil."

"Ripped my heart out," I repeated with derision, swatting his words away like puffs of air. Even Ethan didn't know all the details about Meg. "Whatever. And I know all about evil women."

"I'm not talking about your mom. You can't run from relationships."

"*Run from relationships*," I parroted. "I don't. I never miss one of our meetings." I rapped on the tabletop.

"Meetings." He rolled his eyes. "You're so charming sometimes. I'm not talking about friendships, even if I'm your only friend. You can't just live with your work. Get out of your office, including the one in your home. Live a little!" His dreamy look made me wonder if he was talking to me or himself.

CHAPTER TWELVE

MY EYES POPPED OPEN RIGHT BEFORE FIVE IN THE MORNING. SARAH SNORED SOFTLY NEXT TO me, her head on my shoulder. It was Sunday, and I was dying to get on my bike. I usually rode at least twenty miles every morning, unless Sarah stayed the night. Since she'd started sleeping over most nights a little over a month ago, I'd been feeling restless.

I edged her head onto the pillow, holding my breath. She stirred but settled down right away. Without turning the lights on, I tiptoed out of my bedroom and changed in the bathroom. Part of me felt silly, slipping out of my own apartment. The other part screamed for me to get on my bike and ride.

It was freezing out. Frigid spring wind slashed through my clothes, and my lungs burned when I breathed, expelling a trail of vapor. But it was energizing, and my body and mind craved it. Ever since I could remember, I needed daily doses of strenuous exercise. Hiking used to be my go-to, until I was struck with Graves' disease. It caused leg weakness, making hiking difficult and dangerous since I preferred going alone. I started riding regularly soon after my diagnosis years ago. Riding pushed me to my limits, but not past them. Unless it was snowing out, I was on my bike every morning—until recently, at least. Occasionally, I would hike on the weekends, but never the strenuous hikes I used to enjoy.

Two hours later, I cautiously reentered my apartment, stopping to assess the situation. All was quiet. I slipped into the bedroom, relieved to see Sarah in the same position she had been in when I left. How was that possible? I was an insomniac. Any slight movement or sound woke me, and even when I was asleep I tossed and turned.

Not wanting to crawl back into bed sweaty, I stepped into the shower. The hot water burned my frozen fingers and toes. Normally, I let my body temperature regulate before getting in, avoiding the tingling pain of boiling water on frozen body parts. After a quick rinse, I shut the water off, wiggled my digits to counteract the tingling sensation, and then toweled off and slipped into my pajamas. Hopefully, Sarah would have forgotten I'd fallen asleep naked next to her, like I did even on the nights we didn't make love.

I pulled back the covers and slid into bed as best I could, trying not to jostle her.

"Why is your hair wet?" she said, in a voice thick with sleep.

"I took a shower," I explained, hoping she was groggy enough to doze off again.

"Why?"

"I, uh … went out for a bit, and when I got back, I took a shower to warm up."

"It's Sunday. Where'd you go?" She sat up in bed.

Was I in trouble? "I went for a bike ride."

"This early?" she asked in an incredulous tone.

"I usually go every morning."

She frowned. "This is the first time since I've been here that you have."

"Well, I thought it would be rude."

"Rude? How?"

"It's bad manners to ditch a guest in your home."

"Guest." She chortled. "You're funny." Sarah eyeballed me. "Go on your bike rides. I love the results." She winked and attempted to pinch my ass. Too quick for her, I pinned her to the bed.

"Really?" I said.

"Yes. Very much."

I leaned down to kiss her, but she dodged my lips. "Morning breath."

"I brushed and rinsed." I breathed into my hand to reassure myself.

"Not you. Me."

"Ask me if I care."

"I do." She covered her mouth with the back of her hand.

I nodded. "Okay. Can I do this?" I kissed her forehead and then the tip of her nose. Skipping her mouth, I worked my way down her neck and found her nipple waiting for me. It sprang to life in my mouth. I bit it gently and then harder. Sarah writhed under me, urging me further down her body. Peppering her stomach with kisses, I licked her clit briefly before continuing my trek down her body. Her moans suggested she was angry and excited all at once. I loved taking my time with Sarah. There wasn't an inch of her body I hadn't explored, but each time felt fresh. It was hard to imagine not wanting to make love to her over and over again.

She also loved to tease me. While I trailed kisses down the inside of one thigh, I watched her massage her clit with a finger, curious to see how far she'd take it. She noticed my interest. I'm not sure which of us felt more aroused as she slid a finger inside herself.

I sucked in air, gasping as Sarah fingered herself deeper, seductively plunging in and out. Her other hand concentrated on circling her clit. I could not tear my eyes away from her smooth, sexy motions.

"Join me," she whispered, her voice breathy.

I moved to lap at her clit, but Sarah shook her head. "Please touch yourself."

I froze. I'd never done that in front of anyone before.

She smiled. "Come on. Do it for me?" All the while, she never stopped fucking herself. I was bursting for release.

Two could play at this game. Hovering over her face, I started to rub myself. Sarah's eyes widened. Encouraged by her response, I shoved one finger inside, the rest focusing on my pulsing bud. Sarah's fingers moved even more frantically below, and I reciprocated.

"Come for me. Oh God, come!" she exclaimed. Her hips rose all the way off the bed, and I pleasured myself with fury, throwing my head back, equally close to coming. Beneath me, Sarah's body trembled and bucked.

"I need to taste you," she growled before tossing me onto my back and planting her head between my legs.

The first lick of her warm tongue sent a sensation jolting through me that I swear I'd never felt before. It was as if she was the first person to ever make love to me.

"Oh," I moaned, my head lolled over the side of the bed, my eyes closing. "Please don't stop, whatever you do."

Sarah's hands gripped my thighs as her tongue continued to explore.

The orgasm hit me hard. My entire body shook and arched as if I'd just stuck a finger in a light socket. Sarah still never stopped licking me. A second wave hit and then a third. Finally, she held her tongue absolutely still as I came again.

"Jesus fucking Christ!" The words slipped out of my mouth.

She entwined her arms with mine. "I love it when you come."

Exhausted, I managed to gasp out, "Why?"

"Because you let me in completely."

I had a feeling she didn't mean her fingers and tongue. I knew she'd just felt a connection to my soul, because I had too, although I didn't say it.

I shivered.

"Aftershock?" She giggled.

I said nothing. Let her think that.

Later that day, we popped into the Starbucks next to the theater. Our movie wouldn't start for another forty minutes, and the lobby was crammed with screaming kids, so we'd opted to wait outside, staying warm with our hot drinks.

"What other secrets do you keep?" Sarah asked out of the blue. She fished in her coat pocket for the sugar packets she'd stuffed in there.

"I'm sorry?"

"Besides bike riding." She stirred raw sugar into her coffee.

"Going for bike rides counts as having secrets?" I tapped the side of my chai.

"Not telling me that you ride, yes." She tickled my thigh, letting me know she wasn't overly concerned.

"I'm an open book," I said with as much conviction as possible.

"Ha! Let me see your eyes."

I leveled my gaze on her lovely face.

"Nope, you don't even believe that hogwash."

I had to laugh. "What can I say? I don't open up quickly."

"Let's start with the basics. Tell me about your family."

"Ah, you see, there's not much to tell. We're not close."

She shook her head, exasperated. "I know. But why?"

Why? What good could come from opening that Pandora's box?

I sighed. "They don't like me much, and vice versa." I shifted on the ledge where we sat.

"Is it because you're gay?"

"Partly," I replied, evasive. "Let's talk about something cheerful."

"Such as?" She waited expectantly.

"Puppies and kittens," I offered, knowing full well I had just failed one of her tests.

Luckily for me, a gaggle of girls rushed out of the lobby, each one wearing a red wig, distracting us.

"What's that about?" I asked.

"They probably just saw *Brave*." Sarah waited a moment, before adding, "The movie."

"Ah," I said as if I knew what she was talking about.

Her phone beeped. Out of the corner of my eye I tried determining her mood as she quickly scanned the text. I couldn't. There went my career as a spy. Sarah slipped the phone into her back pocket.

Part of me wanted to point out that she was slightly hypocritical. She'd just questioned me about the so-called secret bike rides, but she never told me who was calling or texting her twenty-four seven. Of course, I didn't expect her to. Meg used to interrogate the shit out of me about any human contact.

She nudged my arm. "I think we can find a spot inside now," she said, her words sending a puff of vapor into the air.

"Great. Let's get some popcorn." I stood and swung the door open for her.

"What if we eat it all before the movie starts?"

I waved the silly thought aside. "I'll get more, of course."

"It still amazes me how much you can eat," Sarah made of show of checking out my ass, "and stay so skinny."

I smiled. "Quick, grab that bench over there. I'll get the snacks."

"Don't forget the Milk Duds," she shouted after me, and I acknowledged it with a wave.

After getting the loot, I took a seat next to her on the bench. I tended to arrive ridiculously early for things, and now Sarah was being patient even though earlier she'd teased that I wanted to hurry up to wait. "I thought of something while in line. It doesn't count as a secret, but . . ." I shrugged. "I once told a woman about my illness and she said I was lucky to be able to eat so much. It was back when my Graves was in high gear. I was eating seven to eight full meals a day, and I always felt like I was starving to death. I wanted to pop her in the nose. I know my illness isn't well-known, and I won't die from it, but it still changed my life . . . drastically. For her to say I was lucky . . ." I shook my head and took a sip of my chai.

Sarah placed a sympathetic hand on my arm, gave it a squeeze, and then shoved popcorn into her mouth, flashing a guilty smile. "Were you awfully sick?" she asked in a sweet, concerned tone. Her fingers stroked my knuckles.

I nodded. "It wasn't fun. I asked countless doctors for help. When one doctor reported that the latest round of tests showed nothing, I broke down in tears in his office. He asked me if I'd *wanted* something to be wrong with me. As if I wanted to be sick." I snorted, remembering the frustration. "I didn't know how to explain to him that I *knew* there was something wrong with me, but he and the rest of them just didn't care enough to find out what it was."

"Is there a cure?" Sarah set her coffee down on the bench, intent on my answer. She didn't seem to notice or care that we were sitting in the lobby of a crowded theater discussing my thyroid disease. I wasn't one to open up much, and now that I'd opened the door, Sarah showed no intention of dropping the subject.

I shook my head. "Treatment with the chance of remission."

"Are you close to remission?"

"My numbers are improving. I have a blood test in a couple of weeks. Cross your fingers."

"I will." Sarah's eyes grew misty, which made me feel miserable. She'd wanted me to share, and I had, but I'd told her something that made her cry.

"Who was taking care of you when you were ... sick?"

I laughed. "Me. It all came to a head after the big breakup." Meg never accepted that I was ill. Instead, she'd accused me of faking it to make her feel guilty. I responded by hiding my symptoms and ignoring signs, such as a rapid heartbeat and dramatic weight loss. I dropped twenty pounds in a little over a month. "More than likely, the problem surfaced during undergrad, but it didn't become full-blown until years later."

"Do you think the stress from the breakup pushed it along?"

I hitched a shoulder. "It probably didn't help; that's for sure. And being a grad student adds to my stress levels." I didn't like that we were veering into uncomfortable Meg memories.

"You really do need someone to care of you." Her face told me I'd found that someone.

Then I saw something that made my head spin.

Meg. Surely I was imagining her.

I blinked.

It couldn't be. Was the money-grubbing psycho stalking me?

She stood on the other side of the lobby, watching me intently. *This can't be happening.* The last thing I needed was for Sarah to meet Meg-the-Destroyer again. I wasn't a dating expert, but having the ex and current girlfriend in the same building spelled disaster—even for someone as inexperienced as me.

"Would you excuse me for a moment?" I sprung up like a jack-in-the-box on speed.

Sarah nodded. I placed a hand on her shoulder as I passed and then focused on Meg.

She was inching closer. I dashed right by her, headed for the restroom. Under my breath I muttered, "Come."

When I reached the door to the bathroom, I rounded to see Meg standing in the same spot. She looked to Sarah and then back to me, repeating the action a couple more times before she followed.

Fortunately, Sarah was too engrossed in reading movie blurbs on the brochure we'd received when purchasing our tickets.

I pushed open the door and motioned for Meg to go ahead.

"Aren't you full of manners today," she said.

Miraculously, the bathroom was nearly deserted. One occupant was in the far stall, about fifteen doors down.

"Hi, Meg." I stared at the open stall behind me, imagining dunking her head in the toilet. How many times had I held her hair back? A hundred too many.

"Aren't you happy to see me?" she said through gritted teeth.

Totally below the belt. When I'd met Meg, she was a couple years ahead and I was fresh off receiving my master's. She was beautiful, intelligent, witty—everything I always wanted in a woman. I'd idolized her. At first, I even thought I could "save" her. But Meg didn't want to be saved. She wanted to obliterate everything in her path: her career, her family, me. In hindsight, I should have walked away after that first year.

But I hadn't. I'd thought she was the one.

She was a nightmare.

An absolute nightmare.

Not only was Meg an alcoholic, but she was also a mean one. The drunken invective that flew out of her mouth had scarred me for life and reminded me too much of my mother.

Even Ethan hadn't known the whole story. He knew she'd broken my heart, but he had no idea she'd also broken me. It was too hard to admit I'd been conned by her in the beginning—duped by her fake sweetness, intellect, and beauty. She'd made me feel special when no one else in my life ever had. It took me a full year after the relationship to realize she'd seen me as weak. I was easy prey for the likes of Meg.

All of this was way before she started demanding money from me. That didn't happen until after we split. At first, guilt urged me to give in to her demands. Was there such a thing as survivor's guilt when it came to leaving an alcoholic? The demands for money kept coming, and the amounts continued to increase. When I started hedging, Meg set me straight, so to speak. Actually she scared the crap out of me. All it took was one rumor about plagiarism or an inappropriate relationship with a student, and all of my hard work would be flushed down the toilet. Neither ever happened. That didn't stop Meg from threatening. The woman had no conscience. Now that she'd seen me twice with Sarah, I knew she had fresh ammunition against me.

Most people who knew me thought I was brilliant—clueless, sure, but still book smart and rational—but the whole Meg debacle proved I was just a weakling, desperate for love and acceptance.

After I left her (I told everyone she'd left me, hoping they would pity me enough to not ask too many questions) I'd been determined never to fall in love again. To avoid questions about what happened, I pretended to pine for Meg. I'd even told Ethan, on several occasions, that I would be with her again if given the chance. I can't remember how many times I pretended to be lovesick, when in reality I never wanted to see Meg again.

That didn't mean I forgot about her. I couldn't. Sometimes, when I saw a woman who reminded me of Meg, sadness would roost in my chest. There were times I missed the old Meg, the loving Meg —the one who made me feel special. The con artist Meg. She needed a chump like me to control, and I was desperate for someone to think I was worthy of love. It was a perfect storm, really.

For some time, I didn't think I would ever go on a date again. Then, when I saw Sarah in Dr. Marcel's office...

"Are you on a date?" Meg's question snapped me back to reality.

I didn't respond right away. Finally, I said, "What do you want? Money?"

"What's her name?"

"Doesn't matter."

"Does she know she doesn't matter?"

I remained mute.

A woman rushed past and slammed a stall door shut. Moments later, I heard her pissing. Seriously, could my life get any worse?

Meg tugged at a string on her sweater. "I'm thinking of coming back to school."

"That's wonderful." I forced a fake smile; all the while, the room was spinning. "I'm glad to see things are turning around for you."

She let out an angry snort. "Yeah, things are looking up. How about you? How's your dissertation?"

"Good, thanks." I'd long ago learned it was best to answer Meg's questions with the fewest words; it gave her less opportunity to twist things.

"Does she know about you? What you did to me?"

Meg always insisted I broke her. Before me, she was fine. She could handle everything. Somehow, I'd converted her into the monster she became.

"It was nice seeing you. I'm leaving." I wheeled around.

"Wait!" The desperation in her voice snared me back into her web.

I stopped, waiting for her to explain.

"I do."

Confusion clouded my vision.

"I do need money." At least she had the decency to avoid my gaze.

"Ah. Right. Text me." With that, I stormed out of the restroom. I should have known the real reason she cornered me in the john. If only I could detect a pattern to Meg's demands. Sometimes she'd ask a couple of times a month, and other times I wouldn't hear from her for weeks. Did she really need money this time, or was our run-in just too good of an opportunity to pass up? It didn't matter really as long as she left Sarah out of our situation.

Sarah remained on the bench. "You okay?" she asked when I sat down.

"Yeah ... no. I think I'll get a Sprite."

She tossed my chai in the trash can. "Let me get it. Why don't you wait outside and get some fresh air?"

"That's okay." I peered at the exit where Meg stood. "I'd rather be near you." I flashed a weak smile.

Sarah hooked her arm through mine and walked us to the shortest line. "You want to leave?"

It took much restraint not to glance over my shoulder to see if the coast was clear. "Nah, I'll be fine in a minute or two. Besides, I'm super excited to watch a movie about a talking teddy bear."

She whacked my arm. "Hey! That's not fair. When I suggested *Ted*, you said sure."

I leaned my head against hers, comforted by the fragrance of her shampoo. "Next time, I demand full disclosure. You knew I had no idea what it was about."

Oddly, her sweet, evil giggle put me at ease.

God, I hoped she was nothing like Meg.

If she was, it would crush me.

But Sarah never acted like Meg. Since we started spending almost every night together, I looked forward to seeing her each and every day. When Sarah had a glass of wine with dinner, she stopped before getting tipsy. And if she did get drunk, I never worried about my safety. Not once had she raised her voice. No threats. Never a shove. No arm on my throat while reading me the drunk riot act.

If she was running late, she'd let me know. If I was late, she'd say "poor baby" and offer to give me a shoulder rub, not interrogate me about who I was with or accuse me of seeing someone on the sly. Sarah trusted me. I was learning to trust her. Mostly. The fear of Sarah finding out about my trust fund lurked in the recesses of my mind.

CHAPTER THIRTEEN

Meg texted me several days later, asking for money. I knew I shouldn't have agreed, but I couldn't say no. For once, Ethan had other plans at our usual time, so I didn't tell Sarah and, instead, arranged to meet Meg at Frankie's in a small town north of Fort Collins, in the hope no one would see us. I didn't need any more rumors swirling about Meg. The past few years, with everyone thinking they knew everything, had been torture enough.

"Next time, maybe we could meet in Cheyenne," Meg said as she took her seat across from me.

How many more next times would there be?

"Sorry." I didn't know what else to say. She was the one who always insisted on cash. I didn't have PayPal or anything, but I'd set up an account in an instant if it meant not seeing Meg ever again.

Meg's beguiling green eyes bored into me. Her fake scarlet hair was swept into a ponytail. Her smile was false. I tried to remember whether her smile was always false.

"How are you?"

"You mean am I drinking?" She fiddled with a fork. "From what I saw that one night, you can't criticize. Never again."

I sighed.

"Your girlfriend is pretty."

"Thanks."

She cleared her throat. "So, you two are dating?"

I nodded. It was no use denying it. I feared if I did and Meg discovered otherwise, she'd make me pay through the nose.

"That's good. I'm happy for you." Her eyes told me the truth.

"What about you? Dating anyone?"

Meg snorted. "Nope." She looked away. "Just having fun and making ends meet."

Her demeanor set off alarm bells. "Having fun and making ends meet" — I didn't even want to fathom what that meant. Who else was she blackmailing?

I stifled a sigh. How was it that years ago I'd been with this woman and now we couldn't get through the basic pleasantries that arise when seeing someone after a long absence?

"I have your . . ." I placed the envelope on the table.

She didn't move to take it.

"You're different."

I covered my mouth. Through the cracks of my fingers, I asked, "How so?"

"You seem happy. At peace."

I wish I could have said the same about her, but it was clear that angst controlled her.

I smiled awkwardly. "Thanks."

Meg didn't reply or move a muscle. It was unnerving.

"Have you spoken to Dr. Marcel yet?"

She tapped her manicured nails on the table. That was new. I'd never seen her wear nail polish … and it was the black nail polish Janice mentioned. I almost laughed out loud thinking of Janice's outlandish thought that Meg was turning tricks. "Not … yet."

I couldn't imagine what that conversation with Dr. Marcel would entail. "I think it's great you want to move forward."

Meg stared into my eyes and then looked down at my hand. "Move forward? Is that what you call it?"

I flinched as though I'd been zapped.

"What do you call it?"

"I don't know what else to do with my life." She half shrugged.

"You're brilliant. No one can take that away from you." I had no idea why I was giving her a pep talk.

She tsked.

We stared at each other.

"Well, this was illuminating, as always." Meg snatched the envelope. "Have a great life, Lizzie."

After she left, I sat stunned in my seat, pondering whether I would ever see her again. Her last sentence held a touch of finality, but a sense of doom hung in the air. Nope, I was certain that wasn't the last of Meg, unfortunately. The money would run out, like always. Five hundred here and three hundred there didn't last long in today's world.

"Can I get you anything?" the waitress asked with kindness in her eyes. Maybe she'd sensed the emotional toll on me.

"Another chai, please."

"Coming right up. How about a cinnamon roll fresh from the oven?"

That made me smile. "Yes, please. And can I have two to go?"

Soon after I returned home, Sarah bounded through the door.

"You're a sight for sore eyes."

"I missed you." I nuzzled into her arms. "I got you a treat."

Sarah disentangled herself. "What?"

"Cinnamon rolls from Frankie's."

"Yum. I'm famished."

"I'll make tea for us while you get settled." I waved to all her bags.

Minutes later, I heard, "Lizzie, come here, please."

I couldn't decide whether I was content or not that Sarah felt so at home in my apartment.

The front room was in complete shambles—bags and other items were strewn everywhere. Why did she love shopping so much? Shopping was an activity I avoided at all costs. I'd rather get a Brazilian wax; I wasn't entirely sure what that involved, but I had an inkling it was something I'd regret signing up for. Still, it was heads above shopping in my book. And I could afford it.

"What's up?"

She took my hand. "Come sit on the couch." I did. "Close your eyes."

"Why?" I didn't obey the last command.

"I want to try something. Close your eyes."

I regarded her warily.

Sarah laughed. "I'm not going to hurt you. Sheesh! Trust me, and close your eyes."

I wasn't happy she'd used the trust card. "Fine." I closed them.

"Sniff."

My eyes flew open, and I saw her whisk something away behind her back.

"You're so weird sometimes." She wandered to the back of the apartment, and I heard her in the kitchen and shouted for her to turn off the kettle. Moments later, she returned with an eye mask she occasionally wore to combat puffiness. "Put this on."

I held it like it was a rattlesnake about to strike my face.

Sarah laughed it off, and I wondered if she thought I was being playful. With the mask firmly in place, she ordered me to sniff again. I did.

"Smells good. Cinnamon apple?" I asked.

"Good." She still didn't explain the game, and I was completely clueless. "Now this one."

"Uh, Christmas," I guessed.

"Yes, it's called Christmas Memories." She sounded thrilled.

Sensing there was a new thing to smell, I inhaled deeply. "Lavender," I answered smugly. I didn't understand the point, but at least I was scoring well. *God, I'm such a nerd.*

Sarah waved three more items under my nose, and only the last one stumped me. I scratched the top of my head. "I don't know. It smells clean."

She ripped the mask off my face. "Wow! I'm impressed you know your Yankee Candles."

I tilted my head. "What?"

Instead of answering, she gestured to the tiny glass containers aligned on the coffee table, mimicking a hostess on a game show. "I picked up all these candles for the apartment. Which is your favorite?"

"The last one."

She handed it to me. "Clean cotton." I nodded. "I do like the smell of clothes fresh out of the dryer."

"Fitting—for you."

"What does that mean?" I asked, not insulted but curious.

"You're the most fastidious person I've met. Do I need to mention Miranda? Whom I've never met, by the way. Does she really exist?"

"Oh, she exists. The shine around here proves it. I've only seen her a couple of times myself. She has a key, and I leave the money on the kitchen counter."

"That surprises me." Sarah slumped down in the chair opposite the couch. "You're so guarded, yet she has a key and can come and go whenever she wants."

"Come and go? Why would she want to come here on her non-scheduled days?"

Sarah studied the bookshelves. "Good point. From the snooping I've done, you don't have any DVDs besides black-and-white flicks, your TV is ancient, and no CDs, unless you count audiobooks. You log on to your neighbor's Wi-Fi." She quirked an eyebrow. "The only type who would break in would be a neo-Nazi in search of Hitler's manifesto."

Her assessment was harsh—spot-on, but harsh. I nodded. "So, you've snooped."

"Not intentionally. One night while you were in your office, I was cooking dinner and wanted to put a CD in. I scanned your collection and saw you didn't have any music. Luckily, I had my laptop so I didn't have to cook in silence. I didn't want to interrupt my favorite workaholic." Her smile teased me.

I walked over to my CD collection. "What's wrong with this?" I tossed her a box.

Sarah read the title. *"To Kill a Mockingbird."*

"You are an English teacher, right?"

She laughed. "True. But unlike you, I like to unwind, not work or try to improve myself every waking moment."

"I don't do that."

"Really?" She stood, strode to the mantle, and pointed to the one-a-day calendar. "Define today's word." She snared the calendar. "Sinecure."

"A well-paying job that requires little work."

She flipped the page over and nodded. "Correct. Let's look at tomorrow's."

"Wait!" I shouted. I darted off the couch, snatching the calendar from her before she could utter the word. "Don't ruin the surprise." I placed the calendar next to a picture frame Sarah had purchased last week and filled with a recent photo of us.

"You are an odd one. What's a fancy word for odd?" She smiled as if she knew I couldn't resist.

"That depends on the definition. If you mean unusual, you could say *peculiar, atypical,* or *deviant.*" She shook her head playfully after I said deviant. "But if you mean *abnormal,* you have many more options: *aberrant, eccentric, heteroclite, heteromorphic, queer.*" I made a circular motion with my hand. Being this close to Sarah, I was incapable of controlling myself. I leaned in to kiss her neck and then flicked her earlobe with my tongue. She let out a soft sigh.

"Vocabulary gets you hot?" she joked.

"Yeah." I pulled back. "It doesn't work for you?" Smiling, I popped open the top button of her silk blouse and leaned down to kiss her chest as I worked to undo the rest of the buttons. "Your breasts are sublime."

"That's a fancy word for the girls."

"Really? It isn't really that fancy."

"Go on, keep talking dirty to me," Sarah murmured.

"One could say breasts this perfect are *recherché*." I unclasped her bra and took her perfect pink nipple in my mouth.

"What does that mean?" she whispered.

"Rare."

"I see." Her chest rose and fell beneath my mouth; she was breathing so heavily.

I fell to my knees and unzipped her jeans. They slid down her slender legs and billowed around her ankles on the ground. Sarah stepped out of them and kicked them aside. I licked her satin panties, right on her sweet spot, making her sigh.

Not wanting to waste time, I tugged her underwear down, my tongue still teasing the inside of her thighs. Sarah spread her legs to give me full access.

"Seems someone is titillated." I waggled my eyebrows.

She laughed. "Who knew vocab could be hot?"

"I did, of course. It turns all the women on." I peered up to gauge her response.

Sarah navigated my head between her legs. "No more talking."

I agreed and took her lips into my mouth. Spreading them with my tongue, I explored, enjoying her taste. She let out a tiny squeal and swayed against me.

"Here." I patted the carpet in front of the fireplace. I smiled when I spied the unnecessary firewood bucket that Sarah had purchased two weekends ago. The fireplace was electric. She'd filled it with cedar scented pinecones to add a personal touch and apparently to counter the mustiness from my book collection.

Sarah yanked my head to her lips. The fire was raging now, but I felt hotter. I gazed up into Sarah's eyes. From the look on her face, three fires raged in the room.

Shucking off my sweater and T-shirt, I lay down on top of her, my right hand trailing up and down her slender body. Her hips rose, grinding into mine.

"My cooter needs you," she whispered in my ear.

I pulled up. "Cooter?"

"What? Ms. Vocab doesn't know that definition of pussy?" She ran her fingers through my hair.

I smiled. "Can't say I've heard that one before."

"What about fur pie?"

I shook my head. She grinded against my hip again.

"Poontang," she whispered as I inserted a finger, eager to be inside her. Sarah continued, "Honey pot."

I added another finger and dove in deeper. Soon, my entire hand was slick with her juices. Her back arched, and I moved up to kiss her deeply, my tongue exploring her mouth as my fingers simultaneously penetrated her. When I came up for air, Sarah panted, "One of my least favorite terms is fuckhole, but right now Lizzie, I want you to fuck me. Oh God, fuck me hard."

I plunged in as deep as I could. She was so wet. Her nails scored my back, but when I lapped her clit, both of her hands gripped my hair, holding me right where she wanted me. No teasing today.

She didn't have to hold me in place. I wanted to be there—taking her into my mouth, feeling her wetness dribble down my chin. No one tasted as good as Sarah.

Her body began its pre-orgasm quiver, and my fingers and tongue worked together to carry her completely there, to that place where her nails gripped my skull and her back arced. I pushed in deeper.

"Oh fuck!" she bellowed.

I held my fingers in place.

"Oh fuck. Oh fuck. Oh fuck," she chanted. Her body shuddered for several moments before she slunk into the plush carpet. I rested my head on her still-quivering thigh. The lower half of my face was slick, but I was too spent to care.

Sarah guided me up again, my mouth to hers, relishing tasting herself. Before I knew what was happening, she had me on my back and she was tugging my jeans off. Once my panties were dispensed with, she didn't waste any time. I let out a yelp as I felt her fingers inside me.

Her mouth eagerly explored my fuckhole. Funny to think the crass term was now turning me on. The sensation between my legs proved it, or it could have been the stunning woman there. I lifted my head and watched her. Her eyes met mine, and the emotions emanating from them matched my own. How peculiar that such base acts—fingering and licking—could be the ultimate way to show someone how much you care for them.

She plunged in deeper, and all thought spilled from my head. I teetered on the brink of orgasm, each flick of her tongue bringing me one dizzying step closer. "Jesus!" I shouted, immediately following it up with, "Don't stop."

Sarah knew how to bring me home. Her fingers quickened, and she paid attention to my clit. It pulsed with each brush of her fingertips. Not wanting to close my eyes, I forced them to stay open to watch her. I wanted to tell her I loved her, but something made me hold back.

Then it hit me. Lights danced before my eyes, and I felt them roll back, making it impossible for me to stay focused on Sarah.

Sarah.

I was falling in love with her.

How could this be?

Love and I didn't work out. Pain would inevitably follow; it always did. But I couldn't control my emotions.

An earthquake rattled through my body as Sarah stilled her tongue and fingers. After a couple of aftershocks, I lay perfectly still while she worked her way back up, tenderly kissing my body along the way. For several minutes, neither of us spoke as she nestled against me. I was thinking about love: cruel, exciting love.

"What does that frown mean?" She snaked her fingers over the creases in my brow.

I smiled and gazed into her eyes. "Fuckhole? Really?"

CHAPTER FOURTEEN

"I RAN INTO MEG THE OTHER DAY." I CROSSED MY LEGS.

"What's Soy Sauce Meg up to?" asked Ethan.

He wasn't referring to Meg's ethnicity. He'd nicknamed her that after an incident that occurred after we broke up. Meg had tried to use every excuse in the book to wheedle her way back into my life. At one point, she'd called to tell me she'd left some soy sauce at my place. It wasn't even a large bottle. Maybe if it had been Costco size, I would have understood. She hounded me for days until I finally told her to come by my place and get it. Not wanting to see her, I'd placed it outside my apartment door minutes before she was due to arrive.

Meg hadn't taken too kindly to that. She'd pounded on my door, insisting I open up. Luckily, my neighbor Carl walked by and asked her if there was a problem. I knew that because I was standing on the other side of the door, peering through the peephole. It was obvious she was drunk, and Carl had threatened to call the cops, which spooked Meg. She left, but she'd continued to call for several more weeks and didn't stop until she entered rehab. Now, most of our communication was done via text to set up clandestine money handoffs.

At one point, I'd slipped up and mentioned the soy sauce incident to Ethan, but I hadn't told him I was visibly shaking while Meg was pounding on my door. Dealing with an alcoholic was not for the fainthearted. I also neglected to tell Ethan it was one of Meg's pathetic attempts to wheedle her way back into my life. Instead, I insinuated it was one of her cruel games—for me to be at her beck and call in hopes of rekindling our relationship.

"She cornered me in a public restroom."

Ethan raised an eyebrow. "I take it that didn't go well."

I shrugged. "You know Meg." I knew full well that he didn't—not completely.

He tutted. "It's a shame. She was so intelligent. Why'd she quit history altogether? She could teach."

"Oh, I think her passion ran out. For history, I mean."

Plus, it was nearly impossible to get a teaching job when you had two DUIs and a stint in rehab—and, according to Janice, looked like a prossie.

"Did Sarah see her?"

"Fortunately, no. We skedaddled pretty quickly after the bathroom incident." I hadn't told Ethan about the run-in at the Italian restaurant.

"Probably a wise move. Having exes meet is never a good thing. Both of them would probably pretend to be cool with it, but you know they'd be sizing each other up. Women can be brutal!"

"Oh, please. Haven't you met one of Lisa's exes? I'm sure you're just as brutal, if not more."

"She did have one boyfriend before me, but he died in a car accident when he was sixteen."

"Wow. That's awful. I had no idea."

Ethan scrunched his mouth around the words. "Needless to say, I never bring him up. If she does, I'm sympathetic. It's hard to compete with a dead guy."

I thought Ethan was lucky. I knew it was heartless to think like that, but it would be much easier if I didn't have to live in the same town as Meg. If she came back to school, it would be horrendous. However, the likelihood of Dr. Marcel letting her back was slim to none.

Ethan continued, "One thing that really bugs me is that Lisa's dad always praises her ex. Talks about how he was the quarterback and our high school won state because of him. He wasn't impressed that her next boyfriend"—he pointed to himself—"was an intellectual who never played a sport."

I smiled. "That makes two of us. Half the time, I'm sure people are thinking *nerd alert* whenever I walk into a room."

My comment made him laugh, easing him out of his funk. "It's probably closer to three quarters of the time." He licked his lips, deep in thought. "Whatcha going to do about Meg?"

"Ignore her to the best of my ability."

I didn't mention that I'd met up with her to hand over five hundred bucks in cash. If I thought it'd work, I'd offer her half a mill to leave town.

But I knew that even if I did that, she'd still come back with her hand out.

He flashed his knowing smile. "Ah, Sarah's good for you. In the past you would have been pining away for Meg. Progress!" He slammed down his cup. I gulped my chai. In the Meg department, the only progress being made was draining my trust fund.

After coffee with Ethan, I headed over to the university library. Lately, when I wasn't with Sarah I was in my office, studying, writing lectures, or grading—or at home doing the same. The office was depressing on the weekends. Even though I was a socially awkward, self-involved loner, working in the office when no one was around felt too lonely, even for me.

Home wasn't as bad because I was surrounded by my stuff. But on days when I wanted to be alone while still being in a public place, the library was the perfect solution. People were always milling about, yet few stopped to chat, and if they did, only briefly. So, I wasn't surprised when Janice caught my eye. I waved and then suppressed a groan when she marched over and took a seat at the secluded table I'd selected because it was mostly hidden from view. The table was in the European history section, which was probably how Janice had stumbled upon me.

"Imagine finding you here," she said with a smile. Motioning to my stack, she asked, "How's your dissertation coming along?"

I nodded noncommittally. "Not bad. Yours?"

She shrugged. Janice didn't seem to be in any rush to finish. Secretly, I hated her for that. All my life I'd pushed myself to my limits. It wasn't that she wasn't intelligent — she was quite brilliant — but that her motivation was severely lacking. She knew it, and it didn't bother her one bit. Me, I was hell-bent on finishing my dissertation a year ahead of schedule. Dr. Marcel chided me about rushing, but I didn't want to stop.

"Have you seen Meg lately?" she asked, nibbling on a fingernail. This was becoming a typical conversation starter between us.

"Briefly last week. You?"

She nodded and then peeked over her shoulder to ensure we were alone. "She asked Dr. Marcel to let her back into the program."

I nodded. To keep my emotions under control, I tapped a pen against the side of the table.

Janice leaned back in her chair. "He's thinking about it, according to Meg."

"Really?" I said, not wanting to play my hand.

Her eyes bored into mine, trying to get her point across. It wasn't working. "It's surprising he's even considering it."

I smiled weakly.

"I thought you'd like to know."

"Thanks."

Janice waited for me to say more. I had no intention of doing so.

"How much this time?" she asked after a moment.

"How'd you know?"

"I can see it in your eyes. The guilt. So?"

"More than I should have."

"She got 250 from me," confessed Janice.

I whistled, giving the impression I'd given Meg less than that, not double. "She's a sieve."

"Her latest roommate kicked her out, and she said she needed first and last month's rent." Janice shrugged. "Hard to know the truth with her." She shook her head. "I miss the old Meg."

I didn't say anything.

Janice stood up, now unburdened by the secrets. "I'll let you get back to it." She pointed to my stack of books.

As if I could focus now. "Okey dokey, smokey," I said, hoping she wouldn't worry about me, even though I knew she would.

Janice flashed an odd smile, dipped her head, and then vanished around the corner.

I waited a few moments and then muttered, "Shit." I'd thought for sure Dr. Marcel would instantly refuse Meg's request. But he was thinking about it. Actually thinking about it.

Fucking hell.

CHAPTER FIFTEEN

DR. MARCEL HADN'T MENTIONED THAT MEG HAD APPROACHED HIM. NOT THAT HE WAS obligated to tell me, a grad student, but he'd been the first to tell me she'd been kicked out of the program. At the time, it was no secret we were a couple, so I guess Dr. Marcel wanted me to hear what really happened from him, and only him. I never told him that Meg hit me or that I'd broken it off before she showed up at the conference drunk, but I think he knew a lot more than he let on. Who knew what Meg had said to him when she was inebriated? The night I'd met him at his house after returning from the East Coast, my lip was swollen and my face showed bruising I'd attempted to cover with makeup. When he told me the news, his eyes had seemed kinder than usual.

Now, I anxiously waited to hear from him, or from Janice, about whether he had refused or accepted Meg's request.

To add another layer of stress, Sarah suddenly went MIA. Over the past week, she'd stayed at my place only on Sunday night. For four days, I received texts that offered little information, which was worrisome. On Thursday night, she knocked on my door, balancing two large pizzas.

"Come in."

"I knew you wouldn't turn down food." She kissed my cheek as she breezed by.

"Were you afraid I wouldn't let you in?" I was somewhat peeved, surprisingly. *What happened to the woman who enjoyed her alone time?*

"I would be upset in your shoes if my girlfriend disappeared."

"Girlfriend?" I parroted.

Sarah still held the pizza boxes. "Isn't that what we are?"

"Of course," I stammered. "We just never clarified."

"I've practically been living in your apartment. What'd you think we were?"

"I guess I never stopped to contemplate our status."

"That's so like you." She shook the boxes. "Are you hungry?"

"Yes, ma'am."

After retrieving plates from the kitchen, we settled on the couch.

"How was your week?" Sarah asked as if nothing was wrong, although I gathered she was holding something back.

I shrugged. "Not much to share, really." *Oh, except my evil, blackmailing ex might be a colleague once again.* "You?"

Her bottom lip quivered.

I set my plate down. "Are you all right?"

"It's Haley."

Haley had been Sarah's roommate all throughout college.

Her behavior made me wonder whether Haley was more than an old college friend, though. Or had been in the past. I was close to Ethan, but I never fretted over him the way Sarah seemed to be doing right now over Haley, not even when he'd quit his program.

"I've been staying at her place this week," she continued.

"Oh," was all I managed.

Sarah didn't pick up on the accusation in my tone. It wasn't like we had an understanding or anything. She was free to date, and so was I. Yet, I just assumed that, like me, she didn't want to date others. Shit, I just found out our new relationship status.

"Her boyfriend is such an asshole."

A rush of relief whooshed out.

"How so?" I caressed her thigh.

"He's abusive, controlling—"

I swallowed too much air, thinking of Meg, and felt a lump in my throat. Finally, I was able to force out, "Abusive?"

Sarah's downcast eyes answered my question. She went on to explain. "Normally, he's just verbally abusive. He doesn't actually beat her up, but he trashed their apartment and terrified the hell out of Haley. The neighbors called the cops." She stared up at me. "I've been staying there because she didn't want to be alone."

My expression must have transformed my face into an enormous question mark.

"I know," Sarah said, nodding. "She isn't alone now. Michael is there."

"Is he a friend?"

The sad shake of Sarah's head was my only answer.

"She took him back." I stated needlessly.

"Haley always will, I fear. Michael has some kind of hold on her. I don't know what. And her self-esteem is non-existent."

Thoughts of Meg flashed through my mind. I could relate completely. But I didn't say anything to Sarah. I planned to take that secret to my grave. The shame was too much.

"It's just so hard to watch. Haley's not just a friend—she's like family and I love her." She looked away guiltily. "I'm not one to judge, but . . ."

"What?" I managed to force out the question.

"I don't get it. How she can let Michael treat her that way? Does she have no shame?"

My gut told me Haley had more than enough shame to fill all the oceans in the world, but how could a strong woman like Sarah understand that. When someone beats you down, it becomes your new norm.

Sarah let out a long, cleansing breath and wiggled her arms as if trying to shake off the bad vibe.

I hated seeing her upset. "What can I do to help?"

"Know anyone" — she made a gun with her hand and cocked it at her forehead — "who can take care of it?"

I had to smile. "Can't say I do. Unless Dr. Marcel is a former CIA agent."

That made her laugh. "Oh, wouldn't that be neat! No one would ever suspect such a pleasant man of being a trained assassin. Actually, you'd make a great agent."

"Really? Why is that?" I picked up my slice of pepperoni pizza.

"I have a feeling there's much I haven't learned about you. No one can study that much." She jabbed her elbow into my side.

"You're forgetting my secret bike rides. That's when I meet my contact. On the wooden bridge by the red farmhouse."

"Do you pass notes?"

"Yes, in code. But now that you know, I'll have to kill you."

"Do I get a last request?"

"Depends on the request."

"Take me to bed."

I was mid-bite, but I instantly removed the pizza from my mouth and tossed it back on the plate.

"You did miss me this week." Her voice was velvety.

I extended my hand to help her off the couch. "Let me show you how much."

"Maybe I should spend more time away, if this is how you'll greet me."

I almost said, *please don't.*

What the hell was wrong with me?

At midnight the following evening, there was a knock on my front door. Fear surged through me. I remained at my desk with a stack of exam papers and listened for a moment. Then I took a sip of my steaming hot tea, instantly regretting it — too hot. I was waving a hand frantically in front of my face to cool my tongue when I heard another knock. My hopes that someone had accidentally knocked on my door were squashed. Was it Meg?

Sarah was in Denver with her mom for some event, so I wasn't expecting to see her until tomorrow.

I cautiously checked the peephole. Sarah's head looked ginormous through the carnival-like glass. I laughed with relief.

"Why are you laughing? Open the door." She put her hands on her hips, distorting the image more.

"You looked funny," I said, opening the door.

Sarah cocked her head. "Excuse me."

That was when I noticed she was dolled up for a night on the town. "No, not that. Through the peephole you looked funny. But now ..." I motioned to her plunging red dress, stockings, and high heels. "You look amazing. Simply stunning."

That put a sexy smile on her face. "Good. Let me in." She pushed past me. "I hope you have the fire going. I'm freezing."

"I don't, but that can be corrected." I switched on the fireplace. "So, why are you dressed up?"

"Do you like it?"

The way my staring eyes devoured her should have been answer enough, but I sensed she was fishing. Instead of replying, I pulled her into my arms and kissed her. She responded passionately.

"Warmer?" I asked when we separated.

She nodded, and her hooded eyes suggested the night was only beginning.

"So, did you dress up for me?"

Sarah laughed. "Not really," she confessed, with the most adorable smile. "It was opening night for *The Magic Flute*. Mom and I enjoy the opera."

Shit, I'd never been to the opera, but if Sarah dressed up like this, I considered getting season tickets to the opera in all major surrounding cities. Did they have opera in Cheyenne?

"I've never been," I said finally, realizing I was ogling her—not that she minded.

"I'll take you sometime." She removed her thin, shiny black coat and rubbed her arms in front of the fire.

"Would you like some tea or hot chocolate?"

"Hot chocolate, please. I didn't realize how cold it would be tonight. When is spring officially going to arrive?" She motioned to her jacket, which was more for show than for warmth.

"Be back in a jiffy. I just made a cup of tea, so the kettle should still be warm."

By the time I returned, Sarah had stripped off her dress. She pirouetted around from the fireside, and I almost spilled the hot chocolate when I saw her black-lace cami and garter. She still wore her four-inch stilettos, too. She looked sexier than any *Victoria's Secret* model—not that I perused those kind of magazines frequently, not since high school, at least.

She slunk toward me and plucked the cup from my hand. "You okay?" Her smirk implied she knew exactly what thoughts were racing through my mind.

"I think I've died and gone to heaven," was all I could think of to say.

"I love it when you get all flustered. I thought about texting to warn you, but decided to surprise you instead."

"And what a wonderful surprise. Much better than grading."

"Is that why you're still up? Poor thing. I can go to bed and leave you alone." Her smile said she would, but her eyes indicated she didn't want to go to bed alone.

"Not necessary. I have 'til Monday."

"We can work together on Sunday. I have essays to read." She inhaled the steam from the cup. "Ah, thanks. This is helping."

I watched Sarah sip her hot chocolate, swirling a dissipating marshmallow with her finger. She stood with her back to me, warming herself in front of the fire. Her head pivoted, and she motioned me hither with a jerk of her neck.

She set her cup on the mantle. Smiling like a fool, I rushed to embrace her.

"I was wondering how long you were going to make me wait. Decided it would be easier for me to get the ball rolling," she said.

"I was enjoying the view. One word: A-maz-ing. I'll never think of hot chocolate the same way."

She melted against me. "Sometimes you say the sweetest things."

I peppered her neck with kisses. "I love the way you smell." I sniffed. "Vanilla and gardenia?"

She nodded. I smoothed my hands down her body and traced them back up, unembarrassed by the moan of desire that escaped my lips.

"Take me to bed. I've been waiting all night," she whispered.

All night? I'd been waiting for a woman like Sarah all my life.

"You know"—Sarah rolled over in bed—"if I had a key, I could pop in like this more often and surprise you. How would you like me to wake you up in the middle of the night—naked?"

I whimpered, satisfied. Turning my head on the pillow, I replied, "I'd like that a lot."

"Why'd it take you so long to answer the door earlier?" She flicked a strand of mussed hair out of my eyes.

"Er …" *Quick, Lizzie, think of something plausible.* "I thought someone had knocked on my door accidentally."

Sarah searched my eyes before saying, "What? You don't get a lot of visitors?" She feigned mock surprise.

"Not on the weekends. The women of the night only visit Monday through Thursday."

"The women of the night," she chortled. "Is that how you think of me?"

Ignoring her question, I asked, "How often do you wear that lace thing?"

"I bought it last weekend, just for tonight."

"For the opera?"

"For you."

"I've never liked shopping, but the next time you go"—I motioned to her lingerie on the floor—"sign me up. I'm buying everything you want."

"What I want? I'm pretty sure you'll want it more." She trailed one finger over my lips.

"Most definitely."

"You're on. I'm going shopping with my mom tomorrow—"

"You bought that with your mom watching? And you want me to join both of you?" I couldn't hide my shock.

"Of course not," she laughed. "If you'd let me finish … I was going to say that Mom has lunch plans, so you can meet me in Denver for lunch and some shopping of our own tomorrow afternoon."

"Deal." I made her shake on it, much to her delight. Then I glanced at the digital clock radio on my nightstand. It was after three. "Shall we get some sleep?"

"Not yet."

I cupped her chin. "I could never get enough of you, not even in the early hours."

Her eyes beckoned, and her soft lips welcomed me back. "I hope not," she whispered.

CHAPTER SIXTEEN

THE NEXT DAY, I EAGERLY STEPPED INTO THE TRENDY TEX-MEX RESTAURANT. NEITHER OF US had slept much, but it didn't matter. Images of Sarah, posing before my fireplace in her black-lace garter slip and stilettos danced before my eyes and made me giddy. I closed them to cherish the memory of freeing her from her lingerie, slowly rolling the stockings down her slender legs … pure heaven.

"Can I help you?" asked the hostess.

My eyes snapped open to see the most insufferable forced smile.

"Yes, I'm meeting someone for lunch. The name is Cavanaugh."

The woman beamed. "Oh, you must be Lizzie. I've heard all about you."

I staggered backward, feeling trapped in an *Alfred Hitchcock Presents* episode. "Is she here?"

"Yep. Both of them."

Both?

The hostess looped her arm through mine and led me through the maze of tables, snaking our way through the massive dimly-lit restaurant. Every table was occupied, and the place buzzed with chatter, laughter, clinking glasses, and country music over the speakers. She patted my arm. "Sarah is such a lovely woman. You better behave—if you get my drift." She let out an obnoxious giggle that made her sound like a chipmunk. "Only kidding, of course." But the vise-like grip on my arm said otherwise. What was this place? A lesbian mafia hangout?

I spied Sarah in the back, seated at the best table in the joint. A woman sat with her, but I could only see the back of her head. Noticing me, Sarah waved, and her companion slowly turned. I nearly swallowed my own tongue! She could have been Sarah's twin, only twenty years or more older.

Sarah's mom.

I was having lunch with Sarah and her mom.

If there'd been a panic button in sight, I would have slammed it several times with my forehead!

"Here's Lizzie." The demented woman added six e's to the end of my name.

Sarah stood, brushed my cheek with hers, and gently forced me down into the seat next to her. I was pretty sure she realized I was going into panic mode. My autopilot, which usually took over in such situations, also seemed to be malfunctioning. It would be a miracle if I didn't have spittle oozing down my chin and resemble a stroke victim.

"Lizzie, I'd like you to officially meet my mom, Rose."

Rose nodded, eyeing me.

Sarah kicked my shin under the table.

"It's very nice to meet you, Rose," I said as pleasantly as possible. My tone was robotic, and my body movements matched it. My best hope was that I resembled C-3PO from *Star Wars*. At least he had a certain charm that millions of people adored. I needed Rose to like me just a smidgen, so I could continue sleeping with her smoking-hot daughter.

"Mom's friend cancelled," Sarah said too breezily, giving me the impression I'd been played. Had she and her mom cooked up this plan at the opera last night?

Yes, they had. I could see it in Sarah's eyes.

"Of course, she can't stay for our shopping excursion." Sarah's tone was neutral and not overly seductive, but I got her meaning: play nice and you'll be rewarded later.

"I'm so sorry to hear about your friend canceling," I said. "But hey, it worked out for me. Sarah has told me so much about you."

I could see the tension slipping out of Sarah's body.

Rose sipped her water. "So, Sarah tells me you're a college professor. That's impressive for someone your age."

I cleared my throat. "Actually, I'm a PhD student, but I teach Western Civ classes as part of my scholarship."

"Scholarship. Sarah received a full ride at CU. Not that she needed it."

Did Rose have money? Or was she the responsible type that had started a college fund before Sarah was walking?

Rose picked up her menu. "I recommend the enchiladas. You aren't a vegetarian, are you?"

I shook my head. If I were, I would have lied anyway.

"Great." She snapped her fingers, and a waiter magically appeared. "Ricky, can we start with queso verduras and ceviche? Then I think we'll all get the lobster enchiladas."

"Excellent choices, Rose."

Sarah flinched, but said nothing. I quickly scanned the starters, identifying that queso verduras were sautéed green peppers, mushrooms, and onions. Ceviche was seafood-based. Basically, Rose had just requested everything on the menu that I normally wouldn't touch with a ten-foot pole.

Ricky yanked the menu from my fingers without giving me a chance to amend the order.

"Oh, and three Big Tex Margaritas," Rose added.

"Mom, I'm not sure Lizzie can drink this early."

"Pfffft. From what I saw that night, she enjoys a drink," Rose said in such a friendly, confident way that it even convinced me I could handle the alcohol.

Sarah's tight-lipped smile was adorable.

"Oh, there's John, the owner. I need to say hi." Rose disappeared into the lunch crowd.

Sarah nudged my arm. "I'm sorry, she can be a bit much. But she enjoys showing off, and I think she likes you."

"How can you tell?"

"She's putting on a show … more than normal." Sarah leaned her head against mine. "Mom is trying hard to impress you."

"Shouldn't it be the other way around?" I whispered.

Sarah patted my leg. "It's good to see you. I missed you."

That made me laugh. We'd only been apart for a few hours. "Everyone here seems to know you two."

"We've been having lunch here every Saturday for as long as I can remember. It's a family-owned establishment, and we've become an unofficial part of the group over the years."

"You come to Denver every Saturday?"

"The shopping's better here." She gave me her *duh* look.

"But every weekend?"

"I know. Many people assume that women who love to shop are empty-headed bimbos. But we like it and we're good at it, so why not enjoy it? Many of our friends have asked us to help them snazz up their homes or wardrobes. I know a certain someone who's started to dress better."

She eyed my outfit and feigned disgust. I wasn't wearing anything she'd purchased for me recently.

"Dr. Marcel complimented my work outfit on Friday." I tugged on my silver hoop earring. I still wasn't used to the accessory, but it reminded me of Sarah.

"And your apartment isn't as sterile."

True, but she neglected to mention that I hadn't asked for help.

"Mom and I love to shop for other people. Earlier we were buying birthday gifts for my friend's son. The father was recently laid off," she explained. "Every Christmas we adopt several families who can't afford gifts and we go hog wild—a real tree, full turkey dinner, and gifts coming out of the wazoo. No child should have to go without Christmas gifts."

"Oh. That's nice." Sarah didn't have a car, but she was buying gifts for poor people and clothes for me? This wasn't adding up. I knew she had a heart of gold with all her school activities and Haley, but she needed to learn to take care of herself.

Rose ambled back, and all of our attention swiveled to her. I guessed it was always like that with Rose, no matter where she went. She reminded me a little of the Unsinkable Molly Brown, but with a bit more class.

"How do you like being a grad student?"

Let the interrogation begin.

"I love it, actually. I know a lot of people don't find history very exciting, but I love research."

"You should see her apartment, Mom. She has books everywhere."

"What time period do you study?" Rose's eyes were so much like Sarah's I found it unnerving.

"Twentieth-century European history. My concentration is on World War II, focusing on the Hitler Youth."

"Ah, the German Boy Scouts." She threw it out there casually, but the slight smile on Sarah's face told me she had already filled her mom in on my specialty subject. Rose *was* trying to impress me; this was new. Parents, mothers especially, usually didn't like me.

"How have you been able to afford so much schooling?"

Sarah's eyes widened, but she didn't interfere.

Her question put me in an awkward spot—not because I was poor, the opposite in fact, but because I feared telling people I was a trust-fund baby. I weighed my options. Admit it and impress Rose, but how would Sarah react? Would Sarah treat me differently if she knew the truth? I decided to deflect.

"I'm fortunate. Not only do I have a scholarship, but they actually provide a small teaching stipend. Luckily, I don't require much."

"Except for a housecleaner and having your groceries delivered." Sarah's eyes twinkled. She seemed to be enjoying watching me in the hot seat.

"Ah, necessities. At least the groceries, or I'd starve." I winked at Sarah, who slid her hand up my thigh under the table. I yanked on my collar and cleared my throat.

"Nothing wrong with spoiling yourself a little. I imagine you have your hands full with your studies." Rose looked around the crowded restaurant. "Finally," she said as the waiter set down our drinks.

"I'm so sorry, Rose. The bartender is swamped, but he did add something special to yours."

Rose smiled and took a sip. "Oh, this is marvelous!" She gave it a sizable swig.

With trepidation, I tasted mine. I imagined my eyebrow hairs boinging straight up from my forehead. So much tequila! Willing the tears out of my eyes, I said, "Yum."

The waiter left happy. Sarah eyeballed me, concerned—especially once she sampled hers. I couldn't blame her. I was her ride home, and if I drank even half of this drink, I'd be drunker than drunk.

"You seem like a thinker." Rose placed one hand on the table, her fingers splayed, drumming. "James, her father, was the scholarly type. His health prevented him from pursuing all the degrees he wanted, but James always had a nose in a book. It's nice to see our daughter finally dating someone with some brains. Don't get me started on that one ex of yours, Sarah."

Sarah rolled her eyes for my benefit.

Rose noticed and shook a finger in Sarah's direction and then leaned over conspiratorially. "I should warn you, once she decides she wants something, she doesn't stop until she gets it." Rose let out an intimidating bark of laughter.

Turning to Sarah, I saw she wasn't upset at all by her mother's comments. She was proud.

I knocked back a third swig of the margarita, regretting it instantly as the burning liquid tried to force its way back up my throat. I swallowed, doing my best to hide my discomfort, although I was fairly certain Sarah had picked up on it.

Rose spun around to her daughter. "You see? She loves her drink." She snapped her fingers at the waiter, indicating we wanted another round. This was going to be a long, excruciatingly boozy lunch.

"Oh, there's Milton." With that, she stood again and chased after a man walking the other way.

"She's a social butterfly," I said and then burped.

Sarah swapped my drink with hers, which was almost empty. How was it possible that both of their drinks were nearly finished? Sarah didn't seem fazed at all, which impressed me. She poured water into my new margarita glass instead. The glass wasn't clear—fortunately for the ruse.

"Thanks," I said, avoiding her eyes.

She reached out and stroked my cheek. "I can't have you passing out before we get our shopping done. Of course, I'll have to try everything on for you when we get back."

I nodded, appreciating that she was willing to ignore my inability to hold my liquor. "Your mom seems friendly." I scouted over my shoulder to see Rose chatting with several people at the bar across the room.

"Oh, she's a sweetheart." Sarah cut her eyes upward. "Unless, of course, you piss her off. She doesn't forgive easily."

Was she speaking from personal experience, or was that a warning? I didn't have time to find out.

By the time dessert arrived, I was slightly tipsy. Whenever Rose excused herself to chat or visit the bathroom, Sarah did her best to get rid of my latest drink by continually swapping her nearly empty glass with my almost full one. I'd barely touched my enchiladas, too. Lobsters belonged in the ocean, not in an enchilada. When it came to seafood, I could only stomach shrimp, and usually only if it was fried. As soon as the waiter placed my crispy sopapilla with vanilla ice cream and cinnamon and sugar in front of me, I dug in hungrily. Sarah spoon-fed me several bites of her flan, too, and I didn't refuse.

"Shall we have a shot for the road?" Rose asked. It was clear she was already blotto.

"Mom. You have to drive!" Sarah wasn't playing nice anymore. I have to admit I was impressed by how well both of them held their liquor.

Rose waved her off. "Ricky arranged a car for me."

Sarah looked relieved, but her eyes implored me to say no to the shot. I wanted to. But how did I say no to Rose? The woman scared the crap out of me.

When Ricky arrived with the check, Sarah rushed to thank him before Rose had time to order anything else.

At around two in the afternoon, we finally made it to the lingerie store.

"What is this?" I held up a sexy, lacy red item.

Sarah giggled at my lingerie incompetence. "It's a bustier."

"What does it do?" I whispered.

"Technically, it pushes your bust up by squeezing your midriff," she whispered back.

"And not technically?"

"It turns your partner on."

I nodded, admiring the scarlet contraption. "Will you try it on?"

Sarah glanced around, taking in the scene surreptitiously. No one was near the dressing rooms, and only one door was ajar. I was okay with holding hands and such in public, but sharing a dressing room in a lingerie store was pushing my lesbian comfort zone. Today, no one would be the wiser.

Sarah entered the room, holding several pairs of bras and panties we'd selected together. I followed, gripping the bustier.

Sarah removed her coat, and I helped her take off her sweater and T-shirt. Encircling her, I unhooked her bra, letting my hands linger on her creamy skin.

She slipped out of her jeans. "Just for you, since I won't be trying on the panties," she said, hooking on the first bra. She knew I wanted to see the bustier, but I had a feeling that would be dessert.

The night-sky bra with green embroidery pushed her tits upward in a way that made my breath hitch. Sarah raised an eyebrow, and I nodded approvingly. She held up the matching panties. I was sure the look in my eyes insisted that buying both was a must — an absolute must.

We went through the same routine for all the bras, with me nodding enthusiastically for each and every one. Who knew shopping could be this entertaining?

Finally, she laced up the bustier. Until then, I had been a good girl, but now I couldn't stop myself. Taking her in my arms, I kissed her. Sarah's mouth welcomed my own, her tongue frantically meeting mine. Just when I was working up the courage to take it further, someone coughed outside the dressing room door. Both Sarah and I stifled a laugh. Could the person see two pairs of legs under the wooden door that obnoxiously stopped a foot above the ground?

"I have a plan. Get dressed," I commanded. Sarah didn't seem aggravated by my bossiness. She dressed hurriedly while I gathered all of the merchandise and marched up to the register.

A perky twenty-something woman with dyed blonde hair asked, "Did you find everything all right?"

I couldn't peel my eyes off her dark roots. "Yes. Thank you."

Sarah sidled up to me, and her proximity sent me in a dither.

I wasn't sure if Miss Perky had noticed the sexual tension, but she quickly rang up our purchases and I whipped out my American Express card before Sarah had time to think of reaching for her purse.

Sarah's expression told me she had registered my Amex. I hoped she hadn't noticed it was a platinum card, not the everyday blue.

"Wow. Grad students don't do so badly after all," she muttered with an odd expression on her face.

"I deliver newspapers in the morning on my bike," I joked, keeping my tone light. After completing the transaction, I whisked Sarah out of the store, doing my best to ignore the stab of regret for not telling her the truth about my finances.

"What's your plan?" She seemed calm, her voice soothing but still with a sexual tinge.

I motioned to a bookshop on the corner, the lingerie bag swinging from my arm as I gestured for Sarah to walk ahead of me.

"Books? Somehow I thought you planned to do something else." She ran a slender finger along my jawline before stepping ahead of me.

"Okay, can you entertain yourself for ten minutes? Twenty tops."

"Wait. You're abandoning me?"

"If I take you, it won't be a surprise." I planted a kiss on top of her head.

Sarah pursed her lips, and I could tell she was excited and irked in equal measure at being kept out of the loop.

"Trust me," I said before I disappeared, rushing back to the mall. I needed to get a couple of things. The perky sales assistant in the lingerie shop recognized me and buzzed over to me like a moth to a flame.

"Did you forget something?" Her overly sweet tone made me wonder if she worked on commission.

"Yes." I marched over to a satin kimono. "The woman who was with me earlier—what size do you think would fit her?" I noticed Sarah eyeing it earlier, but, with a look of regret, she'd said it was too much.

The fake blonde searched through their supply. "Ah, I think this one."

"Fantastic. Do you wrap gifts?"

She nodded as she led me to the register.

At the counter, I added a selection of bubble baths. "Can you recommend anything?" I nodded to the selection of perfume and lotions behind the counter.

"Of course." She set out several fragrances and lotions, and I gestured that I'd take it all.

"I'll be back in a few moments," I told her as I paid. "Can you please wrap everything?"

My next stop was a luggage store.

I checked my watch. Ten minutes had passed. Around the corner of Sixteenth Street Mall was one of Denver's swankiest hotels. I rushed in, contemplating the lobby—the marble floors, the *Gone with the Wind* staircase, the elegant vases of white flowers, and all the wall sconces. It definitely made an impression. The clerk, a skinny man with an overly manicured goatee, said, "Can I help you?"

"Do you have a room available?"

"For tonight?" The corners of his mouth curled up.

"Yes. For tonight."

"I'm not sure." He clicked on the computer mouse, frowning at the screen. "Ah, you're in luck. We have one room left."

One room … my ass. The lobby was nearly empty. Pompous prick.

"Fantastic. I'll take it."

"It's one of our most expensive rooms," he said, his elitist air suggesting it was out of my price range. I'm guessing my T-shirt, Columbia jacket, and Gap jeans weren't the normal attire here.

I whipped out my Amex. "Can you have a chilled bottle of Champagne and flowers in the room, maybe some rose petals on the bed? And would it be possible to have this delivered to the room?" I motioned to the suitcase I'd stuffed the lingerie bag and other gifts in.

The expression that crossed his face was just short of creepy. "Of course, Madame." His attempt to sound French was laughable.

Ma-dame. Pa-lease.

"Thanks. Also, can you recommend a romantic restaurant near here?"

The Francophile pulled out a map of the area and circled a French restaurant two blocks from the hotel.

"Perfect. My companion is fluent." I thanked him and marched toward the exit.

"Do you require a cab?" The doorman opened the door for me.

Shaking my head, I thanked him anyway.

Sarah was just finishing up at the register. I sighed. I should have known better than to leave her in a store. The woman didn't understand the word browse. "There you are," she said.

"Sorry it took so long."

She motioned for me to come outside. Curious, I followed. After she'd made sure the coast was clear, she revealed the book she'd purchased: *Lesbian Sex 101*.

"Are you trying to tell me something?" I tried to sound breezy, but my tone was tinged with worry.

"Trust me, you don't have to worry. I just thought it'd be fun."

Relieved, I said, "It does go with our earlier purchase." *And my plans for later tonight.*

"Exactly!"

Sarah gazed at my empty hands and sighed. I knew getting her the kimono was the right idea, but of course I had no idea she'd buy me one right away. "Are you ready?" I asked, hiding my smile.

"Where are we going?"

"An early dinner. I'm starving."

"I knew lobster would be too much for my sandwich lover."

"Sandwich lover — is that a position in the book you purchased?" I attempted to open the bag.

Sarah swatted me away. "You have to wait and see."

"Sounds promising."

"What restaurant were you thinking?"

"The concierge recommended one."

Sarah stopped in her tracks. "Concierge?"

"Thought it'd be nice to stay the night. Unless you don't want to."

She squealed.

"I'm hoping to hear more squealing later tonight."

"With all the lingerie and book, I think that's a definite."

I woke in the middle of the night, realizing Sarah wasn't in the king-sized bed. Groggily, I wiped the tiredness from my eyes and sat up.

"I'm sorry. I didn't mean to wake you," she said from a chair across the room.

I blinked several times to clear the fog from my contacts; normally, I took them out before I went to sleep. I blinked again when I noticed she was wearing only the kimono. It draped over one leg, providing me with a wonderful view.

"Everything okay?" I asked as I positioned some pillows against the headrest, sensing she needed to talk.

"I'm just thinking."

"About?"

She waved a hand. "All this is too much."

"The room? Do you want to switch hotels?" It was more posh than my usual style. If Sarah hadn't been with me, I would be in a Best Western or something along those lines.

She laughed, but it sounded sad. "You don't have to do all this."

"All what?"

"The lingerie, the French restaurant, and now this." She motioned to the empty Champagne bottle, to the room. "How much did this cost you?"

I was relieved Ethan wasn't present. He would be snickering *I told you so.*

"It wasn't that much."

She boosted one eyebrow. "I'm not an idiot."

"I'm not implying you are. I'm just saying don't worry about my finances."

"Why? Because you have a secret stash of cash?"

I looked away and shrugged.

"Do you?" Her tone switched from accusatory to hopeful.

I nodded, not sure I wanted to confess completely. I'd assumed she would wonder how I was affording everything, but hoped she wouldn't put me on the spot. I should have known better. Sarah was much more direct than I was.

"Please, be honest with me."

I met her eyes. "I have a trust fund," I muttered.

Sarah cupped her ear. "Did I hear that right? You have a trust fund?"

"Yes," I said quietly.

Sarah burst into laughter. "This is perfect. I've been hiding mine and so have you."

"Hiding what?"

"Except for our first date, when my car actually did break down, I've had a car. I just didn't want to pick you up in the brand-spanking new Mercedes Mom insisted on buying me as an early Christmas gift."

"So, you have money?" I perked up.

"As Mom likes to say, more than God." Sarah rolled her eyes.

"Ethan says the same about me."

"Really?"

"Loads. People hate me for it."

"Me too! That's why I hid it. But why the Camry with the missing hubcap?"

"I wasn't lying earlier when I said I had a newspaper route. I don't anymore, but during my undergrad days I did. I saved all the money to buy my own car. It felt good to buy something with my earnings for once. You know what I mean? And I don't know … I kinda like the missing hubcap. It would bug the shit out of my mother."

Sarah giggled. "I get it. That's why I live in a shitty apartment in Loveland. I hate touching my trust fund. I live on my teacher's salary 90 percent of the time, not including the shopping, of course. My old car was in even worse shape than yours. Mom called it the coffin—the brakes were that bad. She insisted I accept her gift because she knew that otherwise I'd buy another used car."

"But what about all the times you needed a *lift* to work?" I made quote marks in the air.

Sarah shrugged. "I liked spending extra time with you in the mornings."

"So those late nights you popped over, you drove? I always felt uncomfortable that your mom knew you were shacking up with me."

She chortled. "Shacking up! You crack me up."

I smiled. "What are the odds?"

"That two lesbians in northern Colorado have trust funds?" She tittered. "This is such a relief." She leaned back in her chair. "My past girlfriends have either taken advantage of it or despised it. I could never find a happy medium in the dating world." She wrapped the kimono more snugly around her. "I'm glad I don't have to feel guilty about this."

"You like it?"

"I love it!"

"Do you hide your trust fund from everyone?" I asked.

"Mostly. Haley knows, of course."

"What about the people you buy clothes and stuff for?"

"Oh, they pay me back. What about you?"

"Of course I can pay you back." I reached for my wallet on the end table.

"Not that, silly. Who knows about your trust fund?"

"Ethan knows." And Meg-the-Blackmailer.

"What about the wicked ex?"

I had to stop and think if I said Meg's name aloud. I was fairly positive I hadn't. Shit. This wasn't a path I wanted to wander down at this time of night. Or ever. "Eventually she figured it out."

"Too many extravagant hotels?" Sarah teased.

I shrugged. "What ex of yours took advantage of you?"

Sarah snorted. "Two did, but the worst one was my last serious relationship. Kerry thought she'd hit pay dirt. We dated for a couple of years, and after six months of staying at my place every night she confessed she broke her lease and quit her job."

"You're kidding!"

"Nope. We hadn't even discussed officially moving in together or anything. When my mom found out, she hit the roof! Let's just say Kerry was out of my apartment within the week."

"Did Rose escort her out?" I laughed and shook at the same time.

"Oh, she wanted to. But no. I handled it."

"What'd Kerry do with her stuff? Didn't you notice an extra TV or something in your apartment?"

"She had a furnished apartment and sold everything but her clothes."

"A furnished apartment?" I couldn't stop an involuntary shudder.

"And you thought my place was disgusting." Sarah winked.

"I never said that."

"It was pretty clear when I found you hovering over the toilet."

I shrugged and flashed an apologetic smile.

Sarah tilted her head. "You don't talk about exes ever. How many do you have?"

"Not a lot. A couple of short-lived flings in my undergrad days, but most didn't like the fact that I studied so much, even on Friday nights. Then the one—the big one that crashed and burned not so long ago."

"She broke your heart, didn't she?"

And then some. "You could say that."

"I wondered."

"You wondered if I'm nursing a broken heart?" I asked, unsure if I wanted to hear the full answer.

"You're so guarded. It's okay. Everyone has scars."

The image was more on target than Sarah intended.

Sarah eyed me, concerned. "I don't plan on breaking your heart, Lizzie."

"What do you plan on?"

"Loving you."

I wanted so much to let her. "I hope so."

In six long strides, Sarah made it to the bed and then straddled me. I opened the kimono completely and pressed her skin against mine. Her kiss was more than a kiss—so deep it felt as if she was letting me penetrate her life completely. For the moment, I wanted to let her sink just as deeply into mine.

We woke late the following morning, after nine. I was usually an early riser, but it's hard to wake at six when after only falling asleep at four. After the night's revelations, we'd celebrated by making love until we couldn't stay awake any longer.

"You hungry?" Sarah rested her head on one hand and outlined random shapes on my chest with the other.

"Famished." I tilted her chin to bring her face to mine and kissed her deeply. Even all the kisses we'd shared last night hadn't satiated my thirst for her.

She slapped me away. "I was talking about actual food."

"I had a feeling, but it was worth a shot." I stroked my fingers through her dark, silken hair.

She beamed. "I feel the same. But I know I need food. And if I do, you're probably even more desperate."

I nodded. My pills were keeping my thyroid levels controlled, but I still felt starved almost every second of the day. "What's our plan today?"

"What? You don't have today mapped out?" She used her bedroom voice.

"I did extend our reservation, but it's your turn to plan. I'm exhausted from yesterday. Usually, my days are the same—wake up, school, study, research, bed." I ticked each off on a finger.

"You poor dear. Are you sure you even want to get out of bed today?"

I rolled her onto her back and climbed on top. "Now that's an idea. We can try mastering some more positions." I thrust my chin toward the book on the floor.

"Don't worry. That's on the agenda. But first, breakfast," she said as she shoved me off.

An hour later, we stepped off the elevator into the lobby.

"Wait here, I'm going to ask about a place to eat." Sarah strutted to the concierge.

I leaned against a marble column. The elevator pinged obnoxiously behind me. A corpulent man stuffed into an expensive suit escorted a woman on each arm into the center of the lobby.

Everyone stopped what they were doing to appraise the situation. It was clear the women were hookers, and the three of them were sloshed even though it was morning.

Sarah's jaw dropped as if she'd never seen prostitutes before. Her intense stare forced me to take another glance at the obnoxious trio.

Meg!

Her hair was bottle-blonde again now, and she wore makeup befitting a hooker. She was thinner, too, almost scrawny, but I still recognized her. *Just having fun and making ends meet—*I suddenly remembered the comment she'd made just weeks ago. *No way!*

Her green eyes relished the look of shock on my face. She turned them on Sarah with such a look of glee I wanted to shove her back into the elevator and hit a magic button that shot her out of the building. Luckily, Sarah seemed to have not recognized her.

Breaking free from the man's chubby fingers and arm, Meg tottered toward me.

"What the hell are you doing?" I asked as Sarah rushed to my aid.

"What I have to," Meg said, her voice slurred. "It's not like you left me much choice."

"Me?" I slammed my palm into my chest, almost knocking the breath right out. "You're blaming *me*? For *this*." I pointed to the fat man.

Meg jabbed a finger in my face. "You ruined me," she spat, venom in her tone.

"Stop blaming me. Just fucking stop."

Sarah's sharp intake of air reminded me she was witnessing one of my blowouts with Meg.

I seized Meg's arm and pulled her off to the side.

"Get your fucking hand off me." Meg shoved me.

"I'm taking you home."

Meg crossed her arms. "It doesn't work that way. You can't ruin my life and then act like you care."

"I had no idea that you resorted to . . . this!" I shouted.

"If you had, would you have given me more? The small amounts you pay me here and there don't go far. You wouldn't give a damn if I offed myself. In fact, you'd probably buy the gun, wouldn't you?" Meg screamed, fingers to her forehead, mimicking blowing her brains out.

I glanced over my shoulder at Sarah, mortified she had a front seat to this charade. The confusion in her eyes forced the anger right out of my head. This wasn't the time. It wasn't the place.

A gray-haired man, flanked by an imposing, tall man in an ill-made suit approached. I assumed the more put-together man was the manager.

Meg peered frantically around the lobby. "Shit. He's gone."

"Who's gone?" I asked.

"My paycheck for the week! He hasn't paid yet."

"What? You don't ask for payment up front? You disgust me."

"I disgust you! What about you, Miss Perfect? You have all the money in the world and yet you'd let me starve. If it wasn't for you, I'd be finishing up my doctorate and would have a promising career ahead of me." She pounded both fists into my chest. "It's all your fault!" She staggered back. "I've been kind so far, but I'll destroy you."

"Ladies," the gray-haired man spread his hands wide. "Can I help you resolve your issue peacefully?"

Fortunately, the morning rush of people checking out must have filtered out earlier and only a handful of people in the lobby, including the snobby concierge, stared at us with slack jaws.

"She stole my money." Meg jerked her head in my direction.

"I did no such thing." I defended.

"I'm out two thousand because of you."

I seethed. "Not my problem. You are not my problem. I paid for your rehab and look how that worked out."

Meg shouted over my shoulder in Sarah's direction. "Real nice. I threaten to kill myself and you refuse to help me. I can't pay my rent. Can't eat. I can't go on like this." She clutched my shirt with shaking, black-nail-polished hands.

I'd seen Meg put on shows before, but this was quickly turning into her finest performance.

Before I could say a word, Sarah was at my side with all the color drained from her face. "Give her the money," she whispered.

The manager and the bruiser in a suit yanked Meg toward a back room. Meg looked at Sarah and started to say something, but the imposing man clapped a fleshy hand over her mouth.

"Lizzie, you have to help her," Sarah pleaded.

"What? Why?" I shook my head. "No, I'm done with her." I mimicked wiping my hands clean.

"Done with her? How can you say such a thing? She obviously needs help. Serious help."

"Tell me about it."

Sarah took a step back. "Then why won't you help her?" The pleading in her tone tore me up inside.

"You don't understand. I've done all I can for her."

"For her? Who the hell is she?"

"Uh…"

"Tell me right now, or I'm leaving and not coming back."

"Sarah —"

"What's her name?" Each word was said with force.

"Can we talk about this outside?" I tugged on her arm, but Sarah shook me off.

She was dead set not leaving Meg behind.

"She's … a… She's Miranda!"

"Your cleaning lady is a hot prostitute?"

"I didn't know she was a prostitute until today," I countered loudly.

"Well, you can't leave her here with them."

I puffed out my cheeks, slowly releasing the pressure. "What do you suggest I do?"

"Save her."

"I've tried. Repeatedly. You've got to believe me." This much was true. But I couldn't confess it all. Not even to kind loving Sarah. If I told her about Meg, I'd have to tell her everything and I swore to myself I'd take that shame to my grave. Letting her in about the trust fund was easy compared to exposing the truth about my relationship with Meg. Show her how weak I'd been? How would Sarah ever respect Punching-Bag-Lizzie again?

Sarah's eyes blazed. "I don't even know who I'm talking to right now, Lizzie." She spun around and headed for the door.

I had to stop her. God knows what Meg would say or do next.

"Wait. Let me handle it." I entered the room. Both of the men had puffed out their chests and bruiser's right hand twitched near his side. I wondered whether he was packing. What did they think? That I was Meg's pimp? For some reason, Ethan's comment, "Don't pimp out Miranda," played in my head and I had to smother a laugh with my palm.

Meg smiled victoriously. I wanted to smash her face in.

I studied the trio, realizing I had absolutely no idea what to say to spring Meg.

"They're threatening to call the cops," said Meg.

I nodded, weighing that option. Would that help Meg in the long run? Rehab obviously hadn't. Jail, though? Did that help anyone?

"I'm sure you'd rather not draw more attention to the matter," said the sleazy manager.

That settled it for me. "Of course not," I said.

"She's not allowed back here. Ever." The manager glared at me as if I had control over Meg.

I nodded. Let him think I did. The last thing I needed was more Meg drama. Fucking hell, if this got out at school … And Sarah stood right outside the door. The only person who truly loved me and Meg threatened that.

Meg, probably realizing she had one chance to get out of this mess, hid behind me. I shook the manager's hand. "Thank you."

When Meg and I exited the room, Sarah jumped to attention and I motioned with a palm for her to wait. Meg took the opportunity to slip her arm through mine. I groaned.

Outside, I asked the doorman for a cab.

"Fort Collins," I told the driver when the cab appeared, shoving Meg into the back seat.

"What? That's halfway to Cheyenne. No way." The driver motioned for Meg to get out.

"How much?"

He must have sensed my desperation. "Three hundred."

"Done." I tossed the cash onto the passenger seat. Fortunately, I had stockpiled some dough for the weekend.

"Lizzie —" Meg started, but I sighed to silence her.

"Not now. I'll call you."

The driver slammed on the gas, and I watched the vehicle slip around the corner.

"Jesus fucking Christ," I muttered.

Now what? I needed a moment before dealing with Sarah. I sat on a bench and leaned my head against the wall.

"Women," the doorman said, probably hoping to ease the awkwardness.

It didn't work. Fortunately, a limo pulled up and he left to attend to the couple and their baggage.

Five minutes later, Sarah appeared, tugging the suitcase I'd purchased yesterday for our romantic weekend behind her.

Our first ... and probably last ... weekend away together, I thought.

CHAPTER SEVENTEEN

SARAH SAT ON THE BENCH NEXT TO ME.

Neither of us moved to speak. My mind was flipping through one explanation after another, but when it came down to it, each and every one was useless. *Just tell her the truth. Tell her everything about Meg,* my brain said.

But the truth was too humiliating.

How could I admit to everything Meg had put me through? I kept hearing Sarah's comments about Haley. How she didn't understand how Haley could let someone treat her that way. Did she have no shame?

"We need to talk," Sarah said eventually.

I nodded.

She glanced toward the front door. "Not here, though. I'm sure the manager will be out soon to make sure we've left."

I cracked a weak smile. "I've definitely made an impression on him."

"He's not the one you should be concerned about." Her tone was sharp as she stood and reached for the bag.

"Here, let me." I lugged it to my car. Sarah climbed into the passenger side.

Before I even started the engine, she said, "You remember that night I surprised you after the opera. You made a comment about ladies of the night . . ." Her accusation hung in the air.

"And?"

"I thought you were kidding."

"I was!" I stared at her, shocked. "Sarah, I have never paid for sex. The thought hasn't even crossed my mind. Never."

"Yet you employ Miranda, who moonlights as a hooker."

"How was I supposed to know that? It's not like she listed it on her resume." I threw my hands up in the air, already feeling guilty about the lie.

"You have to fire her."

"I can't fire Miranda!" The entire situation was getting out of control, and at warp speed. I covered my face with my palms.

"Give her enough money and . . ."

I peeked through my hands. Indecision furrowed Sarah's brow. "God, do you really think she's suicidal? I keep thinking about my student and then about Miranda. The desperation in her tone when she said how she can't go on." Sarah rubbed her eyes.

Was this my way out of not firing Miranda? I'd never find another person who could make every surface in the bathroom sparkle. But maybe I *had* to fire her now, because if Sarah ever laid eyes on the real, dependable dowdy old Miranda … That didn't bear thinking about either. God, what a mess!

"Listen. M-Miranda obviously has issues. I knew her from school. She hit a rocky patch and started cleaning to make ends meet. I wanted to help. I didn't know about all the ways she tried to make ends meet. Not until today, I swear, Sarah. But I'm not sure I can fire her. Maybe I can help her instead of—"

"Help her? How?" Sarah said, but her tone was soft rather than confrontational. "Send her to therapy? Pay off her bills? Buy her a place?"

Shit. Did Sarah expect me to foot the bill for all that for Meg?

"Uh…"

"What?" She spun on me, alarm back in her voice. "We have to help her, Lizzie."

"I … she's just my maid … I mean, we were in school together, but how involved do I really need to get?" The words slipped out as if the situation were true and my cleaner really was prostituting herself.

"How would you feel if Miranda actually killed herself?" Sarah's eyes started to brim with tears. "And you had done nothing?"

Was she seriously getting this worked up about a woman she thought she'd never even meet until today? *Jesus, Lizzie! She* hasn't *met Miranda. Focus!*

"Let me talk to her."

"I want to be there," she said.

Oh, my God! I wanted to slam my face into the steering wheel. How had I moved beyond clueless to goddamned stupid so quickly?

"I don't think that's a good idea," I said. "I'm sure she's embarrassed by … everything. I want her to be able to open up to me." I took Sarah's hand and squeezed it. "I'll take care of Miranda. I promise." And by that, I meant I'd take care of Meg. Once and for all. It was time to get Meg out of my life completely.

After a tense, quiet drive back to Fort Collins, Sarah wasn't in the mood to come back to my place, and I was hesitant to drop her off in Loveland alone.

"Is there anything you'd like to do?" I asked as we approached the highway exit. "I'd hate to end the weekend on this note."

She laughed. "You mean finding out that Miranda is turning tricks." She sighed. "It was such a lovely weekend until then."

"It's still early. We can salvage the rest of today," I said, feeling relief rush back into my chest. "You name it and we'll do it."

"Let's see a movie."

I bottled up a groan. "Oh, do you know another movie featuring talking stuffed animals?" I joked, hoping to further ease the strain.

"The Beaver."

"You've got to be joking."

"Nope. Technically, it's not a stuffed animal but a hand puppet."

"Sounds great. I'm in." I reached across and squeezed her thigh.

"I don't think it's playing anymore. Besides I'm not sure I would like *The Beaver*," she said in all seriousness. Her phone beeped with a text message, and she pulled out her cell and checked it in eerie silence. After a minute or two, she said, "Ah, I just googled it. I know what we'll see."

"Are you going to fill me in?"

"Nope. Trust me, you'll love it."

"What'd you think of the movie, Lizzie?"

"I liked it more than I thought I would."

We were snuggled up in Sarah's bed. I wasn't a fan of her place, but I'd be a fool to press my luck today, of all days.

She'd taken me to see *The Artist*, a movie I'd heard others rave about.

"Much better than the last one," I added.

"I thought you'd love it."

I toyed with her nipple. "Really?" We hadn't had sex earlier, but Sarah favored sleeping naked, and I preferred her to.

"Considering all the black-and-white movies you own, it seemed like a sure thing."

I realized she was much more observant than I gave her credit for, and it made a twinge of worry constrict my brain. I needed to fix the Meg/Miranda disaster — pronto.

"You scared?" Sarah's smile confounded me.

"Scared? What do you mean?" Was I frowning? Had she realized I was thinking about what happened earlier?

"I don't think you're used to people paying attention to you," she said. "You're finding it unnerving."

"Oh, please. I'm a lecturer. I'm used to being the center of attention."

"Not in your personal life you aren't. When's the last time you had someone over to your apartment? Not counting your hooker, of course."

"My hooker!"

"Well, I certainly didn't hire her."

It was a relief that Sarah was injecting some humor into the situation.

"Am I right?" She pushed.

I shrugged.

Her bare breasts rose and fell as she laughed. "That's what I thought."

"Whatever." The conversation was making me nervous. I focused on her nipple again as a distraction.

The buzz of her phone interrupted us, and she glanced at the screen and sighed.

"You need to get that?"

"Nah."

I was curious about who was calling, but I didn't want to seem overly inquisitive, so I let it slide. During the movie, sitting with my hand on her thigh, I'd noticed her phone vibrate several times, alerting her to missed calls or texts. Occasionally, I'd spied her clandestinely checking them with a pained expression on her face. It had to be Haley.

"You sure you don't want to take the call?"

She cupped my chin with her palm. "This is what I want to do." Her lips met mine.

I wasn't going to argue.

"Besides the drama earlier, it was a wonderful weekend." Sarah's eyes glistened, and I felt an immediate urge to alleviate her sadness. "Thank you. I really needed to get away for a couple of days."

I nodded, understanding. It felt good to leave my books behind, to relax and do things that had absolutely nothing to do with my PhD program. "We should do it more often—minus Miranda."

"Yes. And now that we don't have to hide our trust funds, it'll be easier to get away."

"What a relief. I felt horrible when Ethan told me the sweater-vest you bought me was cashmere. I almost gave it back."

Sarah biffed the back of my head. "You can't give back a gift!"

I rubbed my head, grinning. "I know. Ethan told me. And then I toyed with the idea of renting a car for you, since I thought you couldn't afford to get a new one." I tickled her side.

She laughed and squirmed, all tension drained from her body.

"God you're beautiful, Sarah," I murmured.

She enveloped me in her arms. "Say it again."

"Say what?"

Sarah bit my lower lip, tugged at it with her teeth. "You know what."

"That you're beautiful?"

"Yes. That."

"You are absolutely beautiful. And your body …" I traced a hand down her side. "Let me show you how stunning I think you are."

Her neck felt warm beneath my lips. She let out a small moan and said, "I love the way you make me feel."

I grazed her nipple, and her sharp intake of breath was all the motivation my tongue needed to work its way down her stomach. "I need to taste you."

Her hips responded, guiding the way, the wetness between her legs gleaming like a lighthouse, navigating the ship of my kiss to safety.

I found my way.

CHAPTER EIGHTEEN

"Before we finish tonight, I want to invite all of you to Mrs. Marcel's annual end of the year barbecue," Dr. Marcel said, handing out the handwritten party invites.

Each May, the Marcels had all the grad students over to celebrate surviving another grueling year.

Mrs. Marcel's loopy handwriting was even shakier than last year. Janice nudged my leg with her toe. "Gosh, you never pay attention when it comes to this stuff."

I glanced up. "What? I'm sorry."

Janice jerked her head to Dr. Marcel.

"As I was saying, since it's only the three of you this year, I think it would be nice if you each invited a guest. The more the merrier!"

"I have a date, and I'm sure Janice will bring her steady," William said.

Janice and I exchanged a glance over his word choice. Steady? Was that East Coast code for significant other?

William frowned at us and continued, "But, Lizzie … no chance." His lips contorted into an evil sneer.

Janice must have kicked him under the table because his knee suddenly whacked the bottom of the seminar desk.

Since it's just the three of us, I thought, *Janice and William are bound to act even more like siblings.* I couldn't think of a single seminar when Janice hadn't kicked William at least once over the last year.

"Ouch! It's no secret Lizzie is completely opposed to relationships." William hissed, leaning down to rub his shin.

"What makes you think that?" I instantly regretted asking. Why did I care what William thought? Why had I voluntarily just entered the Meg danger zone?

"I don't think we need to go into that. Let's just say, you suck at them."

"She does not!" Janice jumped to my defense.

Dr. Marcel watched us as if we were his grandchildren fighting over who would get to eat the ears off a chocolate Easter Bunny.

"Really?" William whipped his head around to meet Janice's glare. "The one with Meg ended in disaster."

"You can't blame Lizzie for Meg's behavior." Janice placed both palms on the table and leaned forward. "You have no idea what went on in that relationship. It's time you let it go, Willy Boy."

"I have no idea! I know when they broke up Meg quit the program. Before that, she'd been the star pupil." He swung around to confront me. "And Lizzie couldn't handle that because she thinks she's better than the rest of us."

Although he was speaking directly to me, he'd referred to me in the third person. It was hard not to laugh right in his face.

"Careful, William. I think your insecurities are shining through again," said Janice.

Dr. Marcel seemed to be watching Janice and William as if they were putting on a play. His eyes shone with intrigue, but his body language was nonexistent. I'd often wondered if he just tuned us out when we squabbled.

William sucked in his cheeks to the point I thought he might swallow them completely.

It was time to enter the fray again. I cleared my throat and uttered, "I have a date."

"What?" Janice and William asked simultaneously. William's brow knitted itself into a perplexed knot.

I returned Janice's smile and then turned to my professor. "Is there anything I can do to help with the party?"

Dr. Marcel waved a hand. "Mrs. Marcel would have my head on a platter if I asked grad students to bring anything. She's under the impression all you three do is teach and study." He winked at me.

On my way out, Dr. Marcel motioned for me to join him in his office.

Dutifully, I followed. I fidgeted in the leather chair, unsure what he wanted to discuss.

"I thought I'd tell you that Meg stopped by."

I bit my lower lip, nodding absently.

"She wants to come back." He folded his hands on top of his desk.

"Meg's a brilliant student," I managed to say.

"That she is," he replied. "Her actions, though, are hard to ignore." He tapped his thumbs together. "Do you have any insight or advice about what I should do? Let her back or give a recommendation, maybe?" His kind eyes bored into mine as if he was demanding evidence, evidence that no one else knew.

Flummoxed, I swallowed. How could I confess all? It was nice that he was treating me as an equal, but how could I admit the whole truth and nothing but the truth? And what would he think of me if I did?

Perhaps realizing what a bind he'd put me in, Dr. Marcel waved one hand. "I'm sorry, Lizzie. You're right. It's a decision I should make. I shouldn't put any pressure on you to say anything."

He didn't show any sign that he was willing to push me on the topic, but I was certain he was hinting that no matter what I said, he wouldn't judge me. But he didn't know everything, so how could he make such a promise?

We stared at each other, not sure where to take the conversation.

"Who's your date?" he asked, putting that unpleasant business behind us.

"Do you remember Sarah Cavanaugh, the high school English teacher you introduced me to last semester?"

A broad smile spread over his face. "Ah, such an enthusiastic, lovely young woman. Good for you." He shuffled some papers on his desk, which I took as a sign I should skedaddle. I stood.

"Safe ride home," he said as I waved good-bye.

In the stairwell, I fell against the wall. How was it possible that Meg was now haunting every aspect of my life?

"What are you doing on the twenty-first?" I asked Sarah. "It's a Thursday."

"Can't think of a thing besides schoolwork. Got a better offer?" Sarah took a slow lick of her gooey, chocolate-chip cookie-dough ice cream.

I'd returned from campus to find Sarah looking adorable in a short skirt and tank top and insisting that we go for a walk. While strolling through Old Town, we'd discovered a new ice cream shop and had taken a seat on a bench outside to eat our desserts.

I licked the trail of mint chocolate-chip that seeped out the bottom of my waffle cone. "Do you remember Dr. Marcel?"

She nodded, enthralled in watching twin boys, no older than five I guessed, who were attempting to walk a golden retriever puppy. The trio would only get a few feet before the puppy entangled one of the boys, or sometimes both, in its leash. It barked happily, and the boys screeched in delight.

"He and his wife throw a barbeque for the survivors of each school year," I continued. "The first year, there were ten of us. Now there are only three."

"Three?"

"Yep. Soon to be only one."

Sarah's gaze turned on me, and her eyes shimmered with worry.

"William is heading back East to finish his dissertation. He got a research internship in Boston. Janice is finally throwing in the towel and marrying Collin to please her parents," I explained.

"That's awful."

I laughed. "Not really. I'm pretty sure she loves Collin. It's just the whole giving-a-woman-away-to-a-man thing that ruffles her feminist feathers. She told me her father made her an offer she couldn't refuse."

Sarah's eyebrows almost met in the middle as she frowned.

"He'll hire Collin to work in his construction firm, buy them a house outright, and pay off both their student loans."

"Will she finish her PhD?"

"I don't know. Her heart was never in it. That was obvious to all, including her parents, I think. For her, it was a way to escape. But who knows? Maybe when she's had some time away, she'll feel like finishing her dissertation. Stranger things have happened."

"You're sure she loves him?"

I bumped Sarah's arm. "They've been together since their undergrad days. You'll get to meet them firsthand at the barbecue, if you want."

"You're inviting me?" Her eyes crinkled up with shock.

"Yes. If you want to go. It's nothing exciting. You might even be bored to tears. Once the liquor starts to flow, we start debating history, and not just World War II. Last year, we had an hour-long *discussion* about the War of 1812." I made air quotes around the word discussion and sucked another smear of ice cream off my knuckles.

"The War of 1812?"

"Yes. It's quite fascinating actually. To this day, it's hard to determine who actually won, if anyone won at all. The Brits hardly batted an eye at the skirmish. But the Canadians and Americans trumpeted their horns about their resounding victories."

"That does sound fascinating." Her tone implied the opposite.

"Hey, you don't have to go."

"No, I'll go. You said there'll be booze."

"Truckloads. Do you like potato salad?"

She nodded enthusiastically, too busy finishing her ice cream before it melted to give a verbal response.

"Good. I've been told Mrs. Marcel makes the best potato salad."

"You haven't tried it?" Ice cream dribbled down her chin as she spoke, and she wiped it with a half-disintegrated napkin.

"Not a fan, but it's her specialty."

"Lizzie! You have to at least try some. Sometimes I'm shocked by how truly clueless you are when it comes to social situations. Yuck!"

I was fairly certain the *yuck* referred to the river of goo cascading down her hand, not my social ineptitude.

I handed her my napkin. "Odd that it's so warm today. Just last week I was still in my winter coat. Of course, knowing Colorado weather, it may snow next week."

Sarah cleaned up to the best of her ability before attacking her cone with gusto, determined to finish it once and for all. Afterward, she ran back inside to wash her hands. When she came outside again, she plopped down next to me on the bench and said, "This year you *are* sampling the potato salad."

Not much got her off track once her mind was set.

I sighed. "How much do I have to eat?"

"One spoonful — just so you can compliment her on it."

I bit my lower lip, feeling like a child who had refused to eat veggies. "All right. Just for you." I leaned over and kissed her cheek.

"Not for me. For Mrs. Marcel."

"Ugh. Don't put that image in my head. Here I was trying to imagine licking ice cream off your body, and you mention Mrs. Marcel."

Sarah whipped around to face me. "You were?"

"Yes. I was. Not now, though."

"How can I get you back in the mood?" She stroked a finger seductively down my bare arm.

"That's working."

She blew a few loose strands of hair off my neck. Her breath was warm and cookie-scented. Standing, I tossed the rest of my cone into the trashcan and reached out to help her up. "Home. Now."

"Yes, ma'am!" She saluted, then marched in front of me and glanced back over her shoulder. "I like this side of you."

I said nothing, just playfully slapped her butt.

CHAPTER NINETEEN

Dr. Marcel and his wife greeted us at the door.

"Lizzie, it's so nice to see you again." Mrs. Marcel hugged me. "And you must be Sarah. Lovely to meet you." She gave Sarah a friendly hug. "Come in, come in." She ushered us into the front room.

Janice and her fiancé, a squirrely-looking man with a goofy grin, stood to shake our hands.

"Hi, I'm Collin," he clasped Sarah's hand warmly and then turned to me. "Lizzie, congrats on surviving another year." His heartfelt handshake enforced his words.

"Thanks. I'm amazed how quickly this year flew by."

A commotion at the front door interrupted, and I heard William's booming voice. I reached for Sarah's hand and gave it a squeeze, noticing a momentary flash of reluctance on her face.

William and his date stood off to the side, and their awkwardness oozed into everyone's body language. Opposed to Collin, William's date made zero effort to fit in, and the two resembled cast-off royalty sent to far-flung territories to interact with the subjects.

"Now that we are all here, let's move out back," Mrs. Marcel suggested, probably in hopes of alleviating the tension. In years past, William and I did our best to rein in our competitiveness for our hosts' sake, but there was always a ripple of unease whenever we were together.

The end of the year barbecues had become such a tradition that it was hard to believe it would be my last with Janice and William. I wouldn't miss William, of course, but it would be hard to say good-bye to Janice. She was like the big sister I never had.

Along the rear of the large backyard was a rock retaining wall that blocked off Mrs. Marcel's garden, which Janice and I helped with every spring. Gardening wasn't my thing, but the Marcels had been so nice to me over the years that I didn't mind getting dirt under my nails a few days a year. In the other corner huddled five aspen trees.

"Help yourself everyone." Dr. Marcel was manning the grill, but he pointed to a large cooler filled with ice, pop, and beer. Next to the cooler, a folding table offered several wine bottles and another folding table held plates, silverware, and napkins. From experience, I knew that within a matter of minutes it would also be piled with heaped platters of food.

I popped the top of a Mountain Dew, and Sarah laughed.

"What? I haven't had one in years," I said.

"You're going to be bouncing off the walls tonight." She selected an Easy Street Wheat, a local beer.

"Is that a bad thing?" I whispered in her ear.

She squeezed my arm. "It depends. Will you be able to stay focused?"

"Stay focused on what?" interrupted Janice.

"Uh . . ." My face felt as red as the wine in Janice's glass.

"Never mind." Janice sniggered and then rounded to Sarah. "How did you two meet?"

Before she could answer, William and his date joined us.

"Hi, I'm Sarah." She extended her hand.

"Sarah. Right." He nodded as if he were the head of the CIA and she was talking in code. "I'm William, and this is Pru."

Pru shook my hand and then Sarah's. Her fingers were ice-cold, and the handshake was the weakest I'd ever experienced.

"Is that short for Prudence or Prunella?" asked Janice.

"Prunella." She didn't say anything else, but her pursed lips and death grip on William's arm told me she was a blue blood from back East who felt uncomfortable around the heathens of the West.

"Pru is an old family friend." William patted her hand, suggesting they were more than friends. They'd probably been betrothed since birth.

"That's neat," Janice replied, not bothering to make it sound like she meant it. Her gaze flicked to me, and I knew we were on the same page: Pru was just like William. Collin wrapped an arm around her waist, a Coors Light bottle clutched in his other hand.

Sarah watched William and Pru with an amused smirk. I could tell she was already warming to Janice and Collin.

"So, Sarah, how did you two meet?" Janice asked again. "I'd ask Lizzie, but she's the type who only gives information on a need-to-know basis." Janice nudged my arm.

"I introduced them." Dr. Marcel entered our circle, still holding his barbecue tongs. He snapped them in my direction and then Sarah's, clearly thrilled with his matchmaking skills.

Janice twirled to face me. "Really? Do tell."

I almost blurted there wasn't much to tell, but Dr. Marcel seemed so pleased with himself that I let him continue.

"Sarah came to my office in the hope of sitting in on one of my classes with a group of her students," he told them.

Knowing the story, I tuned out, taking the opportunity to compare the two couples. Janice and Collin melded together naturally, with Janice leaning comfortably against her fiancé and sipping her wine. William and Pru were the exact opposite. She clutched his arm so stiffly they reminded me of a painting of an aristocratic couple from yesteryear: overly formal, vacant eyes, and not a lick of warmth between them.

Out of the corner of my eye, I noticed Mrs. Marcel bringing a tray of food from the kitchen, and I let go of Sarah's hand to help out. I had to hand it to Dr. Marcel. He was weaving quite the tale, considering there wasn't much to relate. No wonder his students loved him. He could make watching paint dry sound interesting. To be honest, he had to; some aspects of history were just as tedious.

"Here, Mrs. Marcel, let me help you." I took the heavy platter from her frail hands. It was overloaded with bowls of potato salad, pasta salad, fresh fruit, baked beans, deviled eggs, homemade mac and cheese, coleslaw, and chips. She was a thin, birdlike woman, unlike the plump professor. I'd always wondered if she was a few years older than him. I knew Dr. Marcel was seventy-one, but she seemed closer to her eighties.

"Thank you. You're always such a help." She touched my cheek. "Oh, dear, I forgot the corn bread in the oven." Mrs. Marcel settled her hopeful eyes on me, and I almost laughed.

"Of course. I'll be right back."

When I returned with the piping-hot cornbread, the group was congregated around Mrs. Marcel and the food.

"Can I get anything else for you?" William asked. He glowered at me as if I were a younger sibling trying to outdo him. Then he shoved a handful of potato chips in his mouth and munched loudly. I tried to suppress a smile at the thought that he was pretending they were my bones.

"That would be lovely, dear," Mrs. Marcel answered. "In the fridge, can you bring the platter with the cheese, tomatoes, lettuce, pickles, and other toppings for the burgers?"

"Be back in a jiff." He kissed her cheek before rushing off like he'd been sent to rescue a kitten from a fire.

I turned to catch Janice's eye, intending to mock William, but noticed a look of concern on her face. She rolled her eyes sideways, in Sarah's direction.

My girlfriend was staring off in space, avoiding all eye contact.

I sidled up to her. "You okay?"

"What?" She flinched as if she'd forgotten where she was.

"Lost in la-la land?" I said.

"No. Just thinking." She adjusted her floral skirt, plastered a smile back onto her face, and sidestepped around me to thank Mrs. Marcel on the spread before us.

Dr. Marcel, still finishing his grilling duties, gestured for me to join him for a private chat. William, who'd returned just in time to witness that, gave an annoyed sniff.

"Do you need a hand, sir?" I asked, joining him.

Dr. Marcel set the tongs aside. "No. It's come to my attention that Meg's request to return to school isn't a secret."

I scratched my chin, not sure where this was going.

"I know I told you I was considering it, but I've decided it's best for … everyone … if she doesn't come back." He squeezed my shoulder. "You don't have to worry."

He had no idea how much worry I carried.

"I've talked with former colleagues back East. One who now teaches at Yale has experience … with Meg's issues. She might be welcome there, as long as she cleans up."

"That sounds like an excellent opportunity." I resisted the urge to jump in the air and tap my feet together. "Does she know this?"

"Yes. She arrived in New Haven this morning."

"What about the drinking?" I held my breath.

"My friend is recommending a place in Florida. If Meg completes the program, she'll be able to start as a research assistant this September." He squeezed my shoulder. Had he done all this for Meg or me? Both, probably.

Mrs. Marcel called to her husband, and he smiled and went to her, leaving me in a daze.

"I take it he finally made up his mind." Janice, never very far in moments like this, said from behind me.

Still dumbstruck, I nodded. Had Meg's name come up while I was inside? And if it had, what did Sarah know about her?

Janice jerked her head in Sarah's direction. "I really like her," she whispered. Hooking her arm through mine, she led me back to our dates.

Me too, I thought, watching Sarah. Her color had returned, her cheeks now almost as pink as her shirt. She glanced at me, but edged away a little when I came to stand next to her.

So many thoughts reeled through my head. Hopefully no one pulled up a picture of Meg, Janice, and me, The Three Musketeers, on their phone or something idiotic like that. Janice would never do such a thing after everything, and William hated me enough he'd never keep any likeness of me on his phone. However, he'd always had a thing for Meg.

"Okay, folks. Dinner's ready!" Dr. Marcel scooped the last burger onto a tray filled with brats, burgers, and steaks, and we all made a beeline for the serving area.

I selected two brats, a burger, some fruit, pasta salad, baked beans, and mac and cheese.

Sarah pointed to my plate. "Here, you forgot this." She scooped a portion of potato salad next to my brats.

"Uh, thanks."

William and Janice raised their eyebrows at each other. They'd teased me in the past for never tasting it.

Mrs. Marcel smiled. "Why, Lizzie, are you finally trying my potato salad?" She patted my back. "It's my grandmother's recipe," she told Sarah. "I still remember the day she taught my sister and me how to make it, so many years ago." Her eyes misted.

"Lizzie told me it's the best." Sarah ladled a much smaller portion onto her plate.

"Here let me, doll." Collin took Janice's plate from her and started to fill it.

"Thanks. You want another beer?"

He nodded, and Janice fished a Coors out of the icebox and refilled her wineglass.

"Teamwork. That's the secret to a great marriage." Dr. Marcel nodded. "That's how the missus and I have lasted all these years." He pinched her cheek tenderly.

"And learning to tune out the other," Mrs. Marcel added with a bemused glint in her eye.

"What's that, dear?" asked Dr. Marcel without a trace of humor.

Janice and Collin sniggered. William and Pru were too busy picking through the steaks and burgers to notice. William's plate was almost as full as mine, but Pru's held only a steak and some fruit.

Sarah's potato salad sabotage meant that half my plate was covered in it, even though she'd said I only needed to eat a bite. I was in the doghouse, and I knew it. But I couldn't muster up the courage to ask whether the problem this time was Meg or Miranda, or both. Or maybe she got another strange text from Haley and was nervous about the Michael situation. I could only hope.

For the first ten minutes of our drive home, Sarah didn't utter a single word.

"Thanks for coming with me tonight," I said in a weak attempt to break her out of her trance.

She nodded.

"Did you have fun?"

"Yeah. You?"

"I've always liked the Marcels. They're the closest thing I have to family."

"Did you —" Sarah stopped abruptly and stared out the side window instead. "Would you mind dropping me off at my apartment?" she said after a while. "I just remembered I forgot something I need for class tomorrow."

"Sure. Not a problem." I put my hand on her thigh. She didn't pull away, but she didn't rest hers on top like she normally did either.

I pulled into the parking space next to her midnight blue Mercedes. "I'll wait for you," I said.

"That's okay. I'm really tired tonight anyway. Call me tomorrow." She threw open the car door and got out.

I leaned over to say goodnight, but by the time I got the word out, she'd already slammed the door shut.

CHAPTER TWENTY

A KNOCK ON THE DOOR MADE ME LOOK UP FROM MY BOOK AND GLANCE AT MY WATCH. IT WAS well after nine at night, and I hadn't heard from Sarah in twenty-four hours, which was beyond worrisome. My stomach dropped. What if it was Meg? She was supposed to be in New Haven!

"Just a minute," I called.

"Oh, take your time. It's just creepy out here. No worries."

It wasn't Sarah's voice. Not Meg's either.

I opened the door. "Janice?"

"There's a creepy guy in your parking lot."

I peered over the railing to see my neighbor, Carl, standing by his Ford F-150. He was dressed in all black, and if a person didn't know he was a total pushover, he might come across as a serial killer kind of guy.

"What's up?" I asked. It wasn't like Janice to stop by my apartment, especially so late in the evening. Something about the visit still reminded me too much of Meg—too many late night Mayday calls to the only person who'd known the truth. After Meg and I split, I'd deliberately put more distance between Janice and myself. She understood. I think she and I felt the same. Meg had been her best friend in grad school. When Meg left, Janice might have felt abandoned or she might have felt free.

"Where's Sarah?" Janice asked, arms crossed over her chest.

"Uh. Not here. Probably at her apartment." I tried to control my voice. I didn't want to sound concerned that I hadn't heard from her and didn't know her whereabouts. We'd only been together a few months. We weren't married. She didn't have to check in with me.

"When was the last time you heard from her?"

"The night of the barbecue."

Janice nodded crisply. "Right."

"Right, what?"

"You have no idea why she's avoiding you today?" Janice tapped her forehead with an inquisitive finger.

"What are you saying?"

"William said something last night—"

"William's an ass." I cut her off.

"That's an understatement. He's a fuckstick. But you know that, and I know that." She waggled her finger back and forth in a perfect impression of a teacher reprimanding a child in the playground. "But Sarah doesn't."

I rubbed my face with both hands. "What does William have to do with Sarah not being here tonight?"

"I'm trying to save your relationship."

"What do you mean?" She now had my full attention.

"While you were helping Mrs. Marcel, William told Sarah he was surprised she wasn't blonde, since you have a thing for blondes. Then he baited her, saying, 'I hope she doesn't ruin your life as well.' Sarah didn't bite, but William ended with a snide comment about the dangers of dating colleagues."

What William had said made me look like an ass, but at least Meg's name hadn't come up.

"He also asked Dr. Marcel if Meg was coming back."

"How'd he know about that?"

"Oh please. You don't think Meg's been hitting him up for money, too. William's even richer than you."

"He said Meg's name?" Sweat prickled my neck.

"Yes. Why? He even hinted that since you wrecked her life Meg had been forced to … well … to take up jobs that were beneath her, and even 'beneath others too' was his callous little joke."

I waved her off, despite the panic roiling under my calm exterior.

Was Sarah piecing all the clues together? Did she know Meg was Miranda?

"Did Sarah say anything once you left?" Janice plunked herself down on the couch and fiddled with the latest *European History Quarterly*. It was open to an article about Bismarck and the cult of personality in Germany. Janice scanned the article. "Can I borrow this?"

Her sudden change in conversation surprised me. "Sure." I thought she was quitting. Why would she need it?

"Well?"

"Yes, take it." I gestured to the journal. "I finished it this morning."

She swatted her knee with the journal. "Not *this*. Sarah! Did she say anything to you?"

I shook my head. "She was oddly quiet. Then she said she'd forgotten something she needed and instructed me to take her home. I haven't heard from her since." I bowed my head as if confessing to a priest.

"Have you called? Texted?"

I collapsed in a chair next to the couch. "I texted, but …" The reality of the situation was dawning on me.

"You have to talk to her," Janice said.

"And say what?"

"The truth."

"*The truth*," I repeated.

"Yes. I saw the way you were with her last night. I've never seen you look at anyone like that—not even Meg."

"But …" But what? I didn't even know what Sarah thought was true anymore.

Janice leaned forward and placed a supportive hand on my knee. "I know you. You aren't good at letting people in. And the last time you did, it blew up in your face. You've been running since." She grasped my knee. "Meg told me about your family, about how they treat you. Maybe you should tell Sarah about how Meg treated you, about why you put up with it for so long."

I tried to stand up, but Janice's firm grip kept me seated.

Meg was the only woman I had introduced to my family. Afterward, I swore I would never let them meet another one of my girlfriends. It wasn't that they were horrible to Meg—they were—it was that they were despicable people who treated everyone poorly, especially me. Seeing the pity in Meg's eyes made me vow never to put myself in that situation again. But then I had. Meg turned out to be more like my mom than I'd cared to admit.

"It's no surprise," Janice went on. "But you can't close yourself off from people. It's Friday night. I'm betting you were holed up in your dining room slash office working." She stared at me knowingly.

I didn't bother to refute that since she was spot-on. "And you? What plans did you have this evening?"

"I was having dinner with Collin at Coop's when I saw Sarah with another woman, and Sarah was crying."

I bolted out of my chair. "Crying? I need to talk to her. How long ago was this?"

"I came right over."

I extracted my car keys from my pocket and fled the apartment.

"Wait for me," Janice shouted, running after me.

It was a quarter to ten when we arrived at Coopersmith's. The lights in the dining section were dimmed and tiny candles flickered on all the tables. Janice didn't have to point out Sarah. My eyes instantly sought her out in the crowd. She rested her palm against her face and slumped like she'd just received a punch to the gut.

Janice placed a supportive hand on my shoulder as we approached the table.

"Sarah," I said softly.

Accusatory eyes darted up to mine. Janice must have been prepared for such a reaction; her stiff hand on my back prevented me from stepping back.

"Please. Can we talk?" My gaze flickered from Sarah to her companion, who I assumed was Haley, and back again. I'd never met Sarah's best friend before, but from the fiery expression on Haley's face, she thought I was ten times worse than Hitler.

"I'm Janice." She stuck her hand out to Haley. "Can I buy you a drink at the bar?" She jerked her head in that direction.

Haley refused her hand. "I'm not a lesbian."

Janice let out a tinny laugh. "Right. I like a woman who says what she's thinking. Still, can I buy you a drink?"

Haley sunk deeper into her seat, shaking her head.

"It's okay, Haley. I'll be fine," Sarah muttered in a tone I'd never heard before. She didn't sound pissed, only devastated.

Begrudgingly, Haley stood and snatched her purse from the booth like she thought I might be going to rob her after I pulverized her best friend's heart. Janice threw me an encouraging smile and followed Haley to the bar.

"Can I sit?" I motioned to the seat Haley had just vacated.

Sarah eyeballed me, not speaking for several seconds. Finally, she nodded.

Carefully, I slid into the viper's den.

"Why are you here, Lizzie?"

I guess I would be wondering that as well, if I were her. What should I say? Janice told me you were crying? What if she'd been crying about something that didn't involve me? From the heat coming from her side of the table, I was 99.87 percent sure her ire was directed at me.

"Janice told me she saw you here … and that you seemed upset." I chewed on my lower lip. *Jesus, Lizzie. You watched all those rom-coms with Sarah. Think of a sappy line.*

"And that concerns you how?"

I put my hand on hers, but she pulled away.

"Sarah."

Her nostrils flared as if daring me to continue.

"Why haven't you returned my texts?" was all I could think to say.

"Been busy." Her crossed arms implied I had to work harder.

God, Lizzie, think! I mentally smacked my forehead. I should have been apologizing or begging for forgiveness.

"I think —"

"I'm really not sure you do." She bit down on her lip with such force I worried she'd sever it.

I rubbed my face with both hands so hard that my fingers pushed against my nose and blocked my passageways momentarily. "William. He's an ass."

"From what I'm learning, you aren't much better."

I stifled a snort. "But what he said —"

"What did he say?" she cut me off.

"He said I ruined a colleague's career. But he's wrong. So very wrong."

"Not just her career. Her life."

"It wasn't my fault. You have no idea what really happened."

"I'm not hearing an explanation."

"Okay. I know you're frustrated with me right now, and from the glower in your eyes, you want to shove bamboo under my fingernails." I paused to see how that would affect her. Her glare didn't soften at all. This wasn't going to be easy. "It's just not easy for me to talk about…"

"Easy for you. What about Meg? Or should I say Miranda?" Sarah slid her phone across the table and I saw a photo of Meg, Janice, William, and me, all smiles at the Marcel's barbeque in my first year of the program. Sarah must have gone home last night and scoured the university's history website for information. Damn the Internet.

She snatched the phone back, fiddled with it and then placed it in front of me. I studied Miranda's website page, which had a photo of my cleaner clear as day and who looked nothing like Meg.

Sarah scowled in anticipation of my response.

I let out a puff of air. "Okay, I know this looks bad. It's true I dated one of my colleagues. It didn't end well. Actually, it was horrendous—"

"Yeah, it's been horrendous for you. Poor Lizzie. Jesus, we ran into your ex at the hotel and you lied and told me she was Miranda. How can I believe anything you say anymore? She also said you'd given her hundreds of dollars. Have you been sleeping with her? Have you been paying her for sex?"

This again? What? No! I shook my head.

"So, she was lying? I know you hadn't dated anyone for over a year. I'd often wondered how you got your rocks off—"

"Oh my God. I didn't pay her for sex, and I didn't have sex with anyone until you." Was I seriously bragging about this? Could the people in the surrounding booths hear?

"At the moment, I'm more inclined to believe Meg."

"How can you even say that?" I pulled away as if she'd struck me.

Sarah's huff of frustration reminded me she didn't know everything.

"Sarah, I … I …" God, she'd think I was as pathetic as Haley. Could I do this? Could I tell her? Would that convince her to give me another chance? After all, we'd already established the truth wasn't exactly my forte. Then it came to me—the perfect smokescreen. "Me? I'm the liar? You lied about your car and about your trust fund. And then there's Haley."

"What about Haley?"

"You disappeared for a whole week and stayed at her place. And all the text messages. For weeks I thought I was the other woman."

"So now *I'm* a liar and a cheat. Great. Thanks, Lizzie. Why were you with me?"

"Because I fell in love." It was the truth, at last.

Sarah sniffed. "Do you even know what the word means?"

"I know I don't want to spend the rest of my life without it. And I know you're the one person who makes me happy."

"This is happy?" Sarah spread her arms wide apart and gestured to the two of us. "Right now I'm so furious with you I could throttle you. How you can sit there and compare my *omissions*"—she emphasized the word, eyes narrowed—"to your outright lies over the Meg and Miranda situation is … is … I can't think of the word to describe someone cocky enough to pull that crap."

"Attitudinizer."

She scowled at me. "I wasn't asking for a word! But maybe another one that starts with A is more appropriate."

Did she just call me an asshole? Not that I could blame her at the moment.

"I'm sorry," I said, but I still couldn't come out with the truth about Meg. Maybe Sarah was right: maybe I was an asshole, a fuckstick even. It was easier to let her think that and not the truth. She'd made it clear that she loved Haley, but she didn't respect Haley. Not completely. Not for letting Michael treat her the way he did. And Meg. Not only did Meg abuse me, but she had been blackmailing me for over a year. Was there a way to win Sarah back without spilling my guts? "Look, I'm not trying to pretend anything," I continued, my voice catching. "I'm just saying we both kept things under wraps."

A malicious grin appeared on Sarah's face and her dark bob bounced around as she shook her head. "All along I thought you were clueless. You aren't clueless, Lizzie. You're just a fucking manipulator."

The word slashed through me far more than the word *asshole* had. Meg had manipulated me for months. To have Sarah feel the same about me — it was too much.

I reached across the table for her hand. "Sarah, please —"

"You are a piece of work." She spat the words and then stood. "I've had enough," she hissed as she left the table.

I watched helplessly as she marched over to Haley and yanked on her friend's arm. Both of them hotfooted it toward the door, Haley looking back with an expression that warned me I should watch my back. Janice just stared at me open-mouthed and then raised both hands in the air as if to say, *What gives?*

I gawked back, throwing my own hands up in the universal I-don't-know gesture. Around us, several people watched, amused.

I sighed.

"Fuck it," I muttered. Springing to my feet, I immediately chased after her.

Outside, Sarah was nowhere to be seen. I scanned the sidewalk, left and then right, hoping for a clue. Rom-coms told me to look for a scarf on the ground. That's how it always happened in the movies.

Janice rushed up behind me. "Which way?"

"You go right. I'll go left." I didn't wait to explain what she was supposed to do if she found them.

It didn't take me long to realize they hadn't gone in my direction at all. Shit!

I wheeled around abruptly, nearly knocking over a woman in her fifties. Her husband clutched my arm and shoved me aside. "Watch it!"

"Sorry," I shouted over my shoulder as I ran.

Not even fifty yards away, I saw Janice talking to Sarah by the fountain in the middle of Old Town. Hands clasped, Janice resembled an eager defense attorney pleading for the jury not to convict. From my vantage point, I noticed Sarah's squared shoulders softening. Both of them turned when they heard me approach. Haley huffed in revulsion.

"Sarah, please. Hear me out."

CHAPTER TWENTY-ONE

"No," Sarah said, but her eyes were sympathetic, which confused the hell out of me.

"No?" I staggered back a step.

"I want to speak to Janice."

"Janice?" both Haley and I asked at the same time.

Janice put her arm around my shoulder. "It's okay. Let me talk to her," she whispered, walking me a few steps from the group.

"Lizzie," Sarah called out, and I spun hopefully. "Can you please drive Haley home?"

"Yeah, sure," I replied, eyes downcast so she couldn't see my disappointment.

"What? No. I'm not riding with *her*." Haley backed away as if I were Josef Mengele.

"Haley, please. I need to talk to Janice alone," Sarah said.

I wanted to shout, "What the fuck?" but I remained mute. Sarah's body language indicated she was yielding, and I didn't want to jinx anything.

Haley's eyes were imploring her, but Sarah smiled wanly and gave her friend a hug. "Please do this for me," I heard her say.

I motioned for Haley to follow. My car was two blocks from the town square, and I was dreading every moment I had to spend with this girl who obviously hated my guts.

In the car, I wondered how Sarah could be such good friends with someone so morose. Haley clutched her purse in her lap, holding it against her like body armor. Not once did she look at me or speak, except to tell me where she lived. If not for her demeanor, she'd be gorgeous. I wondered what she was like on a good day. Not that I was curious to find out.

Fifteen minutes later, I pulled in front of Haley's building and she leaped out before the car came to a complete stop, slamming my car door with such force that I swear the steering wheel shook.

"No need to say thanks," I grumbled through clenched teeth. I waited for her to enter her apartment, not wanting to have to explain it to Sarah if something happened to her. When she was secure inside, and out of my sight, I let out a long, tired breath.

My phone vibrated: a text from Sarah.

Meet me at IHOP in an hour.

IHOP? That wasn't Sarah's normal type of place. Given the hour, though, it made sense that was where Sarah and Janice decided to chat. Most eateries, besides bars, were closing. Plus, her request made it clear she didn't want to be alone with me. *Is this my last meal? Have a pancake and then never see Sarah again?*

Sarah's car was already in the lot when I pulled in. I sat in the parking area of IHOP for forty-five minutes before I ventured inside five minutes early. Janice sat at a table in the back—by herself. My heart plummeted to my feet with such force I was sure it would crash all the way to China. Had Sarah managed to sneak out the back?

She waved me over, perkier than the last time I saw her. Was she putting on a brave face? Was she preparing to say that she'd tried but failed?

I slid into the booth across from her.

"Cheer up, Lizzie. She's willing to talk to you now."

"What did you say to her?"

"The truth. That William has been after you since Dr. Marcel chose you over him. That Meg was self-destructive. I think Sarah's starting to come around."

"Where is she?" I scouted the premises, not seeing her.

"In the bathroom." Janice got up to leave.

"Where you going?"

She tipped her head back and laughed. "Don't panic. You can do this."

"But—"

She put a hand on my shoulder. "Just be yourself ... but not completely." She winked, but her shoulder squeeze was supportive.

"Hello." Sarah approached the table tentatively.

"Let's do dinner soon," Janice said, hugging her as if they'd been best friends since elementary school.

Sarah nodded but stepped back. "Thank you."

"No problem," Janice said. "Lizzie is special." She didn't make it sound like a compliment, and Sarah got a chuckle out of that, too.

Sarah slipped into the booth, and I watched Janice march out of the restaurant without looking back. My tongue felt swollen, rendering me incapable of speech. At the last moment, Janice turned and gave me a thumbs-up. It made me crack a smile.

"I like her," Sarah said, gazing at Janice's retreating back.

"Y-yeah," I slurred. My tongue was working again, but my mouth seemed full of sand. "You okay?" I asked, noticing her red, swollen eyes. I reached for her hand. This time, she didn't pull away.

"A little better now. This hasn't been a fun night, though." She waited for me to say something. Anything.

"I'm sorry. I never wanted to make you feel ..." I couldn't say *manipulated*.

"Are you hungry?" She picked up the laminated menu.

I shook my head.

"Seriously? You aren't hungry?"

"Not really."

She tilted her head, scrutinizing my face. "I don't know what to say. I shouldn't have jumped to conclusions without talking to you."

I snorted. "How could you not—after everything? Meg. William. Miranda. I'm really sorry."

"I'm pretty sure Miranda is the only innocent party in this whole mess." Sarah smiled.

I tried to return it, but found I couldn't. Janice paved the way for me, but she didn't know it all, and I knew I'd finally have to come completely clean for the first time or it would never work with Sarah.

The haggard waitress approached. "Can I get you two anything?" Her tone implied we should order immediately or leave.

"Tea?" I suggested out of fear.

"Coffee for me. And . . ." Sarah glanced down at the menu. "Can we get the appetizer sampler to start, please?"

The waitress grunted a yes as she waddled off.

"To start?"

"I eat when I'm upset." Sarah's eyes darted away from mine, and she swiped them with her sleeve.

I felt terrible. "What can I do to make you feel better?"

"Talk to me. Tell me about Meg. All of it."

I nodded, blinking away a tear forming in my right eye. I ignored it, not wanting to let on that I was on the verge of crying.

Sarah didn't ignore it. She reached out and wiped it away with the sleeve of her sweater.

"Meg . . ." I started, quickly faltering. I sucked my lower lip into my mouth.

Sarah gave me an encouraging nod.

"I met her when I first started the program. She and Janice were two years ahead of me. I was dazzled by her at first. She was Dr. Marcel's superstar. She could do no wrong. For a long time, I thought she walked on water."

"Until?" Sarah stroked my hand with a finger, encouraging me to continue. "It's okay."

"She wasn't very nice to me." I sat up straighter, placed both hands on my head, and blinked away some tears. "At first she was, but then I got to know the real Meg. The behind-closed-doors Meg. The alcoholic Meg." I closed my eyes tightly.

"The bitch Meg," Sarah said, and I realized she must have finally remembered their first meeting.

"God, she was so fucking mean," I continued. "When she drank, which was often, she was so belittling, blamed me for everything. Janice was good friends with her, but even she didn't know the whole truth at first. Eventually, she saw how Meg treated me. I don't think Janice knew how bad her drinking was until a year or so after Meg and I started dating. Maybe it was my fault."

Sarah gripped my hand. "No, Lizzie. It was not your fault. The only one to blame for Meg's drinking is Meg. Don't ever think it was your fault."

Her forcefulness surprised me and calmed me.

"I know that—knew that," I corrected myself. "At least most of the time. I tried to help her. I really did. I paid for her rehab." I shook my head. "I don't think she wanted my help. Meg was always so stubborn. Everything had to be on her terms. When she crashed and burned out of the program—"

"How?"

"She showed up drunk for a conference Dr. Marcel was hosting. Meg was one of the speakers."

Sarah put a hand on her chest. "Really?"

"Yeah. It was so unlike anything she'd done. Dr. Marcel was devastated. I think he suspected she liked to party, but she'd never let it interfere with school or her research. Never."

"What happened?"

I covered my face with my palm. "The day before, we really got into it. Meg was screaming at me. She got totally out of hand. It wasn't unusual for her to push or shove me. Once she pushed me so hard I lost my balance and I sprained my wrist. When really drunk, she'd corner me to scream in my face. She'd even placed a forearm over my throat …" I covered my mouth and let out a shaky sigh. "It sounds so bad, saying it out loud. But then, I could explain it all away … Make excuses … She didn't mean to hurt me … But the last time … Before I knew what had happened, she'd hit me. Split my lip." I massaged my lip with my fingers, remembering my humiliation. "She didn't stop there. I had bruises …" My voice caught, so I motioned to my arms and chest to finish the thought. "I was supposed to be leaving that night for a different conference back East, so the last thing I said to her was that I was done. I couldn't be with her anymore."

Sarah swallowed visibly, tears welling in her eyes, but she didn't stop me.

"I didn't even know what happened, about her showing up drunk. When I got back from my conference, all her stuff was gone from my apartment. She didn't live with me, but … well, you know … things accumulate over time. And she never had a key, so I still have no idea how she got in. Dr. Marcel broke the news to me that she'd been kicked out of school."

"How long were you two together?"

"Over two years."

"Was it bad the entire time?"

I licked my lips and then rubbed them together, holding everything in. "I …"

"It's okay." Sarah looked down at the table. "You don't have to explain all at once."

"No, I think I should. I was so desperate to keep her in my life. To feel love … My family, well I never really felt I belonged there. And then Meg happened, and she wanted to be with me. But she really only wanted to control me, I think because she couldn't control herself. I flipped through that book you got after the Haley/Michael situation. The one about abusive personalities." She nodded. "It made me feel so stupid. I missed so many warning signs." I rubbed the top of my head. "I kept ticking them off: the interrogations when I returned home late. Her forcing social isolation—I was never one to hang with friends much to begin with, but to be told I couldn't … That was frustrating. She would accuse me of sleeping with everyone, even William. The verbal abuse. The insults. She was a pro at twisting innocent comments into insults. I was constantly afraid to say anything out of fear of instigating an episode. I started to keep track of the episode-free days. Sometimes I could go days without seeing Mr. Hyde. Sometimes Mr. Hyde popped out no matter how hard I tried to behave. I tried so hard not to make her angry." I rubbed my thighs with sweaty palms.

Sarah wiped a tear off her cheek. My eyes brimmed.

"It got to the point where I didn't know which way was up. Janice spent many nights trying to talk some sense into me. I always made excuses for Meg, always explained the abuse away. I didn't want to admit to myself that I was being tormented by my girlfriend. I still don't. Except for that time when she showed up drunk at the conference, Meg appeared perfect to all of our acquaintances. The star grad student everyone wanted to emulate. Even today, William blames me for ruining Meg. For destroying her career. I was terrified to end the relationship because I didn't want all this to come out. Meg threatened on many occasions to tell the truth—*her* truth. I couldn't face it. And then when she beat me"—my voice cracked and I had to recover before continuing—"that changed me. It scared the crap out of me, and the mortification . . ." I covered my eyes.

Sarah sniffled.

The waitress arrived with our drinks. "I'm sorry it's taking so long for your order. It'll be out as soon as possible." With that she left.

I sighed. Sarah smiled meekly as a way to say please continue.

"Since that day, I promised myself I would never let a woman get to me again, for better or worse. The thought terrifies me. And then I met you." I glanced in her direction. "All thoughts of Meg flew out of my head. And there was only you. But. . ."

"But what?"

"I'm still scared."

"Of what? I'd never hit you." She placed a hand over her heart.

"Being hit only hurts for a bit. But not being enough for someone . . . that frightens me." I stifled a sob, and Sarah handed me a napkin to dab my eyes.

"Even after you found out about Haley you didn't say anything. Why didn't you trust me?"

"You've been telling me all along I'm clueless, so very clueless. Besides, you may not remember this, but when you told me about Haley you said. . ."

Sarah rested her hands on mine. Tears dripped down my cheeks. "I remember, but Lizzie . . . if I had known—"

"Then you'd be there for me as a friend like you are for Haley. Not judge, but not understand and secretly question how I could be so weak."

"I'm so sorry. It wouldn't have been like that. I'm here, now. And I'm not going anywhere."

"You don't know it all yet."

Sarah swallowed.

"Since the breakup, Meg's been blackmailing me."

"How in the world?"

"She's threatened to tell Dr. Marcel that I've plagiarized parts of my master's thesis. Or to say I had sex with a student. She's threatened telling William everything—the sex, the abuse. God knows what other devious plans she's concocted now that she's seen you on more than one occasion. I've been living in dread."

"We'll figure out a way to deal with Meg. I promise."

She looked earnest.

"Dr. Marcel is helping," I said.

"Does he know everything?"

"I'm sure he's guessed plenty, but no. I've never told a soul about all of this. Not even Janice."

"Then how is Dr. Marcel helping?"

"He's helping her get into a program in Connecticut. She just has to clean up her act."

"You don't sound so confident."

"She left rehab early last time." I held up my heavy head with two fingers.

"Let's not think about that, just yet. Maybe the hotel situation was her rock bottom. One can only hope."

"Hope," I stuttered. "What about us? How can you respect me after all of this?"

"Oh, Lizzie. You have no idea how strong you actually are. And no matter what, I'll never stop loving you."

I knew we had only brushed the surface of all the things we needed to say to each other, but fatigue swept over me. "Can we go? I'm exhausted." I had to force my eyelids to stay open.

"Of course," Sarah motioned to the waitress for the check.

"I had them wrap it up for you. Sorry about the wait." The waitress set the box down, stared at me and then at Sarah, and gave a supportive nod. I wondered how many times a week she witnessed people at their worst.

Sarah took out her wallet, threw some cash on the table, snatched up the box, and whisked me outside to my car. Taking my keys, she drove us straight to my apartment.

As soon as we stepped inside my apartment, I couldn't fight off my body's desire to sleep. Sarah held me as I drifted off, her warmth beside me in the bed as I slept. She was still beside me when I jolted up in the early hours, clutching at my shirt and trying to steady my breathing.

Sarah stirred. "You okay?"

"Yeah. Just a bad dream."

She lifted the covers. "Come here."

I nestled into her arms.

"Tell me about your nightmare." She stroked my hair.

"It was nothing. Just about Meg." I hid my troubled eyes, burrowing my head into her bare chest.

"I won't let her hurt you again," she promised, kissing the back of my head.

She held me tight, completely unaware I'd just lied to her again.

I'd dreamed that I lost Sarah and was all alone in the world.

CHAPTER TWENTY-TWO

SARAH STIRRED A SPOONFUL OF SUGAR INTO HER COFFEE. AFTER WAKING UP TERRIFIED, I'D fallen sound asleep in her arms and skipped my bike ride. We decided to have breakfast at home before she went shopping with her mom, and I went on my coffee date with Ethan.

"How much does Ethan know?"

I quirked one eyebrow.

"About Meg? The money?" Sarah took a sip, but kept her eyes glued to mine.

I shook my head. "He knew things with Meg were difficult. He has no idea about the money."

Sarah paused, waiting to see whether I would continue. I didn't. I gathered she was weighing her next words carefully. "Why haven't you told anyone the whole truth? What a burden to carry."

I rubbed the back of my left hand with my right. "I'm an independent person, or so I thought. I had to be. Meg took that away from me. It was like she owned me … and … and I had to prove to myself I could be independent again. But…"

"What?" Her voice was soft and compelling.

"I'm scared it might happen again."

Sarah's expression was understanding, compassionate.

"I'm not saying I want to be alone, but I'm scared of being like that again. It's an ongoing battle." I pointed to my head.

"So, what you're saying is that I should be on the lookout for self-sabotage?" She squeezed my hand to show me she was only joking — partially, at least.

I let out a snort of laughter. "Ethan has already warned me, but it might be prudent for you to stay vigilant, too." I suddenly felt a strong desire to tell her the truth about my dream. I forced down some tea to bury that urge deep inside again.

"What do you mean you had to be independent?" Sarah doused her eggs again with pepper, her brows hoisted as she awaited my response.

"I feel like I've been on my own since I can remember. I spent a lot of time hiding from my family." I looked away again, eyes downcast. "Let's just say they weren't the nicest people to be around."

Sarah nodded. "You have a lot in common with Haley."

I grunted. "I think she hates me."

"Don't worry. She's like that with everyone. It takes time for Haley to warm to people. And you aren't the most open person yourself." She forked some omelet rather aggressively.

I wanted to say I couldn't anticipate hanging out with Haley much, but I thought better of it. I'd only just gotten back into Sarah's good graces. It probably wasn't wise to suggest I thought her best friend was a bitch.

"How are you doing?" she asked. "Last night was long for both of us."

I flashed a half-hearted smile. "I'm okay." I reached for her hand. "But the next time I see William, I'm going to give him a piece of my mind. He's such a fuckstick! Never trust a man who doesn't open his mouth when he speaks."

Sarah choked and covered her mouth with her napkin. "Fuckstick! I never thought I'd hear you say that word."

"Janice calls him that, and it suits him perfectly."

"I really like her."

I swallowed a massive bite of toast. "Yeah. I'll miss her."

"I know I just met her, but there's something about her that pulls me in."

"Then maybe it's a good thing she's leaving. Not that she's gay, but I don't want to take any chances." I smiled. "It's weird, though, that I'm the only one left. Even Ethan quit his program once he completed his master's."

"Well, you still have me and Ethan, even if he isn't in school anymore. And I can tell you I'm not leaving." She squeezed my hand back.

I was positive I must have been grinning like a fool.

"That reminds me; give me your keys." She put out her hand, palm up. "I want to get a copy of your apartment key made today."

I blinked and then stared as if the floor beneath me had just disappeared. I managed to say, "Yeah, good idea," without alerting Sarah to the panic rising inside of me. It confused the hell out of me. I didn't want to lose Sarah; in fact, after this morning's dream, I dreaded it. But the thought of her having a key terrified the crapola out of me, too.

"Have you talked with Meg since the incident in the hotel?" Sarah asked.

"Not yet. I'm sure she'll call or text soon to demand more money. Probably for rehab again."

Sarah slammed her coffee cup onto the table. "Oh, hell no!"

"But I thought you wanted me to help her."

"That was before I knew the whole story and thought she was Miranda. I won't let her hurt you or take advantage of you. Not on my watch."

My phone buzzed, and both of us jumped.

"That better not be her," said Sarah.

"Nope. Ethan. He can't make it today. Stomach flu."

"That gives me an idea." Sarah whipped out her phone. "I have the flu as well."

"Do you need me to run to the store for crackers and Sprite?"

Sarah stopped texting and stared at me slack-jawed. "That's what I'm telling Mom. I don't want to leave you alone today."

"So you're lying?" I teased.

"Not really. Maybe just a little. Just saying I feel tired and there's a flu going around school. Mom hates being around anyone who's ill."

"Ah, I see."

"I don't have to send it," she said, her fingers hovering over the keys.

She had me right where she wanted me.

"Please, send it," I said. "I need you."

CHAPTER TWENTY-THREE

IT HAD BEEN THREE WEEKS SINCE I CONFESSED ALL TO SARAH, AND IT HAD TAKEN ME THIS LONG to work up the courage to meet Ethan for coffee. I slumped in my chair and said, "I think I'm in trouble."

Ethan placed a concerned hand on mine. "Don't you worry. We'll get through this together. Who's the father?"

"I'm not pregnant!"

Everyone in Starbucks gawped at me, and Ethan howled with laughter. Holding his sides, he managed to say between gasps, "Sarah shooting blanks?"

I leaned over the table. "Oh, you think you're so funny."

He waved one hand in front of his face. "Okay, I'm sorry. What's the problem?"

"Do you know what I did yesterday?"

"Ran a marathon? No—a bikeathon?" He slapped the table. "Cured cancer?"

"What's wrong with you today?" I peered into his coffee cup. "Did you add whiskey?"

He shook his head, all smiles. "It's summertime! No classes until August. I'm a free man."

"Yes, that's my problem. Sarah isn't in school either, so she's decided we need a project to keep busy. She's forcing me to redecorate my apartment. She made me box up all the books I'm not actively reading for research. I'm only allowed one bookcase. Five shelves!" I stabbed the air with a solitary finger. "She's allowed to have flowers in every room, even in the bathroom, but I only get one bookcase."

Ethan drummed his fingers on his chin. "I wasn't aware you decorated your apartment in the first place. At least, you don't seem the type who would."

"That's what she said!"

He closed one eye and inspected my face carefully with the other. "I think you're missing my point. It's nice of her to fix up your place, make it homier. It won't kill you to grow up some."

"B-but ..." I stammered unable to think of a counterargument.

Ethan took a thoughtful sip of his coffee. "What's really bugging you?"

I yanked on the elastic band that kept my journal shut. "Nothing, really. It's just weird now that she's not in school. We're always together. She's always at my place."

"Your place? Has the U-Haul arrived yet?" He attempted to hide his smile with his cup.

"Nope, just several trips back and forth from her apartment bringing most of her crap over."

"Talk to her. Don't let this fester."

"Talking isn't my strong suit." I knew deep down he was right. Sarah suggested therapy, but I wasn't sure about that. It killed me telling *her* everything. How would I talk to a stranger?

"No, really?" He stretched his legs, and they nearly reached past the next table. "It was bound to happen."

"What?"

"The newness in every relationship wears off. It's hard to maintain that level of excitement."

"It's only been a few months."

"You lesbians move fast. Now you have to decide."

"Decide what?"

"Whether she's really the one you want, or whether it was just the newness that attracted you."

"How do I figure that out?"

He laughed. "Relationships aren't easy. If they were, there'd be no wars, murders, domestic abuse …" He circled his finger in the air.

I ignored him, especially the last bit. "I just need to get through the summer. In the fall, we'll both be busy, and it'll be easier."

"If you say so. In my experience, turning a blind eye to a problem only leads to more problems. But…"

"But what?"

"You're the type who has to find out the hard way. I just hope I get front row seats to what's going to happen."

"What do you think will happen, smarty-pants?"

"No clue. Only time will tell. It's no secret you'd rather run than deal with your issues."

"What issues do I have besides trust and commitment?" The thought of losing Sarah scared me. Yet, the thought of settling down wasn't pleasant either. Why did things have to change so suddenly? I was finally (hopefully) free from Meg. Couldn't we just enjoy our time together without contemplating our futures? I needed baby steps and Sarah wanted to dive in headfirst.

His phone vibrated. After reading the text, he said, "Goodness, they don't have enough coffee in this joint to get us through that conversation."

"Maybe you and Sarah should hang out this summer," I said. "Both of you are so giddy about not being in school. Some of us like school and feel lost without structure and deadlines." My mind tortured me with thoughts when it had too much free time. If it wasn't getting me worked up about Sarah's need to settle down, it plagued me with thoughts of losing her, as if she'd finally realize I wasn't worth the effort. Maybe therapy was needed. Or a diversion.

He picked up his phone. "What's her number?"

I swatted the idea away. "No way. You and Sarah — not going to happen."

"I'll only say good things. I promise." He crinkled his brow. "You might be right. I can't think of anything good to say."

"Whatever. You've been in couple's therapy for over a year now."

He nodded. "And you know what I've learned?"

I motioned for him to tell me, since I knew he would anyway.

"It's best to talk things through and not run."

"That's what you do? Talk?"

Ethan pointed to his chest. "Me? Hell no. All she does is talk. And talk. And talk."

"And you're implying I'm bad at relationships."

"That's TBD, really." Ethan's smirk didn't alleviate the sense of dread forming in my mind.

To be determined. I guess it really was unknown: the future. Sarah and me. Me and Sarah. Nothing was set in stone. It was a relief to a certain degree. A terrifying relief. I've always hated not knowing where something was going.

That night, we had dinner plans with Janice. Collin had already flown back to San Francisco, and she was leaving the next day.

"So, you all packed?" I asked, placing a napkin in my lap.

She nodded. "Everything is on the truck, all heading home as we speak."

"Are you going to miss Colorado?"

"Some. Not the winters, though. I never got used to the snow."

"I know she won't say it, but Lizzie's going to miss you quite a bit," said Sarah.

Janice giggled. "Lizzie admit that? No way." She pinned me with a frown and then grinned. "I'll miss you as well."

I swallowed.

Sarah placed a hand on my leg, giving it a tender squeeze.

"I will admit I'm sad I never got the chance to sit in on one of your lectures," I said.

Janice flashed me a funny look. "You didn't know?"

"Know what?"

"Why Dr. Marcel asked us to sit in on your class?"

"No."

"It was his way of forcing William out. He already knew I was leaving. After your stellar performance, it was pretty much settled that any teaching positions Dr. Marcel had influence over would be offered to you, not William. Dr. Marcel sat in on William's class before yours. From what I gleaned from eavesdropping, Dr. Marcel pointed him in a different direction." Her eyes crinkled with humor, making it clear she wasn't sorry for eavesdropping yet again.

"That's why William is moving?"

"Yep. Dr. Marcel helped him find a position he'd be more suited to while he wraps up his dissertation."

I sighed. "That man has always had my back."

"He loves you. And he believes in you." Janice patted my hand. "Just like me."

Everything was starting to fall into place. A sense of calm washed over me.

Sarah and Janice plowed on into wedding conversation. For a woman so against the concept of marriage, Janice had a lot of ideas about her own wedding.

"So, you two are coming?" Janice asked.

Sarah answered for us. "Wouldn't miss it for the world."

"Who knows, it might inspire you, Lizzie." She regarded me curiously.

"Inspire?"

The two of them cracked up. "You never know. You might find your inner romantic sooner rather than later." Janice laughed.

Inner romantic? Marriage equaled romance? The conversation was bounding into dangerous territory. I knew I had to put a damper on the mood, so I brought up a topic I thought would stop Janice cold.

"How does Collin feel about not having kids?" I asked. She'd always said she would never have kids—hated them actually.

Janice flushed three shades of red. Then she grinned from ear to ear.

"You aren't?" gasped Sarah.

She nodded. "Found out last week." Her expression registered happiness with a tinge of fear.

"Found out what?" I looked between the two of them.

Sarah tapped my leg, rolling her eyes. "She's pregnant."

"What? When? How?"

Both Janice and Sarah shook their heads, staring at me wide-eyed.

"Sometimes I really wonder about you," Sarah said. "How did you even survive before me?"

"Oh, she was barely surviving, and not living," offered Janice, a shit-eating grin on her face.

"Oh, whatever." I frowned at both of them until Sarah leaned over and kissed my cheek.

"Don't let this one go," Janice instructed me. "No one else will ever get you like Sarah does."

I knew right then and there that Janice was right.

Sarah understood me, and she still wanted me.

It was a peculiar feeling—one I wasn't used to.

I shifted a little in my seat, Sarah's hand still warm against my thigh. "Trust me, Janice," I said. "I have no intention of ever letting her go."

A WOMAN LOST

A novel by
T.B. Markinson

CHAPTER ONE

"Hello."

"I'm getting married."

"What?"

"I'm getting married."

"Peter, it's" — I rolled over in bed and looked at the clock — "five in the morning, on a Sunday. I'm not in the mood for a prank." My entire body ached; I'd been awake most of the night.

"It's not a prank, Elizabeth. I am getting married."

I sat up in bed.

"We're flying in next week to have dinner with Mom and Dad. She wants you to join us."

"What?" I rubbed my eyes, wondering if I was dreaming. My brother and I were not close in any way. I didn't even know he had my home phone number. Was my number listed? And I was shocked that he'd admitted to his bride-to-be that he had a sister.

"Madeline wants to meet you. Oh, and bring Meg." He sounded upbeat. It was four in the morning in California, an hour later here in Colorado.

"We broke up." I tried to keep my voice calm and quiet.

"Oh, my gosh. When did that happen?"

"Two years ago."

A long, awkward silence followed.

"Oh … wow … that's too bad. Well, is there someone else?"

I wanted to tell him that girls, let alone love, just didn't fall from the sky. Instead, I looked over at the naked woman in my bed and chuckled. Well, maybe girls did fall from the sky. Good grief, she could sleep through anything. She always said her mom was intentionally loud during naptime so she would be a sound sleeper; apparently, it worked.

"I'm not ready for that." I didn't mean I wasn't ready to date. Obviously, there was a woman with me, but he didn't know that on the other end of the phone. I meant I wasn't ready to introduce anyone to my family … again.

"Hopefully you will still join us. Maddie is so excited to have a sister."

I thought to myself *fuck no. No way.* I wasn't going to have dinner with Mom, Dad, Peter, and now a fiancée. *No fucking way. I'd rather gouge out my own eyes and then eat them.*

"Um … sure … where should I meet all of you?"

"At the club."

Of course! The club. I should have known. Why would they go anywhere else?

I grabbed my chai from the barista in the coffee shop, and announced, "Peter called."

"Who's Peter?" asked Ethan, and poured an insane amount of sugar into his coffee before we sat down at the table. He always ordered the special of the day, never a fancy drink with a shot of this or two squirts of that. He loved coffee with sugar and none of the hoopla.

"My brother, you ass."

"Oh, my god! How is God?" He straightened his starched shirt. To say he was fastidious would be an understatement.

"He called to tell me he's getting married. Oh, and get this: he wants me to join him, his fiancée, and my parents for dinner." I blew into my steaming cup of chai. The vapors fogged up my contacts, and I had to blink several times to see again.

"You said no, didn't you? Tell him you have a violent case of the clap and if you sneeze they'll get it."

"I'm meeting them Monday night."

"Jesus! You do like your public floggings."

"He asked me to bring Meg."

Ethan giggled as he stirred his coffee. "Talking to you about your family always makes me feel better about my own messed-up situation."

"Yeah. When I told him we broke up, he actually said, 'Oh, my gosh.' Like he gives a crap."

"He did not! He always was such an ass. *C'est la vie.* So bring the new girl."

"Sarah? Are you kidding? She's not ready to meet the family. And besides, I insinuated I wasn't seeing anyone, so I can't bring her now. It will seem desperate."

"Don't you mean *you* aren't ready to introduce her to the family, and other things, I might add?" He gave me a knowing look.

"That could be the case." I smiled and took a huge gulp of my chai.

Sarah and I woke up before the alarm trilled, but neither of us wanted to crawl out of bed yet. She reached over and ran her fingers through my hair. "What are you doing today?"

I rolled over to face her, gazed into her quizzical brown eyes. "Not too much today. I have to teach." I stroked a strand of hair off her cheek. "Tonight I am having dinner with my family. Oh, and I'm meeting Ethan for coffee today before I head down to Denver. You?" My finger moved down her face to stroke her breasts.

She stared at me for a moment in disbelief, and then she bolted upright. "We have been dating for almost a year, and you have never had dinner with your family. I didn't think you were even in contact with them."

I ignored the comment that we had been together almost a year; actually, it was closer to six months. And the first three or four months included only a few casual dates. However, it was not the right moment to remind her of that.

"My brother is in town with his fiancée. We're having dinner to welcome the poor girl into the family."

"Oh." She stared at me with sad doe eyes. "I better get ready for work."

I watched her walk into the bathroom and step into the shower. Then I rolled onto my back and placed the pillow over my head. "Shit, shit, shit."

Normally, Ethan and I met at the coffee shop on Saturdays. But when he couldn't make it, we rescheduled. Meeting him would help take my mind off my impending family dinner.

"My god, Ethan, she looked at me like I had just run over her dog and had then backed up and run it over again." I sipped my chai and stared out the window at College Avenue, the main street of Fort Collins. "I'm so screwed."

He nearly choked on his coffee. "Can you blame the girl? Not only did you plan dinner with your family and not mention it for a whole week, but you are meeting your brother's fiancée. She has to be wondering why you didn't invite her. Hasn't she moved in with you?"

"N-no," I stammered. "Not completely. She's still paying rent at her place. She just stays with me every night … and most of her stuff is at my place, but it isn't official. We have not moved in together." I turned away from his knowing glare and stared at the other patrons in the coffee shop.

"How long are you going to string this girl along?" He shook his head. Not a hair was out of place.

Ethan and I had been *really* good friends at one point. We worked together part-time at the college library. I was just starting my PhD program in history, and he was starting his in English. Since we studied the same time period, we talked a lot about our classes. After working together for two years, Ethan quit the program on completion of his Masters. He opted for teaching at a high school in a neighboring city, and we didn't see much of each other.

But then, out of the blue, we met for coffee. We had so much fun we started to meet for coffee once a week, and continued to for two years. Then both of us hit rough patches in our lives. His marriage was on the rocks. My relationship fell apart completely. We became therapists for each other.

Our weekly meetings switched from discussing our research and learning, to bickering, fighting, and calling the other person on their shit. We had fun doing that, too. No matter how brutal we were to each other, the next week, both of us would be right on time. Dysfunctional: yes. Bizarre: yes. But we needed it. Or at least that was what I told myself.

We would tell each other things we wouldn't dream of telling our loved ones or partners. We knew each other better than our significant others did, indulging in an odd, sometimes intrusive intimacy that never went beyond our coffee dates.

"I don't know what you mean." I eventually answered his earlier question, staring across the table at him, watching his nervous habit of pulling at the corner of his neatly trimmed moustache. *How does he make it so narrow and precise?* I wondered. We sat in the back corner, hiding from a gaggle of college students in the shop. "I'm not stringing her along." Again, I avoided his eyes. Instead, I stared over at the barista, who was making a Frappuccino.

Ethan took off his Coke-bottle-thick glasses and cleaned them on a serviette. "Yes you do. Don't try that shit with me, Lizzie."

"I don't know what to do, Ethan. I care about her, but when I look at her—sometimes, I don't feel anything. When she's sleeping at night and I've got insomnia and can't sleep, I get annoyed that she is in my bed. The other night, I was on my back and she was up against my left side with her leg draped over me and her arm around my chest."

He frowned impatiently and motioned for me to get to the point.

"Wait, that's not the weird part." I continued. "She was holding my earlobe! The arm she had draped over me—she was holding my earlobe. And I started to think: *why?* Why was she holding onto my ear? Then I couldn't stop focusing on the fact. I mean, who does that? Who holds their girlfriend's ear while she sleeps? Who?" I threw my arms up in the air in exasperation. "She wasn't rubbing it. Not feeling it. Just holding it. I don't think I slept at all until she rolled over. Who holds someone's ear?" I took a nervous sip of my chai, embarrassed by my rant about Sarah. Why did it even bother me so much?

"I'll admit that it's a little weird. But it doesn't seem like something you should obsess about. She probably didn't know she was doing it. Do you think maybe it had something to do with your insomnia? When you can't sleep, you focus on anything and everything you find annoying. You're a freak, and so is she. You two are perfect for each other." He gave his southern smart-ass smile.

"Very funny. You might be right." I took another sip and said, "Oh, have I mentioned that she has started to say 'I heart you' now."

He raised his delicate eyebrows.

I shook my head. I really didn't want to tell him why she had started saying that, but then I caved. "We'd only just started saying 'I love you' and I wasn't very comfortable saying it, and then I saw this hanger in the bedroom, from the drycleaners. Anyway, I noticed that it had an advertisement on it that said 'We love our customers' but instead of the word love, it had a heart. What is up with that?" I detoured again, hoping he'd forget I mentioned it. "How did the heart come to symbolize love? . . . Really, it's just a muscle."

He motioned for me to stop stalling. "Oh, all right. Right after seeing the hanger, she was getting ready to leave, and I said, 'I heart you.'"

Ethan burst out laughing.

"She thought it was adorable. Now it's kinda our thing . . . I guess." I rolled my eyes.

"Lizzie, I didn't know you were such a romantic." He batted his eyes at me.

"Yeah right . . . " I took a deep breath. "Are these feelings and thoughts I have about her . . . about us . . . are they normal?"

"Not after this long. Maybe after twenty years, but you two should still be in the honeymoon phase. You should be running home from classes so you can rip her clothes off. Staying up all night talking in bed, naked bodies intertwined." He wrapped his gangly arms around himself in a weird contortion.

Ethan was slim, tall, effeminate—the kind of man everyone thought was gay. He adamantly refused he was, but being such a scrawny, open-minded Southern boy did not help his cause.

"Naked bodies intertwined," I mocked. "Tell me something, oh relationship guru, why should I listen to you? You hate your wife."

Ethan had been married for four years. A year ago, he confessed to me that he wanted to leave, but he hadn't told his wife yet. Deep down, I think he's afraid his friends and family will think he is gay for sure.

"Low blow. Very low blow, Lizzie." He pulled his keychain from his pocket. A nail clipper dangled on the chain. Ethan proceeded to clip one of his nails, and then he carefully put the keychain away.

"Do you expect anything else from me? I despise my own girlfriend. Why would I treat my best friend differently?" I raised my chai in his direction in salute, and said, "Yes, my friend, I am a bitch."

"Oh, I never doubted that. That, my dear, is why we are best friends. You are a bitch, and I am a stuck-up bastard from Mississippi. Neither one of us has any morals or standards."

Despite being a Southerner, when he moved out west, Ethan had soon discovered it was better to lose his southern accent—especially as an English major. His department was full of snooty kids who believed they were elite students. His accent made them look at him like he was a Neanderthal who had married his sister.

I took another sip, and watched the traffic crawl past. "She wants us to go to therapy," I confessed. "Apparently, I don't open up enough. She wants us to learn how to communicate effectively— whatever the hell *that* means." I waved one hand in the air.

Ethan spat out his coffee. "Are you serious?" He wiped his mouth with a napkin and then used it to mop the coffee off the table. "You're just now telling me this. What did you say?" He couldn't stop laughing.

"I said I would think about it. Who do you and Lisa see? Is it working for you two?"

He threw his stir stick at me. "God, you *are* a bitch!"

"And you, my friend, are a wimpy intellectual. Throwing a stir stick at me … Ooooo … I'm scared." I threw it back at him.

My cell phone interrupted. "Speak of the devil," I said, as I looked at the caller ID. "I better get it." I opened the phone, and said in an overly cheery voice, "Hey, baby, how's your day going?"

Ethan whispered, "Don't overdo it."

I quickly covered the mouthpiece and kicked Ethan in the shin.

He yelped louder than necessary to get back at me.

"Yeah, I'll be leaving in a few minutes. I don't want to be late. My mother can be a bitch sometimes."

"That's where you get it from." Ethan giggled. I kicked him again, much harder this time.

"Ok, honey. I won't be very late tonight." I mumbled, "I heart you," and then I closed my phone. "You can be such an ass," I told Ethan. After chugging the rest of my chai, I stood up. "So what's the excuse tonight? A pulled groin muscle so you don't have to screw your wife?"

Ethan stood too. "Nah, I used that one last week. I may have to slip her some sleeping pills."

I stopped in my tracks on the way to the trash can. Turning back to him, I asked in disbelief, "You don't actually do that do you?"

He winked at me and threw his cup away.

"So," Ethan asked, as we walked to our cars, "when was the last time you saw your folks?"

"Christmas, or one of those holidays. I'm not sure if it was last year or the year before."

"It's August. Are you going to be okay tonight?"

I shrugged. "Don't know. My mother can be brutal. She'd have no qualms about ripping the heads off of kittens."

"Well, good luck. Call me if you need to talk. By the way, I dig the pinstripe power suit. You look hot." One hand leaning on the roof of his car, Ethan gestured with the other to my clothes. "I wouldn't worry too much about losing Sarah. You're beautiful, and successful, and I think she loves you. Oh wait … she hearts you." He snickered.

"Thanks. I think." I shook my head. "Are we on for Saturday?"

"Of course. You know Lisa thinks we are having an affair?"

"So how long are you going to string her along?"

"*Touché.*" He stooped and climbed into his car, turned the engine on, and then rolled down the window. "I heart you." He waved limply and smirked as he drove out of the parking lot.

I watched him pull away. Briefly, I stared at my key in the car door. Was I sure I wanted to do this?

CHAPTER TWO

WHEN PULLING INTO THE PARKING LOT, I TRIED TO REMEMBER THE LAST TIME I HAD BEEN TO the country club. I used to eat there all of the time as a child. The food wasn't even that good, but that didn't matter to my folks. All that mattered was that people saw us there several times a month. I always hated it. We lived in Colorado, not on the East Coast, for Christ's sake. Our family didn't come over on the *Mayflower*.

The hostess watched me approach and asked in a snotty voice, "May I help you?"

"Yes I'm meeting the Petrie family for dinner?"

"Oh, are you a friend of the family?"

"I'm the daughter." I smiled wearily and straightened my blazer to look more presentable. I had my hair down, instead of in my normal ponytail, and I had put on eye shadow and mascara. Usually, I only did that when I was out with Sarah, but even then, I preferred the *au naturel* look—or at least that was my excuse.

The hostess tried to soften her bitchy look. "I didn't know they had a daughter."

I'm sure she didn't. My parents didn't really spread the news about my existence.

"I think I am early, though." I changed the subject.

"You aren't early. Your party is already seated." She tilted her head like a confused puppy.

I looked at my watch and noticed it was a quarter to seven. *Nice, Peter—telling me the wrong time.*

I followed the hostess through the maze of tables surrounded by overdressed, pompous asses. I recognized several of them—women who had been under the knife and hadn't changed in the past ten years. Or maybe I didn't recognize them. Rich women were a dime a dozen here. It was how they made it known they had money. How they made themselves feel superior whenever, in fact, they felt inferior.

"May I ask what time my party arrived?" I quickened my pace to keep up with the lanky hostess.

She turned to me, obviously puzzled. "I think they've been here thirty minutes."

Bravo, Peter. Bravo. Tell me 7:30 p.m. and then show up a little after 6:00 p.m. I should have known.

As the hostess led me to the table, she asked, "Do you live far away?"

"Not really. I live in Fort Collins."

"Oh … you're right. That's not very far." She looked disappointed in me.

"I'm working on my PhD. I don't have a lot of free time to hang out." Why was I justifying myself to this girl?

"That makes sense."

Well, thank goodness the hostess accepted my excuse. As if I needed that haughty girl's approval for my absences from family dinners at the club. We reached the table.

"Here's the last member of your party." The hostess plastered a huge fake smile on her face.

"Right on time, Elizabeth." My brother stood to shake my hand. I'd never understood why he always insisted on shaking my hand, or on using my full name. Everyone else called me Lizzie.

"Hello, Peter. I thought dinner was at 7:30." I stared at him angrily. Then, following a deep breath, I blurted out, "Hello, everyone. I hope you haven't been waiting long."

Mom answered, "Half an hour. That sounds about right for you." She took a sip of her scotch.

"Peter told me dinner was at 7:30 p.m." I threw him another nasty look. Mom's statement had already pissed me off. I was usually the annoying person who showed up early for everything. Whenever I went to a party, I had to wander around the neighborhood so I wouldn't show up too early and annoy the host. Yet, Mom preferred to think of me as a complete and total fuck-up.

Peter smiled at me, his usual backstabbing, shit-eating grin. It was one of those charming smiles that could make most women believe anything. His clean-cut appearance helped. Tonight, my brother was going casual; his tie was loosened. "I remember telling you 6:30 p.m."

I turned to the woman I assumed was my brother's fiancée. My mouth fell open; I think my jaw may have even hit the floor. Oh, my God! She was stunning, easily the most beautiful woman I had ever seen. Finally, I found my voice again. "Hello."

I reached out to shake her hand and she rose graciously and accepted it. Long blonde hair. Stormy, ocean-blue eyes. Flawless skin. Very little make-up. And arched eyebrows that suggested a devious side.

My brother's fiancée flashed me a smile that almost made me wet. "I'm Madeleine," she said. "But my friends call me Maddie."

Madeleine. What a beautiful name.

"Very nice to meet you, Maddie. People close to me call me Lizzie." I shot a look at Peter, hoping he'd get the hint. I despised being called Elizabeth.

"Geez, my bad. I'm sorry I didn't introduce you two. I don't know where my head is." Peter kissed his fiancée before sitting back down and placing his napkin in his lap. Why he had stood that long in the first place baffled me.

"I apologize for my tardiness," I said.

"Always the schoolteacher, Elizabeth." Peter tsked.

I took my seat opposite my father. A man of few words, my father gave me a nod of acknowledgment. I knew he wouldn't talk much, if at all, during dinner. My mother, unfortunately, hadn't learned from him.

"Oh, it doesn't matter," stated Maddie. "I'm just glad that you made it here. I hope the drive went well."

"Yes. Quite pleasant. It's always good to get some time to relax."

"I definitely know what you mean. I love to drive. Whenever I'm stressed out or need time to think, I jump in my car and drive my worries away."

"I hate driving. Too many fucking assholes on the road," said Mom, following her statement with another swallow of scotch.

"Maddie, do I detect a southern accent?"

The blonde flushed and looked over at Peter and then at my mom. "Well, I was born in Alabama, but my family moved to California when I was in high school."

My mother bristled. Not only was she from the South, but she was also from California. My mother always believed herself to be a great woman, ranking herself among the Rockefellers and Carnegies. The idea was preposterous, of course. She was a small town girl from Montana who had married a man who became wealthy. Before that, they lived in a trailer. It was hard not to say anything to ruffle my mother's feathers, but I didn't think that was the best way to get to know my future sister-in-law. Everyone else in the family already hated me. It would be nice to have one ally in the bunch. I wondered why Peter had taken such a risk. He had to know Mom wouldn't approve of a Southerner. I bet her family had connections to his work.

The waiter came over to take my drink order.

"Don't bother offering her alcohol," said Mom. "She can't drink." She raised her scotch glass and took another slug. Then she set the glass down and smoothed her navy suit.

The suit covered the whitest shirt I had ever seen, and a pearl necklace ringed Mom's over-stretched neck at the collar. The pearls and shirt were stark against her olive skin. The combined effect was Mediterranean.

I ordered a Coke. "It's not that I can't drink, Mother. I don't like to drink when I have to drive." Her statement embarrassed me. My mother always referred to my preference for drinking only at home. I was such a lightweight that one drink gave me a buzz and forced me to find a cab. In Fort Collins, there was no cab service; hence, I never drank in public.

After the waiter left, Peter said, "Seriously, though … a Coke? Come on, Elizabeth. Why don't you try some of this wine? It's one of the best they have to offer."

Peter always pretended to be a wine connoisseur, swirling his glass, sniffing it, and doing all of that annoying rigmarole to show off his knowledge. I hated wine. Every time he offered me wine, I reminded him that I loathed the stuff.

"Peter, you know she shouldn't drink wine," Mom scolded. "She's already been pulled over for a DUI." Another gulp of scotch.

"I was not, Mother!" I looked over at Maddie, horrified of what she would think. "I used to deliver newspapers when I was an undergrad, to help pay the bills. To save time, I rolled the papers while I drove my route. There wasn't much steering going on, so I got pulled over. Once the cops realized I was just working, they let me go. I was never arrested or cited for anything."

"They never gave you a ticket? Not even for reckless driving?"

"Nope. They were very nice about it. It was almost like we had a bond of some sort, since we all worked really crappy hours. The hours were brutal."

I watched my mother raise the scotch glass to her lips again. I had once seen her drive away and lap the house eight times before she was able to get out of our neighborhood. She kept driving by the house as I watched from the front window. She hit the same trash can twice. And I was the fuck-up with alcohol?

Peter asked, "You can't stay the night?"

"No. I have class first thing in the morning. It'll be easier to head home tonight."

"I thought college professors got to pick their own schedules." His smile was truly smeared all across his face.

"Professors do. Doctoral students do not. We have to teach the classes no one else wants to teach." I tried not to bristle. His condescension got under my skin, but I had learned over the years not to show any weakness around my family, or they would pounce.

"What classes do you teach?" asked Maddie, giving me another bedeviling smile.

"I teach Western Civ," I said, gazing into her gorgeous blue eyes.

"I have to admit that history wasn't my best subject." Her smile this time was shy, sexy, but she never took her eyes off my face.

I reciprocated. "I hear that a lot. It surprises me that people aren't fascinated by it. But I think the problem is that too many teachers concentrate on the facts—you know dates, places, and names. I want my students to appreciate that history is the greatest story ever told. It has violence, sex, love, romance, adventure, betrayal, drama, comedy. It has it all."

"You teach your students about sex?" sniggered my mother, The Scotch-lady. The extravagant diamond on her ring finger nearly blinded me as she raised her tumbler to her mouth again.

Out of everything I had just said, *that* was what Mom honed in on.

"I don't get out the dolls or anything." I rolled my eyes. "But sex is important to history." I swiveled my head in Mom's direction. She took another sip of her drink and looked away.

"What do you do, Maddie?" I turned back to the blonde.

"I'm an interior designer."

"Really? One of my good friends studied interior design at CSU. Her program was tough. She pulled all-nighters all of the time."

The waiter arrived with my Coke and I took a sip. Secretly, I wished I could add a shot of rum, maybe two shots … or three.

"Yeah, a lot of people think all we do is put pretty throw pillows on a couch. They have no idea how complicated it is." She laughed.

"You should see her work; it's beautiful." Peter leaned over and kissed Maddie's cheek. I wasn't sure if he was marking his territory or being affectionate.

Could he be jealous that Maddie and I were hitting it off? I wouldn't say that fireworks shot into the sky for all to see, but there was a connection. Was it apparent to all?

"I'd love to see your work. Any chance you brought your portfolio?"

She laughed and shyly rolled her napkin. "Yes I did. I have an interview here in Denver."

"Maddie and I are moving back home," Peter casually blurted out as he reached for a roll from the middle of the table.

I looked at him, curious. "Oh? I had no idea."

He had been living in California for the past five years. I only saw him for the occasional holiday, and even that seemed excessive. During all those years, I had not visited him; nor did he visit me.

"We want to be closer to family now. We're hoping to start our own family soon." He raised his glass to our mother.

I looked at my mom, then at my laconic father, then back at Peter. Poor girl. Poor kid.

Then a thought crossed my mind. Could I seduce Maddie?

The waiter came over and took our food order. While the others ordered, I took in Maddie's charms. Madeleine. Captivating. A name befitting such a magnificent creature. Her beauty could rival the Greek goddess Circe. How did Homer put it in *The Odyssey*? Circe was the most beautiful of all gods. Yes, Maddie could rival this goddess.

Seducing my brother's fiancée would normally be a repulsive thought to me. Yet, I wasn't repulsed. Did Maddie cast a spell on me? What would my mother say? I bet it would be priceless.

CHAPTER THREE

I HELD THE STEERING WHEEL WITH MY LEFT HAND AND DIALED ETHAN'S PHONE NUMBER WITH my right. I hoped no cops were around, but it was after ten at night on a Monday, so there wasn't much traffic on the highway.

"She's gorgeous."

"What?"

"She is, without a doubt, the most beautiful woman I've ever seen."

"Lizzie, who in the hell are you talking about?"

"My brother's fiancée. Ethan, she's hot. No, wait. Hot is too vulgar for Maddie. She's a goddess who should be fed grapes while reclining on satin sheets."

"Then why in the hell is she with your brother?"

I could tell I had woken him up; he wasn't coherent yet. Maybe he had taken the sleeping pills by accident. "Beats me. I still think he's a total ass. Are you already in bed? You didn't give your wife sleeping pills, did you?"

"No. I didn't have to. Are we still on for Saturday?"

"Yeah, I'll give you the full report then. Good night, my sissy of a friend who can't tell his wife that it's over."

"Bitch."

I smiled and pressed my foot down on the gas pedal. I wanted as many miles as possible between me and my family.

Back in my own bedroom, I leaned down and kissed the top of Sarah's head.

"How was dinner?" Her voice sounded like ice that had started to crack but had refrozen instead.

I kissed her crown again. "I survived. Sometimes I forget just how much I despise those people."

"What's she like?" Sarah was in bed, lying on her side with her back to me, flipping through the TV channels.

"She seems nice. Cute, funny, charming—like all of the other women Peter has dated. How was your night?" I stripped down to my underwear and bra and climbed into bed behind her.

"Pretty quiet. I worked on some reports."

She smelled of lavender. "Did you take a bath? You smell good."

"Yeah. I had a stressful day."

"I'm sorry." I kissed her neck, felt her body respond as I worked my way up to her ear. She pressed her body closer to mine. I ran my hand down her body and slid it back up slowly. Sarah's breathing became heavier. Rolling her onto her back, I kissed her lips, slowly at first, then passionately as if our lives depended on it. I climbed on top of her, slowly rubbing one hip between her legs. She arched her back and moaned.

"You're so sexy." I gazed into her chocolate-dark eyes and brushed the hair off her face. Then, I leaned down and kissed her again. Her neck. Her nipples. All the way down her stomach. When I reached her lower stomach, she moved her pelvis urgently, arching her back. I quickly peeled off her pajama pants. When I tasted her, she moaned again. My lips moved over the inside of her right thigh, then her left. The thrusting of her hips told me she wanted more. I wanted her to want it, so I continued to kiss her thighs. Then I found her clit—darted my tongue across it. She dug her nails into my shoulder as I took her in my mouth. I slid my fingers inside her, thrusting them in and out of her slowly, tasting her simultaneously. Sarah's hips thrashed more urgently. There was no holding her in place. It took some work to keep my tongue lapping at the right spot, but I knew she couldn't come unless she was gyrating like mad.

Her hips were moving so fast now, grinding into my face, so that it took everything I had not to stop. I loved that she got so fucking wet, literally pouring into my mouth as my fingers slid in and out of her so easily.

Her nails scored my back again and then she arched completely, her legs shaking. I stopped licking but kept my tongue against her clit to heighten the sensation of her orgasm. Slowly, her body began to relax. I slithered up her body and lay next to her, wrapping my arms around her.

"Feeling a little less stressed?" I whispered into her ear.

She laughed, her sexy bedroom laugh. "Yes, but I'm still mad at you."

I kissed her head. "And you have every right to be. I was an ass, a self-absorbed ass."

"At least you can admit it." She pushed me onto my back and climbed on top of me, leaning in to kiss me. She whispered, "Don't ever do that again."

"I won't."

"How early do you have to get up in the morning?"

"Don't worry about that. I'll skip my bike ride. What else do you have in mind?"

She smiled, but didn't answer with words.

"Elizabeth?"

The clock read six in the morning. "Yeah, Peter, what's up?"

"Apparently, not you. I thought you had an early class." I could almost smell his smugness. My brother was the type who wanted others to know he was a very busy man. He would tie his shoelace without stopping, too busy to pause for something so insignificant.

"I think eight o'clock is early. Is everything OK?"

"Yeah. Maddie and I enjoyed having dinner with you. I have to take care of some stuff today and it will take all day. Maddie has never been to Fort Collins, so I was wondering if you would show her the town. How many classes do you have today?"

I rubbed my eyes. "My last class is at eleven. I can meet her after that."

I gave him directions to my office and then hung up. Rolling over, I noticed Sarah was not in the room. I listened, and heard the shower running. When I wandered into the bathroom, there was no sign that she had heard the phone. In an instant, I decided not to tell her about my afternoon plans.

The classroom door opened and I watched as Maddie slid in and took a seat in the back row. Carefully stepping over the cord to the overhead projector, which displayed my lecture outline, not wanting to stumble in front of her, I asked, "Can anyone tell me what the word *defenestration* means?"

A sea of blank stares.

I chuckled. "Of course no one can! That would mean one of you actually *did* last night's reading. I should give you guys a pop quiz on the material." I paced back and forth in front of the class before settling behind the podium.

"Nah, you don't want to do that. It would be more work than just telling us. You would have to think of questions, then grade them, record them, pass them out," said Joshua, the most talkative student in the class.

"But, Joshua, you forget that teachers love work, especially historians. We love to read, write, grade—you name it. We love tedious stuff." I glanced at my lecture notes to focus my attention on my class, and not on Maddie. "Defenestration means to throw someone, or something, out a window."

"Are you going to throw one of us out a window?" joked Joshua.

"Don't tempt me, especially after last week's tests, which I have graded and will return after class." I saw some looks of panic. Good. "But we are only on the first floor, so it wouldn't be much fun to toss one of you out. Besides, I am not that strong.

"In 1618, some noblemen, upset after King Ferdinand violated their religious beliefs, went to the royal palace and threw two of the king's advisors out of a window. The gentlemen survived by landing in a pile of manure. Yes, manure." I stopped and looked out at the students. Some smiled. Others just looked like they wanted the whole thing to be over. I didn't dare look at her. "This incident started what became known as the Thirty Years' War, which goes to show how some wars came about by really inane incidents. But any one of you who has been in a relationship knows that most fights start over petty things. So, the next time your significant other gets angry when you yawn at the mere mention of his or her parents, and he or she flips out because you think they are dullards and what's going to happen when you have children, etcetera, etcetera, etcetera, just remember wars have started over such trifling matters. And remember what Winston Churchill said: 'Those who fail to learn from history, are doomed to repeat it.'"

I looked at my watch. "All right we'll go into the details about the Thirty Years' War next time. Remember to do the reading. You should have the novel *The Adventures of a Simpleton* read in its entirety. It will behoove all of you to read it. I am not going to say any more on the subject." I walked over to the whiteboard, wrote the words Pop Quiz, and underlined them. "Now, if you want your tests back, come and get them."

After spreading the exam books on the table, I stood back for the feeding frenzy. Maddie sashayed towards the front, and I felt my heart flutter wildly. I had thought she looked amazing last night, but today she was in jeans and a white T-shirt that didn't suggest a good figure—they downright proclaimed it for all to see.

"Lizzie?" One of my students, Jill, interrupted my fantasy. "Can I set up a time to go over the test with you?"

She got a D, I remembered, and I gave her an encouraging smile. "Of course, Jill. I won't be in my office today, but will you be on campus tomorrow? I can meet with you then. What time works for you?"

"I'm done at two tomorrow. Does that work?" Her head drooped in shame.

"Yes, I'll be there. Please bring in your exam so we can go over it together." I gave her a pat on the back.

I turned in Maddie's direction and smiled, but a few more students gathered around, wanting to talk about the test results. I answered their questions patiently, all the while staring at Maddie out of the corner of my eye. If only my students knew what thoughts I was having, they might not think of me as a stuffy historian.

Finally, we were alone.

"I'm so sorry to keep you waiting."

"Gosh, don't apologize. It was fun watching you with your students. They seem to like you."

"The feelings are mutual. I adore all of them, even the smartasses." I gathered the uncollected exams and placed them in my bag.

"Hope you don't mind my barging in on your class."

"Not at all. I hope you weren't bored."

"Did those guys really land in shit?" She chortled.

"Yeah, they did. There are some things that you just can't make up." Realizing I was staring, I said, "Do you mind if we stop by my office before we skedaddle?"

"Lead the way, professor." She motioned for me to walk in front of her. *God, did she know how sexy she was?* I picked up my bag and slung it over my shoulder. Then I led her outside. It was a little after noon and the campus was packed with students and professors, running to and fro.

Fall had come early, and I could smell it in the air, but it was still seventy degrees outside. Colorado was known for having the most days of sunshine during the year; today was no exception. To the west, the Rocky Mountain foothills were set against a brilliant lapis sky, scattered with clouds. The leaves were beginning to speckle yellow and red.

"Where did you go to school, Maddie?"

"I went to a small college in California. This campus is huge. I'm amazed by the number of students." Maddie gazed around with her mouth slightly agape.

We walked past one of my favorite spots on campus, and she stopped to look. I watched her as she read the quote carved along the top of the bench. "If I have been able to see farther than others, it was because I stood on the shoulders of giants," she said, her tone curious. Her eyes moved to the sculpture adjacent to the quote. It was a pendulum.

"It's about the scientific revolution," I offered.

"What does he mean?" She gawked at the glittering pendulum.

"It's Newton. He's exclaiming he would never have been able to discover gravity if it weren't for all of the other scientists who paved the way for him. He's giving credit to a long line of people who asked questions and who risked their lives by challenging the Catholic Church." I paused and looked up at the pendulum again. "This is one of my favorite places on campus."

"Because of the scientific revolution, or because of pendulums?" She smiled as she spoke.

"The revolution, in a way. You have to admire people who stood up to the leaders and said, 'I think you are full of shit.'" I hesitated for a second, and looked away from her, up at the puffy white clouds. "I have personal reasons as well."

Her eyes returned to my face. I could tell she was expecting me to continue. Commanding me to.

"I'm grateful to those who have advanced science and medicine. I have an illness." I didn't like sharing this weakness with people.

I noticed a flicker of panic in her eyes. "N-no … it's not terminal," I stammered. "But it's an illness nonetheless. Before the medicine was developed, the outcome wouldn't have been fun. Now, all I have to do is take a pill each night. Simple as that."

"I didn't know. Peter never said anything."

"I never told them." I never referred to Peter or anyone in my family as an individual. They were always a "them" for me. I glanced away from her penetrating stare and motioned which direction we should take to my office. "It's not too much further," I said.

She smiled, but a hint of sadness crept into her eyes.

We walked on, to my office.

"You'll have to excuse the mess," I said as we entered my office. "I can only work when surrounded by chaos." Papers, open books, and journals were spread everywhere, including the floor and all available chairs.

"I can tell you spend a lot of time here." She pointed to all the teacups and dirty plates.

"You could say that. I'm trying desperately to finish my dissertation. I would like to close this chapter of my life. And I work better here than at home." *I would like to close this chapter? Come on, Lizzie! Who in the hell talks like that? Stop being such a pompous ass.*

"Your girlfriend must get jealous?" She gestured to the framed photograph on my desk.

I'd never really considered that the picture made it clear we were in a relationship. Sarah had given the picture, with instructions to put it on my desk. It finally clicked why.

"It has been the source of a few fights. She thinks I'm a workaholic."

"What do you think?" She crossed her arms.

"Oh, I know I am … but I love what I do. Researching makes me happy, even more than teaching, and as you can see" — I waved to all of my crap in the office — "I immerse myself in my work." I paused to set my bag down and put in a couple of books I needed to take home that night. "You know what else makes me happy?"

"What?" She uncrossed her arms.

"Eating. How 'bout grabbing some lunch?"

"You're the boss."

We sat outside on the patio at Coopersmith's, my favorite restaurant in Old Town, Fort Collins, talking, laughing, and sharing funny childhood memories. It had been a long time since I had laughed this much with one person — and, the whole time, I could not take my eyes off her.

"So, how long have you and your girlfriend been together?"

"Not very long, only six months … wait … " I started to count on my fingers. "Maybe it's getting closer to eight months. What about you and Peter?"

"Over a year. You aren't close to your family at all?"

"Was it that obvious?" I chuckled. "Let's just say I'm the black sheep of the family. I keep to my own most of the time."

"Your mother doesn't seem to like you."

I was somewhat taken aback by her bluntness, but I tried not to show it. "We have our differences."

"Do they know you're gay?"

"You don't hold back, do you, Maddie?" I smiled at her. "Yes they know, but we all chose not to discuss it. Let me guess, Peter never brought it up?"

"No. I didn't even know you existed for quite some time. Then he brought up your existence very casually. I was a little surprised. He dropped hints about you, but never proclaimed he had a sister."

Peter had a way of inserting things into the middle of the conversation, as if he had already mentioned it and the listener just forgot or ignored him. If anyone questioned it, he made them look like an insensitive ass.

"Huh, Peter and I are a lot more alike than I thought." I explained what had happened the previous day.

"Yes, you two are a lot alike. You don't open up much." She punched me lightly on the shoulder. "It can be very frustrating you know."

"Why are you hitting me? I have my own angry woman at home." I rubbed my shoulder.

"Peter isn't here, and I'm sure if you're like him at all, you deserve to be hit — and much harder, I might add. Am I wrong?" She looked at me with those incredible eyes.

I whistled through my teeth a little. "This is a difficult position to be in. If I say yes, I'm an asshole, then you'll always think of me as an asshole. But if I say no, you'll know I'm lying, and you'll always think of me as a liar. If you were me, what would you do?" I flashed my most cunning smile.

She burst into a loud guffaw. "Oh, my God! You two are so much alike it's fucking scary. Did your parents teach you two never to answer a question directly? Are they CIA?" Her head bobbed up and down in excitement as she spoke.

"You met my father … he could be." I motioned to the waiter that we needed refills. A Coke for me, and a merlot for Maddie. "I can't remember the last time that man and I had a conversation. So who knows? Maybe the vice president of a financial company thing is all a ruse. At least that would make him more exciting."

"I think he hates me."

"He's not the one you have to worry about. Watch out for Mother. And, just a warning, Peter adores her." I wanted to mention that I thought it was sick how he pandered to her, but I didn't.

"I know, but thanks for the tip." A look of worry marred her lovely face.

"So are you ready to join this crazy family?"

She looked away for the first time. "I guess." She shrugged.

I couldn't help but chortle. "You guess? Geez, I hope when I decide to take the plunge with a woman, she doesn't say, 'I guess it's the right thing to do.'"

She hit me again. "Shut up."

Her look was bewitching. No wonder Peter was enraptured with this young creature. My guess was that she was twenty-four years old. Peter was seven years older than me, nearing thirty-five.

"What about you? Have you considered, as you so elegantly put it, taking the plunge?"

"No." I paused. "Not recently."

"Not recently? So, who is the girl who broke your heart and made you so bitter?"

"Bitter? Me? Bitter? What gave you that impression?" I said.

"You know, you and Peter both have that incredible smile. You two flash that smile and you think you can convince anyone of anything. I think that's why I agreed to marry your brother."

I didn't know what to say.

"Well, that and that I love him," she mumbled.

"Here you are. I was beginning to worry."

I looked up to find my girlfriend standing outside the railing of Coopersmith's with her best friend, Haley. "Hey, sweetheart. What are you doing here?" I stood, leaned over the railing, and kissed Sarah's cheek. For an instant, I felt like vomiting.

"Haley and I came for dinner. I tried calling you to see if you wanted to join us, but I kept getting your voice mail. I just assumed you were holed up in your office with your nose buried in some book."

I saw her glance over in Maddie's direction. Then she gave me an accusatory look.

"Shit!" I reached into my left pocket and pulled out my cell phone. It was still turned off. "Honey, I am so sorry. I forgot to turn my phone back on after class." I didn't even try to flash my smile this time. Her eyes told me that wouldn't work. I didn't think even a night of fucking was going to save me from the impending argument, either. I tried a diversionary tactic.

"Maddie, I'd like you to meet Sarah and her friend Haley. Sarah, this is my brother's fiancée." I stepped away from Sarah, in case any punches were thrown in my direction.

"I hope you don't mind me stealing Lizzie for the day," Maddie said. "Peter had some business to take care of, and he thought this would be a great opportunity for me to get to know my future sister-in-law." She stood up and hugged Sarah, and then shook Haley's limp hand. Haley wasn't the hugging type, and her demeanor let everyone know that.

Sister-in-law. The words suddenly made me feel ill. For the past several hours, I had been doing my best to imagine her naked. I was such an ass.

"It's very nice to meet you," Sarah said, as pleasantly as possible, considering she wanted to rip my head off.

"So, you two are having dinner. Do you guys want to join us?" I asked.

"That's a great idea. We've been sitting here so long, I'm famished. You won't believe this, but we came here to have lunch." Maddie paused and then blurted out, "Sarah, Lizzie is quite the storyteller. She must keep you laughing all the time."

Sarah smiled and tried to relax. She and Haley walked through the side gate and then sat down at the table. One thing I really admired about her was that she would never fight with me in public.

"Oh yes, I think that's why I fell in love with her," Sarah said. "She can be quite charming. And there is that smile." She touched my cheek briefly.

For an instant, I thought she was going to sock me. Her eyes told me that was what she really wanted to do.

Instead, Maddie hit me again. "You see, I told you about that smile of yours." She laughed her sexy laugh.

I smiled, and then I looked over at Sarah again. I was in for a very long night. Did she just say she was in love with me? We had barely said I love you to each other. In love? Was that the same thing, or was there a deeper meaning? I made a mental note to discuss it with Ethan.

CHAPTER FOUR

"I CAN'T BELIEVE YOU! AFTER YESTERDAY ... AGAIN? AGAIN, YOU DO IT. DO YOU JUST NOT CARE? Obviously, you don't." Sarah paced back and forth waving her arms in the air while I sat on the couch.

For the past five minutes, she had been ranting and raving, uttering short sentences or fragments, and not making much sense. "And then, last night. I can't believe I fell for that. So what did you think, you could come home, fuck my brains out, and all would be forgotten?" She picked up her pacing. Her arm-flailing reached a manic level. "And I have never known you to have your cell phone off all day. Jesus, on our first date, you kept checking it whenever it rang. Even if you didn't answer, you still checked it. You thought you were so smooth about it, but I knew." She stopped and pinned me with a glare. I noticed she was breathing heavily.

"Sarah, it was such a last minute thing. Peter called this morning to arrange it. It's not like I thought to myself, hey, it was so much fun hurting her the first time, I'll try it again."

She stared right at me and for a second she looked like a puma ready to pounce. Then she said in a somewhat calmer, but still shaky, voice, "So you admit that you hurt me."

I stood up, walked over to her, and looked her right in the eyes. "Yes, I admit that I hurt you yesterday. And I admit that I hurt you again today. I don't know what I was thinking. But I was going to tell you when I got home. I had no idea it would turn into an all-day affair." She winced at the word affair and I instantly regretted my word choice.

"Why are you so mysterious all of the time? Sometimes I feel like I don't even know who you are. Why can't you just let me in? Half the time, I wonder if you even want to be with me."

I remembered what Maddie had said and it took everything I had not to smile when I pictured her punching my shoulder.

"I'm so sorry." I took Sarah into my arms. "I don't try to keep you out of my life. God, Sarah, who knows why I'm so private? It just happens. Can we just agree that I'm a moron?" I held her really tight.

She whispered, "Sometimes, I don't like you."

For the first time in quite some time, I felt something for Sarah. I looked at her and my smile was genuine. "I'm so sorry, sweetheart. I'm so sorry I hurt you."

She looked shocked. At first, I didn't know why. Then I felt her wipe a tear from my cheek. She kissed my forehead and rested her head against my shoulder. "Please, Lizzie," she whispered. "Just let me in every once in a while."

I nodded and kissed her. "I will." At that moment, I meant it. I really meant it.

Sarah's eyes hardened. "Lizzie, I love you, but I won't be with a liar. No more lies."

I promised.

"I truly meant it, Ethan. When I said it, I meant it." We were sitting in our usual spot, the coffee shop, on our usual day, Saturday. I had just finished explaining the past few days to him.

He stared at me while he sipped his coffee.

I downed a significant amount of my chai and then exclaimed, "Damn! That's hot, hot, hot."

Ethan chuckled. "Man I used to love that song."

"What are you talking about? A song about a girl burning herself while drinking a chai?" I waved my hand in an attempt to cool my burning tongue.

"No, you idiot. The song 'Hot Hot Hot' by The Cure. Check it out. It's a fun song. You can't always listen to audiobooks, you know."

"Why aren't you saying anything about the real topic instead of some stupid song?"

"Lizzie, there's nothing I can say. You have painted yourself into quite the corner." He was staring at the barista.

"What, are we going to talk in code today? The man with the yellow hat owns a monkey."

He chuckled. "I loved *Curious George* when I was little, too." He placed both hands behind his head and leaned back in his chair.

"That's great, Ethan. Let's not talk about my situation. Let's discuss children's literature."

He could tell I was upset. "Don't get mad at me, Lizzie. You should be mad at yourself."

"I … I know. How do I get into these situations?" I banged my hand on the table and almost spilled my chai.

"You do have a knack for it. I don't know what to tell you. It took you forever to let me in, and I know you haven't even let me in completely. It's just how you are. Sarah will have to accept that about you. The question is: do you want to stay with her?" He stared at me intensely.

I stared back into his Coke-bottle glasses. "What do you mean?"

"You convinced her that you love her by squeezing out a few tears. But ask yourself why there were tears. Were you sad? Or were you just so overwhelmed with the situation that you didn't know what to do? I've seen you almost cry here when they were out of chai. You're so wound up all of the time that sometimes you crack. What made you crack that day? Also, you aren't the most honest person. You have a way of telling people what you think they want to hear and not how you feel."

Right then, my cell phone rang. I stared at it for a second before I answered. "Hello."

"Hey, Lizzie. It's Maddie. How are you doing?"

"Hi, Maddie. I'm doing well. What are you up to today?" I looked at Ethan to keep him quiet.

He stared at me in disbelief.

"Hey, we're leaving town on Tuesday," Maddie said. "Would you like to get together for lunch tomorrow?"

"Yeah, sounds great. How about I come down there this time?"

Ethan started to wave his arms frantically in the air and mouthed, "No."

I hushed him. I didn't think Maddie even noticed the commotion.

She continued, "I have a better idea. Why don't we meet in Boulder? Peter tells me that they have good shopping along Pearl Street."

"Sounds good. I know some superb restaurants there."

We quickly arranged where to meet, and I hung up.

Ethan shook his head in bewilderment, "Are you going to tell Sarah?"

"Tell Sarah what, Ethan?" I looked him right in the eye.

He laughed. "You're playing with fire, Lizzie. Be careful. Is Peter going to be there?"

"I didn't ask, but I have a feeling we'll be alone."

"So, what's it like going on a date with your future sister-in-law?" He furrowed his brows.

"I'll let you know."

"Well, it's a good thing you turned your phone on today." He reached for his coffee and started to sip it, but then paused. Holding the cup close to his mouth, he added in a sinister voice, "Or is it?"

I smiled.

"Don't try that with me. I don't think your smile is all that cute."

I pretended to be hurt. Ethan laughed and I turned my attention to the window and watched the cars drive by.

After a minute or two, I said, "Sarah mentioned to Maddie that she was in love with me. What does that mean really?"

Ethan stared at me like I was a dingbat.

"I mean, I know we say I love you, but is 'in love'" — I waved my hand — "oh, I don't know, even stronger?"

"Well, it isn't as deep as saying 'I heart you.'"

"Come on, I'm being serious."

"So am I, Lizzie. Sometimes you sound like a relationship idiot. You analyze everything. People who think there's a difference between love and 'in love' are only fooling themselves. What are you so scared of?"

I stared back at him and watched him tug at the corner of his moustache. I didn't have an answer for him.

Did love scare me? Could I spend my life with just one person? Or would I end up like my parents, hating my partner? I pictured them at the club when I had met Maddie. My father hadn't spoken to any of us. My mother never said a word to my father, but I had felt her hatred seething inside. The thought terrified me. Would I be like my father and Sarah like my mother? I shivered.

That night, I took Sarah out to dinner. Afterwards, I planned on taking her to a movie she had wanted to see. For the first half of the meal I kept trying to come up with ways to tell her that I was meeting Maddie in Boulder but that I wanted to go alone. Usually, we kept Sundays just to ourselves. I was obviously struggling to find the right words.

Instead, I chattered on and on about my students and the papers I had just graded. She talked about her students. Sarah taught English at one of the local high schools. For the most part, it was a pleasant evening, which made me feel even more like scum. There we were, having a pleasant meal discussing our work, and all I could really think about was how to ditch her on Sunday, our day together, and spend it with Maddie.

"Oh, I almost forgot to tell you. Matt called and he's coming to town tomorrow. I hope you don't mind, but we are going to have lunch with his parents." Matt had been her boyfriend in high school. They had remained close friends throughout college. He was a cool guy, but he always felt slightly uncomfortable around me.

I nearly dropped my fork. Doing my best to regain my composure, I said, "Really … it's supposed to be nice out tomorrow." Slicing off a piece of steak, I continued. "Maybe I'll hook up my bike and go for a ride in the mountains." I placed the chunk of steak in my mouth.

She smiled. "Geez, it will be such a lovely day for a bike ride. I wish I could go."

I didn't want to risk her changing her plans, so I said nothing; instead, I motioned to the waitress for our check.

"What do you want to do now?" Sarah looked, and sounded, relaxed, as though all of the week's earlier events had never occurred. I marveled at her way of compartmentalizing problems in her head.

"I thought we could go see that movie you've been dying to see. It's playing at the Cinemark on Timberline."

"Which one?"

"*Moonrise Kingdom*."

She squealed and clapped her hands. "I've been dying to see that. It's been out for a while." She smiled. "I thought you'd forgotten that I wanted to see it."

I grinned back at her and led her out of the restaurant and to the car.

CHAPTER FIVE

THE NEXT DAY, I STOOD AWKWARDLY ON THE CORNER OUTSIDE ONE OF THE STORES ON PEARL Street and watched Maddie wait for the crosswalk sign. She stood there smiling, looking radiant, until finally, the light changed and she approached.

"How was your drive?"

"Oh, my gosh, Lizzie, I got so lost on my way here." She was breathing heavily. "Is there always so much construction in Colorado? Every major road has some detour. It's crazy. And the people here do not understand the concept of merging. This one guy actually stopped while trying to get on the highway. Who stops when getting on the highway?" She flipped her hair back. "If he tried that in California, someone would have hit him out of spite, or shot him." She hugged me and kissed my cheek. Her perfume made me giddy.

"Yes, there is always construction here, especially when the weather is nice. And I have to agree that people are idiots behind the wheel. I try to stick to the back roads out here. Not so many blockheads. Plus, you get to look at horses and cows."

Really? Really! Was I this much of a moron all of the time? Horses and cows! She was a California girl, why would she want to look at horses and cows?

"I better get used to it … I got the job." She jumped in excitement and let out the cutest little squeal.

I hugged her, overcome with excitement, fear, and anger. She would now become a permanent fixture in my life. For the first time in my life, I was jealous of Peter. Everyone had always assumed I was. He had everything: good looks, charm, wit, intelligence, and confidence. But I had never wanted to be like him. At that moment, I wanted to *be* him.

We pulled apart and I looked into her eyes. "That's great, Maddie. Peter must be so happy for you."

"I think he is. He bought me a new car last night. The BMW I wanted." Another squeal.

I laughed and said, "That's so my mom."

I immediately regretted it. She didn't deserve such a callous remark.

But she just laughed at me. "I knew you would say something like that. It's almost like you can't help it. You just say what you think, especially when it comes to your family. Your mouth opens and the words spill out even if they are words others really don't want to hear. I love it. I love your verbal brutality."

"Verbal brutality? That seems a bit harsh. But I like it. It's very to the point. In fact, it's something I would've said."

She did a little curtsy for me and we laughed and started walking along Pearl Street.

We sat outside a little fondue place. The weather was gorgeous, and when the sun shone at that time of year, Coloradoans flocked to alfresco venues. We sat at one of the tiny tables squeezed onto an even smaller patio. Maddie's bags, squashed under the table, made it hard to get comfortable, but I didn't mind.

She held her wineglass against her cheek, propping her head up with her other arm, her elbow resting on the table. "Tell me something you haven't told anyone else."

I thought for a moment but didn't question why she was asking. I wanted to find the right answer. "I really enjoy riding my bike—"

"And I really enjoy chocolate chip cookies," she interrupted.

I smiled. "Now hold on and listen to what I have to say before you make a smartass comment."

She nodded in acknowledgement and sipped her wine. "Okay, but you'll have to make it more interesting than 'I like to ride my bicycle.' Or I won't divulge my deep, dark desires." She ran a finger along my arm.

Her suggestive wink made me swallow hard. It was too late to come up with something sexier. *Shit!*

I swallowed again and forged ahead. "For the past few years, I was pretty sick. For a while, the doctors couldn't figure out what was wrong with me. All that time, I didn't work out at all. So, as you can imagine, I got out of shape. Now, I'm doing everything I can to get back into shape.

"Have you ever been told you have an illness that's trying to kill you? Fortunately, mine is treatable. I take a pill each night. But when I first heard the diagnosis, I went online and looked it up. One hundred years ago, this disease was a death sentence. Well, that scared the crap out of me. I know I won't die from it, but I want to get into the best shape of my life, just in case I get something else. I want to be ready."

Maddie's eyes darted towards a couple walking by. She casually asked, "What illness do you have?" She continued watching the man as he pulled out a chair for his wife.

I stifled a laugh. Her smooth way of inserting the question impressed me. She didn't want to seem too eager to learn my secret.

"Oh, I hardly mention its name. When people learn you have an incurable illness, they romanticize it. Why they do this astounds me. Many immediately think of cancer and chemo treatments. My illness isn't glamorous. If you can call cancer glamorous."

"Poor, Lizzie." She laughed. "Stuck with a sub-par ailment. As a Petrie, that has to bug the piss out of you. You all like to excel at everything, even being sick."

Her reply stung, but it intrigued me. Maddie wasn't like other women I flirted with. Her honesty cut to the quick. If I wanted to pursue anything, I had to pick up my game.

"Okay, smartass. I have Graves' Disease."

"Ha!" She slammed her hand down on the table. "I knew that would get you to spill the beans. You are more like your brother than you would like to admit."

My blood boiled, but I smiled. She was playing me. Not that I would admit that to her.

"Seriously" —she put her hand on mine and squeezed— "are you okay? I haven't known you long, but I would like to keep you around. Besides, you can't let me fend for myself. Your family is—"

"Full of assholes." I interrupted.

"Exactly!"

I didn't have the courage to ask if she included Peter in that category. Or me.

Diverting the conversation away from my family, I said, "Once, when I told a woman I had Graves' Disease, she asked if they called it that because I would end up in a grave."

"Is it?" She leaned closer, concerned.

"No. Of course, that would make my illness cooler." I teased.

"Don't you mean more tragic. Then, when you tried to seduce women, you could say, 'I don't have long to live. Before I go, I would like to know the true meaning of love.'" She sighed dramatically and coughed like someone on his or her deathbed.

"Would that work with you?" I perked up in my chair.

"Of course not! I would only sleep with a cancer patient." She winked at me.

I shook my head. "You are terrible. Now I need to come down with cancer."

Smiling, she squirmed in her chair, and asked, "How often do you ride? Your bike, that is." Her face reddened.

"Almost every day." A breeze blew some of my hair into my mouth and I casually pulled the strands off my lips, wishing I had a hair tie to pull it back into a ponytail.

She looked at me like *so what*. "This is your big secret?"

"I've turned it into a challenge. I am determined to ride my bike 3,000 miles during the next six months."

"3,000 miles . . . are you insane?"

"Of course! But that isn't the point. I figured if I ride at least 20 miles each day, it would only take me five months to reach 3,000. Some days I go for longer rides. Those days add up to at least two days worth, which gives me some wiggle room for days it snows and stuff." Saying this out loud for the first time made me feel rather silly.

"You've put a lot of thought into this."

"Yes." I fidgeted in my chair. Why did I share this with her? Now she would probably think I was batty. A bike challenge, what, was I five?

"So why haven't you told Sarah?" Her accusing eyes watched my every move.

I shook my head slowly. "I guess I didn't even think of telling her. She knows I go riding almost every day. I don't know why I haven't told her the rest. Most people don't want to hear about illness or be reminded about it. At first, they're sympathetic and want to hear the details, asking how you're feeling, but that fades quickly. People don't want to hear about it. They certainly don't want to be reminded of it. It scares them, even when it isn't cancer."

Again, she changed the subject. "Is there a reward or something for reaching 3,000 miles?"

"A dog named Zeb."

She choked on her wine. "A dog named Zeb . . . what are you talking about?"

"I figure that if I can stay focused on the challenge, it'll show reliability and prove I'm responsible enough for a dog. A dog is a lot of responsibility."

She chuckled. "You're very different from how I thought you were going to be."

"What do you mean? What did you think I'd be like?" I slumped down in my chair.

"Don't get me wrong, you and Peter are very alike in some ways. You two are almost identical twins. It's scary sometimes. You are both secretive. And you are both very driven individuals. But something else drives you ... not just success." She paused and took a sip of wine. "Challenge. Yes, you love a challenge." Another sip of wine. "However, I haven't figured out if you like to conquer things as well. Or people." She patted my arm, letting her hand linger a few moments.

"Now, your turn." I looked eagerly at her.

"I'm not sure you can handle my secret," she said in a demure voice.

"Oh, come on! Or I'll think you're rodomontade."

She set her wine glass down. "A what?"

"Rodomontade. Someone who's a pretentious braggart." I flashed a cunning smile.

"How long have you been holding onto that one?" She poured more wine into her glass. "Do you use such impressive words all of the time or just around those you are trying to impress?"

I didn't want to admit that I saved them for those who intimidated me.

"Stop stalling." I dipped a strawberry into the chocolate fondue.

"Okay. I wouldn't want you to think of me as a rodo-thingy."

"Rodomontade."

"You can keep saying it, but it doesn't make it sound any cooler." She took a sip of her wine. "This secret isn't a big secret. I mean many people know about it ... but I haven't told your brother. And, I should add, I don't intend to."

I waited anxiously. *What could it be?*

She looked away and blurted out, "I'm bisexual."

I choked on my water. Did I accidentally swallow an ice cube, and was it now lodged in my throat? Beating my chest with one fist, I imagined my face turning a vivid violet.

Maddie started to stand to help me, but I motioned for her to stay seated.

Still gasping for air, I said, "You got me on that one."

"What do you mean?" She looked puzzled.

"You're joking, right?" I sipped my water gingerly to relieve the tickle in my throat.

"Are you against bisexuality?" She looked miffed.

"What? N-no. Of course not. I—" I looked around, searching for the right words. "I only thought you were trying to one-up my 'I like my bike' secret."

She laughed angrily. "A child could top that one without even trying."

"You're serious, aren't you?" Peter would not take this news well. Oh, and my mother. Maddie was playing with fire.

"Yes. I thought I could share it with you. Obviously, I was wrong. Dead wrong." She crossed her arms.

"Oh, Maddie. I'm so sorry. I never meant to imply anything. I'm just shocked, that's all … not that you are, but you're with Peter … " I hesitated. "Really, you can never tell him. Or my mother. Never my mother."

She looked terrified. "I know. That's why I wanted to talk about it. It's killing me, this secret."

"Shit, Maddie. I'm so sorry." I reached across the table and patted her hand.

"Shit. What? You don't have some fancy word for that." She pouted.

"Excrement, but that doesn't quite suit the conversation. And it's not that fancy." I picked up my fork and tapped it against the table.

I sensed she regretted telling me. Let's face it; I did a horrendous job of handling the situation. Really, I don't think I could have bungled it more.

"Listen. I'm here for you. If you ever need to talk, I'm here."

Her eyes softened. "Thanks, Lizzie."

"Ah, Peter hasn't mentioned a prenup or anything has he." I put up my palms. "I know it's none of my business, but I was just thinking out loud."

"Ha! No. Trust me, Peter won't ever mention a prenup. Let's just say my father can make or break Peter's career."

I knew there had to have been a reason Peter risked marrying a southerner.

"That's good. That's perfect, actually." I smiled weakly at her.

She looked more confident. "I warned you."

"Warned me about what?"

"That you wouldn't be able to handle my secret," she teased.

It was a real corker. One to keep — in my family.

CHAPTER SIX

"How was your day?"

It was Monday night and I had just walked into my apartment. The front room was right at the entrance, and Sarah was sitting on one of the chairs in front of the television. She picked up the remote and muted the show. Glancing at the screen, I saw that she was watching a favorite of hers, *The Bridges of Madison County*.

"Very long," I answered. "How was yours?"

Sarah stared at me. She had this weird look in her eye. Was it fear or anger? "Have you been working all day and night?"

"Yes. I guess I lost . . . "

"Track of time?"

"I'm sorry, Sarah. I probably use that excuse a lot."

"About three or four times a week."

I sighed, dropped my bag, and slumped down on the couch next to her. Rubbing my eyes, I asked, "Why do you stay?" I wasn't trying to be mean or cold.

"That's the stupidest question you could possibly ask me at this moment." She watched me, intent on what I would say.

I sat up and leaned closer. She kissed me before I had a chance to say anything. Before I knew it, we were both naked on the floor.

Afterwards, she rolled over and looked me in the eyes. "You've never been like that before."

"Like what?"

"It's hard to describe. It's like you wanted to possess me. Not only were you in control, but it was like you were dictating all of it."

"I'm sorry, baby."

"It wasn't bad, Lizzie. In fact, it was fucking hot. But you have never been like that before."

The next morning, I rolled out of bed at five and hopped on my bike. I rode as hard and as fast as I could. It was like my legs became part of the machine, pistons pushing me further and further on the trail. The pain of exerting myself beyond my normal speed and distance disappeared. All I saw and felt was the path in front of me. After carrying the bike upstairs, I checked the odometer — 341 miles so far.

When I walked into the bathroom for a shower, Sarah said, "Is it that hot outside already? You're dripping with sweat."

I pulled my shirt off and looked down. Sweat poured down my stomach. Even with all of the riding I had been doing, my stomach was still a little paunchy. I suppose I am almost thirty, but it still bothered me.

"Don't get too close to me." Sarah backed away. "I just got out of the shower and you, Lizzie, need to get in."

I stepped closer and pulled her to me. She tried pushing me away, but when I kissed her, she gave in. Her towel fell to the ground. I moved us both toward the shower and turned on the water. She did not fight me when I pulled her in with me and fucked her up against the wall.

Afterwards, while Sarah was getting dressed for work, she said, "I don't know what has gotten into you these past couple of days, but I really like it."

Maddie and Peter left later that afternoon. I didn't call to say goodbye. Neither did Maddie.

"I can't even tell you how much our sex life has improved. It's like we can't get enough of each other."

Ethan stirred more sugar into his coffee. "You can't have the one woman you want, so you're trying to possess the other."

I stared at him, giving that a thought. "Sarah told me that one night—that I fucked her like I wanted to possess her. Is that what I am doing?"

He wiped some crumbs off the table with a napkin. "What do you think?"

I shook my head. "The other day, Maddie commented that I love a challenge, but she wasn't sure yet if I liked to conquer things as well. I don't really know what she meant by that."

Ethan laughed. "Yeah, right."

I looked at him. "What does that mean?"

"Let's just say that you are an extremely driven individual."

"Well, what's wrong with that?" I pushed up my shirtsleeves.

"Nothing. As long as you don't hurt the ones you love while striving for perfection."

"I don't strive for perfection." I scoffed.

"No … really? When's the last time you received a grade lower than an 'A?' Have you ever received an A minus? I doubt it. How many honor societies do you belong to? I know you're Phi Beta Kappa. I'm surprised you haven't joined some bike-racing challenges yet."

"Listen, smarty pants, I got a 'B' once." I pointed my stir stick at him.

Ethan chuckled and shook his head. "Once. Wow, I stand corrected." He put his palms up mockingly.

"I'm not that uptight, you know."

"Oh, I know. Like you would never cry if this place ran out of chai and you didn't get your way." He laughed.

"Whatever, Ethan. You know you're more uptight than me. Have you driven home lately during work so you can take a crap in your own home?"

When Ethan was in high school, he would drive home to take a shit. He was never very comfortable with his bodily functions, or anyone else's. Sex was a big issue for him, since it involved fluids that grossed him out — even his own. I wondered if he ever masturbated.

"I live across the street from the school. I can walk there."

We both laughed. "So we both have our issues."

"Fair enough. I'm going to grab another coffee. You want another?"

"Sure. But doesn't coffee make you want to poop? I'll understand if you have to make a mad dash for your car."

"Knock it off, wise guy, or I won't get you a chai."

"All right. Let's call a truce, for the day at least."

"Sounds like a plan, Miss Perfect. What class did you get a 'B' in?"

"Astronomy. All I wanted to do was look at the stars, but the professor wanted me to do mathematical equations."

"Are you saying there's a field you haven't conquered?"

"Oh, shut up. Go get our drinks, and I hope your coffee gives you the shits. I would love to see you run out of here holding it in and then drive twenty minutes to Loveland."

"My car is souped-up for those types of emergencies."

"Maybe I'll get you a police siren for Christmas."

"That would be awesome."

He wandered over to the counter to get our second round of drinks.

CHAPTER SEVEN

"I SEE THAT YOU'RE STILL RIDING YOUR BIKE. HOW'S THE GREAT BIKE CHALLENGE GOING FOR you?"

I didn't have to turn around to know it was Maddie. I knew it by her voice, and besides, she was the only one who knew my bike challenge secret.

"Really well, actually. How's the new job?" I slowly turned around and gazed into those beautiful blue eyes. It had been weeks since we had seen or spoken to each other.

"I love the job. They're starting to trust me with my own projects." She paused. "How far did you ride? You're dripping in sweat."

Neither of us mentioned how odd it was that she'd showed up outside of my apartment. She'd never been here before. How did she find out where I lived? I wasn't sure she had forgiven me yet for the conversation we had at our last meetings. I hoped both of us could forget the incident.

"I had a lot of energy, so I went longer than normal. I rode to LaPorte and back." I tugged at my T-shirt, which was sticking to my skin. "Geez, look at me — I'm a mess! Do you want to come in? I'm dying for a hot shower. You can hang out while I get cleaned up."

"That sounds nice. Hope you don't mind, but I won't hug you until you shower." She waved her hand in front of her nose. "Stinky."

"Smelly McGee, that's me."

As soon as the words left my mouth, I froze. What had compelled me to make such a nincompoop out of myself?

Maddie snapped her head up to eyeball me. "Oh, wow. That's pretty dorky, even for you. I wouldn't suggest trying that one on the ladies." She snickered.

"Come on, smartass." I led her up the flight of stairs to my apartment, searching for my pride with each step.

"Is Sarah home?" Maddie asked.

Had she sensed my embarrassment and wanted to divert the conversation away from my gaffe?

I laughed, feeling more at ease. "She doesn't officially live with me. But no, she isn't here right now. She and her mom are bonding today. They're having breakfast, and then they'll shop till they drop. They are definitely shoppers. When I go with them, I have to take energy shots just to keep up."

"Two women after my own heart. You don't like to shop?"

"I prefer to have someone else do it for me."

"So you always have a girlfriend to take care of you?"

"You're spunky today."

We walked into my apartment. She looked around and said, "Not what I was expecting."

"Really? What did you think my apartment would look like?"

"I wasn't expecting a feminine touch." She gestured to the fresh flowers and candles on the table.

"Thanks—I think." I fiddled with my hoop earring.

"I mean you aren't a bull dyke or anything." She laughed. "But you aren't super fem either." Color flooded her cheeks. "I'm sorry. I tend to put my foot in it. To be honest, when I met you, I wasn't sure what to expect. Peter doesn't have any photos of you and you don't come up during family gatherings. I thought you were a raving feminist and all of them were embarrassed by you. I was taken aback when you walked up to the table, looking normal, like a female version of Peter. But you were wearing makeup. I had envisioned a woman with a shaved head and covered in tattoos." She stepped from side to side nervously.

I watched her eyes wander over every crevice.

"Don't tell Peter that we look alike," I warned.

"Oh, I won't!"

She turned back to me. "I thought you would have a very sterile apartment. No unnecessary items. No personal touches." She motioned to photos of Sarah and I on the mantle.

It was my turn to blush. "I can't take the credit for the personal touches or for the flowers. Sarah loves to decorate. She has a fetish for fresh flowers and Yankee Candles. I can't even guess how much she spends each week on them." I chuckled. "I swear, as soon as she started staying the night, she began putting her mark on my place. And maybe she didn't like the smell. I have to admit, I do like the smell of the clean cotton candle."

We stared at each other, awkwardly.

"Make yourself comfortable. It won't take me long to clean up." I went straight to my bathroom, turned the water to hot, and stripped down. Before stepping into the shower, I frowned at myself in the mirror and said, "Behave, Lizzie. This is Peter's fiancée." But I didn't want to follow my own advice. I felt compelled to pursue Maddie.

I usually take an extravagant amount of time in the shower, but that day I rushed through the routine. It wasn't that I didn't trust Maddie in the apartment—actually, I didn't care what she got into—but I didn't want to waste any time. I didn't see her that much.

She was perched on the couch, reading one of the history books I had been perusing for my research.

"What did you get yourself into while I was in the shower?" I said, towel drying my hair.

"Your sex toys, of course," she quipped. She winked and flashed an arch smile. Then she gestured to the book. "The Hitler Youth, from the excerpts I have read, they don't sound like a fun bunch to hang out with." She sat up. "I mean, I assumed they wouldn't sit around the campfire singing 'Kumbaya' and shit. But from what I read, some of them were monsters." The color drained from her face. "And at such a young age."

"I think a lot of people don't like to think that children can be evil. It's cool in a horror story, but in real life, it makes many people tremble. You have to remember, though, these kids were indoctrinated at an early age.

"And not all of them were like that, of course. There are stereotypes. Actually, membership in the Hitler Youth was mandatory." I walked over to my bookshelf and grabbed a book. "Here's a memoir of a boy who had to join the Hitler Youth in childhood. He was a weakling, and he didn't fare too well. In fact—" I stopped mid-sentence. "I'm sorry, but sometimes it's hard for me to turn off the historian in me. Do forgive my transgression." I bowed slightly.

"Your transgression? You and Peter are the only two people I know who talk like that."

I felt slightly uncomfortable about the mention of my brother's name, and about yet another comparison to Peter.

"Well, Mom beat us if we didn't ace our vocabulary tests. By the way, how is the old biddy?" I sat down on a chair, heavily.

"She seems like her old self." She looked out the patio door.

"So, still demanding, demeaning, and full of debauchery, but not the fun kind?"

"I guess you could say that. How is it that I know how your mother is and you don't?" She turned to me, staring hard.

"I haven't spoken to her since we all had dinner together. We aren't, shall I say, a close-knit family." I intertwined my fingers and then pulled them apart to enhance my point.

"I'm not so sure about that." Maddie sighed. I could only guess that Peter and Mom were pushing family and duty crap on her. I had no idea why Peter agreed with such antiquated notions of what the wife of a well-to-do businessman should be like.

"Anyway, I have something for you." She jumped up and went to the counter, where she had set her purse.

I was extremely curious about what that "something" was.

She pulled out a small box and handed it to me.

"What on earth are you up to, Miss Maddie?" I opened the box. A bracelet. It was silver, and it reminded me of those chain-links we used to make in school to decorate the Christmas tree, except the links were much smaller and were not made of colored construction paper.

"When I saw this, I immediately thought of you. In your office, I noticed you had a copy of *Atlas Shrugged* on your desk. The bracelet isn't a blue-green, but it symbolized something else for me."

I gazed into her eyes and replied, "This I am dying to know. Do tell."

"Seeing you in your domain, aka your office, I saw how you're chained, in a way, to your studies. I've never seen so many books and articles piled on top of each other in such a tiny office. Really, Lizzie, you need a designer." She laughed and added, "And a candle, or some incense or something. It's very stale in there. Maybe your fave: clean cotton."

I started to laugh.

She looked at me, unsure whether she had offended me.

"Bravo! Bravo. No one has pegged me so quickly. Not only that, but no one has realized I don't mind being chained to my studies. I love that I am. Would you help me put it on my wrist, please?"

She smiled and looked relieved.

"But shouldn't I be the one getting you gifts … to help you celebrate your upcoming nuptials?"

"Oh, you aren't getting out of buying me a gift or two. Trust me. I'm a girl who likes gifts."

"I don't doubt it. Well, since you drove all the way up here to give me this." I rattled the silver chain. "Can I take you to lunch, madame?"

"Why, yes, of course you can."

We both laughed together. It was so easy to be around her. I couldn't explain it, except that it was easy. Usually, I didn't get along with people all that well. I preferred books. Give me Dickens any day. But maybe not today.

Sitting at Coopersmith's, both bundled up in sweaters this time, we chatted.

"Does your dad ever talk?" Maddie asked.

I wiped a smudge off my water glass. "No. Not much. And when he does, it's more like barking orders. He usually starts every sentence with a verb. Not a statement — a command."

"I feel like I can't make a connection with the man — see, I just called him 'the man,' not my future father-in-law, or by his name, Charles."

"Don't take it too personally. 'The man,' as you say, doesn't communicate all that well. He doesn't communicate with anyone, unless it's a computer.

"I remember a time when my father tried to throw away a trash can. It was an old one, so it was pretty beat up, with holes and a stench that would kill a rat — maybe a rat had died in it — anyhoos, he placed it in a much larger trash can. When the trash guys came, they carefully pulled the beat-up can out of the other trash can and set it on the curb with the remaining cans. 'The man' was furious. His face was beet-red and a vein in his forehead was popping out. I could tell he was having a temper tantrum, even if he didn't say anything. The next trash day, he hid it inside one of the larger trash cans under a lot of wet, stinky garbage. But when he came home from work, there it was again, sitting on the curb with the other trash cans.

"The following week, he set it next to all of the others with a note that read: 'This is trash, please take it.' When he came home, he saw they'd removed the note, and presumably threw it away, but left the can. It outraged Dad beyond belief. He doesn't speak much, but when he does, and when he's angry, it is a sight to behold. The next week, he was determined to be rid of the can.

"That next trash day was a little windy. When it was like that, sometimes one of the trash cans would wind up in a ravine in the hogback. One of us would have to traipse down there and retrieve it. When I left for school, I didn't remember seeing the old trash can. But when my father came home that night, he was ecstatic it had finally gone, but so had another one. My father walked down to the ravine and retrieved one.

"For some reason, I decided to walk down there, too. I just had this feeling. And, of course, I saw the old trash can down there. He must have seen it too, but decided this was his only way of getting rid of the damn thing."

Maddie laughed while I told the story. I didn't realize right away, but that was the most I had ever said to her at one time. It was the most I had said to anyone in a long time actually, unless it was a lecture, or to Ethan.

"I can't believe they threw the note away but left the can. That's one of the oddest things I've heard in a while."

"Wow, you must be hard-up for stories right now."

"Well, I hang out with your father. I'm in a drought."

"*Touché.*"

"Actually, I'm surprised your father sets out his own trash. Peter would never do that."

"Mom always wanted servants, but my father has always refused. He grew up poor. He's cognizant of his upbringing. Of course, he did concede to having a nanny, but I always wondered whether he just wanted to ensure we would survive our childhood. Mom wasn't the nurturing kind, if you know what I mean."

We sat in silence for some moments. Then Maddie asked, "Is that why you hate your family so much?"

I set down my knife and fork and watched the light drizzle outside slide down the window. "You know, Maddie, at one point I could give you a whole laundry list of why. But all of the memories are fading. To be honest, I can't pinpoint the reason I decided to go my own way. At one point, I had a reason, or reasons. Now it's just more of a feeling. Whenever I'm around them, I don't like them."

"Is that why you never told them you're sick?" She took one of the flowers out of the vase on the table and smelled it.

"I never even thought about telling them. No one likes to hear about other people's troubles. Even Sarah tunes out when I mention feeling ill. I figured that they would care even less. At least Sarah loves me."

Maddie sipped her wine, her eyes on the busboy who was clearing the table next to us.

We sat in silence again. Maddie seemed to be mulling something over.

"That settles it. Peter is picking up this check." She pulled out a credit card and set it on the edge of the table.

"What are you talking about?"

"I'm tired of the bastard not caring."

I could tell the wine was kicking in. Although I wanted to push her on her declaration, I was torn about doing so. Were my intentions to help a friend? Or were they to drive a wedge between my brother and his incredibly gorgeous fiancée? I sat silently while she, or Peter rather, settled the tab.

Before we left, Maddie handed me the flower she had confiscated earlier and patted my cheek tenderly.

Later that night, I was on the couch with Sarah, watching one of her stupid comedies. I had never been an Adam Sandler fan, or a fan of movies like that, but Sarah loved them, so I agreed to watch one with her. She was stretched out in front of me, my arm wrapped around her stomach. I felt her touch my wrist.

"What's that?"

I looked down at what she was touching—the bracelet Maddie had given me.

"Oh, I was cleaning out a box in my closet and I found this bracelet I used to wear during high school."

She fidgeted with it a little, and then said, "It looks weird. Is it a chain of some sort?"

"I'm not sure, but I've always liked it, so I put it on." I shrugged and turned my attention back to the movie.

That was that. I didn't know that lying to my girlfriend would come so easily, and without regret. I reached for a handful of popcorn and ate it. Sarah didn't suspect anything odd. She snuggled even closer. I squeezed her waist and kissed the back of her head.

CHAPTER EIGHT

"She gave you what?" Ethan choked on his coffee.

"Ethan, don't be so dramatic. You can see with your own eyes."

He reached out and stroked the bracelet, as if he thought it would disappear at his touch. "I can't believe it. Why would she give you a piece of jewelry? You don't give jewelry to someone you barely know. What do you think it means?"

"Come on, Ethan. Focus here. I'm telling you that I lied to my girlfriend. That's the issue right now. I lied, and I didn't feel bad about it. Right after I lied, I held tight and kissed her head, as if I felt closer to her. *That* is the issue; not that Maddie gave me this." I shook my wrist.

"But what does it mean that you're wearing it, and *you lied*! You lied to Sarah!" His eyes grew big behind his glasses. He waggled his finger in my face. "You lied to her *and* you are wearing it."

"Thank you, Captain Obvious." I saluted him.

He stared at me; I mean he *really stared* at me. Then he looked down at his coffee cup. Speaking more to his cup than me, he said, "She bought you a bracelet. You not only accepted it, but you continue to wear it. And you lied to Sarah about it." He turned his eyes back to me. "Have you taken the bracelet off since she gave it to you?" He arched one eyebrow.

"Um ... no. No, I haven't. Why?" It had been too much trouble taking it off to shower, so I had showered with it on. Laziness was the reason I hadn't removed it, I told myself. "I have clumsy fingers that can't work the tiny clasp, and I don't want to ask Sarah each day; that would seem wrong."

"That's it! You don't have a crush on her." He looked back at his cup. "Crushes are innocent. We all know they won't go anywhere. But you ... you actually like her."

Sunlight streamed in through the window. "What are you talking about, you crazy little man?" I snatched my sunglasses from where they were perched on top of my head and put them on.

"Yep! I'm right. You only call me 'little man' when you feel threatened or on guard and you want to knock me down." He rubbed the whiskers on his chin triumphantly. I could picture him as a child in the playground, outwitting one of his bullies in front of the prettiest girl in school. When did he decide to grow a beard? I had never seen him unshaven.

I sipped my chai. "She's my brother's fiancée, Ethan."

"And you are wearing her bracelet."

"Do you know her? Do you know her pattern of giving gifts? She's probably trying to get one of the family members, one who isn't crazy, on her side. We can't assume that just because she gave me this" — I touched the bracelet and tried not to smile — "she likes me."

"Interesting. I wasn't talking about her just now. I said that *you* like *her*. But you just hinted that she likes you as well."

I shook my head in frustration. "Oh, you are twisting everything so it will turn out like a Jerry Springer show. Why do you like drama so much?"

He smiled and sipped his coffee. For once, he didn't say anything. He just kept smiling at me. I sat silently and drank my chai. Every once in a while, I caught him glancing at the bracelet. He tapped his fingers on the table, causing me to grimace. His nails were cut too short for my taste.

Finally, I said, "She's Peter's fiancée. There is no hidden meaning behind the bracelet."

"I disagree."

"And what evidence do you have?"

"The proof is in the bracelet."

I laughed.

Ethan beamed at his own cleverness, or what he believed was cleverness.

"What's it like in your little world?" I queried.

"So you are threatened, or is it confusion?" Puzzlement spread across his face.

I shook my head, frustrated.

Ethan said in a grave voice, "Be careful, Lizzie."

"What do you mean? I'm sure Sarah won't ask about the bracelet again."

His face plainly showed that I missed his point. "I'm not talking about that. I've seen you sabotage your life on more than one occasion. All I'm going to say is look before you leap."

"I have no idea what you're talking about." I fiddled with a pen that sat on top of my leather-bound journal.

"You run away instead of dealing with your issues."

"Issues … issues … I don't have issues!" I bounded out of my chair and hotfooted to the bathroom.

"You see!" he bellowed.

CHAPTER NINE

I SAT IN MY OFFICE, BEHIND MY MESSY DESK, GRINNING WOOZILY AT MADDIE, WHO HAD STOPPED by to fill me in on her latest misadventure.

"Oh, my God, Lizzie! The most embarrassing thing happened to me the other day. For lunch, I had sushi. And let's just say it didn't settle well." She winked at me. "So there I was, in this meeting with a prospective client in their home. They wanted to redo their bedroom." Maddie paused and waved her hand in the air. "But that's beside the point. I was sitting there in their home, discussing their needs, when all of a sudden I felt something. You know when you start to get diarrhea you get a sharp pain in your stomach. Well, I got this cramp. I tried to push it out of my head and focus on the conversation. I started to fidget in my chair.

"So there I am, trying to wrap the meeting up as soon as possible. But the husband kept going on and on about how he doesn't want a really feminine room. The entire time, I'm trying to hold it in.

"Then, I just couldn't hold it in anymore. I had to ask them if I could use their bathroom. I walked as fast as I could down the hallway—without looking like I was about to shit myself. When I sat on the toilet, I exploded. Seriously, I couldn't believe how fast it shot out of my ass. And I'm sitting there hoping they couldn't hear me. But I could feel I wasn't done, so I flushed the toilet, so I wouldn't clog it. And then I braced myself for round two.

"That's when I noticed the toilet didn't flush completely. I started to panic. *How in the world can I go out there and tell them that I had the shits and I clogged their toilet?* I thought. So, I jumped up and saw that there was a plunger. Picture this: I'm standing there with my pants around my ankles, plunging like a mad woman, squeezing my ass cheeks so I wouldn't shit myself.

"And then I sensed I wasn't alone. I looked over my shoulder and saw that the blind was up and the window was open. Their neighbor was watching me with his mouth open. You better order a coffin."

"What?"

"I'm gonna die from embarrassment."

I smiled, "Could he hear you?"

"Oh, Lizzie, I don't even want to think about that." She shook her head and laughed. "I was completely mortified."

She laughed so hard she squeezed out a fart.

"Did you just break wind?" I asked, floored.

"Break wind!" She roared with laughter.

Trying to recover my composure, I said, "Careful. You might do it again."

Maddie had started to pop in more and more at my office. I was only too eager to set aside my work to be entertained by her. Afterward, we wandered over to the Lory Student Center and grabbed a bite to eat.

I couldn't help but think that she was coming up with reasons to see me. I would never tell that story to anyone. Maybe I would tell Ethan. Maddie's carefree attitude drew me in. No one in my family would admit to that story. I was learning how much she trusted me with her secrets.

I let out a sigh when I heard the phone ring. There was only one person I knew who would call at this hour. I rolled over in bed and picked up the phone. "You are aware of the time?"

"Good morning to you, little sis." He sounded cheerful, but in a condescending way. "It must be nice to be a student. I've been up for hours working."

I looked at the clock. It was six in the morning. Peter had always been a liar.

"To what do I owe this wake-up call?"

"Maddie and I would like to invite you and—I'm sorry, I don't know your girlfriend's name—to dinner tonight. What do you say, can you make it?"

"Well, I can. I'll have to ask Sarah."

"Put her on the phone. I know I can convince her."

I could almost see his sleazy smile. "She's in the shower. Don't worry, I'll ask her."

"All right, my address is 1648 Quentin Road. Mapquest it. Be here at 7 p.m., Elizabeth. I gotta go. I'm getting another call."

I didn't bother saying goodbye, since I knew he had already hung up. I stared at the bathroom door. Should I invite Sarah? The last two times I hadn't, she'd flipped out. If I got caught again, it would be over for sure. But did I want her to go?

She walked into the bedroom, drying her hair with a towel. "Did I hear the phone?"

I laughed. Sometimes I thought she had special powers. "Yes, you did. Peter called to invite us to dinner tonight. Would you like to go?"

"What?" She stopped in her tracks and dropped her towel on the floor.

"Do you want to go to Peter's for dinner tonight? You know, my brother," I teased.

She ran over to the bed, straddled me, and leaned down, holding my arms above my head.

"Are you asking me to a family function?"

I smiled. "Well, he invited you, and it would be rude if I didn't extend the invitation. And I remember you telling me that you wanted me to let you in more. I'm warning you, though, it's like stepping into a viper's den."

"Don't be a jerk right now. This is groundbreaking for you. The mysterious Lizzie is letting me into a part of her secret world." She leaned down and kissed me.

I brushed her hair out of her face. "It's not a secret world. I don't like them much, and I'm surprised that anyone would want to subject themselves to my family." I shrugged to the best of my ability, since she was still holding down one of my arms.

A puzzled look crossed her face. "Why did you laugh when I asked if I heard the phone?"

"What?" I ran my free hand over her breasts and down her torso.

"You laughed when I asked the question. Why?"

"I don't know. I just did." I laughed again. "Come here." I pulled her closer and kissed her. Then I asked, "Can you be ready by five? I know you'll have to leave practice early, but we have to be there early." Volleyball season had started, and Sarah was the girl's JV coach.

"What time is dinner?"

"Seven."

"We'll be really early." She looked perplexed.

"Trust me."

She smiled. "Of course, I trust you, and I'll be ready at five."

CHAPTER TEN

WE ARRIVED AT PETER'S HOUSE A LITTLE AFTER 6 P.M. PART OF ME WAS SURPRISED WHEN I SAW his house. The other part thought, *Typical Peter*. Simply put, it was ostentatious. He had a four-car garage. Floodlights pierced the sky near every tree. And from the looks of the neighborhood, it was newly built. The house was reminiscent of a plantation home.

"What does your brother do?" Sarah gasped.

"Investments of some sort. And he kisses Dad's ass."

"It seems to work for him." Sarah leaned closer to the windshield to get a better view.

I parked the car on the street and we trekked to the front door. We had to climb a winding stone staircase to ring the bell. Where in the hell did my brother think he lived, the old south?

Before I rang the bell, I gave Sarah my are-you-sure-you-are-ready-for-this smile. She smiled back at me, but her expression lacked confidence. For a brief moment, I felt bad for her. Then again, she had been asking for this, so here she was. I turned to the door and pressed the bell. I could hear church bells chiming. *Oh God, Peter. Do you think you're Jesus?*

Maddie opened the door and immediately threw her arms around me. "I'm so glad you are here." She let me go, and then threw her arms around Sarah just as enthusiastically. "Sarah, I'm glad you could make it."

She whisked us past the foyer and into the kitchen. Peter was standing at the bar, preparing a scotch. That was when I knew my parents were in attendance. *Nice, Peter. Real nice not to give me all of the information.* I should have suspected. His nose was so far up their asses it would require surgery, and massive amounts of therapy, for Peter to stand on his own two feet.

"Hey sis, you made it. And you must be Sarah. Maddie told me you were quite lovely. Well, that figures. Elizabeth is of the same stock, and boy do we catch fine-looking women in our family." He nudged me with his elbow, winked, and lifted his glass to toast Maddie.

Sarah obviously didn't know what to do after this little performance. She chose to go with a deer-in-headlights look. It was the best choice, considering.

"Don't mind him, Sarah. He just pretends to be crude. Deep down somewhere, there's a nice guy … or I keep hoping there is." Maddie patted Sarah's arm.

"*Touché*, Maddie." Peter took a swig of bourbon and then left the kitchen, carrying the drinks. I turned to Maddie and asked if my parents were present.

"Your mother is. Your father hasn't arrived yet. Something at the office held him up." She fluttered to the other side of the kitchen. "Really, Lizzie, what does he do? There is always some emergency. And now Peter is always held up as well. This is the first night in weeks that I've seen him before ten." Anger flashed in her eyes.

"You got me. We don't talk much." I shrugged.

"Yes, that's right, the mysterious family. Sarah, have you noticed that about Lizzie? Like she tells you just enough about herself, but deep down there's so much more." Maddie laughed and continued preparing a salad.

To my surprise, Sarah came to my defense. "She does have a mysterious side, but when she comes home late, I know what she has been up to. It's usually because she's had her nose buried in some book and has lost track of time." She leaned over to kiss my cheek. Right then, both my mother and brother entered the kitchen. It took a trained eye, but I could see my mother flinch when she saw the kiss.

Peter smiled. I could practically see him counting the extra money he would inherit.

"Look, Mother, for once Elizabeth is on time for dinner." Peter helped Mom to a barstool.

Sarah glanced at her watch. I looked at the clock on the microwave. It was six-thirty. Sarah looked at me and chuckled. I think she was starting to see why I did certain things, like show up so early for everything.

"Maddie, is there anything I can do to help with dinner?" asked Sarah.

"You are a dear, but to be honest, most of it is done. I picked up dinner from this darling restaurant down the street." She smiled at Sarah. "I hope neither one of you is vegetarian or I'm afraid all you will be eating is this salad." She tossed it some more and then set it aside.

I could tell she was nervous. Why? Because of Sarah, perhaps?

"Fear not, we are both carnivores." I smiled at Maddie and she reciprocated.

As she reached for a serving platter on top of the fridge, I saw a large hole in her sweater. It looked like it had been well worn and the hole was testimony to that.

"Maddie, why do you insist on wearing that sweater? That hole is the size of the Grand Canyon. We are not paupers, my dear." Peter waved his arm to point out the luxury of their lifestyle.

"I love this sweater. It's the most comfortable one I own, so I'm sorry but you'll just have to endure seeing me in it." She flashed a stubborn smile at Peter, who turned away to say something to our mother.

The Scotch-lady did not look impressed by Maddie's determination to be comfortable. I couldn't remember the last time I saw Mom in a pair of jeans or shorts. She would always tell me, "It is better to always dress nice, because that one time you wear sweats, the whole world will stop by to see you."

Of course, I never lived by that mantra, but Peter did. On the rare occasion he wore jeans, they were guaranteed to be of the nicest quality and the most expensive. Even then, they looked starched. What was the point of wearing formal jeans? Especially when they resembled "mom jeans."

"How's your job going, Maddie?" Sarah asked, an obvious attempt to divert attention from the sweater.

I looked at Sarah. Usually, she was so quiet she would hardly ever engage in conversation with a group of people she did not know. I stopped to wonder whether she was trying to impress me or support me, or whether she just felt comfortable with Maddie's southern, carefree attitude. It was like they were old friends.

"Well, should we sit down and start dinner?" said The Scotch-lady before Maddie could even answer Sarah's question.

"It's all ready. I was waiting for Charles," Maddie explained.

"Oh, he can eat the leftovers." Mom looked at her watch. "Serves him right for being late again."

"Mom, I'm sure something important held him up at the office." Peter looked troubled.

Was he upset that he would have to choose a side? He was never good at that when it came to our parents.

"How 'bout I get you another drink?" he told her.

"I would never turn that down, but I'm famished. And I have to leave soon."

I was sure that was a lie. I examined her thin, persnickety face. Yes, she was fibbing.

Peter's face was priceless. He looked as if he might cry. I reveled in the moment, wondering whose side he would take: Mother's or Father's. *Come on, Peter. Make a choice for once in your life.*

"Hello all."

Goddamnit! Why did he have to show up right then? I turned to find my father standing there, his expertly tailored three-piece suit hiding his belly.

"Dad, you made it!"

For a second, I thought Peter was going to wet himself with excitement. He reminded me of my neighbor's cocker spaniel, who peed whenever he was excited.

The Scotch-lady took another sip of her drink, but she didn't even look in her husband's direction. Was this why I was so screwed up about relationships? I glanced over at Sarah. To my astonishment, she showed no reaction to the scene at all. Was she just overwhelmed by it all?

"Sorry I'm late … got held up, you know," he said in a deep voice.

Maddie's jaw almost hit the floor. She looked at me, and I could tell she wanted to shout, "Oh my God! That's the most your father has ever said."

Peter must have seen the expression on her face too, because he said, "Maddie, do you think we can get some food on the table and feed all these hungry people?"

I wanted to hit him.

She retorted, "I could if you would get your lazy buttocks out of my way."

To his credit, he didn't rebuff her. Did he know he would lose the battle? Her southern charm didn't quite take the sting out of it, but gave her words the illusion of being heartfelt.

I could tell my father was impressed. He loved a woman with a spark. That explained why he hated my mother: her spark went out years ago.

"If you'll take a seat, I'll bring out the salads?"

I followed my father into the dining room. He was the man to follow. His girth announced that he never missed a meal.

The dining room, considering the size of the house, was quite modest. The table could seat eight comfortably. In the middle was a beautiful yellow rose centerpiece in what I assumed was a Waterford vase. No paintings graced the wall; instead, an elegant candelabrum hung on the wall behind the table. And, of course, all of the votives were lit.

Sarah and I took a seat together on one side, and my parents sat at the ends of the table. I found that surprising, but maybe they figured they paid for the house so they might as well have that honor. I was pleased. At least I didn't have to stare at them across from me all night.

Maddie walked in with the salad and seemed to wince a little when she saw the seating arrangement. Peter gave her his not-right-now smile. She shook her head and said, "I'm happy that all of you could join us this evening."

After placing the bowl by the man of the house, Charles, she sat down. "Peter and I have an announcement." She placed her hand on Peter's.

Panic overcame me. I stopped breathing.

"That's right. After much finagling we have finally got our schedules squared away, and we have set a date for the wedding."

What a relief! I thought for sure she was going to say she was pregnant. I didn't think I could handle that.

"That's great news. When's the big day?" asked the romantic, Sarah.

"July fourteenth," replied Peter.

I started to panic. *Please Sarah, don't say anything.*

"Did you say July fourteenth? That's Lizzie's birthday." Sarah sounded baffled by Peter's oversight.

I wasn't shocked at all.

"Peter, you didn't tell me your sister's birthday was the fourteenth." Maddie genuinely seemed upset. I hoped she'd throw the salad bowl at his head.

"What? I thought … that's right it is. I got so caught up on scheduling I totally spaced it. It's not easy you know, coordinating mine, yours, Mom's and Dad's schedule." He threw his fork down on top of his salad defensively. Coordinating with my schedule obviously wasn't important to him.

"Well, I guess we'll have to come up with a different date," Maddie said, scowling at him.

I was glad we had come to dinner; the drama was pure entertainment.

I stammered, "A-are you kidding … keep it on my birthday. That way I won't forget it. I'm horrible at remembering things like that. You have to keep it."

"Doesn't say much about you as a historian, if you can't remember dates." Maddie laughed and took a sip of wine. I could tell she was seething but was trying to regain control.

"I told you history is the greatest story ever told, remember … not just dates."

She nodded, but the anger was still present.

"You wouldn't mind?" Peter seemed relieved. "Because we already started reserving everything and making initial plans."

"Nah. I don't really celebrate my birthday anyway."

Sarah squeezed my leg under the table. I could feel her nails digging in. We had planned a trip to the Tetons that week. I glanced at her again, but didn't know what to say. What could I do? Say, "No way, Jose, that's my birthday?" Wouldn't that be childish?

"Good. It's settled then. The date is July fourteenth," declared Peter. "And we won't have to buy Elizabeth a cake, since there will be wedding cake."

What a nice thought, Peter. I tried to remember if I had ever had a cake on my birthday.

Maddie looked at me, but I couldn't tell what she was thinking. I smiled and raised my water glass in her direction. A weak attempt, I know, but it was all I could do at the time.

She smiled and turned to Sarah. "How are your classes going?" she asked.

"What? Another student?" cackled The Scotch-lady.

"No, Mother. Sarah teaches high school English."

"My classes are good. They're always good this time of the year … wait and ask me in December and my answer will be quite different." She giggled.

"High school, huh?" Peter looked at me. "They don't pay you guys much. Would you consider yourself more of a volunteer?" He chuckled.

"Peter, what an awful thing to say." Maddie's beautiful face scrunched into a frown.

"All that I'm saying is that teachers don't make much." He paused, looked briefly at Mom and Dad, and then said, "It's a good thing Elizabeth has a trust fund, since she didn't go into the family business."

Family business. What were we — gangsters?

My mother bristled. I often wondered if she had tried to cut off my trust fund. My father just looked bored, but that was normal, so I wasn't sure how he felt. He would be great at Texas Hold 'em.

"Peter, thanks for your concern. But I have my own trust fund." Sarah's expression was one of triumph.

Maddie glowered at Peter.

"What? I was just making a joke. She gets so touchy about these topics. You know, Maddie, I'm starting to think you aren't a Democrat at all, but a hard-core liberal." Again he chuckled, but it sounded nervous this time.

"How can you be a Democrat? You're from the south? Aren't all Democrats supposed to be from the northeast?" asked my mother.

"I thought Arkansas was a southern state?" I quipped.

"You know, I'm not from there, but I think you are right, Lizzie," Maddie replied, a huge grin on her face.

"Wasn't one of their governors … oh, what is his name … a Democrat?" I went further. "And didn't he become president?"

"And didn't he marry a lesbian?" My mother pronounced it Les-Bi-An. Some words she liked to enunciate for dramatic purposes. Lesbian had always been one of them, for obvious reasons. However, she only did it in certain settings; in public, she ignored me completely. Even when I was a child she acted like I was a stranger. One time, when I was small, I accidentally knocked over a display in a store. I turned my beet-red face to her. She looked me up and down and said, "You better go find your mother to clean up this mess." I was devastated.

I squeezed Sarah's leg to give her some support. She placed her hand on my knee. Peter, technically the host of the meal, stayed out of it and refused to make eye contact. Maybe he felt that, since he was denied the host position at the head of the table, he wasn't the host after all. Father, seated at the table head, didn't really accept me anyway, but he appreciated anyone who could ruffle my mother's feathers so he looked on with a smirk.

"Jesus, Mother! She isn't a Les-Bi-An. Just because a woman is powerful, doesn't mean she is gay."

"That's obvious." Mom raised her drink in my direction.

Bravo, Mother. Bravo.

Maddie caught my eye. "Maybe we should start on the entrée? Anyone else hungry?" She stood and started for the kitchen.

"You know me, Maddie. I'm always hungry." Peter nearly shouted after her as she rushed away. He patted his stomach to emphasize the point. I noticed that, for the first time, it was starting to bulge a little, which made me smile. The only one who didn't have a belly in our family was The Scotch-lady, but only because she kept to a strict liquid diet.

CHAPTER ELEVEN

"LES-BI-AN!" ETHAN LAUGHED WHILE SAYING IT. "I CAN'T BELIEVE SHE SAID THAT ... AND AT the dinner table. How rude! No one in my family would say it during dinner." He continued to giggle.

"Well, we aren't from the polite south, my friend." I stared at the hot barista while she made our coffees. *Was I a pig? Or did I just appreciate beauty?*

"What did Sarah say about it?" He flipped the pages of a book that sat on the table. It was *The Da Vinci Code.*

"You know that book is riddled with historical inaccuracies." I gestured to the novel.

"Oh, I know, professor." He raised one palm in the air. "But somehow I'm persevering. Have you ever looked up the word 'stodgy'?"

"Hmph!"

"Oh, don't get your panties in a bunch. Loosen up, Lizzie! Now tell me how Sarah reacted to your mom." He placated me with a smile.

"To be honest, she was really quiet on the ride home. And when she was getting ready to go shopping with her mom this morning, she barely talked to me."

"Does she go shopping with her mom every Saturday?" He looked at his phone, its insistent beeping telling him he had a text. "Dammit, I've only been here ten minutes and she's already getting on my case." He slammed the phone down on the table.

His wife hated that we spent so much time together.

"What do you think her silence means?" he asked while he fired off a text to his wife.

"Got me? Maybe she realized I'm a much bigger challenge than she thought."

"Or she felt bad for you." He paused to read his wife's return text. "Her family is accepting, right? Maybe Sarah doesn't know what to say to you. She's been pushing you to let her into your family, and now she sees how they treat you."

"Maybe. It's a possibility. But she should know me. I don't care what they think." I leaned on the table and propped my chin in my right hand.

"Not at all? Come on, Lizzie, deep down most of us want acceptance, especially from our families."

I tilted my head in my hand and leered at the barista, ignoring Ethan. Seconds passed and I noticed he followed my gaze.

Ethan casually said, "She looks like your ex."

Holy shit! I thought to myself, bolting upright. *He's right.* She had long blonde hair, deep green eyes, and a beguiling smile. "I thought she looked familiar."

He laughed. "Maybe Maddie is good for you. Before, you would have made the connection right away and gone on and on about it." He made limp-wristed circular movements in the air.

"Don't you mean Sarah?"

"Nope. I mean Maddie. You have been so different these past few weeks—more relaxed, happier, and easier to talk to. You've always opened up after some coaxing, but now you don't need any prodding."

"I don't know what you're talking about."

My phone beeped. A message flashed up on the screen. "Oh great, Sarah wants me to have dinner with her mom tonight." I paused before sending a text back.

"Are you going?"

"Don't see how I can say no. She had to put up with my family last night. Besides, her mom is nice." I shook my head. "You know me, I just hate family dinners ... I'm not good at things like that. Geez, Sarah and I hardly go to dinner, let alone with other people."

"And you say my marriage is bad."

I chuckled. "I guess people who live in glass houses shouldn't throw stones."

"Especially you! You wouldn't hit a thing. How is it you never played softball as a kid? Don't all dykes play in college? Sorry, I mean *Les-Bi-Ans.*"

His joke caught me by surprise, and chai almost streamed out my nose. It burned like hell.

"Have you been drinking long?" He smirked.

After coffee with Ethan, I decided to hit the Poudre River bike trail. One thing I love about Colorado is that even in late October the weather can be gorgeous. I looked at the mountains to see if any clouds were rolling in, but all I saw was clear blue sky.

For the first ten miles, the vibrancy of the red, orange, and yellow leaves contrasting the lazy river awed me. I had always loved being surrounded by nature. Since it was late in the season, there weren't too many people out on the trail.

I pulled off the trail at my favorite spot and sat by the river. Sunlight glittered on the ripples of the slow, meandering stream. This time of year, before the winter snow melt, it was more like a dribble. In the spring, it gushed.

Picking up a smooth stone, I tried my best to skim it all the way across. It jumped twice and then sank to the bottom. Infuriated, I tried again. Skip. Skip. Then nothing. I had seen countless fools skip stones here. Why couldn't I?

"Lizzie, stop it." My words floated through the thin air.

I picked up another stone, lined it up carefully, and released. Jump. Jump. Then I saw it no more. I laughed mirthlessly at my ineptitude.

Giving up, I sat there, contemplating life, love, and the kind of stuff one thinks about when sitting next to a river, until I noticed the weather beginning to change. A strong gust of wind sent my bike clattering to the ground. My metal water bottled popped out of its holder and clinked as it rolled over the rocks to stop at the river's edge. The weather could change fast in Colorado at this time of year. Clouds had already started to roll in over the foothills.

Righting my bike, I then jumped on and started the trek home. The wind came in gusts, and when it did, I had to use all of my strength to stay on the bike. At points, the wind picked up my front tire and turned it perpendicular to the rest of the bike. Colorado weather—you never knew what was going to happen. The saying was, "If you don't like the weather, wait ten minutes and it will change."

After struggling for over an hour, I finally made it back to my apartment. As I lifted my bike up onto my shoulders to carry it up the flight of stairs to my apartment, a familiar voice behind me said, "Only you would be crazy enough to go for a ride in this wind."

I turned my head. "It was beautiful when I left ... no wind at all."

"Oh my gosh, Lizzie, you're bleeding." Maddie sounded concerned.

I looked down. Blood dripped from my shin down into my sock. "Yeah, a tree branch hit me. I tried avoiding it, but as you can see"—I gestured to my shin—"I wasn't successful." I laughed.

She shook her head. "And what about your arm?"

"What?" I looked at my left arm and then my right. Sure enough, my right arm had a gash as well. "I don't know what happened." I paused to think. "But that does explain why my arm started to hurt. I just thought my arms were tired from struggling to stay on the bike."

"You're a mess. Let's get you upstairs and get you cleaned up." She took the bike, lifted it onto her shoulder, and started up the stairs. Her manner told me not to mess with her. When we reached the landing outside my door, she noticed the computer on my bike. "792 miles. Not bad." She flashed her sexy smile.

At my front door, she put her hand out for my keys. I sighed and handed them to her. She opened the door, hung my bike up, and then turned to me. "All right, I hope you have a first aid kit."

"I do. You look like you would ream me if I didn't." I walked into my bedroom. Maddie followed. It felt weird for a brief moment. Then she followed me into the bathroom.

"Wow! This bathroom is spotless. Who cleans it, you or Sarah?" She eyed me.

"Uh ... we have a cleaner. I wipe down the sinks and counter each morning, but the sparkle is Miranda's doing." I opened the cabinet under the sink, searching for my first aid kit.

"Peter wants me to hire a cleaner, but, oh, I don't know ... it feels weird to have a stranger in my home." She fidgeted with some flowers on the counter.

I stood awkwardly, not knowing what to say. Did she think I was a snob?

She smiled. "Maybe I should. I hate sticking my hand in the toilet."

I crinkled my nose in disgust.

Wanting desperately to change the subject, since I didn't want her to think of me as a prig, I handed her my first aid kit.

"Good." She laughed. "I don't have to beat you now."

"You wouldn't pick on the injured, would you?"

"Yes! If they're stupid enough to go out in this wind." She gently whacked the back of my head.

"Ouch!" I stepped back in case she struck again. "It wasn't windy when I left." I pouted.

"Didn't you look at the weather channel? I thought for sure you would be the type to check that out."

"What do you mean 'the type to check that out'? Just because I study history doesn't make me a dork."

"I'm finding it doesn't make you smart, either. It's a good thing you weren't seriously injured. The wind is gusting up to 60mph. And there you were, out there riding, you moron." She laughed as she dabbed hydrogen peroxide on the cut on my shin.

I tried not to react, but my leg jerked away.

"You and your brother are such babies." She started to dab my elbow. "The cuts aren't bad at all. All you need is a couple of Band-Aids. I'll put them on after you shower. How can you sweat so much in the cold? I can't believe you are in shorts and a tee when it is only 50 degrees outside."

"I'm not impressing you at all today, am I?"

"Are you trying to impress me?" I wondered what arcane thoughts her smile concealed.

I ignored the question. Or was I scared to answer it? "Is Peter working today?" I asked instead.

"Of course. Saturday is just another workday. Is Sarah shopping with her mom?"

"Yes. Our partners are quite predictable."

"Well, then, get in the shower and then take me to lunch. I'm famished. And I will tell you about this crazy appointment I had this morning."

I gave her a look.

"I know … I know." She put her palms up in the air. "I bust Peter's balls for working on a Saturday, when I made an appointment as well. But wait until I tell you about it. It was so worth it. Now, get into the shower." She turned and left the bathroom.

I turned on the water—hot, since I needed to warm my bones. The wind had chilled me all the way through. My cuts stung when the water hit them. Rushing through my routine, I pulled on a shirt and some jeans.

When I walked into the front room, Maddie shook her head. "Did you put a bandage on your shin?"

"Um … sure."

"You're such a liar. Come on, back into the bathroom."

I felt like I was being scolded.

"Wow, you do like a hot shower." The mirror was still steamed. "How am I supposed to put the Band-Aid on with your jeans on?" She smiled.

I fidgeted.

"Would it make you feel better if I closed my eyes?"

"Yes, it would. But I don't think you'll actually do it." I started to undo my jeans, feeling relieved that I had shaved recently and had put on clean underwear that didn't have any holes. That could have been extremely embarrassing. Standing there with my jeans around my ankles, I prayed that Sarah wouldn't walk in. Normally, I wasn't religious, but at that moment, I was.

"Okey dokey." She patted my leg. "Let's see your elbow."

I pulled my jeans up so fast I almost ripped the bandage right off.

"Easy, tiger. You are injured enough. Don't rip off more skin."

"But I'm receiving such top-notch care, so why not?"

She didn't respond right away, just took care of my elbow. Then she looked me in the eyes. "Someone has to take care of you."

She smelled of orange blossoms. No words came to me. I just stared back. The look only lasted a few seconds, but it seemed much longer.

"Are you going to take me to lunch now? I'm starving. And I am dying to tell you about my appointment." She looked at her reflection in the mirror and messed with her hair.

"All right. All right. I guess it's the least I can do after you played nurse today."

"I still can't believe you went riding in this wind. Do you hear it now, you ding-dong?" She hit my shoulder. "Good thing it isn't trash day or your dad would have to go to the ravine to retrieve his trash cans."

She was right: the wind was howling.

"Oh, my God." After we were seated at Coopersmith's, Maddie grabbed my arm. It was obvious she could no longer keep the story bottled up inside. "So I went to this client's house. At first, everything seemed normal. I sat down with a man and his wife and they started to tell me what they envisioned and stuff. Then the husband cleared his throat and said they had one challenge. His sister, who is mentally challenged, lives with them and has a habit of breaking things, so they wanted stuff that couldn't be thrown or easily broken.

"At first I thought, *Wow, what a great couple. I don't think I could do that …* yada, yada." She waved her arm in the air. "Anyway, we started taking a tour through the house. They want to re-do the entire house. And they are quite well off, so it'd be a large project, which I was stoked about. Ka-ching!"

She paused to take a drink.

All I could think was: *Wow! She might be up here a lot more.* This was fantastic news! I tried to hide my excitement by taking a sip of Coke.

"When they started to show me the sister's bedroom, the wife mentioned that the sister wasn't there. At the time, I didn't notice any apprehension, but now, looking back, it was there." Maddie paused, her eyes glowing. "Yeah, it was definitely there."

She wiggled in her chair and waved her arms again. "But I'm jumping ahead of myself. The couple told me the sister is almost completely non-verbal. She only says a handful of words, such as big wheel, peanuts, and her own name.

"We were almost done with the tour when we went down into the basement. I finally met the sister" — Maddie took a deep breath — "Lizzie, I kid you not. She was sitting in a recliner completely naked, with her legs up in the air, masturbating." Maddie started to laugh uncontrollably. She took more deep breaths and said, "And she kept saying the words 'big wheel' and 'peanuts.'

"I didn't know what to say or do. All of us just stood there dumbfounded. Finally, the husband ushered us up the stairs.

"I know it's not the PC thing to … to" — she paused for a second to laugh again and then sucked in some air so she could talk — "to laugh at that. But when I got into my car … " Maddie was gasping for breath. "I couldn't stop laughing. I laughed so hard I almost peed myself."

I laughed too, not just at the story, but at Maddie. Her face was scarlet but she looked so beautiful and serene, even while struggling for air and laughing so hard.

After she settled down a little, I asked, "How in the heck did you end that meeting? I mean, what did you say, 'Nice meeting you, but I'm sorry this didn't work out'?"

She was still laughing as she said, "Oh, I took the job."

Fuck yeah. She took the job. Oh my god, this was the best news ever. "You did? That's great. A job like that must pay a fortune … not to mention how great it will look for your portfolio."

She smiled. I could tell she was proud of herself, and she deserved it. "What did Peter say when you told him?"

Maddie muttered, "Oh, I haven't told him. We're supposed to have dinner tonight, so I'll probably tell him then." Her tone turned serious. "Are you mad at me?"

I almost choked on my Coke. "What? Because you laughed at a person with a disability? No … no, not at all."

"No, you idiot." She lightly slapped my arm. "Not because of that. Are you mad at me for the other night?"

I racked my brain. "Maddie, I have no clue what you are talking about … unless you mean wearing a sweater with a hole in it."

She swatted my arm again. "Not that, you moron. You know, the other night when your mom was so rude to you. I didn't say anything. It's been bothering me since."

"Really? Why?" My voice cracked a little.

"Because she is such a bitch. I'm sorry, Lizzie, I know she's your mother, but God, what a cunt."

I laughed. "Don't worry. You can say whatever you want about my mom and you won't hurt my feelings or make me mad. I've never called her that, though. I call her The Scotch-lady."

It was her turn to chuckle, covering her mouth with her hand so she wouldn't spit out her food. "You're right. She always has a scotch in her hand … Scotch-lady … I like that. Who else calls her that?"

I paused and thought. "To be honest, I've never told anyone I call her that."

She put her hand on my arm and whispered, "Your secret is safe with me." Her wink gave me goosebumps.

For the rest of the meal, all I could think about was that Maddie had taken the job. I didn't know much about interior design, but I believed she would have to be up here quite a bit until it was done. Maybe I should start expecting more pop-ins … wait, was that an oxymoron? How did one expect pop-ins? Oh well … who cared. This was the best day ever.

CHAPTER TWELVE

I TARRIED AS LONG AS I COULD WITH MADDIE, BUT I HAD PROMISED TO HAVE DINNER WITH Sarah and her mom, and Maddie had to drive back to Denver. We said our farewells and I sped home to arrive before Sarah returned from shopping.

By the time Sarah entered the apartment, I was sitting on the couch with a book and a pen. I had read a few pages, but the thought of Maddie working in the same town preoccupied my mind. I glanced back at the pages I had read and saw I hadn't marked any up at all. I knew it wasn't sinking in.

"My, you are engrossed in your book."

I smiled. "It looks as though shopping was a success today."

Sarah stood in the doorway, five large shopping bags garlanding her arms. I noticed there were smaller bags tucked inside the larger ones. "You could say that. One of these days, you'll have to join us again. I'll pack you some energy drinks." Sarah set the bags down and came to the couch. I lifted my legs so she could sit and then placed my legs on top of her.

"I got us the coolest blender. Now we can have bona fide margaritas." She stroked my leg, running her hand up my shin beneath my baggy jeans. Of course, she felt the bandage. "What did you do to your leg?" She started to lift my pant leg up so she could look.

"Oh, it's nothing. I was riding my bike and I was struck by a blowing tree branch."

She stared at me. "You rode your bike in *this* wind? Are you crazy or something? Let me take a look, God knows you wouldn't have taken the time to bandage it properly."

Before I could protest, she ripped the bandage off. Sarah paused. "This one must have hurt you. You actually put Neosporin or something on it." She secured the bandage again and leaned down and kissed it. "Do you need Tylenol or anything? Does it hurt?"

"Nah, I'm good. Thanks, though." I didn't want to talk about it, so I quickly changed the subject. "So, what amazing treasures did you find today?"

"Oh, the usual—some clothes. And mom and I found some of the cutest things for you. I found some jeans that will show off your ass." She pinched my butt. "Might as well show it off. You work so hard having a nice one, with all of that bike riding and hiking. I still can't believe you went riding in this wind." She shook her head.

I mentioned once, early on in our relationship, that I abhorred shopping and that I'd love to have someone do it for me. Ever since then, whenever she went shopping with her mom, Sarah picked out clothes for me if she saw something she liked. It was sweet really, that she and her mom took the time to help a fashion-impaired person. And, to be honest, I had started dressing better.

"I should have known. Honey, I'm going to have to give up this teaching thing and work with my brother so I can build a closet the size of a house for all of your clothes."

She smiled a huge smile. "Well, maybe we should stop paying rent for two places and pool our resources for a larger place together."

Holy fucking shit, I walked right into that one. No way. No how. I was not ready for that. I looked into her eyes and saw anticipation, hope, and fear. I couldn't do it. "Uh … we can talk about that. But if I'm not mistaken, we have to meet your mom for dinner. What outfit did you buy for me tonight? And by the way, how much do I owe you?"

She slapped my leg and then said, "Oh, my gosh, did I hurt your shin?"

"No, you're good." It did sting a little. "Geez, I get injured and then my girlfriend hits me." I sat up and kissed her cheek.

"You look fabulous." Sarah's mom gave me a hug and eyed my black pinstripe pants and shiny purple shirt. "I have to admit that we did a great job picking out that outfit."

"Thanks, Rose." I stepped back from her and my hand flew to the fabric. The shirt was very soft, silky almost. If I knew anything about clothes, I might know the fabric, but I didn't. I made a mental note to look at the tag to see what it was made of.

Rose said, "I checked in with the hostess and our table is almost ready."

Fort Collins was one of the largest cities in Colorado. But since it was a college town, there weren't many nice restaurants. On most occasions when we dined with Rose, we went to Jay's Bistro, one of the classier joints.

Sarah and Rose chatted while I looked around. Mother and daughter looked so much alike: short dark hair in a fashionable cut, penetrating brown eyes, beautiful skin, and large smiles. And both always dressed impeccably; family money paid off for both of them.

Rosalind Cavanaugh, who hates her full name and prefers Rose, married young. Sarah told me her father had swept her mother off her feet and they married right after Rose graduated from high school. He was a year older. James Cavanaugh was the only child of a wealthy couple and he had never worked. Instead, Sarah's parents traveled all over the world. After six years of marriage, they had Sarah. James's health started to fail soon after her birth. He died before Sarah was three. Rose and Sarah grew really close. Consequently, when Sarah moved to Colorado to attend the University of Colorado in Boulder, Rose followed. They acted more like sisters.

While they gossiped about one of their distant relatives, I scanned the restaurant and noticed a professor who had taught me during my undergrad days. For a brief moment, I panicked. I hated socializing and kissing ass just to aid my career, and I was so awkward and shy in those situations that it made both parties uncomfortable. He obviously didn't recognize or remember me. Thank goodness.

After we were seated, Rose looked me directly in the eyes. "So, Lizzie, I heard you are a Les-Bi-An."

I looked at Sarah, her expression mortified.

Then I started to laugh. I laughed so hard my cheeks hurt. Finally, I said, "I take it Sarah told you about her first, and maybe last, meeting with my family."

"It better not be my last." Sarah crossed her arms and glowered at me.

"Well, I can't see why you would want to endure them again."

"They are your family, Lizzie … unfortunately," she mumbled the last word. Around her mom, Sarah let her guard down completely.

"You're telling me. You know what they say: you can't choose your relatives." I shrugged.

"That's a bunch of hogwash. Family is what you make it. And as far as I am concerned, you're more part of our family than your own. How often do we all see each other? Once, maybe twice a week." Rose winked.

Of course, we met only briefly on Saturdays before their shopping excursions. From my first introduction, Rose had always accepted me as one of her daughters.

"I'm glad you feel that way, Mom, because Lizzie and I have something to tell you." Sarah took a deep breath and turned to me. "We are moving in together."

We are what? Oh no, she didn't. She did not just put me in this situation! I looked at Rose and then at Sarah. Their faces were glowing. Did they plan this?

The waitress came by and announced the dinner specials. She departed quickly, giving us more time to think over our choices. Maybe she sensed the awkwardness. I'm sure my face was a brilliant scarlet, and I was gasping for air.

Rose was the first to speak. "Well, it's about time. It's no secret Sarah spends every night at your house. You two are going to buy a house, right? There's no sense throwing away your money on rent."

Sarah took a sip of her wine and left me to respond.

"I guess so … we really haven't talked about the details yet … but I guess you're right … only making someone else rich by paying rent." *Oh shut up, Lizzie.* I knew I was digging an even bigger hole for myself. I swayed in my seat, dizzy from the oppressive air.

"And Sarah, didn't you tell me Lizzie's brother is marrying an interior designer? If you ask me, all of the signs are pointing to home ownership."

Someone please throw me a fucking rope.

CHAPTER THIRTEEN

After dinner, I texted Ethan and begged him to meet me the following day. Both of us arrived at the same time. Distraught, I couldn't wait to sit down and tell him the news. While we waited in line, I explained what had happened.

"You're buying a house together?" blurted Ethan.

I put my fingers to my lips to shush him. As I guided us towards the back of the store, away from the crowd, I said, "I don't know what happened. When you think about it, Sarah played a masterful hand to do it in front of her mother. She knew I wouldn't have the gumption to say anything. And now it's too late. They practically have an interior designer hired." I collapsed into a seat.

Ethan sat down too, and whispered, "Did they call her?"

"No, but it's only a matter of time. These people don't mess around, Ethan." I looked nervously around the store. Why? I don't know. Was I expecting Sarah and her mom to pop out with brochures advertising homes for sale? "Once they have an idea, they strike like a king cobra."

He started to laugh. "Like a king cobra?"

"I don't know. I saw a show the other night about this crazy guy who tracked down a king cobra in some jungle so he could touch its head … it was on one of those nature channels."

"Was it Animal Planet? I love that channel." He rubbed the top of his head and I noticed that he needed a haircut, and that he had a few gray hairs.

"Focus, Ethan. I'm about to make the worst mistake of my life. How do I get out of this?"

"I should have known something was wrong when you texted me. We've never had coffee two days in a row. My wife was pretty upset."

I banged my head on the table and almost spilled my chai. "You are not helping me."

"All right. All right." He laughed. "I've never seen you like this. Sorry, I was just having fun."

"I guess it isn't so bad. At least she didn't say we were getting married. I hate those gay commitment ceremonies; what a joke." I scoffed.

"Yeah, Lizzie, you're right. It's much better to sign a thirty-year mortgage together."

I groaned.

"Geez, Louise, you are easy pickings this morning. You're a mess, Miss Lizzie." His eyes sparkled.

"Listen, southern boy, you better help me."

"That's better. I was starting to miss the threats. All right, you want me to give it to you straight? Just tell Sarah you aren't ready to buy a house."

"You're right." I straightened up in my chair. "That's all I have to say: 'Sarah, I love you, but this is too much, too fast.'"

"Do you love her?"

I kicked him in the shins and he squealed.

"It's a simple question, either yes or no." Rubbing his shin, he inched his chair away from me.

I glared at him. "What's wrong if I want to take things slow?"

"Slow, huh? How long have you been dating?" He tugged on his frayed collar.

"Almost a year." I paused. "Oh, shit! I think our anniversary is this week."

"Oh, how romantic, Lizzie! You're buying your girlfriend a house for your first year anniversary. What will you buy her on your tenth? A small island or something?"

"Hardy har har, Ethan." I slurped angrily at my chai.

"Seriously, though. It would behoove you to go the whole nine yards for the anniversary. Trust me, women hate to be blown off, and your track record has been horrible lately." He shook his head and tsked.

"Thanks for the tip."

"I'm always here to help." He raised his cup in cheers.

"Any suggestions?"

"How 'bout a ring? You're heading down that path, little miss homemaker." Ethan placed both elbows on the table, rested his chin on his hands, and batted his eyelashes at me.

I would have kicked him in the shins, but he was right. Sarah was playing her cards well. I needed to pick up my game. At least I could learn how to bluff better. Why did she feel the need to trap me?

"One good thing about this whole house business is that Sarah has stopped mentioning we should go to couple's therapy."

"Oh, that's right. I forgot she thought you weren't opening up enough. Well, buying a house is opening your wallet, so maybe she just wanted more gifts the entire time."

"Oh, shut up."

"Good one. I'll have to remember that comeback."

I shook my head and then laughed.

After coffee with Ethan, I took his advice about going all out for our anniversary. I didn't buy a ring, but I decided to head home for my car so I could visit the grocery store. I hardly ever cooked for Sarah. Boiling water was a challenge for me. The one meal I'd made her before hadn't gone over well. But I wanted to try again. Problem was, I had no idea what to cook.

I hoped I would find some inspiration while wandering aimlessly around the aisles in Whole Foods. I didn't.

After thirty minutes, I was still clueless. I didn't want to make something simple, like spaghetti. I wanted to show a little more effort than boiling some noodles and warming up sauce. And there was no way in hell I was going to try to make my own sauce. I didn't think Ragu was anniversary dinner material. Yet I knew I couldn't veer too much away from a simple meal. Before Sarah started staying over every night, I didn't even own any spices other than salt and pepper. And cinnamon—I love cinnamon toast. She was the one who bought us a fancy spice rack with spices I had never heard of. Why did I think this was a good idea?

I wandered over to the butcher and peered down into the glass case. Veal seemed too hard. Finally, I spied some steaks. That was when the idea hit me. I asked the butcher to pick out his two best fillet mignons. Sarah loved asparagus, so I picked some up, along with potatoes. I thought about buying a cake, but then I thought she might think it was cute if I made cupcakes. I added some sprinkles, to decorate the cupcakes, to my basket. On the way home, I stopped at a hardware store to buy a small grill to cook the steaks.

As I drove by the mall, I heard Ethan's voice telling me I should go all out for this anniversary, so I ran into a jewelry store and picked out a necklace. It was nothing too fancy, but I had a feeling she would love it. Sarah loved amethysts.

It wasn't until I got home and set up the grill that I realized I had never cooked on a grill before. For the life of me, I could not light the darn thing.

Before I knew it, Sarah was standing behind me on the balcony, chuckling. "What's the matter: you never took a class on how to light a grill?"

I spun around and smiled bashfully. "They actually teach that in college?"

"No, you nerd! Weren't you in the Brownies or Girl Scouts or something when you were a kid?"

"Nope."

"Have you ever been camping?"

"Camping? You mean that thing that involves tents and washing in the river."

"Yeah, that thing."

"Nope."

"Do you want to tell me what you're up to out here then?" She cocked one eyebrow.

"Would you believe I wanted to burn my dissertation?"

She crossed her arms.

"Oh, all right. I was trying to surprise you. I know our anniversary isn't until Wednesday, but I thought I would make you dinner and I got this grill to cook the steaks and asparagus. I wasn't expecting you this early. Why are you so early?" My voice squeaked.

"Don't interrogate me. You're the one sneaking around," she teased.

Panic seized me, but then I realized she meant buying the grill and making her dinner.

Hiding my crimson face, I lit another match and dropped it onto the stone-cold coals. Nothing.

Sarah snickered at my ineptitude. "You were going to cook me dinner. Wow … you've never cooked me dinner before." She seemed touched.

"That's not true. I made you dinner once, but you laughed at me." I pointed a useless match in her direction.

"You made me Frito pie! You heated up refried beans and mixed it in Fritos, cheese, and salsa. That isn't cooking, my dear."

"You have to admit it was delicious."

She laughed. "Yes, as a great snack, but not a meal."

"Okay, wise guy. Help me light this grill so I can throw the steaks on."

As she walked to the grill, Sarah said, "By the way, I'm pretty impressed you remembered our anniversary. And all of this is sweet." Her delicate lips brushed my cheek, and I got a whiff of her perfume. I loved the smell of jasmine.

"Ah … wait until you see the cupcakes."

"You bought cupcakes? I love cupcakes."

"No, I bought cupcake mix and things for us to decorate them with."

I watched her lean over the grill. Her skirt hitched up and I caught a glimpse of her pink satin underwear. Excitement coursed through me and I felt like I was seeing her the first time. Sarah always wore sexy lingerie.

"Are you looking up my skirt?"

I beamed. "Ab-So-Lute-Ly."

Casually, she glanced at me over her shoulder, teasing me with her eyes. "I felt your leer."

"Leer!" I scoffed. "You make me sound like a dirty old man … or like one of your students. If you bent over like that in class I bet all of the boys would *leer* at you."

"And a couple of the girls." She winked at me. "Does it make you jealous? Thinking that some of my students might have the hots for me."

"*Moi*! Jealous!" I acted hurt. "What about you … do you ever get jealous … that … er … some of my students might have the hots for me?"

Sarah stood up and walked slowly towards me. Her confident stride turned me on, and she knew it. She leaned in to kiss me and I felt her hot breath. Suddenly, she pulled back. I stumbled forward causing her to laugh.

"Elizabeth Petrie, I know what I want. And no, I don't get jealous." She placed a finger on my mouth. When I tried to lick her finger, she pulled that away as well.

Feeling foolish, I asked, "And what do you want?"

"Oh that's for me to know and for you to find out." She kissed me, deep and passionately. My fingers slid up her skirt, but she didn't let me explore. "The coals should be hot now." Gently, she pushed me away.

That isn't the only thing.

"Okay … I see how you want to play it today," I teased.

"That's another thing, Lizzie, I don't play with people."

Did she know about Maddie?

Regaining my composure, I changed the subject. "Come on, let's get this failure of a dinner on."

"Trust me, this is not a failure. This is perfect, and nicely timed, I might add." She gave me a devilish grin.

I pulled her necklace out of my pocket and dangled it in front of her. "I might as well give you your gift as well."

"Lizzie! It's beautiful!" Her eyes glistened.

"Turn around so I can put it on."

She obeyed. I clumsily got the necklace on, and then wrapped my arms around her petite waist.

Sarah touched the amethyst gingerly. "I have to admit that you're getting warmer."

I cocked my head. "What do you mean?"

"You're starting to figure out what I want."

I thought I had a pretty good idea—a house with a white picket fence. *Would it be so bad?* I peeked down her shirt. God she had a sexy figure.

"You're leering again."

I blushed. "I can't help it. You look stunning today."

All of her muscles relaxed and she melted against my body. "I really do love you, Lizzie."

"And I heart you."

CHAPTER FOURTEEN

After a day of classes and working on my own research, I called it a night around eight. All I wanted to do was to take a hot shower and crawl into bed. These long days were starting to kick my ass, and I was regularly avoiding going home at all.

The crisp night air cleared my head and invigorated my muscles as I rushed home. The bike computer inched past 1,000 miles. Smiling, I peddled harder.

As I put the key into my door, I heard giggling inside the apartment. Was Sarah on the phone? I panicked. Maybe she was talking to Maddie about decorating the new place.

I entered to find Sarah and Haley sitting on the couch, a pizza box, two wineglasses, and an empty bottle of wine on the table before them. It took a second for this to sink in. We hadn't even moved in together yet, but she was already inviting friends over for pizza and drinks.

"About time! What do you do all day and night without calling?" inquired Haley.

Second shock of the night: here she was, a guest in my house, and she acted like this.

"Be nice, Haley. Lizzie has to work hard so she can get a good teaching position once she finishes her dissertation. It's not easy you know." She slapped Haley playfully on the leg.

"Ouch. I was only kidding." Hayley sniggered. It was obvious she was inebriated.

Sarah's hand lingered on Haley's leg. I stared at her hand, trying to fathom what it meant. Sarah observed me and stood up quickly, but there was a faint smile on her face. Why?

"Are you hungry, baby? I saved some pizza for you. It's your favorite."

"Actually, I'm famished," I said, pushing my thoughts aside.

"I'll get you a drink." Haley started to get up.

Sarah must have noticed my look of 'Did your friend just offer me a drink in my own home?' and pushed Haley back onto the couch. "Haley, you're drunk. Sit down," she said. Turning to me, she smiled. "Lizzie, what would you like to drink?"

"Do we have any Coke?"

"Yes, we do. One rum and Coke coming up. And, from the looks of it, heavy on the rum." She kissed my cheek on her way to the kitchen.

I sat on the loveseat next to the couch. "So, Haley, what's new with you?"

"Men fucking suck. You're so lucky you are gay. Women would be so much easier. I fucking hate men." She grabbed her wineglass and dramatically gulped the rest of her wine. "Sarah, we need more wine," she shouted.

Haley was never happy. She always had drama in her life, and when there wasn't any, she stirred it up. Her verbally abusive boyfriend had a temper like a clap of thunder. Haley knew he was an asshole, but still she stayed with him. Two or three times a week I would get an update from Sarah. Michael did this; Michael did that. Each time, Haley would swear it was over, but all of us knew she wouldn't end it. Michael had no reason to end it; he treated her like shit, and then he got to fuck a hot woman when they inevitably had make-up sex.

Haley stared at me. I focused on the bookshelves. I could tell she was waiting for my prompt so she could divulge her woes. Instead, I yawned and stretched out my arms.

She sighed dramatically. I continued to ignore her.

"Honey, how was your day?" Sarah returned with my rum and Coke and sat next to me on the loveseat.

"Thanks, baby." I took the drink and pecked her on the cheek. "I really need this tonight."

"I thought you didn't drink." Haley's tone was accusatory.

"Not usually. Only when I'm in my own home."

"Oh. You are one of *those*. Never drink in front of your friends, but when you're at home, you tie one on in the dark. That's cool. I get it."

Neither Sarah nor I responded. Instead, I turned to Sarah and asked her about her day.

"Lizzie, I tell you, I am so ready for winter vacation. Today, one boy burned another boy with a lighter right in my classroom. The burned boy didn't even tell me. Another student told me what happened."

"Are you fucking serious? What the fuck is going on with kids today?" Haley waved her empty wineglass in the air and nearly dropped it. She overcorrected and almost fell off the couch.

I wasn't surprised that Sarah hadn't already told Hayley the story; I knew better. When you talk to Haley, you talk only about Haley. She didn't care to know the details of anyone else's life.

I turned back to Sarah. "Are you okay?"

"I guess so. College doesn't prepare you for these types of situations, you know."

"What did you do?"

"The security guys took him to the SRO."

"What the fuck is an SRO? He should go to jail," Haley muttered.

"An SRO is a cop. School Resource Officer. And the boy was arrested," retorted Sarah.

"I'm so sorry, honey. Can I get you a drink?"

"Oh shit, I forgot to bring the wine." Sarah jumped up off the couch and rushed into the kitchen.

Hayley set her empty wineglass down on the coffee table. "Jesus! After hearing about that, I wasn't going to mention that she forgot the wine," proclaimed Haley-the-Wonderful. Then she hiccupped.

Sometimes, I really wanted to slap some sense into her. How could Sarah be such good friends with Haley? What a selfish ass! Surely, Sarah wasn't attracted to her. Yes, Haley was beautiful, but would Sarah be so blindsided by that? *No. No, Sarah wouldn't be taken in by such a twit. A puerile twit.*

Sarah returned and filled Haley's wineglass, but not her own. Turning away from Hayley, she sat next to me on the loveseat. I offered her my drink and she took a generous gulp.

I spied a copy of the novel *Fifty Shades of Grey* on the coffee table. "Haley, are you seriously reading that crap?" I gestured to the book with my glass.

Sarah blanched. "Actually, I am. Haley said she loved it and gave it to me to try. I thought I'd find it funny, but for some reason, I can't seem to put it down." Color rushed back into her face—too much color.

Why had Haley given my girlfriend a sex book? And why did Sarah accept such a contemptible gift? What reprehensible plans did Haley have? Now, if she had given Sarah a copy of *Lady Chatterley's Lover*, I might have considered her a worthy adversary. But *Fifty Shades*? It was rubbish for the masses. Pedestrian. No, worse! Imbecilic.

I put my arms around Sarah, marking my territory. It didn't go unnoticed.

"Ah, isn't that nice. You two look like lovebirds," muttered Haley.

I resisted my urge to hurl my glass at her head.

Sarah stood up. "Haley, I think it's time I drove you home."

I darted out of my seat. "Sarah, wait! You've been drinking. I'll drive her home."

If Haley had any nefarious scheme, I planned on thwarting it.

There wasn't an argument, but Haley looked disappointed.

She didn't live too far away, so I was home within ten minutes. I found Sarah in the bathroom brushing her teeth.

Pulling the toothbrush out of her mouth, she said, "I'm sorry about Haley. She isn't normally that bad."

I shrugged and grabbed my toothbrush.

Sarah spat out a glob of toothpaste. "She doesn't understand how hard you work." She rubbed my back. "I know how stressed you are about finding a teaching position."

My mind latched onto her last sentence. I wondered … *That might work!* I might have found my bluff.

CHAPTER FIFTEEN

I DECIDED TO RUN MY PLAN BY ETHAN AT OUR NEXT COFFEE "DATE."

"What do you mean?" Ethan plucked a cat hair off his shirt and peered over his glasses at me.

"What if I tell her it's not a good time to buy a house because we don't know where I'll get a job. When she told Haley I have to work long hours so I can get a good teaching job, it struck me that, more than likely, I will be moving in the next year or two."

Ethan stirred his coffee. "I don't know, Lizzie. Maybe you should just be honest with her."

"Does honesty work in your marriage?"

Ethan's nostril's flared slightly and he shot me a nasty look.

"Listen, it would be great to be honest, but you know how much I hate hurting people's feeling. Let's be 'honest'"—I made quote marks with my fingers—"I'm a wimp. Sometimes, it is just easier to lie."

"You don't have a problem hurting my feelings," he said, snarkily. "And you don't have any problems kicking me in the shins either," he added.

"That's the beauty of our friendship. Neither one of us can tell the truth to anyone else. It's like therapy for us. But once we leave this coffee shop, the honesty stops."

"And we're both trapped somewhere we don't want to be." Ethan let out an audible sigh.

"That's not entirely true." I corrected him. "I'm not sure what I want."

"Oh, I forgot, you are only honest with me here, and not even with yourself."

I went to kick him again but hit his chair leg instead.

"Ha! I knew you were going to kick." He looked smug.

"Seriously, though. I'm not sure what I want." I rubbed my toes. "Sarah is a great catch. She's cute, funny, and sweet. I don't mind spending time with her. I'm sure I can get used to the idea. There are worse relationships I could end up in. Hell, I've been in worse relationships."

Ethan set his coffee cup down and looked me in the eyes. "Lizzie, do you hear yourself? 'I don't mind spending time with her,'" he mimicked. "How can you do that to yourself? And most importantly, how can you do that to her? You are dealing with another life here. Fine, screw up your own, but don't screw hers up as well."

I didn't know what to say. I could say the same about him, but we weren't talking about him. Trying to change the subject was pointless.

Afterwards, I drove down Drake Road towards the foothills. I didn't want to go home; I knew Sarah would be waiting for me. Instead, I headed to one of my favorite hiking spots. At one point on the trail, I could veer off and head up a steep rocky climb. I knew I would be huffing and puffing by the time I reached the top, but I loved the climb. At the top I could sit on a bench overlooking the city and be alone with my thoughts. I made most of my important decisions there.

Am I not only ruining my life, but Sarah's as well? I wondered. *Am I even ruining my life? Aren't relationships built on mad love? Can't two people who get along fine be happy for the rest of their lives? And, the sex is fantastic. Am I just experiencing cold feet?* I evaluated the questions from several angles. Even employing the logic I used in my studies when attempting to unravel contradictory historical research findings, I came up with a blank. I just didn't know.

I didn't know. Wasn't that awful? Here I was, considering buying a house with my girlfriend, and I didn't know if I wanted to. I cared about her—that was true. But did I care enough to make such a commitment? Did I care enough to consider spending the rest of my life with her?

The sun started to sink below the mountains, and I realized I better get my butt off the hill or I would have to hike down in the dark. Winter was coming, and it was getting darker earlier. Besides, Sarah might begin to wonder where the fuck I was, and I didn't want to have that conversation again.

"Wow, that was the longest coffee ever." Sarah's smirk marred her beautiful face. I hated that my actions caused her grief. She deserved better, and I wanted to be worthy of her.

"I'm sorry, honey. I stopped by the office and got caught up on some research." I didn't want to explain that I had gone hiking without her. The look on her face already told me I was in trouble. "Can I take you to dinner to make up for being a jackass?"

"That depends. Where are you taking me?" She set Haley's book down on the couch.

"How about Phoy Doy?"

It was Sarah's favorite restaurant. She loved Vietnamese food. And right then, I needed to get back into her good graces.

She smiled. "At least you know you're in trouble. Good. I've been waiting all day for you to come home." She hit my shoulder. "Serves me right … you told me on our first date that you were a workaholic."

"Tell you what, no more work this weekend. You have me all day tomorrow. I won't leave your sight."

She looked suspicious.

I held up my hand. "Scout's honor."

"You must feel guilty about something. All right, let me go change."

"I have a better idea." I pulled her close. "Let's take a shower together, and then we can both get ready for dinner."

She laughed. "Maybe you should blow me off more, Lizzie. I like it when you feel bad." She kissed me.

I laughed. "Come on, smartass. I want to get you naked, and all wet."

She pulled her shirt off. I took her hand and led her into the bathroom.

CHAPTER SIXTEEN

"GOD, I LOVE IT WHEN WE SHOWER TOGETHER," SARAH WHISPERED AN HOUR LATER, AS THE hostess sat us at our table. "You have an incredible way of lathering me up."

"Is that what you call it?" I raised an eyebrow.

"In public places, yes." She placed her napkin in her lap.

I suddenly felt uncomfortable. "Have I ever told you I used to be afraid of using too much soap?" I desperately wanted to change the subject.

She cocked her head and looked puzzled. "What do you mean?"

"When I was little. I used to be scared of using too much soap. One time, in the tub, I told Annie I was going to use heaps of soap so I wouldn't have to bathe for a month. Annie laughed and said if I did that I'd get hideous sores all over my body and I'd smell wretched."

"I misunderstood. I thought she meant that if I used too much soap I'd get sores. It wasn't until years later I figured out what she meant. For years, I used only the smallest amount of soap. I was obsessive about it. Every day, I'd spread a very fine layer of soap all over me and then I'd rinse it off as fast as I could. I didn't want any sores."

"Oh, my gosh!" Sarah covered her mouth and laughed. "I can't believe you! You must have been an adorable kid." She paused, crinkling her forehead. "Who's Annie?"

"She was my nanny."

"You had a nanny? I didn't know you had a nanny."

I fidgeted with my napkin. "It's not something you go around telling everyone. I'm not my brother."

I could feel her eyes on me, and I could tell something was brewing.

Our waitress approached to take our drink order. Sarah ordered a chardonnay and I asked for a Thai tea. It tickled me that a Vietnamese place served Thai tea. I suspected that the owners weren't even Vietnamese, since I overheard them speaking Korean to each other.

As soon as the waitress departed, Sarah pounced. "Do you feel like we are getting closer?" she asked, all trace of humor gone from her voice. "I mean, these past couple of weeks I've felt an even stronger bond with you. Have you noticed?"

Why play that game? I wondered. Of course, I couldn't say, 'Why, no, I haven't noticed that.' I'd come off as a bitch. I swear sometimes she phrased things to hear exactly what she wanted to hear.

I had no choice. I cleared my throat and responded, "Now that you mention it, I see what you're saying." I nodded my head slowly in confirmation.

Sarah reached across the table for my hand and began to lightly rub her fingers along my arm. "Lately, I feel like we are closer than ever. I mean, you never would have told me the story about the soap. But now, you just tell me these stories openly." Her voice dropped to a whisper again. "And earlier, in the shower, you have never touched me like that before."

I racked my brain, trying to remember what she was talking about. Yes, we'd had sex in the shower, but it was just a fuck. At least, that was how I thought of it. Obviously, Sarah felt differently. How was that possible? How could two people do something together and have two completely different experiences? I had told her the soap story because I wanted to change the subject. It was a diversionary tactic, not a "let me tell you a childhood memory story" moment.

I smiled and squeezed her hand, unable to think of anything to say. Staying quiet was the best course of action for this particular pickle, I decided.

"What would you two like to order?" The waitress tapped her pen nervously against her notepad. Was she uncomfortable around lesbians?

"Ah ... " Sarah glanced at the menu. "I think I'll try the noodle bowl with salmon."

"And you?" The waitress looked at me, expressionless.

"The noodle bowl with steak and shrimp, please."

I handed my menu to the woman and turned my attention back to Sarah. Her expression confused me. She was smiling, but there was an air of sadness about it. After a few moments, she said, "So, when will you have time to start looking at houses with me?"

"Um, shouldn't we talk to a mortgage guy first? No real estate agent is going to take us seriously without proof we can qualify to buy." I took a sip of my water. "By the way, have you been reading the papers? They all say this is a horrible time to buy a home. The rate of foreclosures is skyrocketing due to variable interest rates. And banks don't want to give mortgages to new homebuyers. So much for the American dream." I shook my head and tsked about the sad fact, all the while wondering: *Am I laying it on too thick?* I knew we would actually be a wet dream for a mortgage broker — two lesbians with trust funds, and both with steady work histories. But I didn't want to point that out.

"I really haven't been following the news. Do you think we should wait for the market to improve?" Sarah squinted a little and looked up from her placemat, which had a map of Vietnam on it.

Holy shit ... I didn't expect this. My spirits started to rise. "Honestly, I don't know much about the situation. However, I do have one major reservation about buying a house right now ... "

Sarah grabbed her wine and took a swig. It was obvious that words failed her. She nodded, clearly urging me to continue.

"W-we both know I won't be working at CSU for much longer," I stammered. "As scary as it seems, I'll have to start looking for a teaching position at a different university. If we buy a house now, what if we have to turn around in less than a year and sell it."

I could immediately tell by her expression that she had already thought of a way around this. "Oh, Mom and I talked about that. We think it would be best to find something inexpensive now, and when you find a teaching job at a different university, we can rent out the house. It would be a great start to diversifying our portfolio."

"Our portfolio ... " I mumbled. *Our portfolio.* The words rolled around in my head like a pinball. *Portfolio ... our. Our portfolio.* I had certainly never considered that phrase before. She really wanted to settle down together. Co-mingle our finances. What was next? A child?

I realized Ethan was right. Here we were talking about buying a house together, yet we hadn't even discussed our future. I was becoming one of those people I hated: the ones who get involved with someone and then have a nasty separation after a few years because they didn't talk about what they both wanted out of life. One of the two always seemed so surprised that the other didn't want everything they wanted—the house, the kids, the picket fence, etcetera.

I had always lectured Ethan for not communicating that, and here I was—a steel trap. How could I do this to her? How could I do this to me? *Nothing good will come of this,* I thought, and looked up into her eyes. They twinkled with happiness.

I smiled back. I did love the way she looked at me with those eyes. No one had ever looked at me like that before.

Over the next few days, Sarah and I didn't talk much about the house situation. I spent most of my waking hours at the office, working on my dissertation. That was when I received my first email from Maddie. Late one night, my computer dinged, letting me know I had received a new email. At first, I thought it was either a student sending a last-minute request for an extension on a paper due the next day, or a professor burning the midnight oil.

To my surprise, it was from Maddie. It read: *Hey, I found your email address online. Hope you don't mind that I'm writing you. We haven't talked in forever. Are you free tomorrow night for dinner? I have a late afternoon appointment with that family. Maybe I'll have some new stories for you.*

I stared at the computer. One line in particular piqued my curiosity: "We haven't talked in forever." Earlier that evening, I had stopped working and pondered when Maddie and I had last spoken. I was starting to miss her. I wondered if it could be possible she felt the same way?

It took me a few minutes to craft the perfect response: *Hey, stranger. It has been way too long since I saw you. Dinner tomorrow sounds great. What time?*

I hit the send button before I could over-think it. Email was one of the best inventions ever for someone who hated to talk on the phone. It was perfect. I was always much braver via email. I could tell people exactly what I thought and not have to see how they took the news. It worked well with my students and colleagues, and that was what I usually reserved it for. I didn't even have the Internet on at home. I had never bothered, since I had it at work.

A few minutes later, my computer dinged again. I glanced up from my book. Sure enough, it was Maddie again. I opened the email immediately.

Does 6 p.m. work for you? Let's meet at our usual place. Why are you still at the office?

Our usual place, huh? That had a nice ring to it. I quickly dashed off another email:

Six at Coops is perfect. I'm just wrapping up at the office. Why are you up so late?

Her response came faster this time.

10 p.m. isn't that late for me. I'm a night owl. Are you working or avoiding home?

No matter what she said or wrote, Maddie always had a way to make me smile. I responded: *I guess you could say that. Sarah and I have been having a lot of deep discussions about the future and things. I need a break from all of that. So, can I assume the same about you? Are you on the Internet to avoid things at home?*

I instantly regretted sending it. What was I thinking? I hadn't even included a happy face. *Lizzie, get a hold of yourself,* I told myself. *What happened to the serious intellectual who didn't have time for such trifling things?* That was the problem with email: words could be taken the wrong way.

My computer dinged again. Cautiously, I opened her email, as if the process might affect her response. I knew right away that I was okay.

It read: *Very funny, wise guy … or should I say 'touché.' But you are wrong, I'm not ignoring Peter, since he isn't even home yet … wait, does that make you right? Am I ignoring the fact that Peter isn't home? God damn you, Lizzie! Why do you have to make me think? It makes my head hurt.*

Again, the happy face at the end of the email. This time, I wasn't going to blow it. I made a happy face first, and then inserted my text before it, so I wouldn't forget.

I wrote: *Hey, I'll trade you. I know Sarah is home waiting for me so we can discuss where we see the relationship going. How am I supposed to see where the relationship is going? I'm not clairvoyant. I don't even know what I am doing tomorrow, so how do I know where I'll be next year?*

Her response made me smile again:

Um … excuse me, but I thought we established we were having dinner tomorrow night. So, you do know what you are doing tomorrow! Does that mean you are also lying about where you will be next year? I have to wonder. Besides, I thought you people knew your history so you would have a better idea of where you were heading …

No happy face this time, only the dot dot dot of ellipsis instead. What did that mean? Fuck. I needed to be more email savvy to interpret this shit.

I wrote back: *Very funny. Are you insulting my skills?*

Maddie's response was teasing: *You'll never know.*

I decided to wing it: *Yes, Maddie, you are correct. I do know what I am doing tomorrow, and therefore, I do know what I am doing next year. I have decided to create a portal enabling me to travel throughout different time periods. Just think of it—time travel for a historian. No one will be able to question my theories because I will see how things happened firsthand.*

Maddie didn't respond for at least ten minutes, during which time I tried reading my book, but it was hopeless. I kept looking up at the computer. Maybe I had missed the ding, or maybe I silenced it accidentally.

Then I heard it. I pounced on the mouse and opened up the email.

LOL … time travel for a historian. You are such a dork sometimes. I love it. Can I travel with you? I would love to see the world throughout history. Oh dang, I hear Peter downstairs. Off to greet the busy worker bee. See you tomorrow.

I did know that LOL meant "Laugh Out Loud." Did she really think I was funny? And why did she call me a dork? I decided to write her back, knowing she wouldn't respond right away but might respond before tomorrow night. I wished her sweet dreams and told her I couldn't wait to catch up with her tomorrow. After I sent the email, I shut down my computer and called it a night.

CHAPTER SEVENTEEN

THE NEXT MORNING, I POPPED OUT OF BED BEFORE THE BIRDS HAD A CHANCE TO ANNOUNCE the arrival of a new day. Even though I hadn't slept well, I was full of energy and ready to get rolling.

"Wow … you look great. Why are you all dressed up?" Sarah wrapped her arms around me and kissed the back of my neck.

"The history chair is sitting in on my class today. I figured I better try to look like a professor. What's on your agenda today?" I ran my fingers through my hair.

Of course, the history chair was not sitting in on my class. But I didn't want to tell her I was having dinner with Maddie; I couldn't. I hadn't been home the last few nights; I couldn't say I was taking the night off to hang out with my brother's fiancée. It didn't seem right.

"I'm sure you'll do fine. We should go to dinner tonight to celebrate."

"Um … I can't. Didn't I tell you we have a late meeting today? Gosh, I tell you there is so much drama in the history department. These meetings take forever. So many professors are long-winded." I paused for a moment. "Can I take you to dinner tomorrow night, baby? Or maybe we can meet today for lunch." I hoped I didn't sound desperate.

"Really, you would take me to lunch? You've never done that before. That sounds great … but shoot … we are on assembly schedule today, so all of the periods are shortened. Let's do dinner tomorrow night. How about some place romantic."

"I'll see what I can come up with." I kissed her on the cheek and left for the office.

When I logged onto my computer, I checked my email immediately. No emails from Maddie. I didn't open the emails from my students, preferring to surf the net to find a romantic restaurant for tomorrow night — until I heard my computer ding.

As quickly as I could, I opened my email. Sure enough, it was Maddie.

You are so sweet. I hope you had sweet dreams as well … geez, how many times can I write sweet in one email? I'm going to hit the road. See you tonight, sweet Lizzie.

Her email elicited a smile.

I floated through the rest of the day, anticipating dinner with Maddie. Not once did I think how wrong it was for me to have butterflies. The closer the hour came, the more fluttering I felt in the pit of my stomach.

Finally, it was time for me to leave my office and head to Coopersmith's. I arrived thirty minutes early and decided to camp out at the bar. Briefly, I considered ordering a stiff drink, but there was no way in hell I could call Sarah to come and pick me up, so I settled for the house ginger ale. I was living on the edge.

"Holy moly, you guys are two peas in the pod. Peter showed up early for every date for the first six months." Maddie set her purse down on the bar next to me and took a swig of my ginger ale. "Except, he would be drinking bourbon or something." She held up one finger to get the bartender's attention and ordered a merlot.

"How was your day?" I asked, noticing she looked gorgeous in a black pantsuit with a shiny silver belt that looped around and hung down like jewelry.

"Just glorious," she answered, but her voice and aura told me all was not well.

It was the first time I had seen Maddie visibly upset. "Oh no, did the woman do more than masturbate this time?"

"What?" Maddie took a sip of wine. "Oh that." She smiled for the first time. "No, the appointment went well. There were no masturbating mishaps."

I stared at her for a few moments while she took a seat at the bar next to me. "So are you going to tell me what's bugging you?"

She waved dismissively. "Oh, I just got off the phone with your charming brother. He can be such an ass sometimes." She laughed.

I squirmed in my chair. I was treading uncharted water. How could I push my brother's fiancée to tell me the juicy details about their relationship? Words started to form in my throat, but I pushed them back down and then forced my own silence with a gulp of ginger ale.

"Easy there, tiger. Are you riding your bike home tonight?" She winked at me.

I was relieved to see the old Maddie, which bolstered my courage to ask what Peter had done.

"He stopped showing up early for dates for one thing. Oh, where should I begin?" Her voice trailed off.

Her demeanor told me I wasn't going to get the information I craved, so I dropped the matter.

"Shall we get a table? I'm starving." I patted my belly and then immediately felt ashamed. Ever since I started treatment for my illness, I could not get rid of my belly. I missed my flat stomach, even if it was an indication my thyroid was trying to kill me.

"Of course you are."

Again, I could not tell if she was cross with me because I reminded her of Peter, or if she was just in a bad mood. I examined her face—not a trace of malice. In fact, she seemed somewhat concerned, which confused me.

The hostess seated us in a secluded corner in the back of the restaurant. Of all the first dates I'd had at Coopersmith's, I'd never had such a romantic set-up. It was even snowing outside. A candle flickered on the table, and the lights were dimmed. Why did I get *that* set-up on *that* night? It was like the hook-up gods were reveling in the fact that I could never have her. Or could I?

Neither of us looked at the menu, both ordering our usual favorites. The only difference was that Maddie ordered a bottle of wine instead of a glass.

When the waitress left, I asked, "Does the bottle of wine mean you'll be sleeping on my couch?"

"What? Do you mean you wouldn't let me sleep in your bed?" she said, and I thought her voice even sounded sultry.

It took everything I had not to blush like a beet. "Of course you can sleep in my bed. I'm sure you and Sarah will be quite cozy."

"I have no doubt." Maddie laughed. "She seems like a cuddler. But sorry to disappoint, I'm checked into a hotel around the corner."

"Oh … that's nice. Do you get to write it off as a business expense?"

"I could, but Peter is paying for this place. He's hardly ever home, so why should I be." She looked out the window and then she straightened up in her chair and set the wineglass down. "Besides, I have an appointment in town first thing in the morning."

"With the people you met with today?"

"Nope. I'm meeting a potential client."

"Another one in Fort Collins? That's great." I was so excited for her that I wanted to order champagne, and I didn't even like the crap.

Our meals arrived. I picked up my fork and wiped it with my napkin before plunging it into my mashed potatoes. I had a feeling she wanted to talk about Peter, but I didn't know how to broach the subject. It wasn't like there was a *Dummies Guide to Stealing Your Brother's Fiancée*. Not knowing what to do, I started to shovel bangers and mash into my mouth.

Maddie looked at me with an odd expression as she sipped her wine and picked at her food.

I was having a horrible time reading her mind.

Then she finally looked right at me. "Can I ask you a question?"

I gave her my most confident smile and said, "Of course." Inside, I was bracing for the worst.

"How come you still haven't told your family about your illness?"

It was not the question I had been expecting. I started to laugh, which felt like the wrong response. "Um … well, at first, when I found out, the thought never occurred to me. After I had time to let it sink in, I didn't want to bother with it."

"You didn't want to bother with it … what in the fuck does that mean?" It was clear the wine was going straight to her head.

"Ah … I'm not sure what I meant. I didn't feel like telling them. I knew it wouldn't change a thing." I paused and then said, "I was already dealing with the illness. I didn't want to deal with them not caring."

She nodded and gazed out the window. The snow was really coming down now. Most of the other customers were packing up and heading home.

"It really bothers you that I haven't told them. That's the second time you've asked me. Do you want me to tell them?"

She smiled at me. "Oh no. Unless you want to. I'm just baffled by your family, Lizzie. I'm so close with my parents and aunts and uncles, and you guys are all strangers." She laughed. "Then there are all of those secrets all of you keep."

I smiled at her. I wondered what secrets Peter kept. I knew hers.

She started to speak, but then stopped abruptly. A strange expression crossed her face. "Would you ever cheat on Sarah?"

I froze. My hand hung in the air, my fork overloaded with mashed potato, which dripped onto the table. Flustered, I set the fork down.

"Ah ... I have to admit, I wasn't expecting *that* question." Why did I say that?

She reddened. "Oh, of course ... I wasn't insinuating you were ... I know you love Sarah."

Fuck!

There was my opportunity, and I blew it. *I fucking blew it!*

Someone opened the front door and a frigid breeze blew out the candle on our table.

"Y-yeah, of course I love Sarah," I stuttered.

Shut up, Lizzie. Shut up! I felt my face turn crimson, and I wanted to throw ice water on my face to temper the burn. I had never felt so awkward and utterly ridiculous. Foolishly, I asked, "Do you want any dessert?"

Maddie's face brightened. "You know, Lizzie, I just might. Screw looking good for Peter." She perked up in her chair and seemed content once again, and then she changed the subject to a concert she was planning on seeing over the weekend. I appreciated the diversion. While she prattled on, I took off my blazer, unbuttoned my shirtsleeves, and rolled them up.

When we left the restaurant, I didn't bother putting my jacket on. I was impervious to the cold.

CHAPTER EIGHTEEN

ALL OF THE PRESSURE FROM MY DISSERTATION, BUYING A HOME, AND MY BROTHER'S WEDDING was starting to get to me. I had been in a horrible mood for days.

"It's not so easy you know!" I laid into Ethan when he asked me if I had told Sarah I didn't want to buy a house.

"Really? Then why have you been riding my ass for years?" Ethan looked frustrated as hell.

I turned away, rubbing my eyes.

He continued. "We have a mortgage, financial accounts, cars, loans, the cat … " Ethan counted their commitments on his fingers before trailing off.

"And I fart in my sleep."

His hand dropped swiftly from the air and into his lap, like a bird shot out of the sky. "What?"

"What?" I shook my head. Had I said that aloud?

"You just said that you fart in your sleep."

"Oh yeah, that." It had just popped out. I never meant to say it.

"You fart in your sleep?"

"I guess so. I'm asleep. But Sarah told me I do."

"That's why you're staying with Sarah, because you fart in your sleep?"

"She loves me. How could I stay the night with someone else? I wouldn't be able to sleep for fear of farting. And you know I already have problems sleeping."

"Are you fucking serious?" He slammed his cup down on the table.

"What are you so angry about?"

"You want to ruin this girl's life because you fart in your sleep?"

"What do you mean ruin her life?" I raised an eyebrow.

"You can't stay with someone you don't love for such a stupid reason."

"Why do you stay with your wife? Because you are too lazy to figure out the financial issues or to decide who gets the cat?"

"Because we've been best friends since elementary school. We respect each other, which is the basis for a good relationship."

"I respect her."

"Really … ? Then why don't you start acting like it?" he hissed.

I wanted to get up and leave, but I had already acted like a child earlier. Besides, two of my students were in the back of the coffee shop. Our conversation was already heated. I didn't want to draw even more unwanted attention.

We both sat silently, sipping our drinks.

After several minutes, I broke the silence. "So tell me really, why do you and your wife stay together?"

"Because we love to hate each other … I don't know how to explain it, Lizzie. We are used to each other, and we respect each other. We both love to fight. But in the end, we still respect each other. Are you even friends with Sarah?"

"But what about the sex part?" I asked, avoiding his question.

"We've worked that part out." He looked uncomfortable in his own skin.

"What do you mean?"

"I don't want to go into particulars, since it really isn't your business." He flashed his southern-boy smile. "But we both know I don't like sex. We've come to some agreement."

"Are you all right with the deal?"

"It's not the most ideal situation, but we are both living with it. That's where you are wrong. Sarah deserves to have some say in the decisions made about your relationship. Stop keeping her in the dark. She's not a mushroom."

"What?" I crinkled my face.

"A mushroom. You keep it in the dark and feed it shit. Stop treating her like that."

I sighed. "She's going to hate me." And I didn't want to hurt her. She was the last person I wanted to disappoint.

"Yes. She'll hate you at first. But, over time, she will appreciate your honesty. If you keep stringing her along, she'll resent you even more. That won't be good. She'll be mean to you, but most importantly, it will tear her up inside. Resentful women are not happy people, and once they reach a certain stage, they never get over the bitterness. Don't be the cause of that."

"I'm not good at this honesty thing."

"No shit? Really?" He chuckled and shook his head. "No one is, Lizzie. But it's part of being an adult. It's time to grow up."

The next day, there was a package in my mailbox at work. I didn't see a return address. Undeterred, I took it to my office and opened it.

Inside, I found a plaster statue of a mouse under a large mushroom. I looked in the box for a note, but there wasn't one. None was needed.

I set the mushroom on my desk and stared at it for several minutes.

A few days after my dinner with Maddie, guilt was still eating at me. I had been avoiding Sarah and working late almost every night, including nights I didn't have to be on campus. By Thursday, I sat in my office wondering what to do. I decided to shut down my computer at a decent time and head home before Sarah was due to arrive at the apartment. I couldn't remember the last time I had been there to greet her after her long workday.

On the way home, I stopped at a florist and picked up a beautiful bouquet. I didn't feel like going out to dinner, so I decided to order food from her favorite Chinese restaurant. Fortunately, it arrived before Sarah.

I busied myself with setting the table, getting the drinks ready, lighting candles, and putting the flowers in a vase—things to make me feel better about myself. If Haley were trying to steal her away, well I wasn't going to let that happen. I would not lose to Haley.

Sarah entered the apartment as I entertained the last thought.

"Hello?" she called out, obviously surprised to find anyone home.

"In the kitchen," I shouted back. I poured a glass of wine and handed it to her as she walked in.

"Oh, my God." She looked at all of the food and then over at the table. "You got me flowers … you even lit the candles." She looked flabbergasted.

At first, I smiled. Then I saw Haley standing right behind her. Goddammit. I tried not to flinch. Casually, I grabbed another wineglass and poured some for Haley.

"Someone's feeling pretty guilty."

"Shut up, Haley! Lizzie … " Sarah's voice trailed off and her eyes glistened. "This is perfect," she continued. "Haley and I were just talking about ordering in."

"Good thing I ordered enough for an army." I smiled my best fake smile and indicated all of the food.

Sarah looked radiant as the two of us carried the takeout to the table.

Haley couldn't contain herself. "So, what is it? An anniversary or something?"

I took a deep breath. "No, I just thought it would be nice to have a quiet dinner with my girlfriend. I've been working too much, and I've missed our time together."

Haley either didn't take the hint or chose to ignore it completely. She sat down and began heaping fried rice onto her plate.

Sarah grabbed some silverware while I took a seat across from Haley. I knew I should have gone for the silverware, but I was seething over Haley's behavior. She was quickly ruining my happy feeling.

The three of us ate in silence for a few minutes. Sarah and I ate with chopsticks, while Haley-the-Barbarian used a knife and fork.

"Where did you get the food from? It's really good." Haley broke the ice, mumbling through her mouthful of sesame chicken.

I directed my answer to my girlfriend. "I ordered from that cute little place you introduced me to," I told Sarah. "You mentioned it was your favorite Chinese place."

She smiled. *It really doesn't take much effort to impress her,* I thought to myself. *So why don't I do it more often?* I made a mental note to pick up a card to send to her at work. After all, I couldn't mail it to her home, since she was never there. And I didn't want to mail it here. No, definitely not here. That would have given her the wrong idea.

"Wherever you got it from, it's got my stamp of approval." Haley stood up to snatch some of the egg rolls from across the table.

Sarah quickly thanked me, as if she were trying to distract me so I wouldn't hit Haley. *They were just best friends,* I told myself.

"Hey, I set up an appointment this weekend to get wireless Internet." I changed the subject. "They should be here between 11 a.m. and 1 p.m., hopefully."

Sarah set down her chopsticks and stared intently at me. "But I thought we were serious about finding a new place together."

I panicked. "Oh, I thought of that … I made sure they could easily transfer our service. Besides, I thought it would be nice to be able to work from home more. And you could check your email and stuff … " I had no idea what I was talking about. I never found out about transferring service. I saw an ad on TV that had mentioned it, but I wasn't sure if that was the company I had signed up with.

Sarah thought about it for a minute. Then she said, "So you will be home more?"

Jackpot. Somehow, I hit the right chord. "Yeah … and you can too. Can you access your work from your laptop? We can both work at the same time."

Maybe that way she would spend less time with Haley.

"That is a thought. And you said it was easy to transfer the service … hey we can look at homes online as well." Her face lit up again.

Well, Lizzie, you can't win them all. "That's a good idea," I said, unconvinced. I didn't even want to think about that."

Haley gave me a weird look. Did she know something? With any luck, she was just choking on an egg roll.

CHAPTER NINETEEN

It was 7:30 in the morning and I was already in my office preparing a lecture for the following week. Usually, I tried to stay two weeks ahead, but lately my life had become so chaotic that I couldn't get ahead. Since I wasn't teaching and I only had office hours from one to three, I decided to hole up in my office and put my nose to the grindstone.

I briefly considered not checking my email. If Maddie emailed, would I be strong enough to resist chatting online with her all day? I checked it. *Obviously not.* No emails from her. I was simultaneously relieved and disappointed. No matter, I had work to do.

Half an hour later, I heard the familiar chime that heralded a new email. My eyes darted to the screen and then quickly back to my mound of work. *Screw it.* I read the email.

Maddie wanted to know if I could play hooky today. Of course, she knew I wouldn't be teaching today, and that I had no classes of my own. Maddie was quick to learn my schedule.

I replied that it depended on what she had in mind. Several minutes passed before there was a knock on my office door. Irritated that a student couldn't wait until my appointed office hours, I gruffly answered, "Come in."

Maddie's gorgeous face popped around my door.

I was flabbergasted. "I-I-I just got an email from you," I stammered.

"I know. I got your reply." She held up her phone and laughed. "You're like a grandma sometimes. Cell phones are amazing these days. I can email from it."

That explained why she could always email me on the fly. I was glued to my work computer or my laptop all day and night. I briefly considered upgrading my cell phone, but I had made a big deal to Sarah that people had survived hundreds of years without twenty-four hour access to email. She would smell a rat right away if I suddenly bought a fancy phone to replace the cheap phone that came with my plan.

"So what do you say, professor, do you want to play hooky today?"

I smiled. "I was planning on getting a lot of work done today." I gestured to all of my books and journals.

Maddie was undeterred. "Bring it along, if you must. You can do it where we are going."

Instead of asking questions, I packed up my things. Maddie wasn't one to divulge all of her information at once. She was a strictly need-to-know basis type of gal. Telling me the plan was superfluous. On leaving my office, I stuck a post-it note on my door, canceling my office hours for the day.

Maddie led me to her car. I knew it was going to be a long day when she turned the car onto the highway and we passed a sign for Estes Park. Estes was forty-five minutes away, so people didn't drive there just to run errands for a minute or two. It was one of the many tourist traps in the Rocky Mountains and sat at the base of the Rocky Mountain National Park.

Neither of us spoke much on the drive there. I watched the scenery flash by—horses, cows, and fields reeling past like an old-fashioned movie, all surrounded by an immensity of space.

When Maddie pulled into Estes, it was obvious she knew where she was going. We would be hanging out at a bookstore, and one I had gone to on several occasions.

We camped out at a large table to accommodate all of my books and notes. After ordering a chai, I sat down while Maddie wandered through the store. She returned with several interior design books and flipped through them quietly.

From the way she was thumbing through them, I knew her mind was elsewhere. But where? I had no idea. She jumped out of her chair and wandered back to the bookshelves.

Half an hour later, she came back to the table with a copy of *The Thorn Birds*, another coffee, and a pastry.

There she sat for hours, reading the book, only getting up to go to the bathroom or to get something else to snack on.

That was how we spent the entire day. It was heavenly. Not only did I catch up on my work, but I also got a little ahead. The only dark cloud was Maddie. She seemed out of sorts. I couldn't tell whether she wanted to talk, or whether she wanted to stew in company. I figured she would talk if she wanted to.

She wandered around some more, this time returning with a CD. "Look what I found."

It was an Aerosmith CD, one of their greatest hits compilations. I glanced at the song titles but said nothing. I couldn't think of a song of theirs that I knew. Smiling, I handed it back to her and then took a sip of my chai.

Maddie started to laugh. "Oh goodness, don't tell me you are another one. All your brother listens to is the news, and market updates."

"I don't give a crap about the stock market," I said.

"Then what type of music do you listen to?" she asked.

"You know … whatever is on the radio." I couldn't think of any of the music Sarah liked.

"Wow! What a cop-out answer. Can you name some songs?" She crossed her arms and stared at me.

I paused. There was no way I could bullshit my way out of this situation. We were sitting too far away from the music section for me to see any titles. "I don't listen to the radio much." I gestured to the books spread around me.

"Do you listen to anything? Or do you just read?"

Why did she have to put it that way?

"Hey, now! No reason to be snotty … I listen to things. But they happen to be books." I tried my cute smile.

"You listen to audiobooks?" She tried not to laugh.

"Yes … yes, I do. You were reading *The Thorn Birds* earlier," I said meekly.

"I didn't find it on CD, so I had to resort to the old-fashioned method," she retorted. "When do you listen to them?"

"When I go for walks, or hikes, or sometimes on my bike."

"Not in the car."

"Rarely. Sarah is usually with me in the car."

"What? Are you saying Sarah isn't as hip as you?" That time she couldn't help it; she started laughing. "I thought only grandparents listened to books on tape."

"Watch it, missy. They now come on CD."

"So, do you download them onto your iPod?"

"No. Not exactly." I fidgeted in my chair. The last ounce of my feigned coolness melted.

"You still have a discman? Get out!"

"It still works, you know. And most of the books come on CD. Why download them?"

She laughed again and then stopped. "Hey, wait, most of the books. Do you still listen to books on *tape?*"

I took another sip of my chai. "Well, the library does have some audiobooks on tape."

"Wow. Well, that's a whole different ball game, now isn't it, grandma? You even have a sweater vest on today."

I stared at her and she chuckled. Then she wandered away from the table again. Looking down at the vest Sarah had purchased for me, I wondered if my girlfriend intentionally dressed me like a stodgy old fusspot. At first, I had loved the vest. My office was so cold and drafty, and sometimes I found sweaters too confining. The vest was the best of both worlds: warm and freeing. Now, I wanted to tear the vest apart.

At around four, we packed up our things. Maddie purchased *The Thorn Birds* and the Aerosmith CD, and we headed back to Fort Collins. Again, she was silent, except for one instance when she asked if it were possible to have a happy marriage if one person was never around.

Alarm bells jangled in my head. How was I supposed to answer a question like that?

I uttered a few ums and ahs. Then I asked if everything was okay with Peter. I didn't want to know, truly. The less I talked or thought about Peter, the better, but I couldn't just ignore her mood.

"Yeah, everything is good. You know, he just works a lot." Then she said cynically, "Just like your father." She gripped the steering wheel as if she wanted to strangle it.

After several minutes, she said, "Lizzie, you really don't listen to music? Can you name one song that you like?"

"The 'Monster Mash.'"

She looked at me out of the corner of her eye as she navigated around a pothole in the road. "Really? The 'Monster Mash'?"

"It's a graveyard smash."

"Can you sing any of the lyrics? Come on, bust it out Ms. Crypt-Kicker-Five." She smiled to encourage me.

"Sorry to disappoint, but I can never remember the words to songs." I shrugged.

"Recite the Gettysburg Address."

"Four score and seven years ago our fathers brought forth on this continent, a new nation, conceived in liberty and dedicated to the proposition that all men are created equal." I continued the speech in its entirety, even though I knew she was making fun of me. It was better than the awkward silence.

"Wow. That was impressive. Do you know any others?"

"Just the usual."

"The usual?"

"You know, the Preamble to the Constitution and the Pledge of Allegiance, and stuff."

"Oh … of course."

She paused. "So what do you do in your office all night by yourself?"

"You can't expect me to reveal my dark side to you. Besides, what do you think I do all night?"

"To be honest, I picture you in front of a microfiche machine browsing through World War II newspapers."

"Wow … that was harsh." I tried to smile.

Maddie slapped my leg. "Chin up, tiger, now I know you listen to the 'Monster Mash' while you do it."

"What does Peter do all night?"

Her face clouded over. "Ah, that is a very good question."

I asked if Maddie wanted to grab some dinner, but she said she had to get home to Peter. I was sure Maddie was lying, but I didn't say anything. The rest of the ride home was silent. When I wanted to be alone to think, I wanted to be alone. I figured she felt the same way. And I didn't feel comfortable pushing her on anything.

CHAPTER TWENTY

I BEAT ETHAN TO THE COFFEE SHOP, SO BY THE TIME HE ARRIVED I ALREADY HAD MY CHAI. I watched him walk in the door, all the while pounding away on his phone. He walked up to the counter and ordered his coffee and I peered over my book and noticed the back of his neck was a vivid purple.

He sat down, looking as if he wanted to explode.

"Trouble with the missus?" I closed my book and set it on the table.

Calm gradually washed over his face as he sipped his coffee, which, as always, he had spiked with a ludicrous amount of sugar. "What gives you that idea?"

"Well, your face looks like an eggplant."

"It's just hot in here." He tugged at his collar.

"Uh-huh, keep telling yourself that."

I stared at him but he turned away, looking towards the back of the store.

"What have you been doing?" I asked.

Ethan stared at me long and hard. Then he shook his head. "You know, I don't know. And to be honest, I don't care anymore."

His apathy troubled me. I missed the young grad student who once bubbled with energy and enthusiasm; there was just an empty shell left.

"Alrighty, then. You are coming with me to shop for CDs."

"Really, Lizzie, I'm not in the mood to pick out audiobooks." He removed his glasses and rubbed his bloodshot eyes.

"Why does everyone associate me with audiobooks?"

"What's on your iPod right now?"

"I don't have one." I stuck out my tongue.

"Oh good lord! You still have a discman, don't you?" At least this image got a smile out of him.

"That isn't important right now." I flipped some of the pages of my book. "I want you to come with me to pick out some music. I printed some stuff off, but I thought you could help me round out my selection."

I handed over my list.

"So, Maddie likes music and you want to impress her." Ethan continued to stare at my notes of must-have albums.

"Oh whatever, Ethan." I waved the idea away.

"You should get tickets to Iron Maiden."

"What? Maddie bought an Aerosmith CD. Do I need to add Iron Maiden?"

Ethan sniggered. "So it *is* about Maddie. I figured." He shuffled through the papers. "What did you do? Google 'must-have albums' or something?" He looked over the names. "Do you even recognize half of these bands?"

I nudged his foot under the table. "No, that's why I need you. So drink your coffee … we have some shopping to do."

"What are you listening to?" Sarah shouted from the front room. I hurried out of the kitchen to greet her, carrying a cup of hot chocolate. Steam danced around me.

"Hey, I thought you would be shopping all day." I kissed her on the cheek. Then I grabbed the stereo remote and turned down the music.

"Are you listening to Pink Floyd?" Doubt and surprise were both evident in her tone.

"Yeah … at least I think that's the CD I put in." I picked up the CD case. "Yep, it's Pink Floyd."

"Since when did you start listening to Pink Floyd?"

"Ethan and I went to the music store today."

She burst into laughter. "Music store? Who still says music store?"

I shrugged and sipped my hot chocolate. "I guess I do." Then I smiled. "Can I get you a drink or something? Here"—I handed her the cup—"you must be cold."

The wind had been howling all day. I went into the kitchen to make another cup. A few seconds later, as I was filling the kettle again, Sarah bounded in. "You bought twenty-something CDs?"

"I think the number is twenty-seven."

"And not one of them on this receipt is an audiobook." She stared at me in disbelief.

"Do you want marshmallows in your hot chocolate?"

She nodded.

I put the kettle on the stove and lit the burner. "We have large and small ones." I stuck my head out of the pantry. "Which would you prefer?"

"What?" She scrutinized the receipt.

"Large or small marshmallows?"

"Oh, I'm trying to process this information." She looked confused.

I stared at her in bewilderment. *Who can't figure out which size marshmallows they want in their hot chocolate?* "I think the small ones would be best," I say, grabbing the bag and smiling at her. "Do you want to pick out the next CD?" I shouted as I walked back into the front room.

Sarah followed me and handed me a Pearl Jam CD from the stack. I looked at the title: *Vitology*. I slipped it in and we both sat on the couch, sipping our hot chocolates, listening to the music.

Several songs later, Sarah paused the music.

"So you didn't buy any audiobooks?"

I shook my head and sipped up a sweet swirl of marshmallow. She stared at me with an addled look and then hit play again on the remote. She looked shell-shocked. I rather enjoyed that.

CHAPTER TWENTY-ONE

IT WAS THE DAY BEFORE THANKSGIVING AND SOMEHOW I HAD LET MADDIE TALK ME INTO staying with her and Peter for several days. Sarah was with me, too. We arrived Wednesday morning and were soon preparing to watch a marathon of Christmas movies. Sarah and Maddie were feverishly setting out an array of snacks, Peter was upstairs working, and I sat on a barstool, reading a book.

"Oh, shit! I forgot to grab the peppers for the nachos," Maddie said, frowning.

Sarah started to fossick around under bags, plates, dishtowels, and God knows what else on the counter. "Are you sure they're not under something?"

"No. I plumb forgot them. I would remember." She patted her pockets.

We had been to the store a few hours earlier. *Why would they be in her pockets?* I thought. "Can you make them without the peppers?" I asked, glancing at her over my book.

Maddie shook her head adamantly. "Nope. I want those peppers."

"Okay." I grabbed my car keys. "Tell me what kind and I can go get some."

Maddie's eyes sparkled and then she turned to Sarah. "Sarah, would you mind if I went with Lizzie? She can bore us both, reciting historical facts or the Gettysburg address" — she batted an eye at me — "but a cook she's not. Besides, I don't know the names of the peppers, I only recognize them." Maddie grabbed her jacket and purse.

Sarah laughed. Surprisingly, she seemed happy that Maddie was going with me. She never showed any signs of jealousy, and that bothered me. For days, she had been so excited to be included in my family time over the holidays. When Peter invited her mother, too, I thought she was going to piss herself. I wondered if Maddie had convinced Peter to invite Sarah's mom. Rose had already been booked on a cruise with friends, so she couldn't make it, although she was relieved Sarah and I had some place to go. The past couple of weeks at home had been completely stress-free and enjoyable. And there was no chatter about buying a house. Gotta love the holidays. Cheer was everywhere.

Maddie climbed into the passenger seat. "Sarah seems so different this visit."

"I think she's really enjoying being included in my family." I checked the rearview mirror and pulled out of the driveway. "For so long I think she thought I was an orphan or something."

"And I'm sure you didn't fill her in or anything. I wish I could get Peter excited about something … anything." Her voice trembled a little.

Not knowing what to do, I gripped the steering wheel tighter and concentrated on the icy road ahead. It had been snowing lightly for most of the day.

Maddie rescued me. "I think it's great you drive an old Toyota Camry … and the missing hubcap is so you." She chuckled.

I knew she wasn't being rude; she had a knack for saying what she thought.

"Hey, this baby is paid off, and it has gone all over the country with me." I patted the steering wheel. "This is the best road-trippin' car around."

"I didn't know you liked road-trips. Peter wants us to fly everywhere—first class, of course. But I love to hit the road—see the country for myself." She pretended to drive, turning an imaginary wheel and making a vroom-vroom sound. Sometimes, I wished I had an ounce of her charisma.

She hit the eject button on the CD player and I noticed her manicured nails. Then she laughed. "Just checking to see if it was an audiobook."

"I told you, I don't listen to them when Sarah is with me."

It was Sarah's Kings of Leon CD.

"Any good?" Maddie asked.

"Sarah really likes it. They aren't too bad."

"Do you think she would mind if I ripped it?"

I turned to her. "What?"

Maddie giggled at my innocence. "Not literally. I mean if I made a copy of it."

"Oh … yeah. That shouldn't be a problem at all. Isn't that stealing?" I peeked at her out of the corner of my eyes.

She patted my knee. "You're so adorable sometimes."

I felt color flood my face.

We pulled into the parking lot. Not being much of a shopper, I stopped to look at books while Maddie headed for the produce section. As I rifled through the latest book on Lincoln, she rushed up behind me, grabbed my shoulders, and whispered, "We need to leave. *Now.*"

"But what about the pepp—" I started to ask, but she shushed me. I put the book down when she started pushing me out of the store.

Both of us slipped and slid across the ice and over to the car. Finally, when we had both taken our seats, I asked what was going on.

She smiled and pulled a bag out of her jacket pocket. Inside it were two small peppers.

"You *stole* the peppers?" My voice cracked. I felt so uncool.

That made her giggle. "Yeppers! I stole the peppers."

"Why did you steal the peppers? Did you forget your wallet?"

She waved that idea away. "Nah, I never pay for these peppers." She held the bag up in my face.

"What do you mean you never pay for peppers?" I looked at her, amazed.

"I usually only need one. Why pay for such a small pepper?"

"But there are two peppers in the bag."

"I plan on making a lot of nachos. Come on and start the car. Let's get out of Dodge."

I did as she said. "What other things do you steal besides peppers and music?"

"Nothing. Just peppers. And copying a CD isn't stealing. Everyone does it." She opened my glove box and grabbed some Kleenex. "Ha! I knew you would have tissues, grandma."

I didn't let her off the hook. "How in the hell did you come to that? Why peppers?"

"I don't know. They are so tiny. I don't want to pay for something so tiny." She blew her nose.

Her logic was so flawed that I didn't know where to begin. Why didn't she steal diamonds? They were small and they were worth more. "Does Peter know that you steal peppers?" I asked.

"Are you crazy? That guy is so uptight."

I was still struggling with my sense of ethics, so I barely had time to consider the notion that Maddie didn't think I was as uptight as Peter.

"I would love to get you high. I mean, Lizzie, your mind would be like … holy shit."

I stared at her. *How did we move from hot peppers to pot?* I shook my head.

Before I knew it, we were walking back into the kitchen. Peter was standing over the stove, tasting the chili for the nachos.

"Did you get the peppers?" Sarah looked up.

Maddie held up her stolen booty. I watched my brother. *How did these two people end up together? Does either of them know the other?* So many secrets.

"That's great." Peter placed one hand on Sarah's shoulder and said, "Maddie makes the most extraordinary nachos. You will never eat anyone else's nachos ever again." He looked adoringly at Maddie, who patted him on the cheek as she walked past.

"Hey, mind if I rip your Kings of Leon CD?" Maddie asked Sarah, as she waved the CD in the air. I hadn't even noticed her taking it.

I was about to explain what she meant when Sarah readily agreed. I felt somewhat deflated, but I did enjoy the look of confusion on Peter's face.

My mouth was on fire. The four of us sat on the floor, watching *A Christmas Story* and devouring nachos. After each bite, I took a swig of water and then another bite. Swig. Bite. Swig. Bite. Maddie had placed a box of tissues on the table, and Peter had to keep dabbing at his nose.

"Maddie, what kind of peppers did you get? These are hot." He licked his lips.

The two of us burst out laughing. Maddie was in mid-swallow and her laugh turned to a cough as a wedge of corn chip lodged in her throat. She continued laughing, pounding her fist on her chest to dislodge the offending nacho and swallowing the food down.

Peter and Sarah looked at each other quizzically, neither willing to hazard a guess as to why we were laughing so hard.

"Do you smoke?" my brother asked her. "I know these two goodie-goodies don't." He nodded in the direction of Maddie and me.

"Sometimes I enjoy a cigarette. Let's ditch the giggle twins." Sarah hopped up to go get her sweater.

"Don't worry, I'll pause the movie so you won't miss anything while you relish your cancer sticks," Maddie shouted, as Peter and Sarah stepped out on the back deck.

"Do you think they went for a walk?" Maddie asked once several minutes had passed.

I couldn't imagine Peter exercising in the fresh air. He was a gym kind of guy. What was the point of working out unless people saw him doing it? I rose and looked out the window. Sarah was walking towards the door, holding something in her arms. Peter was right next to her.

As soon as she entered, I saw that she was cuddling a black kitten.

"Oh, my gosh!" Maddie hightailed over to Sarah. "Where in the hell did you find this guy?" She petted its head.

"Damndest thing. Sarah heard this weird noise in the open space. We went out to investigate. Neither of us could see anything, but we heard this quacking sound around our feet. No wonder we couldn't see it; it's as black as midnight." Peter paused and pointed to the kitten. "Sarah scooped it up, the mangy-looking thing." He looked disgusted.

He was right. The kitten did look like it had mange, and its hair was matted and filthy.

"Well, what do you think, Lizzie?" Sarah put him in my arms. I knew that, somehow, I had just adopted the kitten.

I held it up, gazed into its face. The kitten batted at my bracelet. "I think we should call it Hank."

"What if it's a girl?"

"Won't matter much after we get it fixed."

Sarah took it back and hugged it close to her chest.

I turned to Maddie. "I guess we're off to the store again. We need to buy Hank a bathroom, and some food."

Sarah seemed stunned that I had given in so quickly, but I had to admit that the tiny black ball of fur was adorable, in a tossed-out orphan kinda way.

Plus, I was on a mission to be nice to Sarah. I wanted her to be happy. If she was happy, I was happy. How much trouble could a cat be?

The next morning, I woke up early and rolled over to look out the window. It was still dark outside. I stayed in bed, unsure what to do. Sarah was snoring next to me. Should I get up and wander around in Peter's house? I had my bike in the garage, but the roads were icy. I was contemplating risking it when the kitten pounced on my head. Oh well, I was on track to finish the 3,000 miles by the end of January anyway.

I pulled the scrawny thing off me and sat up in bed. Sarah, the cat lover, didn't even move. I rolled my eyes and whispered, "Come on, Hank. Let's get you some breakfast."

Cuddling the kitten close to me, I made my way downstairs to the kitchen. Hank purred in my arms. I noticed one of his ears was torn, an injury that looked to have happened a couple of days ago. After his breakfast, I would do my best to clean up the wound.

"Uh-oh, is Mr. Reardon hungry?" Maddie was in her pajamas, already pulling stuff out of the oven.

I hadn't told her I'd named the kitten after Hank Reardon from *Atlas Shrugged*. As usual, her instincts were dead on.

"I guess so," I said. "He tried to eat my face a minute ago. How long have you been up?"

"Not long."

I poured some kibble into his food bowl. "Liar. Did you even sleep last night?" I looked around the kitchen.

"Why? Do I look awful?" Maddie patted her hair.

Actually, I had never seen her look more lovely, but I didn't say that. As I watched Hank chomp his breakfast, I said, "No, you don't. But from the aroma in here, you've been cooking for quite some time."

She flashed a guilty smile. "I don't know why, but your mother, I mean The Scotch-lady, scares the fucking crap out of me."

Her laugh only made me sadder. *Damn Peter for not caring.* "Well, don't fret. Hank and I are here to help."

"You're a doll. Both of you." She smiled at Hank.

I hoped I looked better than the kitten did. It would take several weeks of food and care to get him in good shape. Not that he noticed; he acted like a prince. I wondered how he ended up on the streets.

CHAPTER TWENTY-TWO

"WHAT IN THE HELL IS THAT THING?" HISSED THE SCOTCH-LADY LATER THAT AFTERNOON.

"Oh that?" Peter glared at me. "That's Lizzie's new kitten."

Funny, last night Peter was much kinder to the little furball. Now, Hank was sitting in the chair my mother wanted to occupy.

As I walked over to pick Hank up, I heard an ice cube chink against the side of Mom's first scotch of the day. She would rather take a drink than pet a kitten.

Hank jumped out of my arms and scampered upstairs. Maddie, Sarah, and I watched. More than likely, all of us wished we could have hidden upstairs, too—and the parents had only just arrived.

My father hadn't said a word on entering the room. In fact, he hadn't even said hello, just nodded to acknowledge Sarah and Maddie. Charles Petrie didn't deign to greet his progeny. Peter and I didn't matter. *Did we ever?* Then he waddled over to the chair farthest from the group. I was baffled that he hadn't just wandered straight up to Peter's office. Maybe this was his way of spending quality family time with us—sitting in a leather chair drinking whiskey and reading the *Financial Times*.

I never understood why that paper had pink newsprint.

There they sat: my father reading his paper, my mother sucking down her scotch. No one spoke. Maddie and Sarah slipped into the kitchen to put the final touches on dinner. Peter stood by the fireplace. I leaned against a bookcase. Uncomfortable with the silence, I pulled a book off the shelf and started to flip through it. The clock suggested only five minutes had passed since their arrival.

Several minutes later, Maddie's head appeared around the door. "Dinner is ready," she announced. Even Peter looked relieved. Mister charisma could not get a conversation going.

All of us took our seats and started to dish out the food. The girls had all the fixings for a gourmet Thanksgiving dinner: glazed carrots, mashed potatoes, gravy, asparagus, sausage and bread stuffing, sweet potatoes, turkey, ham, and homemade rolls.

"What are these?" My mother held a pair of tongs over the parsnip tray.

"Those are parsnips," Maddie casually responded.

I thought I detected some fear in her voice.

Mom poked them with the tongs. "Like I said, what are these . . . stringy things?"

"What? You've never had parsnips, Mother?" I forked one, a little viciously, from off my plate. "They're related to the carrot."

"Oh please, do go on," Mom said condescendingly.

I smiled. "Certainly. They were quite popular in ancient times. Until the potato entered the scene, they used to be a staple. In fact, the Romans believed parsnips were an aphrodisiac." I chewed my parsnip and stabbed another with my fork.

Mother set the tongs down and passed the plate to Maddie. "Fantastic. Not only do I get served these disgusting weeds, I get a history lecture as well."

Maddie picked up the tongs and heaped a pile of parsnips onto her plate before passing the tray to Peter.

My brother peeked out of the corner of his eye to see if The Scotch-lady was watching. She was picking through the slices of turkey to find the best ones. He quickly put some parsnips on his plate and then set the platter down next to our father. To my surprise, Dad loaded some onto his plate.

"So, Sarah, how are your classes going?" Peter looked desperate to bury the parsnip controversy.

Sarah smiled and continued serving herself some asparagus. "Oh, they're okay. I think the kids and I are ready for winter break. Each year, the semester seems to get longer."

"You teach math right?" asked my mother.

Peter burst out laughing. Then he stopped abruptly.

Sarah, surprised by the question since The Scotch-lady didn't really speak to non-family members, quietly answered, "Uh, no. I teach English."

Maddie turned to Peter. Her tone confrontational, she asked, "Peter, why did you laugh?"

"Come on, Maddie! It's well known that boys are better at math. I've never had a female math teacher."

"God, you're such a sexist pig sometimes. And for your information, I've had several female math teachers."

"Grade school doesn't count, Maddie." He winked at her as he buttered a piece of his roll. He popped it into his mouth, and smiled as he chewed.

"Excuse me, I took math classes after grade school."

"You're an interior designer." His voice was too high.

Maddie visibly blanched. "I double-majored. My second major was business."

Peter paused and took a sip of wine. "I didn't know you studied business."

"I thought it might be wise, in case I wanted to start my own design business."

"Oh." He pushed mashed potatoes around his plate.

"Please, tell us, oh history sage, who was the first female math teacher?" My mother stared at me.

"Allegra Calculari Abacai."

Maddie and Sarah laughed while I scooped more parsnips into my mouth. My mother snorted and took another nip of scotch.

I wasn't positive, but I thought I saw a slight smile play on my father's face.

Peter went out of his way to avoid eye contact with everyone.

Then The Scotch-lady stared at me and blurted out, "So are you into bondage now?"

Maddie snorted and nearly choked to death on her wine as she tried to stop herself from laughing. Peter, in the act of cutting his turkey, froze, his knife and fork skewed in midair. And Sarah, poor Sarah, I didn't have the heart to look in her direction.

"How does liking parsnips equate to being into bondage? I'm curious about your definition." I stared at my mother.

She motioned to my arm.

I raised my left arm.

"Not that one. The other one."

Sarah, Peter, Maddie and I all stared at my arm. No one said a word.

"All right, I give in," I said eventually. "What about my arm suggests bondage to you?"

"The bracelet." The Scotch-lady gestured to the bracelet Maddie had given me.

Even Peter couldn't help himself. "What's wrong with it?"

"It's hideous." She sighed and took a long swig of scotch. "For her to even wear it I thought it must be for something else."

The mute man who was my father motioned for someone to pass him the parsnips.

The rest of the meal was eaten in silence.

CHAPTER TWENTY-THREE

I STARTED TO SKIP GOING TO CAMPUS A FEW DAYS AFTER WE RETURNED FROM THANKSGIVING.
Since I now had high-speed Internet at home, I sat on the couch with my feet on the coffee table,
my laptop on my knees and the TV tuned in to CNN. I was addicted to news updates.

I felt a newfound freedom, released from slaving away in my cramped office. The entire day, I
kept telling myself how much I loved working from home, but as I gazed around my apartment, I
started to wonder whether I could still call it "my apartment." Should I start thinking of it as "our
apartment?" Should I just accept the inevitable? My eyes wandered over all of the changes in the
front room: candles, flowers, framed photos, books, DVDs, and so on. Yes, my place looked better.
But was that the point.

The debate raged in my head for several minutes until Hank jumped onto the table, skidding on
books and knocking over a cup of tea. All of my papers slid off the table and reshuffled themselves on
the floor. Startled, Hank hissed and ran out onto the deck.

I chased after him and scooped him up before he realized he could jump off the second-story
deck and explore a whole new city. Cuddling him tight, I took him back to the couch. I loved how
my cat purred when I held him, but he only let me hold him briefly before he skittered off on another
adventure. I started to wonder if Hank was "my cat" or "our cat?" Sarah found him, so maybe he was
"her cat," even though he was living at my place and I was the one who took care of him.

I decided to head to Petco and get Hank a nametag, just in case he did escape. I picked out a
bright purple collar and a nametag and had it engraved with his name and my phone number.

By the time Sarah returned from work, Hank was "my cat." He hated the little bell that jingled
every time he moved, so he had hid himself in the bathroom.

Sarah and I fixed some drinks and sat on the couch to watch a rerun of *The Office*. Hank
stepped tentatively out of the bathroom. He had developed a habit of sleeping on the rug in front of
the heat vent, but this time he immediately jumped in Sarah's lap.

She absentmindedly scratched his head. Then she felt the collar. For an instant, I thought she
might get angry I didn't let her help pick out the collar. Plus, her phone number was not on the
nametag.

"Oh, my God. Did you pick this out?"

I nodded and hid behind my glass, waiting to see how it would play out.

"It's adorable . . . and he has a nametag." She scrutinized the tag.

Hank dashed off her lap, launched off of the back of the couch, and scurried out of the room.

I looked back at Sarah. Tears sparkled in her eyes. Not knowing what to do, I kissed her cheek.

"You make me so happy sometimes. I love the collar you picked out for our boy."

I guess that settled it. He was our cat.

I sat across from Ethan in the coffee shop, feeling hopeless. "I'm getting tired of it, Ethan," I blurted out. "Everything I do now she twists into something that I'm doing for 'us.'" I made quote marks in the air.

"What are you complaining about? My wife spends ninety percent of her time telling me how much of a screw-up I am. At least Sarah praises you."

"But how does buying a cat collar equate to settling down? I didn't even put her cell phone number on the tag. In fact, I went to buy the collar to stop thinking about our situation."

"What do you mean?"

"I was driving myself crazy, sitting at home thinking about how I can no longer call my apartment my apartment anymore, and then Hank dashed out onto the deck." I explained my fears that I would never find Hank if he escaped and how I had wondered whose cat he was.

"Maybe Hank wanted to go to Taco Bell."

I paused, but didn't ask what he meant. "Everything I do, she sees as me settling into our relationship."

Ethan tugged at the corner of his moustache and considered my words.

"If I go to the grocery store and pick up food she likes, I am shopping for us. If I pick up food on the way home, I am providing for us. I feel so trapped."

"She isn't trapping you — you are."

I ignored his comment. "She's even thrilled with our sex life. Lately, I've only put out for quickies, but she saw this expert on a morning talk show who said quickies are good for a relationship. So, once again, she thinks I'm a hero."

"I need a refill. Do you want another chai?" He gestured to my empty cup.

I nodded.

Ethan made his way to the counter while I stared at the foothills of the Rocky Mountains in the distance. How could I feel so trapped when there was so much space out there? I needed to move. I needed to move far away.

He handed me my chai and took his seat again. "So, how's the hero?"

"I'm not a hero. I'm a cad. No … wait … I am a piece of shit."

"I don't think you are."

"Seriously, Ethan. Is this all life has to offer? Do all of us settle down just because we are too scared, or too tired, to go after what we want? Do we buy a house, buy a car, and get a pet?"

"And what do you want?"

"Not to be a piece of shit, I guess. Hey, do you think Starbucks sells courage? I could use a few shots in my chai."

"Can I ask you a question?"

I nodded.

"Is being with Sarah so bad? What is it you dislike so much?"

"She likes me, and I don't deserve it." I shrugged. "I'm not used to being liked. What do you dislike so much about your marriage?"

"I can't provide everything she needs and wants from me."

Both of us fell silent and sipped our drinks.

Then I smiled. "Why did you have to bring up Taco Bell? Now I'm craving a bean burrito."

"You better not cave in. You might fart more than normal in your sleep."

I laughed. "Don't be a jerk. Can I tempt you with a taco? It's right across the street. My treat."

"Sure, why not? I don't have to worry about farting in bed; I *want* to turn her off."

Sitting down at a table with our burritos, I asked Ethan, "What did you mean, about Hank wanting to go to Taco Bell?"

"It's a song." He bit into his burrito and cheese oozed onto his hand.

"There's a song about a cat going to Taco Bell?"

"No. A beaver."

I whipped my head up to meet his eyes. "A beaver!"

He laughed and dabbed his hand with a paper napkin. "The song is called 'Wynona's Big Brown Beaver.'"

Shaking my head, I said, "Seriously, Ethan. You listen to weird shit."

"Oh, don't be so uptight all of the time. I'll bring the CD in next week. You might like it."

"Okay, I'll give it a listen … would you mind if I ripped it?" I removed my second bean burrito from its wrapper and doused it with hot sauce.

Ethan placed his hand on my shoulder. "Look at you tossing around new lingo! I've never been prouder."

I threw a hot sauce packet at him.

CHAPTER TWENTY-FOUR

"ON YOUR RIGHT, YOU'LL SEE THE NEW HIGH SCHOOL. THIS IS A GREAT NEIGHBOURHOOD FOR KIDS."

"Oh, that's great. I teach high school English. Wouldn't it be wonderful to get a job across the street from home?" Sarah turned to me and smiled.

Sarah's real estate agent prattled on about the neighbourhood. I sat silently in the backseat of the agent's car as we drove from one house to the next. Sarah and the woman chatted incessantly about this and that. I stared out the window, pretending to care about the surrounding neighborhood. Inside, I was fuming that we were looking at houses on a Friday night, but I would smile and nod occasionally when Sarah turned to look in my direction.

When we wandered around the houses, I feigned interest. Sometimes, I asked questions, but I mostly just kept a huge fake smile plastered across my face.

Afterwards, I took Sarah out to dinner to her favorite Vietnamese restaurant. She was glowing, immensely happy, but I was suffocating inside. I kept pouring Sriracha hot chili sauce into my noodle bowl. Each time, Sarah would laugh at me, because I was already in tears, my mouth was on fire, and my nose kept running. The more she laughed, the less we talked about finding a place together, so the indigestion would be well worth it, I figured.

The next morning, I rolled out of bed early for what turned out to be an extremely cold bike ride. I stayed out long enough to avoid Sarah until she left to go shopping with her mom. Rose's car pulled out of the parking lot just as I was carrying my bike upstairs. She honked, smiled, and waved. I waved back.

I stripped down and stood under the hot shower for as long as I could stand it, stepping out only once my entire body was parboiled and red.

Dressing in sweats and a sweatshirt, I then went into the front room. Despite the hot shower, I still felt chilled to the bone, so I sat in front of the fireplace with my laptop. CNN was on, but I had it muted. Sometimes I preferred reading the scrolling news at the bottom of the screen.

Sarah had asked me to look up some properties online while she and her mom shopped. I was not sure why, since we were working with a real estate agent anyway, but I'd said I would. Instead, I found myself surfing random sites—reading about cities on the East Coast. I had always considered moving out east, which had so much more to offer history lovers. Fort Collins was not a place in which I wanted to settle. Colorado was steeped in Western history and Native American history, but neither of those fields floated my boat.

By the time Sarah arrived home, I hadn't completed anything for her; in fact, I didn't even hear her enter.

"Don't you look studious over there." Her smile was wide, sincere.

"I'm sorry, honey. I didn't hear you come in." I slammed the laptop shut and rose to help her with her bags. "Wow, did you guys leave anything in the stores?" I gave her a peck on the cheek.

I grabbed all of the bags and carried them into the bedroom. After poking around in the bags a little bit, I returned to the front room—and stopped in my tracks. Sarah was looking at my laptop.

I had slammed it shut without closing the window I was looking at, but I still decided to act quickly. "Hey there, you snoop, what are you up to?" I sat on the ground behind her and put my legs around her.

"I wanted to check my email. Are you going on a trip or something?" Her voice quivered.

I wrapped my arms around her tighter. "Kinda."

"Oh. What do you mean 'kinda'?"

I paused, and then took the plunge. "You've always mentioned going out of town for a long weekend. Valentine's Day is on a Thursday this year. I thought we could go out to New York, or Boston or something. I'm leaning towards New York, since you love to shop." I gave her a squeeze.

Sarah just sat there, silent. I couldn't tell if she bought the act or not.

"It was just a thought. We don't have to."

"What? Are you kidding? Of course I want to go. I just didn't expect this." She turned around and kissed me.

"Can you take that Friday off? I'm sure my kids wouldn't mind not going to class that day. I'll tell them I'm going to a conference. I thought we could fly in late on Thursday night. That would give us two full days. Then we can come back on Sunday."

"We should start planning. It's only a couple of months away." She grabbed the laptop and her smile conveyed a sense of urgency.

Before I knew what was happening, I was handing over my credit card to pay for airfare and hotel charges. I had never been to New York City. First time for everything, I guess.

"I think I'm going to move to Boston."

Ethan stirred his coffee well, and then responded, "Have you told Sarah yet?"

I glanced out the window and tried to spy the mountains through the falling snow.

"No, I haven't. She may have suspected the other day, but I think I got around it." I told him about the impending trip to New York City. The entire time I was talking, he stared at me directly but never said a word or showed any emotion.

"Why New York in February?" he finally asked.

"Unfortunately, I was looking at cities out east. I couldn't say 'Let's go to Mexico.' She wouldn't buy that. Besides, it has Broadway and lots of shopping for her."

"So why are you going to New York if you want to move to Boston?"

"I don't want her to know anything about Boston."

"It is a secret location that not many know of … " he remarked dryly. "So are you going to disappear one day? Will you tell me, so I don't have to sit around wasting a day waiting for you?" Something in his tone dripped with anger, or was it jealousy?

"Well, smartass, I haven't thought about all of the details yet. But I'll be sure to send you a memo."

He put his hands up, palms out. "Don't get mad at me. You're the one being a coward. You're willing to uproot your life and move 2,000 miles away rather than break it off. It's pathetic."

I felt my temperature rise. "For your information, I'm looking into colleges out there. There're more teaching opportunities in Boston. I plan on finishing my dissertation within a year, and I'd like to get some connections out there. I've already been talking with some professors I met at conferences."

"That's right, Lizzie, keep telling yourself that. Soon enough you'll believe it."

"At least I'm not scared to chase my dreams. How's your dissertation going? Oh wait, you quit your program and you are teaching high school English. You're a babysitter." I tucked some loose strands of hair behind my ear and glowered at him. Surely, my comment would get a rise out of him.

"Because teaching freshmen in college is a huge difference. People in glass houses, Lizzie."

"I wish I had a glass house. I would throw the biggest rock through it and smash it all to pieces."

"You already have a rock, you idiot. You are just too scared to heave the damn thing."

"What are you talking about?" I pulled my jacket tighter around me to combat the chill in the air.

"Tell her the truth. Are you really *this* stupid?"

"What should I tell her? 'Hey, I really like you, but I'm not sure about this long-term thing. In fact, it scares the crap out of me.'"

He rubbed his chin, and studied my face intently. "If that's how you feel, then yes."

"But I would miss her." I could tell that my words shocked both of us.

"Would you miss *her*, or would you miss having someone there?"

"How do you know the difference?"

He shook his head. "Only you can answer that question."

I've always hated that response.

Later that night, I considered asking Sarah to move with me. What if she said yes? Wouldn't that bind me even more? True, we wouldn't have a mortgage together, but would I feel even more obliged to stay in the relationship, no matter what. If she moved, she would have to change her life completely. We would both be more dependent on each other. Dependent. I hated that word.

If she would agree to a long-distance relationship, that would be ideal. There would be an adjustment period when I moved to Boston, sure, but I thought it would work. Of course, convincing her might take some time.

CHAPTER TWENTY-FIVE

SNOW FLUTTERED OUTSIDE THE WINDOW. THERE WAS NOT ENOUGH ON THE GROUND TO stick, so once the flakes hit the wet cement, they blended into the sidewalk.

"Are you guys sticking around for Christmas this year?" Ethan causally glanced in my direction and then watched the snow falling again. "We're going to my parents' house. Are you guys going to Sarah's mom's house?"

I shook my head. "No, we're going to Peter's." I never referred to the house as Maddie's. The house was definitely Peter's. It was large, over-bearing, and in poor taste; I couldn't associate Maddie with those qualities.

"My, my, my, you're spending a lot more quality time with your brother." He gave me a knowing smile.

"Don't you insinuate anything. Sarah's mom is taking another cruise with friends, and Sarah insisted on accepting the invitation. Apparently, she prefers spending the holidays with any family, instead of just with me. I'm not sure whether to be insulted or not. I suggested spending the week in Breckenridge."

He stirred his coffee. "What, you don't want to go?" he said mockingly.

"I'm dreading it more than ever this year."

"Why's that? Did you and Maddie have a fight or something?" He chuckled.

"No. It's nothing like that. I just don't want to go."

"Spill it, Lizzie." Ethan set his cell phone on the table, accidentally bumping his coffee. He reached for my napkin to wipe up the splotches.

How could I tell him what I was afraid of? I was too old to be worrying about such silly things. Ethan's eyes bored through me.

I pointed to my bracelet.

Ethan shook his head. "I'm not following you."

"Come on. She gave me a bracelet right away. What kind of gift will she give me for Christmas? What will Sarah think? And what if Sarah finds out about the bracelet? She'll catch me in a lie. Then our relationship really would be over."

Ethan shook his head. He sauntered back to the counter, refilled his cup, and then came and sat back down. "I wish I had your problems."

"Why is that?"

"Seriously, Lizzie! Do you think Maddie is that stupid? And so what if Sarah finds out? All along, you've wanted to find a way out. I don't understand why you fight so hard to stay in a relationship you don't even want! I wish I had your problems—because they're all imaginary." He pushed his chair away from the table, causing me to wince as the chair legs scraped along the floor.

"What problems do you have that are real?" My voice quivered with anger.

"She wants to adopt a child. We've started the process. Soon, I may be a daddy."

For an expectant father, he didn't look too happy about it. He looked so unhappy that I didn't even try to joke that at least he wouldn't have to sleep with her to father the child.

"Does she know you hate kids?"

"I don't hate them." He sighed. "I just don't want any. They poop and piss in their diapers. And they cry. They smell. And we don't make a lot of money. Not all of us have a trust fund and can go to Breckenridge for the holidays."

Ethan had always struggled with bodily functions, I knew. Piss, poop, and sweat grossed him out. All sexual acts repulsed him. There were times when I thought his wife must have loved him more than any woman had ever loved a man, history or no history. How could she be with a man who was repulsed by not only her secretions, but also his own? To my knowledge, Ethan never masturbated, let alone fucked. Kissing was probably out of the question as well. I imagined oral sex certainly wouldn't be an option. It was as if he and his wife would live like siblings for the rest of their lives. No wonder she was desperate for a child.

I let the trust fund comment slide. I've lived with that stigma all of my life, and while I resented people thinking I was a typical trust fund baby, few people knew I received a scholarship for my studies. Also, instead of asking for money, I worked my way through my undergrad years. But I also knew that I couldn't pursue a degree in history without a trust fund. Not many people get rich by studying history. It helped that Sarah also came from money. One of us could always suggest an expensive dinner or a weekend away without making the other feel bad. If Sarah had been a boy, my mother would have been so proud of me; she could have bragged to her friends at the club about me dating someone of "our" status.

"What are you going to do?" My instinct was to offer Ethan money. I always had that instinct. I hated watching people suffer because they didn't have what I had too much of. But experience has taught me that people don't like to be reminded they are struggling and I am rich—and not rich from my own endeavors, but rich because my parents are rich. People really hated that.

"I can't really refuse her now, can I? She's been making all of the sacrifices, and I think I owe her."

I stared at a table of high school students. They were trying to act dignified, drinking lattes and discussing a movie they had seen the night before.

After a pause, I asked Ethan, "Do you think that's fair?"

"Fair to whom? My wife? Yes. Me? No. And the child? Well, it's not fair to the child at all. But then again, how many fathers really want their children?"

His coldness was a cover; I could tell by his eyes that the prospect weighed on him. Ethan never wanted to hurt a soul. He was tormented enough about ruining his wife's life, which was why he would never leave her. She never had to worry about him cheating on her. And now he would have to account for another life. It was too early to know if that life would be ruined, but it didn't look good. It definitely didn't look good.

CHAPTER TWENTY-SIX

CHRISTMAS EVE ARRIVED MUCH FASTER THAN I WANTED IT TO. SARAH AND I WERE EXPECTED AT Peter's for dinner, and since my parents would be at the house on Christmas morning, Sarah and I decided to exchange our gifts on the morning of Christmas Eve.

We had decorated a small tree, which pleased us both; our mothers had always gone crazy with Christmas opulence during our childhoods—all white lights and sophisticated ornaments. I had always loved the simplicity of bubble lights and could stare at them for hours and be completely at peace, but they were never deemed dignified enough for my mother. Sarah had chosen our ornaments, cute little decorations from all of her favorite childhood Christmas shows—the kind her mother despised. Sarah loved the *Mickey Mouse Christmas Carol* the most, and you could tell by looking at our tree.

The tree made me smile. I wish I liked my mother enough to invite her over and rub her face in it; her disdain would be priceless.

Sarah and I had also agreed on a budget for gifts. We were not allowed to spend more than three hundred dollars on each other. But while shopping for my mother's gift in Tiffany's, I found a stunning amethyst ring. As soon as I saw it, I knew Sarah would love it. I bought it for her without thinking. With one purchase, I had blown the budget out of the water. Not wanting to let on, I purchased other gifts, too, and wrapped them separately.

As we unwrapped our gifts, I kept the Tiffany's box in my pocket. Sarah had already started to get up to clear away the wrapping paper when I handed her the box.

Her eyes lit up and then she slapped my arm playfully. "I can't believe you! We had a deal—no more than three hundred dollars." She slowly opened up the box. "Wow. It's beautiful. You even remembered my birthstone." Sarah hugged me and then slid the ring onto her finger. She kept admiring the amethyst, smiling, for the rest of the day.

Both of us sighed when we pulled out of the parking lot and hit the road for Peter's house. For so many years, I had avoided the family on holidays or had made only the quickest of appearances. I never understood the incessant need to be with family on special days. All families did was fight, bicker, belittle, and abuse each other.

Yet that year, Sarah and I had agreed to spend several days at Peter's. Sarah didn't have any siblings or other close family, apart from Rose, so when Maddie invited us, Sarah had jumped at the chance. It seemed her desire to be with family—even one as dysfunctional as mine—overcame her desire for a peaceful holiday. I said yes only because Maddie asked, and to make Sarah happy. But once we started heading to the house, both of us had reservations.

No one should make plans for Christmas months ahead of time, I thought. *Or even weeks ahead.* Christmas always seems so far off when you agree to attend, but when the day arrives, it's as if you'd rather be kneecapped than go. Sometimes, I wished I were an orphan like Hank.

One solace was that Maddie had insisted Hank come too. He sat in his carrier in the backseat and meowed, or "talked" as Sarah called it, the entire car ride. I had become unashamedly, if not surprisingly, attached to the little guy.

We arrived before my parents, so at first the evening was relaxed. Peter seemed at ease. Maddie had a cheese and sausage platter out, and all of us sat around nibbling and chatting. In the background, *It's a Wonderful Life* was on TV. All in all, it wasn't a bad night.

When I slipped into the kitchen to get another cocktail, Maddie followed.

As soon as we were out of earshot, she slapped me on the back. "Why didn't you tell me you got Sarah a ring for Christmas?"

I filled my glass with some vodka and mixed it with cranberry juice. "You never asked."

"I can't believe you didn't spill. It's a huge deal. And nice job with the ring. It's beautiful." Maddie grinned.

It struck me that her smile was too wide. She looked too happy. I had hoped that she wouldn't notice the ring at all. "Thanks," I said, feeling suddenly awkward. "It's her birthstone. Why is it a big deal, though? It's not a diamond."

"It's a piece of jewelry. Women love jewelry. And it's a ring. She put it on her ring finger. Seriously, how do you not know this?" Maddie crossed her arms, waiting for me to respond.

I gulped my Cape Cod and stared at her. The bracelet Maddie had given me jangled on my wrist as I took another gulp. "She didn't say much when she opened it. She just gave me a hug."

"Have you noticed she keeps staring at it? She never even told me you got it for her. I could tell by the way she looked at it, and then at you."

I made another Cape Cod. Why did some women have to make such a big deal about things? I had seen the ring and thought she would like it, end of story. But no, Maddie and Sarah had to ponder the meaning. What did the ring signify? What were my intentions? It was a gift—that was the intention. Why can't people just give a gift? When Maddie had given me the bracelet, I hardly knew her. But I had been with Sarah for more than a year. I bought her gifts all the time. It was just a gift. She should know it was just a gift. Plus, it matched the necklace I got her for our anniversary.

My racing thoughts were interrupted by the doorbell. Maddie's face paled and my stomach flipped. Enter The Scotch-lady.

"Well, I guess the fun is over." I made another drink for myself and one for Sarah, even if having another drink was probably a mistake.

I walked into the front room, still carrying the drinks, to see Peter fawning over my mother's new outfit—yet another navy blue power skirt and blazer. Her white shirt looked so crisp it might crack in half. I shook my head. *No one wanted to see that,* I thought. Her hair was pulled back too tight in a bun. I wondered if she'd recently had work done.

"Oh great, you brought the cat."

Hank took one look at the brittle Scotch-lady and jumped into Sarah's lap.

I walked over to them and handed Sarah her drink before taking a seat on the armrest of her chair. Hank purred as I scratched his head. I still hadn't said hello to my parents, and I wondered if I should even bother.

My father sat down on the couch and opened a magazine. Peter chatted to Mom. Maddie, sitting near us, said nothing.

Yes, I loved the holidays. The tension was so worth it. I tried not to remember that I could have been sitting in front of a roaring fire in a cabin in the mountains instead, absorbed in a good book, a drizzle of snow covering the ground. *Stop it, Lizzie. You're only torturing yourself.*

After dinner, my parents stayed longer than was normal. I kept staring at my watch. When my mother left the room, I got up to get some quiet time in the kitchen. Maddie and Sarah were deep in conversation, so I didn't think anyone would miss my company.

I stared out the window. The house was on a hill, overlooking Denver. Beyond, the city lights twinkled in the cold, cloudless night.

I heard the pad of feet entering the room, but ignored the intrusion. The person opened the back door of the kitchen. While trying to stay focused on the lights, I heard a weird *shooshsing* sound.

Turning, I saw my mother trying to push Hank out the door.

"What are you doing?" I rushed over and scooped the kitten up.

"I just thought he would like some fresh air."

"Bullshit!"

Her eyes glistened with hatred.

"Hank is an indoor cat. There are coyotes and foxes everywhere out there."

"What, you don't want your precious child to make new friends?"

"He's part of the family now. We don't associate with those beneath us remember? You taught me that?"

She sniffed. "Well, he certainly didn't learn that from you."

"Meaning?"

"You know perfectly well what I mean. You're always throwing it in my face." She moved closer to me. "It's because of you we can't have bigger functions this time of year."

"By all means, throw bigger functions. I don't give a fuck if I don't associate with you or your friends."

"Come now, you two, play nice." Maddie entered the room, hands on hips. Her voice was firm. Sarah was right behind her.

I glared at my mother for a second longer. Then I said, "Thank you Maddie, for the reminder. I wasn't taught that by my parents." I turned my back on Mom and prepared to leave the room.

My mother retorted, "I don't even understand half of the stuff you say. If you want to say it, say it. Don't hide behind snide remarks."

I whirled to face her. Her words were bursting in my mind like bubbles. Bitch, coward, liar, cunt, two-faced whore—I wanted to shout. How I despised her. How I hated being related to her. How I wished she would—

Sarah took Hank from me, and I melted at her sorrowful eyes. No. It wasn't the right time. I stalked out of the room and headed upstairs.

No one spoke. I heard the footsteps of their dispersal. A few minutes later, Sarah came upstairs and we went to bed.

Sarah's final words for the night were, "Gotta love family time."

I buried my head in the pillow. Hank jumped off the bed and hid in the closet, curled on a pile of clothes.

Surprisingly, the next morning went well. The four of us exchanged gifts. Peter and Maddie had opened their gifts for each other the day before as well.

I was surprised by the thoughtfulness of the gift Sarah had purchased for Maddie and Peter — a personalized basket that included wine, cheese, crackers, and other delicacies. She had also included a day spa voucher for the two of them. It was to the new, trendy spa that was all the rage. Even I had read about it in the paper, and I remembered Sarah and her mom talking about it at one of our dinners at Jay's Bistro. I made a mental note to send Sarah and her mother to the spa for a day.

Maddie handed us our gift with a smile and said, "I guess we had similar ideas."

Disappointed, I let Sarah open the gift. I didn't want to go to a dreadful spa. Sarah took the lid off the box and squealed.

Dammit! I was sure we were going to the spa.

Sarah pulled a piece of paper out of the box and waved it at me. It wasn't a spa. The gift certificate was for a weekend for two at Vail.

"I thought, since the two of you are out of school right now, you could use some time together." Maddie smiled.

I was relieved. Getting a pedicure before sitting in a sauna did not appeal to me. And what's up with drinking weird fruit, veggie, bee pollen, and wheat germ concoctions. No thanks!

"This is great! I can't wait to get Lizzie on a pair of skis," exclaimed Sarah.

Peter laughed. "She's never skied in her life."

"It's true," I told Sarah. "I haven't. Can we snowshoe instead?"

"You'll fall down no matter what, Elizabeth. You might as well go skiing and not be a pussy."

I glared at Peter.

Sarah's lips brushed my cheek and then she left the room with Maddie. Peter and I just glanced at each other, neither of us saying anything. My brother went into his office and I followed Sarah and Maddie into the kitchen to help them finish preparing dinner — prime rib, Peter's favorite.

The three of us chatted, whiling away time.

"Maddie, I hope you don't mind, but I brought Lizzie's favorite." Sarah went to the fridge and pulled out a bag. Then she plopped the parsnips onto the counter.

"She won't go skiing, doesn't listen to music, but she loves parsnips. You got yourself a weird one, Sarah."

"Oh, I'm sure she has some positives. I keep hoping I see them some day." She smiled at me.

"Really? I know she's a workaholic, absorbed in her research ninety percent of the time."

"That's true. And the other ten percent she's asleep. But I have to admit, she does clean Hank's litter box every day."

"Well, I'm obviously not appreciated here." I interrupted. "If you'll excuse my workaholic-self-absorbed ass, I'm going to hang with my cat and read about the Hitler Youth."

Maddie called out after me as I left the room, "You can both be pussies together."

I heard Sarah laugh. "And don't forget to clean his box."

Those two becoming closer made me uncomfortable. They seemed like old friends.

CHAPTER TWENTY-SEVEN

THE TWO OF US SAT BY THE FIREPLACE IN OUR ROOM IN VAIL. MADDIE HAD SPLURGED ON A really nice condo in the heart of the town. Blanketed with fresh snow, Vail reminded me of a quaint, Dickensian village. Everyone was merry and enjoying themselves. The town bustled with activity, people running to and fro to the slopes, shops, and restaurants.

Everyone except us.

"Will you stop giggling?" I squirmed in my chair, trying to get comfortable. The fire was raging, but I was still freezing. "Can I take the ice bag off? I'm chilled to the bone."

Sarah came over and took the ice from my elbow. "Wait until Peter hears about this." She laughed again.

"Sarah! You better not tell Peter."

"Don't you think he'll find out?" Her words had the whiff of betrayal. "We're going to their house on New Year's. It's only a few days away."

"I don't have a cast. I can put the brace on my arm and cover it with a thick sweater. I don't use my left arm all that much."

"Lizzie, you grimace every time you move it."

I looked at my elbow. When we had arrived, Sarah immediately wanted to go to town for lunch. Famished, I readily agreed. My mistake; I have never been known for my grace and adding ice to the mix made for a potentially dangerous situation. People in my family should only be around ice in cocktails. We were not athletes.

As we had hurried out of the condo after unpacking the car, I hadn't even noticed the ice on the steps. My feet flew out from beneath me and my body flipped into the air. Hanging in midair for a second, I grabbed the handrail with my right arm, which caused me to come crashing down on my left side, or, to be more exact, my left elbow. Pain stabbed through my arm as soon as I hit the ground, but extremely embarrassed, and knowing several people were around, I had instantly popped up off the ground and brushed myself off. After reassuring Sarah I was fine, we had gone to lunch.

We spent the afternoon shopping, and I hadn't even let on to Sarah that I was in pain. In one store, I secretly bought some Advil and took it when she wasn't looking.

Later that evening, when I was changing for dinner, Sarah had seen it.

"Lizzie!" she had exclaimed, hurrying over to look at my arm. A bruise was already forming, and it was quite swollen.

Instead of going to dinner, we went to Urgent Care. I refused to go to the emergency room. For some reason, Urgent Care was less damaging to my wounded ego. Only pussies went to the ER.

After several hours and some X-rays, the doctor determined I had a hairline fracture. Not even a real break—a wimpy hairline fracture. Just like my wimpy illness.

Fortunately, they didn't cast for such injuries; instead, I had a lightweight brace that slipped on my arm under my clothes, and I was ordered to rest my arm and ice it. The good news was that I didn't have to get up on skis. Another winter and I still hadn't skied—that was quite a feat for a Coloradoan. I'm still not sure why I was so proud about that.

"What's wrong with your arm?"

"Nothing. Why?"

Ethan stirred his coffee. "You're holding it funny. Usually, you have your arms on the table, and you gesticulate when you talk. But today, you have it in your lap, and you keep rubbing it with your other hand."

"Hmmm … that is odd. I didn't know that I was doing that." I left my arm in my lap but held onto my cup with my good arm. "So how was your Christmas?"

"Oh, the usual. The parents kept hinting they're ready for grandkids. Kept making comments like, 'Wouldn't today be great if there was a little one to spoil.' Between them and my wife, I was going crazy."

"How's the adoption process going?"

"To tell the truth, I'm staying out of it. She's taking care of it. She likes to keep me informed, but I tune her out."

I chuckled. "We are two peas in the same pod."

Ethan nodded. "So seriously, what's wrong with your arm? Are you wearing a brace under your shirt?" He reached over, but I swatted his hand away.

I looked down at my arm, but I still didn't move it. Sarah had promised me she couldn't see the brace. I would have to wear an extremely thick sweater so people couldn't see it. I told Ethan the whole story.

"You are the only person I know who goes to the ER so much."

"It was Urgent Care."

"Oh, sorry, Urgent Care. And who breaks their elbow? Forget about living in a cold climate. You need to live in a desert. Do you remember when you broke your knee? Hobbled to your classes on crutches for weeks, looking pathetic. They even had a service that would have escorted you to all of your classes on a golf cart, but no, not Lizzie; you had to act tough. You've broken two bones that are almost impossible to break. How in the world did you break your elbow?"

"It's a talent of mine. Falling is easy. Landing—now that is the key part."

"Maybe you should take ballet classes, football players do it to learn how to fall, so they don't get injured."

"Are you serious? Or do you just want to see me in traction?"

"Actually, I would love to see you in a tutu." Ethan giggled.

I grimaced at the thought.

"Why didn't you just tell me, instead of trying to hide it?"

"Oh, I don't know. I had hoped people wouldn't notice it. It was embarrassing enough. I don't want to relive it each time someone sees me."

"Maybe you shouldn't wear the brace."

"I've tried. Sarah forces me to."

"Forces you to! For such an independent person, I find it funny you're scared of her."

"I wouldn't say I'm scared of her. I just don't want to listen to her jibber jabber about it. It's easier to wear the brace."

"She's not here now. Why don't you take it off?" His smiled was designed to coax me.

"I tried that, but she found out." I rubbed my elbow. The chill in the store made it ache.

"How in the hell did she find out?"

"I forgot to put it back on. And I had to hear about it the rest of the night."

"What's with our women? They always find out what's going on." He laughed. "So does it hurt?"

"Not too bad. It's a small fracture. Mostly it just aches. But if I bump it on something, that's when it feels broken."

"How long do you have to stay off the bike?" He stuck his stir stick in his mouth.

"A few weeks. The doctor said it would heal pretty quickly." Fortunately, I was ahead of schedule. I only needed 300 more miles to finish my challenge.

"How about your ego?"

"Luckily, only Sarah and you know about it. And you two already know I'm a fucking moron."

"True."

We both raised our drinks. "Cheers."

CHAPTER TWENTY-EIGHT

The good news about New Year's Eve at Peter's was that our parents had other obligations. My father always spent New Year's Eve with all of the top brass of his company. That year, the president was hosting one of those Murder Mystery Who Done It parties. All of the participants had to dress up as if they were in the roaring twenties. I would love to see my mother dressed as a flapper. Peter said Dad had to dress as a baseball player. Oh, to be a fly on that wall. I wondered if they gave Dad that role because he didn't talk. He would just have to carry a bat around and look stupid: not much of a stretch for him.

The bad news was that we were spending New Year's Eve at Peter's house with his friends. But Maddie's parents were coming as well and I was curious to see Peter around his future in-laws.

The afternoon started off okay. Maddie and Peter were frantically getting everything ready, so Sarah and I offered to help.

"Take it easy," Sarah whispered in my ear.

Peter had other ideas in mind. Before I knew it, I was helping him transport tables and chairs from the basement.

Sarah looked horrified, but said nothing. She and Maddie disappeared into the kitchen. Several minutes later, they returned and Maddie started helping with the lifting. I was hustled into the kitchen where Sarah placed a frozen bag of peas on my elbow. No words were spoken. I helped Sarah prepare some appetizers with my good arm.

When Sarah and I went to our room to shower and dress for dinner, Hank was curled up on the bed. I spread out next to him.

"Don't be mad, but Maddie knows about your arm." Sarah joined us.

"I figured."

"She promised not to say anything."

"Yeah, I don't think she will tell him." She was good at keeping things from him. "To be honest, I don't care who knows, except Peter and my mother." I paused. Here I was, late in my twenties and I still felt the need to hide any weakness from my childhood tormentors. "I'm tired of them not being nice to me."

Sarah rolled over onto her side to face me. I was still on my back, unable to roll over and prop on my elbow.

"You know, that's the first time you ever said anything about the way they treat you."

"I don't like to think about it much. I thought about it too much in my younger days."

"What were they like?" She brushed some wisps of hair out of my eyes, letting her fingers linger on my cheek.

"Pretty much how they are now. The only difference is that I used to get really upset all of the time. What you saw last week was a cakewalk to the way it used to be. I would either get so angry that I'd rant and rave, or I would storm out and cry. I learned to turn my emotions off."

She stared at me. Hank rolled onto his back and stretched, and I smiled. "You're really lucky, Sarah."

"What do you mean?"

"You love your mom. I don't even like mine. I'm envious of how you guys get along. I try not to interfere too much with you two."

"What do you mean by that? I thought you didn't want to spend time with us."

"Why would you think that? What you have with your mom is special. I didn't want to intrude."

"You wouldn't be an intrusion. In fact, I know Mom would love to have you hang out more. She always wanted more daughters."

I thought about it. How was it possible that Rose wanted more daughters when my mom hadn't wanted me at all? Maybe Mom just would have liked a different daughter?

"How did she take it when you told her you were gay?" I asked.

"My mom? I didn't tell her. She told me."

"What?"

"She sat me down one day and said it was okay to be gay. She knew I was, and I guess I wasn't dealing with it well. I would date guys, but I hated it. Is that why your mom doesn't like you?"

"I don't think that's the only reason. It's a big part, but I think mostly my mother thinks I'm weak. I never had a hard exterior as a child. I cared about animals, the environment, people … you name it. And I didn't go into business. I studied history. For her, liberal arts mean I'm extreme liberal. In her mind, I am an intense flower child, which makes me weak *and* an embarrassment."

Maddie's parents arrived early for dinner, before the other guests arrived. Peter seemed somewhat anxious, puffing his chest out more than normal until he resembled a small bird roosting to stay warm on a chilly winter day. I thought I even saw a trickle of sweat on his brow.

The six of us sat in the living room, and during a lull in the conversation, I studied Maddie's parents. They did not surprise me at all. From the beginning, I could tell they were kind, loving people.

"So, Peter, how are the Broncos doing this season?" asked her father.

"Uh … " my brother looked flushed. Our family did not follow any sports, and neither of us played team sports. Peter had played tennis, but quit when he determined he wasn't the best player. Lately, he had started to play golf, but only in an attempt to further his career, not because he loved the sport.

"Well, Tom, from all of the grumbling I hear around the watercooler I'd say they aren't doing all that well," Peter responded. "But you know the Broncos." He chuckled meekly.

Tom laughed. "Yeah they have a way of starting off so good and then crumbling right before the playoffs. Fortunately for us, the Chargers are peaking at the right time." He sipped his beer. "Who's your pick for winning the Super Bowl?"

I couldn't tell whether Maddie's father knew Peter was faking it, or whether he was trying to have a father–son moment with his future son-in-law, but out of the corner of my eye I could see that Maddie was enjoying this football grilling just as much as I was. She had to know Peter knew nothing about the sport, let alone the names of the other teams.

"It looks like a tough field right now . . . " Peter's voice trailed off and he took a sip of his bourbon.

None of us knew what he meant by that; the season was almost over and the teams were narrowing down quickly. Tom shook it off and tried a different approach. "Now, this is a good beer." He held it up and looked at the label. "Fat Tire, huh? Is it a local beer?"

I waited for Peter to implode. He was a bourbon man, probably because he thought it was a more manly drink. In family and his business circles, at least, it was a more manly drink. This conversation was fast demonstrating that he couldn't talk to Maddie's father about simple "man subjects" — football and beer. Even I could bluff on those topics, but not Peter.

"Fat Tire is from our hometown, Tom. They brew it in Fort Collins," Sarah jumped in breezily, unwilling to watch Peter suffer anymore.

I chuckled to myself in the knowledge that Peter had to be rescued by a girl. Tom looked at the beer label again and then took another swig.

Maddie's mom saw a break in the conversation and turned to me. "We have heard so much about you. How long have you two been dating?"

I stared in disbelief. Never had a parent asked me how long I had been with anyone. On most family occasions, I was completely ignored. And Sarah was sitting right next to me, so it was clear she knew I was dating a woman. Several seconds rushed by before I composed myself enough to smile. I answered, "Over a year now." I looked at Sarah, who smiled back at me. *At least I got that answer correct*, I thought.

"I think the Giants have a good shot this season, Dad. Eli wants to prove he's better than Peyton." Maddie looked smugly at Peter — a look that said, "Fuck off," or was I imagining that?

Tom turned in his chair to face his daughter. "Well, the Colts are out of it completely this year, with Peyton's injury."

While Maddie chatted with her dad about sports, her mom asked Sarah and me about living in Fort Collins. Peter sulked in his chair. Normally, he dictated the conversation.

Even though I had dreaded attending a party with Peter's friends, the evening turned out to be less painful than I thought it would be. For the most part, Peter stayed with his friends, and Sarah, Maddie, and I hung out with Maddie's parents. The conversation flowed easily, and the love and attention they showed their daughter surprised me. It shouldn't have, since Sarah had a loving relationship with her mother, too, but I had always thought Sarah was the exception.

I assumed everyone interacted with their parents like I did with mine. After interacting with Sarah's mom, and now Maddie's parents, I was starting to wonder if only a few people hated their families.

While I pondered this, Peter and one of his buddies crashed our inner circle, standing there clutching their bourbons, awaiting a break in the conversation.

When he sensed a pause, Peter pounced. "Lizzie, how was the skiing in Vail?"

I paused to think up a believable story, and Maddie interjected, "Peter, why don't you introduce your friend?"

Peter looked flustered. Regaining his composure, he said, "My apologies. Samuel, I would like to introduce you to my sister Lizzie, Sarah, and Maddie's parents, Tom and Joan."

Samuel smiled, or at least I think he did. His lips moved for a second.

"So, Lizzie, how was the skiing? Samuel has a holiday home in Vail. He's heading up there tomorrow and would like a ski update. Did you get your pussy ass up on skis?" My brother laughed maliciously.

Sarah came to my rescue. "Actually, we decided to rent some snowboards. By the end of the weekend, Lizzie could have given people lessons."

Maddie seemed to glow with happiness.

Peter stammered, "I-I don't believe it. You don't seem like the snowboarding type."

"Snowboarding, huh? I guess that is good and all," Samuel chimed in, "but I prefer skiing. If it was good enough for my ancestors, it's good enough for me."

None of us knew what in the hell he meant by that, except Peter.

"I concur, Samuel," said Peter. "Snowboarding is for hooligans. Lizzie … I guess … well, I guess I'm not that surprised by such behavior considering … "

Sarah muffled a laugh.

Was he implying that because I was gay I was also a snowboarding hooligan?

"I tried snowboarding a few years ago." Maddie's dad joined the fray. "I couldn't stay up on the damn thing. Not only that, but by the end of the day, my armpits were on fire from pushing myself up off the ground every few seconds." He turned to me. "Bravo, Lizzie, for trying." He raised his beer glass in my direction. I used my good arm to raise my cocktail.

Out of the corner of my eye, I saw Maddie rise and whisper in Peter's ear. Blushing, he abruptly left the group.

Samuel stood there briefly before excusing himself. Before he left, he did that weird lip thing again. Another attempt to smile?

"What did you tell him?" Sarah turned to Maddie as soon as Peter had left.

"I told him he had a bat in the cave," said Maddie, her words drowned out by Sarah's snort of laughter.

Sarah quickly covered her mouth and Maddie's parents chuckled and politely veered the conversation in another direction.

Casually, I pulled my phone out of my pocket and texted Ethan, asking what Maddie meant.

He replied: *LOL … Lizzie, it means you have a booger in your nose. Happy New Year.*

I glanced at Maddie and then at Peter, who had just returned. He threw Maddie a look I knew was designed to be intimidating, but she kept smiling anyway. It took everything I had not to laugh. My esteem for her skyrocketed.

Peter approached our group slowly. His fake smile alerted me that he was ready to attack.

"I do love your sense of humor, Maddie." His voice was strained.

"I don't know what you're talking about." She gave him a peck on the cheek.

I knew this wouldn't appease him. Peter never could take a joke.

He turned to me, nudged my arm, and started to say something. He stopped. I felt him tug at the brace.

"What are you wearing? A brace!" He laughed. "What'd you do, hit a tree while snowboarding?" Merriment danced in his eyes.

I was a deer in the headlights. If he found out now, I knew he would take all of his aggression out on me.

Sarah laughed. "You won't believe this, Peter. After amazing me with her snowboarding skills, on our last run, an out-of-control skier took her out at the bottom of the slope."

Maddie's smile bolstered Sarah's bravado.

Sarah continued. "It was quite terrifying, actually. This poor chap ended up seriously injuring himself when he finally collided with a building. But before he stopped, he mowed down three people that I saw." She took a sip of her beer. "Who knows how many more he hurt. Lizzie saw him coming and ran to push a child out of the way. In the process, Lizzie got creamed. The mother was so appreciative. She wanted to give your sister an award!" Sarah turned to me and added, "But you know Lizzie, she didn't want to be in the limelight."

"I didn't know we were in the presence of a hero." Tom raised his glass to toast me yet again.

Peter seethed.

Maddie glowed.

Sarah smiled at me. A sense of relief flooded through me and I kissed Sarah in front of all of Peter's guests. I don't know who was more surprised by that, me or Peter. At that moment, she was my hero.

CHAPTER TWENTY-NINE

ON THE THIRD THURSDAY IN JANUARY, I FINISHED MY BIKE CHALLENGE. IT WAS A COLD BUT tolerable day for riding. Sarah and I had quarrelled about me getting back on my bike just two weeks after falling on my elbow, but I was undeterred. Eventually, she had given in. I think she saw it was a battle she would lose. And really, how much more damage could I do to my elbow?

Still, I didn't want to rub her face in it, so I rode when she was at work. She must have suspected it, but I never confirmed her suspicions.

On that particular Thursday, I had hopped on my bike around noon and made my way from campus to my favorite bike trail. It was fitting to finish my challenge on the same trail I had started riding during my illness. The trail felt like a close friend who had helped me through the challenge of getting back in shape. No matter what, it was always waiting for me; actually, it beckoned me.

Mile 3000 came and I paused for a moment on the trail, a smile creeping across my face. I had an urge to drink a glass of champagne; instead, I peddled on.

Once I got back in my office, I changed my clothes and rushed home to shower. Instead of celebrating alone, I drove to Sarah's school, parked next to her car, and waited.

When she spotted me, a radiant smile lit up her face.

I rolled my window down. "Can I take you to dinner?"

She looked curious, and then glanced over at her own car.

"Never mind about your car," I said. "I have time to drive you to work in the morning."

I had never seen her look so surprised, so happy.

"Where are you taking me?"

"I was thinking of this tapas place in Boulder."

She opened the car door and climbed in. "I like where this evening is heading."

"What can I say, Sarah? I heart you." A thought flashed through my mind. "How would you like to stay in a hotel tonight? We can check into a nice hotel, have a fancy dinner, and neither one of us will have to drive home."

She leaned against the car door to look at me. "Lizzie, are you trying to sweep me off my feet?"

"I haven't before now?" I teased.

"It's coming more naturally for you these days." She rubbed my thigh. "I like it."

After dinner, Sarah and I returned to our hotel. Fortunately, the tourist season was over so we were able to check into a posh room. The view of the Rocky Mountains made the cost of the suite well worth it.

I had arranged for the hotel to chill a bottle of champagne for us. I wasn't a big fan, but Sarah loved the stuff. We sipped our champagne while partaking in a bubble bath. The bear-claw tub fitted both of us with plenty of room to spare. Leaning against Sarah, I played with the bubbles on her leg.

"What are we celebrating tonight?" asked Sarah.

"Why do you think we're celebrating anything? Maybe I felt spontaneous." I squeezed her thigh.

She tipped some of her drink on my head. "Spill it, Lizzie."

"Hey, now!" I laughed. "If you dump it all on me, I won't give you anymore."

I ducked my head under the water. As soon as I surfaced, she wrapped her arms around me. I felt her hard nipples press against my back.

"Come on. I want to know."

I glanced over my shoulder to study her face. "Okay, if you must know, and kill the romance, I reached a personal goal today."

"Which was … ?" her voice trailed off.

"I—"

"What?" she shouted, splashing water on me.

"It's silly, that's all. I'm embarrassed to tell you."

"Lizzie, you fart in your sleep. How can you be embarrassed to tell me anything?" She joked.

I slapped her leg gently, causing a spray of bubbles. "Careful now! Or I'll fart in the tub."

"You better not!" Sarah laughed.

I flipped around to kiss her. Then I settled my back on the opposite side of the tub so I could watch her face.

"I set a goal, about six months ago, to ride my bike 3,000 miles. Today, I reached it." I shrugged.

She giggled.

I reddened.

"What's embarrassing about that?" She looked bewildered.

I ducked my head under the water again. Popping back up, I wiped the water out of my eyes. "Oh, I don't know … it seems kinda childish."

"I wouldn't say that. To be honest, I'm not surprised at all. You love to challenge yourself." She sat up, exposing her exquisite breasts. "I'm proud of you."

I looked away.

She turned my face and stared into my eyes. "Seriously. When we first met, you were still struggling with your illness. Remember the first time you took me hiking?" I tried to turn away, but she tightened her grip. "You could barely hike a mile. Your heart raced, your legs almost gave out, and you huffed and puffed. Now, you've ridden your bike 3,000 miles. Sometimes you amaze me. I love the fight in you."

I didn't know what to say.

"Now it's time for me to confess." She wiped some bubbles off my nose. "I thought you'd been offered a teaching position today, and you were going to tell me we had to move."

My muscles tensed, and I couldn't draw a breath.

She continued. "I know that we may have to move, but … " She looked out the window at the mountains. Only a faint outline against the purple-black sky was visible. "It'll be hard."

I felt a window of opportunity. Maybe now was the time to suggest a long-distance relationship.

I started to speak, but she interrupted. "But I'd rather move with you, than be away from you." She leaned in and kissed me. "We should start celebrating things more. I like your style."

A devilish look came across her face, and then she dumped her entire glass of champagne over my head. Before I could react, she hurtled out of the tub, sprinting towards the bed. I chased her, sloshing water all over the bathroom floor. We landed on the bed together, laughing.

She pinned me on my back and looked around. "We've made a mess of this comforter. It's all wet."

"I'm hoping to make an even bigger mess." I attempted to prop myself up, but she held me.

"Patience, Lizzie." Her eyes wandered all over my body. "Yes, all of the bike riding has been good for you."

"Has it now?"

She licked her lips. "Very much so." Her eyes continued to devour me.

"I'm glad I can still turn you on."

"Maybe if you paid more attention to people, you'd notice how often people check you out."

"Oh, please!" I waved away the idea to the best of my ability, since she had my wrists pinned.

"Maybe it's a good thing that you don't notice."

"Trust me, I notice all of the people who check you out." I gave her a knowing look.

"Good." She flashed a sexy smile.

"Good? What's that supposed to mean?" I tried to wiggle free.

"It means good." Slowly, she bent down and took my nipple in her mouth, sucking it, occasionally biting it. I ran my fingers through her short, wet hair. After visiting my other nipple, she moved lower —kissing and licking my stomach on her way down. Her hands gently ran along my body, her fingertips soft and graceful. Down she went.

My eyes closed and my back arched slightly when I felt her tongue on my clit. I loved that first touch every time. It sent a rush of excitement pulsing through my body. No one had ever made love to me like Sarah did.

I let out a small gasp.

Sarah heard me and moved further down to my thighs, teasing me. Pleasurable teasing. And excruciating. Minutes passed. My hips moved more urgently.

"What's the matter, Lizzie? Is there something you want?" Her tone was seductive.

I pulled her head back to where I wanted her, and her tongue darted inside me. Searching. Tasting. Flittering in and out.

She moved back to my clit and took my swollen lips into her mouth. Slowly, she slid a finger inside me. Then two. I wanted it. I wanted her. More. Harder.

Sarah relished being inside me. Leaving her fingers inside, her body moved up. Her lips found my mouth. I tasted me on her tongue as her fingers continued to move in and out of me, frantically.

My fingers dug into her back. My back arched further. I started to see flashes of light behind my eyelids.

"Harder." I whispered in her ear. "*Harder!*"

I felt all of her fingers inside now.

Again, I felt her tongue on my clit.

Oh, my fucking God!

I moaned, much louder. Sarah held my hip down with her free hand.

Bright flashes of light burst in my eyes, causing them to roll back.

My entire body tensed, and then trembled.

Sarah stopped her lapping tongue and held it in place.

A second wave hit me.

Then my body relaxed.

She laid her head on my stomach, both of us sweaty and content. Not content—blissful.

At that moment, I never wanted to lose her. Life without Sarah . . . I couldn't imagine it right then.

My body shivered again.

"Aftershocks." She giggled.

"Come here." I pulled her up into my arms. "I love you, Sarah."

"Good."

I laughed. *God! What a woman!*

CHAPTER THIRTY

On the last day of January, I was sitting in my apartment when I heard the squeal of tires spinning in the parking lot. It had been snowing nonstop for a couple of days, so the parking lot was one huge ice-skating rink and tenants were struggling to pull in and out of their parking spots. Ignoring the screeching tires, I turned back to my reading, only to be interrupted by the phone ringing.

Irritated by all the distractions, I glanced at the caller ID: Maddie.

"Hello."

"Hi. What are you up to?" She sounded overly perky.

"Not much. Just reading a fascinating article on wanderlust. What's up with you?"

"What the hell is wanderlust?"

"It means a desire to wander. It was part of the back to nature movement. Youths wanted to leave the cities behind and wander around in nature."

"Oh. Who would have thunk it? Speaking of nature . . . how about all this snow?"

"I know. It's been crazy. It hasn't snowed like this in years. We've been stuck in the house all weekend. Are you and Peter surviving?"

"I'm not too sure about Peter. He's on a business trip, and he can't make it home. And I got cabin fever, so I decided to visit. Can you help me get my car unstuck?"

I paused and stepped out on my balcony. Sure enough, Maddie was sitting in her car, which was wedged on top of an ice chunk.

She smiled and waved at me.

With a sigh, I went downstairs to help.

Maddie rolled down the window and said, "I thought if I gunned it, I could force the car into the spot."

"How did it work out for you?"

"Great—if you don't count getting stuck." She laughed.

I called Sarah on her cell, for help. After twenty minutes of trying to push and rock Maddie's car into a parking spot, our neighbor Evan appeared, tied a chain to her car, and used his F250 to pull her car off the iceberg.

"I'm starving!" Maddie exclaimed as the three of us walked upstairs. "It took me more than four hours to get here."

When we entered the apartment, Sarah offered her a hot drink and I was put in charge of ordering enough Chinese food to last three people a few days. I cringed at the thought of some poor kid delivering the take-out in this weather, but Sarah and I had not planned for the storm and our cupboards and fridge were empty.

The food wouldn't arrive for an hour, so Maddie, still tense from her drive, opted for a hot bath and a glass of wine.

While Sarah and I scrounged in our closet for some warmer clothes for our guest, I pondered why Maddie had risked her life to come to Fort Collins wearing nothing but a dress. No coat. Nothing. In the middle of a blizzard! Was she insane?

"I think she's terribly lonely," Sarah whispered.

"How long has Peter been out of town?" I asked.

Sarah looked at me, her head cocked. "That's not what I meant, exactly."

We didn't have a chance to finish our conversation.

Maddie burst into the room. "This is great. I haven't had a sleepover in years." She was wearing Sarah's bathrobe and I suspected she didn't have anything on underneath.

Maddie didn't appear flustered at all. And Sarah beamed with happiness. I felt like vomiting.

The following Saturday, I met Ethan for coffee and told him all about Maddie's visit and her car.

"How in the world did she get her car on top of an iceberg?"

"Beats me. Seriously, Californians should not drive in the snow. I'm surprised she wasn't killed." I set my cell phone down on the table. Ethan eyed it and sniggered. "I know. It's ancient."

As he grabbed my phone to get a closer look, he steered us back to our conversation. "Lucky that guy was there."

"Yeah, if it hadn't been for Evan, her car would still be there in April."

"Thank heaven for Evan." Ethan chuckled.

"You're such a nerd."

"You should talk. This coming from someone wearing a shirt with actual portraits of all of the Presidents of the United States on it, and not even the band — the actual politicians."

"There's a band called the Presidents of the United States?"

"Yeah they sing that 'Peaches' song."

"Oh. I like peaches."

"So, you've heard the song?"

"What? No." I shook my head.

Ethan rolled his eyes. "Why do I even try?"

"They sing a song about peaches?" My voice filled with disbelief.

"Yes. It's about how much they like them."

"You listen to strange crap." I leaned back in my chair and stretched my legs out under the table.

"Because a biography on Alexander Hamilton is much more thrilling."

"He wasn't even a president, so there." I stuck my tongue out.

"Yeah, I know. I went to elementary school, remember."

I looked down at his shirt. "Whatever. You have a *The Great Gatsby* shirt on." I noticed, with some surprise, that it had a small stain near the collar.

"Let's agree that we are both nerdy. But I'd rather be a nerd than a dork."

"What's the difference?"

"Literally, a dork is a whale's penis. Figuratively, it's a geeky person who is socially awkward."

"And a nerd?"

"I feel a nerd is just someone who is passionate about his or her subject, or something, like you are passionate about history. Every day you have some nerdy history T-shirt on. Even when you're teaching, your undershirt says something or has a historical quote."

I shook this off. "Sarah made a comment that I didn't understand," I told him.

"Was it a three-syllable word?" He smiled.

"Oh, Ethan, you're on a roll today. Anyhoos, as I was saying, she said she thinks Maddie is lonely and unhappy."

"Uh-huh."

"Well, do you think it's true?"

"Lizzie, please tell me you aren't *still* trying to steal your brother's fiancée."

Was I? If I was, I wasn't doing a splendid job. Something was holding me back. *What?*

Ethan studied my face. "Let's face it: your brother is an asshole. He works all the time. He dotes on your crazy mother, and he thinks your father is a banking god. That would be a difficult household for anyone to live in."

"But she always seems so happy ... well, most of the time. And she's pretty funny."

"You crack me up. Funny people can be sad. A lot of funny people hide their sadness behind their humor. Think about it, Lizzie. She's never home. She practically lives up here. For someone who is about to get married, she spends very little time with her soon-to-be husband."

This bothered me. Yes, it would be incredible to hook-up with Maddie. She was the whole package. Beautiful. Smart. Sexy. Confident. But she was more than that. Maddie wasn't the type to be put on a pedestal to admire. She demanded respect. Was that holding me back from trying to seduce her? Would she want a relationship and not a casual fling?

CHAPTER THIRTY-ONE

"ARE YOU GETTING EXCITED ABOUT YOUR TRIP?" ETHAN IMMEDIATELY IGNORED MY ANSWER AND instead looked at his phone, reading the latest text message from his wife.

"I guess so," I told him. "I've never been to New York. I want to see all the historical stuff, and Sarah is excited about seeing a show."

"Why are you going to New York again?" He glanced up at me.

"Because I want to live in Boston." His questioning annoyed me. Surely, I had already explained this to him! Was he actively trying to annoy me?

"So why not go to Boston? I bet you'd love all the tea party history and all that jazz."

"I didn't want Sarah to find out I want to live in Boston."

Was I sure I wanted to live there?

"Does she know you want to move at all?"

"She knows it's my last year at CSU. And she knows I will have to move when I find a job."

"Are you looking for a job?" Ethan glanced sidelong at his phone again.

"No. I've decided to take some time off and finish my dissertation. I'm thinking of writing a book. I don't know if working a regular job is my thing."

"And you want to live in Boston to do this? Why can't you do it here?"

"I think a change of pace will help me concentrate more." I was making crap up as I went along.

"Have you ever been to Boston?"

"Nope." I was tiring of his interrogation.

"But you want to live there?"

I knew what he was doing. Ethan always lectured me about running away from my problems. What did he know? He quit his program early.

The move to Boston may be perceived as rash to outsiders, but I felt that I needed to do it. Life was getting too comfortable. Too predictable. Stifling, in fact. What would become of me if I stayed?

"I'm not being a coward?"

"Would I say such a thing?" Ethan raised his eyebrows in mock amazement.

"I know what you're trying to do, Ethan."

"And what's that, Lizzie?" he asked, searching my face.

"I'm not running away."

"Of course not. You are just picking up and going to a city where you know no one, you don't have any job prospects, and you don't have a place to live. It all sounds perfectly reasonable to me."

I mulled this over. *No prospects. No, don't listen to him, Lizzie.*

Stay strong.

Do not let yourself get tied down.

"Fuck."

I rolled over in bed. "What's wrong?"

"I think something bit me."

I fumbled for the light switch on the hotel nightstand. Our flight to New York had been delayed, so we hadn't settled down into our room until well after one in the morning.

"Let me see."

Sarah held out her hand and pointed to her ring finger. I could see a slight red mark. That didn't concern me as much as the fact that her finger was swelling. When I tried to remove the ring, she winced in pain.

"Here, let me try." Sarah yanked on the ring, but it wouldn't budge.

I called the front desk for a cab to the hospital.

"What are you doing?"

"Honey, we have to get that ring off your finger. I didn't know you were allergic to insect bites." I rushed around getting dressed and threw a pair of jeans and a sweater for Sarah to put on.

"I didn't either. Will they have to cut the ring off?" She sounded deflated and tenderly rubbed the ring I had bought her for Christmas.

"I don't know, baby. Let's get you to the hospital, okay? We'll see what can be done." I kissed her forehead and whisked her downstairs to the waiting cab.

When the receptionist in the crowded ER department saw Sarah's finger, a doctor was called immediately. Within one minute, she was receiving treatment. No rooms were available, so they led her to a gurney in the hallway. As she was being seated, a nurse jabbed a needle into her arm. Sarah hadn't even seen it coming. She jumped about a foot and cursed, but the nurse was too busy to apologize. The doctor explained he would have to cut the ring off. He was holding something I assumed was a ring cutter.

Tears filled Sarah's eyes. "Don't let them cut the ring off." She pulled her hand away from the nurse.

"We have to get this ring off." The doctor eyeballed me like it was my responsibility.

"It's okay, honey," I coaxed. "We can get this ring fixed or we can get you a new one. But look at your finger; it's turning blue."

"But you gave me this ring."

"And I can get you a new one. A better ring. Just let the doctor take care of your finger."

"What's wrong with this ring? Why would I need a better ring?"

I was astonished that she chose this moment to quibble about my word choice.

"There's nothing wrong with this ring, but I don't want you to lose your finger! All you have to do is tell me whether you want it fixed or whether you want a new one, and I'll make it happen."

"When can we replace it?" She looked up at me, tears streamed down her face.

The nurse looked at me like I was an idiot, and her eyes screamed, *Hurry things up!*

"We can go shopping first thing tomorrow. I promise." I placed my hand on her shoulder tenderly.

Sarah let them cut the ring off.

After several hours of observation, she was released from the hospital. I wrapped her up in my coat and took her back to the hotel. I had requested that the bedding be changed completely, but the hotel staff felt so bad they had upgraded our room. We now had a fantastic view of Times Square, and an extra night if we wanted. Sarah fell asleep at seven in the morning. I noticed the swelling on her finger had finally subsided, and I fiddled with the damaged ring in my pocket. Exhausted, I leaned against the wall and watched her for some time before I joined her in bed and closed my eyes.

"You did what?" Ethan exclaimed.

"I bought her a ring."

"No … No! Wait." He shook his head. "You bought her a diamond ring?"

"I know. I know. But what was I supposed to do? Her finger was turning blue, and I promised I would buy her a new ring. Ethan, her finger was blue … and the nurse—she looked like Nurse Ratched, by the way—was staring at me with a look that said I needed to act fast. So I acted: I promised her a new ring."

As soon as Sarah had woken up after sleeping off all the medication they gave her at the hospital, she had asked when we were going shopping. Before I knew it, we were at Tiffany & Co.

"How big is it?" Ethan was clearly baffled.

"It's not that big. It's only two carats."

"Two carats!" He slammed his cup down on the table. His high, falsetto voice rattled me.

"Is that big?" I felt helpless and stupid when it came to these things.

"I got my wife a one-carat, and I thought that was nice. How much did it cost?"

"Let's just say it was a lot more than the amethyst one."

"I bet." He shook his head. "Did it come in a blue box?"

"What?"

"My wife told me that if the ring wasn't in a blue box, it wouldn't be good enough."

"Did you have to buy a blue box?" I saw a silver lining. I didn't buy one.

Ethan laughed. "Boy, you are a moron when it comes to this stuff. Tiffany & Co. has blue boxes. All women want their engagement rings from Tiffany's."

"Engagement ring? What the fuck are you talking about?" After purchasing the ring, I had done my best to banish this thought from my mind.

He stirred his coffee, smirking. "Did you buy the ring from Tiffany's?"

"Yes."

"It's a diamond ring?" He examined me over the rim of his glasses.

"Yes."

"What finger is she wearing it on?"

"Her ring finger." I whispered, deflated.

"Yep, you're engaged." He got up for a refill.

I pondered the new pickle I was in. When he came back I said, "But I didn't ask her to marry me. Don't I have to ask?" I was grasping for straws.

"I seriously doubt she's taking that technicality into consideration." He laughed. "Can I be your best man?"

"But we can't get married! It's not legal here, thank God." I was suddenly flooded with relief.

"It's legal in Massachusetts, and you are thinking of moving there. It will be a legal marriage if you get married there." His expression told me that he relished my situation.

"But she doesn't know that."

"You better tell her. If you pick up and leave, that will be considered abandonment." He laughed some more. "You know, for someone who doesn't want to commit, you sure know how to tie yourself down. A mortgage, a cat, and now marriage—a legal marriage, I might add. What's next, a kid? I know a good adoption agency." He winked at me.

So much for not getting tied down. I pulled my sweater off.

"What's the matter? Is it getting too hot for you?" He howled with laughter.

"Oh, you're so funny." I rubbed my face.

It was getting hot. I groaned.

CHAPTER THIRTY-TWO

ETHAN WAS RUNNING LATE, SO I SAT AT A TABLE AND LISTENED TO MY NEW IPOD. WHEN HE walked in he started to laugh.

"What?" I pulled the headphones from my ears.

"You were actually rocking out. I didn't know you could do that."

"You didn't know I could bob my head?"

"Nope. I didn't think you had any sense of rhythm."

"Well, show me your moves." I wiggled my butt in my chair in an attempt to dance — a pathetic attempt, because I nearly toppled over.

"No way. The only time I showed my moves was on my wedding day. Never again. And I wouldn't suggest using that move you just did." He shook his head gravely. "By the way, has Sarah picked the song yet for your first dance as a married couple?"

"What are you talking about?" I asked, startled.

"You are a relationship idiot. Don't you know you'll have to dance at your reception?" He waggled his finger in my face.

"Reception? Dance? What are you talking about? This isn't what you call a traditional wedding."

"For some reason, I don't think Sarah will see it that way. I think she'll want the whole nine yards. I'm going to grab some coffee. Do you need anything?"

I stared out the window. "What? Uh? No, thanks."

When he returned, I asked, "So you think I will have to help pick out a cake, china patterns, a dress, and all that shit?"

"Yes, you knucklehead. You're getting married. What did you think? You could just stand under the stars and make a promise. Weddings are a lot of planning and work. Who put the music on your iPod? I have a feeling it wasn't you." He pushed his glasses higher on his nose.

"Sarah gave it to me as a gift. It's great. She put music and audiobooks on it. And she even put the 'Monster Mash' on it. I love it."

"The 'Monster Mash'?" He stared at me as if termites were swarming out of my skull. "You know that's a Halloween song, right? When was the last time you dressed up on Halloween? Did you even go trick-or-treating as a child?"

"Yes, you numbskull. I know it's a Halloween song and I think I went trick-or-treating once or twice in my life. I like the song. Why does everyone question why I like the song? It's fun, light-hearted."

"Okay, besides the 'Monster Mash,'" he shook his head in disbelief and curled up the corner of his moustache. "Have you listened to all of the music?"

"No. There are hundreds of songs on it."

Ethan picked my iPod up and started to scroll through playlists and artists. I sipped my chai and tried to fathom the mess I was in. A wedding?

He chuckled. Then he placed the iPod on the aluminum-topped table in front of me. I looked at the screen, at a mix labeled "Our love songs."

"How did you find that?"

"I've been married a lot longer than you, Lizzie. I know how love-starved women act. I bet those are the songs she's considering for the big day."

I was flabbergasted. "But we haven't even set a date yet."

"Doesn't matter."

I sighed, rose, and went into the bathroom. Staring at the mirror, I splashed cold water on my face. Then I went out and sat down again.

"Feel better?"

"No."

"Oh, you got your shirt all wet." He indicated my collar. "I haven't seen you this messed up since you started grad school. You going to be okay?" Ethan's face wore his "Cheer up, tiger" look, but I could tell he was enjoying my misery.

I shrugged.

"Do you think she wants kids?"

"Oh, God." I put my head in my hands. "I think I'm going to puke."

"Do you remember when you puked minutes before your orals after your first year of grad school?"

I could tell Ethan was really enjoying himself now.

"I bet you puke before you walk down the aisle. Or better yet, I hope you puke right when they ask you to say your vows. Will she make you write your own vows? I bet she does."

I pushed back my chair with a screech and ran to the bathroom. When I returned, a bottle of Sprite sat bubbling away on the table. I sipped it slowly, the bubbles and sugar nice and sweet in my mouth. "Thanks."

"Anytime, puker. So when should we start writing your vows? I wrote mine. Maybe you could just borrow mine but change the name."

I ran back to the bathroom again to the sound of Ethan's chuckling.

By the time Sarah had returned from her shopping excursion, I was recovering on the couch and watching a Cary Grant movie. I had vomited non-stop for several hours and I was struggling to keep my eyes open, let alone to follow what was going on. Hank was curled up next to me.

268 A WOMAN LOST

"Hi, honey. I thought for sure you would be riding your bike. It's such a beautiful spring day." Sarah bubbled with perkiness. She pulled a candle out of one of the bags and placed it on the coffee table.

I grunted.

"Uh-oh … is someone crabby today." She sat down next to me. The movement of the couch made me ill.

I bolted to the bathroom, and Sarah followed.

"Jesus, I'm so sorry. I didn't know you were sick."

When I finished vomiting, I leaned against the bathroom wall while Sarah wiped my pale face with a wet cloth. I closed my eyes to stop from puking again.

She sat with me for several minutes. Finally, she said, "You ready for bed?" Her voice was so sweet. I wanted to crawl into her arms, but I was too weak.

"Yes. Thanks."

She helped me out of my clothes and tucked me in. Then she went into the front room, where I heard her rustling through bags. She returned to set a new clock on the nightstand.

"I got us an iHome, so we can listen to your iPod at night. What do you want to listen to?"

"You decide, honey. I'll fall asleep pretty quickly."

I prayed she wouldn't play the love songs. Luckily, she chose jazz. Then she crawled into bed with me until I fell asleep.

CHAPTER THIRTY-THREE

AS SOON AS I HEARD THE FAMILIAR "PING" ON MY COMPUTER, I KNEW MADDIE COULDN'T SLEEP as well. It was well past midnight, and Sarah had gone to bed hours ago. After she had fallen asleep, I had crawled out of bed in an attempt to get some work done. Instead, I ended up surfing the web, looking for places in Boston. Pipe dream or not, I still looked. It relaxed me.

I opened up the email and read: *Congratulations, you rat! I ran into Sarah and saw the rock! Nice job with the ring. I guess you decided to take the plunge after all. Why didn't you tell me?!*

I sighed. I couldn't write back that it was all a horrible misunderstanding. What kind of impression would that make? I was positive Sarah hadn't disclosed all of the details as to why the ring had been purchased. I wrote back: *Howdy, my fellow night owl. To be honest, I can't take much credit for the ring. Sarah picked it out. What's new with you?*

She fired a response right back: *Don't try to change the subject. Seriously, we need to have a party to celebrate your engagement. We can call it the "Plunge Party" and everyone can bring you a plunger.*

I tried to think of a stalling tactic, and wrote: *Hey now, you have enough on your plate. We can think of a party after your wedding. Besides, Sarah and I haven't worked out all of the details.*

Her response: *Details ... what do you mean details? You're getting married, right?*

Goddammit! Why did she insist on cornering me on the subject? I replied: *I guess I mean we haven't set up a timeline for the event.*

I felt better writing "event" than wedding; it seemed like that gave me a way out.

Several minutes passed before I received her response: *LOL ... timeline ... you are such a historian. I'm off to bed. I'll discuss the party with Sarah the next time I see her. Sweet dreams!*

I shut down my computer and went into the bedroom. Sarah had kicked off all of the covers. My eyes lingered on her naked body for several minutes.

Was our relationship what she wanted? Was it satisfying for her? Was it what she dreamed of when she started falling in love with me? Did reality ever fulfill our dreams? Or do dreams just continually set us up for failure and disappointment?

Our engagement was clumsy at best. I hadn't really whisked her off to New York City to propose. In fact, I still wasn't convinced our engagement was even official. Sure, a ring was exchanged, but is that all it takes to seal the deal?

I heard a mournful train whistle off in the distance.

Finally, I got undressed, crawled into bed with her, and embraced her. She smelled of lavender, sweet lavender. I never liked the smell until I smelled it on her. I kissed the back of her head and drifted off to sleep.

"What if she thinks you're having an affair with Maddie, or with anyone else for that matter?" Ethan rubbed the stubble on his chin.

"Wouldn't that be a good thing?"

"How in the *world* would that be a good thing?"

"Wouldn't it be better for her to despise me? I'm no good for her. I can't be what she wants me to be."

"And what does she want you to be?"

"Oh, I don't know … a character in a Jane Austen novel, or something."

Ethan frowned. "I seriously doubt Sarah wants you to be like Mr. Darcy. She doesn't seem to be putting that pressure on you. I think, my friend, you are putting that pressure on yourself. Stop watching Hugh Grant films. They aren't real. And when have you read any Austen?"

"All I'm trying to say is that I don't think I am good enough for her. I'm not romantic. I don't rush home every day with flowers and such. I like to work long hours. I like being by myself."

"Name any couple you know who does that—and Valentine's Day doesn't count."

"Not my parents, that's for sure."

"So, because your parents have a bad relationship, you are doomed, as well. That's a good theory to live by. That way you never have to try and you avoid any type of failure. Have your history studies warped your personal life that much? Let me guess: if you don't know your past, you're doomed to repeat it. So, since Lizzie's parents have a bad marriage, Lizzie should avoid marriage or it will be a horrible union that will ruin everyone. Grow up, Lizzie, and take responsibility for your own life."

"Ethan, there are days when I think I should fake depression. Just imagine. I could mope around all of the time and she'd be too afraid to press me on the house thing, or anything for that matter."

He fidgeted in his chair. "Wow. I thought I was an asshole, but you take the cake on this one. That plan sounds awful."

"I didn't say I was going to do it. Sometimes I just think about it, that's all."

"Lizzie, you're right. It would be much better to fake suicidal thoughts and torture the poor girl over a long period of time instead of just being honest with her."

"Why can't she be the one who leaves?"

"Are you serious? God, you are the most self-indulgent person I've ever met. We meet here every week and all we do is talk about your problems. Every fucking week. Oh, every once in a while, you poke fun at my life, but you don't really care. Not everything is about you, Lizzie."

"Me? I've been talking about Sarah this whole time." I barked.

"No you haven't. You've been talking about you disappointing Sarah. She loves you—you moron. Love isn't perfect. You have to accept that. Or you'll have a miserable life. A fucking, miserable, lonely life."

Sarah crashed into the apartment, rushed up to me, and kissed me passionately. She was holding a paper bag, which crushed up against my chest when she leaned in. Then she said breathlessly, "Hi beautiful!"

"Well, hello. Boy, you look happy."

A grin split her face and her eyes danced merrily.

"I am happy."

"Okay, happy girl, can I pour you a glass of wine?"

"Sounds perfect. I picked up some Chinese for us. Would you like to have a picnic with me in front of the fireplace?"

"I was going to grade some papers tonight," I said in a teasing voice.

She set the bag on the kitchen counter. Then she took her shirt off and started to kiss me. She smelled wonderful. Orange blossoms? Was that the scent?

"Oh, all right . . . I guess my students can wait."

"There's one rule for this picnic."

"Really? And what's that?"

She smiled as she pulled off her bra. "No clothes allowed." Her fingers flew to the zipper on her jeans. Then, changing her mind, she started to unbutton my shirt instead. As she reached around to undo my bra, I returned her kiss. Sarah tugged at my shirt with urgency, keen to get me in front of the fireplace. Even though she rushed the act, it was not a quick fuck. We went at it repeatedly for several hours; by the time we finished, and lay in front of the fire picking at the Chinese food and sipping wine, I was exhausted. Neither of us spoke. I placed my head on her stomach and she ran her fingers through my hair.

"Come on, Lizzie, dance naked with me."

"What?" There was no way I was going to dance naked.

Sarah popped up from the carpet and tugged on my arms. "Come on, grandma! Loosen up a little." Her eyes sparkled; she looked radiant. I couldn't refuse.

Afterwards, we settled back down on the floor, Sarah said, "Oh I forgot to tell you, Maddie called me today."

I tried not to react. "Oh, really. How is the troublemaker?"

"She sounded good. She mentioned you two talked a few nights ago about an engagement party. She's so sweet."

"She's very thoughtful." My heart started to race. So that was why Sarah had planned this romantic fuckfest.

"Oh, she said you were quite formal." Sarah paused and then put on a southern accent, "We don't have a timeline yet." She laughed and continued to run her fingers through my hair.

I didn't respond, still hoping the whole thing would go away.

"I told her we could wait until after her wedding. There's enough family drama right now … well, on your side. My mom wants to take us to dinner."

I licked her nipple, not lingering long; I inched my way down toward her navel. Her soft skin and scent beckoned me. I worked my way down. Down. Down. I didn't stop until she came again.

CHAPTER THIRTY-FOUR

It took all of my energy to open the door to the coffee shop. I wasn't sure if Ethan would be waiting inside. I thought back to our last meeting and couldn't help feeling that our friendship was teetering on a precipice. Would it survive? Should it?

"Well, look what the cat dragged in?"

"Sorry, Ethan. I was running late." I fell into the chair opposite him.

"Geez Louise! You look beat."

I nodded slowly.

"What the hell happened to you? Did someone slip you some Special K or something?"

I laughed mirthlessly. "No, I've been burning the candle at both ends. Between teaching and Sarah, I'm exhausted."

"Okay, I'm following the teaching part. How does Sarah fit in?"

"Ever since New York City she has been a fuck machine. I mean, she wants sex all night, and then again before work. Man, I'm beat."

"You mean ever since you gave her the ring?" he teased.

"Yeah. And she's much more assertive about it. Passionate even. It's pretty hot, but I am tired. I could probably curl up on the floor right here and go to sleep." I gazed down at the filthy floor. Even that wouldn't have deterred me right then.

"Oh man, that's too bad, Lizzie. You sit right there and I'll get your chai." He stood up.

"Thanks."

He paused. "You really are tired. No comeback whatsoever. And you said thanks." Ethan wandered to the counter and then returned with my chai.

I took a gulp, which burned all the way down.

"So, my tired friend, are you going to go through with this marriage?"

"I don't see a way out of it." I fidgeted with my earring.

"Are you serious?" He sounded flabbergasted.

"What can I do now?"

In a firm voice he said, "Tell her the truth."

"And what do you propose I say? 'Hey, I said I would buy you a ring because I was scared of the nurse and I panicked to save your finger.'" I paused. "Maybe I could throw in, 'and I like what you can do with your finger.'"

"Is that the truth?" He stared through me. What did he see? Himself?

"Sort of."

"What do you mean 'sort of?'" Ethan crossed his arms and tilted his head.

"Let's face it, Ethan, I am a relationship idiot. I don't know what I feel or what I want. Right now, I can barely remember my name."

"Poor little Lizzie. She's been cornered into marriage. Everything is out of her hands." He frowned with melodrama and his moustache drooped. I noticed it was smeared with cappuccino froth.

"I think I will put that on my tombstone." I smiled.

"You are an idiot. And not just with relationships."

"How's the adoption process going?"

He sighed. "It's out of my hands."

Both of us burst out laughing.

"No seriously, Ethan. How's it going?"

Ethan discussed his trials and tribulations for once while I downed three chais.

When I got back to the apartment, Sarah was already home.

"Hi, honey. I wasn't expecting you to be here." I sat next to her on the couch, slouching against the cushions.

"Yeah, I told Mom I wanted to take a nap. I'm beat." She rested her head on my chest.

"Tell me about it. I just drank three chais."

"That explains why you look so flushed. And your heart is racing."

"I'm shocked. You didn't shop at all?"

"Oh, we did for a couple of hours. I bought a new painting to hang over the couch, but I was too tired to hang it." She gestured to the painting that leaned against the far wall.

I didn't say anything.

She kissed my forehead. "Do you want to take a nap with me?"

"Sweetheart, I would love to."

We crawled into bed, naked, and she held me while we slept for hours. I awoke feeling wonderful. Sarah also woke up refreshed—so refreshed that we went at it again.

"You have to go to the office?" Sarah looked hurt.

"I know. I know I installed the Internet so I would be home more, but I have a lot of grading to do, and I have to enter information at work," I told her, lying my ass off. I didn't even think my story made sense. I just wanted some alone time. "I'll come home as soon as I can. I'll be counting the seconds until I get back."

"Until you'll be back with me, you mean." She wrapped her arms around me and began to lay delicate kisses up my neck—my major weakness. She knew that if she kissed my neck just right, I would be hers for the night.

"I better go, sweetheart, so I can get back as soon as possible."

She pulled me toward her and slid her hand down my pants. I felt the feather-light brush of her fingertips, then the grasping hardness of them as she fingered me briefly, her eyes hard on mine. She pulled her hand out and sensuously licked her finger. "Hurry back. I heart you."

"I promise." I kissed her goodbye. I briefly considered staying. Then I saw the painting against the wall. No. I needed space.

I didn't go to the office. In truth, I'd never had any intention of going. Instead, I texted Maddie, hoping she would be in town. She was staying at the hotel near Coopersmith's and agreed to meet me for a late lunch.

When I walked into the restaurant, I saw her sitting at the bar chatting with two guys. Two good-looking guys. Jealousy burned inside me. I approached with every intention of whisking her away.

"Hey!" Maddie jumped off her barstool and hugged me tightly. "You got here fast." She held my hand and turned me towards the two men. "I would like you to meet my friends, Joseph and David. They just adopted their first child." She turned to me and announced, "Lizzie and her girlfriend recently got engaged." She let go of my hand. "You should see the rock Lizzie sprung for. Wheweee! I was jealous when I laid my eyes on it for the first time." Maddie nudged me with her arm.

Joseph and David congratulated me and I reciprocated, feeling silly that I thought they were putting the moves on Maddie. Sarah has always teased me about not having any gaydar.

Their buzzer trilled and they excused themselves, leaving the two of us alone at the bar.

"Can I tempt you with a drink? Will Sarah pick you up if I get you drunk?" Maddie didn't wait for an answer and motioned to the bartender.

Ignoring the Sarah part, I responded, "I could really use a drink."

Maddie ordered a rum and Coke for me and another merlot for herself. The drinks arrived promptly, and Maddie raised her glass. I sipped my drink—no, I inhaled half of my drink.

"Everything okay, Lizzie?"

"Y-yeah," I spluttered. I knew my face and my voice betrayed me. Try as I might, I could not fake a smile.

"Come on, there's a table in the back. Let's talk." Placing her arm around my waist, she guided us to a dark corner.

She smelled of peaches. I envisioned running my hands over her body, tasting her sweet nectar, exploring every inch of her with my tongue.

"Do you want to tell me what's bugging you?"

Her voice shattered my fantasy. I sighed. I didn't know where to begin. So, I didn't.

"Did you and Sarah fight?" She queried.

"N-no." Why couldn't I talk to her? Openly.

"Hey, you texted me, remember?" She joked. "Come on! Tell me what's going on." She placed her hand on my leg and gave me an encouraging squeeze. The warmth spread, igniting a tingling sensation that delighted and frustrated me.

How could I be happy with Sarah and still lust after Maddie?

"Oh, I don't know." I tugged at my Northface vest. "I'm feeling … stifled."

Maddie laughed. "Let's get you out of your vest. You must be roasting." She helped me undress.

"I remember when your brother and I got engaged. For weeks, I couldn't breathe," she babbled. "I think what you're feeling is normal."

What I was feeling was not normal! I wanted to fuck her right then and there.

"Trust me," she continued. "It gets easier. This is a big change for you. All your life, you've been independent. You never were close to your family. Now, you're asking Sarah to spend the rest of her life with you. That's a *big* deal. No wonder you're flustered. You have no experience of letting someone in." She put her hand back on my leg, higher up this time.

I chuckled. Maddie was trying so hard to put me at ease, yet I felt myself getting hotter, more desperate. Frantic. I wanted to taste her. To feel her legs wrapped around me. Be inside her. Feel her body convulse after experiencing an exhilarating orgasm. God, I wanted her.

"Have you talked to Sarah about this?"

"No!" I didn't mean to shout, but for a moment, I thought Maddie knew what thoughts I was entertaining.

She put her fingers to her lips. "No reason to shout. I wasn't going to tattle on you. You can trust me with your secrets. I've trusted you with mine."

I wondered if it were possible to have an orgasm from her touch alone. *What if my eyes suddenly roll back into my head? Will she think I'm having a seizure? Will she call 911?* The thought made me smile. It emboldened me.

"How do you do it?" I asked.

Confused, she replied, "Do what?"

What did I mean? I had to say something. "Act happy."

"Trust me, I have my dark days." She pulled away from me and sat back in her chair.

"Like in Estes."

She nodded.

I wanted her to elaborate. I needed to hear her thoughts. I needed a signal to pursue her.

Maddie gave me nothing to go on.

We sat there in silence.

Flustered, I offered to buy her another glass of wine. She accepted. When I returned to our table, I noticed her happy demeanor had returned. As I handed Maddie her glass, our fingers touched, and I saw a sparkle in her eye.

"Drink up, Lizzie. I feel like dancing."

"Dancing? Where?" My eyes scanned Coops for a new dance floor.

"Not here, you idiot. Around the corner, there's a new gay club." She downed her wine.

Unable to resist her allure, I drained my glass as well.

Sure enough, there was a new gay club right around the corner. Not that I would have gone on my own. Only Maddie could get me there.

Inside, Maddie bought another round of drinks. At first, she danced with some gay boys. It looked like they all knew each other.

Maddie disappeared for a few minutes, and I leaned against the wall, focusing on the handful of people dancing. My drinks were going straight to my head.

Maddie popped up before me. "It took some doing, but you have to dance with me during the next song."

I set my drink down. "And why is that?"

"Just wait." She cocked her head, waiting to hear the music.

That's when I heard it: the 'Monster Mash.'

"Are you serious? How does one dance to this?" I asked, but I didn't wait for an answer, just followed her to the dance floor.

The drinks worked their magic. Or Maddie did. She twirled around me and made me look halfway decent. Afterwards, we danced to several more songs until a slow song came on and Maddie maneuvered me off the dance floor.

My entire body felt relaxed. "Would you like something to eat?"

She nodded, thinking. "But not at Coops. I can't handle another meal there. I dine there more than I do in my own home."

"Shall we go to your room and order in?" I looked hopeful.

"Yes! Let's get pizza." She bounced in her seat like a child.

Her excitement set all of my nerve endings afire.

We didn't finish our drinks. Both of us wanted to leave—and fast.

When we entered Maddie's hotel room, my bravado started to falter. I excused myself and hid in the bathroom. While dousing my face with cold water, I heard Maddie on the phone, placing our order. I thought briefly of Sarah. *Stop!*

"Hope you don't mind, I went ahead and ordered." She flashed me her confident smile.

"Not at all." I walked to the window. "This is quite the view. You can even see the gap from here."

She got off the bed and joined me, standing close. "What gap?"

"Horsetooth." I gestured to the hills, but I could tell she didn't see it. Pulling her in front of me, I placed my arms around her but didn't hold her; instead, I pointed to the gap. "You see that part of the foothills that looks like a horse's tooth?"

She nodded.

I took in her scent.

"That's why half this town is called Horsetooth."

She rested her head against me. "I had no idea!"

My arms enveloped her. She didn't resist. Finally, the moment I had longed for had arrived. Not wanting to waste a second, I leaned down and kissed her neck.

It was pure ecstasy. Her salty but alluring skin electrified my tongue. A fire burned inside me. My face felt hot. My cheek stung like a bee sting. Several seconds passed before I realized that Maddie had whipped around and smacked me across the face. Hard!

"What the hell do you think you're doing?" she shouted.

Dazed, I asked, "Why did you hit me?"

"Why did I hit you?" She pushed me away. "Why in the fuck did you kiss my neck?"

"What?" I rubbed my cheek, pondering. "Why did you invite me to your room?"

"Invite you? You invited yourself, remember." She glared at me. "I thought you needed a friend."

Her comment smarted. A friend — that's all I was.

"I know you aren't yourself today, but this —" She started to hyperventilate. "Th-this is unacceptable!"

I went to her, to comfort her.

She slapped me again.

"Stop hitting me!" I staggered back against the window.

"Stop coming onto me!"

"Isn't this what you wanted?" I screamed.

"Are you insane, Lizzie? Why would I want Peter's sister to kiss me? I thought we were friends. My one ally in the family. And now I find out you want to get into my pants. Lizzie, you may distance yourself from your family, thinking you're better than them, but you are just like them!"

Stunned, I said nothing.

"Don't just stand there looking stupid. Get the fuck out of my room!" She threw my vest at me and then shoved me out the door.

"Maddie —"

She slammed the door in my face.

A couple walked by in the hallway. Pulling my shirt collar up, I scurried to the staircase. The elevator seemed too slow, too confining. I wanted outside, and quick.

As soon as my feet hit the asphalt of the parking lot, I received a text: *If you don't tell Sarah, I will!*

I threw my phone down. It didn't shatter completely. Exasperated, I stomped on in it until it was unrecognizable.

Seriously, Lizzie. You thought Maddie tried to seduce you by playing the "Monster Mash." Are you that much of an idiot?

CHAPTER THIRTY-FIVE

EVEN IF IT WAS JUST WEEKS BEFORE PETER'S WEDDING, I DECIDED I BETTER TELL SARAH. I TOOK a long bike ride first, to clear my head, and then came home and showered quickly. I wanted to talk to her before I lost my nerve.

"Hi," I said, walking into the front room and looking her directly in the eyes.

"Hi," she replied, looking puzzled.

Already, my nerves had started to falter. I could feel my heartbeat in the hollow of my throat, right where I imagined Sarah's hands would be when she heard the news. Fighting the instinct to run to the bathroom and vomit, I settled beside her on the couch and fumbled with the drawstrings on my pajama bottoms. Then I mumbled, "Can we talk?" I pulled the drawstrings tight, watching the thread slip in and out of my fingers.

"Honey, what's wrong?" Sarah put her arm around my shoulder and I rested my head on her arm.

"I ... "

How could I say that I tried to fuck Maddie?

I nuzzled closer to her and she kissed the top of my head and held me tight. It felt good, which made me feel worse.

"What's wrong? You're starting to scare me."

"I don't know how to tell you."

She squeezed me tighter.

Sitting up, I looked her in the eyes. "I'm not sure I want to buy a house."

Sarah took a deep breath. "All right. We can talk about that." She straightened on the couch and looked me in the eyes.

"I just don't know if I am ready for such a huge step. And now that I'm taking a year off to finish my dissertation, I don't think staying in Fort Collins is my best option."

She continued to stare at me. I could see her mind grappling with what I had said.

"Are you saying you want to move from Fort Collins to finish your dissertation?"

"Yes, but—"

"But what?" She pulled away from me.

"There's something else. Something you should know." I braced myself.

She crossed her arms. "I'm waiting."

Oh, shit! What have I done? I looked into her eyes, which welled with tears. *Why have I hurt the one person I love?*

Yes, I was in love with Sarah.

Finally, I was at peace with that — just when it was ending.

"I—"

"You what?"

"I may have … " I couldn't get the words out. I swallowed. Then I blurted out, "I made a pass at Maddie."

"You what!"

"I—"

"You fucking asshole!" She sprinted off the couch.

I bowed my head. "If you knew how sorry I am."

"What? Is that supposed to make me feel better, Lizzie? You know what makes me feel better." She yanked her ring off and chucked it at me. I ducked and it slammed into the wall. "Fuck you and your ring, Lizzie."

"Sarah, please, let me explain." I moved towards her.

Her eyes showed no love. All I saw was coldness. Icy anger.

"You asshole! You fucking asshole!"

She drew nearer to me. I had my back against the wall, trapped. Sarah balled her hands into fists. Preparing for a one-two strike, I turned my head and closed my eyes. She fell against me, fists first, into my chest. All of her strength dissipated. Her shoulders heaved and I felt the wetness of her tears on my neck. As I tried to embrace her, she quickly shoved away from me, staggering back.

"You asshole," she whispered.

I stood motionless. My heart shrieked inside my chest, telling me to make it better. My head knew better. I couldn't fix this.

She charged past me to the front door. "I'm going to my mother's!"

She slammed the door as she left.

I stared after her until all I could see was the closed door.

Several tense days passed before I received an email from Sarah.

Please let me know when you won't be in the apartment so I can pick up my stuff. I have thought long and hard, and I don't want to see you. Please respect my decision and don't try to contact me, other than letting me know when I can come by.

She didn't sign the email. I'm pretty sure she wanted to tell me to fuck off. Maybe her mom helped compose the email to rid it of all vitriol. But I knew Sarah. She was not calm about the situation. If she had the chance, she would throttle me. I also knew that I deserved it. God, I was a fuck-up.

I sat on the couch all night and watched old movies, Hank curled in the crook of one arm. I didn't cry—I was numb. No thoughts, feelings, or anything else, pulsed through me that night. Occasionally, I would flip the channel, but the rest of the time I just petted Hank—until he bit my hand. He didn't leave my lap, but even he didn't want me to touch him.

Finally, my eyes closed, but as my thoughts drifted off, the sudden realization hit me: Sarah was gone. Forever. I had done it. I had pushed her away.

I *was* a fucking idiot!

CHAPTER THIRTY-SIX

"What do you mean you don't want to be without her?" Ethan's coffee cup was reflected in his thick glasses as he stared owlishly at me over the cup's rim.

"Just that … I don't want to be without her, Ethan. I think I screwed up big-time." I did the best I could to fight back tears, but I felt them forming anyway.

"You have been trying to brush her off for almost a year now. Please help me understand this." He sounded angry, and a little baffled.

"Really, I don't know how to explain it. I'm just as shocked as you. But I want her back." I gripped my cup of chai tightly.

We sat in silence and watched a toddler throw a tantrum because her mother did not want to buy a Starbucks bear that was dressed up in Fourth of July clothes. The child screeched non-stop for more than a minute. Finally, the mother relented, beaten. She purchased the bear before pulling the tear-streaked child out of the store by one arm while the brat waved the bear victoriously with the other.

"So why did you do it?" He stroked his chin, musing.

"What?"

"Why did you break up with her?"

"I didn't. She broke up with me."

He laughed, but it sounded hollow. "Yeah, that's right. You only tried to sleep with Maddie. What did you think? You could keep Sarah and have Maddie on the side. The best of both worlds. Or did you purposefully sabotage and now regret your idiocy?"

I chuckled and wiped away some tears. "Well, I've never claimed to be the brightest."

His eyes softened. "Seriously, though. Why did you do it? Was all the talk just bluster, so I wouldn't know you cared for her — that you care for her, I mean? You cared for her the whole time. Are you that caught up on being the tough guy that you pushed the right one away?"

"I screwed up." I shivered.

"Yes, you did."

I put my head in my hands. "Do you think I can make it better?"

"Sweetheart" — Ethan put a hand on my arm, gave it a little squeeze — "I have no idea. A lot of damage has been done."

"What would you do?" I looked hopeful.

"For one thing, I wouldn't have tried to fuck Maddie."

I laughed. "No shit, Sherlock. Is there anyone you would willingly sleep with?"

He squirmed in his chair and said emphatically, "No!"

"I wish I felt the same way."

"Trust me, it adds different complications." He looked away.

"I'm sorry, Ethan. That was insensitive."

He waved my words away and said with his southern accent, "Miss Lizzie, I'm not the one you should be apologizing to. You need to come up with a plan."

"A plan." I nodded my head. I loved plans. Challenges.

He leaned across the table and placed his slender fingers on mine. "If you love her as much as I think you do, fight for her, Lizzie. Fight!" He then slapped my hand. "If you don't, you'll never forgive yourself."

CHAPTER THIRTY-SEVEN

I HAD NO IDEA WHERE TO BEGIN TO MAKE THINGS RIGHT WITH SARAH. AND I ALSO KNEW I HAD to talk to Maddie. The wedding wasn't too far off. I couldn't delay talking to her. Using the text function on my new cell phone, which had all the bells and whistles, I informed Maddie that I had told Sarah. It was a gutless way of communicating, but I still didn't tell her that Sarah had left me. I didn't see a need.

Not a minute passed before I received a reply: *Thank you. Can we talk?*

I groaned. How much crow did I have to eat? Of course, I couldn't say no; she was going to be my sister-in-law. I asked where and when.

To my surprise, she wanted to meet in my apartment in ten minutes. Quick — like a Band-Aid.

Ten minutes had never felt longer. I waited in my front room, like a child waiting to get immunized. Full of dread.

There was a knock on the door. For a second I considered jumping off my balcony and running for the hills. Who would really miss me?

Get it together, Lizzie. You did this to yourself.

I stood, swaying a bit, and answered the door.

"How's my future sister-in-law?" Maddie set the tone right away.

What could I say? I just stared, mutely.

"Are you going to let me in?"

"Are you going to slap me again?"

"Are you going to try to kiss me?"

"Never. Never again." I rubbed my cheek. My jaw was sore.

"Good. I'm glad we cleared this up." She pushed her way into my apartment.

I turned. "Is that it?"

"What? Did you want to talk about it *ad nauseam*? That doesn't seem like you." Her tone was accusatory.

"Seriously, I tried seducing you and you don't want to rip my head off?" I was bamboozled.

"Lizzie, you aren't the first person to make a pass at me. You aren't the first to misread my friendliness. My friends and family always tell me I'm too footloose and fancy free." She paused. "However, I didn't expect it from you."

"Not the first nitwit —"

"Goodness, no!" she interrupted. "But I had thought that since we are going to be family, I would be safe around you." She laughed. "A gay guy even made a pass at me once. And nitwit? Seriously."

"Maddie, I'm so sorry … not about the gay guy … you know what I mean. I —"

"You better be. And don't worry, I won't tell Peter."

I pushed my hands deep into my pockets. "Thanks." I knew she couldn't.

Maddie's face softened. "How did Sarah take it?"

My instinct was to shout, "How the fuck do you think she took it?" Instead, I shrugged. "Not too good. She left."

"Is she coming back?" she asked, and I detected a spark of hope in her voice.

I shook my head. "I don't think so." Tears formed.

Maddie looked torn. Was she afraid that if she hugged me I might kiss her again?

"Lizzie, I'm so sorry."

I stifled a sigh. "It's all my fault."

She laughed. "I wish I could tell you you're wrong."

"Oh, don't worry. I've sat around for hours ruminating on my actions."

Maddie chortled. "Ruminating! Lizzie, get off your high horse. Maybe if you spent less time ruminating and more time living, you wouldn't be in this situation. What's with you Petries? Why can't you act like normal people?"

I started to answer, but she shushed me.

"What's your plan?"

"My plan?" My voice sounded hollow, even to me.

"To win Sarah back?"

"She's asked me not to contact her. She wants me out of the apartment so she can pack up her stuff. In fact, I'm leaving tonight. I'll be gone for at least a week. I don't want her to feel rushed." I motioned to my suitcase in the corner. "I'm taking off for Jackson Hole."

Hank came crashing into the room, upsetting my books on the coffee table.

"Who's watching him?" Maddie gestured to the rambunctious kitty.

"I'm dropping him off at a kennel. Sarah's mom is allergic, so he can't stay there."

"A kennel!"

For an instant, I thought she was going to whack me again.

"Hank, pack your bags. You're coming home with me."

Hank darted out of the room.

"Maddie, that's kind of you —"

"Lizzie, we're family. He's coming with me, and if you try to stop me…" She made a fist.

"Okay." I backed away. "Thank you."

I waited a few minutes after our farewells, and when I felt certain Maddie had left, I went back inside, grabbed the photo of Sarah and my bags, and skedaddled.

It had been some time since I had been on a highway that didn't involve traveling to a family member's house. I felt free, exhilarated. There was an endless road before me, and I wanted to conquer it. The sky was brilliant blue and the horizon beckoned to me.

Six hours later, my body started to revolt. My eyes wanted to shut and my back and legs screamed. I couldn't remember getting much sleep lately, and I had been on my bike at six that morning.

When I spotted a hotel with a vacancy, I pulled into the parking lot. After settling into my room, I went to the diner and silently jumped for joy when I saw they served breakfast day and night. I ordered hash browns and a mound of greasy bacon and relished the junk heading right into my belly. Still hungry, I followed it by polishing off four large pancakes.

Afterwards, I wandered around outside, but there wasn't much to see. No matter. I would be in Jackson Hole the next day.

The next morning, my eyes popped open at four. I knew immediately that I would not be able to fall back asleep. The only good thing about these highway hotels was that the restaurants were always open. Once again, I gorged myself on pancakes, hash browns, and bacon. Then I packed up my meager belongings and hit the road. Thank God Sarah bought me a GPS unit or I would have been hesitant to hit the road in total darkness.

"You couldn't find your way out of a paper bag," she had told me when she gave it to me. It was a little harsh, but not too far off the mark. My sense of direction was severely lacking. I should always go the exact opposite of my gut feeling; however, I was too stubborn to ignore my intuition.

I wanted to be as far away as possible, and the car could not take me fast enough; yet, a part of me didn't want to be gone. I listened to the playlists Sarah had compiled for me on my iPod. Maddie would have been proud—I didn't listen to a single audio book. For hours I held off, but I finally listened to the love mix Ethan said included the songs Sarah must have been considering for our wedding. I listened to all of them—several times—to see if I could pinpoint which one she might have chosen for our first dance.

But I was at a loss. Most of the songs sounded the same. Anyway, I told myself, there was no need to concern myself with that anymore. I sighed. God, I was turning into a mushy sap. *Snap out of it, Lizzie.* I glanced down at Sarah's picture by the odometer.

After locating a hotel that had a vacancy for at least a week, I checked into my room, showered, and dressed. Soon, I was wandering around the city square. The quaintness of the Old West made me smile. For an hour I wandered around staring at cute shops, the antler arch over the street, and the stagecoach in the street, until some of my loneliness left me. I found a spot in the tiny park in the centre of the square and watched the locals and tourists pass back and forth.

When my insatiable appetite overwhelmed me, I found a cafe with patio seating so I could continue people watching. Once again, I was gluttonous. I inhaled a massive bacon cheeseburger with fries and a chocolate malt. I longed to hop on my bike afterwards, but I had left it at home. I hit the shops instead, wandering in and out, checking out all the trinkets and novelties for tourists.

It didn't take too long to purchase a couple of T-shirts, fudge, and chocolate. It also didn't take long to notice that most of the shops were the same. Not wanting to look at T-shirts anymore, I changed tactics and wandered into a jewelry store. That was my mistake.

As soon as I started peering into the glass cases, I could not stop thinking of Sarah—thinking that she would have liked this bracelet or that a certain necklace would look incredible on her. The thoughts invaded my mind. I started envisioning her wearing them. *God, what was I thinking in chasing her away? What a fool.* Sarah was perfect for me in every way—pretty, smart, funny, caring, and most of all, she let me be me. I could work late hours and go for long bike rides. She rarely bugged me about spending more time with her.

Get a grip, Lizzie, I told myself. *Concentrate. You are here to forget, not to beat yourself up. Pull it together.*

I made a break for the exit, confusing the poor salesperson who had pulled out all the merchandise for me. I felt like an ass. But how could I explain? I knew I had acted like a jerk, and that I was wrong. I didn't need a stranger to tell me that too.

How could I say sorry? How could I take back my actions over the past year? Just telling her I loved her wouldn't cut it. You can't put a Band-Aid on a gaping wound. Attempting to change her mind with nothing more than words, or hugs and kisses, seemed impossible. I had to demonstrate that I loved her. And that meant owning up to my feelings and my failings—I was never good at that either. Plus, there wasn't evidence any of my attempts would work. I usually only set goals I knew I could attain. Buying jewelry wasn't going to help me.

I needed to find something to occupy my mind, but it was too late in the day to hike. Instead, I found a used bookstore. That was it: I would buy an enormous book and focus on the words. Force my mind to wrap itself around something else. I didn't want to think about my life. And I certainly didn't want to think about Sarah.

I considered buying a thick book on economics, something that would require all my brainpower to understand, but I knew that wouldn't work. My mind would inevitably wander.

Instead, I headed for the fiction section. I wandered up and down the aisle until I spied a copy of *The Thorn Birds,* and I chuckled, remembering Maddie reading the book in Estes. But I didn't want a book about a forbidden love affair. I continued scanning the shelves and found a fantastic old copy of *David Copperfield.* From the wear and tear the book had endured, I knew it had entertained many people. It was perfect. I also glanced at a copy of *The Witching Hour,* another monster of a book. I purchased both. Who knew how quickly I would read them? There were too many hours in one day. I needed to keep my mind off my regrets. Hiking would occupy part of the day, but what would I do at night?

My next stop was the liquor store. I would need plenty of gin and tonic, my new favorite vice. Too much rum and Coke gave me the jitters. Back in my hotel room, I filled the ice bucket to chill the tonic water. Sipping a gin and tonic, I opened to the first page of the Dickens book, looking forward to the suffering—the orphan boy tossed out into the world. Please Charles, give me some solace. I needed an old friend to spend time with, a friend who wouldn't judge, talk, or look at me like I was a fool.

Several hours later, I could no longer ignore my grumbling stomach. I tucked Sarah's photograph into the book to keep my place, found another greasy spoon restaurant, and ate until I thought my stomach would burst. Then I returned to my room, curled up on the bed with my book, and drank.

The next morning, I woke up early once again. I did not remember falling asleep, but then again, I did not remember much of the night before. I had plans to hike all day, so I found an early-bird restaurant, an easy thing to do in an outdoorsy town, and wolfed down a hearty meal. The place was kind enough to pack me a couple of sandwiches and apples for lunch.

I purchased a yearlong pass to the park, and at that moment, I never wanted to return to Fort Collins at all. Everything I knew and loved was over. Maybe I would buy a place here and live in hiking, biking bliss. I made a mental note to check out available real estate. Part of me felt foolish, thinking like that. How could a reasonable adult run away? The other part of me thought: *Why the fuck not? What was keeping me in Fort Collins, or Colorado for that matter?*

It was beautiful, but it did not compare to the beauty of northern Wyoming. Would Boston be better? Did I care about teaching that much? I was an outdoor girl. I loved research. I loved quiet and being left alone. Being alone in a city would not be hard, but it wasn't the type of alone time I wanted.

The thought of leaving Colorado energized me. I couldn't wait to get to the trail and explore. I had decided to hike around String Lake, so I wore my bathing suit underneath my clothes. I wanted to test how chilly the water would be in June. Usually, I came to these parts during late July or August.

Just being on the trail, surrounded by nature, eased the tension from my body. I sucked in the fresh air, heard the rustle of the breeze through the treetops, like the whisper of Nature itself.

It didn't take long to work up a sweat, and I started to peel off some of my layers. By ten in the morning, I was famished again. I stopped and unhitched my rucksack to eat one of my sandwiches.

Turkey and cheese, stacked high on fresh-baked bread—the type of sandwich I imagined loving mothers made for their children each day before sending them off to school. I sat down on a log and watched the chipmunks grow braver and braver. I knew I shouldn't feed them; nevertheless, I enjoyed watching them.

The buzzing sounds of insects invaded my ears. I couldn't see them, but occasionally one whirred near my ear. Swatting at the invisible assailants, I wished I had remembered to pack bug repellent. Sarah would have remembered. *Stop it.*

I shut my eyes on Sarah's image and listened to the wind whistling through the leaves. A deep breath reinvigorated me. I could live here.

Whack!

I sneered at the squashed bug on my arm.

I should have brought some spray. Dammit! A butterfly flitted past me. I gazed at the cerulean sky through squinted eyes. What had Lewis and Clark felt when they first stepped foot here? Did they want to explore? Conquer? Tame?

The possibilities were endless then. Now, tourists crawled over the land, despoiling the sense of freedom. From my vantage point, I spied at least twenty people on the trail below, winding their way to my spot. Their prattle shattered the tranquility.

I shut my eyes again, relishing the sound of the wind, the insects, and the chattering chipmunks.

The sound of something crashing at my feet forced my eyes open.

"I'm sorry," said a man, as he leaned over and picked up his water bottle, which sat near my foot.

I nodded and watched him amble away with his wife. They looked happy. Not alone.

I sighed and scrambled to my feet. I needed to focus on the trail.

As long as I kept moving, I could keep my mind off Sarah. Physical exertion had always been a way to distract myself from trouble or sadness. I relished pushing my muscles to the point of exhaustion, and the beauty around me made the pain more bearable.

After hiking all day, I made a reservation for dinner at the Jackson Lake Lodge. I was dying for a steak. I requested a table by the window, so I could watch the moose come to drink at the watering hole.

Back at my hotel, I showered before climbing into bed and reading until I fell asleep. My body was so relaxed from all of the exercise that I didn't even bother to make a drink.

I kept this schedule for the next three days: up early and hiking until I could barely walk, and then finishing my day by eating steak while watching the moose at the watering hole. On day five, I woke up early and could barely move my legs. My entire body rebelled against any physical exertion, and a slight limp made me look like I was suffering from hemorrhoids. Hitting the trails alone in that state was not advisable — even my stubborn-ass knew that.

Instead, I wandered the square once more. Again, everything reminded me of Sarah. When I passed a real estate office, I stopped to look at the properties. Maybe Boston was not the right place for me. Maybe I should be in the mountains, isolated, so I could finish my dissertation. And on the days I didn't want to work, I could disappear on the trails. The idea appealed to me. It appealed so much that I made an appointment with an agent.

Afterwards, I wandered about the square again. *Screw it.* I marched into the jewelry store and bought all of the crap I thought Sarah would love. The salesclerk patiently boxed and wrapped each item. Finally, I had some peace of mind. Sarah never said I couldn't send her stuff. She didn't have to know it was from me. I just wanted her to have it.

CHAPTER THIRTY-EIGHT

As soon as I got back into town, I called Maddie to let her know. I had stayed two days longer than originally planned. Of course, she had said that minding Hank was no problem, but I didn't want to trouble her any further. Besides, I missed the scamp. I'd offered to pick him up, but she had insisted on bringing him to my apartment and planned on dropping him off after work.

My apartment seemed empty. All traces of Sarah were gone, even the candles. The large picture she had bought the day I met Maddie at Coopersmith's no longer leaned against the wall. I had hoped it would still be there, as a sign that things could get back on track. She even took the fancy new margarita blender. I couldn't blame her, but still.

The barren apartment closed in on me. I needed to get out on my bike. After my ride, which helped loosen my taut muscles from hours spent in the car, I unloaded my luggage. I had ended up buying a lot of bric-a-brac for my new place, as well as Sarah's gifts. I stopped unpacking for a moment to look at them, piling the boxes on the table. As soon as I had, Maddie knocked on the door.

I let her into my apartment and freed Hank from his carrier. He immediately disappeared around the corner, into the back of the apartment.

"I guess he didn't miss me all that much," I said, watching his tail vanish around the door.

Maddie was staring at the pile of boxes stacked on the table. "I see Sarah rubbed off on you. It looks as though you hit every store in Jackson."

I reddened.

"Can I see what you bought?" Of course, she didn't wait for an answer. She mumbled to herself as she snapped open the jewelry boxes. "For some reason, I don't see you wearing any of this."

"I thought I would get some Christmas shopping done."

"Of course. You're always thinking ahead." She paused and started to say something, but then didn't.

I changed the subject by asking if she wanted to go to dinner. She accepted, but wanted to change first, so we decided to meet at Beau Jo's Pizza. Coopersmith's was off-limits now.

When she left, I hopped on my bike to ride to Old Town. Being alone in our apartment was not what I needed. The next day, I picked out one of Sarah's necklaces and mailed it to her mother's house. I didn't include a note.

Ethan sat across from me with his arms folded. "So, did you find any answers while wandering aimlessly in the woods?"

"Yeah, I did, unfortunately."

"What does that mean?" He looked skeptical.

"All this time, I've been trying to prove myself. Trying to be a survivor. I didn't need anyone. No one was going to get in the way of my success." I stirred more sugar into my chai. "I wasn't going to be a waste of space. I was going to push myself and push myself to the top. Fuck Peter and my mom. I would be better than them. They would finally have to admit that I wasn't a loser. But it didn't feel right. Deep down, it didn't feel right."

"What didn't?"

"All along, all these conversations and all those bike rides and hikes, I was searching for answers. What did I want? Why did I feel so lost and trapped? And the entire time, the answer was right there: Sarah was the answer."

"Then why did you push her away?"

"Because. Is the answer *that* simple?"

"What do you mean?" Ethan cocked his head.

"Is that what life is about? I've worked so hard all of my life. Does anything I've done or accomplished matter? Or am I like everyone else, and all I want is someone to go home to? Someone to love me? What if she decides one day that she doesn't love me anymore? Then what do I have? What if she decides that I wasn't the person she thought I was?"

"Oh, honey. Is that what's been driving you crazy? You don't feel like you matter to the world? You need to stop thinking on such a cosmic level. Fuck the world! You don't need to be a pre-eminent scholar. Just be you. Why do you try so hard to prove yourself? Stop turning your life into a challenge. Sit back and enjoy it. Sarah wasn't going to leave you if you didn't perform on a grand scale."

"She did love me, didn't she?" I felt tears dripping down my cheek and I looked away so he wouldn't notice.

"Yes, Lizzie, she did." He hesitated. "I'm betting that she still does. What are you going to do about it?"

"My head is spinning." I closed my eyes and pictured her naked, dancing with me in front of the fire. I loved her so much.

"Life is so cruel, Ethan. I thought I was fading away or drowning in the relationship, that I was becoming normal. Buying a house. Settling down into a routine. I was afraid my life would become boring, or like my parents' life. But now all I want is to have it all back. Sarah was the only thing that made sense."

I fidgeted in my chair, not sure if I should get up or stay and finish my train of thought.

Stop running.

"Growing up around my mom and Peter taught me that in order to survive I had to be strong and stay one step ahead. I focused so much on that thought, that I didn't realize not everyone is like them." I let my head fall back and stared at the ceiling. "All my life, my family let me down. Then, when I got sick, I felt like my body let me down. I kept waiting for Sarah to let me down. Ironically, I let her down. And I drove her away. Stability scares the hell out of me." I looked at him. "What's wrong with me?"

"You want me to tell you everything? Or just the top three?"

"Can you name the top three right now?" I smiled and wiped a tear off my cheek.

"You're a workaholic. You are self-absorbed. You always think you're right." He checked them off on his long, effeminate fingers, and grinned.

"Huh. You didn't even have to think about it." I stared out the window. "And I wasn't even referring to any of them."

"What were you referring to?" Ethan flashed a smile. Then he sipped his coffee and grimaced. "Jesus!" He sucked his bottom lip a little. "Too hot."

"Why don't I have more people in my life? I can count on this hand, one hand"—I pointed to my left hand, the fingers splayed—"how many people I care about. I see people, and I know people, who have an endless supply of friends and loved ones they care about and who care about them."

"An endless supply. That's funny." He blew into his coffee. "You have an odd view of human beings."

"Seriously, what's wrong with me?"

"Lizzie, ask yourself if these people with an 'endless supply' really care about all the people they know. There is nothing wrong with being independent and not addicted to collecting Facebook friends, but if you are pushing people away . . . " his voice trailed off.

"Go ahead, say you told me so." I braced for it.

"I would love to. But I can't. I've been fucking up, myself."

Ethan's furrowed brow spurred me to inquire. "What? Is there something wrong with the adoption? With you and Lisa?"

He sat up straight in his chair. "Actually, it's going well." He ran his fingers through his hair. His nails were meticulous. "While you were gallivanting in the Tetons, I was doing a bit of soul-searching. Oddly, I have *The Little Prince* to thank for that." His eyes sparkled.

"The children's book?"

"Yes. I was preparing a lesson and I pulled my copy off the shelf. When I opened it, I glanced at a note I had written to Lisa years ago when I gave it to her before I left for college." His voice faltered and his eyes glistened.

I felt my eyes moisten, watching him. "This is a fine mess. Both of us are a wreck."

He laughed. Then his face became serious. "We have to stop. I know I can't keep coming here each week, bashing my marriage and Lisa. It's—"

"Not helping either one of us. I know. You told me before that I needed to grow up." I squeezed his hand. "I'll always be here for you, Ethan. But you're right. I need to get my life back together, and you need to focus on Lisa."

"And on the baby."

I stared. Everything went quiet. Then all of a sudden it hit me.

"When?" I asked, feeling a sudden rush of excitement.

"Any day."

Ethan looked giddy. He reminded me of the grad student I had met years ago. Full of life. Love.

"Wow!" I sat back in my chair. "Wow."

"I know … I never thought I could be excited about having a baby." He giggled girlishly.

"Oh, Ethan. I'm at a loss … I really do wish you the best."

He removed his glasses and wiped his tears on his starched shirt. "Thanks, Lizzie."

We stood and made our way to the parking lot. I gave Ethan a hug. He held on tight. I stiffened.

"You hug like a man," he teased.

"You hug like a girl."

"This isn't goodbye, Lizzie." He placed his hand on my shoulder.

"Yes, I know. Until we see each other again." I paused. "Maybe we should meet at the top of the Empire State Building in a year."

He chuckled. "And I thought you couldn't be romantic. Look out, Lizzie. Once you release your inner romantic, there's no stopping it." He looked down, into my eyes. "Don't give up, Lizzie. You love her. For once in your life, do not run away."

A couple of days later there came a knock on my door. Few people stopped by my apartment without calling first. My heart jumped into my throat, strangling me. Sarah? Had she liked the flowers I'd sent?

I rushed to the door and yanked it open.

My hopes were suddenly squashed.

Maddie stood there, a concerned look on her face.

"Hi," I said, and invited her in.

She surveyed the place with a glance. "Well, this is a little better than I was expecting."

"What?"

"It's a little messy, but I was expecting a total wreck … dishes and dirty clothes from your trip."

The mess consisted mostly of my books and journals spread all over the coffee table. I was intentionally drowning in work. When work wasn't occupying my mind, it always wandered to thoughts of Sarah. And when I thought about her, it was nearly impossible not to call her.

Maddie walked over to my bike, which leaned against the wall. Since Sarah had left, I had never bothered to hang it up out of the way. Maddie examined the odometer. "You're still riding. That's good news, I guess."

She walked into the kitchen, and I followed. "Have you eaten anything since you got back?" she said as she opened the fridge.

"I've been eating out."

"Where are all of the takeout containers? The leftovers? This kitchen looks like no one has been in it for months. Nothing has been used or is out of place."

I didn't say anything.

"All right, missy, get out of your sweats. We're going to lunch."

I tried to protest, but the fire in her eyes stopped me dead. Quickly, I turned and went to the bedroom to dress.

Within half an hour, Maddie and I were seated at Beau Jo's. Maddie placed our food order and asked for a glass of wine for herself and a rum and Coke for me without even giving me a chance to turn it down. Then she ordered two large pizzas with all the fixings. "You can take the leftovers home."

I sipped my water and avoided eye contact.

"So what are you going to do?"

"What do you mean?"

"Are you going to call her?" Maddie fixed me with a glare.

"She asked me not to."

Her eyes softened. "But you miss her?"

"Of course I do."

"You love her?"

I nodded.

"That is all I needed to know."

I laughed. "Are you gathering intelligence?" I stared out the window at the mountains, so solid, so permanent. I had convinced myself I didn't need that. I was attempting to squeeze out the last drops of my youth. For me, finishing my PhD marked my official entrance into adulthood. I would no longer be sheltered by my student status. It was time to grow up. Happy memories with Sarah slowly flooded my mind.

Maddie put a hand on my arm and I noticed I felt nothing. No frisson of attraction. She was a friend, nothing more. "Stop thinking so much," she told me. "Don't let your brain dictate your life. Open up your heart and chase your dreams. Everybody has dreams, but not everyone has the heart to plunge in headfirst. Take the plunge, Lizzie. You may not always succeed, but you won't die wondering."

Our pizzas arrived. "But don't worry about that right now. I need you to finish your drink so you can have another one."

"Really? Why?"

"You have a wedding to attend, and I'm betting you haven't given a thought to what you'll wear."

"What's wrong with what I'm wearing now?" I smiled.

"That's what I thought." She winked. "After we finish up here, we're going shopping for a dress. If you don't dress appropriately, your mom won't let you in. And you don't want to miss the show."

"The show!"

"Trust me, it won't bore you. Do you think I could get your mom to dance on top of any tables? We could spike her scotch with acid or something."

"My life is bad enough right now. I don't need to be traumatized by a strip show featuring my mother."

"Oh that would never happen. I think she sews those navy suits to her skin." She laughed.

"Can't you just pick out the dress and send it to my place," I whined.

"No! And I don't want to hear any complaints, missy."

"Good luck with that."

"Oh, don't worry. I brought some duct tape. I'll tape your mouth shut. Now I know why Sarah did all of your shopping for you." She passed me a napkin and gestured to the corner of her mouth. "You've got sauce on your chin," she said, smiling as I dabbed at it. After a few quiet moments, she said, "Oh, by the way you have a hair appointment the morning of the wedding. Don't miss it."

She flicked me a card with the appointment date and time. The directions were scrawled in her long, looping handwriting. I sighed and put it in my back pocket. Then I shoved a piping hot slice of pizza into my mouth.

"Now that's a good girl." Her eyes sparkled. I didn't have to heart to tell her that I had been eating all along, gorging even, and that the reason there were no leftovers in my apartment was because my appetite was out of control. I wanted Maddie to feel she was accomplishing something.

CHAPTER THIRTY-NINE

THE DAY OF THE WEDDING FINALLY ARRIVED. WITHOUT SARAH AS MY BUFFER, I FELT MORE OUT of place than ever. Full of nervous energy, I stood outside, staring at the flowers that enlivened the grounds of the posh hotel. Peter had rented all of the rooms of the small hotel to accommodate all of the out-of-town guests. It was located just outside of Denver and specialized in weddings. Maddie had insisted the wedding be outside, rain or shine. Mom insisted that the Californian in her made her want to get married outside rather than in a church. According to The Scotch-lady, Californians were barbarians who preferred living in the wild. Fortunately, the weather was beautiful and the summer flowers were in full bloom.

I stood awkwardly off to the side while the other guests trickled in. Not only did I feel out of place standing there, but I also looked stupid. Maddie had chosen my dress, and while it wasn't taffeta, thankfully, dresses never did fit me right. My left shoulder is an inch higher than my right, so the dress hung on my frame at a slant. To make it worse, I kept catching myself slouching to offset the slant. I felt like a hunchback in pink Chiffon and contemplated scratching like a monkey to round out the picture.

"Hello there."

It was a voice I hadn't heard in weeks. And for the first time, it sent shivers down my body. Slowly, I turned around. Sarah.

She stood there wearing an off-white strapless satin dress, stark against her golden brown skin. She had a sassy new haircut, with highlights, and her neck was encircled by one of the necklaces I had sent her.

"Hi." I paused for a moment, not knowing what to say. Not knowing whether to say what I wanted to. I decided to go for it. "You look fantastic. I love your new haircut."

She blushed, and looked down at her feet. I stared at the flowers behind her, feeling like we were on a second date.

Several seconds passed in silence.

"How have you been?" It had only been weeks since she left, but it felt like years.

She smiled and shrugged. Then she started to laugh, which caught me off guard. "Maddie didn't tell you that she called me last week to insist I come?" She shook her head. "You know, Maddie, she has a way."

I laughed with her. "Tell me about it. I'm wearing a pink dress." I held out a part of the chiffon skirt.

It made Sarah laugh even harder. She had never looked more beautiful.

"By the way, how did she convince you to come? She pouted to make me wear this dress. And she got me drunk."

Sarah's eyes softened, and then she looked at the ground again. "She said you would be lost without me, and that you needed me. Don't worry, I know those were her words not yours; you would never say that." She smiled.

"She's right, though," I said quietly. "I am lost without you."

A few people approached and I played the hostess and directed them to the seating area. Sarah never took her eyes off me and I saw they were wide with pure shock. When we were alone again, she asked bluntly, "Did you mean that?"

"Yes." I stared directly into those beautiful brown eyes. "You know that phrase 'You never know what you have until it's gone.' Well, I learned the true meaning of it."

"Please, Lizzie, this is hard enough. The wedding … you … Maddie. Please don't play games with me." Her voice and eyes were pleading with me.

"I know you have no reason to trust me, but I'm not playing games."

Another couple approached. Sarah and I rushed through polite conversation and then I took her arm and directed her away from the wedding area. Screw being nice to my mother's friends, who couldn't even remember my name. Most of them didn't even know I was a member of the family.

When we found a private spot, Sarah pushed my arm away. "I don't understand you at all. If you felt that way, why didn't you try to call me?" The threat of tears choked her angry words.

"Sarah, you asked me not to contact you. I thought that after all I put you through, I could at least respect your last wish."

"I didn't want to talk to you."

I laughed but stopped myself, and looked at her, suddenly panicked that I had blown it again.

But a smile inched across her cheeks. "This is a fine mess. I'm crying, you look miserable, and your brother is getting married in less than an hour."

"True." I felt like we were in a soap opera. I fidgeted and then came to a decision. "How about we just enjoy this day together? You're here because Maddie gave you a guilt trip. I'm here because I have to be. Let's just make the best of it. At least there'll be cake."

Sarah smiled. "I do like cake."

I took her hand and we strolled back to the guests. A few heads turned, and for the first time, I didn't give a shit. I hoped my mother saw us holding hands at my brother's wedding on my birthday.

Sarah made pleasant chitchat with more arriving guests. She could charm the pants off of the pope, I thought, if he wore pants under his robe.

Out of the corner of my eye, I saw Maddie hiding behind a tree, waving for my attention. I whispered in Sarah's ear and gave her a kiss on the cheek. She smiled and continued making small talk with some of Maddie's guests.

Grabbing my arm, Maddie began to pull me frantically into her room. For the sake of tradition, Peter and Maddie had separate rooms the night before the wedding. Before I could say anything, she blurted, "I'm not going through with this."

I smiled briefly. The thought of my brother being stood-up at the altar pleased me.

"Calm down, Maddie." She was pacing back and forth. I thought for sure she would crash right through the wall.

My statement pissed her off. "Calm down … " She turned on me. "Calm down? Why should I calm down? What a fucking asshole. He had the gall to tell me to get used to it. That she wasn't going away." She kicked a trash can across the room. "What a fucking asshole!"

Dumbfounded, I asked her what she was talking about.

"Like you don't know. Everyone knows. He isn't very secretive about it."

"Seriously, what are you talking about?"

Maddie stopped suddenly and looked taken aback. "You really don't know."

I shook my head.

"He's cheating on me."

It all made sense instantly. That was why he was never home. That was why she would get a forlorn, lonely look sometimes. That was why she spent so much time in Fort Collins. How could I be so stupid and insensitive not to notice? In her hotel room, she said I was more like my family than I knew. Now I understood.

"Honestly, Maddie, I didn't know. I'm so sorry."

"I thought for sure you knew but were too nice to mention it." She collapsed into a chair. "He wants everything to be perfect. A perfect career. A perfect wife. Perfect kids. And a perfect mistress. I was just another piece of the perfect puzzle. He needed a beautiful wife to go with his perfect life. No one wants to marry the mistress. But this isn't the 1800s. Wives don't just look the other way anymore. I'm not your mother."

"What?"

"Really, Lizzie? Are you that oblivious to everything? Your father has been having an affair for years. You can't possibly think he works all of the time." She threw her arms up in the air, exasperated.

"I guess I never gave it much thought." I shrugged. The news didn't affect me. I felt no pity for my mother, no anger at my father. I had cut them from my life long ago. Their actions no longer had any impact on me.

"Peter even told me I should learn from his mother. She had everything she wanted: money, houses, rich friends, expensive vacations. But look at her, Lizzie, she's miserable. I don't want to be miserable." Her eyes screamed bloody-murder.

I wished Sarah were here; she would know what to say. I stood awkwardly and offered to tell Peter the wedding was off.

Maddie looked up at me. "No," she said.

"You don't plan on going through with it, do you?"

She laughed. "No, I don't. But I don't plan on telling him that. Let him stand up there and look like a fool. See how he likes it."

The image was delightful. I smiled and nodded.

"I saw Sarah with you."

"Yes, she told me you guilt-tripped her into coming."

"You really are clueless, aren't you?"

Instead of being offended, I answered, "Yes."

"Don't mess this up, Lizzie."

My confused look must have urged her to continue. "Yes. I guilted her, but she came, didn't she? She came. She still cares. Yes, she wants to make you suffer for a while. But she's a woman; that's what we do. Don't mess this up again. Are you ready to take the plunge?" She hit me in the arm.

I couldn't believe that one minute she was telling me she was not going to get married, and the next she was calling me a moron for ruining my relationship with Sarah.

"I hope not to ruin anything. But right now, what are we going to do?"

"I think I am going to leave."

"Where can I take you?"

"Lizzie, if you go with me, I think Peter will figure it out."

"Um, Maddie, I don't know if you noticed, but I'm not particularly close to my brother, or to anyone else in my family. I don't give a fuck what they think."

She threw me a look of relief and said, "Let me change out of this horrible dress." She rushed behind the changing screen.

"Okay, let me go get Sarah."

She popped back into view. "Bravo, Lizzie. You might not fuck this up after all."

"I hope not." I disappeared out of the room.

Sarah was in the same spot, talking to a new couple. I approached quietly, and when there was a break in the conversation, I excused us and directed her to Maddie's room. On the way, I quickly explained we were leaving with Maddie.

Sarah didn't even bat an eye. "Thank God," she said. "Your brother is such an asshole."

I almost said that it runs in the family, but decided against it. How had I been so oblivious to everything? It astounded me. Ethan was dead-on. I was self-absorbed.

By the time we got back, Maddie was ready to go. She had left the dress hanging in the room with a note that read, "Give it to her."

As the three of us exited the room, The Scotch-lady approached. For once, she didn't have a drink in her hand. She looked naked, vulnerable.

"Going somewhere?" she hissed.

At first, I wanted to tell her to go to hell. Then I looked at her—looked at her properly for probably the first time in years. She looked small. Weak. Sad.

"Mother—" *What to say?* "I didn't know. I'm sorry."

She misunderstood. "Don't apologize. I'm happy to be rid of both of you." She glared at Maddie and then at me. "Really, I thought this would be one of the worst days of my life, but now I've killed two birds with one stone, wouldn't you say?" She cocked one thin eyebrow.

Her ire did not hurt. I felt sorry for her.

I considered giving her a quick hug. Maybe Maddie sensed this, because she yanked my arm away to save me from my mom's reaction if I did.

"That's right, Elizabeth. You better leave with your harem." She clenched her jaw. "It looks like we can have a proper Christmas party this year—just like I've always wanted. With you gone, things can be normal again."

I looked at her and bowed my head. Hopefully, that would make her happy, even if it were a fleeting happiness.

We piled into my car. It was only noon, and it was so nice out that I decided we should go to the mountains. Maddie was wearing jeans and a T-shirt, but Sarah and I were still wearing dresses. Not digging the pink dress, I had packed a bag of clothes to change into at the first opportunity. However, Sarah had planned on heading back to Fort Collins later that night, so had nothing to change into.

I pulled off I-25 at the nearest mall.

"Sarah, I think it's time I bought you clothes for once."

"Why? Where are we going?"

"If it's all right with you two, I thought we could go to Breckenridge for the weekend."

"That sounds fantastic, but I can't use my credit cards, or at least I don't think I can. I'm sure Peter will have them cancelled within minutes of finding the dress." Maddie looked despondent.

"You can count on that. No worries, though. He doesn't have access to mine. And since we are on summer break, Sarah and I don't have any classes on Monday. So we can make it a long weekend."

"I'm supposed to be on my honeymoon, so I don't need to be at work on Monday." Maddie sighed and looked out the window.

When we parked, Sarah hopped out of the car first. Maddie squeezed my arm and gave me an encouraging look. She whispered, "Happy Birthday."

Was my gift Sarah? Or was it Maddie jilting Peter at the altar? Maybe both.

Later that day, the three of us sat at a restaurant in Breckenridge. It was happy hour at The Whale's Tail, and that included ten-cent shrimp and cheap booze. All of us were gorging ourselves on shrimp and beer while Maddie filled Sarah in on the details. Even on the second hearing, I was kicking myself for being so stupid.

When Maddie had finished, Sarah said, "I suspected he was cheating, but I wasn't sure."

"Really?"

Both of them stared at me as if I were an idiot.

"What? Am I just totally blind or am I a fucking moron?"

"Yes," both of them said in unison and then laughed.

Maddie turned to Sarah and asked, "How's Haley?"

"What's wrong with Haley?" I wasn't sure I wanted to know. What if Sarah said they were dating? How would I handle *that* right then?

Sarah ignored me and answered Maddie's question. "Oh, you are sweet to ask. She's doing better. And she got the restraining order."

Maddie looked relieved. I stared at her face and then Sarah's. "What's going on? Why did she need a restraining order?"

"Michael beat her up. I knew it was only a matter of time, but I couldn't convince Haley of that." Sarah looked on the verge of tears.

"Jesus . . . Sarah, I'm sorry. Are you okay?" I placed my hand on hers.

She flicked a tear off her face. Maddie rubbed her back. How in the world did Maddie know about this when I didn't? Then it hit me: Maddie and Sarah were friends. I mean, they must have met up, like Maddie and I did. And I'm betting Sarah never considered that Maddie was hitting on her. Sarah probably knew that Maddie needed a friend and was there for her, like she was for Haley. When Sarah needed a friend, she turned to Maddie, not to me.

"I'm so sorry . . . I didn't know how serious it was. Seriously, I feel like an asshole right now." I squeezed her hand more, hoping she would know how awful I felt.

"You're just extremely self-involved," Sarah said in a loving way, but her voice informed me that it hurt her.

Maddie's cell phone interrupted. She stepped outside to speak to her parents.

When I thought Maddie was out of earshot, I said, "Sarah, you thought Peter was having an affair?"

"Lizzie, how can you be so brilliant and yet so stupid? Of course! It was obvious. You just didn't pay attention. You really should pay more attention to the people around you." She withdrew her hand.

"I don't think I paid enough attention to lots of things I should have. Most importantly: you."

"Wow, you are being honest today, or a sweet talker. Am I a fool to believe anything you say?" She pushed her chair away from the table.

"I've had a lot of time to think." I fidgeted with my beer coaster. "Even Hank doesn't like me right now."

Sarah's eyes filled with tears again. "How is he?"

"He's good. He's been very bitey lately, though. Every time I pet him, he chomps my hand."

"Good! You deserve it." She slapped my shoulder.

Maddie came back to the table. "My parents are going to the house to get all of my stuff."

"Will Peter give them any trouble?" asked Sarah.

Maddie laughed. "Gosh, no. Peter is terrified of my father. He's big in the industry. It's how we met." She paused for a few seconds. "So, does anyone need a roommate, or know anywhere I can stay?"

"Well," I smiled, preparing to divulge my secret. "I'm buying a cabin in Idaho, an hour away from Jackson Hole. You're welcome to stay there for however long you want."

Sarah stared at me. I couldn't believe I'd suddenly blurted this out in front of her. After all the looking at houses we had done together, I went away for a week and bought a place.

Then she surprised me. She laughed. "Hmmm . . . I guess you are capable of buying a home. Or is it less scary if you call it a cabin?"

"Maybe." I chuckled and met her eyes. "Or maybe I liked that it is just a summer home. I'll have to close it up for the winters."

"Why Idaho?" Maddie asked.

"The area is beautiful. The cabin overlooks a lake. Also, I couldn't justify spending millions of dollars for a place next to the Tetons."

She nodded. "Thanks for the offer, but I still have to work."

Sarah stopped staring at me and said, "You can stay with Mom and me. She has a huge house."

Her response stung. I wanted Sarah back home, but the way she said it made me feel as if staying with her mom was a permanent thing. But I couldn't blame her. A few nice words wouldn't wipe away what I had done. The betrayal. It was going to take more. Much more. And it wouldn't be quick. My plan was to persevere and to take baby steps to show her how much I wanted her in my life.

"If you need a car, you can use mine. I'll ride my bike."

"Thanks, Lizzie, but my car is in my name. I insisted on that. And, Sarah, I'll take you up on that offer. Now, let's not talk about that asshole for the rest of the weekend. I'll have plenty of time after Monday to dwell on this. What did I miss while I was gone?"

I raised my beer and hid behind it while I drank. Sarah answered, "Apparently, every time Lizzie pets Hank he bites her." She couldn't help laughing.

Maddie hit my arm, too. "Good. You deserve it. What's this I hear about you thinking of moving out east and not telling Sarah about it?"

I slouched down low in my seat. "It was just an option I was pondering. And I admit, I was an asshole for not telling Sarah about it right away."

"Damn right you were an asshole. Seriously, Lizzie, that's a move Peter would have made." Maddie looked disappointed.

I started to defend myself but thought better of it. She was right. It was a smarmy move. And I was realizing I was more like my brother than I cared to admit. Neither of them had brought up the elephant in the room. How had Maddie convinced her to come to the wedding? Maddie must be more persuasive than I thought possible. Maybe the enormity of Maddie's decision had pushed aside the event from their minds. I wanted to believe that they would forget it entirely, forever. But life wasn't that easy. I was learning that. And I was learning that Maddie and Sarah were the best of friends. I had hit on Sarah's friend. Jesus, I was an imbecile.

"You were considering?" Sarah asked meekly, bringing me back to the conversation.

"I've decided there are other aspects of my life that I need to concentrate on, besides my research and career. For now, that choice is out of the hat." I answered, looking between the two of them.

"Out of the hat? What the fuck does that mean?" Maddie muttered as she shoved another shrimp smothered in cocktail sauce into her mouth. It was hard to believe she had stood Peter up earlier in the day. *Had she planned on doing it all along?* I wondered. If she had, the plan was brilliant, in a crazy, bitchy way. I remembered her referring to the wedding as a show.

"It means that, right now, I am not considering moving. And now I have a place to get away for weekends and stuff."

"So, down the road you may move?" Sarah stared at me earnestly.

"I don't know, Sarah." Having Maddie there helped me open up. Her candor and point-blank questions made me feel good, for once, about answering Sarah honestly. I was finally tired of hiding behind bravado. My family had hurt me so many times that I had started to lie about my feelings to everyone. To Sarah. To Maddie. To Ethan. And to myself. I was like an iceberg, with ninety percent of my real feelings submerged so no one would know how vulnerable I truly felt. I lied so much, and so often, that even I didn't know my true feelings anymore.

"No I don't plan on moving away." I looked at Sarah. "Who knows what next year will bring? But right now, I want to stay put. I have some shit to work out."

Sarah continued staring into my eyes for what seemed like an eternity. Then the muscles in her face relaxed and she looked at peace. "So, ladies, I am in the mood to shop," she said.

Maddie readily agreed, so I settled the bill and the three of us hit the main street of tourist shops. Most charged exorbitant prices for a Hanes T-shirt with some stupid slogan like "Don't Feed the Bears" and depicting a bear holding the sign with the word "Don't" crossed out, but I didn't even mind.

We wandered from store to store, laughing and giggling the whole time. That evening, we had a fancy dinner and stopped at a candy store on the way to the hotel to splurge on homemade fudge. Sarah picked out five different flavors and five pounds of fudge in total. I also bought her some chocolate-covered strawberries, which she had always liked. I couldn't remember ever having bought her any before.

Then we sat in the hotel room drinking wine and eating fudge until shortly after midnight, when we all collapsed with full bellies.

Maddie slept in a single bed, and Sarah and I shared. We both changed separately in the bathroom and then crawled under the covers, both aware of the excessive space between us in the bed.

I reached out and took Sarah's hand. She didn't pull it away.

That was the best day of my life.

On Monday afternoon, I drove Sarah and Maddie to Rose's house. Sarah had arranged for Maddie's parents to drop off her stuff and her car, and all the junk that didn't fit was put into a storage unit. I marveled at how wonderful Maddie's parents were. Not only did they not mind helping out, they actually wanted to help.

Her dad was flying out on the red-eye to get back to work, but her mom was going to stay for at least a week. Maddie wanted to have dinner with both of her folks before her dad left town, so she rushed inside to change.

Sarah sat in the car with me for a moment.

"Does she know where she's going in the house?" I asked.

Sarah laughed. "Yes. Mom and I had her over for dinner a few times." She paused. "You aren't the only one who had secrets." Her voice sounded triumphant, cunning even. It was sexy.

I laughed. I wanted to say, "I'll tell you mine if you tell me yours." But I didn't. We said our goodbyes and I watched her saunter into the house. She stopped at the door, turned, and waved goodbye. I waved back and sat in the driveway, staring at the door she had just walked through and envisioning myself running through the door, scooping her up and kissing her. I really wanted to kiss her.

Telling myself not to be stupid, I grabbed my cell phone and dialed her number. She didn't answer. I closed my cell phone. *Don't be stupid, Lizzie.*

I dialed again. Still no answer. I left a voicemail saying I would really like to take her to dinner sometime.

Then I hung up and sat in her driveway, staring at my phone. She didn't call back.

Later that night, I heard my cell phone vibrate on my nightstand. I rolled over in bed and read the message: *I'll think about it.*

Smiling, I rolled onto my back and stared at the ceiling. She'll think about it. I petted Hank and told him the good news. He bit my hand, and I laughed.

"You will believe in me," I said. "I'll make her believe in me again."

Two weeks passed before I received another text from Sarah. It simply read: *Pick me up Friday night at 7 p.m.*

She didn't ask if I was free. She didn't even ask if I wanted to go. Her boldness turned me on.

I showed up promptly at five minutes to seven and waited in the car with the candy I had picked up for her. At one minute to seven, I got out and walked up the driveway. A slight breeze kicked up some dirt and I watched an empty Coke can blow casually in several different directions.

An urge to run overwhelmed me.

I stopped dead in my tracks.

A car drove by and smashed the Coke can into smithereens.

Chuckling at the timing, I conquered my need to run and continued my journey to the door.

I heard laughter behind the door.

Sarah opened the door. Maddie and Rose stood behind her, laughing.

"We weren't sure you would get out of the car," Maddie exclaimed.

I smiled. Then I handed Sarah the candy. She wore a tight T-shirt and jeans, and her body had never looked so good. She turned to take the candy into the kitchen. While she was gone, her mother said, "Don't make me want to run you over with my car again."

I stood there awkwardly, wanting to explain but not knowing how to, until Sarah came back and we excused ourselves.

"Where are we were going?" Sarah asked as we climbed into the car.

"I thought we would go to dinner in Denver and then catch a late movie. There's a great foreign film theatre near the restaurant. I've heard good things about this French film playing there."

Sarah was fluent in French and loved French films. We never saw them, though, since I didn't like them.

"Really?" I detected excitement in her voice. "I thought for sure we would go to Phoy Doy again."

I guessed she had seen through much of my bullshit in the past, when I had attempted to appease her without really trying.

I smiled at her. "I thought a change would be nice. You might be out late, though. Will your mom send a hit man?"

"Oh, Lizzie, it's not Mom you have to worry about; it's me."

And she was right. It was her. It was finally all about her.

A WOMAN IGNORED

A novel by
T. B. Markinson

CHAPTER ONE

"Lizzie, I think you should sit down." Sarah, my girlfriend — I mean wife (Why can I never remember that?) — motioned to a chair on the opposite side of the room. I did as she instructed.

Sarah, along with her mom Rose, and Maddie, my brother's former fiancée who had ditched him at the altar, sat across from me, staring at me with blank faces. Too blank. They were really trying not to scare the shit out of me. It wasn't working. I started to squirm in my chair like a child sitting in front of the school principal.

"Um, what's going on?" To say I felt uncomfortable would be an understatement.

"We wanted to have a chat with you," explained Sarah with forced nonchalance.

"A chat—oh…" I didn't finish my thought. I feared one of them was sick. Rose? Cancer? I flashed a concerned smile at Sarah's mom.

"No, dear. This isn't about me, but thanks for assuming that, since I'm the oldest." Rose's narrowed eyes suggested she was still pissed at me for something I had done a few years back. Even though Sarah had forgiven me, Rose clearly hadn't, and I wasn't sure she ever would, not completely. Sarah, an only child, was Rose's sole purpose in life.

I looked away. "So, what is this, an intervention?"

I thought my behavior had been on the up-and-up lately. That hadn't been the case when Maddie first entered our lives a few years ago. The year of my brother's engagement wasn't a stellar year for me. Sarah called it my lost stage. I didn't know what I wanted, and I made some stupid mistakes, including trying to seduce Maddie. Sarah left me, rightfully so, and I had to pull my shit together — fast.

Until Sarah left me, I didn't realize I was madly in love with her. I knew I loved her, but I couldn't see how much, let alone comprehend what life would be like without her. Since winning her back, not a day went by that I didn't thank my lucky stars.

Her mother, however, still seized every opportunity to remind me how fortunate I was to receive her daughter's forgiveness. I took Rose's abuse. If I were Sarah's mom, I would have wanted to kill me as well.

"I wouldn't say an intervention…" Sarah turned to Maddie for help.

When I'd hit on Maddie, she put me in my place as soon as I made a pass, slapping me across the face — hard. But I knew that she also felt sorry for me. Maddie knew better than most what it was like growing up in the Petrie family. Eventually, Maddie had helped me realize why I had pushed Sarah away.

Since then, all of us had moved past the unfortunate incident and mended our relationship. Thankfully, Rose never held anything against Maddie; I was the only one she glared at menacingly. Sometimes, when only I could hear her, she imitated a car sound: reminding me of her threat that if I ever hurt her daughter again she would run me over with her Cadillac. She made that threat a few years ago; I believed it then, and I still believed it now. Sarah didn't entirely believe me when I said her mother wanted to mow me down. And sometimes I wasn't sure if I'd actually heard Rose revving a car engine, or whether my guilty conscience caused me to imagine it whenever Rose was around. It was difficult to link Rose—always dressed immaculately, always so put together—with homicidal tendencies.

"Let's just say it's an informational get-together," suggested Maddie, her storm blue eyes twinkling mischievously.

"Yeah, informational." Sarah didn't sound so sure.

Rose gave me a wink, implying I was in for it now. At least someone was enjoying this.

I felt clammy and wondered if my forehead was breaking out in a sweat. I envisioned sitting in a police station, being interrogated by a team of detectives—a light bulb dangling over my head, swinging precariously for added effect.

"Okay, what kind of information involves the three of you sitting across the room staring at me like I'm in trouble?"

"You aren't in trouble," explained Sarah.

"Not yet, at least," said Maddie with a sardonic smile.

"Will someone just tell me what's going on?" I was close to my breaking point, which was never a good thing. I could be an ass when I felt threatened, and I didn't want to take it to that level.

"Lizzie…" Sarah started, and then faltered.

Maddie gave her an encouraging smile.

"Lizzie, I wanted, with the help of Maddie and my mom, to tell you something. Something that I've been wanting for a while."

Wanted? What did she want? She had already convinced me to marry her two years ago and to buy a house together: the two issues that first sent me into the tailspin I explained earlier.

"I want to have a baby."

The room grew silent—the type of silence that fell when a judge walked into a courtroom to pronounce a death sentence.

I opened my mouth, but I couldn't speak. I was fairly certain I had stopped breathing. There I sat, frozen in confusion, words unable to penetrate my feeble mind.

A baby!

What is a baby? Think, Lizzie! You can figure this out. Think! You know what a baby is. For Christ's sake, you have a PhD, admittedly in history rather than biology, but still! Baby—small, right? Cries a lot? Baby!

"Should we get her some water or something?" asked Maddie, obviously concerned, although she never stopped grinning.

"Is she having a stroke?" pondered Rose. The corners of her mouth quivered oddly, making me wonder if she was trying not to smile.

"Lizzie...Lizzie..." Sarah rushed over and kneeled down before me. "Sweetheart, it's okay. Are you okay?" She patted my knee.

"Are you fucking insane!" I sputtered.

"Whew! I thought we'd lost you for a moment," declared Maddie, obviously completely satisfied with my response.

"A baby? What would I do with a baby?" I jumped out of my seat and began to pace. "A baby?"

Sarah laughed and returned to her seat. She crossed her legs. One flip-flop swayed, about to fall from her foot. "Love it, of course."

Oh, of course! Love a baby.

Like it was that easy.

"I know this is a big shock for you. That's why we decided to break the news to you together."

I stopped mid-stride and glared at Sarah. My head spun. I slumped back down in my chair.

"I think this is going pretty well, considering," Maddie told Rose.

Rose nodded. "For Lizzie. She's handling it much better than I thought she would."

"I'm still in the room. I can hear you," I said, snarkily.

All three of them sat there grinning, watching me like I was a three-year-old throwing a tantrum.

Maddie turned to Rose. "Pay up."

"Not yet. This isn't over."

"Mom, what did you bet?" Sarah flashed Rose an accusatory stare and crossed her arms, but I could tell there was no real threat. Sarah enjoyed her mother's feistiness, and why not? She was never the brunt of Rose's spiteful comments or stunts.

"I bet her that Lizzie would faint." Rose, not ruffled at all by her daughter's demeanor, glanced in my direction. "From the looks of her, she still might. She doesn't have any color in her face."

I gritted my teeth and forced an angry puff of air out of my mouth. "And how do you suppose we acquire this baby?" I asked Sarah.

"Acquire? Lizzie, we're talking about a baby—a living thing. You don't acquire one like a sack of potatoes." Sarah laughed nervously.

There was much more to this, and I totally feared what was to come. "Are you suggesting what I *think* you're suggesting?"

"By Jove! I think she's coming around," crowed Maddie.

"For the love of God, Sarah. I'm not getting pregnant."

"You!" Sarah screamed, before breaking into hysterical laughter.

Maddie's jaw hit the floor before she immediately joined in the hilarity. Even Rose cackled some.

"Oh, Lizzie, I do love you. But, you are hopelessly and completely clueless." Sarah wiped away some tears. "I would never ask you to do such a thing."

"So, you want to adopt, then?" I pushed. I might be able to live with that.

"No. You're missing the obvious." Maddie eyeballed me as though her stare might force the right idea directly into my stubborn pea-brain.

"Surrogate?" I whispered, as if it was a dirty word or a despicable concept.

"No, silly." Sarah sashayed over to me and sat on my lap. "I want to get pregnant."

"Oh." I stared, stone-faced. "How?"

"Really, Lizzie? You can't be this stupid."

"Don't underestimate her," said Rose.

I wanted to tell Rose off, but she was right: I was clueless about Sarah's plan.

"Okay, how can I say this? I want to get pregnant using a sperm donor and one of your eggs."

I stood up abruptly, grabbing Sarah before she toppled off my lap entirely and setting her upright. "*My* egg? You want to suck some of my eggs out of *me*. Why would you want *my* egg?" I paced the room again.

"Because I want to have *your* child." Sarah said that like it was the most natural thing in the world.

"B-but, you said it yourself: I'm an idiot…completely clueless. Why would you want to perpetuate my genes? You've met my family. Hateful people. Despicable." I stopped pacing and set my legs firmly apart. "No. We can't do this to a baby. No one deserves that. Not even a baby." I started pacing again, afraid that if I stood still they'd corner me.

"Not even a baby! You're funny." Maddie turned to Rose. "Pay up. She's not going to faint now. She's far too worked up."

Rose sighed and reached for her purse where it lay on the coffee table.

Sarah stepped into my path. Both hands on the sides of my face, forcing me to stop and stare into her eyes, she whispered, "I love you. I want to have your baby."

Speechless, I stood there, staring into her shining chocolate eyes.

"This is so exciting!" Maddie clapped. "I'm going to be an aunt." She rushed over and threw her arms around us both.

Rose stayed seated, smiling. "And I'm going to be a grandmother."

Sarah grabbed one of my hands and placed it on her stomach. "Just think, we're going to be parents, Lizzie."

I staggered backward. Before the room went dark, I heard Rose say, "Pay up, Maddie." I wasn't positive, but I thought she followed it up with, "Timber!"

After I recovered from my humiliating fainting spell, Rose and Maddie left us alone. I lay on the couch while Sarah pampered me, fixing me a cup of tea with extra sugar—even if she had lately forced me to forego sugar altogether—placing a pillow under my head, rubbing my forehead. Maybe I should consider fainting more often.

"Are you feeling better?" she asked.

"Yeah. I feel silly, though." I dipped a shortbread cookie into my tea.

"You went down like a ton of bricks." Sarah stole one of my cookies and plunged it into my cup. "Are you ready for your second shock of the day?"

"Second shock? Are you trying to kill me?" I sipped the tea again, thinking she was joking.

"Not just yet. If I wanted to bump you off, I would amp up your life insurance policy first. Then I'd have to wait a few years, so I wouldn't be a suspect." Her expression was deadly serious.

"Very funny, wise guy. You need to stop watching *Law and Order*," I said, hoping she actually was just joshing.

"We're having dinner with Ethan and Lisa in a couple of hours." She said it casually, as though we had dinner with them all the time; Sarah had only met my best friend, Ethan, for the first time at our wedding. Lisa wasn't able to attend, as their daughter, Casey, had fallen ill. Which meant that I, in fact, had never met Lisa either—and now I was having dinner with her this evening.

"You have been busy, haven't you?" I raised an accusatory eyebrow.

"Why, Lizzie, whatever do you mean?" she feigned ignorance.

"Don't act all innocent. First you set me up today—"

"Set you up!" Sarah cut me off. "You make it sound like I framed you for a crime or something."

"I think having me as a parent is a crime—a crime against humanity." I was only partially kidding.

"Oh, stop it. You'll be a great parent." She tried to placate me with one of her winning smiles.

"Oh, please. How did you get Ethan and Lisa to agree to dinner?"

"I just called him and asked."

"That's it? You didn't have to trick him?"

"Trick him? Why would I have to do that? Have you ever considered that it might be nice to have dinner with your best friend and his wife?" Sarah pinned me with a glare, one eyebrow arched.

Baffled, I replied, "I've never met her."

"You've never met Lisa, not in all these years? How long have you known Ethan?"

"We met in grad school, over eight years ago." People skills weren't my strong suit. In the past, on many occasions, I had been accused of being self-involved.

"You continue to shock the hell out of me."

"You say it like it's a bad thing," I winked. "How long do we have before dinner?"

"Two hours." She peered at me suspiciously, leaning closer. Her ample breasts strained against her tight Broncos T-shirt as she eyeballed me. "Why? Are you going to try to squeeze in a bike ride?" She made no attempt to hide her feelings about that, just sat back away from me, one manicured nail picking at the side seam of her jeans, which were even tighter than her tee.

I was an avid bike rider and generally logged at least twenty miles a day, but bike riding was the last thing on my mind. Sarah looked sexy as hell.

"I hadn't considered it, but now that you suggested it . . ."

Sarah pinched my side and growled, "Don't be an ass."

"Don't pinch me." I rubbed my side dramatically, even though she had barely touched me.

"God. You can be such a baby sometimes."

"Baby," I repeated quietly to myself.

I must have sounded scared to death, because Sarah placed a loving hand on my cheek. "Are you okay? I didn't mean to startle you again."

"No, it's fine. I'm—"

"I know. You don't handle change all that well. We'll go slow, Lizzie. I promise. Just not too slow. My clock is ticking."

I stood up and extended my hand. "Care to join me in the bedroom?" I asked with a suggestive wink. I knew I must have looked a fool, compared to her. I was the type who wore sweater vests, and sweater-vest people weren't usually associated with sex appeal or charisma.

"I suppose," she joked. "Only if you feel up to it."

"Hey, if you aren't interested, I can still hop on my bike and take that ride." I playfully tossed her hand away and started to march to the garage.

Sarah grabbed my arm and yanked me around, kissing me to both shut me up and lure me back. I considered it the best way to be told off, and she had perfectly mastered this shushing technique.

"And, since you're so worried about my health, I'll let you do all the work this time." I kissed her again cutting off any protest.

We sat at a table in a new trendy restaurant in Fort Collins: the kind that served the same food as Applebee's or Chili's but gave each dish a fancier name, a sprig of garnish, and a ten-dollar price increase. Sarah's newest fascination was locating *it* restaurants. Ethan and I usually met at the same coffee shop whenever we got together; however, we hadn't met in ages, not since he and his wife adopted their daughter and Sarah and I got hitched. I had the feeling that this dinner was just one weapon in Sarah's ongoing battle to convince me that having children was grand.

"I still can't believe you haven't met Lisa." Sarah placed a napkin in her lap.

I shrugged while I filled her water glass and mine from the fancy water jug on the table and replaced the glass stopper. The joint had ramped up the hip factor by adding slices of cucumber and weird, unidentifiable green twig things to the water. It didn't look appetizing, but I was thirsty enough to give it a try.

"Never really gave Lisa much thought," I shrugged.

"That's so like you."

"Hey, Ethan didn't meet you until our wedding day, and that's only because he was my best man."

When Sarah and I got engaged, Ethan had joked he should be my best man. You should have seen his face when I asked him for real. I didn't subscribe to the notion that a bride should be confined to a maid of honor. Anything goes at a lesbian wedding. Ethan actually cried during his toast—well, we all did. Of course, I later refused to admit that I had cried, too. To this day, I swear I had something in my eye.

"Do you even know what she looks like?" probed Sarah.

"Now how would I know that, given I've never met her?" I pulled my best "don't be an imbecile" face and took a sip of the water, bracing for something horrible. "Hey, this isn't bad. Refreshing, actually." I pulled the glass away from my mouth to inspect it for weird objects swirling inside like sea monkeys. Not seeing anything unusual, I took another swig, enjoying the flavor.

"You've never seen a picture of her?" Sarah ignored my antics with the water.

I wasn't the type to check out social media to find out what people looked like. "Nope." I rubbed my chin, feeling a hair that needed plucking. I tugged at it. I scratched it unsuccessfully. "Ethan showed me a picture of the kid, but not the wife." I wondered if Ethan had a pair of tweezers with him. I knew for a fact that he carried fingernail clippers. Would that work?

"What's the kid look like?"

I whispered, "She's black." Then flashed my *only joking* smile. Sarah knew their child was black; she also knew I didn't give a hoot about race, color, creed, or any other hoopla.

Sarah laughed. "You're impossible. And completely self-involved."

"Oh no, not that one again." I winked.

"You're in a good mood, considering." She ran a finger up my thigh.

"Considering you nearly killed me today with your announcement."

"Come now, it can't have been that much of a surprise. Do you remember when we purchased the house—the real estate lady and I kept searching for a house with a nursery, and one that was close to a school." Sarah looked smug.

"I thought you meant a nursery for plants, and you teach high school—how was I supposed to put those clues together?" I leaned over and gave her a peck on the cheek.

"Careful, you two, you might scare the homophobes." Ethan's voice was louder than normal, slipping into the Southern accent that he typically tightly controlled. A woman sitting nearby pursed her lips, looking downright insulted that Ethan had classified her as a gay basher.

I stood and gave Ethan one of my best "man hugs." Hugging or touching people, besides Sarah, made me extremely uncomfortable.

Ethan stepped to the side and motioned to his wife.

I had expected Ethan's wife to be frumpy, considering all the conversations he and I had engaged in about him not wanting sex with her. He hated body fluids, which made sex an uncomfortable obligation for him, rather than something he enjoyed. Knowing that, I assumed his wife would be ugly as sin, a woman desperate to have a partner, any partner, in her life. I was wrong.

Dead wrong.

I nodded at the stunning, slender redhead who stood before me. Back in my single days, I would have made a complete fool of myself trying to impress Lisa.

Ethan must have sensed my thoughts, because he flashed me a knowing smile.

Sarah came to my rescue. "It's so lovely to meet you, Lisa."

Sarah, who had no issues with hugging or bodily fluids, threw her arms around Lisa, who was about three inches taller, and gave her a welcoming squeeze. I shifted awkwardly from side to side before putting my hand out for a handshake.

Lisa didn't seem insulted at all; she almost looked as if she expected me to be ill at ease. Ethan had prepared her well, no doubt.

I motioned for the waitress, so we could place our drink orders. Sarah ordered two bottles of wine. "I'll be on the wagon soon, so why not?"

"Did you know that on the wagon comes from the days when they hanged people in England? Prisoners were allowed one last drink on the wagon that transported them to the gallows." I smiled, proud of my ability to share such a fascinating and random historical tidbit.

"I take it you dropped the bomb," said Ethan matter-of-factly.

"What is that supposed to mean?" I directed my question to Sarah.

"Only you would refer to having one last drink before being hung, today of all days." Sarah patted my cheek tenderly. "And to answer your question, Ethan: yes. We told her this afternoon."

I whipped my head around to glare at Ethan. "You knew!"

Ethan was nonplussed by my accusation. Over the years, he'd become quite used to my idiocy.

Sarah shook her head at me before turning to Lisa. "You have the most stunning hair. Oh, how I would love to have hair like yours."

Lisa blushed. "I've always wanted straight hair. We should trade. People don't know how hard curly hair can be."

"It takes her hours to get ready each morning." Ethan tsked, but his eyes beamed as he admired his gorgeous wife.

Again, I wasn't expecting that. He obviously loved her. For years, I'd thought he was a miserable man trapped in a horrible marriage; now I knew it was his aversion to fluids that drove him mad, not his wife. Maybe I had been too self-involved. Maybe I still was? How could I not know this about my best friend?

I picked up my menu, disappointed with the selection. I wanted simple, like bangers and mash from my favorite restaurant in Fort Collins. I was excited to see they offered mac and cheese until I saw it came with lobster. Why would I want lobster with mac and cheese? Could I order the mac and cheese and ask them to hold the lobster? No, Sarah would not appreciate that. I opted for the filet mignon. It sounded fancy but essentially was just a hunk of meat with roasted potatoes on the side.

Sarah actually ordered the mac and cheese with lobster and I was relieved I didn't make an ass out of myself by saying, "Hold the lobster, please" like a child. Ethan followed my lead and had the filet. Lisa ordered short rib tacos.

"Oh, I saw Bobby Flay make red chili short rib tacos just the other day on the Food Network, and they looked divine," said Sarah.

I tried not to roll my eyes when she said divine.

"So how did Lizzie take the news?" Ethan grinned.

I could tell he was bursting at the seams to humiliate me.

"Oh," — Sarah flashed me a devious smile — "as expected. She fainted."

Lisa looked concerned, but Ethan immediately burst into a gale of laughter. Sarah joined in, encouraging Lisa to finally push her concerns aside and laugh along.

I had never enjoyed being the center of attention, especially when I was the brunt of the joke.

My chair scraped the tiles as I stood, somewhat dramatically. "Ethan, let's go out for a smoke."

"Lizzie! You don't smoke," exclaimed Sarah, who occasionally smoked but quit for good recently — right around the time she cut me off from sugar. Were those clues I missed?

"Didn't you tell me the other day that I should pick up some new hobbies? No time like the present." I stormed off.

Ethan joined me outside after a few moments. I sat on a bench in the middle of Old Town and observed the full moon, which illuminated the dark as if we were in a creepy Hitchcock film. The sky in Fort Collins always seemed endless, because no tall buildings obscured the view. I remembered being in New York City a few years back, feeling trapped by the skyscrapers.

Even though it was a beautiful spring night, the town center was deserted, giving me the heebie-jeebies. On occasions like this, I always wondered if the apocalypse had happened without my knowing.

"So, you're going to be a mommy." Ethan pulled out a cigarette and handed me his pack of Marlboro Lights. I didn't intend on actually smoking…but on second thought, why not give it a go? Ethan bowed slightly to light my cigarette. Inhaling, I waited for the coughing fit, given that was what happened in the movies. I didn't cough; instead, I whacked my chest as if I had a neurological tic.

Ethan placed one foot on the bench and leaned closer. I stared up into his eyes, inquisitive behind his thick glasses.

"I guess so," I replied.

He sat next to me and slid an arm around my shoulders. "I know you're freaking out, and you're trying hard not to, considering your past with Sarah." Ethan gave me a squeeze. "What you're feeling is normal. Give yourself some time."

"What happens if I don't change? How can I do this to a child?" I sucked on the cigarette and then whacked my chest again.

Ethan chuckled. "I've never seen anyone have that reaction to smoking for the first time before." He blew out a perfect smoke ring. "I know you, Lizzie. You're stubborn, selfish, and annoying."

"Thanks for kicking me while I'm down, buddy."

"I wasn't finished. But, deep down, all of those qualities are for show. You're a loving person and you feel weak when you show your true self. You need to learn that's not a weakness but your greatest strength."

I sat there, speechless. The silence was killing me. "Wow, what's in these cigarettes?" I pointed it at him. "Because that's the biggest crock of shit I've heard in some time." I tried to laugh but couldn't.

Ethan ignored my childish attempt to avoid the heart of the matter.

Both of us sat motionless except for our hands, smoking and admiring the moon.

Finally, Ethan stood. "We'd better go back in. Not sure we should leave our wives alone for too long. Who knows what they're plotting?"

As I walked back in, I saw the worry in Sarah's eyes. Ever since we had got back together, I sensed she was constantly waiting for the other shoe to drop—for the old Lizzie to reappear and take over for good. The look in her eye was like a swift kick to the shin.

Ethan, being the perfect Southern gentleman, pulled out my chair. "Well, now. I think Lizzie is a natural at smoking."

Sarah leaned over and sniffed me. "You *did* have a cigarette!"

"Today marks a new beginning." I raised my wineglass. "To getting pregnant!"

Sarah almost fell out of her seat, but she quickly recovered and grabbed her wineglass, clinking it to mine with "Cheers."

Ethan gave me an encouraging smile and Lisa looked puzzled. I wondered what Ethan had told her about me.

"So how does this work?" asked Ethan, immediately turning three shades of scarlet. "I mean, whose egg are you using?"

I stopped myself from making a joke about Ethan not knowing the first thing about the birds and the bees, considering his troubles.

"Lizzie's egg, of course." Sarah glowed with happiness.

"I heard getting an egg extraction hurts like hell," Ethan said. "More than actual labor." He winked, but it didn't put me at ease.

"Hey now, don't discourage her, Ethan." Sarah swatted his arm as if they were lifelong friends, even though I could count on one hand how many times they had interacted.

I tugged on my shirt collar, feeling stifled and, to be completely honest, terrified. Lisa noticed. I couldn't discern whether she felt sorry for me or for the child.

My child.

Our child.

Shit.

How did this happen?

Looking at Sarah's face I knew how it happened. I loved her more than I thought possible. And no matter what, I was determined to love our child.

Later that night, Sarah opened a bottle of champagne she had put on ice before we left for dinner. The woman was always prepared, yet it still amazed me. Cold nestled over the city, and I lit the fireplace to combat the nip in the air. We sat on the sofa near the fireplace, with Sarah huddled against my chest, sipping the bubbly.

"Thank you, Lizzie."

"For what? Lighting the fire?" I was enjoying the extra pizzazz that pomegranate seeds added to my drink.

"No. For keeping an open mind. I know I took you by surprise today."

"I'll say. It's been a while since I fainted." I rested my chin on her soft chestnut hair.

"When was the last time? Yes, when we signed the mortgage papers. Later that night you had the worst panic attack, and then — boom! — out cold on the floor." Sarah chuckled over the memory.

"Hey, you don't have to enjoy the memory that much."

Sarah sat up, gazing into my eyes. "Besides the minor incident today, you've handled it much better than I thought you would. You actually seem open to the idea."

"I'm not sure if I'm there yet."

Sarah pulled away from me.

"Wait, don't do that. Come here." My arm over her shoulder pulled her back. "I love you, and I would do anything for you. But you have to understand: I need time to get used to the idea. I have inner demons to battle, mainly my own crappy childhood. I won't lie. I'm petrified."

"And that's exactly why I think you'd make a great mom. You're scared of letting your child down. Not many people feel that way in the beginning, or ever."

"Well, most people don't have our luxury."

"What do you mean?"

"We get to plan when we want to get pregnant. No oopsies. I imagine most parents are scared for different reasons."

"I had thought of that—getting pregnant and then telling you."

"You wouldn't dare! Would you?" Even to me, my voice didn't sound confident.

"Unfortunately, it'd be hard to get one of your eggs without you noticing." She peppered my neck with soft kisses.

"Are you sure you want my egg? Who knows how my genes will play out?"

"Don't worry. We'll use mine for our second child."

I shot off the couch. "Second child!" My heartbeat skittered like a trapped animal.

Sarah sat on the couch, a mystifying look on her face; then, the most beautiful smile illuminated her eyes, and all of a sudden I felt calm.

"That's my girl." Sarah drained her champagne. "Now take me to bed. Let's put your nervous energy to better use. Enough baby talk for today."

CHAPTER TWO

SINCE FINISHING MY PHD A FEW YEARS AGO AND BEING TECHNICALLY UNEMPLOYED, I HAD woken up early every day, including Sundays. I wasn't the loafing type, not even after I quit teaching. Once I acquired my doctorate, I concentrated on my true passions: research and writing. I published my first book within the first year of not teaching, and I was working on my second. As much as I had loved teaching, I enjoyed researching and writing more. And my trust fund allowed me to do just that.

By five each morning, I was itching to hop out of bed. That morning, Sarah was dead to the world, as usual. She taught high school English, a frustrating and draining job, so I didn't want to disturb her. I knew how much she loved sleeping in on Sundays.

By the time I got on my bike, the sun was making an appearance. The birds were already announcing the start of a beautiful morning. The chill in the early spring air gave me instant goose bumps. No matter, within ten minutes I'd be warm and riding along Poudre River on my favorite bike trail. Not many people were out, so I felt like I had the river to myself. The water gurgled on my right, and on my left I could see a fox scurrying off to bed. Frost speckled the wild grass, the sun illuminating each strand and making the ice glimmer like gold. Only in nature did I feel this relaxed. Not once had the baby issue popped into my mind. It was as if yesterday hadn't happened. All I felt was tranquil.

I didn't notice much of anything—until I realized I was pedaling past Laporte High School. Glancing at my watch, I saw that it was still early, and I was famished. I decided to head up the road and pop into Frankie's for breakfast. The diner's claim to fame was having the best cinnamon rolls in Colorado, and I agreed wholeheartedly.

After locking my bike outside, I slid into a booth in the back. The waitress was obviously a morning person—or was damn good at pretending she was. Her dishwater brown hair was piled high on top of her head in an old lady bun. Makeup caked the cracks of wrinkles, and her leather skin clocked too many hours in the sun.

"What can I git ya, sugar?" Her raspy, smoker's voice belied the youthful flicker in her eyes.

"Tea and a cinnamon roll, please. Oh, can I also have a big glass of ice water?" I shook my empty water bottle.

"Sure. Looks like you can use it. Are you riding through the canyon after this? Now that the weather is warming up, we've seen loads of bicyclists and motorcycles."

I almost shouted yes, but then thought better. It was tempting. I loved riding in the canyon, but I knew that if I avoided Sarah today, of all days, she'd flip out.

"Nah, I'll head home after this. Too many things to do today," I lied. I had nothing to do. Maybe I'd take Sarah to Denver to catch a foreign flick and then head to Sixteenth Street for dinner. I was still adjusting to not being in school. Sure, researching and writing was demanding, but my schedule was mostly determined by me now, not by professors. I enjoyed the freedom. Occasionally, I was invited to colleges and conferences to speak, which satiated the teaching bug that reared its head from time to time.

The waitress nodded and waddled to the beverage area to prepare my tea and water.

I thought I felt my cell phone vibrate in my pocket. Surely I was imagining it. Who in her right mind would be calling me this early on a Sunday? Just to be safe, I pulled out my phone. Sure enough, I had a text message from Sarah. Odd—usually she called.

"Where are you?"

I texted that I was at Frankie's, having a cup of tea.

"I'll meet you there."

I read the text a couple more times. Why was Sarah up this early on a Sunday? Did she think I was freaking out about yesterday? Actually, I was feeling pretty smug about it. Sure, I had fainted, and then almost fainted again when she mentioned using her egg for our second child, but other than that, I was handling it pretty well. For me, at least.

I told her I was fine, not to worry, and I'd be home soon.

Again, she texted that she was on her way to meet me at Frankie's.

Wow. And she said I had trust issues. Jeez Louise, I only went out for a bike ride, like I did every other day of the week. I wasn't freaking out. And I didn't like the insinuation that I was. So in the past I hadn't handled things all that well. Okay, I had tried to sabotage my relationship with Sarah by attempting to seduce Maddie, who was not only my friend but also my brother's fiancée at the time.

I bobbed my head, understanding how bad that sounded. And it was. But did it warrant always being reminded of that every time something monumental happened in our lives?

Had her announcement shocked the hell out of me yesterday? Hell yes!

Had I fainted? Check.

Had I acted immature? Somewhat.

But had I gone over the edge? Not at all.

That was a good sign for me.

The waitress set my cinnamon roll down in front of me.

"Thank you," I said, smearing melted butter all over the top. There was nothing like a Frankie's cinnamon roll on a spring Sunday morning after a beautiful bike ride.

Why did my girlfriend—*fuck, I mean wife*—have to ruin it for me? Shit, she acted like I hadn't changed one iota.

By the time Sarah strolled into Frankie's, I was ready to give her a piece of my mind. Seriously, she had to stop treating me like a delicate flower that might go to seed each time something popped up. But then I spied Maddie, hot on Sarah's heels. They both looked blank, like something had happened. Something bad. Did someone die?

All I wanted to do was enjoy my Sunday morning. I looked down at my half-eaten roll and selfishly thought about asking them to wait until I had finished. Wasn't there a rule: no bad news on a Sunday before nine?

The two messengers sat down at the booth, and I motioned to the cheerful waitress to bring two cups of coffee.

"Righty-O. Coming right up!"

"How was your bike ride?" Sarah didn't look me in the eye; instead, she fidgeted with the drinking straw in my water glass.

"Very enjoyable. A bit crisp, but a gorgeous start to the day." I tried to maintain a happy demeanor, hoping the two doomsayers wouldn't panic about the news they had to break to me. I was trying—maybe too hard. I saw Maddie give Sarah a worried glance.

"That's nice. You'd think that after two years you'd be able to sleep in past five."

I smiled—unhappily, but doing my damnedest to be convincing. Happy as a clam. A clam that was ready to snap its shell shut and ignore whatever news they brought. Wait—was that what they were worried about?

Pull it together, Lizzie.

"So, why are you two out of bed so early on a Sunday?" Maybe if I just kept thinking or saying the word "Sunday," the happy-go-lucky feeling would stick around, no matter what.

"Peter called me," said Maddie.

Peter? My brother, and her ex-fiancé. Hey, maybe this news wasn't about me at all. Maybe Maddie was having a bad day and she needed me. Things were looking up—for me, at least. I took a cheerful bite of my cinnamon roll and motioned for Sarah and Maddie to help themselves. Neither did. Shit! That was bad.

"What's up with Peter?"

"He wanted to let me know something, so I could tell you." Maddie leveled her gaze on me.

"Why didn't he just call me?" Ever since I had left the wedding with Maddie when she jilted him at the altar, my brother hadn't spoken to me. Not that we were close before that, but his obvious avoidance since then still irritated me. I wasn't the one who ruined his relationship; he was. He'd been having an affair, with no intention of ending it, even after Maddie found out. I was sure that in his warped mind it was all my fault. My family blamed me for everything.

Lizzie the Les-Bi-An destroys all in her diabolical homosexual path.

"Well, you know that's not going to happen." Maddie crossed her arms. "He has to talk to me. He has to play nice so my father won't ruin his career."

"My father can ruin his career as well." I said, even though I felt childish. Peter and my father were in the same business: finance. They made shitloads of money while I was content making a lot less but doing a job I loved. My mother hated that about me. She never could understand why I loved studying history. Dead people didn't pay much.

"Yeah, but your father doesn't like you." She smiled to offset her bluntness.

"Thanks, Maddie, for keeping it real. So, what's the news that has you two so worried?" I motioned to their faces with my fork.

"Worried? We aren't," Sarah said, in her "pretend everything's fine" tone.

"Uh-huh. That's why you look like I'm about to go off the deep end. Go ahead, just tell me." I mentally prepared myself for the annoying tidbit about my family, something that would make my skin crawl. To say I was the black sheep was an understatement. If I didn't look so much like my brother, I would have demanded a DNA test to prove I wasn't related to anyone in the hateful Petrie clan.

"Your mom's sick." Maddie stirred the coffee the waitress had just placed in front of her; I suspected only because it gave her something to do, since she hadn't added any sugar or cream.

"Like the flu sick?" I couldn't see the big deal. It wasn't like I was about to rush out of Frankie's to whip up a batch of chicken noodle soup for my mom—the woman I liked to call The Scotch-lady since that was the only beverage she ever consumed.

"Actually, it's a bit worse than the flu." Sarah jumped into the fire.

Worse than the flu? Well, I hated colds more than the flu for the simple fact that colds lingered for days, if not weeks. The flu made you shit your pants or puke up your guts for a few days, and then it was done. I preferred that.

"Can one of you give it to me straight?"

"Okay—" Maddie looked to Sarah for help.

"She has cancer, Lizzie."

I gazed at Sarah, not comprehending. My mom was one tough broad. Nothing could kill her. Cancer and my mom didn't add up. I mean, if Death arrived on Mom's front doorstep, she'd let out a hiss that would make him tremble and tell him to crawl back to hell.

Cancer?

Cancer—and my mom?

No, simply not possible.

"Breast cancer?" I probed.

"No. Colon."

Of all the cancers, she would get colon cancer.

Jesus, Lizzie. Stop being such a heartless bitch.

This was not the time for asshole jokes.

None of us spoke. Their expressions told me it was true, but I was having a hard time digesting it.

The big C.

I was never close to Mom, that much was true; yet I wouldn't wish this on my worst enemy. Cancer didn't mess around. Before I was diagnosed with Graves' Disease, I was tested for cancer. And I was scared shitless. Seriously! I didn't intend for that to be a pun.

Fuck!

The word echoed inside my head, even though I sat mute at the table. Sarah and Maddie passed questioning looks back and forth.

Finally, I broke the silence. "Did they catch it early?"

Maddie shook her head. "I don't think so. You know your mother. Peter said she refused to go to the doctor, even though he kept encouraging her to."

"So there's no hope?" Damn it was hard to keep my voice from cracking. Why was it so hard? I wasn't close to my mother, but that didn't stop me from feeling like my whole world was crumbling down around me.

"Your father wants to have a chat with you." Maddie didn't take her eyes off her coffee. She continued to stir. Did she feel less helpless staying busy?

"Peter called you to give me the news and to have you set up a meeting with my father, is that the gist of the phone call?"

Maddie nodded.

Sarah put her hand on my arm. "Are you okay?"

I looked at her, confused. My reply sounded like it came from far away. "I don't know," was all I could say.

My father wanted to meet at a restaurant near his work, not at home. I wasn't surprised, considering I wasn't a frequent guest. I knew where they lived, of course — I grew up there — but I wasn't itching to visit, and they weren't itching to have me over for dinner; up until this point, that had worked well for all involved.

My father sat in the bar. The lights were dim, and a small candle flickered on the table, which sat between two leather chairs. Even in the gloom, I could see that he was troubled. He stared down at his bourbon, the glass containing the honey-colored liquid gripped in both hands. Dad looked old. My dad, Charles Petrie, had always given the impression of a businessman who was used to being in charge, used to being right. Now, my father looked feeble. His wrinkled three-piece suit suggested a confused man. His scarlet tie was tugged loose, and the top button of his blue silk shirt was undone. I couldn't ever remember seeing my father's tie loosened so haphazardly. I spied pink pages tucked into the side of the chair. He didn't even have the energy to read *The Financial Times* while waiting for me.

"Hello." I slipped into the leather chair opposite, feeling underdressed in jeans. I knew the establishment, but I still hadn't been able to bring myself to dress appropriately — not that the staff minded. The clientele was a mix of business people and other, more down-to-earth folk like me, family members of the professional types.

"Hello, Lizzie. Thanks for joining me this evening." Dad sat up straighter, cultivating the illusion that he was in charge.

I nodded. Was this going to be a business meeting? Item one on the agenda: your mom has cancer. Item two: what's new with you?

Dad swirled the bourbon in his glass. A waiter approached and asked if I would like anything to drink. I ordered an Earl Grey.

"If you would like a drink, I can have Matthew drive you home."

Matthew was my father's driver. About ten years ago, my mother insisted my father must have someone drive him to and from work. It was a ridiculous notion, but my father didn't put up much of a fight. Maybe he enjoyed the peaceful ride. I pictured him with a cup of coffee in the morning, rustling through *The Financial Times,* and then sipping bourbon on the evening leg while checking his emails. My father always worked. His downtime was reading financial reports. International finance never stopped; neither did Dad.

"Is it that bad?" I asked. Maybe I would take him up on the idea. I wasn't the type of person who could have one drink and be fine to drive. A whiff of alcohol made me feel tipsy.

"It's not good. Do you know anything about colon cancer?" He sounded tired, beneath the businessman composure.

I shook my head and poured milk into my tea.

"At first, the doctors weren't too alarmed. She had a colon resection —"

I cut him off. "Resection? As in removal?"

"Yes. They removed seventeen centimeters."

I turned my head to the side and let out a long breath. "I didn't know she even had surgery."

Dad looked as though he was about to say something unpleasant, but he swallowed some bourbon instead. "Peter didn't know about it at the time, either."

That was so my mother. She wouldn't want anyone to know she was sick or having surgery, let alone of the colon. I bet she was even pissed off about the word itself — "colon." Prim and proper, that was my mom. I wondered if she'd insisted on wearing one of her navy suits throughout the procedure. Imagining her in a hospital gown was. . .well, it was unfathomable.

"Was the surgery successful?" My voice sounded small, which made me flush, heat creeping up my neck.

"Yes." Dad took another sip of liquid courage. "And no. It's metastasized in her liver. She has Stage Four colon cancer."

"How many stages are there?" Four didn't sound great, but was it out of ten?

"Four."

I rubbed my forehead, shielding my eyes. Come on, Lizzie, don't lose it in front of him.

Him.

I didn't want to cry in front of my father — how fucked up was that?

Dad leaned all the way back in his chair and placed both arms firmly on the red leather armrests. His knuckles were fish-belly white. "I know you and your mother haven't always seen eye to eye."

Like, never.

"But I know she needs you right now." He stopped, staring over at me to ensure I was looking at him. "And I need you."

Now they wanted me to be a part of the family. It was suddenly okay to invite the lesbian back into the family fold.

Shit no! I didn't want to forget everything and play the loving, dutiful daughter.

Actually, that wasn't a fair assessment. My father spoke so rarely that I never knew whether he was bothered by the fact I was a lesbian. My mother always spoke her mind. She made it very clear that having a lesbian daughter was the worst thing that ever happened to her. My father? Well, I didn't know him at all. To this day, I couldn't tell you whether he was religious, Republican or Democrat, or anything personal about him.

"What do you need?" I couldn't stop the words from escaping my mouth.

"I've hired a nurse to take care of her at home. But your mom doesn't want the nurse to take her to and from appointments." He squirmed in his chair; it didn't become him. He was too serious a man to fidget. Clearly, Mom's illness was getting to all of us.

"She has her first appointment next week, but I'm sure she'd like to see you before then."

I didn't think my mom wanted a friendly chat. She wanted to make sure I would toe the line, act like a doting daughter. All she ever cared about was keeping up appearances.

The last time I saw my mother, I had just learned that my father had been having affairs for most of their marriage. I felt sorry for her, briefly. After some thought, I realized she put up with it so she could be a rich man's wife and enjoy all of the glory that went with it: money, vacations, social status. She cared more about what other people thought about her than she did that the man supposed to be closest to her was a cheater. Some days, I felt sorry for her; others, angry.

Now, sitting across from my father — the cheater — I didn't know what to think. It wasn't like my parents had ever been a doting couple. I can't remember them ever acting like they were in love, or like they were even friends. It was always business in our home. Appearances mattered above everything else.

When I came out as a lesbian, my mother went into a tizzy. Before, she tolerated me somewhat. I wasn't the best daughter, but I wasn't the worst either, in her opinion. Mostly, she put up with my weaknesses, such as being shy, an animal lover, an environmentalist, and a historian. It wasn't as if she was kind to me. She was not a kind woman. But, after I came out, it was all-out warfare.

And now my father had the gall to tell me my mother needed me. I wanted to tell him to fuck off. How dare he? How dare my mother? Why couldn't Peter, the favorite, take her to appointments? Peter, the good son, the one always idolized in our family. The one who went into business, not history. The one who would settle down, marry a respectable woman, and have grandchildren my mother could brag about at the country club.

If Sarah and I had a child (or when, I guess), I had no plans to tell my parents. No way would I put my child through what they put me through. I gritted my teeth.

But now that Mom had cancer, it was supposed to be a game changer. I would come back home. I would be the good daughter.

Fuck that.

Stage Four colon cancer. Why did this have to happen?

I wanted to scream, to throw my teacup across the room, to stomp out of the place and forget all about them. They sure hadn't ever tried to track me down just to say hi, not even when my book was published. I didn't get a phone call saying, "Congrats. We're proud of you."

Ignored.

That was all they ever did. Ignored me. Swept me under the rug.

"Would you like to order another drink?" The waiter broke the silence.

My father motioned for more bourbon. Then he shocked the hell out of me. "Would you stay for dinner? I could use the company."

I nodded and ordered a gin and tonic; then I excused myself to call Sarah and ask her to pick me up. The drive would take her more than an hour, and I figured we'd be done with dinner by then. Dad wasn't one to linger after a meal.

My father and I sat at a small table, out of view of the entrance. My mother would have shit a brick if the hostess had tried to seat us at a table where the Petrie family couldn't be seen, together. My father was different. He enjoyed the best of the best, but he liked to be out of the spotlight. I started to realize how different they were. And how much I was like my father.

We didn't chat much, and Dad barely touched his rack of lamb after it arrived.

"Are you okay to drive?" he asked as we exited the restaurant. "Matthew wouldn't mind."

"Thanks, but my w—" Shit! I almost said my wife. Most days, I forgot she was my wife, but tonight, of all nights, I'd called her my wife. "Sarah is picking me up," I rushed to cover my mistake. I had consumed two more gin and tonics over dinner, and the lights outside were starting to blur.

Dad placed a hand on my shoulder. "I always liked her. A beautiful woman. Intelligent."

I stood there, dumbfounded. Never had my father acknowledged a woman I was involved with. He'd met Sarah on a few occasions, but I didn't remember him ever speaking with her. Now he was speaking about her.

Dad put his hand out, and I shook it.

Were we sealing a business deal?

Then he walked away, to his car. Matthew held the door open, and my father disappeared into his domain. Matthew nodded at me before getting behind the wheel and pulling away from the curb. I stood on the sidewalk, near the valet stand, waiting for Sarah to pull up.

When she did, I noticed Maddie was in the car, too. She hopped out, gave me a hug, and put her hand out for my keys. "We thought it'd be easier to drive your car back tonight, instead of coming back in the morning. Where are you parked?"

"Thank you," I said, pointing to my car. Why hadn't I thought of that?

Maddie threw me a quizzical look. "Must have been an odd dinner. You okay?"

"She has Stage Four colon cancer." They were the only words I could think to say, as though no other words in the world mattered.

Maddie nodded and led me to the passenger side of Sarah's car.

"How are yo—" Sarah started, but I shot her a look that told her I didn't want to answer an unanswerable question.

Okay? Who would be okay right now?

My mother despised me, and I reciprocated; yet she had requested that I take her to all of her doctor appointments. Why? I rubbed my face with both hands, hoping that when I opened my eyes, everything would be clear. Sarah placed her hand on my knee while she waited for Maddie to pull out. I opened my eyes slowly. Clarity didn't return.

Soon, we were on I-25 heading north to our home in Fort Collins. All I wanted to do was crawl into bed. All I wanted to do was forget everything.

Sarah's alarm trilled.

I pictured her groaning and slamming her hand down to silence the alarm's shrill intrusion. She wasn't much of a morning person. She never understood why I habitually hopped out of bed early to ride. This morning, though, I wasn't on my bike. I sat at our kitchen table, nursing a lukewarm cup of tea. On the drive home last night, all I had wanted to do was crawl into bed. However, once there, I couldn't stop my mind from bouncing all over the place, rendering sleep impossible.

I decided to be useful and set about making Sarah a cup of coffee. She was still in the shower by the time it was ready, so I carried it into the bathroom and opened the shower door to say good morning. She needed more than a sip of coffee to jumpstart her brain in the morning; Sarah was usually a zombie until her second cup.

"Jesus Christ, Lizzie!" She placed a hand on her chest and sucked in a breath. "You scared the crap out of me."

"Sorry. Just thought you'd like some coffee." I raised the cup so she could see the vapors, mingling with steam from the shower, enticing her.

She shut off the water and wrapped a towel around her body, stepping out and placing a kiss on my cheek. "Thank you." She took the cup from me and gave it a greedy slurp. "I thought you were out riding."

I waved the idea away. "Couldn't sleep so I got up late. I didn't realize the time until I heard your alarm."

Her face softened, as if struck by the memory of picking me up last night, after my dinner with my estranged father. "I'm sorry. Is there anything I can do for you?"

I wanted her to stay home from work, but I knew she couldn't. Sarah hardly ever missed a day of teaching. Shaking my head, I said, "Not really."

She let her towel drop and walked toward me, hips swaying seductively. "Nothing at all?"

Sometimes, when I looked at Sarah completely naked, I had to pinch myself; this was one of those times. "You might be late," I teased.

She kissed my neck, her lips still wet from the shower. "I'll drive really fast," she whispered, pushing me backward into the bedroom.

We tumbled onto the bed.

As it turned out, to fall asleep all I needed was a roll in the hay. I vaguely remember Sarah getting up afterward, rushing around, getting ready. Before she left, Sarah flicked a strand of hair off my forehead and replaced it with a tender kiss.

A few hours later, my phone beeped. Even rubbing my eyes with the palms of my hands couldn't clear away the fogginess. When my eyes finally focused, I checked my text messages.

"You have twenty minutes to get ready."

Maddie — letting me know she was playing hooky and she expected me to join her.

I grunted. All I wanted to do was to stay in bed all day. I set my phone aside, intending to ignore her. My cell beeped again.

"I'm not kidding."

"Jeez, Maddie," I muttered as I pulled myself out of bed and into the shower.

She arrived five minutes early, brandishing a Starbucks chai latte.

"Thanks." I ripped the cover off and sucked in the delicious steam. "What time did Sarah call you to check on me?"

"Suspicious much, Lizzie?" Maddie's hands formed determined triangles on her hips.

I tilted my head, waiting.

"As soon as she left. She said you didn't sleep at all last night."

"Couldn't turn my brain off."

"You finally found it, then." She smiled and arched an eyebrow.

"Oh, so funny." I took a long swallow. "Well, since you're my babysitter today, what's the plan?"

"The zoo."

"You've got to be kidding. I'm not five," I jeered.

"Have you ever been to the zoo?"

Maddie had me there, and she knew it.

"So don't knock it until you try it. Besides, once you have a kid, you'll need to know how to get there."

Kid. I'd completely forgotten about the baby Sarah wanted. Shit! How must Sarah be feeling? Overwhelmed? Or disappointed? She'd announced she wanted to get pregnant, and then, all of a sudden, Mom reenters my life with colon cancer. What rotten timing.

Would Sarah wonder whether I'd planned this somehow? Or whether I was fibbing, that none of this was real. No. The outlandish thought made me smile.

"That's the first time you've smiled at the mention of your child."

Maddie looked so impressed with herself that I didn't have the heart to confess the truth. Instead, I steered the conversation to a topic I knew she loved. "Can we grab some breakfast first? I'm ravenous."

She gave me that knowing smile of hers. "Did you two get naked earlier?"

"Maddie!" I stormed out of the room, calling for Hank, my cat, to say good-bye. Not that he cared when I came and went, as long as his food dish was full and his cat flap was open during daylight hours. But even after we moved to a quieter neighborhood, it took me weeks to trust him on his own outside.

When I returned to the kitchen, Maddie was still giggling. She and Sarah could talk about sex all day, and often did around me. Not me. Maddie told me once that Peter was the same way: he couldn't discuss it. I think I went into shock. Who in their right mind wanted to know they were as sexually repressed as their brother? Sometimes, I thought Maddie brought the subject up to distract me. This morning, it was working.

I fidgeted in the passenger seat as we traveled back to Denver to go to the "magical" zoo that was meant to take my mind off my disaster of a life.

"It's okay, you know," Maddie said.

We hadn't spoken for miles, so I had no clue what she was talking about. "What is?" I placed my empty chai cup in the holder.

"Feeling conflicted, about your mom?" She tapped the steering wheel in tune with the radio.

I stared out the window. I did my best to concentrate on some cows coming into view in the distance. If I didn't, tears would fall. "I don't know what to think or feel. All night I wondered why I couldn't feel sad. I mean, I am sad, but I'm not devastated." I leaned against the headrest. "I'm such a crappy person."

"That's true, but not about this, at least." Maddie's voice gave no indication whether she was teasing or not. She could be a difficult person to read. She had a knack for saying things that, in her Southern tone, could mean anything.

I opened one eye and saw her smile. "Thanks."

"Let's face it, Lizzie. Your mom would never win any Best Mom awards. You haven't spoken to her since the wedding, and now, all of a sudden, she wants you to be there for her. It's fucked up."

"So you wouldn't do it?" I felt hopeful.

"Oh, no. I'd take her." Maddie took her eyes of the road briefly to make eye contact. "No matter what, she's your mom. Maybe this experience will be good for you two. If you turned your back now, I know you'd let it tear you up inside."

"Why is it I only feel two emotions around my mother: guilt and anger?"

"Families. Gotta love them."

"I need to pee."

Maddie cocked her head, insinuating she knew I was using it as a diversionary tactic. To my surprise, she didn't object. We pulled off at the next gas station. I hid in the bathroom for several minutes, feeling silly. A gas station bathroom wasn't the best place to gather one's thoughts. Before I was ready, I stepped outside.

The sun blazed above. I couldn't help but feel a tad excited about the zoo. The Petrie family didn't do the regular family things: zoos, soccer games, bowling, movies. Maybe having a child with Sarah would give me the chance to experience the things I'd missed out on as a child. Goodness knows Maddie and Sarah wouldn't let me miss out on those types of events. Was I ready to spend every weekend doing something new? Would Sarah insist on taking tons of photos and then spending hours scrapbooking, like she had after our wedding? I had only just recovered from all of that insanity.

Maddie honked the horn and stuck her head out the window. "Move it, or lose it."

I laughed. Was she serious? I was pretty sure Maddie wouldn't actually mow me down in the gas station parking lot? But knowing her, I decided not to press my luck.

Turned out, otters were the most adorable creatures I'd ever seen. I stood outside, watching one little guy float on his back and slam a rock into a clam. I couldn't get enough. Two more chased each other in the water. Maybe this was why Mom had never taken me to the zoo: it'd prove to her that I was completely hopeless. For Mom, animals weren't cute; they were a nuisance. I wouldn't be surprised if she signed a petition to do away with all animals and zoos.

Maddie stood off to the side, talking on the phone with one of her clients. It always amazed me that she could be away from the office and still manage to get work done. If I didn't lock myself in my office at home, I wouldn't accomplish a thing.

My latest research project—the role young women played in the Third Reich—was fascinating, but I still often found myself staring out of my window instead of pouring over my books, researching, or writing. My publisher had pitched the idea after I completed my book on the Hitler

Youth, the Nazi version of the Boy Scouts. For the most part, women, especially young women, had been excluded from the history books during that time period.

Oh God, if my mother found out about my new project, she'd be irate. "So now you're a feminist, too! It's not bad enough you're a lesbian. You have to be the voice of Nazi women. Nazis! What will they say at the club?" The opinion of the ladies at the club was all that mattered to my mom. Did they know she was sick? Let them take care of her.

I was so busy having this mental discussion that I jumped when Maddie tugged on my shirt.

"Come on, let's check out the baby animals."

When we exited the zoo, I asked Maddie if we could stop at the Tattered Cover bookstore in Cherry Creek. I had spent many a day there when I was in high school. The store was massive, with so many wonderful nooks and crannies that a book lover could get lost there and completely forget about the outside world. On most visits, I went straight for the history or audiobook section. Today, I had a different mission: parenting books.

If nothing else, today had proved I was clueless. Shit! I hadn't even been to a zoo before! At thirty years of age I was, until very recently, a zoo virgin. My child deserved better. I considered asking Sarah to go bowling later.

Maddie appeared around the corner, a stack of books piled in her arms—mostly chick lit and romance. All of the covers were either pink or purple. "I've been looking everywhere for you, but never thought to check here." She eyed the shelves, but said nothing.

"Research," I said, ashamed I couldn't admit the whole truth. I was terrified I'd be a shitty parent—just like mine. "Are you ready? Sarah should be home in a couple of hours."

Maddie nodded and followed me to the registers.

"You busy tonight?" I asked Maddie as she pulled the car off the highway, onto Harmony Road in Fort Collins.

"Why? What do you have in mind?"

"I thought the three of us could go bowling." I said it as if we went bowling all the time.

"Bowling?" she chortled. "Oh, this I have to see." Before I could change my mind, Maddie hit a button on the steering wheel and the phone started dialing. Sarah's number on speed dial, I guessed. Maddie always made or answered hands-free phone calls to and from clients while driving. "Sarah, Lizzie wants to take us bowling."

"Are you in the car?" Sarah replied. I could sense a smile in her tone.

"Yes, so I can hear everything you say," I said. "Go ahead and laugh. Maddie already did."

I heard muffled laughter. "I'm not laughi—" she couldn't get out the rest of the word.

"Shall we meet you at home?" Maddie said.

"Ye—" More giggling.

This was going to be a long night. Why had I thought it was a good idea? Could I really squeeze a whole childhood into one day?

CHAPTER THREE

SEVERAL DAYS LATER, I PULLED MY NEW SUV INTO MY PARENTS' DRIVEWAY. SEVERAL MONTHS back, Sarah had insisted we needed the car. I realized this was another clue I had missed.

It was eleven in the morning, and I knew my father would be at work. Mom's condition wouldn't change his work routine, not one bit. More than likely, Peter would continue his seventy-hour working weeks as well.

I had tried calling Peter to talk about Mom. He finally responded to a text and told me she'd more than likely be home on Tuesday. More than likely. She had cancer. Did Peter think she was out on the town, shopping?

I sat in the car, deciding what my next move should be. I felt chickenshit. My instincts screamed at me to put the car in reverse. To tell everyone that I had stopped by but Mom was out. Simple as that. I tried, really tried, to be there for her, I could say, appeasing the guilt. Maybe I could even actually convince myself that I had tried.

My hand started to pull back on the gearshift. All I had to do was pull it back to R. My nanny used to say, "R is for rocket." As a kid, I spent more time in cars with Annie than I did with my own mother. It was probably safer that way, since my mother was hardly ever sober.

Why should I be there for her?

Because she has cancer, you douchebag.

I put the car in park again and opened the door.

Just get out of the car. Baby steps, Lizzie. Baby steps.

Goddammit, just go and ring the front doorbell. You're better than this. Just fucking do it.

I trudged up the front steps and raised my hand to press the bell, suddenly realizing how ridiculous it was that I had to ring the bell to enter my parents' home. I grew up here. Why didn't I just walk in?

The thought angered me. I turned around and started back to the car, stopping abruptly when I heard the front door open.

"What'd you want?" My mother bellowed.

Shit! Now I looked like a coward: the exact image she always had of me.

I turned around slowly, snapping my mouth shut so I wouldn't look completely asinine. "I just —"

"Oh, it's you. I thought...well, it doesn't matter." She waved an arm limply, erasing her thought.

"Hi. I just stopped by to say, well. . .hi." I shifted nervously from one foot to the other.

She looked twenty years older than the last time I had seen her. She wasn't wearing one of her usual navy pinstripe power suits; instead, she wore royal-blue silk pajamas and a matching robe. I couldn't remember ever seeing my mom in pajamas. I was under the illusion that she slept in her skirt and crisp white shirt.

"Do you want to come in, or do you want to continue standing outside, looking foolish?"

Mom still had a way with words.

Keep it together, Lizzie. Remember she has cancer, for Christ's sake.

"Thanks. You look good, Mom."

"I hope you're a better historian than you are a liar," she scoffed.

I gawked at her. She turned her back on me, and led me to the family room. I hadn't been in the Petrie family home for years. Besides a new coat of paint on the walls, everything looked the same. An overstuffed burgundy leather couch with matching chairs took up most of the front room. Off to the side of the fireplace stood a small bar, home to several crystal decanters. The coffee table was glass, and spotless. A book sat on the floor by one of the leather chairs, and I was shocked when my mom nestled down into the chair. Was she reading a book? I knew she could read, but I couldn't remember her ever reading much. I glanced at the cover and almost fell over. It was a copy of my book.

"Would you mind making me a cup of tea?" It was a question, but her face told me it was also a demand.

"Uh, sure." I needed to be alone for a moment or two, to pull myself together. My mom had not only purchased a copy of my book (and not many people had), but she was also actually reading it! Why? A book on the Hitler Youth wasn't exactly uplifting material for a person dealing with chemo treatments. Then again, maybe she liked depressing, survival-of-the-fittest shit at the moment. It did fit her acerbic personality.

I placed the teapot, cups, creamer, and sugar bowl on a silver tray and carried it into the front room. "I wasn't sure if you wanted milk and sugar."

My mom nodded. "Yes."

I fixed her a cup and handed it to her, making sure I didn't forget the saucer.

She didn't say thanks, just sank further into her chair. It engulfed her, diminishing her meanness. I glanced down at the floor and saw that the book was now out of view. Had she shoved it under the chair or tossed it in the trashcan off to the right of the room?

"Peter called," I started, not knowing where to go with that conversation.

"I assumed. It's not like you to stop by." She sipped her tea without flinching, even though I knew it was blistering hot.

I poured more milk into my cup.

"Oh, you made yourself a cup."

I couldn't tell from her expression whether she had meant to say that out loud, or whether she even noticed she had verbalized the thought. How dare I enjoy a cup of tea? My mother never wanted me to have an easy life. She despised that my father had set up a trust fund for me. She made it perfectly clear that I was an undeserving disappointment—a humongous stain on her happiness.

And now I had waltzed into her home and helped myself to her tea supply. Lizzie the Les-Bi-An strikes again.

I didn't respond. I was trying to be the bigger person. "How are you feeling?" I asked eventually.

She sighed, nostrils flared. "How do you think I'm feeling?"

Mental note: don't ask The Scotch-lady how she feels.

"I—"

"Don't pretend you care. I'm sure Peter told you to visit, to say your piece so you wouldn't have to live with guilt and all that hippie crapola Oprah preaches about. So you did. Don't expect me to be grateful. I don't need pity. Not Peter's. Not yours. No one's."

Hippie crapola. What decade was this? And didn't Oprah retire or something?

I ignored her tirade. "Will you have someone looking after you…when you start your treatments?" I already knew the answer, but I couldn't think of anything else to say.

"Yes. Your father hired a nurse. That's who I thought was at the door." Her voice dripped with revulsion at "father."

I could tell the war hadn't ended. My parents didn't scream or shout at each other, but they did things to each other that hurt like hell—like not being there when your spouse was undergoing chemotherapy.

I shuddered at the thought of living my life with someone I hated. Neither of them ever mentioned the D-word. Divorce didn't happen to nice families like ours. My mom's definition of a nice family was a wealthy family.

Mom had no siblings to help her out. I was sure Peter would stop by every evening, but he wouldn't actually do anything to help. My father and my brother preferred to hire help to deal with things they didn't want to do personally. But Mom wasn't a chore—or, at least, she shouldn't be. Regardless, being around her was hell. I wasn't about to offer my time to take care of her. Maybe I was just as bad as the other two.

"Is there anything I can do for you?" I asked.

"Yes, I would like some books to read. The one I'm reading now—it's so dry." She turned dry into a two-syllable word.

I didn't flinch. "Okay, what type of books?"

"Whatever's popular these days." Her eyes dulled. She'd already lost interest. I think she only mentioned the idea so she could take a dig at me.

"Anything else. Food?" I almost asked if she wanted me to pick up some scotch, her favorite drink. Actually, until today, I don't think I'd ever seen The Scotch-lady drink anything else.

"No. We can afford to have our groceries delivered," she barked.

Another dig. I could afford it as well, but we opted to do our own shopping.

"Sure." I guzzled my tea. "I'll be back soon." I needed to get out of there before I lost my temper.

"Wait." She shifted in her chair. I could tell she was having a hard time keeping her eyes open. "Why don't you bring the books by tomorrow, or the next day?"

Shit. I had hoped this would be a one-time thing. Surely my father didn't expect me to chauffeur Mom to all of her appointments and spend "quality" time with her.

The Scotch-lady's eyes flickered with an idea. "Actually, next Wednesday. Then you can take me to my appointment."

Holy shit. Did she just ask me to take her to her appointment? From her demeanor earlier, I assumed it was my father's idea for me to take Mom to and from her appointments and that she wasn't on board or didn't know about the plan. But she was on board.

Jesus, I wasn't ready for this. I just wanted to buy the bitter woman some books, appease my guilt, not be her nurse, or her daughter.

"Sure, I can do that. What time?"

"Nine." She forced her eyes open. "So be here at eight, since you're always late." Mom closed her eyelids once more, and I knew sleep would overtake her soon.

I didn't bother saying good-bye; it would be superfluous. I had been dismissed, as if I were a member of the household staff, but not before I was given my orders: buy books and take Mom to her appointment.

My one problem—well the most pressing concern, at least—was finding books my mom would like to read. I felt as though it was a test. Most of the books I read were about Nazis, but Mom made it clear that not only was my book a letdown, but also that my specialty was too dull for her.

I needed help.

Ethan and Sarah were English teachers. I shot Ethan a text asking if we could have a coffee date at Barnes & Noble in Fort Collins. His town, Loveland, had no bookstore, and Fort Collins was only a ten-minute drive from his house.

What types of books would a crabby woman with colon cancer read? I suddenly realized I didn't know. I did not know the first thing about my mother. If Sarah asked me to buy her a book, I would know exactly what she'd like: sappy, something with a pink cover. But my mom? I had no fucking clue.

My SOS worked. On Saturday afternoon, Sarah and I sauntered into the coffee section in Barnes & Noble on College Avenue and found Ethan, Lisa, their daughter, and Maddie waiting for us. Ethan and Maddie were embroiled in a comical conversation, and Maddie was trying not to choke on her latte. Ethan gently patted her back, doing his best not to pee his pants over her antics. The woman didn't suffer quietly.

"Anyone need a refill?" I asked, gesturing to their coffee cups before slipping into the line to order drinks for Sarah and myself.

Usually, I couldn't stand waiting in line, but I didn't want this one to end. Once it did, I would have to start searching for books for a woman who had given birth to me—that was pretty much all I knew about her. I felt like I was meeting my biological mother for the first time. It wasn't far from the truth. Mom didn't give me away at birth, but she did basically give up on me shortly thereafter.

Thirty years later, she was dying. It took her getting cancer for me to recognize that I didn't know my own mother, and that I might want to learn more about her.

I slumped down into a chair, ready to face the book inquisition.

"So, give it to me straight, how screwed am I?" I stared at each blank face. The only one not paying attention was Lisa. She was busy entertaining Casey, who was three-going-on-sixteen. The child wore a princess outfit including sparkling gloves, a tiara, a boa, and a wand. God, I really hoped Sarah and I had a son. How would I handle my kid dressing up like a Disney princess in the middle of spring? On Halloween, I could live with it, maybe.

"What did you tell me once" — Ethan knitted his brow and his Coke-bottle glasses hitched up — "your mother has no qualms about ripping the heads off kittens."

"Yeah, I'm toast." I slurped my chai.

"Now hold on you two. Let's not get all dramatic. I think it's wonderful that your mom wants you there." Sarah plastered a supportive grin on her face. It was phony as hell, but I appreciated the effort.

Maddie looked away and started humming the theme song from *Jaws*, making Ethan giggle uncontrollably. Maddie laughed so hard she had to excuse herself and step outside. I watched her wiggle her arms frantically and wipe the tears from her face. Before returning, she checked her reflection in the glass door to ensure her mascara wasn't smudged.

Casey climbed into my lap, as if it was the most natural thing in the world. "Do you like Ariel?"

"Ariel?" I asked unsure if that was a real word.

"The Little Mermaid," explained Ethan.

"The what? The statue in Copenhagen?" Why did they name her Ariel? It didn't sound Danish to me.

"Seriously, Lizzie. You're such a dork sometimes," Ethan shook his head in amazement and smoothed the top of his perfectly styled hair.

"Ariel — from the Disney movie." Lisa pushed a book into my hand and spoke slowly, as if I was the three-year-old here.

Sarah observed me closely, concern etched on her face. I was sure she was realizing I needed some major education about raising kids. Would she come home tomorrow with a bunch of Disney movies for me to watch?

"Read to me," Casey demanded as she snuggled against my chest.

Ethan raised his eyebrows over the rim of his glasses.

"That's a great idea." Maddie obviously saw it as an opportunity. "You read to Casey, and the rest of us will look for books for your mom. I'm pretty sure she doesn't want anything that would catch your eye."

Everyone but Lisa stood. Ethan gave an almost imperceptible shake of his head, and Lisa reluctantly left her child with me: the person who didn't know Ariel.

Casey tapped the book, and I started to read it aloud, although as quietly as possible. I didn't want the entire store to think I was a loon. Two minutes in, Casey hopped off my lap and began to wander in the store. I followed, uneasy about her wobbly legs, eyeballing strangers who might be child-stealing kooks. People smiled as she weaved in and out of the crowd. I gave each one a curt nod and then got back to my guard duty. There was no rhyme or reason to her meanderings.

Spying the children's section in the back, I swooped Casey up in my arms. "Let's go play."

"Yippee!" she shouted, tapping me on top of the head with her magic wand and giggling madly. I wanted to throttle Ethan for saddling me with his demented fairytale kid.

On the way, a book caught my eye. I grabbed it off the shelf.

I had never set foot into the children's section before. Maybe I had when I was a kid, but I had no memories of ever being there.

The place was a disaster. A cursory glance revealed seven kids running amok. Two of them crashed into each other—hard. But not hard enough for either of them to start crying, I noticed. Then I noticed they had light sabers, but they weren't using them Luke Skywalker style. Instead, they were jousting like medieval knights. One of the knights noticed Casey in my arms.

"The princess is here!" Both of the boys bowed dramatically.

Casey clapped her gloved hands together and somehow managed to wiggle magically out of my arms.

"The enemy, your highness, is attacking!" said one little boy—I mean "knight." He raised his light saber and shouted, "Charge."

The other boy followed suit. Casey squealed in delight.

Seconds later, she was distracted by a massive dollhouse, leaving the two knights, who didn't even notice that their highness had forgotten about them, to fight it out. They were already trying to overthrow another boy, who was hiding behind a beanbag.

The scene was chaos. I was certain I had never acted like these buffoons a day in my life. Did they have any decorum? And their parents, where were they? All I could see were employees doing their best to tidy up after each wave of children blew through like a tsunami. To their credit, the employees didn't look mad. I would be grabbing kids by their ears and throwing them out of the kids' section—*wait a minute, Lizzie. You can't throw a kid out of the kids' section.*

What was wrong with me? Sighing, I sat down on a miniature chair next to Casey.

"Would you like a cup of tea?" She'd now forgotten all about the dollhouse in favor of a tea set perched on the table in front of her.

"Uh, sure."

Her caramel eyes glowed as she pretended to pour me a cup. "Sugar?"

I nodded.

She prepared her own cup and sat down at the undersized table. The chair suited Casey, was designed for her even, but my knees jutted up above the table. I felt like an ogre.

"We went hiking this morning. Do you know what hiking is?" Casey tilted her little head, curious.

"Um, yeah sure, it's when…" Why in the world couldn't I answer a simple question? I hiked all the time. It wasn't a foreign concept to me.

"It's when you walk on dirt," she stated matter-of-factly.

I sat there, astounded. What a simple definition. Kids really got to the heart of the matter. *Walking on dirt.* I chuckled, and raised my tiny cup of pretend tea to my mouth.

"Next week, we're going to my grandparents." Casey was a chatty kid.

"That's nice. Do you like your grandparents?" I had no clue what else to say.

"I'm going to puke in a bucket!" she shouted with glee.

I looked around for a bucket. "Do you feel okay?"

"In the car. I'm going to puke in a bucket!" Again, Ethan's daughter looked thrilled with the idea of puking in the bucket.

"She gets car sick." Ethan sat down at the table with us, grinning at the sight of me sitting at a kid's table and enjoying a cup of tea with his daughter.

"May I?" I motioned to the teapot.

"Yes, please." He ruffled the top of Casey's head, beaming at his princess.

I pretended to pour him a cup. "One lump or two?" I held out the tiny sugar bowl.

Casey giggled.

"Two, Miss Lizzie."

Casey sniggered some more. I had to admit it was catching. Trying my best not to join in, I bit my lower lip.

Ethan raised the cup and feigned burning his tongue.

"You're silly, Daddy." Casey was out of her seat like a shot. The knights were back, fighting for her honor once again.

"How's the book hunt?" I queried as I fished in my messenger bag for my bottled water.

"Oh, I think you'll be impressed by the stack. Maddie keeps trying to sneak in erotica, but Sarah is dealing with her."

"Who sent you: my wife or yours?" I crossed my arms. I knew he was checking up on me, not on Casey.

"Mine."

I raised an eyebrow.

"Okay, they both sent me. They were worried." He flicked the pages of the book sitting in front of me on the table. "I don't know why." He grinned.

I glanced at the cover of the book: Mein Kampf.

"Not many people sit in the children's section reading Hitler's manifesto." He suppressed a chuckle by tugging on one corner of his expertly manicured moustache.

"I saw it on the way in, and I remembered I needed to check something."

"A Mein Kampf emergency?" His expression was pure amusement.

"Very funny, wise guy. Sarah made me get rid of my copy, so this seemed like a good time." I shrugged.

He let out a loud guffaw. "You really are a piece of work. Just be careful. Don't get arrested."

"Hardy har har. By the way, she's kinda funny." I motioned to Casey.

He rolled his eyes. "Wow, that was charming."

"No, I mean it. Did you know that hiking is walking on dirt? She asked me to define it and I couldn't, but she had the definition without even thinking about it."

"Kids are like that. They see things how they really are." He smiled at his daughter, who was sprinkling pretend fairy dust over the knights. "It's a shame we lose that."

"I'm not sure I ever had that."

He smiled wryly. "You? Probably not."

"I'm not sure I can do this," I warbled. "Since all of you abandoned me, I've been a nervous wreck, afraid I'd break your child or something."

Ethan placed a hand on mine. "Sure you can. Just don't think about it. If you overthink it, you'll drive yourself crazy. It'll be the best thing you've ever done. Trust me, Lizzie. And if you don't trust me, trust Sarah. That woman loves you more than you deserve."

I couldn't help but laugh. "Thanks, buddy."

"Just keeping it real for ya."

A boy dressed as Spiderman came crashing into the kids' section, running full speed before throwing himself against the wall.

I was too stunned to move or speak. No one in the room reacted. The other kids ignored him. His parents, or the people I assumed were his parents, gazed around the section and then turned to leave their insane child with all of the other innocent children, and me.

The parents paused and waved to Ethan, who gave a friendly wave back.

"Do you know them?" I whispered.

"Yes. Why are you whispering?"

"I sure hope that doesn't happen to our kid," I whispered again.

"What?" He jutted his chin out, waiting for my answer.

"You know." I fidgeted on the small chair and nearly fell out. "Having a *special* child."

Ethan burst into a fit of laughter. "Nate isn't special. He's just a boy."

"Who thinks he can scale a wall like Spiderman! Did you see the way he threw himself at the wall and then bounced back three feet? No normal person would do such a thing."

Ethan shot me a serious look. "What about Casey, do you think she's special?"

"What? No! Why?" My voice cracked more than I cared to admit.

"She's dressed as a princess."

"Uh…that." I gasped for air.

"Lizzie, calm down. I was just giving you shit." He smiled, relieving my stress a little. "Kids are kids. You can't explain what or why they do things. But you need to loosen up."

I glanced over at Casey. She was chasing Spiderman, having the time of her life. I just didn't get it.

By the time we left the store, I had eight books for Mom. Maddie tried to sneak in Fannie Flagg's *Fried Green Tomatoes at the Whistle Stop Café* at the last moment, but Sarah was watching her hawkishly. As the cashier rang up the books, I saw *Tipping the Velvet* fall into the bag and gave Maddie the evil eye.

"It's for me," Sarah explained.

I assumed the lesbian parenting books were also for her. I hadn't shown Sarah the books I bought the day Maddie took me to the zoo.

I better make sure none of those accidentally slip into my mom's pile. I'd never hear the end of that. I could hear her now, "Oh great, Les-Bi-Ans raising a child. Just what the world needs—more gays."

After Barnes & Noble, Sarah had plans with her mother, so I opted to go for a bike ride. My legs, however, weren't into it, or maybe my mind wasn't. After five miles, I turned around and headed for home. I plopped down on the sofa, flipped open my laptop, and picked up my cup of Earl Grey.

For some reason, the image of Casey in her princess outfit popped into my mind. Who did she say she was? Ariel.

I googled Ariel.

Being a nerd, I read some articles on *The Little Mermaid*. Turned out Ariel was one of Disney's most iconic characters, based on a Hans Christian Andersen fairytale, and I didn't have a fucking clue. How could I consider becoming a parent if I didn't know Ariel? Shouldn't I know that? God, I was going to be the worst parent ever.

At least I'd recognized Spiderman, although I still couldn't believe the way that little boy had thrown himself into the wall. How did he think that'd turn out? Could the child be so clueless that he actually thought he could scale a wall like Spiderman? Were boys really that stupid?

Hank jumped into my lap and swatted at Ariel on my laptop screen. Purring, he started to rub up against her. Shit! Even my cat knew more about Disney princesses than I did.

"That's it, Hank, we're going to watch *The Little Mermaid*." I streamed the movie from Netflix. If everyone else on the planet knew about this chick, so would I.

I paused the movie during the opening credits. If I was going to watch one of the most iconic Disney characters of all time, I wanted to be in the right mood. I zapped some popcorn in the microwave, grabbed a bag of M&Ms from the pantry, and settled down in front of our new sixty-inch HD TV, which Sarah had insisted we buy last week. Sixty inches! If you'd asked me before last week whether we needed such a large TV, I would have laughed in your face. But after one day, I was hooked. Usually, I read at night while Sarah watched TV or graded papers. But this week we had settled down on the couch to watch movie after movie. And Netflix—what a brilliant idea. Thank God I didn't have this TV and Netflix when I was in grad school, or I wouldn't have finished my program.

A thought struck me. Did Sarah think I'd have the time or inclination to take care of the baby while she was working? My heart started to flutter. I felt all the blood drain out of my face.

Get a hold of yourself!

Closing my eyes, I counted to ten like my therapist had taught me. I calmed myself down.

Then I hit play and lost myself in the movie.

"Are you watching *The Little Mermaid?*"

"Shit!" Sarah's voice scared the bejesus out of me. I placed a hand on my heart. "Are you trying to kill me?"

"I'm sorry, I didn't mean to startle you." She laughed over my antics, as though I was being playful. I wasn't. If I had heard her coming in, I'd have turned the damn movie off. Now I'd never hear the end of it.

"Jeez, you could have knocked or something."

She shook her head disapprovingly. "Why would I knock to enter my own home?"

"To give me some warning."

"Why, do you plan on having an affair?"

The word "affair" hung in the air. Neither one of us knew how to handle the situation.

Finally, I joked, "No, but when I'm watching crap TV I would like some notice so I can shut it off before you arrive."

"*The Little Mermaid* is not crap!" Sarah crossed her arms, ready for battle.

"Well, it's not good for kids. Do you know the chef dude says *merde*? That's *shit* in French. How can parents let their kids watch this trash?" I felt silly saying it. Of course Sarah knew; she was fluent in French, after all. She was constantly dragging me to Denver, to her favorite theater, to see foreign films. The theater was fancy, serving cocktails and scrumptious desserts, so I didn't complain too much.

I refused to admit that I actually thought *The Little Mermaid* was pretty darn cute for a cartoon, let alone that I was on my second viewing. Next time I saw Casey, I planned to give her a run for her money. I'd show her who was an expert on *The Little Mermaid*.

Sarah motioned for me to raise my legs so she could sit down on the couch. "Lizzie, has anyone ever told you to lighten up."

"Not in the past five minutes."

"I can't believe you don't love this movie. I remember seeing it when I was a kid."

"Have you seen it since then? I bet you don't like it now."

Okay, how shameless was I? I didn't want to admit I had wanted to watch it again, so I concocted this plan. Pitiful!

"I bet I do!" She tapped my legs playfully.

"Bet you don't." Was I pushing too hard?

"Well then, go make more popcorn so I can prove you wrong."

As soon as I stepped out of view, I gave myself a high five. Instead of making popcorn, I decided to put out some cheese, chorizo, and crackers on a plate, and then I uncorked a bottle of wine. I hummed as I prepared the food, which wasn't like me one bit. I wasn't sure where the inspiration came from.

"Liar!"

I looked up to find Sarah propped against the kitchen doorframe. "What? I'm sorry. I thought this would be better than just popcorn."

"Not that." She sauntered over to the platter I had prepared and snagged a piece of chorizo. After popping it into her mouth and chewing, she said, "This looks good."

"Then why did you shout *liar*?"

"You were humming the song, 'Under the Sea.'"

"I was not," I lied with as much conviction as I could muster.

"Yes. You. Were." The look of satisfaction on her face annoyed the hell of out me.

"I don't even know what you're talking about." I whisked past her with the snacks and wine. Glancing back over my shoulder, I asked, "Can you bring the wineglasses, please?"

Sarah strode into the room after me, carrying the new wineglasses she and her mom had picked out at Pier One. "You can lie to yourself, but you can't lie to me."

I rolled my eyes. "Whatever. Can we watch this lame movie yet, or do you want to continue your jibber-jabber?"

There was no way I was going to confess that I liked the movie. No way in hell.

CHAPTER FOUR

WEDNESDAY MORNING ARRIVED MUCH FASTER THAN I EXPECTED. I HOPPED OUT OF BED AT FIVE, anxious to get going so I wouldn't be late to pick Mom up for her appointment.

I was brushing my teeth in the bathroom when Sarah slipped her arms around my waist. "You going to be okay today?"

I shrugged.

She rose on her tippy toes and kissed the back of my head. Then she turned and stepped into the shower.

Mom had told me to be at her house by eight, but I was in her neighborhood by seven. Not wanting to disturb her, I stopped at Starbucks to kill time. I fidgeted at a table, one hand nursing a chai latte and the other shakily holding open a book—an account of a young Englishwoman living under Nazi tyranny. My eyes kept darting back to paragraphs before, my brain unable to wrap itself around the words. Every few seconds, I peeked at my watch. I wanted to ensure I wasn't late, but I also secretly kept hoping time had magically stopped.

Chemo.

I pondered over the word. Just the thought of it made me shit my pants. I couldn't imagine what my mother was going through.

At 7:55 a.m., I rang the doorbell. As I waited, I straightened my shirt and swore at myself for being stupid enough to wear jeans. I could just hear my mother: *Jeans, Elizabeth? I'm dying and you wear jeans.*

The door swung open, and my neck cracked a little as I did a double take. My father held the door open for me. Since when did he go to work this late?

"Morning," he huffed, motioning me inside.

"Good morning," I mumbled, as he shut the door behind me.

The mood in the house was chilling. Maybe if we had been a closer family, it wouldn't be so tense, but I doubted it. Nothing in life prepared anyone for this.

My mother was perched on the leather sofa. One of her navy blue skirts had been paired with a starched white blouse and matching navy blazer. Her purse sat on her lap.

"Lizzie's here," my father announced—needlessly, as I was standing in plain view.

My mother opened her mouth and then snapped it shut, resembling one of those turtles you see on a nature documentary, with her wrinkled neck, thin lips, and beady eyes always on the lookout for prey.

"How you feeling?" I asked. She looked as scared as I felt. The last time I asked her that question, Mom had nearly bitten my head off, yet I couldn't think of anything else to say.

"Fine."

I lifted the bag of books. "I got you some books."

"Good. Set them by my chair," she commanded. She didn't bother saying thanks, but this time I didn't really care.

"You ready to go?" she asked.

I wanted to ask her the same thing — not in the same way, though. I meant mentally.

"Call me when you're done," my father instructed, directing his statement to me, not her. "The nurse will be here when you get back."

I nodded. He studied Mom for a split second before retreating to the safety of his chauffeured car, his mountain of work. I wanted to shout at him. Coward!

When we arrived for the appointment I braced myself for the sterile environment beyond the door. I wasn't sure what I expected, but I didn't think the entrance would scream welcome, yet it did. A floral arrangement was the first thing that caught my eye. Colorful prints adorning the walls gave the impression this would be a cool place to have a cup of joe and catch up with friends. I hated the place immediately. The attempt to be overly cheerful was an insult to reality. People didn't come here to have coffee. They came in hope of cheating death.

My mother strode to the front desk like a cavalry officer riding into battle: full of confidence and bravado. I admired the front she was putting on.

The nurse handed her some paperwork to complete; Mom handed it straight to me. We took a seat opposite an older woman wearing a headscarf.

Jesus! I don't need to see that!

Mom's expression suggested she felt the same. She nodded at the woman, but didn't speak.

"Your first time?" the woman asked her.

"What?"

"Is this your first appointment? I can tell. I've been around for a while." The woman smiled, her expression supportive under drawn-on eyebrows. How she managed that was beyond me.

"Yes." My mother's tone was cool. She was never one for chitchat.

The woman eyed me. "It's wonderful that you're here for her."

I nodded, not knowing what to say. It was obvious she didn't have anyone, or maybe the person tired of the appointments. *How long does it take,* I wondered, *until a patient's hair falls out?*

"I need your insurance card," I told Mom, motioning toward the intake form.

When she pulled out the card, I saw that her hand was shaking, her eyes averted. I didn't say or do anything to reassure her. Knowing Mom, that wasn't what she wanted anyway. Being human wasn't her thing.

Several minutes later, I returned the forms to the woman at the front desk. A nurse appeared in the waiting room, glancing at her clipboard and calling my mother's name. Both of us sat there, frozen. Finally, I stood and put out my hand to Mom. I half expected her to swat it away; she didn't.

It was icicle cold.

"I'll be here when you're done."

She acknowledged me with a slight tilt of her head and then strode off briskly, once again a cavalry officer.

I pulled out my book. Words blurred the page. That was when I noticed that my eyes were filled with tears. I dabbed at them casually and wiped my cheek on my shoulder. I needed to hold it together. My mom needed me to be strong.

A table offering tea and coffee sat to one side of the room. I poured myself a tea and wandered back to my chair, opening my book, pretending to read for I don't know how long until the door that led to the back opened and the nurse ushered Mom out.

"Here she is," the nurse announced, as if my mother was a child who'd just had her teeth cleaned for the first time.

"Is there anything I need to do?" Mom asked her, in a not-so-confident tone.

"Nope. You're all set. We'll see you in a couple of days."

We drove home in silence.

"I'll see you in two days," she informed me when I pulled into her driveway. Without another word, she stepped out of the car. Her nurse opened the front door of the house.

Just like that, I was dismissed. Dad's assistant took my message to let him know that Mom was back home and that everything went well. Actually, I wasn't sure what had happened, let alone whether it went according to plan. Mom left me in the dark.

I arrived back in Fort Collins before noon, feeling like I just biked one hundred miles. I sat in my SUV, unable to open the door, let alone move my arms or legs. I put the car in park. I left the seatbelt on. I stared at my driveway. I felt numb. Numb.

By the time Sarah walked in the front door, I was in much better shape, even if I'm pretty sure my splotchy cheeks and puffy eyes screamed, "I've been crying!"

My conflicting emotions confused and baffled me. Why was I was feeling overwhelmed, confused, sad, angry, and alone when Mom and I were never even close. Peter was much closer to her, even if not involved in actually taking care of her. My brother never could face reality. He was always too busy putting on a show, one that assured everyone how successful he was. I doubted it had ever occurred to him that no one cared. *People care about actions, Peter, not impressions.*

Ironically, my mother, if she didn't have cancer, would have been one of the few people impressed by the way Peter was handling things.

"How'd it go?" Sarah set her bag down. Papers brimmed out of the top, and I knew she had a full night of grading to do.

"Um, it was...surreal. I don't really know how to describe it," I said in barely more than a whisper.

"Did she get sick?" Sarah sat down next to me on the couch and rubbed my back.

I shrugged. "Not sure. She only let me take her to the appointment. When we got back to the house, she didn't even let me get out of the car to help her up the stairs. It was like I'm only good enough to take her to the hospital, or she wanted the staff members to know her daughter cared enough to take her, which implies she was a good mother. Why couldn't she just pay someone to act like her daughter and leave me out of it?"

Sarah sighed. She had never let on to me, but deep down I think she was worried about this turn of events, worried I would let Mom take advantage of me in the hope of finally earning maternal love. I knew I was worried about that as well. Why, at the age of thirty, was I still desperate for acceptance? Given that I had let my childhood memories interfere with my relationship with Sarah in the past, I admired her ability to support me silently, without giving voice to her concerns. Perhaps she sensed I had enough on my plate.

"If she's anything like you, she didn't want to show you that she's vulnerable. Give her time, Lizzie."

It made sense. I wouldn't want people watching me puke my guts up either.

"I will," I said, finally. "I'm taking her to her next appointment. Actually, I think I'm on the hook for all of them. I know Peter won't think to offer." I paused. "My father was home when I got to the house. I can't remember a time he was home after 7:00 a.m."

"Maybe this will bring them closer. Your mom is a tough bird. She'll survive this."

"That would be just like her. Goodness knows she's not done torturing me yet." I let out a relieved snort.

"Now, I want you to take me to dinner. Maddie texted. She wants to join."

I gestured to her bag. "Don't you have to get caught up on grading?"

Sarah waved the idea away. "Nah. Half of my students don't turn their stuff in on time, so why should I?"

I reached for her hand, where it rested on my shoulder, and gave it a squeeze. "Thank you."

She leaned in and hugged me, saying nothing. What was there to say: *Sorry that your Mom, who has always been a bitch, is dying and you don't know how to process your feelings?*

"Where are we meeting Maddie?"

"A new Mexican joint. And I probably should warn you to be on your best behavior."

"Why? You afraid I'll break down and cry or something?"

She swatted my shoulder, as if appalled that I thought so lowly of her. "Not that. She's bringing a date. Do you remember the last guy you met?"

I did. He was a complete and total asshole who didn't respect women and wasn't smart enough to pretend that he did, not even while having dinner with three women. I had given him a piece of my mind—and then some. "I didn't say anything that you didn't want to say," I pouted.

"You didn't have to tell him he was an asshole to his face."

"Hey now, Maddie burst into laughter when I did. He asked us how lesbians had sex, for Christ's sake, and if we shaved our pubic hair off to avoid getting hair in our teeth while eating each other out. He's allowed to do that, but I can't say, 'You're an asshole.'"

"You do shave, by the way."

"Because I'm a neat freak, not because I'm worried about you getting hair in your teeth. It's more hygienic!"

"So it's not for my benefit at all?"

I groaned. "Good twist on that. Nicely played."

She smiled, and then started into me again. "And then you proceeded to tell Maddie's date that if he didn't understand lesbian sex, he'd never satisfy a woman."

"Well, he won't!" I stood firm on this point.

Sarah smiled. I'm sure she was relieved to see my spark back. "Just go easy on this one, okay. Maddie really likes him."

"What does he do?"

Please say teacher or something along those lines. A profession I can respect. Even a mechanic.

I admired a person who could take an engine out and put it all back together; plus, it would be nice to have one I could call.

"He's a weather forecaster on a local news channel." Sarah turned her back. Was she deliberately avoiding my glare?

I gawked at the back of her head as if she had cockroaches crawling all over it. "You're joking."

"No, I'm not. And you won't make one crack about it." She flipped around and waggled a finger in my face.

"It must be nice to have a job where you don't have to be right—ever. Talk about job security."

"Yeah, don't say anything like that, Lizzie." She pinned me with a stern look.

I gave a Boy Scout salute and determined that I shouldn't say anything at all, just to be safe. Weather forecaster—please! Did he have to train for that? I sincerely doubted it. All the dude had to do was stand in front of a blue screen and point to the right areas. At the least, maybe he had to study geography.

We ran into Maddie and her date in the parking lot. After I had been introduced to Doug the weatherman, Maddie pulled me aside. "You okay?"

"Yeah, I'm fine. Where'd you find Doug the weather dude?"

"Don't be an ass tonight. I like this one." She shot me a look that suggested she'd take me out back and pummel my ass if I was rude.

"He better not ask me about lesbian sex, then."

Maddie rolled her eyes and rejoined her date. Doug was only about five foot nine with dark hair, eyebrows that appeared to have been trimmed, a wispy goatee, and curious eyes. His nose was huge. Maybe that was good for his profession. Maybe he could smell rain or snow in the air like a bloodhound. Was I allowed to ask that question?

The hostess seated us right away. The restaurant was almost deserted. Either the food sucked, or the place was too new and no one had heard of it yet; my money was on the former, but my gut was cheering for the latter. After the day I'd had, I really wanted something to go right.

I imagined crappy Mexican food would taste how dog food looked. I'm not saying Mexican food is only fit for dogs, just that the cheap shit, like refried beans in a can, looked like dog food. The weird watery/oily substance on top of canned beans always freaked me out.

"One of my colleagues recommended this place, so I hope it's good," Doug said, disappearing behind the oversized laminated menu.

The menu wasn't a good sign—laminated. But now that I knew Doug had suggested it, I knew I would have to pretend to love it, just to stay on Maddie's good side. I wanted to avoid an ass kicking. I think she was still a bit peeved about the last guy. But that wasn't my fault! I didn't ask him about heterosexual sex. Couldn't he be a normal guy and just watch lesbian porn, instead of interrogating the first lesbian he met in real life? Fucking creep.

"You look deep in thought, Lizzie. Care to share with the group?" Maddie always enjoyed putting me on the spot.

I straightened in my chair, ready to spill until I felt Sarah's hand on my thigh, giving me that you-better-not squeeze. Could the woman read my mind?

Maddie laughed. Doug, still engrossed in the menu, didn't notice a thing. Typical male.

"How's work been lately, Maddie?" I asked instead, biting back words about how rude her last boyfriend had been, even though I was the one being blamed for that double date crashing and burning. In our little group, I was always the fall guy. Okay, so I usually wasn't entirely blameless, but why did I have to turn the other cheek when straight people asked insulting questions? Why should they receive a pass for being noble enough to have dinner with me without having a clue how to act or what to say? Why should I just ignore their stupidity? No way.

Maddie shrugged. "Same old same old." A year ago, Maddie had opened her own interior design business, and it was growing at glacial speed. She was talented—Sarah and I had hired her when we bought our house—but the economy in this part of the country was still in the shitter. There were signs of life, but that didn't mean people were rushing out to redecorate their homes. Luckily, Maddie had her parents helping her out.

"Have you seen her work?" Doug set aside his menu and smiled like a schoolboy.

I nodded.

"That's how we met." He beamed.

Maddie colored. "Doug is one of my clients—former client." She raised a finger at me.

As if that was going to stop me.

"Are you allowed to fraternize with clients?" I arched my eyebrows, ready for battle. "Jeez, ouch!" Both Sarah and Maddie had kicked me in the shin under the table, each striking a different leg. "I was only kidding. No need for both of you to kick me."

Sarah and Maddie glared at me for outing their behavior.

Doug just chuckled. "Be glad it wasn't my sister. She can pack a wallop."

"Are you two close?" asked Sarah.

"Oh yeah. She's one year younger than me, and we've been inseparable almost since she was born."

I couldn't think of anything jerky to say about that. I had only dealt with siblings who hated each other. Both Sarah and Maddie were only children, thank God. I struggled enough with my own family; I didn't need to add any more relatives who would be disappointed in me or piss me off.

"What about you?" Doug directed the question to Sarah.

"Oh, the only sibling I have is through Lizzie, and he's an asshole."

Doug sat there with his mouth open, waiting for me to reply.

"Sarah, no reason to be shy." I looked Doug straight in the eyes. "My brother is a fucking asshole. Just ask Maddie." I pulled my legs up quickly so both Sarah and Maddie kicked each other accidentally. "Ha!"

"Why do I get the feeling I'm missing something?" Doug put the menu back down on the table.

Tilting my head, I flashed an evil grin at Maddie. "You want to field this one, boss, or should I?"

Maddie let out a long, angry breath. Shaking her head, she explained, "I met Lizzie through her brother."

"Oh, you two dated," Doug probed.

"You could say that." Maddie looked to Sarah for help, but she didn't receive any. "Truth be told, I was engaged to Peter."

Comprehension flooded Doug's face. "I wish I could say I'm sorry it didn't work out, but it worked out well for me." Maddie hugged his arm and rested her head on his shoulder. Then she stuck her tongue out at me.

Damn. I thought for sure that would get to him. I needed new ammo. "So, Doug, what do you do?"

Fire shot out of Sarah's eyes, but I did my best to free my face of all judgment.

"Meteorologist. Maddie tells me you're a history nut. Do you know who founded meteorology?" He looked innocent, even though he'd just put me on the spot.

"Uh…" I fiddled with my fork. "Can't say that I do."

"Aristotle."

Shit! How could I say something snarky about Aristotle?

"Is that so," was all I could think to say.

Sarah and Maddie were clearly tickled pink over my inability to be an ass.

When the waitress interrupted to take our food order, I was never so happy to see a server. To make matters worse, Doug and I both ordered tamale platters—like we were two peas in the same pod. It pissed me off. Would this day never end?

"Lizzie, Maddie mentioned your mother's situation. I'm so sorry to hear it. My grandmother had colon cancer. If you ever need to talk…" He left the rest unspoken.

I sat there, frozen.

"Thanks, Doug." Sarah patted my arm and then said, "Today was her mom's first chemo session."

Why was that necessary? Why did he have to be a nice guy? I needed to vent, and the best way for me to do that was to rip other people apart. Just like my mother. Fuck! Was I turning into my mother?

Maddie directed the conversation to safer waters: the three of them discussing spring training. The Broncos lost big time in the Super Bowl earlier in the year, and everyone in Colorado hoped the upcoming season wouldn't be such a dud.

I didn't care. I just appreciated that I didn't have to speak. I really didn't think I could. Dealing with my mom and then Doug…my eyelids felt heavy. Change wasn't my forte, and I was facing a lot of it, all at once. It was best for me to tune everyone out.

Minutes later, the three of them burst into laughter. It soon became obvious that the joke involved me. I flashed a fake smile.

"I knew it. You have no idea why we're laughing, do you?" Maddie put me in the hot seat yet again.

"Maddie, you don't expect Lizzie to admit that, do you?" Sarah grinned, relishing the moment.

"I'll give you a clue: turkey baster."

I blinked foolishly, utterly clueless. Were they deriding my lack of cooking skills?

The three of them broke into a loud guffaw once again.

"Maybe Doug's sister can teach you," offered Maddie.

"How to cook?" The words spilled out before I could stop them.

Maddie roared with laughter, tossing her head so hard that it whacked the high-backed seat. She rubbed it gingerly, but she didn't stop chortling.

"My sister and her partner recently conceived their first child," explained Doug, doing his best to control his laugher.

I still wasn't connecting the dots. Partner? That was lesbian speak for girlfriend. Was his sister gay? Damn! Was there nothing I could hate about this dude? Why did Maddie have to introduce the perfect guy today, of all days?

"Maybe I should explain this to you later," said Sarah.

Maddie laughed even harder, now gasping for breath.

"Here we are," the waitress cooed, her arms laden with plates. She set the tamale platter down before me, and I did my best to ignore Maddie's ongoing giggles by starting to eat.

To say I was miffed would be a euphemism. Sarah patted my leg, so I knew she had noticed. I bristled, moving my leg away.

She leaned over and kissed my cheek. "Don't be mad," she whispered.

I responded by shoving an overloaded fork of tamale into my mouth and chewing dramatically. As soon as I swallowed, my attitude softened.

"These are good," I mumbled, forking in another mouthful.

Doug nodded. He was chewing as enthusiastically as I was.

Sarah and Maddie, taking that as an invite, plunged their forks into our respective platters.

"Back off!" Doug uttered the exact same phrase as me and pretended to defend with his fork, just as I did. It was like we were fucking identical twins — except I didn't think my nose was as large as his.

He eyed me, brow crinkled, and gave me *the look*. Simultaneously, we each dug our forks into our date's plate and scooped up a large bite.

"Hey!" The girls protested in unison.

Doug and I high-fived. Okay, maybe I could get along with this one.

Later that night, Sarah slipped under the sheets, naked, and joined me in bed. She rested her head on my chest.

"Do you mind telling me about the turkey baster?"

She giggled and hid her face with the sheet. "Do I have to?"

"Yes." I tickled her side.

"All right, but don't flip out. Maddie was joking that you'd get me pregnant with one."

"How is that —? Oh." I didn't like the image in my head. "Um, is that how you want to…to do it?" I didn't. Not one bit.

"Don't worry. We can't do it that way, since we're using your egg. The doctor will have to implant the embryo."

I'm sure my relief was evident.

"Gosh, you're such a weirdo when it comes to this." She poked me in the ribs.

"Comes to what?" Getting pregnant wasn't an everyday thing, at least not for lesbians.

"Gay stuff."

"What do you mean? I am gay."

"That doesn't mean you're comfortable with the topic. Not one bit." Sarah waggled a finger in my face.

"Really." I wasn't in the mood for this conversation again. My family hated that I was a lesbian, and my wife and best friend complained I wasn't gay enough; it was a losing battle.

"What about this subject instead?" I lifted her chin to kiss her. "And this one?" I rolled her on her back and licked one of her nipples.

"You happen to be quite good with this particular lesbian subject." She grinned.

"Good. Now be quiet, so I can focus."

CHAPTER FIVE

Sunday morning arrived, and I had to pinch myself to prove that the week was nearly over. Taking my mom to two appointments had really done a number on me. I knew the appointments were harder on her, and I was trying to stay focused on that, rather than on me, but as everyone loved to point out, I was self-involved. My therapist and I were working on that.

On Friday afternoon, I had received a text from The Scotch-lady. I didn't even know my mom could text!

"Pick up some more books for me. Audiobooks."

So, I had to drive to Denver once again. I wasn't one for driving—I preferred to ride my bike most places—so three round-trips from Fort Collins to Denver seemed overwhelming. I'd also hoped for a two-day reprieve from Mom. All I wanted was some time to myself, or with Sarah. That was all. Nothing more.

I rolled onto my side. The clock read seven o'clock. Seven!

Sarah nestled up against me. "You're still here."

"Yeah, I must have been more tired than I thought." I rubbed my eyes, trying to force my eyelids to stay open; they weren't cooperating.

"I kinda like it. I can't remember the last time we woke up together. I thought when you finished grad school and started working from home, I'd see you more." Her voice was still thick with sleep.

"Don't you get tired of seeing me all the time?" I knew as soon as I finished speaking that Sarah would take this the wrong way.

She bolted upright. "Why? Are you tired of me?"

I swear Sarah could twist anything to make me look bad—not that she had to twist that statement all that much.

"That's not what I meant at all. You're a good person. It's me. For the past five minutes I've been feeling sorry for myself because my mom is sick and she's relying on me. I'm the selfish shit, not you."

That appeased her a little, but I knew I'd be walking on eggshells the rest of the weekend anyway. Just what I needed. When would I learn to keep my foot out of my mouth? Probably never.

"Can I take you to breakfast? Will that help repair the damage?"

"Do you only want to take me to breakfast to shut me up?" Sarah crossed her arms over her naked breasts. God, I loved that she always slept naked, not just in summer.

"That depends. Will it work?"

She grabbed her pillow and whacked me with it.

"Is that a yes or a no?" I tossed her pillow aside and pulled her on top of me. "Since I skipped my bike ride, how about some exercise?"

She opened her mouth to say something snarky, but I quieted her with my lips. It usually didn't take much to get her to see my line of thinking.

But today, I didn't get very far. My phone vibrated. With everything going on, I stopped to check the message, to make sure—to be blunt—that my mom hadn't died. Since I had learned about Mom, whenever I got a phone call or a text, that was my first thought.

The message was from Maddie.

"You back from your ride yet?"

Sarah sensed my drastic mood change. "Is everything okay?"

I let out a sigh of relief. "Yeah, it's just Maddie. Would you mind texting her back for me? I need to pee."

Standing in front of the sink, dousing my face with frigid water, I listened to Sarah on the phone. Texting wasn't her thing. She preferred the old-fashioned phone call. I mostly opted to text or email: the less human connection the better. How odd that my mom felt the same way.

Nope, Lizzie, block this line of thinking from your brain!

Sarah's soft footsteps sounded behind me. "Can you be ready in thirty minutes?"

"For what?" I grabbed a hand towel and dried my face.

"Breakfast with Maddie and Doug."

"She's already fucking Doug? Maddie doesn't waste any time."

"Oh, please. You slept with me right away. And, nice language," she smirked.

I sneered back at her. "That's not the point."

"What's the point, then? It's been a long time since Maddie was in a relationship. You should be happy for her." Sarah stepped into the shower and pulled me in after her.

Normally, I liked showering with her, but not when she was arguing with me. "I just don't want her getting hurt, like last time."

"Not everyone is like Peter."

"Point taken. I'll try to be happy for her, but…"

"But, what?" She lathered shampoo into her hair. This was the most dangerous part of showering with Sarah. She took the lathering process seriously and really got into it, flinging shampoo everywhere. If I didn't close my eyes, I risked being blinded by TRESemmé, or whatever brand she used.

Clenching my eyes shut, I rubbed shampoo into my own hair with much less gusto. "Doug seems nice, and you know what they say about *nice* guys." Some shampoo flew into my mouth, and I spat it out instantly.

"You think Maddie will dump him because he isn't like Peter." Sarah stood under the water to rinse, and I felt somewhat safer. Her conditioning routine wasn't so zealous. "Turn around, I'll wash your back."

I complied. "That, and…have you seen the guy? He's not that good-looking."

Sarah smacked my ass. "Maddie isn't an asshole, like someone I know."

"Shouldn't you take that as a compliment?" I glanced over my shoulder to see her reaction.

Sarah quickly wiped a satisfied grin off her face.

"He has hairy knuckles," I continued.

"He's half Greek. He can't help that."

"Does he have a hairy back?" I pondered aloud.

"How would I know? Seriously, Lizzie! You're just trying to find things wrong with him. You can act this way all you want, but I know you like him." She raked my back with her nails. It felt good, even if she was trying to punish me.

"And he's a weatherman—they're never right about anything. He makes a living lying to people." I ignored her previous statement.

Sarah shook her head in disgust and shut the water off. "We need to hurry."

When we arrived at the Creole restaurant, located in a yellow house, I spied Maddie and Doug waiting outside with several other small groups of people. This place was always hopping.

"Morning," I said as I approached the two lovebirds. It was obvious they were in the honeymoon stage. Neither of them noticed us walking toward them; they were too busy touching each other, giggling, and sharing tender kisses.

When they did finally notice us, Maddie turned red. Doug put his hand out for a handshake.

"Maddie," a woman stuck her head out the door and called.

"Perfect timing. Our table is ready."

I took Sarah's hand, surprising her somewhat. I wasn't going to let the lovebirds outshine me. I was already on thin ice from earlier. If I didn't act fast, I'd have to listen to Sarah complain that I didn't show enough affection in public, like Doug did.

Doug. I was competing with a man called Doug. What a preposterous name. D-ou-G.

We settled around a table more suitable for two. No complaints from me, though. I was famished. Every time we came here, Sarah ordered blackened salmon with grits and a biscuit. I usually stuck with the French toast, but today I felt adventurous. I picked up my menu, studying all the options.

"What are you doing?" asked Maddie. She rammed her menu into mine to get my attention.

"What do you think I'm doing? I'm reading the menu." I already knew what she was going to say.

"Like you'd ever order something different." Sarah scoffed, looking to Maddie instead of at me.

"Just so you know, I decided, even before we arrived, to try something new, to think outside of the box."

"What brought this on?" Maddie sipped her water, her face registering disbelief. "The craziest thing I've seen you eat are parsnips."

"Don't know. Just feel like it, I guess."

Maddie and Sarah shared a concerned look. Ever since Mom had re-entered my life, they had been sharing this look quite a bit. It was starting to irk me.

"I haven't been here before. Do you ladies have any suggestions?" The man with the ridiculous sounding name tried to come to my rescue.

While the three of them dissected the menu, I regretted my decision to tell them about trying something new. Eggs Pontchartrain. Eggs Sardou. Creole Omelet. Eggplant—what the? What happened to normal breakfast food, like French toast? Oh, wait, there was a waffle. But I knew I'd never hear the end of that one. My eyes continued the trek down the menu. The last item before the sides was sausage gravy on a biscuit with grits or potatoes. Damn. I knew I had to order the grits, even though the potatoes sounded better. Next time, Lizzie, keep your trap shut.

Sarah ordered her usual, which, as usual, put my choice to shame. Doug ordered the creamed spinach, Gulf shrimp, poached eggs and hollandaise—yuck! Maddie went for the fried eggplant with creole sauce. When I ordered, I noticed Maddie and Sarah glance down at the menu to interpret the dish's fancy name.

"Sausage gravy? You're living on the edge today," Maddie snarked.

"Hey now, at least it wasn't the French toast. Give her some credit."

I grinned my appreciation of Sarah's defense.

"Are you two ready for the big storm?" Maddie changed the subject.

I looked out the window—nothing but blue sky. Then I glanced down at my outfit—jeans, T-shirt and a fleece vest. "What storm? It's a beautiful spring day."

"Deceptive, huh." Doug sat straighter in his chair. "But in a few hours, the flakes will be flying."

"Flakes? You mean snow. It's April. How much can we get?"

"We're predicting it'll be as bad as the storm on April 23, 1885." He merrily tapped the table with his fork.

What fucking storm was he talking about? Okay, I was impressed he knew an actual date, but for all I knew he had plucked that date out of his ass. I made a mental note to look it up.

"It's going to be a blizzard." Maddie smiled at Doug, in awe of his "forecasting" abilities.

"Get out." My tone betrayed me. I immediately felt the weight of Sarah's disappointment. I had to learn to control my tone.

Maddie glared at me as if I had just smacked Doug in the face. "Care to make a friendly wager, Lizzie," she managed, through gritted teeth.

"Yeah, I do," I taunted her, waving a fork at the sky.

Next to me, Sarah bristled. Time to bring my contempt down several notches or I'd get the silent treatment for the rest of the weekend.

"One dollar."

"Oh, you are living on the edge, Maddie."

"It's not the amount, but the satisfaction. I might frame it to remind you." She looked tickled with the idea.

To Doug's credit he didn't look put out by my obvious disdain for his profession.

Profession! Puh-lease!

In my estimation, the man licked his finger, stuck it in the air, and guessed what direction the wind was blowing and what that portended. Meteorologist, my ass. I studied his massive nose to see if it twitched.

Sarah steered the conversation away from Doug by throwing me under the bus. "Lizzie doesn't think she has any issues with being a lesbian."

My heart stopped beating. "Thanks for that, Sarah," I said. I tried to stop my jaw from clenching.

Maddie laughed and covered her mouth.

"Anytime." Sarah smiled sweetly at me. This was my payback for being an ass to Doug.

Again, Doug looked comfortable. Was he slow on the uptake? Was that how he stayed calm about everything?

"I take it you had to explain the turkey baster." Maddie wasn't slow about anything.

"Yep. And then I said I wouldn't put her through that, and you should have seen how relieved she looked." Sarah rubbed the top of my head as if I were a well-behaved puppy in training.

Our food arrived, and thank God mine looked edible. Raising my fork to dig in, I responded, "Just what issues do you think I have with being gay?"

"For starters, you just whispered the word *gay*." Maddie was quick to the punch.

"I did not!"

"Yes, you did." Sarah was feeling punchy as well.

I rolled my eyes. "Fine. What else?"

"You don't have any gay friends." Maddie sampled her eggplant. It must have passed the test because she shoveled a much larger piece into her mouth.

"That's not true. You're —"

"Bisexual. Come on, say the word with me." I assumed Maddie knew why I had stopped, but she wasn't going to let me off the hook. "Bi-Sex-U-Al."

"Now, hold on." I held my fork in midair, the tines pointing toward Maddie. "When you told me, you told me in confidence. I have no issue with saying the word."

"If I remember correctly, I said don't tell your family." She grinned triumphantly. "And you still haven't said it."

"Bisexual."

Maddie cupped her ear. "I'm sorry, what? I can't hear you."

I wanted to hurl my glass of water in her face, but two could play at this game. "Bisexual!" I roared, stabbing my diminutive pitchfork in her direction.

Every head in the place turned and stared. Not a sound could be heard.

Uh-oh. I felt the color rush to my face, and for a second thought I might pass out.

Maddie raised her orange juice in my honor. "Good for you. How'd it feel?"

I ignored her question. "So, I take it Doug knows."

Doug responded, "My sister is with a bisexual, too." He whispered the word, but I was pretty certain he did it for my benefit, since he added a wink.

Damn! I wanted to hate Doug, but I couldn't.

"Okay, so everyone else is gayer than me. I'm guessing this is something the two of you" — I stabbed my knife in Sarah's direction and back at Maddie — "have discussed and you have been waiting for the right opportunity to bring it up."

"Maybe." Sarah glanced at me out of the corner of her eye, sheepishly.

"So what? Do I need gay education or something? Do I need to tell everybody I meet that 'I'm here and I'm queer,' or should I blurt out, 'Hi, I'm Lizzie. You can remember that because it rhymes with lezzie, and I am one. Lizzie the Lezzie, pleased to meet you.'"

Sarah knew my breaking point, and she must have sensed I was approaching it. "Honey, it's not that. It's just—" She turned to Maddie for help.

"I think what Sarah is trying to say is that she's worried that when you two have a kid, well you'll raise a *you*."

"What in the hell does that mean?" I threw my fork down on my plate. Somehow, it missed the massive pile of food and clattered off the hard surface, onto the floor. Its clanging invited another round of head-turning and tut-tutting from other patrons.

"Lizzie, you know I love you, but I don't want our child to think there's anything wrong with being gay."

"And you think I'll teach our child that?"

"Not intentionally."

"But I'm too much like my family—that's what this is about, right?"

Not one of them looked at me. Doug suddenly seemed to find napkin origami captivating. Was he making a swan?

"Okay," I said.

"Okay, what?" Sarah didn't look sure what I meant.

"Okay. I see your point. What can I do…to improve?" I wasn't just trying to appease her just so I could eat my meal. Spending "quality" time with Mom made me see signs that troubled even me. I didn't want to be like her, not one bit.

"Uh…" Sarah tilted her head to Maddie and bit her lip. Did she fear I was about to lose it completely and go bonkers? Was this the calm before the storm?

Maddie was speechless.

"So, Doug, when is your sister's baby due?" I asked, as I dipped my fork into Sarah's salmon and tried it. I couldn't stop my lips from puckering; it was horrendous. I grabbed Maddie's orange juice to wash the hideous taste from my mouth. Everyone at the table let out a relieved laugh.

I raised the OJ glass. "Welcome to our crazy meals, Doug. Just you wait, these two will gang up on you soon." I hoped so anyway. I could use some interference.

Everyone finally relaxed enough that I was able to enjoy the rest of my breakfast…that was, until Doug nudged my arm. "Don't look now, but black clouds are rolling in."

I jerked around in my chair and squinted at the sky. Sure enough, the sky was threatening a doozy of a storm.

"Do you want to pay up now?" Maddie asked, her tone sweeter than any of the cakes that tempted from behind the glassed desserts counter.

Nothing was going my way lately.

"How about I pick up the check? Will that suffice?"

She nodded triumphantly.

CHAPTER SIX

MY MOTHER AND I SAT IN THE ONCOLOGY WAITING ROOM. SHE WAS SIX WEEKS INTO HER treatments, and her doctor wanted to have a chat. I didn't think an oncologist should call up a patient and say, "Let's have a chat." It was too broad, too worrisome.

My mom sat so still in the chair that she resembled an ice sculpture. I couldn't even hear her breathing. She stared straight ahead, prim and proper in her navy suit.

Another patient was slumped in a wheelchair off to the side, with a woman I suspected was her nurse. The patient was emaciated, wearing a scarf over her bald head and clothes that hung off a body that didn't contain an ounce of fat. I wondered if that was why Mom stared straight ahead out the window, to avoid seeing the woman in the wheelchair.

"Oh, no!"

I glanced over my shoulder to see what the commotion was about. The nurse jumped out of her chair and strode, briskly but professionally, to the front desk. She leaned over the counter and said something to the lady.

The woman behind the desk bounded out of her seat, too, and disappeared behind a door. She returned promptly, carrying pads of some sort.

That was when I figured out what happened. The poor woman in the wheelchair had peed herself. I inhaled sharply.

Incontinence. I hadn't considered that.

My mother rested her chin on her chest and briefly rubbed her eyes; then she resumed her statue pose. I thought I detected a tiny tear in the corner of her eye.

A nurse came to help wheel the woman out back, to get her out of her soiled clothes. No one spoke. Everyone did their best to pretend that everything was on the up-and-up. Not wanting to, but unable to control the urge, I glanced at the woman. She seemed clueless about what was going on. My heart startled and quivered in my chest. I feared if I opened my mouth, it would lunge out. Jesus! I wasn't prepared for this.

"Mrs. Petrie," another nurse called.

"You want me to come with?" I asked.

Mom shook her head and tried her best to march confidently into the inner bowels of the complex.

I texted Sarah, hoping she had a free period. No reply. She must have been in the middle of class. Maddie was my next choice. She texted right back, knowing I was with my mom. We exchanged a few texts: her, sympathetic, and me, relieved to stay busy and keep my mind off my surroundings. My mom didn't need me to break down right now.

Two more patients, a man and a woman, checked in, and took their seat across from me. They didn't sit next to each other, but that didn't stop them from striking up a conversation.

"How's it going?" asked the man.

"Not too bad, considering. And you? What'd the doc say last time?"

It was obvious they had run into each other before. I wondered when I would begin to recognize other patients.

"Well, I finally know. I'm terminal." The man stated it bluntly. He looked almost relieved.

I couldn't believe I was sitting in a room eavesdropping on this conversation. Weeks ago, everything in my life was going well. I was happily married to a wonderful woman who wanted to start a family. Sure, my friends drove me crazy, but I still loved them. I had published my first book, which had been well received by other historians, even if it wasn't selling. Several universities had invited me to speak about my research, and my publisher was keen for me to complete my next project. A couple of universities were even trying to convince me to join their staff. Things were good.

But now, I was sitting in an oncology waiting room and had just witnessed a man tell a stranger he was dying.

What did it feel like, to know your time was severely limited? Was he in pain? Scared?

Was my mom hearing the same news during her "chat" with the doctor?

My instinct was to run. To call Dad's assistant, have her arrange a car for my mom, and then to drive back to Fort Collins and pretend none of this was happening. To go back to my normal life—a life that didn't involve a woman pissing herself, a man confirming his imminent death, and my mother…

I rocked in my seat, working up the courage to rise and bolt. Both hands firmly on the armrests of the chair, I began hauling my body up. I couldn't deal. And why was I expected to? Mom had treated me like shit most of my life, but now that she needed me, I was expected to take care of her.

Fucking bullshit.

Where was my father?

My brother?

She didn't need me; she needed someone to fill a role for her, to keep up appearances.

I stood. The man and woman nodded in my direction, and both smiled convincingly.

Fuck! Why couldn't I be strong, like them?

I walked out of the office and headed down the hallway. At the end was a pop machine.

I wondered if Mom might want a Sprite to help settle her stomach. I could use a drink. I put in a dollar and punched the button. The can crashed down onto the metal, the sound bringing me back to my senses. I slid in another dollar and hit the button for a Coke. After retrieving both cans, I walked back into the doctor's office. I had to be strong.

My mother stood in the middle of the room, looking for me. I held up both cans, to explain my absence. She actually looked relieved that I was still there. She grabbed my arm and I led her to the parking lot.

"I wasn't sure if you wanted a drink," I said, helping her into the passenger side of the car.

"Thank you." She took the Sprite and popped the top.

Her thank you startled me. After settling into the driver's seat I asked, "Would you like to stop anywhere on the way home?"

Mom shook her head. She stared out the window, avoiding my eyes. I wanted to ask what the doctor said, but I didn't think Mom was ready to share.

I expected her to dismiss me in the driveway, as she had all the other times, but when I pulled up to the garage, she turned to me. "Would you come in and keep me company?"

I nodded, too shocked to speak.

When I walked into my front room later that afternoon, Maddie was sitting on the couch, watching some female talk show. She clicked the TV off and bounded over to me, wrapping me up in her arms. "I thought you could use a hug." When she pulled away, she added, "Come on, I'm dying for Mexican food again. And I bet you could use a margarita or two. Sarah's meeting us there after volleyball practice."

I wanted to say thank you, but I didn't have much of a voice. Not that Maddie expected me to say anything; friends didn't.

CHAPTER SEVEN

By Friday night, I was beat. When Sarah barreled home late, after a night out with teachers from her school, I was in bed reading a book about a colon cancer survivor. That was my go-to whenever a new issue arose: I researched the hell out of it.

Sarah tilted her head to read the book title. "Any good?"

"Not sure yet." I laid the book on my chest. "How was your night? Anyone end up with a lampshade on their head?"

I went out with the teachers one night, and only one night. High school teachers had a special bond, and for some reason, they loved the job—mostly. I taught at a university while I was finishing my PhD. I preferred prep work to lecturing, which was why I decided to write stuffy books few would read. The speaking gigs helped me pay the bills. Then there was my trust fund.

"Well, Shirley got a tad bit tipsy, but nothing outrageous happened." Sarah unzipped her skirt and I watched as it slithered to the ground. "How's your mood?"

"Why?"

"I need to tell you something, and I'm not sure you'll be all that thrilled," she confessed, looking guilty.

"Huh. Is that why I'm getting a mini striptease right now?" I raised my eyebrows.

"Maybe." She began to unbutton her shirt, slowly, like a stripper, and then stopped teasing.

"Don't stop. I'm sure it'll help your cause."

"You're horrible."

"Me? You're using sex to get me to do something."

"And you're complaining. Why?"

I sat up in bed to get a better view. "Good point." I pretended to seal my lips shut and throw away the key.

"That's a good girl." Sarah eased onto my lap, and I popped open the last few buttons on her blouse.

A full moon shined brightly through the windows, so I switched my reading lamp off. The moonlight danced over Sarah's milky skin. I traced the flickering light from her chest to her stomach with one finger.

Goosebumps appeared on her body.

"Are you cold?"

She shook her head, a sexy smile on her lips. "Not one bit."

I leaned in to kiss her. Her lips felt moist, soft; the taste of beer clung to her tongue. "Who drove you home?" I asked, when we stopped for a breath.

Sarah shook her head. "Don't worry, I didn't drive. Now, shush." She smothered my mouth with hers, her passion undeniable. Overcome with excitement, I rolled her onto her back and climbed on top of her.

"Easy there. We have all night."

"I missed you," I whispered. "I feel like I haven't seen you all week, with all the traveling back and forth." I cupped her breast, watching her nipple redden and start to harden. I licked it gently, and it stood to attention in my mouth.

Trailing my right hand down the side of Sarah's body, I stopped at her ass, pulling her hips against mine. Body heat radiated from us, as Sarah slid her arms up to rip off my tank top. I stared into her eyes, unable to contemplate ever losing her.

Maybe she sensed my thought. One hand on my cheek, she whispered, "I love you, Lizzie. I'm not going anywhere."

The words I was desperate to hear. How badly I needed to believe that. We kissed, tenderly but forcefully, as though it might be the last time we ever made love. Everything of late reminded me that it was better to live in the now; who knew what lurked around the corner?

My tongue explored her body, stopping only briefly in one spot as I descended. The insistent movement of her pelvis told me she wanted me there, but I ignored her plea. My tongue and hands explored her long, slim legs, not stopping until I reached her toes, so tiny and perfectly round.

She loved it when I kissed her toes and the soles of her feet. A spot on her lower back also drove her crazy; that was my next stop.

Rolling her over, I massaged her firm buttocks, occasionally placing a kiss here and there, my lips moving up to that special spot, which I kissed and bit tenderly.

Sarah let out a low, satisfied grumble. A pillow over her head muffled the sound. I traced the muscles of her shoulders and neck, and then kneaded them, surprised by how tense they were. My tongue flicked her earlobe and carried on its exploration.

She groaned. She wanted me now. Her hips gyrated and I heard her whisper, "please" from under the pillow.

It made me chuckle. "Okay, okay, roll over again."

Her eyes were huge, dark, and pleading as I lay beside her. She wanted me to make love to her. I ran my hand down over her breasts and stomach and then slipped a finger inside her, slowly, loving how warm she was, how moist. As I pushed deeper, Sarah arched her back and closed her eyes. I added another finger and moved in and out of her with more force, matching the rhythm of her rocking hips, pushing against her movement.

Her reaction to my being inside her always excited me. I moaned and plunged in deeper still. Sarah groaned, and before I knew it, she was inside me, too. Both of us frantically fingering in and out, deeper and deeper. Sarah was slippery with sex, each movement of my fingers against her slickening my hand. I felt the warmth of my own excitement, wet on her curled, constantly fucking fingers.

"Oh, Jesus!" I shouted. She was already taking me there with her touch. I couldn't hold on.

Her body trembled as much as mine, and her moan in my ear was satisfied. Then she collapsed on her back, exhausted, thighs quivering. I fell back too, one arm over her, my fingers still damp. Sex scented the room. I inhaled the intoxicating fragrance of it, deeply.

"Are you asleep?" I prayed she wasn't.

"No," she whispered contentedly.

"Good." I moved down the bed. My hands spread her thighs again, stroking their still-quivering paleness, and then my tongue lapped her clit.

Sarah groaned as I thrust my tongue inside her. She arched her back, circled her hips. It wouldn't take her long to come again, but I wanted to taste her. She reached down until her nails scored my shoulders, but I ignored the pain and continued lapping at her clit. I could never tire of her taste; it made my own clit throb with desire.

Sarah's grip on my shoulders intensified. She pulled me up, drawing my head back to hers, to kiss me. I slid up her body, skin on skin, clit on clit. I rubbed my clitoris against hers, both of us moaning through our kisses. I felt the tension that comes before release, Sarah's body winding itself tight before her orgasm gushed through her body. She dug her head deep into the mattress, pulling the pillow over her face to muffle her scream.

Her scream set me off, and I felt myself coming once again, too. Lights cavorted behind my eyes, and I nestled my face into Sarah's neck, letting out a long, contented sigh.

Spent, I rolled onto my side to reach for my Nalgene bottle filled with ice water. Sarah snatched it playfully, and took a long draw. Handing it to me, she said, "I love it when we fuck like that." With a sigh she collapsed back onto the bed, her hair mussed around that beautiful face.

I nodded in agreement and drank heavily from the water bottle. Settled on the bed next to her, I pulled her close. She rested her tousled head on my breast and stroked her fingers up and down my skin.

"Can I tell you the news now?" she teased.

I laughed. "Sure, I'm your prisoner now."

Resting her chin on my chest, she gazed into my eyes. "I promised Ethan we'd meet him and his family at Chuck E. Cheese's tomorrow, for Casey's fourth birthday."

"That was what you were afraid to tell me." I teased a tangle out of her chestnut hair.

"Yes."

"Dude, I'm so going to kick your ass at Skee-Ball."

"Oh, you're on, missy."

"Can you pretend that you still need to butter me up?" I winked.

"And why is that?" Hooded eyes told me she understood perfectly.

"Because I'm not done with you."

"Good!"

Walking into Chuck E. Cheese's was quite an experience. The door opened onto a cacophony of screams. Three children sprinted by us, chasing each other; a fourth rammed into my leg, bounced off, and then shouted, "Wait for me!" without apology. I wasn't sure if the boy even knew he had collided with a person.

Sarah gestured to me and laughed. "Oh, the look on your face is priceless."

I forced a smile. "I need a drink."

"Lizzie! It's ten in the morning, and this is a family establishment!"

I found her indignation endearing. "Jeez, I was just kidding." I removed my sunglasses and squinted to block out the bright colors. It was sensory overload, especially after spending most of the night languidly making love to Sarah—not that I was complaining about that. Sarah, in a floral skirt and tight tee, looked ravishing. Was that an okay thought to have while at Chuck E. Cheese's, or did it make me a pervert, lusting after my wife? I slipped my arm around her waist and led her in search of the birthday party. Thank God I wasn't hungover, or all the shrieking would have been even more unpleasant.

"Look what the cat dragged in." Ethan stood to hug us.

"Ten o'clock. Really?" I responded.

"Naptime is at 1:30, so we didn't have a choice." He shrugged. "Besides, you're up at five every morning riding that damn bike of yours."

"Not this morning." Sarah gave me a suggestive wink.

"I've always wondered, Sarah. Does frigid Lizzie need any aids to get you going?"

I felt fire radiating up my neck to my forehead. Why did all my friends have to banter with Sarah about sex? Considering Ethan's aversion to bodily fluids, him joking about it was even harder to fathom.

"Ah, how cute. Are you Strawberry Shortcake today?" Ethan patted my back and handed me a red plastic cup filled with Coke. "Maybe this will help. The pizza will be ready in an hour or so."

Casey ran up and grabbed Ethan's hand. "Daddy, I need more tokens."

"Casey, honey. Say hi to your guests," Ethan reminded her.

I squatted on my haunches. "Happy birthday!" I put my hand out to shake.

Casey launched into my arms for a hug. Then she grabbed my hand. "Come on! Let's play!"

I looked over my shoulder. Ethan, Lisa, and Sarah all waved good-bye, smirking.

Why did this kid like me so much? She was like a cat, choosing to rub against the one person in the room who was allergic to cats. The adults sat down at the table to chat while I slipped further and further into kid hell.

"Hey, wait!"

For a moment, I was relieved. Ethan was going to save me. I stopped and turned, only to see him hurrying over with tokens. He shoved them into my hand and then turned and shouted over his shoulder, "Have fun!"

Bastard!

No wonder parents invited childless adults to parties—so we could babysit. It wouldn't surprise me if Ethan was pouring rum from a hipflask into his Coke.

"Do you like Skee-Ball?" Casey tugged on my arm to get my attention.

Skee-Ball. At least that perked me up a little. The kid was in for it now. I briefly wondered why she was dressed as a cowboy and not a princess.

"Let's go!" I squealed with delight. I stopped myself from adding, "I'll clean your clock." That didn't seem like the right thing to say to a four-year-old, on her birthday.

Five games later, Sarah showed up. She glanced down at the pathetic amount of tickets I had won. Then she eyed Casey's stash.

"I thought this was your game, Lizzie," she teased.

I growled, "I'm out of practice."

Sarah crossed her arms over her chest. "And how often did your mom and dad take you to play?"

"Obviously not enough. Besides, my nanny took me. Feel free to take over." I tossed a ball at her.

Casey ignored us. She was in the Skee-Ball zone, giggling and clapping her hands each time the machine spat out more tickets. How was I getting creamed by a four-year-old? Half the time, the ball didn't even make it to the top when Casey chucked it. She was barely tall enough or strong enough for this game, even though she was much bigger than the other kids her age. I envisioned Ethan spending a lot of time at basketball games in the near future.

Sarah pretended she was pitching a softball, and wound her arm up three times before she released the ball. It launched out of her hand and landed in the hundred-point hole. Flinging her arms in the air as if she had just crossed the Boston Marathon finish line in first place, she yelled, "Yeah."

Casey stopped briefly and squealed. Sarah put her hand out for another ball.

"Lucky shot. Let's see if you can do that again." I felt confident she'd fail.

She didn't. A machine opened up next to me, so Sarah started her own game. Within five minutes, she'd won more tickets than Casey and I combined. She ripped off her tickets and placed them in Casey's tiny hand. "Go get yourself a good prize."

Casey grabbed her tickets and then mine. I bristled, but Sarah gave me that look: the glare that said *Don't be an asshole.* It was an effective reminder.

"Come on!" Casey ran toward the prize counter.

"Don't lose her, Lizzie." Sarah pushed me in the child's direction.

I rolled my eyes. When I had a kid, I planned on getting even with Ethan. He was sitting at the table, probably having a relaxing morning, while I was chasing his child around this parent trap.

Casey had her nose and both hands pressed against the glass display case. A million tiny fingerprints speckled the glass, coupled with who knows how much slobber. When she saw me, Casey pointed to a unicorn sticker. I looked to see how many tickets she would need. Two hundred! Two hundred tickets for a measly sticker. Panicking, I thumbed through the tickets. We were seventy-five short.

"Um, Casey. We don't have enough tickets." I braced for a screaming fit in which she would throw herself down on the floor, kicking.

"Okay. Let's win more!"

I started back toward the Skee-Ball.

Casey pulled on my arm again. "Not there. Whac-A-Mole!" And she was off like a shot.

Whac-A-Mole? What the fuck?

The kid wasn't lying. There was a game called Whac-A-Mole. Armed with a club, each of us did our best to whack a mole's head whenever it popped out, smashing it before it disappeared. If we were successful, the machine would spit out part of a ticket. I could see this was going to take some time. Pushing the thought aside, I focused on the game. It would have been easier if it was an adult-sized mole-whacking table, so I didn't have to lean down so much, which restricted my arm reach.

"You're just as bad at this game."

Once again, Sarah magically appeared, just to mock me.

I handed over my mallet. "Go for it. I'm thirsty."

Before she could protest, I made a beeline for salvation. Over at the party table, Lisa was chatting with some of the moms while Ethan was reading a book. What the—? I'd been entertaining his brat while he was reading a book!

"Nice to see you're getting into the spirit." I raised the plastic cup to my lips.

"I have to take advantage of these chances. They're rare, trust me." He set the book aside. "I hear my kid kicked your ass at Skee-Ball." He grinned, knowing that would get under my skin.

"Whatever. I think she cheats."

"If that makes you feel better."

"I think the agency lied to you. There's no way she's four. Has to be five."

Ethan stared at me as if I was insane. "Do you only play Skee-Ball with children under the age of five, so you can win?" He quirked an eyebrow.

"Lizzieeeeeee!"

The voice made me jump. The kid was back, ready to whisk me off again. Ethan smirked as he picked up his book.

"Come on!" Casey shouted.

She dragged me to a pit filled with plastic balls. What was the point of this? Casey climbed right in. "Get in!"

Get in? There was no way I was climbing into that disgusting germ factory.

"Don't be a scaredy-cat!" Casey taunted me.

Scaredy-cat? She did not!

I jumped in, feeling silly. None of the other adults were in the ball pit. Oh well, they were scaredy-cats.

Casey dived under the balls and then popped back up again, just like a grinning little mole, squealing in delight. Honestly, I didn't see the appeal, but her infectious laughter wore me down. Soon, I was mimicking her. I would go under, holding my breath, and then jump out like a monster and try to grab her. Other kids came over. Before I knew it, I was entertaining half a dozen kids, all by acting like a complete idiot. I walked about like a zombie, stumbling through the brightly colored balls, mumbling, "I'm going to get you."

A child would draw near, and then dash off, screaming. Another would approach timidly, running off after I repeated the whole zombie routine. I wish I could say I was bored out of my mind, but I wasn't. Not once in all that time did I think of my mom. All I did was let go and have fun.

"Come on, Casey, time for lunch!" Sarah helped Casey out of the ball pit. "Lizzie, say good-bye to your friends." Sarah was enjoying herself way too much.

I waved to my playmates. They waved back and then began a new game. Jeez, they could have missed me a bit more. Ingrates.

"You fit in here." Sarah looped her arm through mine.

"Are you surprised?" I raised my eyebrows.

"Stunned." She patted my arm. "And thrilled."

I rolled my neck back and forth. "I think I pulled a muscle playing Whac-A-Mole."

"Oh, poor baby. I'll give you a massage later. Maybe more."

"Maybe. But I'm beat."

"One hour playing with Casey and you're turning me down."

"I'm sure you'll be able to rally me later. You do have a certain charm about you."

She walked ahead of me, swaying her hips more than usual.

"How come she's not Ariel today?" I asked as I plunked myself down next to Ethan, gesturing to Casey's outfit.

"*Toy Story* is her new thing."

"*Toy Story?*"

"Seriously, you haven't seen that one either?" Ethan bit into his slice of pizza. A long string of cheese suspended itself from his chin. When I motioned to it, he wiped it away daintily with a paper napkin. "She's dressed as Woody. The cowboy in the movie."

Damn, now I needed to watch another juvenile cartoon.

"How long is this movie?" I asked, not sure why. Did I plan on sneaking off to the bathroom to cram it in, just so I could show up a four-year-old?

Ethan's forehead wrinkled. "How long? I don't know. But I should mention there are three of them."

"Three!"

"The third one was nominated for Best Picture."

"Yeah, right." I rolled my eyes. I wasn't falling for that one.

"I'm serious." He pulled out his phone and brought up the wiki article.

"Shit!" I clapped a hand over my mouth.

Ethan chuckled. "Don't worry. We're teaching her curse words are just words, trying to take the power out of them."

"Let me know how that works out for you," I winked.

"Have you considered joining a soon-to-be parents group?"

I studied his face to determine whether he was kidding. He wasn't. Even the thought of it made me uncomfortable. "Should I?"

"I didn't, but you might want to."

"Uh-huh. Because everyone thinks I'm going to crash and burn," I said bitterly.

"Not true. We want you to succeed. Trust me, we're all pulling for you." He stared across the table at our wives, hesitated, and then asked, "How's your mom?"

CHAPTER EIGHT

My cell rang at four in the morning. Fumbling to grab it, I accidentally knocked it onto the carpet. Sarah flicked on her bedside lamp.

"Who is it?" Her voice was raspy with sleep.

I shrugged, too busy locating the ringing phone. "Hello," I finally said.

"Lizzie?"

"Yes." I sat up in bed.

My father never called me, so I knew the news was bad.

"It's your father. I'm at the hospital with your mom."

I wanted to ask how bad it was, but I couldn't force myself to utter the question.

"Lizzie...you there?"

"Yes. I'm sorry the phone cut out," I lied. "I'll be there as soon as I can."

"Thank you," he said, and then I heard a click.

Thank you. My father wasn't the type to say thank you. This was bad.

Sarah wrapped her arms around me. She had nuzzled up next to me to hear the conversation. Normally, that type of behavior would annoy the shit out of me, but now I didn't mind. It saved me from having to vocalize what was going on.

Was this it?

I rubbed my eyes forcefully and then chastised myself for lollygagging. This wasn't the time for contemplation; it was the time for action.

I jumped out of bed and grabbed up my jeans from where they lay crumpled next to the bed, not even bothering to locate underwear. Sarah followed suit, tugging on a wrinkled skirt. At first, I was going to tell her not to bother, that I'd go alone, but then I realized I wanted her there. My eyes felt briny, tearing over no matter how hard I tried to stop tears from forming.

Before pulling our car out of the garage, Sarah said, "Hang on a second."

She threw open the car door and ran back inside, reappearing with one of my Nalgene bottles, which I usually kept in the fridge for my early morning rides. She plopped the bottle in the cup holder by the gearshift and then backed the SUV out of the garage. Immediately, I reached for the bottle, hoping water might force my sobs back down.

Neither of us had said a word after the phone call. Actually, I was pretty amazed by our efficiency. We were dressed and out the door in less than five minutes. Sarah even managed to brush her teeth. I opted for a quick rinse with mouthwash.

There was little traffic on the way to Denver; few people were up and out the door so early on a Sunday. The GPS led us right to the hospital entrance.

"Do you want me to drop you off?" Sarah asked.

The million-dollar question. Sarah hadn't seen my family since Peter's wedding. So far, Mom seemed content to ignore the big purple elephant in the room, and I wasn't trying to force the issue.

"I'm sure the cafeteria is open. I can hang out there." She was trying her hardest to make the decision easy for me.

All I had to do was nod and be done with it. A simple nod would make it clear Sarah would take no part in my family interactions, and she was giving me the okay to make that decision. I knew Sarah wasn't the type to throw a hissy fit to get her way, not at a time like this. Because the circumstances were different this time around: my mother could be dying, right at this moment. And right at this moment, I wanted Sarah there. I knew I wouldn't be able to do it without her. I had an urge to shout, *Look at me! I'm growing up.* But I still couldn't speak.

I motioned for her to find a parking spot. Then, as we were getting out of the car, I reached for her hand. Together, we headed toward the sliding glass door.

As soon as we were inside, I released her hand; maybe I wasn't growing as much as I thought.

Mom was in the cancer ward. Cancer Ward. Capital C. Capital W. It was still a shock to my system to hear that word: cancer.

I knew it was silly. I had been taking Mom for chemo treatments for weeks, and to the oncologist's office for checkups. But for the most part, I had blocked out the nasty word. I had wiped away the reality and focused on the little things.

Pick up Mom.

Take Mom to her appointment.

Wait for the appointment to end.

Take Mom home.

It was the only way I could avoid the gravity of the situation and still function. Compartmentalizing helped me stay strong. I lied to myself. I said I was doing it for my mother's sake. Mom didn't need to see her daughter breakdown. But I knew deep down that it was more for my sake than hers.

My father stood outside the room. After shaking my hand, he turned to Sarah. "Thank you for coming. It's good to know Lizzie has someone...well, you know."

I didn't know how to handle that statement; from the look on Sarah's face, she didn't either. My father was a man of few words. He had said more to me in the past few weeks than he had during my entire childhood.

"How is she?" I finally spoke. Even to me, my voice sounded thick, like I was drunk.

"She's resting at the moment."

"What happened?" Sarah took over, speaking on my behalf.

"Evelyn discovered some swelling on her arm, near the chemo port. She's being treated for Deep Vein Thrombosis."

I nodded, not absorbing the information. Evelyn! I always forgot Mom had a name. For years, I thought of her only as The Scotch-lady, nothing more.

Evelyn.

Her name made her real to me.

My father continued. "DVT is the fancy term for blood clot. They're worried it can get into her bloodstream and work its way into her lungs, which would cause a pulmonary embolism. Right now, they're doing their best to thin her blood to liquefy the clot."

Pulmonary embolism. Why did all of these medical terms have to sound so fancy and intimidating? *Deep Vein Thrombosis.* Were they purposefully trying to scare the shit out of their patients and their family members?

"When did she notice the swelling?"

I admired Sarah's ability to hold it together and to be able to speak.

"In the middle of the night. She hadn't been sleeping well," he explained. "I would have called earlier, but she didn't want me to." He stared into my eyes, shrugged. "You know your mother." Then he added, "Peter's on his way."

On the inside, I was screaming, but I nodded crisply to my father. His stoic expression never changed. As a distraction, I tried to remember a time when my father had shown emotion, even a tiny flicker. But it was to no avail. I couldn't.

Still, I shouldn't be too hard on the man. He was finally speaking to me—not that he was verbose with Peter either. My father usually let his wife do all the talking. Now that she was sick, he was stepping up to the plate, finally.

"Would anyone like coffee?" asked Sarah.

"Yes, please." My father turned to her, his expression still blank. "Thank you."

"I'll go with you." I looked at my father. "Shall we get Peter one, as well?"

"Two actually. His fiancée is coming with him." He didn't wait for me to respond to the announcement. Instead, he just turned and walked back into my mother's hospital room.

I stared at the door that had just shut in my face. Sarah tugged on my arm, trying to dislodge the fog that had descended on my brain.

Fiancée?

Farther down the hallway, when I thought it was safe enough, I asked Sarah, "Did Maddie mention that my brother was getting married?"

Sarah shook her head.

"Why is it that every time my brother reenters my life, he has a fiancée?"

In reality, it had only happened twice. My brother and I were not best buddies, so it wasn't overly shocking that I didn't know.

"I'm not surprised, really. Peter always wanted a perfect life." Sarah avoided my eyes, fixing her gaze on the signs at the end of the hallway. "I think there's a coffee shop this way." Once again, she had to yank on my arm to get me moving. My brain and my feet weren't on speaking terms.

We discovered a Starbucks' trolley near the entrance, and I ordered four coffees, plus a chai for myself. Sarah was smart enough to load her pockets with different types of sugar packets and creamers.

On the way back, I stopped in my tracks. "Should I get anything for Mom?"

"I doubt she can have coffee at the moment." Sarah didn't sound convinced.

"She's been drinking a lot of herbal tea lately. I'll get one. The last thing I want to do is hurt her feelings."

Sarah gave me an odd look, but said nothing.

Before we turned the corner near my mother's room, I heard Peter's booming voice in the hallway. Jesus, didn't he understand this was a hospital? Sarah's expression said *Just don't say anything rude.*

I smiled at her reassuringly. Inside my brain, *Just be nice, Just be nice* was running on a loop. *Just be nice. This will be over with soon. Just be nice.*

Peter towered over my father, who, surprisingly, looked much smaller than when I had I seen him minutes earlier.

What was this like for my father? His wife of thirty-something years was in a hospital bed and, from what I heard from Maddie a few years ago, my father had been seeing the same mistress for years.

Peter must have heard our footsteps. He stopped talking and eyed me menacingly, a perplexing smile turning up the corners of his mouth. The last time I had seen my brother, Maddie jilted him at the altar. His eyes told me he hadn't forgiven my betrayal in leaving the wedding with Maddie.

"I wasn't sure what everyone wanted, so I hope plain coffee will do."

Sarah handed a cup to everyone, including a woman in a pink sundress.

"This is fine." My father removed the lid and blew into the steaming black liquid. It was odd, seeing my father do this. It made him human, vulnerable. My father, Charles Petrie, had to wait for his coffee to cool, just like everyone else.

"We picked up some sugar packets and creamer." Sarah emptied her pockets and placed the loot on a small table in the hall.

The woman in pink snatched up two fake sugars and dumped them in her cup, swirling them in with a wooden stir stick. Peter, who wore golf clothes—yellow pants with a purple shirt that could only look good on the Easter Bunny—passed on the sugar. I think the Easter Bunny would have been too proud to wear that outfit.

"Hi, I'm Sarah. And this is Lizzie—Peter's sister." Sarah offered her hand to the stranger dressed in pink.

The woman hesitated.

"Where are my manners?" Peter interrupted. "I'm so sorry. Elizabeth, I would like you to meet my fiancée, Tiffany."

My brother always insisted on calling me Elizabeth. I bristled at that, and at the fact that he hadn't bothered to introduce my wife, Sarah. *Just be nice.*

"Hi, Tiffany."

The woman spoke for the first time. "It's Tie-Fannie."

I tilted my head to catch the pronunciation. *"Tiff-*any?" I repeated, knowing full well that was not what she had said.

The pink lady shook her head and gave a fake smile. "No. It's pronounced more like Tie-Fannie."

Tie-Fannie. It wasn't bad enough that my brother was nearing forty and going to marry a chick who looked barely twenty-two, but he had to find a *Tiffany* who was so conceited she made up a whole new pronunciation of her name.

"Oh, how unusual. Is that a family name?" asked Sarah in a sincere tone.

Tiffany smiled, not responding. Maybe she didn't want to ruffle Peter's feathers. I was pretty certain Peter would have filled her in on his version of the jilted-at-the-altar story, leaving out that he was cheating on Maddie. He probably hadn't yet informed his new fiancée that he had no intention of being a faithful husband. No doubt that detail was superfluous to my brother.

"You never could count, Elizabeth," said Peter.

Count? How was this connected to his strange fiancée and the pronunciation of her name? I frowned.

Peter nodded to my mother's tea.

"Thanks, Peter. I completely forgot I got Mom a tea."

"Tea?" scoffed Peter. "Did you add scotch to it?"

Even Tiffany looked at Peter like he was a moron.

"That was very thoughtful, Lizzie. Your mom just asked for a tea." My father took the cup from me and disappeared into the hospital room.

Peter looked triumphant. Both of us knew I wouldn't get the credit for the tea. But I didn't give a damn.

"Dad said only two people are allowed in the room at a time. Would you mind if Tiff and I go first? I have a golf date with some clients." Peter sipped his coffee, an odd twinkle in his eye.

It took everything I had not to laugh in his face. *Just be nice, Lizzie.*

"Not a problem, Peter." I waved him in, and then turned my back on him and headed for a few chairs at the end of the hallway.

"It was wonderful meeting you, Tie-Fannie." Sarah stressed the pronunciation without a hint of mockery.

Sarah and I settled into the chairs. Soon, my father joined us after Peter and Tiffany entered the room.

"Your mother said thanks for the tea." For a second, I thought my father was going to pat my knee, but he pulled his hand away.

"When did Peter get engaged?" Sarah asked.

For a split second, I thought I saw a trace of disapproval in Dad's body language. "A couple of months ago."

"Have they known each other long?" probed Sarah.

My poor father probably wasn't used to being interrogated by anyone, especially about these types of matters. "A year," he grunted.

Sarah stopped her questioning and pulled out her cell phone. Was she texting Maddie? Hopefully not. I would like to break that news to her in person, not that she'd care all that much, not now that she had Doug the weatherman.

The three of us sat silently until Peter and Tiffany approached. "Elizabeth, the nurse said Mom needs to rest for a bit before you can see her."

Sarah and I remained in our seats. I seethed. Why did he always insist calling me Elizabeth, knowing full well I didn't like it?

My father rose and Peter shook his hand, business-like. "Dad, let us know if you need anything. I would skip this damn golf game if it wasn't so important." He puffed out his chest like a soldier. Did he really think a game of golf superseded his mother being in the hospital? How pathetic.

Peter always tried to appear more important than he was. True, he made a lot more money than me, but did that really matter? Both of us had trust funds, and neither of us had to work, really. But he stood in front of us posing as though the entire world as we knew it would collapse if he didn't rush off immediately.

My father escorted them to the elevator.

"What a jackass," I whispered to Sarah.

She covered her mouth, trying to look concerned rather than amused. "You know, Peter."

"Pompous prick." I sat up in my chair and mimicked, "I would skip the damn golf game —"

Then my father stood before me, and I felt the blood rush to my face.

Dad didn't say anything. He sat down next to me and stared straight ahead.

"How long will she be in the hospital?" Sarah tried to bury my *faux pas*.

"A few days, at least." Dad's voice was strong, but it carried a tinge of sadness. I got the impression he wanted to breakdown, except he didn't know how.

"I can stop by the next few days and keep her company," I offered. The idea of my mom alone in the hospital was an unbearable thought. I knew from my own battle with Graves' Disease how scary it was to deal with an enemy that showed no mercy. My thyroid condition was treatable, but it didn't have a cure. And it wasn't nearly as scary as cancer, certainly not in my opinion.

"Thank you. I would appreciate that. I think it'd be all right for you two to visit with her. The nurse said it was okay."

Wait? The nurse said it was okay? Had Peter lied to stall my visit? Was Peter trying to ruin whatever plans I had for the day? Not that I had any. And if I did, I would have canceled them, considering. What a conceited jerk.

Sarah stood and waited for me. I hadn't intended on asking her to actually visit with my mother, but after my father suggested the two of us should head in, I couldn't refuse. I always wondered whether my father really gave a damn that I was gay. He hadn't ever said a word either way. I added it to the list of things I didn't know about the man: whether he believed in God, whether he had a favorite football team, whether he preferred dark or milk chocolate, or, just anything, really? My father was a stranger. The only reason I knew his middle name was because I'd peeked at his passport when I was a child.

My mother. Well, that was a completely different story. I knew how Mom felt about me. Mom voiced her opinion, usually a negative one, all of the time. Whenever she had a chance, she took a dig at me for being a lesbian.

Les-Bi-An: that was how she pronounced it. Akin to an odious disease, like leprosy in biblical times.

Sarah paused right outside the door, and I let out a long breath and steadied my nerves. She gave me a mischievous smile, and all of a sudden I felt confident. I winked at her as we strolled in together to visit The Scotch-lady.

Mom lay in the hospital bed, resembling a shriveled, featherless bird. Her skin was pasty pale. No makeup hid her flaws or wrinkles. Her hair was still in a bun, but strands fell down haphazardly. The only way to describe how she looked was frail. Or, beyond frail, as in knocking on death's door.

Her eyes flicked open feebly, and she saw Sarah standing next to me. Her expression didn't contort with anger, but there was no warmth there either.

Feeling silly that I was gawking at her like she was a specimen under a microscope, I took the seat next to her bedside. "How you feeling?" I immediately cringed, knowing how she would respond. Why did I constantly ask her that question?

"How do you think?" came her curt reply.

I tried to console myself. At least she retained some of her usual anger; that might keep the fire going for a bit longer.

"Is there anything I…we can do to make your stay easier?" I motioned to Sarah. My mother hadn't even acknowledged her. At least my wife wasn't wearing a fucking pink dress and telling everyone they should pronounce her name Sa-Rah.

Mom motioned to the table at one side of her bed. One of the novels I had purchased for her recently sat there, pages down, the spine sitting up. "My eyes are too tired. Can you read to me?"

Tears began to well in my eyes, but I willed them away. "Sure."

"You"—she shocked the hell out me by motioning to Sarah—"can I have more tea?"

It wasn't the best progress, but at least she had admitted Sarah was in the room with us. I wouldn't have put it past my mother to ignore her completely.

"Of course, Evelyn," Sarah said without a glance at me, but her body language told me she thought this was a big step as well. Not that either of us pined for my mother's acceptance, but if we could live without strife, it would be something.

I read to my mother for several minutes before Sarah returned. By the time she peeked in, holding a steaming cup of herbal tea, the patient was fast asleep. Sarah sat down on the other side of the bed, not speaking. We both kept Mom silent company for an hour.

When Dad shook my hand as I said good-bye, I swear he held onto it for an extra second.

Was I imaging all of this? My mother had spoken to Sarah—negatively, sure, but she still spoke to her. My father hadn't exactly said, "Hey, I'm cool with the fact that you're a lesbo." But he had ushered Sarah into Mom's room and he had said he was glad I had someone.

Jesus! Why did I care?

And then there was Peter. What a fucking asshole.

By the time we got outside, I was worked up.

"A pink dress? Who wears a pink dress to the hospital?" I fumed.

Sarah stood back to avoid my flailing arms.

"It's early…on a Sunday. It wasn't like she was out and about and then rushed on over. Nope. She got a phone call just like us, and she intentionally put on a *pink* dress. My brother's bimbo actually got out of bed and slipped into a pink sundress to visit her future mother-in-law in the cancer ward. Un-Fuck-Ing-Believable!" I ranted, walking along the curb, following it as though I was in the circus and it was my tightrope. Spying a pop can in the gutter, I attempted to kick it. My foot soared over the top, causing me to lose my balance. I stumbled off the curb and landed on my ass.

Sarah tried to muffle her laughter.

That annoyed me. Instead of getting up and admitting I was acting like an ass, I lay down and stared at the gray sky above. Clouds threatened rain. Passersby threw me odd looks, and I did my best to return a snarky stare.

"Are you done?" Sarah finally asked.

"With what?" I barked.

"Throwing a fit?" Sarah loomed over me.

"No," I pouted.

"Lizzie, your mother is in the hospital. This isn't the time to act like a child. You're mad at Peter. I understand. But get a grip, will ya!"

"Mad at Peter? What're you talking about? Tie-Fannie is the one who wore pink." I let out a derisive snort.

"Oh, come on, you couldn't give two shits about what she wore. You're mad that Peter swooped in and did his usual Peter thing: acting like he was in charge and super important. He has a wonderful way of making you look like an ass."

"Does not." I tried to stop my face from scrunching up in anger.

"Really? Then tell me the real reason you're lying in the gutter."

"Gutter!" I bolted up.

Sarah tugged my arms and helped me to my feet. "Come on. Let's go get some food in you so we can come back this afternoon for visiting hours."

That night we had dinner plans with Maddie, Doug, and Rose. I wasn't in the mood for company.

"Maybe you should go without me." I tucked my hands into my jeans and stared intently at the floor, searching for an escape route. "I won't be good company tonight."

"Oh, honey. You're never good company." Sarah lifted my chin with her hand. "I don't think you should be alone tonight. You brood all day long when I'm at work." She winked at me.

"Brood—is that what you call research?" I attempted a weak smile, but I couldn't muster the energy.

"Come on. I need your help breaking the news to Maddie."

Her face said that was her final word. I had to go, or we'd be heading for a conversation later. And not a friendly chat—one of those talks Sarah said was supposed to be helpful but was actually anything but. I already knew I had shortcomings. Did we need to have a conversation to point them out? I preferred leaving things unsaid; Sarah didn't. Ever since I almost lost her, I realized that maybe her method was better. Didn't mean I liked it, though. Not. One. Bit.

My therapist agreed with Sarah. She encouraged open dialogue with my wife. Dialogue. It made it sound like we were diplomats trying to solve the Middle East Crisis. Not that our problems were that severe, thank God.

"Shall we order some bottles of wine?" Rose asked, after perusing the menu of the new Italian place the girls had read about in the local paper.

Their mission to try every restaurant in northern Colorado was starting to wear on me. Personally, I could eat at the same place every night of the week and be perfectly content. Once I found something I liked, I stuck with it. But those two loved change. Mixing things up scared me.

When Sarah's best friend, Haley, moved to California two years ago, Sarah and Maddie became almost inseparable. Maddie was still reeling from Peter, and Sarah had lost her best friend. Usually, their need to hang out all the time didn't bother me. But it did tonight. Why couldn't we stay at home so I could mope and eat a gallon of mint-chocolate-chip ice cream?

"Yes," responded Sarah. "I'm thinking red. Mom, you choose. You're so good at pairing wine with food."

While Rose ordered the wine, Maddie eyed me. "How's your mom, Lizzie?"

I shrugged. "She seems okay, given the circumstances. At least they don't have her hooked up to a bunch of machines—not sure I can take that. They've increased her Coumadin dosage, and they're monitoring the blood clot."

Rose and Maddie gave me sympathetic smiles, and Sarah rubbed my back. Then she turned to Maddie. The look in her eye said, *It's time to tell her.*

"We saw Peter," she said.

Maddie did her best not to react, but she did. I was pretty sure Doug noticed, although he tried to remain unperturbed. What an awkward situation. Really.

"How is the busy worker bee?" Maddie asked in a breezy tone.

"He had to rush off for a round of golf," I sneered.

Doug raised his eyebrows. I wondered how much he knew about my family. Probably enough. Maddie was chatty, just like Sarah. No wonder the two of them hit it off so well.

"You're kidding." Maddie chewed her lower lip, not in surprise but in contempt. "That's so Peter."

The waiter arrived and did the ridiculous routine of opening the bottle and letting Sarah's mom sample the wine. I hoped the process might distract Sarah, but knew, deep down, that it wouldn't.

Sarah patted my thigh. Then she dove headfirst into the danger zone. "He wasn't alone."

Rose's face scrunched up. Sarah's mom hadn't met any of my family, and I was fairly confident she never wanted to. The Petries were not high on many invite lists. They attended business functions, but friends? No. We didn't have any family in the state. It was just the four of us.

"Really?" Maddie's face looked curious. "Let me guess…much younger than me."

I laughed, but quickly tried to pretend I was coughing.

"Don't worry, Lizzie. I know your brother. Shall we play a game?" Maddie tapped her fingernails on her water glass. "She's blonde?"

Sarah nodded. Doug withered in his seat. Was he upset for Maddie, or for himself?

"Under twenty-five?"

Again, Sarah nodded.

"Ditzy?"

"She wore a pink sundress to the hospital," I stated.

"Dear me." Rose shook her head in disgust.

Maddie wrinkled her brow, thinking of the next question, but Sarah stopped her. "There's something you should know."

Doug opened his mouth, and I could see bits of half-chewed bread and wondered if he was trying to keep his mouth busy so he wouldn't speak out of turn.

Sarah turned to me, as if I should make the big announcement because Peter was my brother. Gee, thanks. I sat up in my chair and placed both hands on the table, bracing myself for the bomb I was about to drop.

Maddie's face paled.

Rose held a wineglass to her mouth, not sipping it. All eyes were on me.

I cleared my throat. "It seems that Peter is...engaged...again."

No one spoke. No one moved. Doug's mouth stayed open. Rose still held her wineglass to her lips. Sarah watched Maddie.

Maddie stared out the window. I wasn't sure she was breathing, and I tried to see if I could see her taking a breath (without being obvious that I was staring at her chest). Everyone was so still I felt as if we were trapped in a photograph.

"I..." The rest of my words stayed buried inside.

Maddie wadded up her napkin, threw it on the table, and then jumped out of her seat, knocking over her chair. With one hand over her mouth, she dashed out of the restaurant. Sarah leaped to her feet and chased after her. Rose glared at me as if I were the guilty party.

I wanted to joke, "Don't shoot the messenger," but Rose's former threat to run me over with her car popped in my head, silencing me.

Doug stared at the fork in his hand and traced some of the lines of the tablecloth with the tines.

"I think *some* families are more trouble than they're worth," stated Rose, grasping her wineglass, white knuckled, and bringing it jerkily to her lips. Her emphasis was directed at me, of course. I clenched my jaw and remained mute. I had no leg to stand on. I would be the last person to come to my family's defense.

"I'm not sure all families are that bad," responded Doug, weakly.

Rose nodded. "Sarah and I get along well."

"I'm best friends with my sister, and I'm close with my parents." Doug perked up some, straightening in his chair.

So, that left me. Only *my* family was fucked up. My brother was the reason Maddie had run from the restaurant like it was on fire.

Rose studied me closely, waiting for an opportunity to dig in her claws. I felt like a fox in a trap. Would she skin me alive?

"Uh, I think I'll go check on Maddie." I lurched out of my seat and rushed off before Rose or Doug could react.

I found them in Maddie's BMW. It wasn't cold out, but I'm assuming they wanted some privacy.

Sarah rolled down the passenger side window when I approached. I leaned down and patted Sarah's hand, where it rested on the car. "Everything okay?"

Maddie sniffled. "I don't know why I'm so upset."

Her reaction shocked me, but I sensed I should keep that thought to myself. My therapist kept telling me that my childhood prevented me from reacting to things like a normal person. She didn't say it like that, of course. She used much fancier lingo, to spare my fragile feelings. But that was the gist. My family fucked me up, and I cut myself off from others so I wouldn't get hurt.

"Don't be hard on yourself. Your reaction is normal." Sarah rubbed Maddie's back. Maddie leaned on the steering wheel. It made me think of drawings I'd seen of torture devices in the Middle Ages: a person prostrated on a rack and then gutted or quartered.

"Peter's an ass. When I walked out, I had no intention of ever seeing him again." Maddie's voice informed me she was barely in control. "So why do I care?"

I was wondering the exact same thing. Why was she facedown on the steering wheel, moaning about Peter marrying some young gold digger? Good riddance, if you asked me.

"Because you're human, Maddie." Sarah didn't look at me, but I wondered if she guessed my thoughts.

What a shitty day. First the hospital, and then Rose hinting that out of everyone at the table only I had the effed-up family, and now Sarah was hinting that I wasn't human.

Maddie slumped back against her seat, her face streaked with tears and snot. I cringed at the sight. Sarah searched the glove box, locating some tissues and passing them to Maddie, who started to clean herself up.

After a few moments, Maddie opened the driver side door. "Might as well go back in. Poor Doug."

I followed the two women in, feeling pretty shitty. Fuck Peter! He had messed up this whole day for me. The only person who had been civil to me the entire day was my father, and that was because the man never talked much. He had the right idea. I could relate to that; could respect it, in fact.

Doug stood and helped Maddie to her seat. Why was Maddie so upset about Peter when she had a nice guy like Doug? Sure, he had a big nose, but he wasn't wearing purple and yellow together.

"Thank you." Maddie placed a reassuring hand on Doug's shoulder.

"Can I get you anything, dear?" asked Rose. "Would you like a stiff drink?"

"Thank you, Rose. I'm fine. A bit embarrassed, really. Not sure why I reacted that way." Maddie smoothed the napkin on her lap.

"Well, the news could have been delivered better." Rose gave me the stink eye.

Wait a minute. Sarah had started it. She was the one who made me deliver the *coup de grace*. Why place the onus on me? If it were up to me, I wouldn't have said anything at all. Sarah's human need to share had got me into this mess. Maybe it *was* best to be a robot, like my father.

And how else was I supposed to deliver the news? Would sugarcoating it have worked better? Should I have said, "Well, there may be a chance that the two of them may be more serious than boyfriend/girlfriend…I don't mean wedding bells, but, oh, okay, I do."

The news had to be delivered, so I delivered it — at Sarah's prodding.

"Let's talk about something else." Maddie flashed a sad smile. "Something happy."

"I made an appointment with the fertility clinic to get the process started," Sarah said, as if that was normal dinner conversation. Did she really want to talk about sucking my eggs out of me and then putting one in her after mixing in some semen to make a baby cake?

"That's great news," Doug said. He looked like he meant it, as if he wasn't even grossed out by the process.

What was wrong with these people?

"When's the big day?" asked Maddie, obviously relieved that I was now in the hot seat.

"Not until September."

"Wait. What?" I said, without thinking. The months were flying by and September was just around the corner.

Sarah leaned closer to my ear. "I told you I was going to make the appointment." Her tone suggested I shouldn't start a scene.

"I know, I just didn't think…"

"Here we go," said Rose. She motioned to the waiter for another bottle of wine.

Sarah crossed her arms and Maddie eyed me with a look that warned *tread carefully*. Only Doug had kind eyes. Sympathetic eyes. I was starting to really warm to Doug the weatherman.

"Now, don't all gang up on me. It's not what you think."

"Please, Lizzie, tell me what I'm thinking." Sarah's sarcasm shot through me. I knew I was in serious shit now, for the second time that night. And I was innocent. I pictured myself being hauled off by bailiffs. After being sentenced to death, I shouted, "I'm innocent, I tell you. Innocent!"

"Sarah, I'm on board with the whole egg thing—"

"Egg thing? That's how you refer to our child?"

Oh boy. I wanted to say, "Fasten your seatbelts, it's going to be a bumpy ride," to help ease the tension, but one look at her face told me that would be a mistake.

I tugged on my collar and took a sip of water, unsure how to get out of this mess.

"I made sure the appointment didn't coincide with one of your mom's."

I nodded, remembering her asking for my mom's hospital appointment schedule. We kept a calendar on the fridge, so we could keep track of each other's schedules and avoid situations like this. Sarah started writing everything down on the calendar and there was some type of code that I couldn't decipher but never asked about.

"What day of the week is the appointment?" I held my breath.

"Monday."

Whew!

"That's great!" I thought my enthusiasm would make her feel better. I was wrong.

"What plans do you have that you don't want to tell me about?"

"It's not that."

I heard Doug shift in his seat, and Maddie cleared her throat menacingly. I have been known, in the past, to keep secrets from Sarah. "I just spaced it, with everything going on."

The waiter arrived to take our orders. The poor man had been waiting forever, given all of our previous drama. Rose waved him away. I made a mental note to give him a big tip, since we were taking up so much of his time. By now, we should have been enjoying our main course; instead, we hadn't even started eating.

"I've been invited to speak at a conference at a small university in California. The symposium is on a Friday, so I was hoping you could fly in that night, because the university is near Napa Valley. I thought it would be good for the two of us to have a weekend away together, before you're pregnant."

Sarah's eyes softened.

"I'm sorry. I got the call last Thursday, when I was at one of my mom's appointments. I totally spaced out about putting it on our calendar. It wasn't until you mentioned the appointment that I even remembered the commitment. That would have been embarrassing—if I didn't show up." I coaxed her back around with a silly grin.

"Why didn't you just spit it out, Lizzie?" asked Rose, too busy snapping her fingers at the poor server to bother waiting for my response. She was ready to eat, and she was fed up with me.

So Sarah could just spit out news about our medical appointments, but I couldn't spill the news that Peter was getting married? I never knew how to act around Rose anymore. Sarah leaned over and whispered in my ear, "I heart you."

CHAPTER NINE

The next day, I found Tiffany sitting at Mom's bedside in the hospital. Mom was napping. I nodded hello, not wanting to disturb the patient.

"Hi!" Tiffany said.

Mom stirred, but her eyes didn't budge.

Tiffany covered her mouth, realizing her blunder, and motioned for me to follow her out of the room.

"How's she doing?" I asked, gesturing in my mother's direction.

"Huh? Oh, fine. I was wondering if you wanted some coffee." She leaned in conspiratorially, which annoyed me. We weren't close, and I didn't like the implication that we were. "I'm so bored. I'm falling asleep."

Nice, Peter. Real nice gal you snagged this time. I didn't want a coffee. But I did want to get rid of Tiffany for a few moments, so I sent her to get me a chai and a tea for my mom. I stressed that it should be herbal, with no caffeine.

"Sure thing. I'll be back in a jiffy." She smiled at me as if I were a child enjoying a parade. Jesus! Did she even know where she was? I watched her lemon-yellow dress disappear around the corner, listening to the *clip-clop* of her three-inch wedge sandals. Why would anyone wear such preposterous shoes? I half hoped to hear her crashing to the ground.

Back in the room, I settled down in a chair by the bedside—the one Tiffany had just vacated. Mom and I weren't close either, but I still felt I deserved the primo seat in her hospital room.

"Is she gone?" Mom whispered, only one eye open.

"For the moment. She's on a coffee run."

Mom harrumphed.

"How are you feeling?" I stood and bent to take her hand in mine, stopping just before I made an ass out of myself. I pictured her pulling her hand away, like a snapping turtle yanking its head back into its shell.

"I want out of here."

"What did the doctor say? Can you leave soon?" I cursed the hope I could hear in my voice, afraid it would set Mom off.

She waved a bony hand in the air. "Everyone here is an idiot. I feel fine. I want to go home." She pulled her blanket up to her chin, hiding. "I have a nurse at home. She can take care of me."

Not knowing what to say, I went with, "It's nice of Tiffany to keep you company."

Mom rolled her eyes. There was no need to verbalize her thoughts; her body language said it all.

Was it possible that Peter had found a woman who irritated my mother more than I did?

The door sprang open with a bang, and Tiffany appeared. "Goodness, that door is light. I feel like Superman."

For the first time, I noticed her toned arms. Did the woman spend all day in the gym? I wondered if she had a six-pack.

"Oh, you're awake!" Tiffany thrust my chai in my face and then cheerfully presented the tea to my mother, as though offering a diamond ring. "I got you your fave—herbal tea."

I wanted to punch her in the face. I was the one who told her to get the herbal tea, and I was shocked she had managed to remember that for five minutes.

"Thank you," Mom said to me.

Tiffany was too busy being cheerful to notice that my mom had snubbed her. Something gave me the impression she missed a lot of things in life. Had she picked up on the fact that my brother was an arrogant ass who cheated? Maybe it was best if she didn't know.

"So, what did I miss?" Tiffany plunked herself down on the chair opposite me and ripped the cover off her latte, a silly grin spreading over her face.

Mother sipped her tea angrily.

"Tiffany, where did you grow up?" I asked.

"Tie-Fannie," she corrected.

"Yes, I'm sorry." I put my hand up to emphasize my apology. "Where did you grow up?" I didn't bother saying her name correctly. I swore right then and there that I would never call Tiffany by her name ever again; instead, I'd just say, "Hey you."

I enjoyed seeing my mother's scornful frown from behind the cup of herbal tea, mocking the girl.

I should send Peter a thank-you note. Usually, my mother ridiculed me.

"Right here, but I've traveled all over the world."

"Really? Where have you been?"

"So many countries: Mexico, Bermuda, the Caribbean, Puerto Rico, and…Hawaii." She counted each one on her right hand, a glint of pride in her face.

I wanted to correct her, to tell her that Hawaii was actually a part of the States, and that one could make an argument about Puerto Rico, too, even if I was sure the people there felt differently. The puppy dog look on her face told me I'd be wasting my time.

I tried a different approach. "Did Peter take you to these places?"

"Oh no. He's been so busy lately."

I was pretty sure I knew why: he'd been busy avoiding her and being with other women.

"I went to all *those* places for spring break." Tiffany's emphasis was an obvious effort to make herself sound as well traveled as Marco Polo.

"What university did you go to?"

She cocked her head, eying me suspiciously. "College? I didn't go to college."

"Sorry, I just assumed…since you said spring break." A sip of chai helped force my laugh back down my throat. *Where in the world did Peter find this clueless child?*

"My family always goes away each spring. My brothers are in college, so we work around their spring breaks. I considered going to college." She shook her head, giving me the impression she thought it unladylike to seek higher education.

"I see."

I looked to my mother for help, hoping she would say something that might nip all chatter in the bud—she had such a knack for doing that—but instead, she stared at Tiffany with her mouth slightly agape.

"Peter said *you* went to college," she said. Tiffany tried her best to erase the disgust from her face. "And that's why…why you aren't around much." A blush flashed across her face like a lightning bolt.

I could tell she wasn't an experienced liar. It took her some effort to recover from her gaffe. Had Peter told her college turned me into a lesbian? A woman allowed to think for herself apparently led to independence—and lesbianism.

"Yes, I did. I have a PhD in history."

"What's that?"

"A doctorate in history." From the expression on Tiffany's face, I knew I wasn't getting through to her. "I'm a doctor."

"Oh, do you work here?" She waved to the room.

"Nope. Different kind of doctor."

For a brief moment, I got the feeling that my mom was proud of me. Here I was talking to Peter's fiancée, who was dumber than a post, and I could say I was a doctor. Too bad Mom couldn't gloat about this at the club.

"She studies Nazis," Mom offered, her voice betraying no emotion.

Was she proud? Or had I imagined it?

"I've heard of Mengele. Are you a doctor like that?" Tiffany looked hopeful.

Mengele! Did she just ask me if I was a twisted fuck who tortured people in concentration camps?

The blank look on her face suggested she didn't even know it was an insult.

What was it like in her head?

"No. Not at all." I leaned down and pulled a box out of my messenger bag, which sat on the floor. "I got you this, Mom. It's a Kindle. Not only can you read books on it, but you can also listen to books as well." I handed it to her.

A couple of weeks ago, my mother had handed me a note that requested certain titles. I noticed that some of the books were by authors I had already given to her. Sarah and Ethan had done a great job. Her chicken-scratch handwriting was so wobbly and difficult to decipher that, for some reason, it upset me. The fact that it was scrawled with a purple pen disturbed me. Purple and The Scotch-lady? How did I not know she liked purple?

To my surprise, Mom opened the box with a hint of glee. I showed her how to turn the Kindle on. "It's connected to the Internet as well, so you can email and stuff. And when you want to shop"—I pointed to the shop button at the top—"all you have to do is search for any book you want and click buy. It downloads within seconds. It holds hundreds of books." I neglected to tell her that I had my credit card hooked up to her account.

"Hundreds! Who wants to read that many books?" Tiffany slurped her latte. "I tried reading that book everyone was raving about years ago—*Eat, Pray, Live,* or something like that—and couldn't get through the first ten pages. Hundreds? I don't know if I've met anyone who's read that many books. Even the Julia Roberts movie based on that book bored me." Tiffany snatched the device out of Mom's brittle hands. "Oh, it has apps like my cell phone. Does it have Angry Birds? Now that's something worth having."

Mom cleared her throat and motioned for Tiffany to hand the Kindle back. The clueless woman did not realize that my mother was completely unimpressed with Angry Birds.

Mom turned to me. "Will you read to me, Lizzie?"

"I thought you said that it would read to her," Tiffany said to me. Then turned to Mom. "Why make Lizzie waste her time?"

"Lizzie has a nice reading voice. Must be from all her years teaching at a university." She eyed Tiffany. Was she trying to decide whether Peter's fiancée understood her meaning?

"What would you like me to read?" I asked, trying not to enjoy the moment too much. Maybe I should send Peter a basket of cookies to thank him, not just a card.

"*Eat, Pray, Love,*" snapped my mother.

I busied myself with the Kindle, downloading the book and watching Tiffany out of the corner of my eye. It took her less time to make a decision than I thought it would.

"You know, I told Peter I'd meet him for lunch. I better head out." She threw her purse over her shoulder. She held the door handle and spoke over her shoulder, "Enjoy the book. Um, it's really… interesting."

And the ditz in yellow was gone.

CHAPTER TEN

A YOUNG WOMAN SAT AT MY KITCHEN TABLE, WIDE-EYED, WHILE I PUTTERED AROUND GETTING some snacks ready.

"Would you like something to drink? Tea? Coffee? Water?" I mimed etcetera with my hand.

"Tea would be great." She pulled a couple of notebooks from her over-stuffed backpack.

"Sure, I'll put the kettle on. So, where did you complete your undergrad?" I asked as I filled the kettle.

"University of Puget Sound." She doodled on her notepad, patiently waiting.

Steam spewed out of the kettle, and I lifted it off the burner before it had a chance to scream.

Setting the teacups down, I said, "All right, why don't you tell me about your thesis?"

Hours later, I heard Sarah walk through the front door. "I'm home," she shouted.

"In the kitchen."

My companion looked at her watch. "Goodness! Look at the time." She gathered her notebooks and started to shove them into her bag, struggling to cram everything back in.

"You won't fucking believe what I heard today at work!" Sarah sashayed into the kitchen and then stopped in her tracks. "I'm sorry. I didn't know you had company."

My guest looked nervous, which made me smile. When I was her age, everything made me jumpy. And the first week of the school semester always made me jumpier.

"Sarah, I'd like you to meet Jasmine." I motioned to the awkward but stunning graduate student.

"I've heard all about you." Jasmine put her hand out.

Sarah shook Jasmine's hand as if she wanted to crush it, which surprised me a little. Her eyes suggested she would rather throw the woman out of the house than greet her. Sarah must have had a bad day, I figured, but it was only the third day back after the summer vacation, which didn't bode well for the rest of the year.

Ignoring Sarah for a moment, I turned to Jasmine. "I'll walk you to the door."

My wife followed me so closely I could feel her angry breath on my neck, making Jasmine jumpier. "Call me if you need any help, day or night," I said.

"Thanks," Jasmine said. "Thanks for everything. Nice meeting you, Sarah," she added in a shaky voice.

Sarah popped her head over my shoulder, and Jasmine started as if she'd had a heart attack. "You too, Jas*mine*."

I cringed at Sarah's pronunciation.

After I shut the front door, I turned around to face Sarah. Arms crossed, she was tapping one foot expectantly. "What was that about?" she demanded.

"What was what about: your rudeness to my guest?"

"*My* rudeness?" She placed a hand over her heart. "How would you feel if you walked in while I was entertaining a sexy young woman?"

"Entertaining…?" I had to laugh. "Sarah—"

"I don't see anything funny about this." Her angry tone increased with each word she spewed.

"What are you insinuating? That I slept with Jasmine and then, just for shits and giggles, made her several cups of tea so she'd still be here when you got home—at your usual time?" I pinned her with a look of disgust. "You think that lowly of me?"

Sarah just grunted. Her scrunched forehead and bunched shoulders suggested she wasn't willing to let the accusation die just yet.

"Tell me, Sarah, what do you think I did?" I bottled up my fury, stopping it from slipping into my tone.

"Jasmine is a very beautiful woman," she sputtered.

"Yes. I'd noticed that." I flashed my "so what?" expression.

Sarah's expression opened out—an aha moment. I could tell she was thinking that if I'd noticed Jasmine's looks, I must have acted on it.

"And so…that means I fucked her?"

At the word *fuck*, Sarah cringed.

I stormed back into the kitchen to prepare another cup of tea. I didn't really want one, but I needed to stay busy. I didn't want to think. I concentrated on the clicking of the gas burner, and then on the catch of the flame. Next, I grabbed two cups and spooned sugar in each, ignoring Sarah's sugar ban. Not having anything else to do to keep my fingers busy while the water boiled, I started to count to ten.

Sarah watched my every move.

Finally, she said, "Well, why was she here, in *our* home?"

I wasn't ready to let her off the hook yet, even if that little voice in my head said I should.

This isn't worth the fight. Just let it go, Lizzie.

"So, you think that with everything I have going on in my life—my mom, us trying to get pregnant, my research project—you think I have the time, let alone the energy, to have an affair. And you also think I'm either stupid enough or vindictive enough to let you walk in on it." I glared at her, ignoring the whistling kettle; steam rose from it, blurring my vision of Sarah, who stood on the opposite side of the island, near the stovetop.

"You still don't trust me, not after a year of couple's therapy and three years of individual therapy for me."

Sarah sighed, and all the tension left her shoulders. Sadness and guilt filled the void. "Lizzie—"

I put up my hand to silence her words, and then I turned off the burner.

"I'll play by your rules, Sarah. Do you remember Dr. Marcel, my mentor in grad school? That was one of his students. He asked me to help with her dissertation. You do remember Dr. Marcel, don't you? We've had dinner at his home on several occasions. Jasmine is researching growing up in the Third Reich, which happens to be my specialty." Part of me wanted to give my wife a reassuring hug. But the other part felt betrayed. "Did you think…?" I couldn't complete my accusation.

Her eyes widened. If we'd been in a cartoon, a light bulb would have gone off over her head. "Oh, I remember you mentioning that." She looked down at the island bench, guiltily. "I didn't expect a history PhD student to be named Jasmine."

"So if she was named Gertrude, you wouldn't have thought I was having an affair?" It was my turn to cross my arms over my chest.

"Not if she looked the exact opposite of Jasmine." Sarah's tone was tinged with culpability, but she flashed an award-winning smile to cover it.

"Jesus, Sarah! I'm not Peter. That girl is just a child. When I first met her, I couldn't help but remember when I started my PhD program. I don't remember being that young, looking that young. And I also thought thank God I'm not anymore. I'm in a much happier place now, here with you."

That softened Sarah up some. "What did she mean when she said she'd heard all about me?"

I huffed, annoyed. "We got to talking about our partners, and how lucky we are that we both have supportive people in our lives. Jasmine's fiancé moved here from Seattle. She was rushing off to be with him."

"Lizzie" — Sarah took my hand in hers — "I'm sorry."

"Maybe I should be flattered that you think I still have enough game for Jasmine." I glanced down at my waistline. With everything going on, although I still took a bike ride each day, it was a short one, not my usual twenty miles. It was definitely showing.

"I'm going to talk to Dr. Marcel," Sarah said, gazing at me hopefully, as though she hoped I'd forgotten what just transpired.

"Really? What do you intend to say: don't accept graduate students who are attractive? I go to universities all of the time to give lectures. Do you think the entire audience is made up of old men in tweed jackets with elbow patches?"

"Yes, that's exactly how I picture it, plus a few old maids."

I rolled my eyes. "Is that how you picture me?"

"On the outside, no. But you can be a bit stuffy."

"I'm meeting Jasmine in two weeks — am I still stuffy?" I couldn't help needling her a little.

"We should have her over for dinner?"

"After your performance today, I doubt she'll want to see you again. Hell, she'll probably cancel on me." I poured hot water into the cups. Sarah didn't ask for tea, but it was my peace offering.

"Good. Mission accomplished," Sarah pouted resolutely.

"I was at Bed Bath & Beyond this morning, would you like to see what I bought?" I wanted to change the subject, knowing it would go nowhere. It was also possible that I wanted to make her feel worse about the situation.

"You went shopping? And at Bed Bath & Beyond?" She pinned me with a skeptical scowl as she added milk to her tea.

"Please don't hint that I was having another liaison. You only get one false accusation per year."

She saluted me. "So, why were you there, then?"

"I had an early lunch with Maddie, and she needed to pop in there for work. I really didn't have a choice."

She nodded, understanding.

I'm not the shopping type. Sarah bought all of my clothes for me during her weekend shopping sprees with her mom. Those two were born shoppers. Me, I despised it.

"Can you stop judging me for one second and follow me?" I led her to our spare bedroom, which we'd planned to turn into a nursery. "Now, I know I probably should have waited for you, but I saw this and I thought it was adorable." The zoo animal wall decals were propped against the far wall. "I haven't put them on yet, but what do you think?"

Sarah put her hand to her mouth. When she could finally speak, she said, "You picked this out… on your own? Or did Maddie?"

"It was me. If you don't like them, I saved the receipt." I tried to keep the disappointment from my voice.

"Like them…I love them!"

I grinned. I'd made sure the animals weren't blue or pink, since we didn't know what sex our child would be, and Sarah was adamant about creating a gender-neutral environment. The giraffe, elephant, and hippo were lilac, purple, and aqua respectively. I was disappointed that the decals didn't include an otter.

"Oh, Lizzie. I'm so sorry."

"What do you mean? Won't these work on our walls?" I lifted the packaging to read the instructions.

"Not that. I'm sorry I was so rude to Jasmine. Here you were, shopping for the nursery earlier today."

I smiled and wrapped my arms around her. "You have nothing to worry about, Sarah. But, it does mean you have to take me to dinner to make up for it."

Even though we had a kitchen most chefs would love, we hardly ever cooked. I was home all day, but no one wanted to eat my cooking. Sarah was usually too tired from teaching and coaching to want to cook.

She rested her head against my chest. "It's a deal." She pulled away from me. "But will you still find me attractive when I'm as large as a house?"

"You'll be even more beautiful." I smiled. "Hey, Jasmine mentioned she needed a part-time job. Maybe she can be our nanny," I teased, ducking away carefully so I wouldn't spill my tea when she whacked me in the side.

"Stop hitting me and take me to dinner." I kissed Sarah's forehead. "What happened at work today?"

Her expression clouded over. "I'll tell you over dinner. Okay if Maddie and Doug join us?"

I nodded. "Wow, Doug is like her shadow these days. She never spent that much time with Peter."

"She really likes him. After being with your brother, who was never around, I think she likes being in a real relationship."

"Or she's afraid to let him out of her sight. Are all of you women so mistrustful?"

Sarah didn't dignify that comment with a response. "Go shower. You look like hell."

I laughed. "First you accuse me of having an affair. Now you're telling me I look like hell. You need to make up your mind, missy."

Sarah shucked her skirt and tugged her shirt over her head. She shook her head, tousling her hair, eyes lowered. I eyed her crimson bra and panties.

I started to speak, but her lips were on mine in a shot. Her tongue darted into my mouth, while she peeled my shirt up, pushing away from me briefly to get it off completely. Not wanting to make love to her in the future nursery, I led her to our bedroom, leaving a trail of bras and panties behind us.

We fell on the bed, naked, Sarah's urgency apparent. I eased inside her as she again smothered my mouth with hers. I wasn't sure whether it was her earlier fear, or whether something else had happened, but I sensed Sarah needed to feel sexy, needed me to make love to her. And I was more than willing.

"It's unlike you to be late." Maddie's mouth curved into a mischievous smile as Sarah and I slid into the booth across from her.

"Hello, troublemaker," I said. I turned to Doug and nodded. He reciprocated.

"Lizzie, you look like hell." Maddie's voice was full of piss and vinegar, but her eyes showed concern.

"Funny, someone else told me that recently." I winked at Sarah. I wanted to add *before seducing me*, but I thought it best to keep that to myself. Maddie was never shy about embarrassing me. Both Sarah and I had showered before leaving the house, but I imagined I could still smell her on my fingers. I brushed my fingertips over my lips, in hope of catching her scent, smiling at the memory.

The waitress appeared to announce the nightly special: steak with blue cheese crumbles. It won me over instantly. Sarah ordered a Caesar salad, which was totally not her norm. I threw her an odd look, but said nothing.

"So, what's this news?" Maddie pounced, as soon as the waitress flipped her notebook shut and padded away on tiny feet. I wondered how the woman stayed erect on such silly looking feet.

I should have known Sarah had called Maddie about whatever the heck happened to her today before she got home. It was highly unusual for her to be so rude to anyone. I still couldn't believe the way she had acted towards Jasmine. As a peace offering, I resolved to call the poor girl in a few days' time and check on her progress in tracking down some of the sources I had suggested.

Sarah sat up straight in her chair and placed both hands on the table. Her posture told me that the news she was about to break was beyond upsetting. "You remember my coworker Jen, who works in the front office?"

Maddie and I nodded. Doug cocked his head in expectation.

"She's bursting out to here"—Sarah indicated extreme pregnancy—"well, she went home early the other day because she wasn't feeling well." She leaned over the table and whispered, "She surprised her husband—fucking another woman on their couch!"

Maddie covered her mouth. Doug's jaw clenched. He looked like he wanted to punch the husband right in the kisser.

"Can you imagine being seven months pregnant and discovering your husband is having an affair?" Sarah collapsed back into her seat as though she'd been slugged in the face.

"So that's why you accused me of sleeping with Jasmine!" I slapped the table.

Sarah looked away guiltily.

"Who's Jasmine?" Maddie said sourly, staring at me as though she was considering taking me out back and using me as a punching bag. Doug straightened in his seat, too, unsure whether he should wait for my response or be the knight in shining armor.

"Hey now, don't jump to any conclusions like someone else I know." I jerked my head in Sarah's direction. "I'm innocent, I tell you."

Maddie groaned.

"What is that groan supposed to mean?" I was getting pissed all over again.

"Come on, Lizzie. You tried to sleep with me."

And there it was: the elephant in the room that the three of us always avoided. It was the first time any one of us had mentioned it so blatantly in a group setting since it happened. Of course, Sarah and I talked about it in therapy…well, we danced around it, at least.

Doug started to stand, and for a moment I thought he really was going to slug me. Maddie tugged on his arm, forcing him to sit down.

"Thanks for that, Maddie. Much appreciated," I smirked.

"Can someone tell me what's going on?" someone boomed.

I jumped, unused to Doug's voice sounding so manly.

"It happened long ago," Maddie explained.

Doug's jaw kept working. It didn't satisfy him, I could see, and if I were in his shoes, I would want to know all the details as well.

Sarah looked as if she wanted to melt into the cushions of the booth and disappear entirely.

"I made a very stupid mistake—years ago—and I've been living with it ever since."

That got a rise out of Sarah. "Living with it! I never even mention it! I never throw it in your face."

I stared at her. "Until today…"

Doug pinned Maddie with a look that said he wanted answers, right away. "Did you or did you not sleep with Lizzie? And was she dating Sarah at the time?"

I admired his bravery, but his tone was not the way to handle Maddie.

Maddie squared her shoulders, ready for battle. "Excuse me…" She jutted her chin out. "Who in the hell do you think you are?"

"Hold on, everyone!" I snapped my fingers to get them all to look at me. "Let's not drag past mistakes into the present."

"Shut up, Lizzie. I don't want to hear any of your psychobabble—"

"Hey, Lizzie has been making great strides in therapy," Sarah came to my defense.

"Really? Is that why you accused her of fucking someone today?" Maddie somehow managed to eye Sarah while still giving Doug a menacing glance. I wondered if doing that gave her a headache, or eyestrain at the very least.

Diners at surrounding tables stopped talking and turned to stare at our table, some in mid-bite. One older woman left her fork dangling in front of her mouth, watching us intently as if we were a reality television show.

Maddie cleared her throat and stared the woman down until she looked away.

At that, the other patrons lost interest; out of fear, I guessed.

I turned to Doug. "A few years ago, I was really lost. I know it sounds like a cliché, but I was a total mess. And I made a pass—just a pass—at Maddie. You'll be happy to hear that Maddie slapped my face and told me what she thought of me. I now know that was my way of sabotaging my relationship with Sarah because I was scared to death of settling down. Sarah—" I turned to her, full of remorse—"left me. And it nearly killed me." I could feel my eyes welling up. "Luckily, she was willing to give me another chance, and I will never mess up again." I stared into Sarah's eyes. "Never again."

"Then who's Jasmine?" asked Maddie, not entirely convinced.

"When Sarah came home today, there was a woman in our house."

Maddie scowled.

"She's a PhD student, working with my former mentor, who asked me to meet with her to help her locate sources for her dissertation. Sarah strutted in, saw me talking with a beautiful young woman, and assumed the worst."

Sarah smiled sheepishly. "In my defense, Jasmine is hot as shit."

I shrugged, conceding the point. "And she's engaged. How did you not notice the huge diamond on her finger? It's bigger than yours." I pointed to Sarah's ring finger.

Maddie pulled her cell phone out of her back jeans pocket. "What's her last name?"

"No idea. Why?"

"I'm looking her up." Her crinkled brow said *duh*.

"Can't be too many PhD candidates named Jasmine on the school's website."

Maddie snapped her fingers. "Good thinking!" Several seconds later, she uttered, "Whoa!"

Doug whipped the phone away from her and held it in front of his face. He briefly flashed me a look that was all conquering hero.

"You see!" declared Sarah.

Doug and Maddie both nodded.

"So, Maddie, if you came home and Doug was sitting down having tea with Jasmine, would your first thought be, 'That bastard!'"

Doug leaned closer to Maddie, eyebrows raised.

"Here ya go," the waitress interrupted. She plunked her tray down on a stand her coworker had set up and started to dish out the meals.

"Ha! Saved by steak." I winked at Maddie.

Doug's determined smile suggested he'd get his answer later that night anyway.

CHAPTER ELEVEN

SUMMER PASSED QUICKLY, AND I STEPPED OUT OF MY HOUSE ONE MORNING TO FIND MYSELF shocked by the crisp fall air. How had I missed an entire season? Not once had Sarah and I ventured out to our cabin in Idaho. Usually, we spent several summer weeks up there during her school break. My thirty-first birthday slipped by almost unnoticed by me.

With fall came another check-up for Mom. Once again, I found myself waiting in the oncologist's office while my mother was in the back, hopefully hearing encouraging news — not that I ever knew what was said. Usually, my stony-faced mother sauntered out from behind the door and then strode right for the exit. She didn't even bother saying my name or anything. I had to keep an eye out for her, bolting up as soon as I caught a glimpse of her navy suit whisking by.

This time, I saw the door open slightly. A pause. Maybe the person behind the door had dropped something and leaned down to get it, or maybe a nurse had called out to the patient to say something. Or maybe someone just wasn't ready to face the world outside yet.

Filled with dread, I couldn't take my eyes off the door. Then it opened forcefully and an elderly gentleman ambled out, heading straight for the exit. He looked defeated. I'm not the religious type, but I said a small prayer for him. A woman followed him, moving as though the world was rubble around her feet. *Which one received the news?* I wondered.

I sat there, contemplating what would be harder: hearing that I had cancer or hearing that Sarah did? Actually, that was a no-brainer. I would never want Sarah to suffer. I said another prayer. *If one of us is struck, let it be me.*

Finally, my frail mother appeared. This time, she paused and stared at me, her face slack with an expression I couldn't make out. She flashed the tiniest of smiles. And then — poof! — it was gone. I wondered if I imagined it in the first place. Mom marched to the exit, and I followed dutifully, feeling slightly relieved.

When I dropped her off at her house, she mentioned that my dad would be away on business over the weekend.

"If you don't have plans, why don't you come by on Saturday, for lunch? Bring that girl with you."

Before I could answer yes or no, Mom pranced up the staircase to her front door, moving with a lightness I had never seen before.

That girl. My wife.

I wasn't sure whether to be angry or happy. It was the first time Mom had ever asked any of my partners over. Sarah had been to my brother's house on a few occasions, but she had never set foot in my parents' home.

That girl!

I started laughing so hard I had to pull off the highway. Then, inexplicably, tears started falling from my eyes. Something told me Mom's smile wasn't one of victory, but of relief.

Was it over?

And if it was, what: the battle, or the treatments?

Ever since we'd bought our house, I'd spent most of my days in my office, which doubled as the library. When we started house hunting for the second time, after Sarah forgave me, I took it more seriously than the first. Before the whole Maddie situation, Sarah had wanted us to buy a house, but I was too chickenshit to tell her I wasn't ready to take that step. Instead, every time we went looking, I found something wrong with the house. Sarah had assumed I was being overly picky because I wanted our house to be perfect.

When we officially began looking the second time, I had a different goal: to rein in Sarah's desire to spend money, too much money. Yes, we both had trust funds, but I didn't think we should spend willy-nilly. I wanted a relatively small home with no extra bedrooms. Guest bedrooms invited visitors, and I liked my space. Sarah said she agreed, so the first couple of weeks we saw only average-sized homes.

Then I noticed something. Sarah kept inviting me to used bookstores with her, helping me track down wonderful leather-bound editions of classics.

Her explanation was simple, "We can't have a house filled with just Nazi books. The first time I visited your apartment I was terrified by all the swastikas on the shelves. I thought I'd walked into some type of serial-killer trap."

I laughed. "Occupational hazard, I guess."

She had placed a loving hand on my shoulder. "We don't want people thinking you're a Neo-Nazi *and* socially awkward."

"So, just socially awkward is okay?" I asked.

"Not much I can change about that. It is your personality," she retorted, with a wink.

At first, I loved the shopping excursions, which was saying a lot, since I loathed shopping. Then I noticed a second trend. The more books we bought, the bigger the houses we visited. At first they weren't substantially larger, but they gradually started getting out of my comfort zone. Each time, Sarah found something wrong with the house.

My gut told me I was being played, but I couldn't put my finger on how. This continued for a few months. We bought more and more books, and the houses we toured were bigger and bigger.

One Monday morning, while she was getting ready for work, Sarah mentioned that the agent had a home she wanted to show us that evening. "She says it's perfect for us."

I tried not to roll my eyes. Our agent said that every time. "Sure, I'll meet you there."

The house was a mansion. Well, not really, but it was much too large for my taste. When I pulled up at the address, I doubled-checked Sarah's handwritten note with the address on the side of the home.

"She's out of her frigging mind," I grumbled when I opened my car door to greet Sarah and the agent on the stoop. The house was near the old town section of Fort Collins. It wasn't new, but nor was it as old as some in the area.

I wanted a new home; the idea of living in a place that other people had once lived in creeped me out. What could I say? I was both a neat freak and a control freak.

Sarah rushed up to me and threw her arms around my neck, giving me a peck on the cheek. "Isn't this beautiful?" she squealed in delight.

I grinned, knowing she was playacting for my benefit, to lure me in.

The agent walked us around the house. I had to agree it was lovely. The floor plan was open—I hated tight spaces—with four bedrooms. I cringed at the thought of people staying in our house and having to act happy to have them. Acting jubilant was not my forte.

But this time, Sarah wasn't finding fault with the home. As we neared the end of the tour, I wasn't yet sold. But I knew Sarah was. I was mentally preparing for battle.

We don't need this much space for the two of us, I kept thinking. *Too large. Too expensive. And much too pretentious.*

"There's one last room I want to show you two, especially you, Lizzie," said the agent.

I raised an eyebrow, curious.

She opened the door to the library. I kid you not, it was the one I had always dreamed of. Floor-to-ceiling bookshelves, with a few of the quaint little ladders I always found so charming. At the far end, bay windows presented a wonderful view of the foothills. And the room was big enough to accommodate a massive desk, a couch, and leather reading chairs, all without feeling cramped. Hell, I could put a pool table off to the side if I wanted to. Maybe even a Ping-Pong table.

My mouth hit the floor. Sarah and the agent stared at me, waiting.

"How long have you been holding out?" I asked Sarah.

She shrugged and gave me an unconvincing, "I don't know what you mean" look.

I crossed my arms.

Sarah put her palms up. "All right. Mom and I found it weeks ago."

"You played me." I walked to the windows and looked out, keeping my back to both of them.

"What do you think?" asked the agent.

Without turning around, I said, "Where do I sign?"

Sarah let out a relieved squawk and rushed toward me, almost slamming me against the windows as she enveloped me in her arms.

"Nicely played."

She giggled. "Now you have a place for all those books," she whispered.

I nodded. "You aren't getting out of it. We still have plenty of space to fill. Our book shopping trips aren't over just because you got your way."

"Deal." She squeezed me tight. "Maddie's going to be thrilled!"

"I take it she's already seen it."

"Of course. We can't buy a place without our designer's approval." Sarah whisked a strand of hair out of her face, triumphantly.

"I'm surprised you didn't just go ahead and buy it."

"Don't be silly. Your input is important to me." She almost looked sincere. "Plus, I can't forge your signature."

Sarah found me in my office, snapping me back to reality. "There you are?"

I looked up from my gin and tonic, leaving the memories in the past.

"Why are you sitting in the dark?" I didn't hear a hint of accusation in her tone, only concern.

I sighed. "I don't know, really."

Since leaving Mom earlier that day, I couldn't get the thought out of my head that it was over. Just when I was finally getting through to her, it was over. For thirty years that woman had ignored me or tortured me. And then, for a few months, I had a mother, albeit one still completely on her terms.

Sarah flicked on the desk lamp. I hadn't realized that the sun had gone down, and I was sitting in the dark. She left the room and soon returned with a glass of wine. Perching on the leather chair next to mine, she said, "Do you want to talk about it?" Then she took a nervous sip of wine.

She sniffed loudly and I watched her light a Yankee Candle.

Knowing Sarah wouldn't let her question fade away like the smoke from the candle, I finally answered, "Not much to talk about really. I don't know what's going on."

"With your mom?"

I let out a sad laugh, "with anything." I walked to the small bar in my office and replenished my drink, heavy on the gin. My back to Sarah, I asked, "Why do we crave love from those who are most incapable of loving?"

I heard the creak of leather as Sarah stood. Wrapping her arms around my waist, she gave me a squeeze. "Nothing about love is easy."

"Then why do we crave it so much?" I stifled a sob.

As always, Sarah was in tune with my thoughts. "Just enjoy the time you have left with her, Lizzie. This is your one chance. Take it."

I broke free from her arms and slumped against the bar. "Do you know she's never told me that she loves me? Not once."

"Have you told her that?"

I shook my head. "It would mean nothing to her."

"That may be true, but would it mean something to you?"

CHAPTER TWELVE

As Sarah and I approached my parents' front door, I couldn't shake the odd feeling in the pit of my stomach. For years I couldn't wait to leave this place and never return. I wouldn't say my childhood was dreadful; after all, some adults have painful childhood memories such as sexual or physical abuse, or both. Me, I had just grown up knowing I didn't matter to anyone in my family. It sounded like a pathetic complaint. Did I really need my parents to give me a hug and say, "I love you" every day? Was I that needy, that fucking weak?

Simply put: yes.

My mother was never the loving type. Hugs were out of the question. She acted more like a drill sergeant toughening me up for war. It was difficult in the earlier years, as I was a sensitive child. Later on, when I outed myself, it became much worse. She became worse. She no longer tried to toughen me up for battle; instead, she declared war on me.

For years I tried to believe my childhood didn't affect me. I was stronger than that. Independent. Too intelligent to let something so frivolous bother me. I studied Nazis, for Christ's sake. I had read countless stories about people who really lived through hell, stuff that no one could possibly imagine, let alone survive—yet many did.

Why was I letting my parents, especially my mother's lack of feeling, destroy me? Pathetic. I felt feeble. So I pushed it down. All those feelings, or lack thereof, I discounted completely. I told myself not to be a fool. *Push through it. People have lived through much worse. Get the fuck over yourself, Lizzie.*

Then I almost lost Sarah through not dealing with my childhood, through lying to myself that I was okay, that I didn't need anyone to complete me.

My therapist pointed that out right from the start. She asked me if I found it interesting that my research centered on children of the Third Reich. Many of the young boys who belonged to the Hitler Youth were shipped off, isolated from parental influence. Many more were orphaned at a young age. Why was I so fascinated by a generation that had grown up without parents?

I felt like a fucking idiot. The answer was staring me in the face the entire time, yet I never saw it. I could have studied so many different aspects of World War II, but this was the one that pulled me in.

Now Sarah and I wanted to bring our own child into the world at the same time that I was preparing to say good-bye to my uncaring mother. Talk about conflicting emotions. But Sarah was right: I needed to make peace with my mom, The Scotch-lady. If I didn't, I might never be completely whole.

Sarah gave my hand a squeeze before she reached out to ring the bell.

Tiffany opened the door. Shit!

I guess today wasn't the day to have my reckoning.

"Hello, there. We keep bumping into each other." She giggled like a vapid schoolgirl.

"Is Peter here?" asked Sarah. She gave me an "I'm sorry" look, since she knew I wanted this day to be just the three of us.

Tiffany marched off toward the main part of the house, answering over her shoulder, "Nope. He dropped me off on his way to golf." She paused and whispered conspiratorially, "He didn't want your mom to be alone."

"Peter sure has been playing a lot of golf lately."

Did Tiffany know that Peter wasn't really a sports guy? I was positive he played the occasional round of golf for business purposes, but every weekend? No way.

"He's become quite the fanatic," Mom said from her leather throne in the front room. Her beady eyes glinted. I knew she was thinking the same thought as me. Was that why she wasn't as close to her firstborn these days? Before Maddie left my brother at the altar, my mother had favored Peter. Did she know why Maddie had flown the coop? Maybe she read Maddie's note, pinned to the wedding dress: "Give it to her." Had it dawned on Mom that Peter had grown to be just like her husband?

I learned late in the game that my father had kept a woman on the side for years. My mother knew all along, but she looked the other way. Was she angry with Peter? Disappointed? Disgusted? Or angry with herself for not leaving my father?

Quite possibly, she just hated Tiffany.

I wasn't a fan either. I could live with the fact that Tiffany was not the brightest, but her flippant attitude grated on my nerves. Like her comment, "We keep running into each other." My fucking mother was dying, you dingbat.

Could I be jealous of Tiffany? Here she was, engaged to a man who couldn't keep his pants on and being dropped off to keep her future mother-in-law (who despised her) company, and yet she acted like it was a day at Disneyland.

No. I couldn't live that way. As much as my mind tortured me, I did appreciate I wasn't a Stepford Wife. And I wasn't married to one either.

"How are you feeling, Evelyn?" asked Sarah.

Mom set her Kindle aside. I smiled that she was actually using it.

"I'm not dead yet, although I think some treat me like I am."

Was that a dig at Peter?

Years ago, I would have loved to hear her take a jab at my brother. The once-mighty Peter had fallen. Today, seeing her thin body engulfed by an afghan in her massive leather chair, it was disconcerting.

Sarah didn't respond, just nodded sympathetically. What could one say to that?

"You," my mother stretched out a bony finger in Tiffany's direction, "get me a tea," she barked.

Tiffany smiled, as if someone just handed her some cotton candy, and bounded into the kitchen.

I watched, amazed—or at least overly inquisitive. I followed Tiffany into the kitchen on the pretense of making drinks for Sarah and myself. My real goal was to see if Tiffany still wore her happy face.

Much to my consternation, she did. Where had Peter found such a lobotomized woman?

"So, how are things?" I purposefully didn't say her name, since I couldn't bring myself to pronounce it her way. Maybe I should tell her that my name was pronounced Lizz-Aye.

"Fantastic. You?" She plopped a tea bag into a Wedgewood teacup.

I nodded, dumbfounded. "Have you and Peter set a date for the wedding?"

"December twenty-fifth." She set the cream and sugar on a tray.

Tiffany rattled off the date as if she had no clue that date held any other significance. Was she Jewish?

"Christmas, huh? I wouldn't have guessed that."

Peter had scheduled his first wedding on my birthday. He always had to be the center of attention, which made his absences lately decidedly odd. Had he realized he couldn't compete with a woman with cancer?

"Peter says work is slower at that time of year."

So that was it: it was more convenient for him, even if not for the rest of the world.

"We're going to Fiji for our honeymoon. Peter says it'll be warm, but I'm really worried. Won't it be cold in the winter?" For the first time, I noticed a different emotion on her face: concern.

"I think Peter's right. That's their summer."

"What?"

I imagined the concept bouncing around frantically inside her empty head, searching for an anchor.

"It's on the other side of the world. When we have winter, they have summer."

"Really? Who would have thought that?" Joy returned to her eyes.

"Would you like a drink?" I asked, hoping to bury this inane conversation before I insulted her.

"Wine would be great."

I looked at the clock on the microwave. 11:15 a.m. Interesting. Maybe she hadn't had a lobotomy after all.

"Red or white?" I asked, heading for my parents' wine cellar.

She crinkled her brow. "Makes no difference to me."

I was sure it didn't. And neither did anything else. Except for cold weather on her honeymoon.

An hour later, the four of us sat around the table, eating lunch. Tiffany was on her third glass of wine, but she didn't seem overly tipsy. Hard to tell with her, though. What qualified as tipsy and what was just ignorance?

"Evelyn, where did you and Charles go for your honeymoon?" Tiffany said it like she expected some epic adventure.

"Yellowstone," my mom snapped. She stirred some pasta salad around on her plate. I don't think I'd seen her actually eat one morsel of food.

"Where's that?"

I could see Tiffany still expected something luxurious.

My mom looked up from her plate and then back down.

"It's in Wyoming, mostly," I answered for her. "Part of the park is in Montana—where my parents are from."

"Park?" Tiffany's expectations were dropping drastically by the second, and so was her smile.

"It's a national park. When my parents married, my dad was just starting out," I explained. Had Peter claimed we were from old money, that his ancestors were robber barons and his father struck out West to make a name for himself? Did Tiffany know that my parents had lived in a trailer home at one point? I doubt it. Mom was usually desperate to keep all the cool aspects about them under wraps.

"Oh," she sounded beyond disappointed.

To help cheer Tiffany up, I turned to Sarah. "They're going to Fiji for their honeymoon."

Sarah picked up on my motive. "Oh, that sounds romantic. Have you set a date?"

I braced for Sarah's reaction.

"December twenty-fifth." This time, Tiffany eyed me cautiously.

"Christmas! And then Fiji for the New Year. That's wonderful."

Tiffany seemed relieved to find that Sarah's reaction was the polar opposite of mine.

"Marriage is like prostitution," said my mother.

The entire mood at the table slid into a black hole. I had been trying to keep it at even keel, but after that declaration, I was clueless how to yank it back from the brink of complete disaster.

Sarah and I both knew not to react to Mom's statement; that was what she wanted.

Tiffany, however, took the bait. "What do you mean, Evelyn?" she asked.

I really didn't want Mom to elaborate.

"The only reason men marry is because it's good for their careers. They don't love anyone. They put a ring on your finger to take you off the market. Marking their territory. Then they come and go as they please. And if you want anything, you better be willing to spread them." Mom dropped her fork onto her plate. Over the clattering sound, she uttered, "Golf. You think Peter's playing golf today? And Charles is away on business? Please. Marriage is legalized prostitution. You may feel respectable, but no wife is. You might as well get used to it or leave like—"

Tiffany took a healthy slug of her wine. Her body language suggested she knew all along why Peter was absent. Was she playacting the ditz as a cover, a coping mechanism? Shit. I felt horrible. Was she just subscribing to a role Peter defined for her? It would be the type of wife he wanted, after the Maddie debacle: a woman who wouldn't challenge him. Someone who would just be beautiful and not expect too much from him, or from the marriage.

I let out a long breath.

A cloud re-emerged over Tiffany's demeanor, but she plastered another fake smile on her face. I wanted to tell her to stop, that it wasn't worth it. Financial security wasn't worth it. If she didn't believe me, take a look across the table. Look at my mom. Really look at her. Was that what Tiffany wanted out of life?

"You two," —Mom pointed at Sarah and me—"do either of you play *golf*, eh?" She started to cackle, but it turned into a coughing fit.

Neither of us responded.

"That's one thing about Lizzie—she's never cared about what others think. It used to drive me fucking crazy, but now…" Mom rose slowly to her feet. After she steadied herself, she announced, "I'm tired. I'm going to take a nap."

When she was out of earshot, Sarah rose to clear the dishes. At first, I was too thunderstruck to move. Did my mom just compliment me in some weird way? Or was that another veiled insult?

Tiffany filled her wineglass again. She must have seen me eye her brimming glass. "I have to wait for Peter to pick me up. My car is in the shop," she said, clearing her throat.

"Would you like me to drive you home?" I offered. "Does he still live on Quentin?" It wasn't until I asked the question that I realized how ridiculous it sounded. I didn't know where my brother lived, and he didn't know where I lived. God, we were a fucked up family! How did I think I would ever get some type of closure?

"No, he moved after…" It didn't seem like she'd run out of words, just that she was defeated. She had run out of desire. "I should help Sarah." She hopped up, shaking her head from either standing too quickly or from the copious amount of wine she had consumed. My money was on the wine.

"How you doing?" asked Sarah on the drive back to Fort Collins.

I shook my head and gripped the steering wheel. "What an awful afternoon."

We drove in silence for a few minutes. Then I broke it. "I feel terrible for Tiffany. Is it all an act?"

"I think so. She's so young, and Peter…"

"Why does my family chew everyone up and spit them out?"

Speechless, Sarah patted my leg.

"And to watch my mom dig her claws into Tiffany. At first I was thrilled I wasn't the target, but shit, this is worse. I can at least stand up to her. Do you think Peter ever felt this way? Conflicted about not being the target, but feeling bad for me?"

She avoided answering, instead saying, "What do you think?"

"Not a chance in hell. Peter's too much like them, or like my mother at least. To be honest, Sarah, this whole experience is showing me just how much I don't know my father. The man is either mute or not present. How does he feel? Mom is bitter. Beyond bitter. But is he? For the life of me, I can't figure out why they never divorced. For as long as I remember, they've always been like that, always combative. What kind of life is that?"

Two days later, I received an email from my father requesting my presence at dinner. The message didn't say much, but I formed the impression it would be just the two of us. We met at the same restaurant.

Once again, I found my father sitting in the dark, stylish bar in an overstuffed leather chair. He swirled a bourbon, but didn't seem to be drinking. I watched him briefly as he stared blankly out of the window. He didn't move, speak, drink, or anything. It was the saddest I had ever seen him.

"Hello," I said, taking a seat across from him.

He nodded and motioned for the waitress to approach.

"What'll ya have, darling?" Her bouncy attitude didn't fit my father's somber mood.

"Gin and tonic. Double please."

I had prepared ahead of time, so that Sarah and Maddie were in a different restaurant nearby, waiting to take me home. No one said it out loud, but I think we all sensed what was about to happen.

Mom's chemo treatment had ended abruptly. Just yesterday, when I arrived to pick her up, she announced that she wasn't going. Not that day. Not ever. And with that, she'd shooed me away.

"Lizzie…" My father sipped his bourbon. "Your mom has decided to stop her treatment. The last test revealed that it wasn't working and—"

"Here ya go." The bubbly waitress appeared. "One G and T, heavy on the G." She plopped the drink down and rushed off, smiling.

I held the glass, watching condensation slide down onto my fingers before dripping onto the arm of the chair. "I see," I finally said.

"We knew that it was a long shot. It was caught so late…"

A *long shot*. It seemed cruel to refer to someone's life as a long shot, but oddly fitting, too. Mom was always playing games. Until recently, it looked like she'd win by playing dirty. Cancer—the great equalizer. Rich, poor, happy, or sad, it didn't matter. Cancer struck and left death and destruction in its wake.

I let out a long breath and swallowed a mouthful of my drink in an attempt to force my emotions back. I needed to hold on. There would be time for me to fall apart—later, not now. I had to be strong.

Neither of us spoke.

"Another round?" The waitress came by again. My father and I nodded gravely. Our mood finally seeped into hers, and she hurried away less cheerfully this time.

"Is there anything that can be done to make her more comfortable?" I asked.

"I've called Hospice. They'll work with your mom's nurse, make sure she has OxyContin and morphine to ease the pain. She wants everything to be on her terms, like normal." For the first time, I saw a slight smile cross his lips.

"What was she like, when you met her?" The question popped out of my mouth before I could stop it; even I was floored by it.

Dad cradled his tumbler with both hands and stared into his lap. "Strong, determined, not as harsh. The more successful we became, the more her fear took over. She never wanted to return to where we started. Power. She craved power. I loved your mother once, Lizzie." He lifted his haggard face to gaze into my eyes. "Until she stopped letting me."

Dad excused himself, and ambled to the bathroom, looking like an old man. I sat in my chair, stunned, unable to think of what I should do or say.

When he returned, my father asked, "Do you have a ride home?"

"Yeah." I nodded to ensure my meaning got across. I wasn't sure he had heard me; my voice felt stuck in the back of my throat.

He placed a hand on my shoulder. "She would like you to continue visiting," he said, and then he was gone. I guess he had opted not to have dinner, and I wasn't hungry now either.

I flagged the waitress, cancelled the second round, and asked her to settle the bill.

She waved me off. "I'll just put it on Mr. Petrie's tab, honey."

My drink was still two-thirds full. It took me more than an hour to finish it. Tempted to order another, I fished my phone out before I slipped into a miasma I couldn't recover from. Maddie and Sarah rushed inside to retrieve me.

I gazed into Sarah's eyes and whispered, "He loved her. . . in another lifetime."

Past tense. Soon, she would always be in the past tense. It was over. The drill sergeant had lost this battle, and consequently, the war.

Cancer was unforgiving. It didn't care about power. It crushed Mom like a bug smashed into a windshield, only not as quickly. It teased her with the hope of beating it.

CHAPTER THIRTEEN

SARAH AND I SAT IN THE DOCTOR'S CONSULTATION ROOM TO DISCUSS OUR FUTURE *TEST-TUBE baby*—a phrase Sarah forbade me from uttering out loud. She preferred the clinical in vitro fertilization or IVF. Personally, when I heard it put that way, I started to freak out.

The room wasn't overly clinical. A vase with fresh daisies sat on the far table. The wall behind displayed photos of smiling babies and cooing parents. The colors were soothing. Everything seemed purposefully cheerful, except for the schematic of the IVF process; it reminded me of those silly cartoons they showed in elementary school, explaining how a bill was turned into a law. The drawing in the office wasn't very cheerful either. It depicted a female form with a red spot marking her reproductive parts and an arrow pointing to a laboratory dish. I stopped inspecting it even before it detailed two other steps in the process.

I always cringed whenever I saw or thought of a Petri dish. Having the surname Petrie didn't help. I felt like a science experiment, akin to Harry Harlow's experiments on baby monkeys raised by unfeeling mothers.

I took a deep breath in an attempt to calm myself. It didn't work. I was certain Sarah could see my heart pumping inside my chest, so hard I thought for sure it was heaving up and down like an overwrought piston about to explode.

The doctor sat in a chair behind the desk. She had a kind face and appeared to be in her late forties. She in no way resembled a mad scientist, much to my chagrin.

"So, Sarah and Lizzie, I understand you would like to extract eggs from Lizzie, and then you, Sarah, will carry the baby. Is that correct?" Her soft voice matched her caring appearance.

Extract—the word made me shudder.

"That's correct," said Sarah, our unofficial spokesperson.

The doctor jotted something on a notepad before stating, "Wonderful. The process has really advanced since it was first accomplished in 1978."

My brain focused on the year. I hadn't considered researching the history of test-tube babies.

Realizing the woman was still speaking, I checked back into the conversation. "We'll need to chart Lizzie's cycle, and then stimulate her ovulatory process and remove ova, or eggs, from her ovaries. We'll then add sperm to fertilize them in a laboratory. The zygote…" She paused and looked directly at me. I didn't like her assumption that I was clueless about the process, even though I was. "The fertilized egg is cultured for two to six days, and then we'll implant it into Sarah's uterus."

All the words: *ovulatory, ova, zygote, sperm,* and *uterus* bounced around in my head like an out-of-control Ping-Pong ball. The woman was a mad scientist after all. But she was even scarier for looking so unassuming.

Sarah reached for my hand. "How do you extract Lizzie's eggs?"

I could have done without that question. Ignorance is bliss.

Dr. Frankenstein gazed at me sweetly, and replied, "We use a transvaginal technique called transvaginal oocyte retrieval."

I wanted to say, "Come again."

She must have sensed that all I heard was jibberish. "Basically, it involves using a needle to pierce the vaginal wall to get to your ovaries."

I honed in on two words: *needle* and *pierce.*

Sarah squeezed my hand tighter. I would have squeezed back if I wasn't mortified by this sweet woman calmly talking about torturing me with modern-day medicine.

The nut job continued. "Lizzie will be given drugs that will stimulate her ovaries, with the hope that she'll produce several eggs."

I no longer liked the term test-tube baby. And I wasn't fond of IVF either. The cheerful consultation room suddenly felt like a prison, and I felt like a prisoner undergoing outrageous and painful medical tortures, all for the glory of a mad scientist.

If Sarah hadn't had a vise-like grip on my hand, I would have bolted.

"However, quality eggs are still the goal, not necessarily quantity."

So, I wasn't exactly a factory egg producer but more of a free-range chicken.

I didn't look at Sarah or the doctor so my true feelings would remain undetected.

Panic.

I was panicking. All of this was becoming real to me. Soon, I'd be taking egg-inducing drugs and then this crazy woman was going to insert a needle into me to suck them out.

What the fucking hell?

Who in the fuck thought of this?

Any desire I had to research test-tube babies oozed out of me. I imagined seeing a puddle of fear forming around my feet.

By some miracle, I managed to remain quiet for the rest of the appointment. The doctor kept asking Sarah all the questions, like what would we do with the extra eggs: freeze them, or donate them?

The longer we stayed, the more determined I became to never eat another egg in all my life. This whole stealing of eggs was barbaric.

Dates were discussed. Soon, Sarah was standing and shaking the loon's hand saying, "Thank you so much for meeting us. You have been so reassuring, and I know I speak for both of us when I say we are thrilled to be starting this process."

The doctor smiled. I reached down deep inside to yank a smile out. I imagined I was pulling a string connected to the sun on the other side of the earth and forcing its warmth and radiance to appear hours before the dawn.

We made it to the parking lot before Sarah noticed my dazed look. When she plucked the keys out of my hand, I didn't even protest. Our appointment was early in the day, so Sarah had taken the rest of the day off.

It wasn't until we'd been driving for well over forty minutes that I realized we weren't heading home. Instead, we were driving through Estes Park, a small town outside the entrance of Rocky Mountain National Park.

"Are we going hiking?" I asked.

"Not really. We're meeting Maddie and Doug for lunch, and then hopefully we'll explore a bit. Do you know what season this is?"

"Fall," I said with no confidence it was the correct answer.

"True, and it's elk-rutting season."

I rubbed my eyes and swallowed. "What are you talking about?"

"Large numbers of elk gather together and you can hear the sounds of the bulls bugling. Rocky Mountain National Park has more elk than Yellowstone."

"Why?"

"Fewer wolves and grizzly bears," she said matter-of-factly as she pulled off the main street to park the car in the public lot.

We met Maddie and Doug at a small sandwich shop that had a view of Main Street. The place was atypical for Sarah and Maddie. The plastic chairs and cheap tables covered with red-and-white checkered tablecloths made me question why we were eating here.

I must have looked rattled, because Maddie was on her best behavior for once. She didn't crack any jokes at my expense. Normally, I would have minded being handled with kid gloves, but I didn't think I could handle too much joviality today.

"This place has the best meatball subs," said Doug.

It was Doug's place; that explained the décor.

"So Lizzie," he continued, "are you ready to hear the elk bugling? They say it's one of the most unique sounds in nature, like the howl of a wolf."

"Sounds great," I replied not so enthusiastically.

Maddie offered Doug a sweet smile. "Don't worry, sweetheart. I think Lizzie's still in shock from her appointment."

Doug nodded sympathetically.

Sarah's warm hand slipped onto my thigh. "The poor thing had to sit there and listen to words like zygote, sperm, and ova—" Sarah burst into laughter.

"Hey! They're going to stick a needle in me and suck my eggs out," I pouted.

"And Sarah's going to carry the baby and then go through this thing called birth." Maddie arched her eyebrows, clearly curious as to how I would respond.

I didn't.

Just then, I saw a person bolt past the window. Followed by two more. They didn't seem like they were running to catch a bus or something. They were sprinting for their lives. I pointed out the window, speechless.

Everyone looked in time to see a massive elk charging after the runners.

Then I heard the sound. The bull screamed.

"Shit," muttered Doug. "I wish people would respect elk more, especially during rutting season. Those people probably called out to get a better photo or something." He shook his head in dismay.

I had been to Estes countless times, but I had never seen elk roaming through the town. It was like a mini elk apocalypse outside, and we had front-row seats.

"Shall I order the meatball subs?" asked Maddie. Without waiting for our answers, she headed for the cash register.

"This is insane." Sarah's mouth was slightly agape as she watched the madness outside.

Doug agreed. "The males are very combative right now." He turned to me. "Do you know that their urethras point upward, so when they piss it shoots onto their hide? The females are attracted to the scent."

Maddie returned just in time to hear his disgusting tidbit. "You see, Lizzie. You thought you had it bad. At least you don't have to pee on yourself."

Everyone got a kick out of that, and I had to admit that, for the first time that day, I felt relieved. Despite all the mayhem taking place outside, sitting inside with Sarah and our friends and sharing lunch had turned it into a normal day — for me, at least, if not for the people being chased.

"So, tell me, who came up with this idea for today?" I stared directly at Maddie.

Her guilty smile answered me.

"Her first suggestion was taking you to eat Rocky Mountain oysters," said Doug.

My mouth fell open. "Fried cow balls. You wanted me to eat fried cow balls?"

She shrugged. "I thought it was kinda fitting, considering."

I couldn't help but laugh.

CHAPTER FOURTEEN

At the start of November, Sarah surprised me by taking me to Breckenridge for a weekend. The winter tourists hadn't yet arrived in full force. We were sitting in a restaurant next to a roaring fire, Sarah looking radiant in a Norwegian ski sweater she had purchased specifically for the getaway. Neither of us planned to ski because there wasn't much snow to speak of and I had never skied in my life, but Sarah hardly ever missed a chance to shop.

"You're quiet over there," she said, washing the words away with a sip of water, cautious doe eyes gazing at me over the rim.

I smiled awkwardly. "I'm sorry. You take me away on a romantic getaway, and here I am ruminating."

"This doesn't have to be a romantic getaway, Lizzie. I just thought it'd be good for you to get away from everything for a couple of days. Relax, have a little fun, eat some good food." She motioned to the steak that sat untouched on my plate.

Usually, I inhaled every meal that was placed before me. Today, not even a steak could tempt me.

"I'm worried about you." Her voice was soft, supportive. "I don't know how I would handle my mother dying, and your situation has added layers of difficulty."

"'Added layers of difficulty,'" I repeated. "That's an understatement." I sliced off a small piece of steak—for her benefit, not because I was hungry. "I've been reading, I think we should go organic, for the baby's sake."

Sarah set down her water glass, taken aback by the sudden change of topic. Her eyebrows shot up.

"I just think fewer pesticides and other chemicals would be better for us, and for the baby," I continued. "I've been living with an illness that many people believe has environmental causes. And cancer…well…I just think it would be better. Safer." I looked away, feeling foolish. I wasn't the type to support organic food or to change my diet because it was trendy.

"Wow. I don't know whether I should be impressed or check to see if you have a fever," Sarah teased. "Have you considered veganism?"

I had to laugh. "Don't push your luck. Buying organic will be a huge step for me."

"What other changes do you want to make?"

I scrunched up my forehead, thinking. "I don't know. Let me do some more research."

"You're going to be one of *those* parents, aren't you?" She looked amused, albeit slightly concerned.

"What do you mean, 'one of those'?" I crossed my arms, playfully. It felt good to banter back and forth.

"The type who tries new fads. Certain toys, music…" She motioned a never-ending cycle.

"Maybe," I admitted. "I just want…I want our child to have what I didn't."

She leaned closer to me. "Which is what?"

"To feel loved. To have options."

A tear formed in the corner of her eye. I reached over and wiped it away with a fingertip.

"You never fail to surprise me," she said.

"Hopefully in a good way."

"At least forty percent of the time."

I chuckled. "Forty! That's harsh!"

"Honesty hurts."

I waved her words away. "I bet our kid will be smarter than Ethan's."

Sarah shook her head and tsked. "Don't even start. I won't let you pressure our baby to succeed. Nothing good comes from it."

"But I can watch documentaries with our child. What musical instrument do you think? Cello? Violin? What about the trumpet? I always wanted to play the trumpet."

"The trumpet!" she chortled. "Since when did you want to play any instrument, let alone the trumpet?"

Not responding, I changed tactics. "Fisher Price has apps for babies."

Sarah set her fork and knife down methodically, taking extra time to weigh her words. "This coming from the woman who had a flip cell phone when we started dating."

She leveled her gaze at me, and I felt my confidence wilt. I put my palms up. "Okay, okay. I give. But some of them seem harmless, like the animal sounds."

"Lizzie, I'm not opposed to learning tools." Her voice was even but firm. "I'm opposed to pressure and setting unreal expectations."

"So I guess the *Learning Letters Monkey* app is out?" I flashed my cell phone.

"Let me see that," she demanded. "How many apps have you downloaded? You do know I'm not even pregnant yet, right?" We were to attend another appointment with the doctor next week.

I rubbed the crease that formed in the center of my forehead. The other day, I had downloaded a ton of those apps on my phone to try them out. Of course, then I realized the baby would need a tablet, too — thank God I hadn't said that out loud.

"I get it. You need distractions. Maybe you should sign up for a hobby or something."

"A hobby!" I scoffed.

"I'll buy you a trumpet." Sarah pretended to dangle what I assumed was a trumpet in my face. "Deal!"

"One condition, though. You have to practice when I'm at work," she smirked.

"Really! I hope you're more supportive of our child." I raised an accusatory eyebrow.

"I'm hoping our child is more mature than you."

I feigned hurt. "Is it too childish to share a dessert?" I nodded to the table behind her. "The brownie sundae looks very tempting."

Ethan was sitting at our usual table in Starbucks. The door closed behind me, shutting out the street traffic. He didn't bother looking up from his novel. *Usual table*, I'd thought, as if we still met once a week, like we used to before Casey came along. Before I got married. Before. Before—when life seemed miserable and yet less complicated. I fucking hated irony.

I ordered a chai from the young man behind the counter. He looked like he wasn't old enough to drive a car. How was it that young people were starting to look younger and younger while I felt and looked older with each passing second? Earlier that morning, I'd plucked two black hairs from my chin. Seriously, no one warned you about that becoming the norm.

I strolled up to the table.

"Howdy, stranger." Ethan set his book aside.

"Imagine meeting you here," I replied.

He smiled his cynical smile, his thin moustache giving a quasi-intellectual appearance. The Coke-bottle glasses he always wore added to the effect. "I haven't been to a Starbucks in years, not since you."

"My, you do know how to charm a girl," I winked. "Who knew I had the power to ruin Starbucks for you. Me, I still pop in every day. I'm addicted to this." I raised my chai and took a melodramatic sip. "I wish I could kick the habit. It's wreaking havoc on my girlish figure. Just the other day, my thighs rubbed together. I felt like a stuffed pig."

"Are you riding much lately?"

"I try to get out for short rides each day, but I don't seem to have enough hours in the day, and it feels wrong to be riding and doing something I enjoy."

He nodded, but didn't ask why. I sensed Ethan knew that even better than I did. He usually knew what I was feeling long before I processed it.

"Who called you?" I tucked a flyaway strand of hair behind my ear. My hair was thinning, random strands slipping from my ponytail no matter how tight I made it.

"What do you mean?" He looked away.

"Sarah or Maddie?"

Ethan threw his hands in the air. The jig was up. "Both, actually. I'm not sure if they planned it that way or whether it was just a coincidence."

"There aren't any coincidences when it comes to those two."

"You have to admire their methods. I'm still amazed they got you to wear a wedding dress. A white one!" he hooted.

I cringed, recollecting. "Don't remind me, please."

"And the cake. Did you know Sarah intended on smearing the cake all over your face?" His eyes sparkled over the disgraceful memory.

I crossed my arms and huffed. "She promised me she wouldn't."

Ethan cocked one eyebrow. "And you believed her?" he tsked. "Seriously, I would have thought being a woman would have given you a better advantage in a lesbian relationship."

"So, what's your mission today?" I tried to steer the conversation away from our wedding. I hated being the center of attention; even the memories of having to be a "bride" gave me gooseflesh. I'd cried during my toast. How humiliating!

"To see how you're doing. You know, the usual with you. Do you plan on running away, like normal? Or do you plan on pretending nothing is wrong and bury yourself in work?" He motioned to my bag. "How many books do you have in there?"

"Seven, but I went to the library on my way here," I defended myself.

"Why didn't you leave them in the car?" Ethan rubbed his chin and squinted: his best hard-boiled detective look.

"I planned on thumbing through them after…" I pointed to him.

"Is it option two, then?" He grinned, but I could tell he was concerned.

"Is there an option three?"

"Such as?"

"I don't know, yet," I confessed.

"Honesty — that's new."

"Anyone tell ya you're a riot?"

"Come on, I'm just teasing you. Tell me, how do you feel?"

"I'm assuming we're talking about my mom."

"That would be a good assumption. Stop stalling." He waggled a finger in my face. "And while you're at it, I've also been asked to wheedle out how you feel about having a kid, during all this."

"How did I miss that one?" I smiled, but I meant it.

"You should have left the books in the car. We're going to be here a while."

I stood. "What can I get you?" I motioned to his nearly empty cup.

"Just coffee. No frills."

Despite all of the options, Ethan always went for the house blend. Before heading to the register, I added, "I've missed our chats. Thanks."

"Don't try to sweet talk me. I'm going to get you to open up. I'm afraid of those two." He folded his arms, but the twinkle in his eyes said he felt the same.

I shook my head in mock disdain and left to order. Ethan immediately returned to his book. A man after my own heart. No wonder we got along so well.

When I returned, he held his finger up to silence me, and then traced the words near the bottom of the page. Peeking over, I saw that he was finishing up the chapter.

I set his coffee down and spread out the sandwiches and fruit I'd bought.

"Good Lord, you planning for the end of the world?" He snatched up a grape and popped it into his mouth.

"I figured it was the least I could do, since my wife and Maddie pretty much threatened your life if you didn't accomplish your mission. Hopefully this isn't your last meal."

"Let's get to it, then. What thoughts are rolling around in that empty noggin of yours?"

"If it's empty, how could I have any thoughts?"

Ethan shook an apple slice in my face. "Stop stalling. I have my own woman at home who'll kill me if I'm gone all day."

I rubbed my eyes, applying too much pressure, causing flashes of light. "Where do I start? I feel guilty, sad, relieved, angry…" I made a circular motion with my hand. The list was endless.

He latched onto one word. "Relieved?"

"Yeah. That one goes with guilty. The most obvious aspect is that I don't want Mom to suffer anymore. But there's a part of me that is relieved. Even if we haven't talked in a few years, the threat was always there. Mom could pop back up into my life at any moment and continue tormenting me. I know that sounds heartless. I can't believe I'm mentioning it to you." I shielded my eyes with one hand, stopping myself from seeing the expression on his face.

Ethan didn't speak for several moments. Finally, he cleared his throat. "That's why you're beating yourself up? Lizzie, when are you going to realize that you're human, just like the rest of us?"

I uncovered my eyes. "So this is normal?"

"Yes. People are selfish. It's normal. Let's face it, your mom wasn't the best. Is it right to feel this way? Well, that's a different question." He drummed his fingers on the tabletop, lost in thought.

"So it's normal, but not right. You and your riddles." I smiled weakly.

Ethan straightened in his chair, such a skinny, awkwardly tall man. "I think you need to have a come-to-Jesus talk with your mom."

"What the fuck does that mean?"

"I think you need to tell her how she made you feel all those years."

"You want me to confront my dying mother and tell her she was a crappy mom. Sarah wants me to tell her that I love her. What if I don't want to do either?" I was testy, and my voice did nothing to hide it.

"Then you'll never have peace," he stated bluntly. "And while you're at it, tell Peter he's an ass." He smiled, attempting to soften the blow with humor.

"You should meet his new fiancée. She thinks Hawaii is a foreign country."

"It should be."

I looked up from the sandwich I was about to bite into. "What?"

"We stole it. It should be autonomous."

"Jesus, Ethan, do you really think Tiffany—who pronounces her name *Tie-Fannie*—understands that much. And if we went by your logic, none of the US should be the US. Ever since—"

He raised his hand to silence me. "There's the Lizzie I know. I have one more question for you. How do you feel about Sarah and the baby?"

Without thinking, I blurted, "That's the only thing in my life that makes sense right now."

Ethan slapped the table. "Mission accomplished!"

"When do you have to report in?" I teased.

He eyed his watch. "Fifteen hundred hours."

"You're a nerd. What book are you reading? It's massive."

"*Gone with the Wind.*"

I rolled my eyes. "And you wonder why everyone in grad school thought you were gay."

"Narrow-minded assholes," he growled. He chomped off half of his sandwich and patted his mouth daintily with a napkin.

"How's the little one?"

"She said her first curse word the other day." He swallowed, and then grinned mischievously. "It was one of my proudest moments."

"What'd she say? Fuck?"

"Please, my child isn't a commoner like you. *Merde.*"

"I told Sarah *The Little Mermaid* wasn't good for children!" I shook my head.

"Sarah told me you studied the movie for days, just so you could show up my daughter. Then, when she didn't dress as Ariel again, you lost your nerve. Really, Lizzie, are you that competitive?"

I sniffed. "I don't know what you're talking about."

"Yeah right." He shook his head. "You do make your life a lot harder than it needs to be."

After Ethan left, I stayed to get some research done. Armed with a book and pen and paper for notes, I zoned out completely and was quite good at blocking out distractions. I was flipping through a reference text, making notes, when someone behind me cleared her throat in an obvious way, to get my attention. Something warned me about turning around, but I did it anyway.

Jasmine stared back at me.

Thank God Ethan had already left, or he would have reported this back to the girls for sure.

"Hi, Jasmine." I stood awkwardly to shake her hand.

"Sorry to disturb you." She smiled and gestured to the books.

I'm pretty sure she wasn't sorry, since she'd done her best to attract my attention.

"Please, have a seat." I motioned to the chair across from me. "How goes the research?" I asked politely. Historians, myself included, loved to talk about things most people didn't give two shits about. Primary sources, secondary sources, journal articles—it was amazing what got our hearts pumping.

Her face perked up, her timidity dissolving. "Really well. Thanks for all the tips. I actually received a book from the British Library yesterday. I was tickled pink!"

See? Who else would get excited about receiving a book from the British Library?

I had planned to get some work done, but ended up losing track of time and talking to Jasmine for more than an hour.

"*Are you still at Starbucks?*"

I hadn't realized how much time had passed until I received Sarah's text. Obviously, Ethan had already reported in, and she was expecting me home.

"*Yes.*" I sent back, and continued my conversation with Jasmine.

A man ambled past, took one look at Jasmine, and stopped in his tracks. Both of us stopped talking and eyed him, waiting for him to say or do something. He flushed profusely and mumbled, "Did you drop a pencil?" He pointed to a lone pencil on the floor, about three tables away.

"Thanks, but that's not mine," Jasmine replied, dismissing him with a sweet, shy smile.

The man nodded but didn't budge, not for at least five seconds.

Once he was safely in the bathroom, I laughed. "Does that happen to you often?"

Jasmine stared out the window and shrugged. It was cute how she did it. I wanted to tell her about Sarah's reaction, but thought better of it. I could see Jasmine was already uncomfortable with the man's unwanted attention.

"There you are!" I knew, even without turning around, that Sarah had come to retrieve me. Before I had even spun in her direction, I could feel her glaring at Jasmine, who in turn, wilted.

I popped out of my chair and announced cheerfully, "Look who I bumped into after Ethan left. Sarah, I'm sure you remember Jasmine." Maddie strutted through the door, Doug right behind her. I swallowed a groan.

"Jasmine, I want you to meet two of my dearest friends, Maddie and Doug." I turned to the couple. "Jasmine is pursuing her PhD in history, and we both focus on children under the Third Reich." I gave Maddie a steely eyed glare, cautioning her not to be her usual self. Jasmine wasn't comfortable at all.

Doug immediately pulled up a chair next to the young woman until Maddie's cough alerted him that he should first grab a chair for Maddie. Taking his lead, I pulled out a chair for my jealous wife.

Sarah sat down stiffly. I affectionately slid my hand onto her leg, which calmed her down some. "How's the research coming along, Jasmine?" she asked, almost kindly.

Jasmine smiled but said nothing. Doug was actively gaping at her. Maddie was staring at Doug as if she wanted to throttle him. It was time for me to step in.

"Jasmine was just telling me about a book she discovered, a diary that hadn't been published when I was in school. Thanks to Jasmine"—I turned to Sarah—"and to you, I already ordered it on the iPad you got me for my birthday." I turned back to Jasmine. "I can't wait to read it. So, you really think this will change your thesis?"

Jasmine transformed into her confident self again. I could see she would make a great lecturer in a couple of years, once she controlled her nerves. Doug hung on her every word, and even Maddie and Sarah seemed intrigued.

When she finished, I added, "Of course, your findings may blow one of my new theories out of the water."

Jasmine started to interrupt, but I put my palm in the air. "Oh, no worries. That's what's great about scholarship. New things surface, changing the way we think. So many people think history is dead, but it's alive and kicking. Keeps us busy!"

Sarah stared at me. Blinked. Had I just witnessed my wife's realization that Jasmine wasn't a threat? I was too much of a historian to get turned on by Jasmine. The fact that I was giddy about a new diary rather than about the hot woman sitting opposite me didn't help my cool factor, but it did make my wife almost laugh in my face with relief.

Doug, on the other hand, was still in for a long night. I pitied him.

Jasmine looked at her sports watch. "Oh no, I'm late." She gathered her bag and reusable coffee mug. "It was so nice meeting all of you." She rushed off before Doug could hop up to give her a hug. He seemed disappointed, but no doubt that was for the best.

Maddie whacked his leg as soon as Jasmine was out of sight. "Really! Really, Doug!"

He stuttered, "Wh-what?"

"And Sarah thought I was bad." I laughed. "I only had tea with her and talked about Nazis. You were practically drooling, dude."

Doug looked betrayed, as if I should have his back. I felt bad for him, but I wasn't going to join ranks with him on this. Not when it was such a thorny subject in my marriage.

"I don't know what you're talking about." He jumped up and rushed to the bathroom.

"You want me to take him out back and give him a beat down?" I asked Maddie, feigning some boxing jabs.

She laughed. "I would love to see you try."

When Doug returned, Sarah and Maddie were chatting about a new restaurant they wanted to try. They were becoming quite the gourmands. I blamed cable television. They really like the show *Man V. Food*: the one with Adam Richman, who entered all of these crazy food challenges, like eating dozens of oysters in thirty minutes. Yuck!

Doug took his seat tentatively. I gave him the "You're in the clear" look, and he sighed and put his arm on the back of Maddie's chair. She harrumphed playfully before turning to pat his cheek and continuing her conversation with Sarah. But the look in her eye suggested Doug wasn't completely out of the woods.

The drive to see my mother was way too short. As I neared her home, a pressure tightened in my chest; I feared it would strangle me before the day's end. What did you say to someone who had decided not to continue the fight? I couldn't blame her. Her pain and suffering must have been overwhelming. And the chemo wasn't working. I couldn't picture my mother searching for alternative treatments.

Instead of taking her to appointments, lately I had been keeping Mom company a few times a week. Was that what she wanted? Would Peter take any shifts? Or was Mr. Important still too busy?

I sighed. Jesus, I needed to get a grip. Who cared about Peter? I needed to move on. I was pretty sure Peter wasn't sitting around thinking about me.

My mother's nurse opened the door.

"How's she doing today?" I asked.

The nurse pursed her thin lips together. "She's comfortable, for now. That's all we can do."

"What do you mean?"

"She's signed a DNR," the nurse explained, putting her hand on my arm and giving it a gentle squeeze.

"DNR?"

"Do not resuscitate. It means we won't intervene if she stops breathing or anything."

"So you just watch her die?" I was appalled by the idea. Wasn't that against their oath?

The woman squeezed my arm again. "It's your mother's wish."

She tried to walk away, but I stopped her. "Does my father know about this?"

"Of course. I know this isn't easy, but there's nothing you can do." She strode to my mom's bedroom and motioned for me to go inside.

I wasn't sure what to expect. It had been just days since I last saw her, and I knew cancer wouldn't take her easily. It wanted to make her suffer. I knew it could take weeks or months to kill her. It was just a waiting game now.

Mom sat in a recliner positioned in a sunny spot in the bedroom. I almost laughed—a recliner! Not once had Mom ever bought a recliner. It must have been a punch to the gut when she realized she needed one, or had my father or the nurse surprised her? I hoped the latter, at least that would preserve some of her dignity.

Her eyes were closed, and she was listening to a novel on the Kindle. Finally, I'd found a gift Mom actually used. The nurse left us alone, and I stood motionless in the doorway. Mom looked so peaceful. I had never seen her peaceful. Maybe it was because her eyes were closed, rather than beadily searching for something or someone to shred.

That narrator was female and had a soothing voice.

"You going to just stand there?"

Mom's voice startled me, and I jumped as if I'd seen a ghost.

"I didn't want to disturb you," I mumbled, slinking into the room. "What are you listening to?"

"Some book. I don't remember the name." She waved a hand dismissively.

It almost made me smile. She was working hard at being her normal self, but she couldn't quite muster enough rancor in her words and tone. "I need water," she croaked. She motioned to the pitcher and cup by her bedside.

Several pill bottles were lined up next to the water. At least the nurse could still give her pain meds, even if there was a DNR. I couldn't imagine babysitting my mother if she was in excruciating pain. Keeping my back to her, I asked, "Do you need anything else?" I didn't know how to ask if she was in pain. She might infer that I thought she was weak.

"No," she barked, but in a tiny voice.

I handed her the water and settled in the chair next to her. Secretly, I wished it was a recliner, too. My eyelids felt heavy. I would have loved to close them and listen to the book with her. Instead, not knowing what to say, I asked, "How's Peter been?"

"Planning his wedding. He thinks I'll be there." She stared out the window, glaring at the leafless trees.

Peter's wedding was six weeks away. So, Mom thought she had less than six weeks. Something clutched at my throat. Why hadn't I poured myself a glass of water when I had the chance? If I poured myself one now, she'd know why. I couldn't show weakness now.

Just fucking hold on, Lizzie.

"A Christmas wedding. How romantic." I was desperate to focus the conversation on Peter, and not on what was actually happening in that room—the cancer slowly eating away at her, piece by piece.

She grunted. It was hard to decipher whether she approved or not.

"Does Tiffany have a large family?" I looked around the room, as if hoping Tiffany would magically appear and answer the question herself. Deflect. Distract. I was desperate for a distraction. As annoying as my brother's new fiancée was, she did have some benefits.

"Peter always liked being the center of attention." Mom ignored my question about Tiffany.

She hadn't liked Peter being with Maddie either, but back then, she'd hid it more. Maybe Mom no longer felt like she had to hide her contempt. Just let it fly. It was a terrifying thought.

I chuckled softly, hoping it wouldn't offend her. Peter, her precious child—the one who got all her attention. I wasn't sure I could call it love. It was always difficult to associate that word with The Scotch-lady.

"You were difficult to know."

Her words pulled me out of my head. "What?" I wasn't sure I'd heard her correctly.

"Independent. Like your father. Neither of you ever needed me. Peter needed me." She talked as though I wasn't in the room.

I sat mute, my mouth open.

The Scotch-lady rolled her head to eyeball me. "I didn't know what to do with an adult-child. Mother you? Be your friend? I felt robbed."

"Robbed?" I wasn't sure I was strong enough to pursue this conversation, but the question popped out. "What do you mean?"

"Peter was the perfect little boy. Just what I wanted: smart, handsome, friendly. He loved Hot Wheels, Legos. You...you were different. I thought I would be able to dress you up. I thought you would be a little girl. A real life doll for me to play with." She looked away. "I don't know what you were. You'd never wear a dress. One Halloween, I made you a princess costume. You cried and cried when I put it on you. You wanted to be a Smurf. Brainy Smurf," she said with as much venom as possible, a sneer on her face. "You threw such a fit that it was your first and last Halloween."

Brainy Smurf. I couldn't even remember watching *The Smurfs*, let alone remember the princess costume. Had she made me a costume herself, or did she have it made? She must have had it made. How come I didn't remember any of this?

"For Christmas, I would buy you a Madame Alexander doll. Every time you saw what was in the box, you would get this pained expression on your face, but you never told me you didn't like them. You never told me you didn't like me. But I knew it."

"I didn't like you?" My voice started to rise. "What about you? For as long as I can remember, you antagonized me. The only attention I got from you was negative. Attack. Attack. Attack. And your precious boy, Peter, would join in. The two of you ganged up on me. Jesus! I was just a child." I jumped out of my chair.

"No. You were never a child. I don't know what you were. You always had an opinion of your own. Never wanted to be told anything. Never needed anything. You just..." She shook her head, unable to continue.

"I thought that's what you wanted. For me to be self-sufficient and not need you. God knows you tortured me whenever I showed any sign of needing anything from you," I snarled, through clenched teeth.

Mom waved my words away. I was exhausting. Her eyelids drooped. Luckily, the nurse appeared in the doorway, mouthing whether it was okay for her to enter.

I nodded, feeling like an asshole. Why was I yelling at my tired and obviously in pain mother?

"How are you feeling?" the nursed asked in a singsong voice.

"I need more."

The nursed padded over to the nightstand to retrieve Mom's medicine. "Would you like some soup?"

The Scotch-lady pursed her lips tightly, like a child refusing to take its medicine. She shook her head.

I wondered whether she was eating at all. She had never been much of an eater. Before all this, scotch provided much of her sustenance.

"Maybe when you wake up, then?" The nurse waited for an answer, but never received one. She smiled brightly and left us alone again.

My mother hit play on her Kindle again and closed her eyes. I slumped into the seat and listened with her. Our conversation was done. Nothing was resolved, but it was done.

I had an insight, but I still hadn't said my piece. I wasn't sure if Mom had said all she wanted to either. Yet, try as I might, I couldn't force any more words out. What more could I say, really?

She'd made it clear I was a disappointment for her right from the start, not just because I was a lesbian, but also because I was like my father. Did she despise him that much that she had to hate me as well? Everyone always said I looked like my father. Did she see him whenever she glimpsed me? It seemed so irrational to me: to hate me for that.

All these years I had tortured myself and tried to win my mother's approval. And now I knew there was nothing I could have done. My fate was sealed as soon as I popped out. I was like him, and therefore a mortal enemy. And then, when I announced I was a lesbian, well, it really was the perfect storm.

CHAPTER FIFTEEN

THE DOORBELL PULLED ME OUT OF MY STUPOR. I'D BEEN STANDING IN MY KITCHEN, STARING out the window, although my intention had been to fix some lunch rather than to stare uselessly.

I needed to pull my shit together. Seriously, people dealt with tragedy all of the time.

Stop being a pussy, Lizzie.

I swung the front door open with more gusto than I intended and almost whacked myself in the face.

"Easy there, tiger. Don't knock yourself out." Maddie sashayed in, not bothering to wait for an invite.

"Please, come on in." I bowed like a butler letting in a princess.

"I'm starving. Do you have anything to eat?" she demanded.

"Actually, I was just thinking of having lunch. Will a sandwich do?"

"I'm so hungry I might eat Hank. Where is the little bugger?"

"Probably in my office, sunning on a cushion in the window."

Maddie wandered toward my office to give the cat some love. I headed for the kitchen to fix lunch. I guessed the princess didn't plan on helping prepare the sandwiches.

When she eventually joined me, she was cradling Hank in her arms. Usually, he protested being held, but few could ignore Maddie's charm—not even my cat. He enjoyed her attention briefly before launching himself onto the counter, knocking off some papers and then scurrying back to my office.

Maddie replaced the papers and eyed me suspiciously. "What are you doing?"

"Making your sandwich, your highness." I bowed.

"I can see that, but why are you folding the pita like that?"

I stared at her. "How else will the turkey, cheese, lettuce, and tomato stay on it? You want it like a pizza?"

Maddie let out a snort of laughter. "Oh my God! Don't move! I need to snap a photo." She whipped out her cell phone. "Doug's going to love this. He thinks I'm a bad cook!" She grinned, shaking her head.

I gazed at her. What was she on about?

"They're called pita pockets for a reason, Lizzie." She dumped all of the fillings off the pita and sliced it in half before I could stop her. To my astonishment, she separated the pita, creating, well. . .a pocket.

"That's so neat!" I started shoving the sandwich stuffing into it.

Maddie shook her head, chuckling. "Let me guess, Sarah does the grocery shopping?"

"Yep. And we're trying to eat healthier, so she got me these for my lunches." I bit into my pita pocket. "Wow, this is much easier."

"Can we sit down and not eat over the sink?"

"Jeez, you're demanding today," I teased. I pulled two red plates from the cupboard. "What do you want to drink?"

Maddie padded to the fridge and helped herself to a Diet Coke before grabbing a regular Coke for me.

"Sarah filled me in on your latest conversation with your mom." She sat down at the kitchen table and leaned over to place her hand on mine. "I'm sorry. Really. That must have been tough to hear."

"Yes and no. I mean, it's not fun knowing I was a disappointment from the start." I took another bite of my sandwich. Since my conversation with Mom, I'd had a ravenous appetite, my body craving all sorts of food. I made a mental note to make an appointment to get my thyroid levels checked, just to be safe. Whenever my appetite seemed uncontrollable, I automatically feared my Graves' Disease had come out of remission.

I swallowed and continued. "But it was a relief to find out she didn't just hate me solely for being a lesbian or for studying history instead of going into the family biz like Peter did. Not that those two factors helped my cause." I shrugged. "At least I didn't try to be someone I thought she wanted me to be. Marry some dude and work for Dad and then find out that wouldn't have made a difference." I let out a sigh.

"That's a very mature response. I'm impressed." Maddie slurped her soda out of the can.

I flashed a sheepish smile. "Well, my therapist may have helped me realize some of those points. I would be remiss to take all the credit."

Maddie shook her head. "Remiss." She rolled her eyes. "I hope you don't make flashcards to improve your child's vocabulary. The only people I know who talk like that are you and Peter. . .and I don't talk to Peter anymore." She glared at me as if it was my fault that I reminded her of him.

"Flashcards!" I snickered. "Who still uses flashcards?" I pulled my cell phone out of my pocket and showed her my word-a-day app.

She grabbed my phone. "Hir-sut-e," she said, butchering the word hirsute.

"It's pronounced *her-soot*."

"What does it mean?"

"Hairy," I said with a shrug, as if it were common knowledge.

She tsked. "Please don't turn your child into a freak."

I put both palms up. "Sarah already lectured me when she found out I downloaded a bunch of apps for the baby," I confessed.

"What kind of apps?" Maddie finished her sandwich and licked her fingers. I handed her a napkin, but she waved it away.

"Learning apps. She was okay with some, like the animal noises. But she deleted the math and vocab apps."

"You want to teach your baby math before he or she can walk? What's with you Petries? Always so competitive about everything."

"I hope we have a boy." The sentence popped out before I could control what I was saying.

"Don't tell Sarah you said that. She'll kill you. Why a boy, though? To carry on your family name?"

"No. I just don't know anything about girls."

"Lizzie, you've never said a truer statement in your life," Maddie said, before she laughed her ass off, or should I say *derriere?*

The house phone jarred me out of an uncomfortable slumber. I fumbled for the phone, wondering why I was sleeping hunched over my desk in the library. Was it night or day?

"H-hello," I slurred into the receiver.

"Elizabeth?" Peter's voice shook me awake.

"Yes."

"She's dying." I heard zero emotion in his voice.

Before I could respond, I heard a click. Peter had hung up. Why?

And why did he say, "She's dying," and not, "Mom's dying?"

Part of my job was to analyze rhetoric. Word choice was crucial to understanding and interpreting a person's motive. Had Peter been too upset to say Mom? Was he distancing himself? Or was Mom out of the picture already in my brother's path to become even greater than our father?

Sarah's footsteps sounded on the staircase and then she stormed into the library in various states of dress and undress. Tugging a shirt over her bra, she asked, "Why aren't you getting ready?"

"She's dying," I stated.

Her face softened as Sarah tugged on a pair of jeans and crossed the room to reach me. "I know, sweetie. I picked up the phone in the bedroom and heard. We should get there as quickly as possible." She leaned down and kissed the top of my head.

"Why do you think Peter said, 'She's dying,' and not, 'Mom's dying'?"

Sarah's fingernails dug into my shoulders, where she squeezed them. She was restraining herself, was my guess. She often accused me of acting like an intellectual first and a human second. She hesitated for a moment before saying, "Honestly, I don't know. But I think we should discuss it later —"

"I read somewhere recently that when someone says 'honestly,' they're lying."

"Lizzie..." Her voice sounded tense before it died out. She dashed out of the room and returned with my jacket. I was still fully dressed.

She clutched her car keys in one hand. Without speaking, she pulled me out of my desk chair and pushed me toward the door. "Let's go." It was a command.

Neither of us said a single word during the drive. The digital clock on the dashboard announced it was three in the morning. Heavy clouds tinged the sky a vibrant rouge, and if I didn't know the time, I would have thought it was closer to sunset or sunrise, not deep in the night. Snow sprinkled the windshield but left no trace of moisture. The asphalt was bone dry. The first snow of the season usually didn't amount to much.

A hospice nurse met us at the door and led us to Mom's room.

The death room.

I cringed, hesitating before entering. This time, Sarah didn't shove me into action; instead, she gave me an encouraging nod.

My father and brother sat on either side of the bed.

Tiffany stood by the window, gazing out.

"It's snowing outside," she said, to no one in particular.

No one responded.

My father looked up and nodded hello, seeming relieved that we arrived.

Peter didn't seem relieved. He stormed out without saying a word. No words were needed.

I took Peter's seat and reached for my mother's hand, half expecting it to be cold; it wasn't.

"We'll give you a moment," my father murmured. He stood and directed his gaze to Tiffany, imploring her to follow. She finally realized Sarah and I had arrived and smiled a wan greeting before looping her arm through my father's. I didn't think I'd ever seen anyone do that to him before.

When they left, I kept my eyes fixed on the closed door, feeling trapped. Stunned.

Sarah cleared her throat. "Do you want me to leave?"

I shook my head, unable to speak.

My mother remained absolutely still. I felt the urge to place a mirror over her mouth, like they did in the movies. Then she let out a gasp that made me jump. "Jesus," I whispered loudly.

Mom stirred, and then settled back down, still not opening her eyes. The sheet moved up and down, very slowly, almost imperceptibly. At least Mom was still breathing—for the moment.

"Do you have anything you want to say?" Sarah nudged my shoulder.

I felt like I was six years old, standing in front of the class, panicking during my turn for show-and-tell.

My mouth opened, yet no words came out.

I stood and stared out the window. The sky was still red, and I couldn't help but wonder about it. Did the universe know about my mom's impending death?

"I never got the chance to get to know you." My words were barely more than a whisper and were followed by a small, insincere chuckle that held no joy. "We lived in the same house for eighteen years, and I never felt like I belonged. Not in your world. Not in your home."

Sarah shuffled uneasily behind me. This probably wasn't what she'd had in mind, but she stayed mute.

"Did you know I used to call you The Scotch-lady?" I turned, to see Mom's response.

Of course, there wasn't one.

Sarah blinked uneasily, but I continued. "It wasn't until you got…sick…that I felt something. Like you letting me in…well, as much as you could. It wasn't how I wanted it." I sat back down next to Mom and held her hand once again. "But I'll take it," I sighed. "I didn't tell you this before, because I was scared. You always terrified the shit out of me." I paused and sucked in a deep breath. "Sarah and I…we're trying to have a baby."

I felt Sarah's hands on my shoulders. I couldn't see anything through my tears. My voice was faltering, and I knew I needed to say the rest quickly, or I would never finish.

"I learned a lot from you, Mom. Even if we didn't have the best relationship, it never stopped me from loving you."

Finally.

I'd said it.

I twisted my hands in my lap, waiting for a reaction — any reaction.

My mother remained still. I was always late in realizing my feelings. Yet, I'd said it. I would have to be okay if she didn't reply.

I sucked in some air, flinching when I also swallowed some snot. Sarah squatted next to me, and I rested my weary head on her shoulder and flicked more tears off my face.

"Is she —?" Peter barged in. My tears stopped him in his tracks.

I shook my head.

He didn't respond, but I felt his scorn. Determination and control, the two things my brother exuded. I felt the urge to laugh in his face. To slap him, even. His bravado was useless in this situation, and I was starting to realize that it was all he had. Bravado. No human emotion. He'd never be a happy man. Or a complete one.

"Come on, Sarah. Let's give Peter some time with Mom." I resisted my desire to emphasize Mom. He wouldn't understand why. He would never understand much of anything. I'd always thought I was the weak one, the pathetic one. But I wasn't. That was Peter. And Mom.

We found Tiffany and my father sitting at the table in the kitchen nook. Tiffany looked up when we entered and hopped out of her seat. "I'll fix you two a cup of tea."

"I'll help," offered Sarah.

I sat across from my father. He grunted quietly to acknowledge me. The sky outside had turned charcoal; the snow had stopped. I searched for some meaning in that, but couldn't piece it together. Life. Death. Who knew anything, really? Probably, by the time I had it all figured out, I would be on my deathbed. Was that why Mom had started to let me in? Did she have an epiphany? Or was she terrified? The poor woman forced to rely on the one child she had never liked.

Peter ambled in, still exuding control. I glanced at my father to gauge his reaction. There wasn't one.

"I'll go sit with her," Dad said, leaving.

Peter patted him on the back the way football players did after a tough play. There was no emotion in it; he was just going through the motions.

Sarah and Tiffany sat down, cradling their teacups.

The three of us sat in silence while Peter leaned against the window, his arms akimbo.

"We haven't sent out invitations yet…considering…" Tiffany flushed. "But I hope you two will come to our wedding."

That drew Peter's attention. "Tiff, family stuff really isn't Elizabeth's thing." His tone was prickly.

None of us paid him any attention.

"It'll be a small affair, actually," Tiffany continued. "Two hundred or so."

Two hundred! That was small?

Peter cleared his throat and tried to make eye contact with his fiancée. It appeared that Tiffany was intentionally shutting him out. Had something happened between them? Maybe she had caught him red-handed, and this was part of his just desserts? She seemed stronger, more in control.

"We'd love to," said Sarah.

I nodded.

I knew Peter had always wanted a marriage just like our parents', but I didn't think he understood what that meant. He scowled, his handsome face showing his frustration, but there was something else there too. I studied him out of the corner of my eye. Defeat. He looked defeated.

I sipped my tea, its warmth sliding down my throat and into my body. I reached for Sarah's hand and gave it a squeeze.

My mother died a little after midday. All five of us were present when she took her last breath. I had hoped she'd looked peaceful when it was all said and done, but she didn't. She looked tiny and alone under her blanket.

The days afterward passed in a blur. Dad asked me to help organize all of Mom's personal papers. It was the first time I had been in her study. She'd never spent much time in there, so I never thought to snoop when I was younger. I'd forgotten about it completely until my father brought it up.

In the bottom drawer of her desk, I found several historical journals. Intrigued, I pulled them out to study the table of contents. Each one contained an article I had published. Stunned, I sorted them. To the best of my recollection, she hadn't missed a single article I had penned.

Anger welled up inside me. Would it have killed the woman to have said something—just one thing to let me know I wasn't the biggest disappointment of her life. Shit! I'd tortured myself for years trying to get her approval, and spent even more years pretending her words, or lack of words, didn't cut me to the bone. And now this.

"She was proud of you."

I hadn't heard my father enter the room, and I jumped in my chair.

I rested my hand on the stack of journals, tapping my fingers so he wouldn't notice my hand was shaking.

"Your mother was a tough woman to know, and to love, Lizzie." He sat down heavily in a leather chair. "But she was hardest on herself." He handed me a tumbler of whiskey and took a sip of his own. "She didn't allow herself to feel." He raised his glass to his dead wife's honor.

"She didn't want to feel, and I couldn't stop myself from feeling too much!" I paced in my office.

Sarah sat on the edge of one of the couches. "Isn't it good to finally know the truth?"

I paused and glared at her.

She put her palms in the air and her eyes widened. "I know it doesn't take the pain away, but still…"

I strolled over to the bar with one purpose: to pour a stiff drink so I wouldn't have to feel; it had worked for The Scotch-lady. Raising the gin bottle, I shook it in Sarah's direction. She declined a drink. The taut look on her face suggested she thought I'd had too much. I poured a generous swig and added a splash of tonic on top, not sure why I bothered.

Then I sank into a wing-backed chair and immediately guzzled half of my drink. Its burn began, a warm, tingling sensation coursing through my body. I let out a satisfied sigh.

"Is this your plan tonight?" Sarah motioned to my glass.

"Yup!" I answered, too enthusiastically.

She shook her head in disgust and left the room, letting me wallow in my own self-pity.

The next thing I remembered was someone shouting, "You fucking idiot!"

I rubbed my eyes, confused. Did I leave the TV on? Who was shouting?

"What were you thinking, Lizzie?"

I cracked open one eye and shut it just as quickly. Sunlight scorched my retinas.

I felt a weight on the couch and someone grabbed the gin bottle I'd been cradling. I fought, until I realized it was Maddie.

"Maddie, what the fuck?" I snatched the bottle back from her.

"'What the fuck?'" she mimicked. "What did you do last night?"

I sat up on the couch, instantly regretting that decision. The room swirled and the bottom fell out. I held my head in both hands and groaned.

"Drank…! Drank too much." I pushed my palms into my eye sockets, trying to still the falling feeling.

Maddie sniffed loudly. "You need a shower. I'll make a pot of coffee." She raised her hand and pointed to the door. "Go. Now."

"Where's Sarah?" I asked.

"She doesn't want to be around you until you sober up. And Jesus, you reek!" Again, she pointed to the door. "Go!"

When I stumbled into the kitchen half an hour later, Maddie said, "Well, you look a little better." She walked past me and sniffed again. "And you don't stink as much." Shoving a cup of coffee into my hand, she eyed me until I sipped the scorching liquid.

"Shit! That's hot." I waved my hand in front of my mouth.

"I don't care. Drink it."

Her scowl intimidated the shit out of me, so I did as instructed, even if I wouldn't be able to taste any food for a month afterward.

She crossed her arms. "Are you done feeling sorry for yourself?"

I nodded, but Maddie didn't look convinced.

"I'll swear on a stack of Bibles to prove it," I offered.

"Yeah, right. Like that would mean anything to you. Where's your copy of Herodotus?" She bounded to the library and I stumbled after her. I watched her scan the shelves in search of the ancient Greek book, *The Histories*.

"How do you even know about Herodotus?" I surreptitiously searched the shelves for my copy as well.

"You aren't the only one with a brain. Everyone knows the Father of History." She waved my stupidity away.

"I'm pretty sure you're wrong, considering many of my students couldn't name him on their exam paper."

"Students!" She scoffed. "No one knows anything until they finish college. Aha!" She made a beeline for it from across the room. "Here it is. Okay, put your hand out."

I complied.

"Do you swear to stop wallowing and not to drink yourself into oblivion?"

I nodded.

Maddie cupped her ear. "What? I can't hear you?"

"Yes, I swear. Now tell me, where's Sarah?"

Maddie watched the book closely, as if it might burst into flames if it sensed I was lying. "Shopping with her mom," she said. "She asked me to check on you, considering..." Maddie indicated the empty gin bottle on the floor. Her face softened. "Would you like to talk?"

"Not really." Hank wandered in and jumped into his usual spot in front of the window, immediately grooming one of his paws. "It was a shock, really." I wrapped my arms around my chest.

"Why don't we go hiking? I know how much you love to hike in the snow."

I did. I loved being surrounded by untrodden snow, feeling like an explorer seeing a place for the first time.

"It'll clear your head." Maddie left the room to find her coat.

I smiled, feeling fortunate to have such a wonderful friend.

"*I'm awake,*" I texted Sarah. "*And not too hungover!*"

I lied about the last bit.

CHAPTER SIXTEEN

My phone buzzed. Another text.

I blew it off, since it was probably only from Maddie. How that woman found the time to text and email twenty-four-seven astounded me. An hour later, as I was shoving some sprouts into a pita for lunch, I noticed it had no caller ID. And that I'd never responded.

"Would you like to meet me for lunch?"

My jaw nearly hit the floor. Tiffany — my brother's fiancée. Why in the world was Tiffany texting me? How did she even get my number?

It wasn't like we were friends. True, we'd be "sisters" after Christmas, but I never really bought into that. I didn't like my blood relatives, let alone in-laws.

"Yes." I sent a tentative message back.

"Tomorrow???" Within a minute, Tiffany responded.

Shit!

The last time I'd made an effort to befriend Peter's soon-to-be wife, it hadn't gone over that well. Sure, Maddie and I were still friends, but my brother hadn't spoken to me since, not until I'd seen him at the hospital after Mom's cancer. He didn't know I'd made a pass at Maddie, but he knew I'd helped her escape minutes before she was supposed to walk down the aisle to marry him. I was 99.93% certain he wouldn't want me to have lunch with Tiffany.

So I agreed.

I didn't agree just to get under Peter's skin; I was also curious about what she wanted. Knowing Peter wouldn't approve was just an added bonus.

I arrived early at the restaurant the following day. Tiffany was fifteen minutes late. It shocked me. I figured she'd be the type to arrive much later.

"So sorry I'm late, traffic was a bitch."

Again, this surprised me. She didn't just apologize for being late; she spoke like we were old friends. Something was going on, and I wasn't entirely sure I wanted to know what.

"No worries. I always have a book." I patted my Kindle.

"Let me guess, you're like Peter. You arrive early for everything. Except that he spends his time answering emails, not reading." Her tone suggested she preferred my way of killing time, even if she didn't read herself. I wondered if his career was causing issues on the home front. His job was the only thing my brother was devoted to. I used to think he was loyal to my parents, but after seeing how he handled Mom's death, I suspected he was more of an opportunist than I'd thought. People didn't matter to Peter. Business mattered. That and his inheritance.

"How is Peter holding up?" I had a pretty good idea, but I thought it would be polite to ask.

She waved a hand. "You know Peter."

I did. But I wondered if she knew the man she was marrying in less than a month.

The waitress popped into view and scared the shit out of me. Was she a ninja or something?

"What can I get you two?"

I nodded for Tiffany to order first. She glanced at the menu and ordered a salad. How typical.

I ordered a steak and parmesan sandwich, with a side salad instead of fries. Sarah was really on my case lately about eating better. I'd never been a big fan of rabbit food, but I thought I might as well make an effort, especially since Sarah had been buying organic at home.

"So, you're probably wondering why I invited you to lunch." Her frown and smile baffled me.

"Uh…" Should I be honest with her? "Actually, yes I am." I decided to go for it.

"It breaks my heart that you and Peter aren't close. I plan on changing that." Her smile was shrewd; it made her look ridiculous instead of triumphant.

"Really? How do you propose to make that happen?" I lifted my iced tea.

"I want you to be one of my bridesmaids," she declared. She said it like it was the most obvious solution.

I choked on my drink.

"I knew you'd react like that," Tiffany beamed.

Was she trying to kill me?

I cleared my throat, stalling for time to figure out how to respond.

"Don't try saying no. I've already ordered your dress. I guessed at your size, but I think you'll find I'm good at guessing. Plus, you'll have a final fitting a week before the wedding." She shook her head and her blond hair fell perfectly into place. "I'm so glad we have it all worked out."

"Have you told Peter this plan?" I was finally able to speak.

"Peter?" She quirked her eyebrows. "Why would he care about the wedding plans?"

I couldn't determine whether his apathy bothered her or whether that was how she wanted it. I had a feeling this ditz was used to getting her way, no matter what. And I wasn't entirely sure she was a ditz.

"Sarah won't mind, will she?" Tiffany did her best to look concerned.

"About what?" I asked, flummoxed by the turn the conversation was taking. Shit, I was already a bridesmaid in a wedding I didn't want to attend. Now what?

"Well, you'll have to walk down the aisle with a man." Tiffany gave a strange little smile.

Was that guilt or triumph? Was she trying to cure my lesbianism as well?

It took a lot of effort for me to not laugh in her face. I dug my nails into my left palm under the table, to keep myself from cracking up. "Oh, that. Sarah won't care at all."

"Good. I didn't want to step on any toes."

I was pretty certain she didn't care about anyone's toes.

"Trust me, that's something Sarah never has to worry about."

"You cheating, or you cheating with a man?" Her eyes narrowed until she resembled a lioness about to lunge at its prey.

Her question floored me. And her nonchalance was a good indicator that she knew everything about Peter and my father. Just great. Would she watch me too, to see if I was a cheater? I seriously doubted she would make any effort to protect Sarah. She seemed like the type to gather intel for her own personal benefit.

It struck me that perhaps I had seriously underestimated this woman from the beginning. I had thought Peter was playing her, but maybe she had been playing him. I wished I could call Peter to see how he was handling the situation. Then again, why bother. I didn't even like him. Maybe this wedding would be more entertaining than I thought.

"Also, I hope you can give a toast during the dinner," Tiffany said, before devouring a crouton, crunching loudly.

Fuck!

"A bridesmaid! You said no, right?" Sarah leveled her gaze at me.

"How do I say no to that request from my future sister-in-law?" I stared back at her, feeling helpless.

"You just say no." Sarah studied me. "Oh, God, you agreed?" She started laughing. "Wait till Maddie hears this."

Before I could respond, Sarah left the room, dialing her cell. Not long after, she returned to the kitchen. She'd already told Maddie, and I hadn't even finished making my tea. How in the world did those two gossip so much so quickly? I wished I could be as efficient, but with my research, not my gossiping. I would be three times as productive if I were as quick as they were. I would be on my fourth book, instead of my second.

"Maddie wants me to film it all. She's taking bets that you'll fall walking down the aisle, or freeze and say something completely inappropriate during your toast."

"That second accusation doesn't seem fair. She can't give two different scenarios and count it as one." I bit into a scone.

"Is there more hot water?" Sarah gestured to my tea. I nodded.

"Fix me a cup, will ya?"

"Yes, ma'am. Anything else, ma'am?" I tried to mimic a slave's voice, but failed miserably.

"Yeah, don't talk like that." She swiveled around on a barstool, smiling.

Was it just me, or did Sarah have a certain glow about her?

CHAPTER SEVENTEEN

A STRING OF GIGGLES ISSUED FROM THE KITCHEN. I SAT AT MY DESK IN THE OFFICE, WONDERING if I wanted to know what Sarah and Maddie were up to. Something told me their merriment had something to do with me, so I chose to remain hidden.

I should have known it wouldn't work. I also should have installed a lock as soon as we moved in.

"I have a gift for you." Maddie burst through the office door like she owned the place, waving a garment bag at me.

Sarah waltzed in after her, looking full of herself.

"I told you to say no…" Sarah said, her words disappearing into a gale of laughter.

I stared at the garment bag, unable to think of anything to say.

Maddie shook it. "Aren't you curious to see what's inside?"

I shook my head.

"Too bad." She ripped the zipper open to reveal a hideous red and green dress, so disgustingly ugly that no woman in her right mind would ever wear it.

"What the fuck is that? Your prom dress from 1999?"

"Ha, you wish. I wouldn't ever put this thing on, not even then." Maddie's grin made me squirm in my chair.

"Three guesses? What do you think it is?" Sarah chimed in.

"You mean besides a hideous dress?" I needed clarification.

Sarah nodded.

"Uh, something that should be burned," was all I could think of to say.

"Oh, just tell her, Sarah. I've never met a more clueless person." Maddie was doubled over with laughter.

"It's your bridesmaid dress for Peter's wedding." Sarah was enjoying herself—too much, I thought.

I snapped my mouth shut, shocked. "I'll look like a deranged Christmas gift."

"Yeah. It's like something a ninety-year-old grandmother would wear." Maddie flicked the fabric with a finger. "Not only is it ugly, it's also scratchy. I wouldn't be caught dead in it."

"I'll pay you one hundred bucks to wear it to dinner tonight," I said, only half in jest.

"Nope. You'd have to pay me a lot more than that."

"One thousand."

"Where?"

"Old Town."

Maddie scrunched up her face. "So lots of people would see me." I could see her mulling it over.

"That is the point."

"Nope. Not going to do it." She folded the dress over the back of my chair, and brushed off her hands, as though she wanted to cleanse her fashion sense.

"Your loss."

"What about two thousand?" Maddie bargained.

"No way!" Sarah waggled a finger at both of us to stop the madness. "Knowing you two, something would happen to the dress, and how would I explain that to Tiffany? She's put me in charge of you, Lizzie."

"Ah, Sarah, you're no fun," I pouted her accusation away.

"I wonder what type of shoes you'll wear with a dress like this?" Maddie turned serious.

"Maybe we should raid Mrs. Claus's closet," I offered.

Maddie snorted, taken aback that I'd uttered a joke that was somewhat funny.

Sarah tried her best to maintain her *I'm in control* bravado, but it was slipping.

How in the world had I ended up in this situation?

I tapped the side of my champagne flute with my knife. No one in the room took any notice. Actually, I think the din increased, as if everyone was intentionally giving me the cold shoulder. Any pride and confidence I had seemed to ooze out of me. I glanced to my side and caught Tiffany's attention. I had been shocked to discover that Sarah and I were to be seated at Peter's table. I thought for sure he'd stick us in the back, right next to the kid's table.

Tiffany stood and shouted, "Quiet, everyone. Lizzie wants to say something."

Shit, she was annoying. A burning sensation seemed to work its way up my neck to the top of my head. I was sure I looked ridiculous—almost as red as my dress.

I glanced over at Sarah for support. She flashed me her *you can do it* smile. At least my wife looked confident that I could get through my toast without making a total ass out of myself.

"Uh…" I cleared my throat. "Many of you don't know me…or at least…" I stepped from side to side, fighting the urge to bolt from the room. "Or, at least, you didn't know me before today, but I have a feeling many of you will remember me…or at least the dress." I pulled out the hideous skirt to emphasize my point. Laughter floated out from the crowd, bolstering my courage.

Everyone laughed, except for Peter. Even the other bridesmaids nodded their understanding. We all looked ridiculous.

"I probably should mention that I'm Peter's sister."

Some lady uttered too loud, "I didn't know he had a sister."

I raised my glass. "Now you do. How's this for making an impression?" I downed a third of my champagne.

Sarah covered her mouth. For a second, I thought she might pee herself.

The mood relaxed a little; Peter's evil glare, did not. But to tell you the truth, I was enjoying it. The man was insufferable. He didn't know how to relax, not even at his own wedding. He'd been strutting around with his chest puffed out all evening, like a conquering hero returning from war. Every time I heard his booming voice, I wanted to vomit.

"In all seriousness. . ." I paused not sure what to say. I glanced at Peter and Tiffany. She beamed. Peter looked his usual smug self. "I wish both of you the best." I resisted the urge to add, *You'll need it.*

My speech over, I sat down in my seat, completely relaxed. For days I'd been dreading my brother's wedding, afraid I'd screw up my toast. And I had messed it up, big time, but at least it was over. One of Peter's coworkers stood up to add his two cents. He talked about how Peter was the most astute businessman he'd ever met. Was this a board meeting? I sucked, but at least I wasn't shameful enough to stick my nose up Peter's ass.

The following day, Sarah and I joined my father, Peter, and Tiffany for brunch. Tiffany thought it'd be nice to have a family get together before the newlyweds took off for their honeymoon. Sarah had convinced me to go. I found it odd that Tiffany's side of the family didn't attend the meal.

"Sarah, I noticed you aren't drinking your champagne. It's the best they offer." Peter's haughty grin annoyed the hell out of me. Everything he ever ordered was the best — or so he said.

"I guess I'm just not in the mood for bubbly," Sarah declared.

"Bubbly." Peter looked aghast. "This is not the kind of champagne you find at your local wine shop." He shot me a reproving glare. "I bet you've never ordered champagne this divine." He took a careful sip, his expression reverent, as if he was kissing Jesus' feet.

Divine. What drug was my brother on, anyway? Divine, my ass. It tasted like champagne. Good, champagne, yes, but I wasn't having an out-of-body experience with each swig.

Sarah and I hadn't planned on breaking the news that she was six weeks pregnant. We both firmly believed we should wait at least another month. Actually, I didn't ever plan on telling Peter, not if I could help it. My hope was that Tiffany would lose interest in family time once all the wedding hoopla settled down.

"What exotic adventures do you have planned?" I tried to steer the conversation to safer waters.

Peter puffed out his chest. "I plan on eating the finest food and drinking the finest wines." He set his glass down firmly. "Elizabeth, I'm appalled that you don't treat Sarah to the finer things in life. I'm confounded as to why she refuses to try this champagne. I know for a fact she's never had anything this nice. Obviously, you two just aren't used to a life of luxury."

My father stared out the window. I couldn't determine whether he was listening. He was probably lost in his own world.

"She doesn't have to try your fucking champagne, okay," I muttered through clenched teeth. I immediately regretted my word choice, but really, he'd pushed me into it with his elitism.

Sarah put a hand on my arm, rubbing it so Peter could see it. He rolled his eyes, which I suspected was her intention. I wanted to shout, "Homophobe!"

"Peter, I'm not trying to snub you or your champagne. I can't drink," Sarah explained.

"Can't drink!" he jeered. "That's absurd. You mean you don't want to."

Peter missed the meaning behind her words—and the twinkle in her eye. Sarah was positively radiant. I hadn't ever seen her look more beautiful.

"Oh my God!" Tiffany squealed. "When are you due?" She grabbed both of Sarah's hands and swung them about as if she was playing an accordion.

Women had a way of picking up on these things.

Peter frowned at his new bride, both exasperated and clueless.

"We didn't plan on saying anything until you two got back." Sarah took a deep breath. Tiffany let go of her hands, and Sarah flashed me her *prepare yourself* look. "We're due in August."

Tiffany clapped her hands. "I'm going to be an aunt." She turned aunt into two syllables, and I tried to picture our child saying, "A-Unt Tie-fannie."

Realization dawned on Peter's face. It was priceless. I'm sure he never considered that we'd have a kid. And he'd probably never given two thoughts to the idea that we'd be the first to give our father a grandchild.

He scowled. He had been first with everything, yet I had beaten him to one of the biggest milestones in our father's life. Peter wasn't just miffed; he looked like he wanted to commit murder.

My father, on the other hand, turned slowly to face me and then turned to Sarah. His usual poker face carried a faint trace of glee. "Really?" he asked.

My grin answered him, and Sarah confirmed with a resounding, "Yes."

"That's wonderful." He added, almost wistfully, "My first grandchild."

His words floored me.

"August, though, so that means you're only six weeks pregnant? Anything could happen. Isn't it too early to tell people?" questioned Peter.

Everyone ignored him. I felt pity for him. He really just didn't have a clue about life. Not surprising, really, considering who raised us. Part of me wanted to tell him it was all right not to be perfect. The other part said, "Don't bother. He won't get it."

His bride raised her champagne flute. "To new beginnings, all around!"

AUTHOR'S NOTE

Thank you for reading the *A Woman Lost series*. If you enjoyed the novel, please consider leaving a review on Goodreads or Amazon. No matter how long or short, I would very much appreciate your feedback.

You can follow me, T. B. Markinson, on Twitter at @IHeartLesfic or email me at tbm@tbmarkinson.com. I would love to know your thoughts.

ABOUT THE AUTHOR

TB Markinson is an American living in England. When she isn't writing, she's traveling the world, watching sports on the telly, visiting pubs, or reading. Not necessarily in that order.

Her novels have hit Amazon bestseller lists for lesbian fiction and lesbian romance. For a full listing of TB's novels, please visit her Amazon page.

Feel free to visit TB's website at www.lesbianromancesbytbm.com to say hello. She also runs I Heart Lesfic, a place for authors and fans of lesfic to come together to celebrate and chat about lesbian fiction. On her 50 Year Project blog, TB chronicles her challenge to visit 192 countries, read 1,001 books, and to watch the AFI's top 100 movies.

Printed in Great Britain
by Amazon

47158393R00249